‖‖‖ **W9-BVT-780**

...R W. MICHAEL GEAR'S
...MER AND *THE MORNING RIVER*

"...g [person's] historical novel, with crisp, authentic
...ue and strong characterization."

—*Amarillo News-Globe* on *Coyote Summer*

"[A] solid Western. . . . A well-plotted page-turner that
distinguishes itself from other Westerns in its depth and
quality of its historical reconstruction."

—*Publishers Weekly* on *Coyote Summer*

"Gear presents the early American West with a rare, salty
accuracy of detail."

—*Kirkus Reviews* on *Coyote Summer*

"A bold novel of the birth of the American fur trade in 1825.
. . . A good, strong story, the ending will leave you wanting more . . . which you will get in the sequel."

—*American Cowboy* on *The Morning River*

"Gear writes superbly rolling prose with flair, confidence,
wit, an ear for sounds, and an eye for details. . . . And he
has another gift: the ability to teach his readers as he enter-
tains them."

—*Rocky Mountain News* on *The Morning River*

"This is a wonderful book. . . . Well-researched fur trade
setting, cultures in interaction and sometimes conflict. [Gear
has] a special understanding of American Indian mysticism
which provides the stamp of reality."

—*Don Coldsmith* on *The Morning River*

COYOTE SUMMER

W. Michael Gear

A TOM DOHERTY ASSOCIATES BOOK
NEW YORK

NOTE: If you purchased this book without a cover you should be aware that this book is stolen property. It was reported as "unsold and destroyed" to the publisher, and neither the author nor the publisher has received any payment for this "stripped book."

This is a work of fiction. All the characters and events portrayed in this book are either products of the author's imagination or are used fictitiously.

COYOTE SUMMER

Copyright © 1997 by W. Michael Gear

All rights reserved, including the right to reproduce this book, or portions thereof, in any form.

Maps and interior illustrations by Ellisa Mitchell

A Forge Book
Published by Tom Doherty Associates, LLC
175 Fifth Avenue
New York, NY 10010

www.tor.com

Forge® is a registered trademark of Tom Doherty Associates, LLC.

ISBN-13: 978-0-765-35728-1
ISBN-10: 0-765-35728-3
Library of Congress Catalog Card Number: 97-5762

First edition: August 1997
First mass market edition: February 1999
Second mass market edition: October 2006

Printed in the United States of America

0   9   8   7   6   5   4   3   2   1

To

Harriet McDougal

With special appreciation for all of her hard work over the years. Harriet has always challenged Kathy and me to excel and explore new directions in fiction. You're the best, Harriet. Thank you for everything.

CREE

BLACKFEET
(PA'KIANI)

ASSINIBOIN

HIDATSA

MISSOURI

ATSINA

MANDAN

YANKTONAN

YELLOWSTONE

MOUTH of the BIG HORN

CROW
('ANI)

Arikara
Village

MISSOURI

DUKURIKA

GRAND
DETOUR

Fort
Kiowa

YANKTON

TETON SIOUX
KU'CHENDIKANI

PONCA

OMAHA

PLATTE

Fort
Atkinson

RIVER

PAWNEE

KAWS MOUTH

KANSAS R.

MISSOURI

KANSAS

OSAGE

Coyote Summer

Miles 0   100   200   300

C Hubbell
1996

Mouth of the Yellowstone

Yellowstone River

Missouri River

James River

Little Missouri River

MANDAN
△ VILLAGE
(MITUTANKA)

Belle Fourche River

△ BEAR LODGE

BLACK HILLS

North Platte

Pa"ido'aifuaint
(Geyser Basin)

Dicipa'ogwe
(Stinking R.)

Arapaho
Burial
Grounds

We'shobengar
(Devils Tower) △

Bana'ite Lands
(Bannock)

Piague (Big Horn R.)

Nagatusia
(Big Horn Mts.)

Ndoyabi

△ Isa'we'an
(Coyote's Penis Mts.)

Pogushowen r
(Hot Springs)

High Wolf's
△ Camp

Gourd Buttes

Ainkahonobita
Coal Creek Mts.

Meat Poles

Mts.
Ndoyabi
Camp

Red Wall

Pia'ogwe (Big River)

Junangarit
(Copper Mtn.)

Ki'nyatiwener
(Split Rock) □

Wongo'yigwindo'yap
(Green Mts.)

Guyo'ogwe
(Bear River)

Wongo'ogwe
(Black's Fork) □

Detail Map: Wyoming Territory

ONE

Upper Missouri River, July 1825

Predawn mist, like curling wraiths, rose off the smooth surface of the Missouri River. It drifted across the murky swirls of current, over the muddy bank, and into the trees. The eastern sky glowed with the promise of a new day. Against it, cottonwood, willows, and an occasional ash created a lacery of black silhouettes. Birds trilled and warbled as the night creatures retired and those of day stirred. Dew beaded on leaves and grass, and silvered the stems and branches.

In the distant uplands beyond the river, the slopes were mantled by hip-high grass and isolated spears of juniper, while the dark veins of drainages were clotted with stands of bur oak. There coyotes yipped in final salute to the night as four riders pushed a small herd of horses westward. They quirted their mounts across the dawn-still grass as if in pursuit of the retreating night.

One by one, they would snap a quick look over their shoulders—back toward the river and the camp of sleeping White men. Long black hair whipped in the wind of their passing; fringes jerked and flicked to the movement of their horses. As they rode, they flashed smiles at each other, dark eyes glinting. It had been a perfect raid.

Stealing from White men was easy. And, unlike raids on the Blackfeet or Sioux, no stalwart warriors would come riding in pursuit. No, these White men would stay with their big, ugly canoe. Let them sleep late into the morning, for the *Apsaroke* had shown the Whites how brave and clever true warriors were.

◇

Beside the west bank of the river, the keelboat *Maria* floated, her wood sun-bleached and pale in the faint morning light. She lay snugged close to the high bank, tied off by a painter line to a massive gray cottonwood trunk. Dewshrouded and furled, the baggy sail hung from the spar. Oars and poles had been stowed on the big square cargo box. A trick of the lazy current toyed with the rudder, and the long tiller slipped soundlessly back and forth, as though managed by a ghostly hand.

The crew had camped in the tall grass beyond the boat. Blankets, stretched over lines strung between the cottonwoods, created crude shelters in case of rain. Fingers of hazy blue smoke rose from the ashes of last night's fires.

Men lay scattered like ten-pins, rolled in blankets, their

snoring a burr on the still air. Occasionally, one would shift to peer through a slitted eye at the lightening sky, only to surrender himself again to shredding filaments of dream.

Heals Like A Willow had already risen and rolled her blankets. On silent feet she walked into the ghost gray trees, her back bent with packs. Her people were the *Dukurika* band—the Shoshoni Sheepeaters of the high western mountains.

As the dew-wet grass spattered her moccasins, Willow cocked her head, listening to the lilting cry of the distant coyotes.

Among her people, Coyote was the Trickster, and just after the Creation of the world he became the source of all trouble and misfortune. Not that Coyote was evil like the White man's devil; rather, his insatiable desires led him to impulsive acts. Famine, disease, death, war, incest, and all manner of ills had resulted as the compromise between impulsive Coyote, and his counterpart, the wise and logical Wolf.

Recently, too much of Willow's life had been orchestrated by Coyote. Last winter, after the death of her husband and son, she had left the *Kuchendikani* band to travel home to the *Dukurika*. During that journey, the Pawnee warrior, Packrat, had captured her and brought her East as a slave—a gift for Packrat's father, Half Man. She'd waged a war of wills with Packrat, broken his Power, and finally won. A twist of fate had placed her with the White men, who, she had discovered, had a great deal more in common with Coyote than they did with Wolf.

She listened to the last of the coyote's morning song echoing down from the uplands. This time, she promised herself, Coyote wasn't mocking her. She was going home—back to her people, to their distant western mountains.

So silent . . . too silent.

Heals Like A Willow cocked her head and listened. In the

twilight of dawn, she stood like a statue, the packs dead weight on her shoulders. Not even the stamping of a horse's hoof intruded on the morning birdsong.

Placing each foot with care, she approached the camp's picket. The horses were gone. Willow carefully shrugged out of her packs and laid them quietly on the ground. She sniffed, taking in the old smells of manure and urine. The rope was still tied around one of the trees. Her fingers slid over the smooth end. Only a steel knife cut so cleanly.

There should have been a guard, but she could see no sign of the man. After a night of pacing, the grass would have been trampled. Had a guard even been posted? Trudeau would have been responsible for appointing one of the *engagés* to stand guard. But the day before he and Richard had fought, and Trudeau would have been in no shape to attend to his duties.

She bent down, feeling the manure: cold clear through. Brushing her hands clean on the grass, she looked up at the reddening sky and sighed. Today, with a horse, she would have started home for the *Dukurika* mountains.

What a fool you are, Willow. Coyote was indeed singing for you. She picked up her packs and warily retraced her way to the camp.

Lowering the packs by one of the smoldering fires, she crouched down beside a blanket-wrapped man. Despite her stealth, he was watching her through narrowed blue eyes. The dim light revealed a patchwork of cruel scars that crisscrossed his ruined face: the sign of the great white bear. His rumpled dark hair and beard were shot through with gray. He was wrapped in a dirty striped blanket that had once been red, white, and yellow. A heavy Hawken rifle lay within easy reach.

She shrugged and said, "The horses have been stolen. The rope was cut with a steel knife. The shit is cold, Trawis. They have been gone a long time."

He hadn't moved. "Injuns?"

"Are White men that good at stealing horses? I didn't hear a single sound. Not the rattle of a hoof, not a snort or wicker."

"Injuns," Travis growled. "And the guard?"

"I don't think there was one. Trudeau . . ."

"Hell! My fault. As bad as Dick whupped him last night in that caterwauling, I shoulda seen to it." A calculating look filled his eyes. "I'm betting on the thieving Crows. How about ye?"

"*A'ni,*" she agreed. "Crows. They are this good. But far away, no?"

"Their country ain't that far." Travis sat up in his blankets. "Five days' hard ride west . . . maybe six."

"I am sorry they did this. I was going home today." She sighed wearily. "I would have warned you, but I did not know they raided here."

"Shoulda known meself," he growled. "And no, a body don't usually find Crow this far west. They don't savvy the Rees, nor the Sioux, or Cheyenne." He paused. "If it's Crow."

"You can get more horses among the Mandans?"

The soft dawn light left his eyes like pits, but she could read disgust in the look he gave her. "Hell, gal, them's *my* hosses!" He kicked a leg out of the blankets to prod at Richard's blanket-bundled form. "C'mon, Dick. Injuns has stoled the hosses. *Leve!* Let's get at 'em."

Richard muttered sleepily, threw back his blanket, and sat up, but gasped and winced from pain. Even in the half-light, Willow could see his bruised face and swollen nose. Long brown hair hung in disarray, and a wispy beard covered his cheeks. He stretched now, and grunted as he discovered new sore muscles and aches.

She started to reach out, to touch those hurts with tender fingers, but balled her fist instead and asked Travis, "What are you going to do?"

"Go after the damned hosses," Travis growled. "Ain't no

cussed Crows a gonna get this coon's hosses." He gave her a cautious study. "And, without a hoss, ye cain't run off ter them Snake lands ye been a-pining on."

She said nothing, watching him warily.

"So, Dick and me better get yer hoss back, Willow, or it'll be a tarnal long walk fer ye."

"We're doing what?" Richard asked as he stood up gingerly. He grunted and made a face as he tried to stretch. "Dear God, I hurt."

"That was a hell of a scrape ye had with old Trudeau yesterday," Travis reminded. "Tarnation! Ye damned near chewed the coon's ear off. Last I seen, Toussaint and Baptiste was hauling him down ter the river fer a dunking. He's hurt enough he fergot ter set guard on the hosses."

Richard's expression softened and he glanced away, refusing to meet their eyes. "I never thought I'd become a common brawler, Travis."

The grizzled hunter stood, back crackling as he arched it. "Yep, wal, life's full of little surprises, ain't it?"

Willow glanced surreptitiously at Richard. He was young, lanky, and possessed a wiry strength belied by his slim body. He wore a fringed hunting shirt, and a knife and possible sack hung from the belt that secured his buckskin pants. Heavy Crow moccasins covered his feet.

She knew his story. Richard came from a place far to the east, a White-man town called Boston. Richard's father had sent him west to carry money to a man in St. Louis, but on the way, Richard had been robbed. To save his life, he'd indentured himself to Dave Green's *Maria*—and Travis had been his guard.

In Boston, Richard had studied something called philosophy, which Willow had decided was a kind of special medicine knowledge. But since he had come to the river he had become more than a seeker after Power. He'd become a warrior and a hunter.

Richard had saved her life when Packrat would have killed her. He had looked into her eyes and seen her soul, as she'd seen his. Unlike the men of her people, he hadn't been horrified at the idea of a woman using *puha* or Power. It had been at that moment, when their souls touched, that she first had begun to love him.

Fool that you are, Willow. He is going back to his Boston, and his Laura. What you wish will never be. Coyote had tricked her again.

"Willow, I want ye ter keep to Baptiste and Green," Travis said as he headed for the boat. "Give Dick and me time ter get back. Then ye can run off. Promise?"

She slapped futile hands to her sides. "Yes. Promise." Anyone would feel safe around Baptiste, the strapping soot black warrior. He'd been a slave once, and, like Willow, had killed his owner. She took one last look at Richard's swollen eye and puffed-up nose.

Richard was stumbling after Hartman, groaning as he prodded bruises from last night's fight with Trudeau.

Trudeau had tried to force Willow—and Richard had taken him down for it. But then, bad blood had run between Trudeau and Richard since the first days on the river.

She whispered softly, "Good luck, Ritshard. Be very careful . . . and come back safe."

Why? a voice asked in her soul. *When he comes back, you will just leave. Either way, your time with him is running out . . . like water trickling from a snowbank in late spring.*

A square-walled tent stood in the middle of the camp. The white canvas had grayed from months of weather and grimy hands. Inside, David Green, the booshway, or expedition leader, was blinking himself awake and stretching.

He called softly, "Henri? You awake?"

The man who slept before the flap grunted, yawned, and rubbed his face. He sat up in his blankets to stare owlishly around at the sleeping camp. "*Oui, bourgeois.* I am awake."

Henri stood, flexing his muscles against cramps and aching joints. As patroon, he was master of the *Maria,* the man who steered the keelboat. Now he bent over the gray ash in the firepit, flicking the remaining coals into a pile, carefully placing twigs atop, and blowing the coals to life. As the flames crackled up, he added fuel and dug out the cook pot.

As Henri fixed breakfast, Green ducked through the flap, and walked down to check the boat. After he'd assured himself she was snug, he made his way through the waking *engagés* and seated himself by Henri's fire.

The patroon had filled Dave Green's tin plate with steaming catfish and grouse meat. Holding the hot plate by the rim, Dave had just lifted his first forkful of breakfast and was chewing methodically when Travis strode purposefully across the camp. The hunter carried his Hawken in his right hand, his left resting on his possibles, powder horn, and the bullet pouch tied to his belt. His graying hair flowed out over his collar from under a battered black felt hat. Travis wore a hunter's leather clothing, some of the long fringe missing. The only new apparel was the Sioux moccasins on his feet.

"*Malchance aujourd'hui,*" Henri said as he glanced up from spooning his own breakfast onto a tin plate. Coffee boiled in a soot-blackened pot, the aroma rising in the cool morning air.

"I reckon Trudeau was too stove up to detail a hoss guard last night," Travis said as he laid his rifle against the trunk of a cottonwood and hunkered down on his haunches. "And I don't know if'n it'd done any good anyhow. I just come from the picket. Injuns stole the hosses last night."

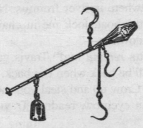

Green stopped in mid-chew. "All of them?"

"Yep. Reckon Dick and me'll go get 'em back." From his possibles, he extracted a tin cup, and pulled his sleeve down over his hand to grab the hot coffee pot. After pouring a cup, he glanced up at Green with cold blue eyes. "Don't call us dead fer at least a month."

"A month?" Green rubbed the back of his neck and frowned. "I don't like it, Travis. A week, you hear? That's all I want you gone."

Travis sipped the hot coffee and made a sour expression. The act pulled all the scars tight across his ruined face. "No telling how far them coons—"

"That's my point, Travis." Green straddled a log and lowered himself. He pulled at his blond hair and shook his head. "I know you, Travis Hartman . . . and I understand. Some Crow snuck in and lifted *your* horses. You think it's a matter of honor now to get them back—come hell or high water. But I'm serious. I can't afford to let you chase off all over the plains looking for horse thieves. Good Lord, by a month from now, we should be two weeks past the Mandan. I need you here, Travis."

"Now, Dave . . ."

"Travis, before you go off half-cocked, think about it. We're almost to the Mandan. We need a license to trade with Indians, remember? We don't have a legal right to be here, and Atkinson and O'Fallon—along with half the American army—are somewhere upriver from us. Now, if they catch us, they'll take the boat, lock me in chains, and haul our arses right back down to—"

"Ye don't gotta *remind* me!" Travis gave him a hostile squint. "Dave, I'll be back when I'm back. Ye can't go a-letting these pesky Crow up and steal your hosses!"

Dave lifted an eyebrow, reading Travis's stony expression. "Please?"

With one hand, Henri twisted the ends of his thick black mustache. With the other, he absently poked a long-tined fork into the cooking pone. "The Rees, I think some of them are up ahead. It would not be good, Travis, if you are gone when we meet them."

"Reckon not," Travis relented. "But, hell, ye got Baptiste fer palavering with the Rees. That coon's worth more when it comes ter Rees than this child."

At a nod from Henri, Green handed a tin plate to the patroon. Henri heaped it with breakfast and handed it in turn to Travis. Beyond them, the *engagés* ate by their fires, glancing curiously at the booshway's tent and muttering among themselves. Word traveled fast. Even hardened boatmen got a mite owly knowing that Indians had sneaked through their camp and stolen horses.

"A week," Travis promised reluctantly as he piled into the food. Between chews, he added, "Dick and me, we'll be back afore ye reaches the Mandan."

"You sure you want to take that pilgrim?" Henri asked. "He will be useless! A burden to you out in the prairie."

"You're wasting your breath," Green growled around a mouthful. "Travis still figures he can make a man outa the Doodle."

"Ye'd a never figgered he'd a whupped up on old Trudeau," Travis reminded Green, a twinkle in his blue eyes.

Green stabbed out with a blunt finger. "And we'd a still

had the hosses if he and Trudeau hadn't tangled. Trudeau checks the horse guards each night, and sets the watches."

"Maybe." Travis cocked his head and spat into the fire. "'Course, if these is Crow, they mighta lifted the hosses no matter what. Ain't no better hoss thieves in the world than Crow."

Travis wolfed his breakfast and stood. He tossed off the last of the steaming coffee and dropped his cup into his possibles. "We'd best be hightailing after them red bastards. I told Willow ter stick close ter ye and Baptiste."

"I'll see that she's safe. God knows, she's worth her weight in furs to us." He paused, "Oh, and Travis, be careful. Watch your hair out there."

"Watch yourn," Travis responded, turning and walking away with a hunter's quick step.

"What do you think?" Green propped his blocky jaw on the palm of his hand.

"I think I will not sleep until he return, booshway," Henri answered. "Baptiste, he ees good man, but none scouts like Travis Hartman."

"Nope. I reckon not. I just hope no one gets killed because of this foolishness." And God help them all if the army caught them clear up here without a permit.

The sun had barely crested the irregular horizon; nevertheless, Richard's muscles complained it was time to rest. Looking back, he could see the line of trees carpeting the bottom land on either side of the muddy brown Missouri.

Chest heaving, he trotted to the top of the rise and broke out onto the rolling flats with their waving stands of tall bluestem grass and hidden patches of prickly pear.

Each deep breath made him wonder if his ribs were splintered. Scabs cracked when he flexed his battered knuckles. Ugly bruises mottled the flesh on his arms and hips. His face hurt; one eye had swollen almost closed. He reached up with his free hand, prodding at the tender flesh. A year ago, back in the warm safety of Boston, the idea of brawling would have sickened him.

How far have I come from that day in my father's office? Who am I now? He'd won that fight with burly Trudeau. A strange spark of pride burned brightly within him. That old rational Richard would have despised him for it.

I beat a man bloody. Was that really me who tried to claw his eyes out? Richard could still remember the rubbery feel of Trudeau's ear clamped in his teeth. He could still taste the man's salty blood.

I was a gentleman once. A scholar, a student of philosophy. So much of him had died since that cold day in January when his father sent him west.

And what a mess I've made of it since then. He'd been robbed, sold upriver by a murderous boatman named François. He'd worked like a common ox, become the animal he'd once accused François of being. He'd killed the young Pawnee, Packrat, to save Willow. And, for her sake, he'd beaten Trudeau in a fair fight. Travis had taught him how to brawl like that. Travis had taught him so many things. But to run down stolen horses? That defied even his wildest imagination.

His lungs had begun to burn, his legs to tremble.

"Rest!" Richard called at Travis's retreating back.

The hunter slowed, shooting a glance over his shoulder. "C'mon, Dick. Them coons got nigh ter five hours head start on us. Hell, we's just started. Ye ain't a gonna let an old man like me outrun ye?"

Richard stared down at the heavy Hawken rifle hanging from his right hand. "Old man? My arse!" And forced his weary legs into a trot.

Sweat dampened his collar and waist; his lungs were pulling deeply as he fell into the dogtrot adopted by Travis. The grass made shishing sounds as his moccasins beat through it.

Step by step, Richard closed the gap until he was running beside Travis. "This is crazy."

"How so?"

"We're gonna . . . run down horses . . . on foot?"

"Yep."

"But, Travis!"

"They's our hosses, ain't they?"

"A man on foot . . . can't any more run down . . . horses than—"

"If'n ye'd shut up, ye'd have a sight more puff fer running." And at that Travis lengthened his stride, outpacing Richard.

He's crazy! But Richard continued to force his legs into the rhythm of the endless trot.

Puffy white clouds littered the western horizon, gradually vanishing into a bright blue straight overhead. Meadowlarks hung from sunflower stalks and other tall weeds. The sun burned white and hot into Richard's back, hinting of the baking midday to come.

His mouth had gone dry, his throat raw. Still he plodded along, his feet pounding in the cadence set by Travis. Well, the hunter would tire soon and they'd take a rest. No one could maintain a pace like this for long.

His arm grew tired, and Richard shifted his rifle from one hand to the other. The aches and bruises from the blows Trudeau had given him still hurt, and running didn't help. If he had any consolation, it was that Trudeau didn't feel any better this morning.

A slow smile built. Hadn't Trudeau been a sight? His nose black-and-blue and bent, his bitten fingers swollen—and that shredded ear had looked like something dog-chewed.

Not that I look any better, with one eye swelled closed and a lip puffed up like a dead fish.

With his tongue, Richard prodded the loose tooth in the side of his mouth, and hoped it would firm up the way Travis had assured him it would.

The bottom of Richard's throat had begun to burn. Pants had turned into gasps. A pain stitched agony through his side.

"Travis?"

The hunter continued to trot onward, following the faint sign left by the horses.

Richard shifted the gun again, and pressed at his side as he slowed to a walk and bent double.

After what seemed an eternity, Travis threw a glance over his shoulder and stopped his headlong charge. Richard hobbled forward, gasping and wheezing as he rubbed the stitch in his side.

"Got a cramp?" Travis scowled, his full chest rising and falling.

"Yes. . . . Hurts."

"Hyar, now." Hartman laid his gun down, squinted, and grasped Richard's side. He squeezed hard, fingers digging deep.

Richard groaned at the way it hurt. "Damn! Easy there!"

"Thar ye be, coon. Mountain medicine. She'll run fer a ways again."

"Rest. We gotta rest."

"A while longer yet, lad." Travis scooped up his rifle and started off in that maddening trot.

Richard cursed under his breath, willing himself to follow. Surprisingly, the cramp was gone from his side.

Morning stretched into midday. Richard and Travis alternately walked and trotted, ever westward toward the endless line of the horizon. Eagles soared overhead, turning lazy circles in the sky. The shaggy gray buffalo wolves gave them a wide berth, keen yellow eyes wary as they panted from the heat. From time to time, jackrabbits shot out from underfoot to sail away in long leaps.

Had Boston really existed, or was it just a dream? He could remember his father's hard gray eyes that long-ago day, his remorseless words: "You will not be returning to the university."

If he said that to me today, I'd beat him the same way I did Trudeau! But that had been a different Richard Hamilton who had stood quaking before his tyrannical father.

Richard frowned as sweat trickled down his hot face. Had the old man been so wrong about him? *Was I really such a silly fool, locked away in my books and philosophy?*

What an arrogant boor he'd been, cloaked in lofty superiority, on that long trip to Saint Louis! Charles Eckhart, the Virginia planter, had tried to befriend him on the *Virgil* as the steamboat chugged down the Ohio and up the Mississippi to Saint Louis.

And I insulted him in return.

Nor had Eckhart been the only one. At Fort Massac, that filthy collection of hovels just above the mouth of the Ohio, Richard had called that human jackal, François, an animal. And for that, François had more than gotten even.

Richard stumbled and recovered. One foot ahead of the other. That's it. Just keep the stride. Step after step, foot after foot.

"C'mon, coon." Travis called. "Top o' the next rise!" Richard struggled up the long slope. "C'mon, coon! We're most of the way there!" And Richard gazed up wearily to see the next rise beckoning from the distant horizon.

But no matter how long he ran and stumbled and trotted, and walked, and ran again, the goal retreated—like the terrible curse of Tantalus.

No water, no spit in his dry mouth, his tongue half gagging him when he tried to swallow. His raw throat burned from the air he sucked in and blew out with each breath.

One foot ahead of the other. One, two, one, two, one, two . . . An endless litany.

The feeling was gone from his trembling legs. He had to use a staggering trot, or they'd go rubbery and limp under him.

One foot ahead of the other. One, two, one, two, one, two . . .

Richard slammed hard into the ground. For long moments he lay there, breath sawing in and out of his lungs. A ladybug climbed along the grass blade in front of his eyes.

Travis asked, "Hurt yerself?"

"Travis?"

"What happened?"

"Fell."

Travis turned his sweat-slick face up toward the sun, squinting in a manner that tightened the pattern of scars. "Reckon we'll catch our wind some, Dick."

Richard coughed, a rasp like splintered wood in his windpipe, then dropped his head face-first into the grass. As he lay panting, he slipped his fingers down to the fetish Travis had given him. The silky long black hair was supposed to bring luck, or so Travis had claimed. From a kind of skunk, Travis had told him. A sign of status.

I feel weak as a kitten. He'd give anything—even his fetish—for a drink of water.

"They's Crows all right," Travis said as his breathing recovered. "Saw a moccasin sign back by that anthill. One of them cussed coons stopped ter pee."

"Is it worth it?" Richard wondered.

"Wal, if'n a feller don't pee, he'll plumb leak all over hisself. So, I'd say—"

"The *horses,* damn it! Are they worth all this?"

"Whose hosses is they? Ours! Yers and mine, coon. Can't just up and let no thieving Crows steal yer hosses. Hell, them's a year's wages gone up in dust, Doodle."

I lost thirty thousand just as quick, and never thought twice about the money, only my life. "I'll buy you more horses."

"With what, coon? Lessen ye wants ter steal 'em from the Rees or Hidatsas up by Heart River. Trouble is, where'd ye hide 'em? Stealing Ree hosses, now, that's a coup feather fer yer hair fer sure, but the Hidatsas and Mandans, they's friends. That'd be poor bull, stealing from friends."

"How about Crow? We'll steal from them."

Travis had pulled a grass stem apart. "Now yer talking sense, lad. And, seeing as how we got us a bunch of Crows up ahead—with our hosses, to boot, by God—we'll just go a-stealing 'em back!"

"Oh, my God."

"C'mon, Dick. Since yer so keen on this, ye can lead the way." Travis gripped Richard's hand and tugged him up.

"Water, Travis. I swear to God . . . I've got to drink something. My throat . . ."

"Just up ahead, coon. Cain't drink till we gets thar, I'm thinking, unless ye can suck water outa a grass stem."

"Up . . ahead . . ." Richard squinted at the endless grass. He locked his legs to keep from falling.

"Yep, just up yonder," Travis said seriously. "C'mon, coon. Let's go. We'll walk a mite ter limber up yer legs. Gotta be fast, or them red varmints is gonna get plumb away."

"This is crazy!"

"That's what we're counting on. That them sneaking Crows think the same thing. If'n they don't, we ain't never gonna get them hosses back."

Richard balanced his rifle over his shoulder, plodding in Travis's tracks. Some of the sap had returned to his bones by the time Travis broke into that infuriating dogtrot, and he managed to pick up the rhythm again. One, two, one, two, one, two . . .

He fingered the fetish, stroking the long black hair as if it were a source of energy.

The afternoon sunlight slanted down out of the clear sky. Richard fell quite often now, each time staring stupidly at the grass.

"C'mon, coon," Travis's calm voice would call down from beyond the haze. Hands would help Richard to his feet, and he'd stagger on in misery.

Everything had a milky glaze to it, like a kind of dream. Voices echoed hollowly inside his head. At times, he was back in philosophy class at Harvard while Professor Ames lectured. Then, he'd hear Will Templeton, his best friend, tell a joke. Laura's gentle voice told him over and over again, "I'll be waiting for you, Richard."

Gone . . . all gone.

Phillip Hamilton's hawkish gray eyes burned in

Richard's rubbery recall. He could see his father's office clearly, hear the *tick-tock* of the ship's clock as he stood before his father's ornate desk. It might have been yesterday instead of last winter. The fire in the hearth crackled and popped, warm against the bone-chilling cold outside the Beacon Street house.

Phillip had sat in his overstuffed French chair, papers in his hands as he looked over his spectacles at Richard. He had asked, *"To what earthly use will you put this 'philosophy' of yours?"*

The question now festered and burned like cactus thorns in flesh.

The greatest blow had fallen later, at supper that evening. In the elegant dining room, Phillip had been devouring a turkey dinner, spearing the steaming meat with a silver fork and chewing mechanically. He raised his eyes and said, *"I've given thought to our earlier conversation. It has become startlingly clear to me that you have no understanding of the world. Therefore, travel is to be recommended."*

How Richard's heart had soared with notions of European cities, learned aristocrats, and cultured conversation.

". . . Your universe has been limited to this house, this city, and the university. A wide continent stretches out to the west of us. That untamed land is your future. . . ."

Dear God, if the old man could only have seen what would come of that statement.

A cough racked Richard's throat. Memories, like darting fish, slipped through the fingers of his mind. *Father . . . you've condemned me to Hell.*

What had he become in this Western inferno? A murderer, a beast of burden . . . a dockside brawler. His dry tongue mocked him with the salty taste of Trudeau's warm blood. They'd fought like dogs, gouged, stomped, and bit, until Richard had clamped a hand on Trudeau's throat. To keep the *engagé* from breaking loose, he'd sunk his teeth into Trudeau's ear, arching his back, heedless of the blood as he tried to rip it from the Frenchman's head.

Philosopher? Was that you, Richard John Charles Hamilton? Or the demonic actions of the animal you've become?

He'd fought for Willow, to protect her from Trudeau's rapacious lust. *And I won. She's . . . safe.*

Precious Willow with her soft skin and encompassing brown eyes—an infinity reposed there, reflected in her soul.

"Mirrors," he croaked. "Eyes . . . like mirrors."

"Ye talking about Willow again?" Travis asked gently. "Hole hyar. Watch yer step, coon. That's it."

One, two, one, two, one, two . . . one foot ahead of the other. Run . . . run . . . run . . .

TWO

◆

The criminal action, whereby the abstract individuality of the person posited for itself is at last realized, is null in and of itself. But in it the acting entity determines itself as rational, yet formally and only by itself, as a recognized law, has subsumed itself through the criminal action, and been at the same time subsumed under it. The manifested nullity of this action and the elaboration of this formal law through a subjective will *is revenge,* which, because it derives from the interest of the immediate, subjective personality, is at the same time only a new injury—and so on to infinity. This progress suspends itself equally in a third judgment which is disinterested: punishment.

—Georg Friedrich Wilhelm Hegel, *Encyclopedia of the Philosophical Sciences in Outline*

Boston was baking under the hot August sun. Had Phillip Hamilton cared to glance over his shoulder through the bay window, he would have noticed that even the trees in the Commons looked wilted. But Phillip's attention was centered on his big ledger book. There he tallied row after row of figures. His concentration was so complete that he didn't hear the knock. Jeffry, his black manservant, opened the office door and cleared his throat, asking, "Master Phillip?"

Phillip leaned back in his overstuffed French chair and made a face as he pulled his spectacles from his nose. He propped his quill in the ink bottle and sighed. "Beastly hot today. And beyond that, I swear, my eyes are getting worse. What on earth will I do when the numbers become too foggy to see any more?"

"Hire a secretary to read them for you, sir." Jeffry strode across the crimson carpet to stand before the ornately carved cherrywood desk. His dark fingers offered a dog-eared envelope, the paper smudged. "This just arrived, sir. A messenger brought it fresh from the harbor."

Jeffry laid the letter on the desk beside the big Bible and the English officer's button—Phillip's trophy from the fighting at Breed's Hill. His leg had been maimed that day, shot out from under him by an English ball.

Phillip picked up the envelope, squinting for a moment until he remembered his glasses and pinched them on his nose again.

In the light spilling through the bay window, he read: "Messr. Phillip Hamilton, Hamilton House, Beacon Street, Boston City, Mass." Phillip broke the seal and unfolded the paper, peering intently at the scrawled words. As he read, he whispered, "March 19, 1825, Saint Louis."

Dear Sir:

I wished to communicate to you that as of this date, I have received no word from your son, Messr. Richard Hamilton. Your agent, Messr. Charles Eckhart, has contacted me several times with information that Mr. Hamilton did indeed arrive safely in Saint Louis on the fifteenth of March on the steamboat Virgil, and did leave the vessel. His luggage was faithfully delivered to the Le Barras Hotel, along with several satchels of books. It is my unfortunate duty to inform you, sir, that neither your son, nor the banknotes which we agreed would be delivered to me at this address, have appeared as of the time of this writing. I have taken the liberty of waiting for several days before setting myself to pen this letter in hopes that some explanation might be found. Mr. Eckhart has been indefatigable in his efforts on your part, but, after consulting with the authorities, and given the paucity of news, we must conclude foul play in some manner.

It is with great distaste that I discharge this duty of informing you of your son's disappearance. Please rest assured that I shall endeavor with all of my resources to discover your son's situation and recover your monetary interests.

> Your Most Obdt. Servant,
> William Blackman.

Phillip stared at the letter, reading and rereading the terrible words.

"Dear Sweet Jesus. Did he run off with the money?" Phillip handed the letter to Jeffry and rapped his fingers on the desk, making the brass button dance.

Jeffry read the missive, then folded the paper. A pensive frown deepened on his face. "No, sir. Not Master Richard."

Defeat, like a barrel band, tightened in Phillip's chest until it ached with each beat of his heart. "Thirty thousand dollars, Jeffry. He could do a great many things with such wealth."

"The books, sir," Jeffry said. "Master Richard would never leave his books behind. Even, sir, if he could buy new ones."

Phillip closed his eyes, his right hand groping for his wife's Bible. He dragged it close—carelessly knocking the ledger to the floor—and clutched it to the pain in his chest. "Dear God in Heaven. Tell me he's run off . . . taken the money. Please, God, tell me that's the way it is."

Yes, run off. Say it's so, Richard. Write me a taunting letter. Tell me how you're spending my money. He tried to swallow down a fist-tight throat.

"Master Phillip? Are you all right, sir?"

All he could do was grip the Bible. "My God, Jeffry, what have I done?"

A hand steadied Richard's shoulder as the world started to spin.

"Easy," Travis soothed him. "Just a little further, coon. Night's coming. Water with it. Just hang on, Dick. Ye can make it."

"My name's . . . name's . . . Richard."

"Yep. If'n ye keeps 'er up, coon, I'll call ye Richard, Dick."

"Richard . . ." He staggered. The terrible sun burned his soul. And he was bulling forward, straight into it, until it

burned him. The roaring wind would blow his ashes back to the cool, wonderful river, where they would slip between Willow's fingers into the delightful water.

One foot ahead of the other. Run. Charge right into the sun. It would burn away the pain, sear the agony like acid.

"C'mon, coon. That's it. Yer making her, Dick. Ye can do her. That's it. Just a little further. Water's just up ahead." Travis's voice carried him onward, like a flame drawing a moth to its deadly tongues.

"The sun, going to burn . . ." He wobbled on his feet, propped up by Travis's quick hand.

"Easy, coon. One step ahead of t'other. That's it. Yer some, ye is, Dick. Ye've a lot of guts, and ye can do her."

"The sun . . ." How odd. It had gone flat on the bottom. He blinked, and it burned into the back of his eyelids.

"One, two, one, two . . ." Travis trotted alongside Richard, steadying him.

Richard coughed, panting, baffled. The sun grew ever more flat, mashing against the world, being sucked up by the distant black line of the horizon.

"C'mon, coon. Water's just up ahead. She'll drown yer fire, sure. Shining water, Dick. Cold, clear, bubbling wet and cool down yer gullet. All ye can drink."

"The sun's dying," he mumbled, stumbling to a walk. "Look—dying . . ."

"Yep. Sunset, she is," Travis answered. "C'mon, now. Let's hustle."

Richard pitched face-first into the dark grass. He just lay there, panting.

Tired . . . so tired . . . sleep now. His body felt feathery, light, as if it floated in a warm current . . .

I stand alone, naked, up to my knees in river water. On the bank above me, the trees sway and thrash as a violent wind tears through the branches. My hair is blown and tangled, my beard matted with filth. I look down at my arms, all smudged and dirty. My hands are bloody, my fingers tacky with it as it dries.

I seek Truth. It's all I've ever wanted.

But here I stand, naked and alone, my hands dripping with a young Pawnee warrior's blood. So much has changed that I no longer know myself. Overhead, clouds scud across the sky. Thunder rumbles.

Yes . . . the river tugs at me. Its soul ebbs and flows past my calves, the current eating the sand out from under my heels in an attempt to topple me. But I have already fallen. Blood drips from my fingers, the crimson droplets vanishing in the water as if they'd never been.

I wanted Truth because my mother died giving me life.

Once I was a student of philosophy. Now, in the murky water, I study my wavering reflection. I don't know this man who stares back at me.

I traveled aboard the steamboat *Virgil* from Pittsburgh to Saint Louis with thirty thousand dollars of banknotes, my philosophy books, and the knowledge of my own moral, spiritual, and intellectual superiority over the loutish frontiersmen.

The money was my father's, to be invested in the growing Sante Fe trade.

At Fort Massac, on the Ohio River, I encountered a man named François—a known cutthroat. He was more than just a thief and murderer. He had a sense of humor. He gave me the choice of signing a letter of indenture, bonding myself for two years of hard labor, or having my throat cut and my body dumped into the river.

I signed.

He sold the contract to Dave Green, who owns the keelboat *Maria*. Now, I am an animal, and François is a rich man.

I wanted Truth because my mother was dead, and my father blamed himself for her death.

I flex my fingers, still so shiny with blood. I was with Travis Hartman the day Packrat rode into camp. I'd stitched up a slice in Travis's side after he'd fought and killed Packrat's father, a Pawnee named Half Man. The hatred in Packrat's eyes sticks with me as surely as his blood on my fingers. He'd taken a slave, a Shoshoni woman called Heals Like A Willow—and she laughed at him just before he would have killed Travis and me.

Packrat turned to beat her, would have killed her before my eyes. That's when I shot him through the chest. So much blood. It pumped out of his body . . . and here it is warm, wet, and sticky on my hands.

Not long ago, a Sioux *wechashawakan*—a holy man—asked me, *"What are you?"*

I bend down and drag my bloody fingers through the water. Streaks of crimson mark their path. The river has become my universe. When I thirst, I drink from the river until the blood beating in my veins is river water. I walk its banks with the cordelle over my shoulder, or pole the *Maria* upstream, my back bent as my feet grip the cleats on the *passe avant*. River sounds fill my ears: the crystalline drips, and waves slapping the hull. Part of my soul belongs to the river.

I try to wash the blood from my hands, but it remains bright red, warm and wet. Does it stain my hands with murder—or salvation?

I saved Willow's life that day. Once, in a camp by the river, her face inches from mine, she looked into my eyes—into my very soul. I began to love her then, though I am promised to Laura Templeton.

I am a philosopher. I belong in Boston. One day I will marry Laura. I am saving myself for creamy white skin and golden blond tresses. I can't love a dark-skinned savage, an Indian woman of uncertain moral values. Willow had a husband once, bore him a child. So what if they're dead now?

From the corner of my eye, I catch movement in the shadows under the wind-lashed trees. A coyote stares out at me with pricked ears.

I look around, suddenly afraid. On the far bank, a wolf is watching me with knowing eyes.

I wanted Truth, because it could give me what my parents could not.

Coyote and Wolf frighten me. They have since the night *Maria* landed at the Sioux village of Wah-Menitu. We traded with the Sioux, and later, they gave us a feast. It shames me that I joined their dancing warriors, leaped and whooped like a savage. It was later that the hideous *wechashawakan*, Lightning Raven, caught me alone. According to the story, he once fought a monster that pierced his eye with poison. Lightning Raven plucked out his own eye and fed it to the monster, killing it with its own venom. However he lost his eye, only a scarred socket remains. But he'd seen inside me, talked inside my head like some living ghost.

"Will you be coyote or wolf?" The *wechashawakan*'s voice echoes in the corners of my mind. Coyote, or Wolf? And now they are both watching me. Coyote is to the east, in the direction of Boston, of my future as a professor of philosophy. My home is there, and so is Laura, with her golden hair and blue eyes.

And to the west lies the wilderness—and Wolf.

I drop to my knees, and warm water rushes around my waist. The river pulls against me. An eagle soars overhead, sunlight flashing from its wings.

I throw my head back and search the blue eternity of sky. Dear God, what do I do?

I close my eyes, and the words of Jean-Jacques Rousseau, Thomas Hobbes, and Immanuel Kant float past my ears. I have traveled into the wilderness, but I have not found Rousseau's man in nature to be pure. Kant's infallibility of pure reason is a lie. Nor do I believe Hegel's phenomenology any more. There is no evolution of intellectual life to a higher order—not in a natural system.

I wanted Truth because it promised me safety.

The flaw I have discovered in philosophical systems is that reality is always lurking in the shadows and slipping through the brush. Reality has never read philosophy.

Now I kneel in the river, looking back and forth between Wolf and Coyote.

Everything I once believed is washed away. I have looked

through philosophical Truth—and seen its horrible other side. I discovered it to be ephemeral.

My soul cries for an answer, but I have none.

The *wechashawakan* told me that the answers lie in the West, with Wolf. But in his vision, he saw me freezing in the snow. He did not know if I survived.

Truth was only illusion.

The *wechashawakan* told me that if I returned to the East, to Boston, and Laura, I would die empty. He said I would find my answers in the West, in the snow and cold.

Now, I hang my head and sink down into the water, terribly alone as the river swirls around my navel.

I wanted Truth. But with each step I take into the wilderness, I lose more and more of myself—of what I believed.

If I keep going, there will be nothing left.

I *must* cling to something. Or was my old life nothing more than a sham, a trick I played on myself? If all those things I believed in were false—who, or what, am I?

Looking down, I see that the water has washed away my flesh. Only my bones are left resting on the sandy bottom.

I open my mouth, but a skeleton cannot scream. The river hears only silence . . .

◆

"Dick?"

"Gone," Richard sighed as the voice penetrated the veils of fatigue.

"Got water, coon. Hyar now, open yer mouth."

Wetness trickled on the side of Richard's face.

"Aw, don't give up the ghost on this child. Hyar! C'mon, coon." Arms wrapped around Richard's shoulders, lifting him. "Hell, yer heavier than I figgered. Help me, coon. Stagger along."

Richard sagged limply in Travis's arms, content to be

dragged along like a sack of flour. When he fell again, it was to splat face-first into cold water.

It rushed into his nose and mouth, brought him to. He kicked and floundered, coughing and splashing so weakly he almost drowned before he could crawl back to shore. Lying there, half in and out of the water, he sucked the muddy stuff into his mouth, gulping.

"Enough," Travis ordered, twisting a fist in the collar of Richard's jacket and jerking him back. "Listen, Dick. Don't drink too much, too fast. It'll make ye plumb sick with the collywobbles, hear me?"

"Sick, yes." He bent down and drank some more, pulling back when his aching lungs demanded air.

"All right," Travis straightened, a dark blot against the starry sky. "Take yer time, Dick. I got ter go back and fetch up the rifles. Hear me? Don't you go chugging on that water!"

"I won't."

Richard drew deep breaths, then bent down, sucking the wondrous water into his mouth. The pungent, smoky taste of mud and humus barely slowed him as he swallowed another mouthful. He tried to spit out the grit, gave it up as hopeless, and crawled out into deeper water to drink more.

He was sitting on the bank, shivering, more asleep than awake, when Travis jabbed a relentless toe into his side. "How're ye doing, coon?"

The whining sound around his ears came from a cloud of mosquitoes that were swarming around him. For once, he didn't care. "I want to die, Travis."

"Yep, a feller always feels better with his belly full of water."

Travis settled beside him, and laid out the rifles. "If'n I'd a know'd I'd have ter carry yer gun as well as mine, I'd had ye leave her ahind." He rummaged in his possible sack. "Hyar's jerky, coon. We'd best eat all we can hold, then suck a heap more of this water."

"Where are we?"

"I'd say nigh to thirty miles west of the river. We made good time today. Do her again tomorrow, and we'll have her licked, I'd say."

"Tomorrow? Travis, I can't."

"Got to, Dick. Ain't no other way out hyar. Lessen ye wants ter head back on yer own."

Richard took a slab of the jerky, ripping it apart with his teeth, savoring the juices. He chewed for a while. "You really think we'll get the horses back?"

"Yep. I done this a time or two afore. Injuns, ye see, they don't figger a white man'll follow 'em out. I'll bet prime plews to poor, that these Crow is gonna slow down come sunset tomorrow, and we'll just sneak in and lift our hosses right back."

"And then?"

"We smoke fer the river, coon. Then she boils down ter a race. We gotta hope our hosses can get us ter the *Maria* afore the Crows can run us down. Now, I'm figgering these Crows is pretty nigh fizzled after running all the way ter the river, then beating hide hell-fer-leather back west. I figger we can push the hosses faster than they can foller."

"And if it don't . . . doesn't work?"

Travis chewed his jerky and shrugged. "Reckon it'll be Katy bar the door."

Heals Like A Willow stood at the edge of camp, gazing off into the western twilight. She leaned on the ax, a half-cut cottonwood log before her. Long white chips littered the grass at her feet. The warm wind rattled the cottonwood leaves and carried the scent of the dry plains beyond the river's uplands.

She closed her eyes and sent her soul flying out into that lavender sky. Where were they? How far away?

She let herself float, seeking, reaching out to touch Richard. If only he'd allowed her more intimacy so that her souls could know his. She'd been able to sense her husband in this manner. He'd never really believed her, just smiled with that warm indulgence when she told him.

Would Richard believe? Did it even matter?

She exhaled wearily, unable to sense him, unable to feel anything beyond an assurance that he was alive.

I'd know if he died. She nodded soberly to reassure herself. *Just as I knew the moment my husband's soul slipped from his body.*

What kind of a gift was that, to sense death? How much better it would be to sense and understand life.

"What say, Willow?" Baptiste asked from behind her.

She started, whirling, the ax swinging up into her hands with a familiar ease. Baptiste de Bourgmont was the strongest man she had ever known, with broad shoulders and arms like pine roots. He wore a white canvas shirt, fine buckskin pants, and tall moccasins. A wide-brimmed black felt hat covered his buffalo-wool hair, and shaded his obsidian eyes. At his belt hung a big knife, a possible sack, bullet pouch, and pistol. His rifle filled his right hand.

The first time she'd met Baptiste, she'd tried to rub the

rich black stain from his skin. Though stories circulated among the *Dukurika,* Baptiste was the first black man Willow had ever seen. She still caught herself studying with fascination his broad nose, the set of his lips, and the angle of his jaw.

Willow lowered her ax. "Baptiste, I didn't hear you."

He suppressed a smile at her reaction. "I'd say it be a right good thing you likes me. If'n I's Trudeau, you'd a split my head wide open with that thing."

"Trudeau might do better with a split head. Each half could argue with the other."

Baptiste chuckled again, the sound rich and deep. He scanned the western horizon with thoughtful eyes. "They ain't gonna be back fo' a while, child. Not with Crows to foller. I reckon we gonna be nigh to the Heart River afore they catches up. Don't pay to worry none, Travis'll bring him back. Worn thin, sure, but in one piece."

"What would it be like, to go to Boston?" She fingered the handle of the ax absently.

He made a face, stretching his broad lips. "Gal, don't go a thinking on it. You ain't white."

"You've been to Boston?"

"Nope. New Orleans, Natchez, Memphis, Saint Louis . . . they's enough. Boston wouldn't be no different. White folks marry white folks. Yor nothing but a nigger Injun to 'em, Willow." He paused, studying her from the corner of his eye. "Why? Dick done gone and asked you to go with him?"

"No." She shrugged. "I was just wondering."

He heard the sadness in her voice and reached out, placing an arm around her shoulders. "Trust old Baptiste, gal. You don't wants to go back there. Dick, I figger he's a hickory down deep. That means a good, solid man. But them other white folk back in the settlements, they cain't see past yor skin, Willow. Dick knows." He paused again. "He ain't been filling you with no stories, now, has he?"

She shook her head. "It's me, Baptiste. I just keep trying to find a way."

"Wal, maybe so he'll come ta his senses and see that the only shining place fo' a coon is out heah, away from them pious damn Christians back in the States." He cocked his head. "And, if'n he don't want you, I could sure take up living in a Snake lodge. Especially if'n someone like you was in it with me."

"You would hate me, Baptiste. Every time you saw the faraway look in my eyes, you would know I was with Richard. It would prick at you like a cactus thorn, and over time it would fester and sicken your soul."

"Aw, I knows that, Willow. I's just trying to ease your mind's all."

She patted the bulging muscles on his right arm. "You are a good man, Baptiste. You will be my friend forever."

He hugged her up under the hollow of his arm. "And yor mine. And ain't no damn white man can tell us otherwise. That's why you gots to believe me when I say you don't never want to go back there. They'll kill yor soul, Willow. That's what them whites do to anybody what ain't white."

"I think I already knew that."

He waved his other arm. "And fo' now, hell, Travis, he'll take good care of Dick. You'll see."

THREE

◇

And therefore philosophers, who tie themselves
to natural reason, suppose that a body can neither be generated nor destroyed, but only
that it may appear otherwise than
it did to us, that is, under different *species,* and consequently be
called by other names; so that
that which is now called man, may at
another time have the name of not-man; but
that which was once called body, can never be called not-
body. But it is manifest that all other accidents besides
magnitude or extension may be generated or destroyed;
as when a white thing is made black, the whiteness that
was in it perisheth, and the blackness that was not in it is
now generated.

—Thomas Hobbes, *Elements of Philosophy*

Richard's head snapped sideways. His ears rang, and
his skin prickled.

"What . . . what?"

"C'mon, ye damned yeller-livered Doodle! I said, *get
up!*"

Richard cried out as Travis twisted a handful of his hair
and pulled his head back.

From the corner of his blurry eye, Richard saw the hand
coming again, flinched just before it hit, and rocked under
the stinging impact. The crack might have been the discharge of a rifle. The world turned silver as his eyes teared.
Unforgiving hands pulled Richard to his feet.

"Leave me," he croaked from dry lips.

"Ter what?" Travis asked. "I ain't even sure the buzzards want ye."

"What happened?" Richard sagged against Travis and dragged a filthy sleeve across his blurry eyes. Damn, he ought to be drinking those tears instead of wiping them away.

"Passed out, coon. Yer water's gone dry's all. Happens. A feller dries out and plumb falls flat."

"And what if there isn't somebody to slap me awake?"

"Aw, ye'd a come to after dark. If'n ye had the sense God gave a grouse . . . Naw, ain't nothing dumber than a grouse. If'n ye had *any* sense, ye'd foller the drainage to water. Drainages always take ye to water. Leastways, they do in this country. Them basins way out west, I hear tell ye can foller one out inta the middle of a desert and die."

They were walking again, Richard hobbling on his painful feet, his legs shaking with each step. The sun hovered no more than two hands over the western horizon.

Dear Lord God, how can I keep this up? "Travis, I feel like I'm going to die."

"Good. Reckon so long as yer miserable, yer hanging on. It's when the whole shitaree gets blurry, warm, and fuzzy that yer arse is nigh to being wolfmeat."

"I could stand a little of that now. And maybe about three weeks of sleep in a big feather bed, with lots of cool fruit juice in a big, ice-filled pitcher. And Willow . . . Willow to pour it for me."

"Cain't take her to Boston, coon."

"And I can't go live like a Shoshoni, Travis. What's left?"

"Saint Loowee until it fills up with farmers. Then maybe the Platte. Hell, I don't know. Some fur post like Michili-mackinac. They got folks what reads books and got Injun wives to boot."

"My God, what kind of life is that?" Richard sucked at his tongue, trying to get enough spit to swallow—and gave it up as a poor hope. "Fur post? I want to be a professor of philosophy. Maybe . . . maybe in Europe."

"Take Willow to Europe?" Travis shook his head. "It'd kill her, coon. She's free out hyar. Her people's hyar. Yer asking her to cut her soul in half. And what? So ye goes to England. They'd treat her like a chained bear."

Blink as he might, he couldn't clear the haze from his vision. "What am I saying? I'm going to marry Laura. Laura Templeton. Will's sister—blond, blue eyes like a morning sky. A lady . . . delicate . . . pretty."

"Take my advice"—Travis pulled his hat off, wiped the sweat from his forehead, and crammed the hat back down until the brim shaded his eyes from the sinking sun—"and come with us ter the mouth of the Big Horn. Hole up with Willow fer the winter. Hell, come spring thaw ye might both be so sick of each other ye'll pack yer possibles and light out like Hell's a-fire just ter be shed of each other."

Richard shook his head to clear the sudden blurring, all of his defenses laid bare. "You mean just live with her? Like . . . like a man does with a wife? Travis, I can't. What would I ever tell Laura? That she wasn't the first? Travis, what sort of cad do you think I am?"

The hunter squinted at him. "Ye ain't never laid with a woman?"

"No! I told you." He squinted hard, struggling to keep his vision clear. "Pure . . . don't you see? I promised myself. Laura will be the first. We'll be able to learn from each other in an intimate sharing of chastity and virtue. A special . . . bond between us . . ."

"Painter crap," Travis said thickly. "I'd spit if'n I had any." He resettled the guns on his shoulders. "Willow's had a husband. Birthed a kid."

"I know. That's another reason I can't . . ." Richard frowned. "She's not, well, mine. Alone. Do you see?"

"I see a hellacious damn fool."

"What do you mean?" The thoughts were losing themselves in the hazy softness that rose around him. If he just concentrated, the thought would . . .

❖

Travis plodded along for another couple of steps after Dick collapsed like a limp bale of cotton, then stopped, holding a rifle balanced on each shoulder.

He made a face, sighed in the hot air, and turned back.

Richard lay on his side, glassy eyes half-open but vacant, one arm flopped into a patch of prickly pear.

"Wal, thank Hob it warn't a rattlesnake." Travis lowered the rifles and grabbed a handful of hair, twisting it painfully. A good hard slap brought Dick back. He blinked away the tears again and groaned.

"Coon, I reckon yer about on yer last legs fer today." Travis licked rough lips with a dry tongue, and scanned the endless grasslands. The horse tracks they followed led up to the ridgetop and disappeared over the other side. Probably to disappear over yet another ridgetop, and another, and so on clear to the Little Missouri.

Damnation, and I promised Dave I'd be gone no longer than a week. What if the Crow had outrun them? Could he really just turn back empty-handed?

"Travis?" Richard whispered, "I'll be all right. One step, then . . . then . . ."

"Another."

"Yeah." Richard groaned and lifted his arm. "Damn. Hurts."

"Ye fell inta the cactus, Dick." *Can't even hold his eyes still. Cuss it all, the kid's given about all he can. Hell. Get-*

ting right close, too. "Tell ye what. They's a ridgetop up yonder. Let's coon our way up there, take a look around. I'll figger where the Crows is, sneak down and lift the hosses, and come back and fetch ye."

Richard nodded, his cracked and swollen lips parted. "Help me up."

Travis hoisted him, then bent for the rifles. Cuss old Jake Hawken for making such a heavy piece of iron, but, by the Lord, it was as good a shooter as could be had, and tough enough that a feller could whack Old Ephraim across the snout and still shoot straight afterwards.

"C'mon, Dick," Travis whispered.

"You know," Richard croaked, "I'm sick to death of hearing you say that."

Not half as sick as I am of saying it. Just how far had they come, anyway? Step by step, they hobbled onward, any chance of trotting gone.

"Yer a game lad, Dick Hamilton, I'll say that fer ye."

Richard's forehead lined deeply as he puzzled on something. "I had thirty thousand dollars. I'd give it all up for another stream of water." A pause. "And rest."

"By Hob, I'd let ye, too," Travis agreed, balancing Richard on one side, the rifles on the other.

"Sorry, Travis," Richard whispered dryly. "I gave it all I had. Just ran out of . . ." He wavered, his head wobbly, and frowned again, searching for the thought.

"Don't make no apologies, Dick. I'm just about tuckered myself, and I been a-humping up and down these plains fer years now. Ye made a sprite try, yessiree."

"Dear Lord God, I'm tired."

"Me, too, Dick. Reckon we'll sleep on them hosses."

"Water'd set me right."

"Me, too, coon." Travis peered out into the yellow light of the sunset as they crested the hilltop. A mound of stone—an Injun cairn—marked the spot. The ones used as eagle traps had hollow centers where a warrior hid under a bait and grabbed a live eagle out of the air to pluck its feathers. Other piles of stone supported poles with spirit helper standards and prayers tied to the ends. Some were for seeking visions; a young man went there to fast, pray, and sing for four days. This one, old and fallen, covered by lichen and grown up in grass, might have been new when God made the world.

Richard sagged onto the rock pile while Travis took his bearings off the blood-red sun hanging bloated over the western horizon. Shading his eyes, Travis made out the black dots of buffalo grazing in the long draws leading westward. Down there, in the bottom, bur oak, buffaloberry, and plum bushes filled the draws. What caught and held his attention was the snaking line of cottonwoods in the valley bottom. And there, right down where the drainages all came together, a line of black dots moved into the trees.

Over such a distance, he couldn't be sure, but . . . the animals moved purposefully; and something about the silhouette was just different enough. Men on horses? Or antlered elk?

"Yer a damn fool child, Travis," he mumbled to himself. "Ain't no antlers on elk, not this time of year. All they got is velvet as long's a man's forearms."

A slow smile curled his cracked lips. "Dick? We got 'em, coon. And thar's water down thar, too. Enough to fill our bellies so full we'll piss fer hours."

❖

The cool darkness instilled a faint throb of life into Richard's numb body. He followed Hartman, grass whipping around his feet. Overhead, a million, million stars glittered and sparkled against the velvet blackness.

Once, just off to his right, a rattlesnake's *shiiiiish* of warning brought a start to his jumpy heart.

"Step wide of the cuss," Travis rasped. "Don't need ter set him off and rustle up the Crows. Just watch yer step. Whar ye gots one buzzworm, they's four or six more."

Richard squinted down at the tall grass, dark under the starlight. *Just watch your step? Oh, right enough!* He picked his way in what he hoped were steps inoffensive to anything with a rattlesnake nature.

Downhill was much easier than up, but still he teetered on the brink of falling—the floaty sensation of being cast adrift hovered with dreamlike certainty just at the edge of his conscious thoughts.

"How ye doing?" Travis asked.

"Stumbling along. Half asleep. Ready to fall on my face."

"Wal, at least I ain't having ter carry ye any more. Reckon that's a hair of improvement."

Richard rubbed his gritty eyes. The shakes were eating at his bones. His belly growled. "Travis?"

"What?"

"What do we do when we get down there?"

"Find a drink. Then we scout the Crow camp and fill our bellies. Cain't fight or think when a feller's this dry and hungry. Then we takes our hosses back and burns a shuck to the river."

Richard stumbled on until they passed into the protection

of the bur oaks. Travis wound through the dark trees, skirting patches of brush, and crossed the thickly grassed bottoms to a small, rush-filled stream. There, he dropped to his knees and flopped head-first into the narrow channel. Richard crawled up alongside and lowered his head to the cool flow, sucking down great gulps before coughing.

"Shhh! Ye want the whole valley wide awake?" Travis smacked him with a balled fist. "Drink slow, coon. Ain't ye larned nothing?"

Richard forced himself to suck up a mouthful of water at a time and hold it in his mouth before he swallowed it down. Travis finally pulled him back.

"Best fill our bellies. Hyar's the last of the jerky. Eat up, and we'll drink again."

They sat, backs to a cottonwood, alternately chewing on dried meat and then slipping off to drink.

Richard sighed as he felt life restore itself to his depleted body. "If Trudeau showed up now, he could kill me with one finger."

"Wal, he ain't hyar. And further, he'd a run off long past. Hell, he'd a barely made it up outa the river."

But I did. Richard chewed thoughtfully. What had he done over the last two days? For almost forty-eight hours, he'd run and trotted and walked and run some more. He'd pushed himself to the end of his endurance, and then found an extra bit to keep going.

"Swaller down, hoss," Travis said, standing. "Go suck up yer fill, and let's be getting on."

Richard got his drink, and reached for his rifle. "Thanks. You've carried it more than you should have."

Travis patted him on the shoulder, then turned and ghosted southward through the trees.

They nearly walked into the Crow camp. Only the white mare gave it away, looking straight at them. Richard's heart hammered, sudden fear tickling in his guts as he realized the dark forms in the grass at his feet were blanket-rolled Crow warriors.

Travis backed away slowly, Richard following until the scrubby oaks hid them again. The hunter leaned his mouth to Richard's ear. "I got this figgered. Wind's from the west. Foller me."

Step by step, they circled until the camp lay upwind. Travis whispered, "I'm going in fer the hosses. I want ye ter take cover ahint a tree. If'n anything happens, I'll holler out that they's surrounded, understand?"

"Yes, but what—"

"When I calls out, ye shout back. Now, peel yer ears, coon. The second ye calls, ye scoot over yonder about another fifteen or twenty paces. If I call again, ye changes yer voice and scoots again. Ye got ter go fast, and ye got ter go quiet 'cause we're making them think they're surrounded. Understand the plan?"

"I understand."

"Ye don't shoot! Not unless they've kilt me and are closing. Ye can always bluff with a loaded rifle."

"But, Travis—"

"Let's go." And he slipped away into the darkness.

Richard took a deep breath, wished he'd checked the priming on his rifle, and followed.

All it takes is one misstep, a snapped twig, and we'll be killed. If anything, the night had turned blacker as Travis walked out into the center of the Crow camp.

Richard settled behind the rough stump of a bur oak; fear tightened like a band in his chest. Swallowing hard, he lifted his rifle and propped it on the stump.

Travis looked like a black blot against the night-shadowed grass. An owl hooted, the call lonely. Richard's nerves pulled tighter than a cat-gut rope.

The horses shifted at Travis's approach, and Richard's

thumb caressed the curved cock with its leather-clamped flint.

Travis bent, his knife flashing as he cut the picket on one side. Then, as if it was the morning ritual, he cut the second side.

"Come on," Richard whispered as his fingers turned sweat-slick on the rifle.

Travis took a step and stopped. He seemed to wait forever. He took another step and stopped.

At this rate, it would be hours before they were far enough way to vault onto the animals' backs and flee.

Richard's lungs had gone tight, his bowels loose. He had to gulp to get enough air into his chest.

And then the Crow warrior sleeping to Richard's right grunted and stirred in his bedroll. The man growled to himself, unrolled from his blankets, and walked to the edge of the camp.

If my heart beats any harder, it'll split my ribs. How can Travis stand this? Richard had frozen like stone. Travis had crouched, no more than a black shadow among the animals.

The Crow warrior calmly unlaced his breechclout and yawned as he urinated into the grass. He barely gave the horses a glance as he found his blankets again, and resettled himself to sleep.

Richard's jaws ached, strained from clenching his teeth. His breathing, gone shallow for so long, slowly returned to normal.

Surrounded by Crow, Travis still hadn't moved. *Come on, man, we don't have all night!* Richard thumped his fist on his knotted thigh muscles. Travis Hartman must have nerves of steel to stand there so quietly.

The Crow warrior had evidently fallen back to sleep, because Travis made another small step.

A bead of hot sweat trickled down Richard's cheek.

FOUR

If now to this natural proclivity of men, to hurt each other, which they derive from their passions, but chiefly from a vain esteem of themselves, you add, the right of all to all, wherewith one by right invades, the other by right resists, and whence arise perpetual jealousies and suspicions on all hands, and how hard a thing it is to provide against an enemy invading us with an intention to oppress and ruin, though he come with a small number, and no great provision; it cannot be denied but that the natural state of men, before they entered into society, was a mere war, and that not simply, but a war of all men against all men.

—Thomas Hobbes, *Leviathan*

The midday sun beat down hot enough to cook an egg on a pan lid. Travis hunched on the back of his horse, his rifle propped across the animal's withers. As he and Richard rode east over the grassy plains, he gnawed on a prairie turnip to draw strength from the starchy root and keep some moisture in his mouth. He'd shown the haggard Richard how to recognize the plants, and they'd dug a mess of roots with their knives, but this late in the year the roots had gone woody and fibrous.

Travis kept glancing over his shoulder at their backtrail. Heat waves, like a silvered dream, shimmered across the waving grass. Weary as he was, vision could play tricks on a man. He blinked, rubbing his gravelly eyes.

I ain't sure, but this beaver's about done clear in. Every muscle ached, his feet burned from blisters and prickly pear thorns, and worst of all, his mind had dulled as though filled with cottonwood down.

"I still don't believe you walked the horses right out of that camp," Richard said woodenly. He sat his Pawnee mare like a limp bag of bones. Dark circles hung under his hollow eyes. With each step the horse took, Richard's head bobbed loosely.

"Wal, ya see, it's like this." Travis choked down a mouthful of root. "Them Crows now, they stole these hosses pretty slick, I'd say. I figgered ter be just a wee bit slicker. Hell, coon, ye can't just up and let 'em out-Injun ye."

Richard stifled a yawn. "I thought we were going to die when that warrior woke up. You don't know how close I came to shooting him down."

"Tarnal Hell! That would have cooked our goose plumb through. Didn't yer hear me tell ye ter keep yer shot till the last?"

"That's *why* I didn't shoot him."

Travis wiped at his mouth, satisfied that no black dots—the sort running humans would make—stood out on the backtrail. "He just got up, loosened his strings, shook out his pizzle, and made water. That notion comes on a man every now and then. So, what did I do?"

"You just *stood* there!"

"Yep. I hunched down in the hoss's shadow, that Crow did his pissing—and then I let him crawl right back inter his blankets."

"You waited half the night."

"Just long enough to hear his breathing go deep and even. Then I took a step, and waited, and took another. The lesson is, Dick, that a feller can get by with a lot if'n he'll take his time and use his noodle."

Travis pulled another of the fat roots from his possibles. With a thumbnail, he scraped most of the clotted dirt off the brown skin. "I reckon I'd a loved ter have been hid up in one of them bur oaks and heard the squalls when them coons woke up this morning."

Richard craned his neck to look backward. "Are they coming after us?"

"'Course they is. Hell, we stoled their damned hosses, didn't we?"

"But they were *our* horses to begin with!"

"T'ain't neither. They's the Pawnee's, and probably the Osage's afore that, and the Sioux's afore that, and hell, who knows, maybe the Crows' afore that. Hosses get a good go around out hyar."

"But the morality of ownership—"

"Haw! I knew ye was gonna up and philos'phy at me the moment ye got yer legs back! By God, Dick, glad ter see yer turning right pert again. Reckon I was getting plumb worried ye'd up and die on me, or maybe come down with the mountain fever or something."

"What are you talking about?"

"Why, Tarnal Hell, coon. It's nigh onto a whole week without philos'phy. I was scared ye was ailing."

"Oh, blessed Lord God!"

"Got religion, too? Yer pap'd be plumb proud . . . 'cept maybe about that thirty thousand dollars ye lost. Reckon that'd twist a coon's gout up something fierce." Travis cocked his head. "Wonder how old François's doing with all that money?"

Richard scowled at Travis. "Can we talk about something significant for once?"

"Ain't thirty thousand dollars significant?" He paused, getting no answer, and added, "Aw, some whore's probably cut his throat fer it by now." Travis chewed off another bite of the root. "How about Willow and ye? We never—"

"No! I want to talk about this horse stealing! I mean, these people have no moral foundations. They just steal and steal. It flies in the face of every convention of society, of . . . of civil order."

"Oh, they got lots of civil order. And, Dick, they don't steal—not from their own people. It's all right if'n I steal Crow hosses, 'cause they'll steal from me first chance they get. So long's no one gets caught, we'll do just fine. Wait and see. Hell, we'll probably meet up with those coons up ter the Big Horn and have us the dangdest . . ."

"Meet up with? You mean *these* Crow?"

"Reckon so. Hell, I got relations among the Crow."

"They'll kill us for what we've done. But, no—I mean, these are our horses. We were in the *right,* for God's sake!"

Travis waved him down, the half-eaten root in his hand. "Pay attention. I'm gonna larn ye this once. Got the wax outa yer ears? Good. Hyar's how she lays. Ye can steal from anybody ye wants to out hyar . . . so long as they ain't yer own people. Now, let's say ye go into a Mandan camp. You don't touch nothing unless someone gives it to ye. Ye don't *admire* nothing, because that beholds the owner to offer it to ye. Understand?"

"Yes, the rules of good manners are the same in Boston. Well, but for the offering part. And you're supposed to comment on nice things."

"Among some Injun folk that's generally a polite way of asking fer something. Don't tell a Mandan he's got a pretty wife. Not the way yer fixing to save yer pizzle fer a holy relic."

"I'm not—"

"So, ye don't steal nothing in a village, *but,* if'n ye's a-riding through the country and happens ter spot a village off in the distance, and yer not fixing ter go in and palaver, why, who'd notice a couple of hosses missing? 'Course, they's gonna try and chase ye down ter get 'em back. And when they do, the shooting starts."

"People get killed when guns go off." Richard glanced over his shoulder as if expecting mad Crow warriors.

"Yep. Unless ye talks yer way out of it. And sometimes ye can. Now, according ter the rules, the Crow took our hosses, we took them back. Each side admires the other's bravery and skill at lifting hosses."

"It's like a giant silly game!"

"Might be ye could call it that. Ain't all life nothing but a sort of game? A feller's just got ter know the rules, Dick."

"But you can still get shot."

Travis glanced sidelong at Richard—his head had bowed, half asleep, nodding with each step the horse took. "Ye can indeed. That's part of what makes it so all-fired interesting. This country out hyar ain't fer no puff-and-struts. Ye can be free, Dick. Be anything ye wants ter, so long's ye've the courage to back it up."

Richard jerked his head up, blinking and rubbing his eyes. "I think I've heard that speech before."

"Uh-huh. Now, what's this foolishness about being a virgin? Is that why yer staying so shy of Willow? Can't stand the thought of sticking yer pizzle in where some red coon's done stuck his?"

Richard gave him a bloodshot glare. "We've had this argument before, too."

"And I ain't never got no straight answer out of ye." Travis shook his head. "Wal, what in Tarnal Hell are ye in love with? The woman? Or what's atwixt her legs? God A'mighty, Dick, yer about the stupidest Doodle I ever seen! There's the two of ye, staring at each other like long-lost fawns, and yer so knotted up with this virgin bed shit ye can't see what's drying up right before yer eyes."

"It's not that!"

"Then what is it? Laura? Hell, she probably thinks yer dead by now. And just what's she a gonna think when she hears ye lost thirty thousand dollars and then vanished, huh?

Why, if'n it was me, I'd figger ye done skipped off ter Paris or London to live like a rich jasper, or something. And if'n ye's just up and robbed, I'd figger ye fer a stupid son of a bitch what couldn't be trusted. If'n I's as purty as ye say Laura is, I'd marry the next feller in line."

Richard's expression soured. "Don't, Travis. Don't even say it. I couldn't stand the thought of Thomas Hanson and her. Not . . . not like that."

"Thomas Hanson?"

"Another of my . . . well, friends. He's tall, muscular, with a nice smile and good family. But he uses people. He's a rake, if you know what I mean. The rumor is that he sees prostitutes. The thought of Laura and him . . ." Richard's head hung.

"Do tell? And ye mean ter say this Laura ain't smart enough ter know what sort of man he is? Hell, then she ain't worth shit herself."

"I *won't* have you talk about Laura that way. I intend to marry her."

"So? Is she a fool . . . or ain't she?"

Richard glared at him with eyes like red pits.

"Wal, I reckon she's from Boston, ain't she? And, if'n ye ain't willing to winter over with Willow, I can tell ye that Laura wouldn't be the only fool in that marriage."

Richard shook his head. "Travis, this isn't my country. I'm going back to Boston. When I get there, I'm going to teach philosophy. So, tell me. What would happen to Willow if I took her with me? Hmm? Wouldn't we be the talk of the town? Professor Hamilton and his little squaw? Can't you just imagine Willow attending ladies' teas? She eats with her fingers and wipes grease off her lips with her sleeve."

Travis glanced at the turnip in his fingers, then at the grease streaks on his sleeve, and lifted an eyebrow.

Richard's fist knotted. "They'd crucify her. And me."

"What about now? Ye've got time afore we reach the Yellerstone."

"What? Share her bed and then just up and leave her? What kind of man do you think I am? For me, lying with a woman is a commitment, Travis. A covenant, if you will. I'm not like you. I can't just *use* her and ride off like that. I'd be no better than Thomas Hanson."

Travis took a deep breath. "Nope. I reckon not. But seems ter me, ye've made all the decisions hyar. What's Willow say about all this? She's half, ain't she?"

"She knows it's impossible."

"Maybe she wants ye anyway. Ever think of that? Or have ye been so wrapped up in yer high and mighty Bible-thumping covenants that yer forgetting she might want all of ye fer the little time she's got?"

"I am a student of *philosophy*—not quaint Hebrew teachings as reinterpreted by transplanted Greeks. I am interested in the moral dimensions of life, *my* life." He paused. "You're disgusting."

Travis jerked a hard nod. "And I eat with my fingers, too. But now that ye've done throwed yer fit, maybe ye otta consider. Shoshoni have different notions about men and women. God made 'em to go together. Now, Willow's a grown woman. She knows what she's about, Dick. And I reckon that given the choice, she'd take yer Laura on head to head, and Devil take the hindmost."

Richard rode on in dejected silence, the hard set of his jaw reflecting his determination.

"Why're ye fighting so hard, Dick? Yer making yerself miserable."

Richard gave him a flinty look from the corner of his eye. "Because, Travis. Damn it, everything's slipping away from me! Don't you understand? Every time I turn around, someone wants to take something away from me!"

"Ain't no one—"

"Jesus Christ, Travis! It started the moment I set foot in my father's office in Boston. He took my studies away—sent me out here. In Saint Louis, I was robbed, beaten, tied up. August made me sign that damned indenture. You and Green have taken away my freedom to go where I want."

"But that ain't it, is it?" Travis chewed thoughtfully on his prairie turnip. It sure was stringy.

"No, it isn't! You've been mocking me for all of my beliefs. You want to destroy everything I believe in!"

"Wal, some of it's plumb silly, Dick. Like Injuns being some sort of red-skinned innocents. Or perhaps ye done fergot old Half Man trying ter split my head because ye asked him some questions about God and such?"

Richard slumped in the saddle. The anger fled just as quickly as it had come. "I just want you to stop picking at me." The haggard brown eyes had turned dull. "You don't know what it's like when everything you believed was wrong."

"Hell, maybe it ain't wrong everywhere. It's just wrong out hyar."

Richard lifted an eyebrow. "Then it's not Truth, Travis. Truth is just that—right everywhere. If I have learned anything from you, it's that life is nothing more than chaos, irresponsibility, and morality that shifts by the moment and one's present company."

"Yep, nope, and yep. Life's chaos, all right. And the way a feller acts depends on who he's with. But ye missed plumb center with that bit about responsibility. Cain't never duck that."

"But you would have me turn my back on Laura to gratify my baser instincts by bedding an Indian woman."

"Is that it? She's an Injun?"

Richard's eyes squinted painfully. "No . . . yes . . . I don't know. I'm tired, Travis, fit to fall over. I can't think now. My mind is turned to mush."

"Just tell me this. Do ye love this Laura?"

"Yes."

"And I know ye love Willow. Don't deny it, hoss. I seen it in yer eyes."

"I guess."

"Dick, hear me. Look around ye. Ain't nothing hyar but what the good Lord made. This is yer chance, boy. Ye've got an opportunity that other coons ain't gonna get. Freedom, hoss. No one ter judge ye but God. This hyar's the last chance fer a feller to live free afore the farmers come. Think, Dick. If'n ye wants ter love Willow, ye can. Hell, marry her, love her, have yer kids, and not a single scandalous whisper or cocked eye from the good pious folk.

"Don't ye see? Civilization's coming, and they's gonna ruin it all. Make it like back there." He waved randomly at the east. "But fer now, fer one shining time, it's yers, Dick. And hers, too. Don't throw it away because of what they believe back there in the East. Ye can rise above that, and I swear, ye'll never regret it."

Richard rubbed his puffy eyes and pursed his cracked lips before saying, "I don't know, Travis."

Travis nerved himself. "I did. Once. Loved, I mean. Married a Crow woman. Calf in the Moonlight was her name."

Richard straightened. "You? Married? What happened?"

Travis narrowed his eyes to keep from looking back into his memory. "She's dead. And ye otta think about that. A feller cain't see into the future. Use yer time wisely, Dick. Sometimes ye can think ye've got forever, and ye don't. It can creep up on a feller and snatch away all that's pure and fine and beautiful in his life. And when it's gone, all he's got left is the empty ache and the memories."

"You must have really loved her."

As if you'd know. Travis straightened his backbone, and gestured with his half-eaten root. "Time's the thing. This country, lad. I had me a vision, a dream. They'll kill it, just like they kilt every other thing. They'll come in with their ways, and there won't be no more coup. No more hoss thieving. Just their damn farms and laws and 'good' folk. Won't be no free niggers like Baptiste. No pretty women like Willow. No crafty coons like Wah-Menitu, or Big Yellow.

"Just ye wait. Come the preachers and farms, why, ye'll have to 'fess the line, then. Wear scratchy clothes, go ter church of a sabbath, and foller the white ways." Travis hawked and spat. "Poor bull if'n I ever heard it. This coon'd rather be wolfmeat."

"Do you really think it'll be that bad?"

"Worse. Ain't nobody so God-holy boring as a farmer. 'Cepting a whole passel of farmers."

"You make it sound like damnation and Hell."

"Yep." Travis squinted into the distance ahead at the patchwork of spots that darkened the far hills. "And this coon's just seen salvation start slipping over yonder hill."

Richard shaded his eyes with the flat of a hand. "Looks like . . . what *is* that?"

"Buffler, coon."

"Buffalo? But they're—good God, they're covering miles! I can't see the end of them."

"Yep. Kick up that old mare. Let's go weave us a trail that'll drive them cock-eyed Crows plumb crazy."

"What if the buffalo stampede?"

"Wal, Yankee Doodle, I hope ye can hang onto that hoss's mane and keep yer seat. Fall off in that mess, and ye'll be stomped inta dust." He glanced across at Hamilton. "Seems ter me it'd be a right shame ter die, and never know what ye had in Willow."

"You always have the answers, don't you?"

"Yep. And since I met ye, I've larned ter write my name. So, tell me, have ye larned anything?"

Willow's agile fingers tied the last knots in the net bag she'd been weaving. Made of slender willow twigs and red cedar bark, the fine mesh would hold most of the berries she'd dried.

"Nice work," Green said, coming to sit beside her on the front of the cargo box. He sighed, wiped the sweat from his blunt face, and stared up at the broiling sun before surveying the river. The water was running smoothly this morning, only the sucking swirls breaking the glossy brown surface. Reflections of the trees and the brassy sky wavered and bobbed with *Maria*'s progress.

On the shore, the *engagés* sang "*C'est l'aviron*" as they plodded along with the cordelle slung over their shoulders. Though a good bow-shot away, their voices carried clearly in counterpoint to the birdsong and rustling leaves in the cottonwoods.

"Thank you," she said, and smiled at her bag. "I learned knots as a little girl. Playing the string game. You know, a loop. With it you can make patterns in the fingers, and then another plucks it off into other patterns."

"We call it cat's cradle."

"Cat's cradle," she said, liking the words.

Green fidgeted, running his hand along the oak deck. He traced the wood's grain with callused fingertips. "I wish you weren't planning on leaving."

She gave him a sidelong glance. "Oh?"

"Well, you're still drying berries, storing jerked meat in your pack, sewing new soles on moccasins." He waggled his hand. "Making containers. And I see you staring off to the west every night before you go to sleep."

She hesitated, smoothing the tight knots. "I want to go home, Dave. I miss my people, my mountains. My souls are not whole here. I want to hear the wind in the trees, laugh with my family, dance, and play double-ball. So, I will go when Travis and Ritshard come back with horses. One is mine. Travis said so."

Green sank his teeth into his lower lip. After a while he said, "I wish you wouldn't. We're two days below the Mandans. This country here, a lot of Rees have come in, driven north after Leavenworth shot up the Arikara villages. West of here, the land's crawling with Crow, maybe Cheyenne hunting parties. You'd be safer with us. We'll get you back to your people. I've given my word."

She laid the netting in her lap and studied him. "I will tell my people about your trading post. I have promised this."

"What will you tell them?"

"The truth. That I think you are a good man, but that I don't know if your White man's things are good for the *Dukurika*. I will also tell them that whether it is you or another trader, the Whites are coming and these things must be dealt with."

He tilted his head back so that she could see the small lines at the corners of his sky blue eyes and thin lips. The sun glinted golden in his beard. "*If* you make it across all that country. So many things can happen to a woman alone. Hell, the Hidatsa love to take Snake women for slaves. There's storms, white bears, fires, lightning, a thousand things could happen. A party of Blackfeet could cross your tracks."

"On the river, your boat could sink, we could be ambushed by Rees, or lightning could kill me dead on your cargo box."

"It's that Yankee, isn't it? Richard."

She said nothing, gazing safely on the river.

"Hell, he's been trouble since I brought him aboard. There's other men besides him."

She caught the tone in his voice. "You?"

"Well . . . why not?"

She folded the netting in her lap. "I have seen the look in your eyes, Dave. I've seen how you watch me. Sometimes, it is as a man watches a woman he wants for his bed. At other times, I think you want me because I can help your trade. The one look I never see in your eyes is the look of the soul."

He grunted, propping his chin on a pulled-up knee. "Maybe with time. It takes a while for a man and woman to get used to each other. There are a lot of advantages to being a trader's wife. You'd never want, not for anything."

Except the soul's love. She chased away the memory of her husband's eyes and leaned back, bracing herself on her arms so the sun could warm her. His gaze kept straying to the thin leather where her dress conformed to the rounded curve of her breasts. A man was a man. "For most women, I think it wouldn't be so bad. For me . . . well, I think it would make us unhappy. You would grow tired of my questions. In the end, you would hate me."

"You know all this?"

"I've read your soul. All people have a desire, something inside them that makes them who they are."

"We call it passion."

"Passion? For you, passion is trade. You wish this post, and what it will get for you. You wish to be treated as an important man. One that chiefs will come to see, and the *engagés* look up to. You want men to know your name."

"I will have that—and you can share it with me, become part of it. That wouldn't be so bad, would it?"

"It's your way, Dave Green. The way *Tam Apo* has made for you. Some men must be warriors, some seek Power and visions. You look for something else, to be a booshway. And trade is the way you will get it."

He fingered his chin and cocked an eyebrow. "All right, you know so much about me, what do you think I really want?"

Do I tell him? "Dave, perhaps . . ."

"Please, tell me. I won't get mad."

She met his stare, looking past the startling blue in his eyes for a glimpse of the soul beneath. "You do not see yourself. You need other men's eyes to see for you. It is that reflection you want. As other men see you, so will you see yourself."

He snorted irritably and stood up. He started back toward where Henri gripped the steering oar, then turned, as suddenly contrite. "I'm sorry. I guess I asked, didn't I?"

She reached out and touched his leg. "That is why I would make you unhappy, Dave. You would ask, and I would tell you."

"Is that . . . I mean . . ."

"You are a good man. A man I would trust in hard times, and call my friend. Don't look hurt or angry. It is who you are, what *Tam Apo* meant for you to be. If no one followed your path, there would be no chiefs. I think you will be a very great trader, a most important man. For that you need a chief's woman, not Willow."

He scuffed the toe of his foot on the sun-bleached oak. "Yeah, I reckon. Tell me, are all Snake women like you? Can they all see souls?"

"No. Most are happy with themselves, with the way *Tam Apo* made them."

"And you're not?"

She shook her head. *How lonely you are, Willow.* Of all

the men she'd met, only Richard might have filled the hole emptied by her husband's death.

Green rocked back and forth. "Willow, I'm asking you. Please, don't go. Not yet. Not until we're closer. I can't make you a prisoner. But I'm asking, as a friend."

"I will think about it. But I must . . ."

At that moment, Baptiste came charging out of the trees, rifle in hand. He waved desperately, fringe swirling with the motion. "Pull up! Beach the boat!" Turning upstream, he shouted, "Fort up, boys! Rees is on us!"

FIVE

◇

Hereby it is manifest, that during the time men live without a common power to keep them all in awe, they are in that condition which is called war; and such a war, as if of every man, against every man. For war consisteth not in battle only, or the act of fighting; but in a tract of time, wherein the will to contend by battle is sufficiently known: and therefore the notion of *time,* is to be considered in the nature of war; as it is in the nature of weather. For as the nature of foul weather lieth not in a shower or two of rain; but in an inclination thereto of many days together: so the nature of war, consisteth not in actual fighting; but in the known disposition thereto.

—Thomas Hobbes, *Leviathan*

Henri!" Green barked. "Put in!"

The patroon leaned hard on the steering oar, nosing *Maria* toward the shore. The cordelle went slack as the *engagés* threw it down and bolted back down the bank.

Green jumped flat-footed to the bow, uncoiling the painter and slinging it toward Baptiste, who splashed into the mud, caught a coil with his free hand, and slogged shoreward through the shallows.

"Henri! Break out the guns!" Green was already scrambling back along the *passe avant.*

The boat's weight caught up with Baptiste several paces shy of the cottonwood he'd hoped to tie off on, and began to pull him inexorably backward as momentum lost the battle with the current.

Willow rose to her feet, heart racing. She scanned the trees, seeing shapes flit through the gaps. Baptiste's feet were sliding as his arms knotted and his face strained.

Wild whoops broke out in the trees. The war cries spurred the running *engagés* into panic. Henri cursed, struggling to steer. *Maria*'s bow slewed out toward the river.

"I can't hold it!" Baptiste screamed as the boat dragged him toward the water.

Green dived over the side, sloshing chest-deep toward shore.

"Merde!" Henri cursed. "We are helpless!"

Willow jumped down to the deck and pulled the Pawnee bow from her pack before slinging the quiver with its arrows over her shoulder.

Toussaint, Etienne, and Louis de Clerk arrived, panting, and caught up the painter as Green waded ashore. All added their weight to the wet rope.

The yells grew louder back in the trees—then came the boom of a rifle. A man screamed in terror.

"Willow!" Green cupped a hand and shouted. "Get the guns! Inside the cargo box!"

She tore along the cleated *passe avant,* and ducked down into the darkness. There, racked along the back wall, stood the line of muskets. She grabbed up two, and scrambled up the stairway.

They'd managed to snub the painter, but even as they tied the knot, terrified *engagés* were throwing themselves into the water, flailing for the boat.

Like shadows, the dust-brown bodies of Rees slipped among the gray-bolled trunks of the cottonwoods. Slivers of arrows glinted as they arched toward the struggling men. Another gunshot banged.

"Go!" Henri shouted. "Take the guns!" He pointed toward shore.

Willow took a deep breath and jumped into the hip-deep water as the *Maria* pulled tight. The mud slipped under her feet; she struggled for balance and to keep the guns dry. Teetering on the slippery gumbo, she almost fell backward at the last moment before stepping ashore.

Green—wet and mud-splattered—ran to meet her, taking one of the muskets. He quickly checked the priming and turned to draw a bead on the closest warrior. Smoke and fire spouted when the musket boomed.

Baptiste had retrieved his rifle, leveled it, and fired.

Toussaint took the second of Willow's guns and threw himself flat on the bank to shoot.

Willow fumbled for her bow, strung it, and slipped an arrow from the quiver. Scuttling forward, she took a position beside one of the thick cottonwoods.

The last of the *engagés* had rushed past, joining the thrashing melee in the water.

"Powder!" Green shouted as he waved his empty rifle. "Henri! We need powder and shot!"

Blessed Tam Apo, *am I going to die now?* Willow nocked an arrow, heart pounding. The Rees charged into the open, shrilling loudly, some firing rifles, others drawing their bows as they dashed to a stop, released their arrows, and charged on. How many? Ten? Twenty, at least.

A shot sounded from the boat, then another. One of the charging warriors pitched head-first into the grass.

Willow took her time, mouth dry, waiting for the right target. A young warrior sprinted headlong toward her, and Willow took her shot. The feathered shaft flew straight—right into the soft hollow under his ribs. The youth stumbled, dropping his gun and grabbing at the shaft as he cried out in disbelief.

She nocked another arrow.

Easy. Take your time. Tam Apo, *help me.* Her hands were shaking, legs trembling. Panting, she lifted her bow, drew, and shot too quickly; her arrow whistled past a warrior's shoulder.

Slow, now. You must aim. Be sure, Willow, or they will kill you. They might kill her anyway. But it would be a release, wouldn't it? The pain would be over.

She steadied herself. A song about *Pachee Goyo*, the Bald One, rose to her lips. As it had soothed her in childhood, so it soothed her now. She drew a bead on a muscular man who lifted a gun to shoot Green, and released, the action smooth. The arrow drove into the man's side and he screamed, gun discharging into the sky.

The blood of the Dukurika *runs in your veins, Willow. Show them. Husband! Come from the Spirit World. Help me! Steady my arm.*

She nocked another of the iron-tipped arrows, drawing the bowstring back to her cheek. *There! That one . . . all painted red.*

The bowstring twanged as the shaft flew home, catching the Ree low, in the soft spot above the genitals. He dropped to his knees, clawing at the wood.

Now, another.

She missed as a dodging warrior skipped out of harm's way.

A bullet whacked into the tree she hid behind, splintering bark. Willow nocked an arrow, drawing and searching for her target. A Ree warrior was pouring powder into the barrel of his gun, casting anxious glances her way as he spat a bullet into the muzzle and thumped the rifle butt down on the ground to seat the load.

Is that who shot at me? Willow shifted, sighting down the slim shaft. The warrior tapped powder into the pan and snapped the frisson shut, raising his fusee. Willow released, and the warrior screamed as he twisted out of the arrow's path.

Willow ducked back behind her tree, pulled another arrow from the quiver, nocked it, peered out from the other side as she took up the tension on the string.

He was stalking forward, a young man wearing a breechclout. Yellow paint streaked his cheeks, and a black line had been drawn down his forehead, along his nose, and over his lips and chin. A patchwork of burn scars covered his right arm. Excitement and fear shone in his black eyes as he lifted the trade gun.

Willow began to raise her bow, to draw . . . Too late. He was sighting down the barrel, squinting as she looked into his eye across the sights. That instant froze, eternally engraved in Willow's mind. The sounds of combat grew distant, oddly muted as she stared at her death.

He jerked and sagged in the instant before the fusee jetted fire-laced blue smoke. The boom mixed with a hissing rip as the ball cut air beside her. Willow stared, paralyzed, watching the warrior collapse onto his left side. His expression was disbelieving, his mouth rounded into an O, eyes wide as he slammed into the ground.

He floundered, trying to rise, then looked down at his leg, bent at an angle and spurting blood and meat where a ball had torn through.

In those long moments, Willow could only gape, as if there and not there.

She willed herself to draw the arrow back to her cheek, her hold wavering. Her body might have been a dream.

More from instinct than skill, she made the shot, her arrow driving deeply into the Ree's chest.

He flinched at the impact, mouth working silently as he clamped his eyes shut and tried to squirm away. One hand gripped the slim shaft, the other propped him. Then he looked into her eyes, his soul pleading with hers.

Willow swallowed hard, shook her head, and tore herself from the horror. Screams and shouts mixed with banging muskets. She plucked another arrow, and scuttled back around her tree.

Wounded Rees were hobbling away from the fighting, but here and there a man lay on the ground. She noted at least two *engagés* with feathered shafts, like oversized cactus spines, sticking from their bodies. Whimpers and frightened screams mixed with war cries and curses.

The breeze blew strands of hazy blue gunsmoke past the milling Rees. They hesitated—and Green saw his opportunity to charge forward, swinging his gun like a club. Another of the warriors jerked, head exploding, as Baptiste's rifle boomed.

Willow's last arrow grazed a warrior's back as he turned to flee.

From the corner of her eye, she caught sight of horses, two of them racing out of the trees, riders bent low, one screaming a howling war cry. *Travis!* He rode into the middle of the Rees, lowered the barrel of his Hawken, and blew a warrior's chest open. Richard cut right, having trouble keeping his seat on the bucking white mare. Taking a chance, he tried to slide off, but was piled on his rear. As he scrambled for his feet, she saw the arrow plunge like a silver streak into his back.

No! Tam Apo, not Ritshard! A cry built in Willow's throat as she dropped her bow and pulled the war club from her belt. In a dreamlike reality, she raced forward, shouting, "Ritshard!"

Richard had found his Hawken, and from a seated position, shot the warrior who rushed at him. Then he was on his feet, swinging his rifle at the Rees who closed around him.

A single warrior stopped, glanced at her, and then at Richard. He raised a short Nor'west gun, the stock studded with shining brass tacks. Pivoting on his heel, he made his choice and aimed at Richard.

Too far! Willow threw her club like a rabbit stick; the weapon—spiraling so slowly in the air—hung in her frantic vision like a thing alive. Then it thumped hollowly on the man's shoulder, bouncing up like a wounded bird and arcing into the grass.

The thunderous boom of the gun deadened her souls as she dived right, caught up the club, and rushed headlong. Sobs tore at her throat as she attacked the half-crouched warrior. His teeth were clamped, face twisted with pain. He jabbed at her with the smoking rifle. She danced to the side. He parried her whistling war club with a forearm, the impact snapping his bone.

Fury boiled within as she rose on tiptoes and swung the club again, and again, splintering the bones in his arms, crushing his face, skull, and throat.

In the corner of her vision, she saw Richard drop to his knees, an anguished expression on his pale face. She howled her rage through gritted teeth as she threw herself at a Ree who charged down on Richard with a raised tomahawk. The man saw her, slashing at her at the last minute. She blocked his first blow, barely blocked the second, and stumbled backward. His black eyes bored into hers as he lifted his hawk.

On impulse, Willow jabbed at his testicles, making him twist aside. She used a side-hand swing, as with the White man's ax. He leaped back, grinning at her, obsidian eyes sparkling with challenge. He jumped at her, feinted, and hammered her war club with an arm-numbing blow that staggered her. Like a cat, he pivoted, raising his hawk high—and a bullet hit him. She heard the meaty slap and snap of bone, watched his body jerk and collapse in a heap. He lay there, facedown in the grass. His feet slipped up and down, as if crawling, and his fingers opened and closed in the dusty grass. With each labored gasp, his lungs gurgled and rattled through the bullet holes torn in his chest wall. When he exhaled, frothy blood blew out the holes in crimson spray.

"We got 'em boys!" Travis shouted. "They's a-running, coons!"

Gasping for breath, Willow backed toward the groaning Richard, her club gripped tightly. She pulled back wild strands of hair and searched for another enemy. Her limbs shook. But the Rees had broken, fleeing back into the trees. Some carried wounded warriors, others tried to drag the dead—and gave it up as Travis whipped his ramrod from the barrel of his Hawken, primed the gun in one fluid motion, and shot one of the rescuers through the back.

As the last of them disappeared, Willow dropped her war club and crouched beside Richard. He was blinking at her, face blanched of all color. He reached up weakly, took her hand, and sighed. Then his eyes rolled up in his head and he collapsed.

"Don't die," she whispered in Shoshoni, easing him onto his side. The arrow had entered his back at an angle. During the fighting, it had snapped off just above his jacket. Willow pulled her knife and slit the heavy leather.

The iron point had cut a gash across his back and embedded in the ridge of the shoulder blade. She grimaced, steeled herself, and prodded the flesh around the arrow. The soft iron had bent when it lodged in the bone. Blood was welling up and dribbling down his back.

"Willow?" Travis leaned down beside her. His hat was gone, gray hair awry. The blue eyes gleamed with excitement, then dulled as he realized what she was doing. "Aw, damn. Not Dick!"

A gun banged behind them as Green shot a writhing warrior. The man jerked and fell limp. One of Willow's arrows stuck out of his groin.

She hunched her shoulders, stomach queasy. "Got to pull this arrow, Travis. It's stuck in the bone. He's . . . how you say? Out? No better time than now."

"Yep, all right."

"Hold him."

Travis rubbed his hands together and put a foot on Richard's arm. "Go fast, gal."

Willow set herself, fingers on the blood-slick shaft. She pulled slowly, harder, and still harder, watching Richard's shoulder move up and out under the bloody jacket.

"Son of a bitch," Travis growled. "Yank hard, gal."

Don't let it break. Willow threw her weight against the arrow, fingers slipping on the clotted blood.

Richard came to and bellowed with pain, his body jumping and jerking like a spitted frog's.

"Have ter cut," Travis said.

"Dear Lord God!" Richard cried out, chest heaving. "Hurts, oh God—oh God!" He swallowed hard, lungs heaving as sweat beaded and trickled.

Another gunshot split the air and a wounded Ree was dispatched. Willow closed her eyes, nodding. "I'll cut. Hold him."

"Baptiste? Anybody! Git yer arse over hyar!"

Willow barely noticed Toussaint as the big man came and clamped his thickly muscled arms around Richard. "Two are dead," Toussaint growled.

"Damn! Dick, she's gonna hurt like all hell," Travis whispered soothing tones into Richard's ear. "Ye ain't dying, child. Hear me? That point just stuck in the bone's all. Willow's gonna dig it out."

"Do it, Travis." Richard panted, eyes gone glassy.

Willow glanced down at the knife in her bloody hand. *His blood. My skill. Tam Apo? Can I do this? Is my Power strong enough?* She met Travis's questioning eyes and nodded.

"Hyar we go, coon. Hold on, Dick. Scream if'n ye got ter."

Willow sliced the skin around the shaft, and Richard made a gurgling sound deep in his throat.

"Sacré!" Toussaint hissed, looking away.

Willow used the tip of the knife like a digging stick, slipping down through the meat to the smooth iron of the bent arrowhead. Where it had driven into the bone, she used the knife to pry. Richard screamed and bucked.

"Be still, coon," Travis soothed.

Willow ground her teeth, eyes closed. *Don't think about it. You can't let yourself think. Just do it, Willow. No other choice.*

She pressed the knife deeper, levering the arrowhead loose from the bone. A blood-curdling shriek tore from Richard's throat.

Sinking back on her haunches, Willow lifted the arrow free, gazing at the clotted mess of bent iron. Sunlight gleamed on bright red blood.

"We're done, coon," Travis murmured, patting the limp Richard. "Yer fine." To Toussaint, he said, "Get pressure on that hole. We got ter stop that bleeding *beaucoup rapide.*"

Willow gulped air, the world around her in extraordinary, perfect focus. Sweat trickled down her skin, and she barely heard the buzzing of the big black flies that came at the first hint of blood. "Spirit water," she said. "Travis. Bring some."

"Fer his wound."

She nodded. "Yes. You know how to tie it up tight?"

"Yep, I know." The hunter stood. "Hell, whiskey's ter be poured inta a coon, not on him."

"It healed you."

"Aw, I remember." Travis gave her a measuring stare.

"Willow?" Green called. "If you're done there, I got another one over here."

She bent down, running a bloody finger along Richard's perspiring jaw. In *Dukurika,* she said, "Live for me, Ritshard. Live."

Standing, she drew a deep breath, and started across the war ground toward Etienne, who grimaced over an arrow transfixing his thigh. Behind him sat Trudeau, blood streaming in sheets down one side of his head. As she passed, she glared her hatred at the dead Rees—especially the ones with her arrows sticking in them.

◆

Travis winced as Willow dribbled whiskey on Dick's wound. He glanced at Dave Green, who stood nearby with his arms crossed. Green's blunt face betrayed his disapproval of the waste. Whiskey was a valuable commodity, not to be squandered on foolishness like wounds, but Willow insisted. If it made her happy and kept her with the boat, Dave would probably have agreed to dump it into the river.

Richard moaned and hunched as the sting brought him out of his delirium.

"Shhh!" Willow said as she bent over him. "Easy, Rit-

shard. The spirit water will burn the evil out of your body."
Then she sang to him, the soft Shoshoni song lulling him.

"Pretty bad," Green muttered. "I've seen wounds like that
turn sour and kill a man."

"Wal, 't'ain't festering yet," Travis noted.

"Hell of a waste of good whiskey," Green growled under
his breath.

The grassy bank slid past as the *engagés* poled *Maria*
against the current. "Two dead, three wounded. Could'a
been a sight worse, Dave. All considered, we been damn
lucky so far."

"Baptiste says there's more Rees up ahead." Green fingered his square chin. "They're watching, you know. Waiting."

Travis narrowed an eye, thinking of the tension among
the *engagés* as they plodded down the *passe avant* behind
their poles. They didn't sing today. They were dwelling on
the two graves they left behind.

Willow sighed and stood up, her gaze on Richard. Her
expression had softened, betraying the ache in her heart.
Travis bit his lip, thinking back, remembering the last time
a woman had looked at him with such love in her eyes.

*No, coon. Forget. Leave the dead buried. Your time for
love is past.*

Willow had turned to Etienne. He lay beside Dick, his leg
bare to expose the ugly hole cut through his thigh by a Ree
arrow. Trudeau sat behind, his back propped against the
cargo box. Willow had sewed his scalp closed where a knife
had laid it open.

"What if ye hadn't turned 'em back?" Travis asked suddenly. "Remember what happened to William Ashley back
in twenty-three?"

"Yes, yes, but that didn't stop him. He took off west with
what was left of his brigade. Travis, Ashley's been out trapping, making plews. We've got to reach the Yellowstone,

establish ourselves at the mouth of the Big Horn. The time is now, or Ashley will have it all."

"If'n he's still alive." Travis chewed his lip. A coldness washed his soul. "Remember that dream I told ye about? The one where Immel and Jones come ter me? Warned me off from going ter the mouth of the Big Horn? Set the colly-wobbles ter this child's bones, it did." He remembered the look in Michael Immel's eyes, so mournful and sad. He and Jones had been killed by the cussed Blackfeet—just up from the mouth of the Big Horn.

"You were wounded, Travis. The fever comes on a man, makes him see lots of nonsensical things." Green placed a hand on his shoulder. "You're not losing your nerve, are you?"

"Hell, no!" Travis brushed off the offending hand and glared. "But in this country, a coon's got ter think. Stop thinking, stop being wary as a lamb in the lion's den, and yer gone beaver. That fight with the Rees, it could'a been a heap worse, ye know. Boats can be swarmed."

Green lifted an eyebrow. "I won't let them have it, Travis. I worked too hard for this."

"What are ye thinking, Dave? I know that slit-eyed stare, and it's plumb shore yer a thinkin' about being bullheaded, or this coon don't read sign."

"I was remembering the *Tonquin*."

"Tarnal Hell, ye wouldn't!"

"Oh, indeed I would, Travis. You know the story?"

"Who don't? Jacob Astor sent the *Tonquin* 'round the Horn to the mouth of the Columbia to meet up with Stuart's Astorians. That Captain, Thorn, got too high an' mighty with the Injuns, and they swarmed the ship. Story is that after the Injuns kilt most of the crew, some coon set off the powder and blew the whole shitaree to hell." Travis shook himself.

Willow straightened from examining Etienne's leg and walked over. "He will be fine. I think he can walk in another couple of days." But worry reflected in her eyes when she glanced at Richard.

Green took a deep breath, shaking his dour thoughts. "Well, at least you're safe. Willow, thank you for your help." He gave her a sheepish grin. "I don't know what we'd have done without you."

"And maybe it's put an end to this foolishness of traipsing off fer the mountains," Travis growled.

Willow stepped past them, her long hair catching the sunlight. She sat herself on the deck, back braced on the cargo box as far as she could get from Trudeau.

Travis settled beside her and manfully avoided staring at the smooth brown leg exposed below the hem of her hide dress.

She sat silently for a while, eyes unfocused. Green stood uncertainly, thumbs stuck in his belt as he rocked back and forth.

"This isn't my place," she said simply. "By now people will have realized that I am missing. They'll be worried. My aunt, Two Half Moons, told me not to travel in the winter."

"We'll take you to your people," Green promised.

Travis caught the tightening around the corners of her mouth and asked, "Why'd ye take the chance?"

Willow shrugged. "My husband's brother, White Hail, wanted to marry me. So did Fast Black Horse, one of the important warriors among the *Ku'chendikani.*"

"Among the Snakes, ain't it accepted that a man marry his dead brother's wife?"

Willow nodded. "Yes. But I did not want White Hail for a husband. I will always love him, but as *teci,* a brother—not as *kuhappi,* a husband. I knew him as a happy young man, brave to the point of foolishness. I would have soured the happiness that now dances between his souls."

"How's that?" Green asked.

She gave him a measuring glance. "Like a hide wrapped around his head, I would have smothered him. Besides, I would have been a second wife—and I can tell you, his first wife, Red Calf, hated me. To marry White Hail would have caused much trouble. I suppose that now I could have dealt with it. But not then, not with my souls hurt and grieving over my husband's death. There are times to fight—and times to leave. That was a time to leave." She smiled wryly. "I usually know when to leave."

Travis asked, "And this Two Half Moons? She wouldn't have stood up for ye?"

A bitter smile crossed her lips. "People are people everywhere. Packrat took me to give to his father—to pay him back for an old wrong. My people are no better than the Pawnee. Red Calf would have made me miserable." She paused. "I fear she will drive poor White Hail to his death as it is. I couldn't stay in my husband's village and watch that happen."

"It doesn't sound like you've got a lot to go back to." Green lifted a blond eyebrow.

Willow said, "Oh, but I do. I miss my mountains, the colors of the earth, the smell of the wind. And I have my father, mother, and family. My souls are dry and wilted, like poor plants under a summer sun. The plant is made well with rain, and my souls will become healthy again when I can dance the Father Dance with my family."

Green smacked his hands together. "Well, if it's dancing you need, we can—"

"Dave, I *need* the high places, to be able to see forever and reach for the sky." The longing grew in her voice. "Way up in the mountains there is a tall rock that stands up like a peg. The sides are sheer, but the top is flat. When I was a little girl, I climbed to the top and saw the world as Eagle sees it. Power filled me there, changed my life. I want to climb that rock again and reach up. Perhaps . . . just maybe, I can touch *Tam Apo* and . . ." She gazed up at the sky.

"And what?" Travis asked gently.

"Heal myself," she whispered.

SIX

Morality requires nothing except that freedom should not contradict it, and also that, although we may be unable to understand it we should at least be able to think of it, for there is no reason why freedom should interfere with the natural mechanism of the moral act, even if taken in a different sense. The doctrine of morality may very well hold its place, and the doctrine of nature may hold its place, too. This would have been impossible if our critical examination had not previously taught us about our inevitable ignorance with regard to things in themselves, and limited everything that we can know in theory to mere appearances.

—Immanual Kant, *Critique of Pure Reason*

W*ho have I become?* Richard lay on *Maria*'s hard oak deck, his blanket the only padding. A soul-burning pain lanced his shoulder. Etienne lay next to him, and beyond that, Trudeau sat propped against the cargo box, a bloody rag wrapped around his head. Despite Willow's stitches, the scar would be a beauty.

Images spun through his mind: Travis fighting for his life with the Pawnee warrior, Half Man. *My fault. I gave Half Man the opening he needed to try and brain Travis.* The Pawnee had feinted at Richard and swung his rifle butt at Travis. Then they had fought there in the grass, battering each other like two animals. In the end, Travis had killed Half Man, his side sliced open by the Pawnee's knife in the process.

I sewed him up. I, Richard Hamilton, gentleman-philoso-

pher, ran a needle and thread through his bloody flesh. He could remember the way the needle had dimpled the skin, the resistance as he pulled thread through living tissue.

Then, as if in a nightmare, Packrat had ridden into the little valley in search of Half Man—and found his father dead. Willow had been with him—a bound slave—a gift for Half Man.

Packrat's eyes had hardened, reading the story in the bloody ground, seeing the tins of whiskey. He'd nocked an arrow in his bow, a killing rage in his eyes as he pulled back to kill Travis.

Then Willow laughed—and Packrat went insane, grabbing his war club, striking at Willow. She'd fallen from her horse, and Packrat had leaped off his mount in pursuit.

Richard winced, recalling his fright. He'd picked up Half Man's trade gun. Out of instinct, he'd fired, the shot blowing a hole through Packrat's chest.

With vivid memory, Richard watched Packrat's body fall limply. Saw the disbelief reflected in his shocked eyes. Blood. So much blood.

Richard clamped his eyes tight, as if to squeeze the vision from his mind. *I killed him. Just as I killed the Ree warriors. What have I become? Is sanity gone from the earth?*

This land was so different from Boston. Here the meaning of death had changed. By killing, he had saved Willow from slavery—saved the boat and the *engagés* from the Ree. What was right any more?

Richard shifted, the pain in his shoulder making him gasp. Thought-numbing pain. He'd spent the last couple of days in a haze of misery and bleary dreams.

But I'm alive.

The unlucky ones had been August Torme and Vincent Saint-Michel. They now lay buried in two shallow graves back at the battle site. If the coyotes didn't dig them out, the current would eventually undercut the bank and topple their bones into the river. As *voyageurs,* perhaps they wanted to be there anyway.

The fight had given birth to a grim determination in the crew that Richard hadn't seen before. Now the *Maria* was snugged to the bank by her painter, the *engagés* ashore cooking the evening meal. The breeze blowing down from the north eased some of the torment caused by the clouds of mosquitoes.

As he lay belly-down on the hard oak, hazy images slipped around behind Richard's closed eyelids: the scene on the riverbank as he and Travis rode in; the popping guns; arrows hissing through the air; and the screams of men in mortal combat. He remembered his mare going crazy, his falling off . . . and the angry pain in his shoulder.

He'd fumbled for the rifle, lifting it, setting the trigger and shooting the Indian who came rushing down like a wrathful demon to kill him. It remained so vivid: The gun's concussion; blue smoke billowing; and the Indian falling away, mouth open, eyes wide with shock.

He'd seen Travis shoot and bellow, crack a head with his Hawken barrel.

So I got up and fought. He remembered the Rees circling, trying to get close enough for coup before they killed him. He'd broken one skull with the heavy rifle barrel, blocked a blow, driven the barrel into another man's face, stepped back, and knocked the teeth out of another man's mouth with the rifle butt.

Then what? He frowned, unwilling to take a deep breath. Filling his lungs turned the throbbing ache into soul-numbing agony.

Then what? Come on, Richard. You were there.

Things seemed to blur. *I fell . . . no, dropped to my knees, the gun . . . so heavy . . .*

. . . And Willow, standing over him, her bloody war club raised to protect him. Yes, that was it. The image had burned into his brain: her leather dress, wet, clinging like a second skin. Blood on her hands, spattered on her face in a freckled pattern. Her hair tumbled around her in wild raven strands. She might have been one of the Greek Furies, teeth bared in her beautiful face as she dared anyone to challenge her.

"You were magnificent," he whispered, savoring the image. "Magnificent."

"Thank ye, coon. I figgered that meself."

"Travis?" Richard started, only to have the pain drop him flat. "Damn!" God, that hurt.

"Ain't every day I get called magnificent."

Richard lifted a weary eyelid to see the hunter settling himself cross-legged and, from a leather sack, dumping out little piles of bloody hide, all bearing long black hair. Fetishes?

"How're ye feeling, coon?"

Richard closed his eye and sank into the anonymous darkness. "I think I'm ready to die, Travis. No more fights, no thirst, no running for days on end. The dead can rest— and by all-merciful God, I've never been so damned tired in all my life."

"Yer a game one, ye is. The way we figgered it, ye kilt three Rees back there. Not so good as Willow, she plumb made 'em come, she did. Now, them's some doings, but then she just ain't any old squaw, neither."

"That's a double negative."

"A duh . . . huh?"

"Double negative. Two no's cancel each other in a sentence."

"Hot damn, yer feeling better!"

"Go away and let me die."

"Cain't. Willow's been a-doctoring ye. She's got ye trussed up like a hog fit fer butchering. And ye otta heard the row she and Green got inter over the whiskey. Green told her no more whiskey, and she like ter lit inta him worse than them Rees did."

"What?"

"Oh, it ain't the way she's using it—though Green and me, we figger whiskey goes in a coon instead of on him—but how much she's using. Why, that gal pours a half a gill on yer shoulder each time she fools with that binding on yer wound. Cuss me if'n I ain't sure it's helping. Ain't a lick of fever in there, and it's healing right pert."

Richard sighed wearily. "You're not the one getting it poured on you. Firewater's right. I'd rather be shot again."

"Reckon ye ain't fergot her digging that arrow outa yer back?"

Richard blinked. "Arrow?"

Travis pointed at him with the knife he was using to scrape the fetish. "Who do ye think carved that arrow outa yer back? Willow, that's who. And she done a plumb fine job of her. Hell, I looked at that arrowhead. Took three of us—and one being Toussaint—ter dig that out. Made a hell of a hole. Now, if'n Green or me'd a done it, I'd figger ye five-ter-one fer wolfmeat by now."

Richard rubbed his cheek against the scratchy wool of his blanket. "Anyone ever tell you you talk too much?"

"If'n it was anyone, it was Baptiste or ye." The rasping sound of the knife continued.

"Willow saved me?"

"Reckon so, coon. Henri saw most of it. Said one of them Rees was gonna shoot yer lights out, and she throwed her war club. Made it shine, she did. Bounced it right off the coon's back and ruined his shot. Then she scooped it up quick like and whacked that coon down dead. Then she fought with another one until I shot a galena pill inta his lights. After that, she stood over ye like a she bear over a cub."

Richard swallowed, wincing. Breathing hurt. Swallowing hurt. He could move his feet, a little, but that hurt, too.

Richard carefully extended his chin, wishing he could lie any way but on his belly. "More fetishes? Those look pretty fresh, like they . . ."

It all came clear.

"Yep. Fresh batch of skunks."

"You *son of a bitch!*"

"If that don't beat all hell? I was plumb magnificent a moment ago." Travis continued to stare down his nose as he scraped human hide with the edge of his knife.

"*Damn you!* I've been wearing a man's scalp on my belt? Why'd you do that to me? To humiliate me!"

"Nope."

"You *knew* how I'd feel about it!"

"Yep."

"Why, Travis?"

"Why? Oh, I reckon I'd never seen a philos'pher with a coup tied on him."

"So, you had your joke?"

"Wal, Dick, ye just kind of set yerself up fer it. Get where my stick floats? All that jawboning about being a gentleman. Made it right interesting ter hear yer hammering on about Kant and Plato—and all the while Packrat's hair was a swinging from yer belt."

Baptiste came up from behind. "How's the sick doing?"

"Hamilton, hyar, he's figgered out about the coup."

"I'm not laughing," Richard growled.

"Why, child," Baptiste crooned, "you know, with all your

talk about jumping ship and running, Travis figured you'd be hair today and gone tomorrow."

Richard gritted his teeth, reaching down with one hand to finger the long hair. Cut from Packrat's skull. *The boy I killed.* He couldn't untie it from this angle. "Get it *off* me."

The hunter gave him a mild look. "I ain't sure I'd do that, Dick. Seems ter me, that coup brung ye a sight of luck. Specially with them Sioux coons, and now, why hyar I've gone and skinned them Ree ye sent under. Hyar's three more fer yer belt. Nope. Ye wants 'em off, take 'em off yerself."

"Why, Dick," Baptiste added cheerfully, "that was one mighty fine Scalp Dance old Wah-Menitu throw'd fo' you. Sure made the trade go slick, and the last thing we needed was that band of Teton Dakota thinking we's like that damned Leavenworth."

"If I could get up, I'd beat the piss right out of you." Richard clenched his fists despite the pain in his back.

"Best be on yer uppers." Travis chortled. "I didn't larn ye all of my fighting tricks. Now, what about these hyar Ree topknots? Want 'em tied on with that cousin Pawnee on yer belt? Reckon the Crows'll see 'em and throw a right whoopee shindig fer ye."

"Throw them overboard."

"He shore don't seem to have no sense of high honor, Travis," Baptiste said mildly.

"Wal, now, he just ain't chipper, Mister de Bourgmont. Ye know how a coon goes a mite sour when his back's all laid open. Collywobbles the mind. He'll come around right quick soon's his meat heals."

"I'm *not* a savage!"

"Nope. Just shot the lights outa that Packrat. Danced the liver outa the Sioux. Beat the hell outa Trudeau. Run down a pack of Crow hoss thieves and snuck yer hosses back, and kilt three Rees what was gonna lift yer hair, kill yer woman, and send yer friends under. Boston doings, I tell ye. Plumb Boston!"

"Why, Mistah Hamilton," Baptiste said in a most reasonable voice, "I still ain't heard a single coon in this heah party call you 'Old Sculplock Dick.'"

Richard closed his eyes and groaned. "You wouldn't."

"Might."

He had to change the subject before Baptiste and Travis had time to think about the Sculplock name, and how to make it stick. "What about the Rees? They've got a village up here, don't they?"

"Passed 'em." Travis looked up. "Baptiste? I'd be mighty obliged if'n ye'd fetch me pipe."

"Reckon I could. Why, I might light a bowl for myself. Dick? You want a smoke?"

"God, I'd kill for a bowl. In my possibles . . . wherever they are."

Baptiste's feet padded down the *passe avant*.

"So?" Richard asked. "How'd we get past the Ree villages?"

"One of the chiefs. Bear. He come down and palavered. Being a Ree, he blamed it all on one of the other chiefs. Said he'd made peace with Atkinson and O'Fallon, but he couldn't speak for the other *Nesanus*. His warriors escorted us past the Ree villages. Tomorrow we'll be to the Mandans. Safe sailing from there up past the Hidatsa villages a couple of days north."

"How long have I been lying here?"

"Three days. Willow's been keeping an eye on ye. Fever's had ye, but mostly ye've slept."

"Three days?"

"Yep."

"And Willow?"

Travis fingered the Ree scalp. "She's gonna see ye through. Then, once we're up past the Hidatsa, she says she's leaving. Going home."

Richard pursed his lips. In a low voice he asked, "Where is she?"

"Setting up camp and cooking a pot of something she dug outa the ground. Smells right keen, it does."

"She's a good woman." Richard swallowed hard. "I wish . . . I wish she'd wait. You know, until you could make sure she was safe. Can't you talk her into that, Travis?"

"Nope. And I ain't gonna, 'cause she don't love me. But then, just as soon as I smoke this bowl Baptiste's bringing me, I reckon I'll go try and talk her inta my blankets again."

"Good." Richard lied and clamped his eyes shut against a different kind of pain.

"What? No lecture about what a snake I be at heart?"

Richard barely shook his head. "No. Because I don't know what's right any more."

Willow sat in her usual place, propped against the front of the cargo box. To either side, the *engagés* leaned into their poles, thrusting *Maria* against the sluggish current. They were singing again, spirits buoyed by their proximity to the Mandan. Faint traces of breeze stroked Willow's cheek in the mildest of caresses.

The boat moved slowly up the river, stilting along on its wooden poles. Overhead, a flight of ducks flapped past in a

flurry of wings. The river seemed closely hemmed by the wall of trees that overhung the banks. The blazing orb of the sun had burned the sky white. Flies buzzed and dragonflies skimmed the water, stopping to hover over the boat before darting away.

Richard and Etienne lay under a sunshade that Baptiste had rigged from a blanket, poles, and line. Both now slept, Richard restlessly, while Etienne snored happily.

Willow's head dropped lower onto her chest. The sun's warmth loosened her muscles, eased the tension in her souls. The gentle rocking of the boat soothed her. The *engagés* sang:

> *J'ai cueilli la belle rose,*
> *J'ai cueilli la belle rose,*
> *Qui pendait au rosier blanc,*
> *La belle rose.*

Her souls drifted with the song, sinking away from wakefulness and into the hazy margins of sleep . . .

. . . Through the misty fragments of dreams, eyes stare at me. I know that face. With recognition comes a terrible unease; it's the Ree warrior who tried to kill me. I shot him as he lay wounded and disbelieving while pain and death crept through his body and drove away his souls.

From the hollows within, Coyote wails and mocks me. I hear shouts, gunshots. Men are running, heads thrown back as they shriek their war cries. Moment by moment, I relive the Ree battle, seeing my arrows slice through warm flesh. I see the warriors' stunned expressions as the realization of death pierces them as sharply as the arrows.

I killed them.

How heady it feels . . . and how hollow. Warrior's blood runs in my veins—as does the healer's. These Rees were enemies who would have killed my people. At the moment of the attack, my blood took over. *Puha*, Spirit Power, guided me through the fighting, and, later, to care for the wounded.

It swelled within me as I grasped the arrow sticking in Richard's shoulder. I look down at the blood on my hands, feel the slim shaft, sticky with Richard's blood.

Once, I would have been horrified by such responsibility for death and life. *What has happened to me?*

In the days before I watched my husband and son die, I would have acted differently, waited for directions rather than leaped to battle.

I have changed, loosened my puha.

It started with the death of my family. And I changed more while I was Packrat's slave. We fought—he and I—a battle of wills and *puha*. In the end I killed his Pawnee soul, broke him, and left him ready to die.

How does it make you feel, Willow, to know that you can kill a man's spirit? A chill wind blew in her soul.

Red Calf, your brother's wife, once called you a witch, Willow. Did she see more clearly than you do?

What effect have these fascinating and dangerous White men had on me? I have seen life through their eyes and experienced their marvels. But what are they? Evil spirit beings? Or good?

When I looked into the eye of Richard's soul, he looked back, unafraid, seeking to touch my souls with his.

Many things have changed me. Pain, grief, fear, and danger have acted like fire, hardening me as flame does the point of a digging stick.

A long howl rises to mingle with my souls. The sound is very clear, as if cleaving through still and frosty air—the howl of Wolf, and all that means after Coyote's mocking laughter.

I hear your call, Wolf. You have done this to me, haven't you? You put me through these trials.

The long howl drifts away until it is nothing but echoes, and I can see him now, staring at me with hard yellow eyes. The round-tipped ears are pricked, the broad nose quivering. His long ruff is frost-tipped, full and soft.

What did you want from me, Wolf? Haven't I given you everything?

And what about Richard? Once I saw him in my dreams, a dancing, white-mist dog. But he has changed, become something different. What is Wolf's purpose with Richard? Or, is Richard Coyote's creature? How am I to know?

As I ask, Wolf's face changes, the eyes darkening. The ruff merges into long black braids. The muzzle flattens, becoming a man's face with high cheekbones and a broad jaw. The nose is broad and strong, so familiar that I . . .

I know you now, High Wolf, puhagan *of the* Dukurika. *Hello, Father. I have missed you.*

He smiles slowly, keen anticipation in his eyes, as if I should know something that momentarily eludes me.

Father, where are you? Why have you come to me in this way?

But he says nothing. The smile grows wistful enough to twist the heart in my chest.

Father? What's wrong?

I know that look of his—have seen it often when I was a girl. He looks this way when something precious has been lost forever.

Is that what you're trying to tell me? Who, Father? Who is lost to you forever? I don't understand.

Father's image fades. I wring my hands, pacing in my dream. *It's not me, Father. I'm coming home. You'll see. I'll be there soon. I promise. Don't mourn me.*

Then I hear the laughter, and turn. My souls shrink back, and I place a hand to my breast. Packrat stands there, haughty, and behind him are the Ree warriors. I try to back away from the ghosts, but there is nowhere to flee. They are pointing at me and laughing . . .

A sharp cry brought Willow out of the dream. She jerked her head up, and blinked. The *engagés* were looking up toward the bank as they poled the craft forward.

Willow winced at straightening her cramped limbs, and stood, shading her eyes with a flat palm as she stared up at the grassy terraces west of the river. Travis and Baptiste rode guard on the horse herd that paralleled the boat's progress. Baptiste threw his head back and bellowed a loud "*Yaaa-Hoooo!*" a call Willow had come to know meant happiness.

Travis was pointing. She followed his hand, and saw six or seven mounted Indians, who charged across the flats in a gallop. Travis and Baptiste trotted their horses out to meet them. Sunlight flashed off their rifle barrels and caught the dance of their long fringes.

Willow's first instinct was fear, for after all, anyone not her own kind was most likely an enemy—and she still didn't understand the portents of her dream.

"Who's that?" Green called from the cargo box.

"*Les Mandan!*" Henri whooped. "We have lived to see the Mandan!"

A joyous cry went up from the *engagés,* and they bent to their poles with new vigor.

The riders had pulled up amidst milling horses and Travis leaned out from his saddle to shake the warriors' hands.

Willow slumped against the cargo box. *Yes, I know these Mandan. They take Shoshoni women . . . and make slaves of them.*

She'd had enough of slavery at Packrat's hands.

The excitement could be felt, electric, like static in the air. It added to Richard's frustration as he lay forgotten on the foredeck. By craning his neck until his back pained him, he could see the *engagés* hustling back and forth from the rear of the cargo box. Busy as ants with breadcrumbs, they were rearranging cargo under Henri's careful direction. Some of the stocks would be traded with the Mandan for food, moccasins, hunting shirts, and other necessities.

Still a half-day's journey from the main village, the *Maria* lay snubbed by her painter to a cottonwood log buried like a crooked thumb in the point of a long sandbar that curled out into the river. It was a defensible position. Despite the well-known friendliness of the Mandan, Green was taking no chances. Guards were stationed on the top of the cargo box.

From his vantage, Richard could see out over cornfields that gleamed golden in the afternoon sun. Here and there, he could make out Mandan women moving among the stalks, sometimes with black-headed children in tow.

Travis and Dave Green had ridden ahead on horseback to talk to an American trader at Mitutanka village. A pre-scout, as Travis had explained it. A way of discovering the current disposition of the Mandan toward whites, and the critical location of the Atkinson-O'Fallon expedition.

Richard gritted his teeth and tried to move his right arm forward. Stitches of pain brought beads of sweat to his face, but he inched his arm ahead. Little by little, he managed to gain some movement, but each inch was bought with pain and tears.

If I can run down Crow horse thieves, I can stand this. And he'd sink teeth in his lip to do it all over again. The trick was to exercise the shoulder without tearing the wound.

I won't be any cripple. That promise circulated around and around in his head.

He ignored the soft whisper of moccasins on the deck until they stopped beside him.

Panting from the effect of moving his arm, Richard looked up. Trudeau stood there, leering down, muscular arms crossed. The garish scab on the side of his head was peeling to expose wound-pink beneath.

"*Bonjour.* You are better, *oui?*"

"Yes, better." Richard stared up at his old tormentor through narrowed eyes. Then it hit him that both Travis and

Green were gone. If Trudeau were here for trouble, did he dare call out for Baptiste?

Trudeau lifted a lip to expose yellow teeth. He fingered his mauled ear, still puckered with scars. Richard quailed inside at the memory of Trudeau's ear clamped between his grinding teeth.

"You 'ave marked me, *cochonnet*."

"You started it."

Trudeau snorted. "Perhaps I kill you, eh? I 'ave not decided." He glanced toward the stern and the working *engagés*. "Some of the others, they no longer hate you." He slitted his black eyes. "But I do. To me you are a *chien sordide*."

Richard licked his lips and shifted, raising on his good arm. "If you want another dose of what I gave you the last time, you just wait until this arm . . ."

Trudeau crouched down, his face inches from Richard's. "I could kill you now, *mon ami*. Who would know, eh?"

"They'd know." Richard bit back the urge to scream for help, forcing himself to meet Trudeau's eyes.

"*Possible*." Trudeau nodded to himself. "You 'ave changed, Reeshaw. Grown tougher. No longer a *poltron*."

"Am I supposed to thank you for your kind comments?"

Trudeau snorted his contempt.

"Trudeau!" Baptiste barked, walking along the *passe avant*. "I reckon you got work you otta be doing."

Trudeau smiled. In a low whisper, he added, "It is not over between us." Then he rose and knotted his fists, thick muscles bulging under his shirt. With a swagger, Trudeau jerked a nod at Baptiste and headed aft.

Richard lowered himself wearily to the deck where he gasped air into his oddly starved lungs. His back prickled and ached as though cactus thorns were being pushed and pulled through his flesh. He barely noticed when Baptiste settled beside him in a swirl of fringes.

"You all right?"

"Yes, just a little tuckered." Richard blinked at the sweat. "And a little spooked, I guess. He could have. . . . Oh, never mind."

"Aw, he just be struttin', showing you ain't got him cowed. He ain't gonna cause no trouble. Not after that whupping you done give him."

"My God, Baptiste, doesn't it ever end?"

Baptiste cocked his head, pensive black eyes on the corn-rich shore beyond the gunwale. "End? What? Life, coon? Hell, no. It just goes on and on, like the river. Ain't no end to it till you fetches up dead."

Richard ran a thumbnail along the wood grain in the deck. "I'm tired, Baptiste. I want to go home where things are sane and normal." He paused. "I never knew how good my life was."

Baptiste studied him from the corner of his eye. "Gonna make up with your pap?"

"Make up? How can I? I lost a fortune when François robbed me. You don't know my father. He keeps a loaded musket in his office. If I turned up without the money, he'd probably shoot me dead." He swallowed hard. "He thinks I'm a failure as it is. Why remove any doubt?"

"A man changes, Dick. You have. Shoa 'nuff, you ain't the same runt I fust met north of Atkinson. You shoah yor pap wouldn't just as soon have a son as his money?"

Richard frowned, remembering those hard gray eyes. But when he looked past the eyes, and saw the sagging flesh on his father's face, the stoop in the shoulders . . . "I'm not sure I know who my father is any more."

Baptiste pulled his hat off and wiped the sweat from his forehead with his sleeve. Sunlight glinted in his thick mane of kinky hair. "How's you raised, Dick? Didn't yor pap take you out, larn you things?"

"I was raised, for the most part, by Jeffry, my father's manservant."

"He a slave?"

"Yes. And a good man, Baptiste. I'll free him when my father dies."

Baptiste's jaw muscles jumped as he ground his teeth. "You didn't tell me yor pap kept slaves."

Richard gave the hunter a sly smile. "Jeffry does have a single-bitted ax, but I think he considers himself too much of a gentleman to use it."

"Secret is, he better keep a good edge on it. Keen, like, you see?"

"That's my father you're talking about."

Baptiste studied him through narrowed eyes. "I ain't got no spot in my heart foah a slaveowner, Dick. No matter who."

Richard nerved himself under Baptiste's hostile glare. "It's different for them. It's . . . well, like they're best friends. Like you and Travis, but more."

There was no give in Baptiste's eyes. *Dear God, how do I explain this?* "They just go together, Baptiste. You'd have to see them. Jeffry—he's my father's best friend. Probably his only friend."

"And he keep his friend a slave?"

A sour feeling churned in Richard's stomach. "Yes. Look, I can't explain it, all right? You'd just have to know them."

The bitterness in Baptiste's eyes didn't give way.

"Baptiste, I'm sorry about my father. I don't approve of

keeping slaves either. But, beyond that, if you got to know him, you'd . . ." *What, Richard? Why are you protecting him?* The thought left him uneasy.

"I'd like him?" Baptiste finished. "Dick, I ain't holding it again' you none, but this child don't see past the slavery."

As if a door had swung open, and he'd stepped into another room, Richard suddenly had an entirely different glimpse of his father. He took a deep breath. "Oh, you'd like him all right. He has as much courage, craftiness, and cunning as you do. He was a brave soldier in the Revolution. And even when a ball crippled his leg, he didn't give up. His father came to America in chains—like yours did."

"But he's lucky enough to be born white."

"He was, but to have what he has today, he had to risk his life, fight for what he believed. Just like you fought for what you believed. He's got the same iron resolve inside him that you do." Richard gave him a crooked smile. "Yes, you're a lot alike. Especially when it comes to being bullheaded."

The sintering glare abated just the slightest. "You teasing me?"

"I'm betting that you wouldn't thrash a cripple, even if he was a slaveowner's son."

"Don't you never make that bet, boy." Baptiste's lip twitched with a smothered grin. "You ain't that same owl-eyed Doodle I fust met."

Richard stared absently at the wood as he thought about Phillip Hamilton. What had it cost the old man to send Richard out into the world? *It must have scared him to death. Was that why he was so unforgiving that last morning in Boston?*

Baptiste shook himself. "Well, hell, I can't free 'em all."

"No, but you can feel for them, can't you?"

The hard glint had finally drained from Baptiste's eyes. "Yep, that I can." He paused. "You tell me. How does yer pap live with hisself, knowing he owns another human being?"

"It's just the way it was, Baptiste. He grew up with the notion that it was all right. But, I'll tell you what, slavery's going to simply wither away and die. My father's an anomaly in Boston, a relic, if you will." *No wonder he hated my philosophy, my rejection of his world.* "Dear Lord, that's it!"

"Huh? What you saying?"

Richard propped his chin on his fist. "What fools we all are. No matter how we want to reinvent the world, we always do it from the pieces of the past. In my father's case, he hated the British gentry enough to go to war, but down in his heart, he envied them so much that he became just like them."

Baptiste lifted an eyebrow.

"Weren't you the one who said, 'Never go against yer pap'?"

"That's afore I larned he's a slaveholder. But that's all right, Dick. I'll try not to hold yoah pap against you."

Richard gave him a sly grin. "I'd appreciate that."

Baptiste stood. "I'd better shinny on back and make sure them *engagés* ain't loafing. If'n Trudeau gives you grief, you just sing out, hear?"

"Thanks, Baptiste." He barely heard the hunter go. *I defended my father. And, yes, if he and Baptiste could see each other clearly, they would like each other.* Richard shook his head, and pain laced his shoulder. *Father, you old pirate, for the first time, I think I understand you.*

In his imagination those terrible gray eyes had suddenly turned oddly brittle. To his amazement, the image left a hollow feeling in his gut.

SEVEN

❖

It may peradventure be thought, there was never such a
time, nor condition of war as this; and
I believe it was never generally so,
over all the world: but there are many
places, where they live so now. For the
savage people in many places in America, except the government of small families, the concord whereof dependeth on
natural lust, have no government at all; and live at
this day in that brutish manner, as I have said before.

—Thomas Hobbes, *Leviathan*

Where's Atkinson and O'Fallon?" Green asked. He
was shoved back in a handmade chair across
from a stone-cold metal heat stove—not that anyone needed heat on the first day of August.

Travis casually inspected the small trading post. He and
Green had ridden ahead to speak with James Kipp, the trader
who lived at Fort Tilton. It always paid to scout the country
first, and Kipp would fill them in on the Indian situation—
chancy at best—and the army's current location. Kipp would
comply, once assured that Green didn't intend on cutting out
a piece of the Mandan trade.

Fort Tilton consisted of a room made of rudely squared
cottonwood timbers, saddle-notched, and haphazardly
chinked with pale mud. Shelving, made of everything from
split planks to pegs driven into the wall and wrapped with
shrink-fit rawhide, hung from each wall. Blankets, tins of
oil, kegs of powder, and bales of furs were stacked, stuffed,

and crammed into every cranny. The only light entered through the doorway beyond the plank that served as a trading counter, and from the rifle loopholes cut through the logs. Kegs and tins were stacked best-luck along the walls.

Travis puffed blue clouds from his pipe as he eyed James Kipp, the trader who manned Fort Tilton and saw to the Mandan trade for the Columbia Fur Company. Unlike Pilcher, or the Chouteaus, Tilton hauled his goods in overland from Lake Traverse, far to the east.

He's a canny old coon. Got ter be to last it out up hyar. The sober-eyed Kipp was a "hiverner," a veteran winter man who'd stuck out the hard days after the Leavenworth disaster when the Rees had made everyone on the river miserable.

Kipp puffed at his pipe, feet up on a pressed bale of beaver. His leather pants had gone grease-black, contrasting to his newly made doe-brown moccasins. He wore a red flannel shirt, the collar unbuttoned to expose curly hair.

Kipp looked down his nose at the blue smoke rising in whorls, and said, "Atkinson and O'Fallon? Aw, they're up palavering with the Crow. They were here. When they weren't fighting with each other over every damned thing, they were making treaties right and left."

Travis relaxed. The worst fear had been that they'd be here, among the Mandan. Travis caught Green's eye, sharing his controlled relief. *Wal, Dave, leastwise we don't have ter run fer the boat, and drop back downriver till we can find us a hiding hole.*

"Fighting with each other?" Green asked, face like a mask. "You mean Atkinson and O'Fallon?"

Kipp slapped his leg as he laughed. "Yep. Atkinson give a bunch of gifts to the Mandan—but O'Fallon, why he's a fire-eater to start with, he wanted to wring some apologies out of Four Bears fer letting his young men side with the Rees when they shot up Ashley back in twenty-three. Atkinson and O'Fallon got so het up at each other they went at it with their dinner forks till the camp aides pulled 'em apart."

"Do tell?" Travis pulled at his beard. *If the leaders is busy fighting amongst themselves, they might not pay much heed ter rumors about a keelboat on the river.* "But they still made new treaties? How'd that work?"

"Like you'd expect. Everybody sat down to a big feast, then they squired that Peter Wilson around. You heard about him?"

"Uh-huh," Green growled. "The fancy new Indian factor or some such. General Clark sent him up to help pacify the river after that mess Leavenworth made of the Ree villages."

"Hell!" Kipp jabbed with his pipestem. "Told everybody he's the new subagent—special for the upper river. He's a damn politician, Saint Loowee thick, if'n ye ask me. Mark me, boys, he'll take right smart care of the upper river . . . a-sitting in a damn office on Walnut Street!"

"Got any idea when they might turn downriver?" Green asked innocently.

Kipp sucked at his pipe, and shrugged. "Depends on how long the river Crow can keep convincing them to give out presents and foofawraw. Couple of weeks. Heard tell they wanted to make the mouth of the Yellowstone. More of that crazy talk of an army fort there."

"Army on the upper river?" Travis shook his head. *Fool's business, fer sure.* "They couldn't even keep them riflemen down ter Cantonment Missouri from starvation. Fort Atkinson's barely hanging on as 'tis. Talk is, they's gonna move the fort south, down toward the Blue somewhere. How in hell can they supply a fort up hyar? Injuns would plumb laugh themselves silly when them soldiers started eating their boots along about February."

"Reckon yer surefired right, coon." Kipp scratched his beard. "Aw, I don't know what the hell good they'd do. Look at what happened to you. Fresh damn treaty, ink ain't even dried, and the Rees jump yer boat."

"But Bear showed up the next day." Green waggled a mocking finger. "Said it wasn't his boys that hit us."

". . . And got the ever-loving shit shot outa 'em," Travis added. He was watching Kipp poke a dirty finger into his mouth. He used the digit to wiggle one of his yellow teeth. "Can't trust a damn Ree, I tell ye. Fight ye one day, wipe yer blood off, and ask ye in fer dinner and a squaw the next."

"They're treacherous, all right," Kipp agreed, staring thoughtfully at the tip of his damp finger. "But, hell, they all are. Assiniboins kilt a couple of Mandans the other day. Party of Yanktonis run off a bunch of horses belonging to some Hidatsa. The Hidatsa talked a couple of Cheyenne into going along fer revenge. They ran across a party of Cree coming in to trade, and damned near killed 'em all. Now everybody's scared the Cree is gonna come down, and maybe join up with the Yanktoni, and who knows who's gonna die."

"Some things never change," Green said, chuckling. "But I'll bet Atkinson and O'Fallon are just happy as little larks at a bug hatching, making treaties right and left."

"Which are good until the feast is over, or the next party of Sioux ride across the horizon." Kipp laughed. For a moment, he made a face as he prodded his errant tooth with his tongue, then added, "Only a madman would try and make sense out of the upper river. Hell, I've seen times when the Mandan didn't have anybody else to kick, so the Amahamis picked a fight with the Mitutankas."

Travis sucked his lips, squinting at Kipp's mouth. *I could just up and pull that loose chomper of his. A pair of tongs and a good yank, and hell, it'd come out right smart, it would.*

"Ain't that the truth," Green muttered. "Hell, I heard about an Assiniboin chief got so carried away double-dealing, shifting alliances, and taking advantage that he found out he'd declared war on himself."

"So, what happened?" Kipp asked, the tooth momentarily forgotten.

"Why, he couldn't resist the opportunity to get one up, so he shot himself in the back, then his right hand hacked off his left just as it reached up to lift his scalp."

Travis slapped his knee. "This hyar Pete Wilson figured this out yet? That these folks like killing each other fer no reason?"

"Nope. Like I said, he's a Saint Loowee puff-and-strut. He's all blowed up with making peace treaties." Kipp knocked the dottle out of his pipe onto the dirt floor.

Then Kipp cut tobacco and tamped it into his pipe. The whole time, his tongue played with that tooth.

'Course, if'n it didn't come loose, a coon might need ter take his patch knife and pry it out by the root. Teeth were always a problem. But then, God had figgered that dodge out early on, which was why he put so cussed many in a feller's mouth to start with.

"Half yer stockade posts look fresh-planted outside in the palisade," Travis noted, to take his mind off the tooth.

"Yep. Moved 'em up a couple of weeks ago. Moved the whole post. Wanted to be a hair closer to Mitutanka village. Figgered I's a goner a couple of times these last years. Probably would have been, if old Four Men hadn't taken me clean into his lodge."

"Mandans are generally good folks." Green cocked his head. "Which brings us to the here and now."

Kipp lifted an eyebrow. "Yer not after my Mandan, are ye?"

"Nope. That's why we come here first. Travis told me you were a coon to ride river with. His word is good. Dealing straight, Kipp, we're going to spend a couple of days here. Rest the crew."

"Uh-huh." Kipp sucked at the offending tooth like it was rock candy. "And next spring they's gonna be another batch of blue-eyed babies born, and I'm gonna have to hear that damned crap about lost Welshmen again."

"That still flying around?" Travis asked.

"Goes clear back to Evans fifty years ago, or some such thing." Kipp turned his head and spat impressively in emphasis. "Some damned fool is born every day, ye know." He gave them a level glance as Travis, in vain, inspected the spittle for the tooth. "And then what, Dave?"

Green leaned back, taking a deep breath. "Then we head upriver."

Kipp studied Green. "How far?"

"Long ways." Green spread his hands.

"Three Forks?" Kipp glanced at Travis. "Naw, Trav. Yer not that fool-stupid. Not after what happened to ye up to the Great Falls, and then Immel and Jones atop that. Ye've a heap more sense than that."

"We'll let ye know where we end up," Travis said with a grin. "That's plew to poor kit, I do swear."

"Sure, Travis." Kipp nodded reflectively. "Let me know when ye get there . . . and leave *my* Mandan alone."

"I give ye my *word*. Now, will ye let me yank that damn tooth *outa* there?"

Kipp gave him an oddly confused look, as did Green, who'd evidently missed the tooth entirely.

"Hell, no!" Kipp thundered. "Yer lucky enough I trust you around my Mandan, let alone around my damn mouth! It's my tooth and I'll do her as I will." He jabbed with the pipestem again. "And it just so happens that fiddling with it gives me something to do of an evening."

"Your Mandan trade is safe," Green said. "But you'd better be making plans, James. The Company's gonna be coming upriver after you. Pilcher's been licking his lips, and Chouteau's been dickering with Astor."

"Tilton and me, we got hyar first," Kipp claimed.

"Yep," Green said. "But the price of plews is going up.

The big outfits have their eyes on the upper river. No telling who will stir up who. Things fall apart here, come on upriver. You never know—in this country, a coon might need a warm post to hole up in. That, or he could bet on which Injuns is fighting which other Injuns this week."

"Not on your life. Hell, just in the time we been talking, the Yanktoni's brokered a peace with the Ree and are planning on wiping out the Crow, who've just made an alliance with the Assiniboin."

"And ye can live like this?" Travis blurted.

"Well," Kipp mused as he returned to sucking his tooth, "Injun trade is like three-card monte. A coon never knows which card'll turn up where. So far, Tilton and me, we've been watching the ace, and turning the right card up."

"Yep," Travis said thoughtfully. "But some coon will always come along with slicker fingers, and the dealer will slip ye a deuce." And he couldn't shake the memory of the dream he'd had. The one where Lisa, Immel, and Jones had told him not to go to the mouth of the Big Horn.

The sun burned in a red-orange ball over the rounded bluffs west of the river. The slanting light softened the grassy slopes. Drainages lay in shadow, dark bur oak and brush creating the illusion of veins in the meat of the earth. Tasseled corn gleamed in the Mandan gardens, tall above squash and bean plants. The golden glow on the rounded Mandan houses within Mitutanka village cast a magical illusion of wealth and peace.

The Mandan had built this, their largest village, on a spur-like ridge that stuck out into a loop of the Missouri. With sheer bluffs and water on three sides, the location was defensible, and could be easily approached only from the southwest.

Richard stared out from where he lay on the *Maria*'s deck. The evening breeze carried faint cries and laughter from the village, and the dry scent of grass and eternity down from the western plains. He'd been out there, beyond the river, in the endless waves of golden grass rippling in the wind. In that vastness, he'd walked under the eye of God.

Was it really me who ran down the Crow? He could recall the fever of his aching muscles, the wretched thirst, the crushing fatigue. *But I made it. Travis kept me going, made me reach down inside to find the will to go on.*

On the bank, upside-down bull boats, like wounded turtles, cast humped shadows over the track-stippled mud. They'd made their landing here, upstream from a creek the Mandan called "Washing-the-Dishes." Just beyond that creek his horses grazed, guarded by three Mandan boys.

One day in Boston, in the comfort of a drawing room, he would look into a crystal glass of sherry and tell the tale to a rapt audience of ladies and gentlemen. Would they believe him?

But he'd done it. Recovered his horses. That stubborn ember of pride burned bright through all the other confusions filling his head.

Willow rounded the corner of the cargo box on silent moccasined feet. He watched her, so lithe and graceful. A white woman didn't walk with that sinuous balance.

He smiled up at her. "I thought you'd be at the feast. That chief, the one they call Four Bears, is feeding everyone. They're going to dance, I hear."

"I came to see how you are before Travis and the others come." She dropped to her knees beside him. Her thoughtful expression betrayed a subtle sadness.

He eyed her warily. "Is something wrong?"

"I went with Travis and Green when we arrived here today. There, in the village, I saw several women. Slaves.

Some were *Agaiduka,* another was *Ku'chendikani.* I knew her family."

Richard pillowed his chin on a knotted fist and stared out at the sun. It was sinking slowly behind the darkening irregular horizon. "Maybe we could buy them? Take them home?"

She raised her face, hollowness in her eyes. "They would not go. They have children here, different lives to live. I talked to one who has been adopted into the Awatixa clan, and has bought rights into the White Buffalo Cow Society. I think these women have become more like the Mandan, and less like the Shoshoni."

She looks beautiful in the evening light. He watched her, trying to engrave the sight into his memory: how the glow accented her bronze skin; the sleek black hair in regal cascades over her shoulders; slim hands clasped in her lap; and her eyes, so large and dark under the perfect brow.

Willow said, "Before I was taken from the mountains, I would not have believed that people could walk so many different paths. Richard, is it so impossible for us?"

He ran a finger along the wood grain of the worn deck. "I don't belong here." The warm lights of Boston, the gaiety and laughter of old friends called to him. "This isn't my place, Willow." He imagined himself in black broadcloth, standing at the lectern. Before him sat rows of bright-faced young men, eager to learn. "I have a different life back in Boston."

She sat silently, head bowed.

"Would you rather that I lied? Told you it would all work out? And then have me leave? Listen, life used to be so clear. I knew right from wrong. My philosophy books gave me everything I needed to make decisions about life. I knew who I was, and what I was. Where I fit into the universe." He pulled at his long hair. "But nothing that I believed seems right any more."

"Maybe it wasn't really right in the beginning."

"Everything has become hopelessly tangled, Willow. I have to find Truth again."

"And this Laura? The woman in Boston? Is your heart for her?"

He ground his teeth for a moment, then said in a wooden voice, "Yes . . . because I have to believe I'll marry her. If I don't, I'll lose the last of what my life was, and what I want it to be." He glanced at her. "Do you understand?"

She nodded stoically.

Voices carried on the evening air, followed by the plank rattling. Travis appeared around the cargo box at the head of a group of young Mandan warriors: muscular men, bare-chested, with bright face paint that accented fierce obsidian eyes. "Howdy, coon. Time's come ter feast and dance."

"What?" Richard gave the hunter a wary look; the warriors lowered a rolled buffalo hide to the deck and spread it out.

"Honor guard!" Travis said proudly. "Fit fer a wounded warrior. C'mon, coon. We're going ter a shindig."

"Travis, I"—strong hands reached down and lifted him onto the robe—"but . . . wait!"

"Hush now, coon. Yer a guest. And do me a favor. Don't moan or groan, no matter how it hurts. These warriors here, they's Black Mouths, soldiers. Each of 'em's been through *Okipa*. That's a ceremony where they run skewers of wood through their bodies. Then they hang till they pass out and send their souls to the Spirit World. Powerful medicine fer only the strongest and bravest. C'mon. And Willow, ye come, too. Uh, as Dick's wife. Otherwise, he'll have ter fight off all the young women wanting ter lay with him."

Richard winced as the stalwart warriors knotted their hands in the buffalo hide and bore him off like a haunch of meat. All in all, it wasn't too painful, except when they thumped him against the cargo box while crossing the *passe avant*.

"Where are we going?" Richard demanded as the warriors threaded their way through the bull boats.

From where Travis and Willow followed, the hunter called, "We're headed up ter Mitutanka, lad. I told ye. It's feast time, and a Scalp Dance ter boot. Celebration fer blizzarding the lights outa that sneaking bunch of Rees that jumped us downriver. As of today, Mandans is at war with the Rees. 'Course, that could change tomorrow, so we'll shindig tonight."

"What do you mean, change tomorrow?"

"This hyar's the upper river, Doodle. Alliances switch faster than cards in a New Orleans poker game."

Richard glanced up at the muscular men carrying the buffalo robe. They looked lean and dangerous, smiling and muttering among themselves in their sibilant tongue. Black Mouths—the warriors who policed the Mandan camps. They looked like savages all right, each bare chest lumped by hideous scar tissue. Nor did they seem to understand the severity of his wound; they flew across the uneven ground at a run.

Just one misstep, a trip and fall, and his back would split open like a mush melon. In resignation, Richard closed his eyes and considered the "wife" business. Travis would come up with something like that—and just after he'd been telling Willow about Laura.

They wound up the trail, past the palisaded wall, and into the village, a maze of rounded lodges, each built within mere feet of its neighbor. He might have been floating in a sea of huge earthen bubbles. After several twists and turns, Richard was totally confused as to their direction.

Square-roofed doorways jutted from the curving walls, some with children or old folks sitting on the roofs. These spectators called down to the bearers, and were answered by the warriors' laughing calls.

A dog yapped at one of the warriors' feet. A hollow thump, and the cur vanished into the shadowed ways, yipping its pain.

"Where are we going?" Richard called. "Hey! Let me down!"

One of the warriors said something in Mandan, but the progress continued at the same breakneck pace.

"I might just as well be a log, for all you care." Richard gritted his teeth as pain shot through his back.

Then they burst into an open space. Through the folds of the buffalo robe he saw an odd column of planks around a cedar tree, a beaten-dirt plaza, and what looked like a chopped-off lodge. Then they charged headlong into a square doorway, and the timbers of the entry passage flashed past. The interior of the great lodge was crowded with Mandan seated shoulder to shoulder.

The Black Mouths slowed to march ceremonially down a narrow aisle to the center of the lodge and laid the robe gently to one side of a bonfire. Green and Baptiste sat beside a scarred Mandan chief. The Black Mouths nodded to him and smiled, before retreating through the crowd to places beside the door.

Gasping with relief, Richard took in his surroundings. Perhaps seventy feet in diameter, the interior was spacious. The log roof arched high overhead, and between the sooty rafter logs he could see the wickerwork of branches that bore the heavy earthen covering. The whole was supported by four vertical tree trunks centrally placed. Stringers ran from each trunk to rafters that ran down like rays to more stringers supported by short perimeter posts. In the highest arc of the roof a huge smokehole opened to the purple light of evening. Directly beneath it, the bonfire crackled and sent sparks upward.

Nestled between the perimeter posts were the beds; each consisted of a leather-hung cubicle, something like a small four-poster. Through openings in the sides he could see the thick sleeping robes. After some of the miserable nights he'd spent in the rain, they looked remarkably snug.

The Mandan watched him with curious dark eyes, the burble of voices making a din. Equal numbers of men and women were present. The place smelled of smoke, leather, dust, and human musk.

Travis and Willow crossed the lodge, and all eyes turned to follow their progress through the throng. Willow walked with a stately elegance, like a queen among the masses. In the firelight, her hair gleamed, and her blanket was held tightly to her slim body. She seated herself beside Richard and quickly checked his wound. The tension in her face added to his unease.

"How's the ride?" Green asked. He gave Richard a mild look, pipestem drooping from the corner of his broad mouth. The booshway was sitting cross-legged on a buffalo robe, his billowy white shirt unbuttoned at the collar. Baptiste sat on the other side of two Mandan chiefs, talking to one with a series of rapid hand signs, his white teeth flashing in a smile.

"Fast," Richard said uneasily.

"Figgered ye'd not want ter miss this," Travis told him as he settled between Richard and Green. "What with yer dancing down ter Wah-Menitu's, this otta be plumb easy. Hyar, ye can sit 'em all out."

The chief beside Green stood, and the babble dissipated into silence. A woman walked forward, her long-fringed dress snow white, glistening with a wealth of beads. She presented the chief with the biggest pipe Richard had ever seen, the stem a full five feet in length. The chief took it reverently and offered it to the cardinal directions. The woman in white snared an ember from the fire and lit the heavy stone bowl. He puffed a cloud of blue and began to speak in the sibilant Mandan tongue.

"That coon's The Four Men," Travis whispered. The Four Men was a large man, almost overweight. He had a round face, prominent cheekbones, and a long, thin nose. His hair was greased and stuck through with feathers. He wore a fox hide over his shoulders like a mantle.

"And the man beside him? The one decked out in the claw necklace and shells? He looks important."

"He is. That jasper's called *Mato-Tope,* Four Bears, the most powerful chief among the Mandan. He's a heap good friend ter have in this country."

Four Bears wore a decorated buffalo robe over his shoulders, and a breechclout with a quilled flap hanging down almost to his knees. The tops of his moccasins were beaded in colorful patterns. A huge bear-claw necklace hung over his scarred chest. A pendant of silver lay beneath. The man's hair was long, oiled, and curled back at the top of the high forehead. Those eyes, dark and shining, might have belonged to a bird of prey.

"Yep," Travis said. "He's a heap of warrior, old Four Bears is. Kilt a Ree in his own lodge once."

"I'm more at ease already," Richard muttered, turning his attention to the speaker. "What's The Four Men saying?"

"Oh, all the usual. About what fine friends us whites is. How we shot Hob outa the Ree, and come hyar like warriors."

Food was carried in by women and placed before them on wooden platters. Richard stared at the lumpy balls with misgiving.

"Four-in-one, they call it." Travis said. "Eat up, Dick. T'ain't more than corn, squash, sunflower seeds, and beans."

Next, steaming portions of roasted buffalo hump and whole tongues were laid out in mountain sheep-horn cups. The flaky white meat in the wooden bowls was sturgeon. Richard's stomach growled. He hadn't realized just how hungry he was.

All around him, people were eating, laughing, dark faces shining. The hubbub grew louder.

Richard licked his fingers and glanced at Travis. "This business of Willow being my wife. It's really for her protection, isn't it?"

It was Willow who answered: "No. For yours. The Mandan offer their women to honored guests. Travis thought it would make you uncomfortable. If I am here as your wife, you can avoid lying with a Mandan woman."

Richard made a face, and cast uneasy glances at the crowd of Mandan surrounding them.

"It is not your custom," Willow said. "But it is theirs, and you are a guest."

"Reckon if'n ye get an offer, Dick"—Travis was chewing on a joint of meat—"ye might want ter refuse politely, and offer to pray fer the feller and his wife. I reckon ye can do that fer 'em."

"Anything you say. But why do they offer their women? A different form of prostitution?"

Travis ran a sleeve over his greasy mouth. "The way a Mandan figgers, a successful man has medicine, Spirit Power. One way a lesser man can get some of that power is ter lend out his wife. When she lays with the first feller, he shoots power inter her. Then, later, her man lays with her and sucks it up. What's the word? Transfers?"

Richard reached for another of the four-in-one balls. He bit into it, savoring the sweet taste. "A transfer of power? But at what price?"

"Folks all got their own ways," Travis replied, already

eyeing the young women in the back of the room. Richard followed the hunter's appraising gaze. He stopped in mid-chew, food forgotten. The women wore nothing but deco-rated buffalo robes—some painted and tasseled, others beaded—over their shoulders.

"If you keep staring like that, your eyes will fall out of your head. Just like they did from Coyote's," Willow remarked dryly.

Richard barely caught the raising of her eyebrow. Her displeasure seemed to be with him rather than the Mandan.

Green continued to talk and laugh with Four Bears, the trader apparently fluent in Mandan.

Richard chewed thoughtfully, trying to imagine how Kant, Hegel, Rousseau, or Locke would have reacted had they been placed in his circumstance. It was so easy to brand the Mandan as savages, licentious in an animalistic way, and dismiss them.

But when I look around, I just see people. Laughing, smiling people—as I'd see at a festival in Boston were it not for the clothes and the setting.

Despite himself, he couldn't help but study the waiting women, seeking to understand the thoughts in their heads.

"Ye might not want ter stare," Travis warned. "They'll be thinking yer interested."

"Prostitution is payment for services. I'm still having trouble accepting the idea that a man would just *offer* his wife."

"In this case, it's religion, Dick. Wal, ye'd best not go a-philos'phying 'em." Travis dropped his gnawed bone and used his knife to slice off a thick chunk of the tender tongue. "Just be polite and pray fer 'em." Then the hunter grinned. "Reckon I'll take up fer ye."

Richard stared at him.

Travis chewed innocently, the scars twitching as his jaw muscles worked.

To change the subject, Richard asked, "What was that column of planks outside? It looked like it had a tree in it."

"It's an altar," Travis said. "According to the Mandan, back just after the world was created, Lone Man—he's kind of like Adam—saved the people. It seems that a huge flood come. Wal, old Lone Man, he built a palisade around the people. Built it high enough that the water didn't come over. Saved everyone. Nowadays, ye'll not enter a Mandan village without seeing that little pillar. The tree inside is the sacred cedar. That represents Lone Man. Mandan make offerings to it. Pray there."

"And the oblong lodge with the flat face?"

"*Okipa* lodge. That's where these coons have their big spree. They calls the buffalo there, do their torture. Mandan believe the *Okipa* keeps the world healthy."

"Real torture?"

"Reckon so. They starve themselves, sweat and sing, set out the skulls. When the time's right the bravest young men are skewered and hung from thongs, like deer from a meat pole. The whole time, they're a-praying to God. It's a test of courage. Finally, a warrior, he passes out, and if'n he be worthy, the Spirits take his soul away fer a vision. In the meantime, the Foolish One—sort of like the Devil—he's driven off, and the world is set right."

"A renewal?"

"Reckon so. Powerful medicine. I seen it once." Travis shook his head. "Ain't no way ye'd hang me up there like that."

Richard studied the scars on the Black Mouths. How could any man bear such pain?

"I know what yer thinking," Travis muttered through a mouthful of four-in-one. "But, tell me, what's a better gift ter God? A prayer? Any coon can pray. Injuns figger the only pure thing ye can give to power is part of yerself."

"The Greeks and Romans used to sacrifice a goat, or chicken."

"Huh!" Travis shook his head. "Seems ter this coon that it's the chicken makes the sacrifice. Nope, Dick, thar's only one thing in the world that's wholly yers, and it's you." Travis gestured. "Look around. Here and there ye'll see folks short of their little fingers. They cut 'em off. An offering to power. Seems ter this child, there's a heap of them Bible-beaters back in the settlements could larn a thing or two from Injuns. Now, if'n yer ready ter hang yerself by the thongs, or offer a piece of yerself, that's an honest gift ter God, I tell ye."

"Maybe." Richard sighed. *And to think I once believed that I understood human nature.*

But, his contrary self replied, isn't the *Okipa* nothing more than a form of crucifixion? And all the more holy by being self-inflicted? From a philosophical perspective, how did one reply?

Professor Ames, his fellow students, they had all debated morality, ethics, the nature of God, man, and the world with such clarity. But here, so far up the Missouri, those ideas had become as murky and fluid as the very river itself.

He glanced down at the scrap of human scalp hanging at his belt. Every time he'd made a resolution to remove it, his will had failed him. What had happened that he wore a man's scalp on his belt—and carried three others in his possibles? Was this person really Richard Hamilton from Boston? Had he once sat in lecture at Harvard, and bowed so gallantly over Laura Templeton's hand in an ornate parlor?

In the middle of this huge Mandan lodge, surrounded by people, he felt barren and isolated. Tonight, men would offer their wives to other men in a system of belief beyond his comprehension. These smiling, warm people hung their warriors from skewers through the flesh. Yet they had brought him here to be honored for bravery.

I am supposed *to understand! I am a philosopher, a student of mankind and thought.*

From the past, Thomas Hanson's voice mocked: *". . . If you really think creatures like Indians are human. Are they, Richard?"*

Was that it? Indians were just a kind of sophisticated beast? His gut crawled at the suggestion. He'd experienced Willow's soul, felt the Power in the one-eyed stare of Lightning Raven, the Sioux *wechashawakan.*

"Indians—and all the primitive races, for that matter—are beasts. They can't be tamed. Just like wolves and foxes can't be domesticated into dogs. They can only make way for civilization with its nobler institutions." Thomas Hanson's voice, from that long-ago Boston parlor, droned on in Richard's memory.

Despite their incomprehensible beliefs, he couldn't see the beast in any of these Indians. At least, no more so than among his white compatriots. And there sat Willow, easily the most beautiful woman in the country. When she looked at him, he could see the hurt in her eyes, because he would not allow himself to touch her.

Beside her sat Travis—a truer friend than he had ever had. But a gap was opening between them.

It's inside you, Richard. From the dim halls of memory came the words of Professor Ames: *"It is within man to seek truth in a world of chaos, to establish a framework within which a man can interpret and deal with the world, with his fellows, and his God. That search is called philosophy, gentlemen."*

Premonition stirred deep in his soul—a sense of impending horror, as if the very Fates were pulling him toward a dark and terrible tempest. The cold fringes of the black storm were brewing just beyond the realm of perception. *And when it breaks, it will destroy all that I was.* And maybe kill him in the process.

The image of the cedar tree surrounded by its planks lingered in his mind. A refuge against swirling waters. But the only thing it contained was the wooden representation of a lone Mandan hero.

EIGHT

❖

> In nature, not only is the interplay of forms unrestrained and unlimited in contingency, but each figure by itself lacks the concept of itself. The highest level to which nature derives its existence is life, but as only a natural idea this is at the very mercy of the unreasonableness of externality, and the individual vitality is in each moment of its own existence entangled with an individuality which is alien to it, whereas in each expression of the spirit is encapsulated the instant of free, universal self-relation. Nature in general is justly determined as the decline of the idea from itself.

> —Georg Friedrich Wilhelm Hegel,
> *The Philosophy of Nature*

Woman of the People." Shoshoni words interrupted Willow's thoughts as she watched the Mandan dancers.

Willow turned to inspect the newcomer who'd walked up behind her and now settled on crackling knees. She was an old woman, perhaps of forty summers. Her glossy braids were still jet black and hung down in front of her rose-beaded dress with its fine fringe, but years of winter winds and summer suns had engraved and burned her face. Lines curved down from the corners of her eyes to surround her chin. They were intersected by starburst wrinkles from the corners of her nose and mouth until her face looked like sand-scoured wood. Squat and sturdy, she had the look of the *Ku'chendikani*.

"Greetings, woman. May Wolf shed his blessing upon you," Willow replied in her tongue.

The elder cocked her head, squinting. "Huh, I know that accent. But it's been so long."

"Dukurika."

"Ah!" The woman clapped her hands. "So, a Sheepeater! They say you are not a slave, but travel with the Whites. This is so?"

"It is. I am Heals Like A Willow. The daughter of High Wolf, of the Rock Sheep clan. My people live in the Powder River Mountains, but sometimes we join our cousins in the Owl Creek Mountains across the Big River."

"Yes. I recall. Here, I am called She Sews the Roses. But once, among the People, my name was High Mountain Rose. My father was *Agaiduka* and my mother was *Ku'chendikani*. Then the Crows, the *A'ni*, took me when I had no more than ten summers. I lived with them for several years before they traded me to the Amatiha Hidatsa. A young man took a liking to me. I've been here ever since."

She doesn't ask if I know her relatives. It's as if her people have ceased to exist. Curiously hurt, Willow returned her attention to the gyrating dancers who shuffled and stomped in a circle around the center posts. With a high-pitched yip, they all leaped and twisted, landing on crouched legs in time to the beat of the big, round drums.

"Quite a dance," She Sews the Roses said, watching the sweat-streaked warriors panting and whirling around the four support posts and its fire. "They do this for you . . . in your honor."

"Then we are most honored." Willow waited, aware of the woman's sly scrutiny of herself and Richard.

"It is said that you killed some of the Arikara yourself.

Many people here are talking about that. Only a very brave woman would act like that."

"Wolf guided my hand and gave me courage."

"And you have no obligations to these White men? None of them own you?"

"No."

She Sews the Roses rubbed her callused hands together and pursed her lips. After a moment, she said, "I have been asked to ask you. Would you stay here?"

Willow lifted a skeptical eyebrow. "Stay here?"

"That man"—She Sews the Roses indicated Four Bears with a twitch of her lips—"is a very powerful chief. He has watched you over the last couple of days. He does not believe that you are married to this wounded White man. I am told to tell you that he would make you very comfortable, give you many presents. Honor you and make you his wife."

"Why doesn't he ask me this himself?"

"He cannot speak your language, and he's worried the White men might become angry."

Willow crossed her arms. "Why would he want me? I'm nothing but trouble. Just ask the White men."

She Sews the Roses laughed and slapped her dress in a very Mandan way. "You ask that? Look at you! Young, strong, too beautiful to be an *Aitani* Snake woman. And you have killed warriors in battle. Taken scalps! When you walk, every man in the village watches the way your hips sway, how your breasts fill your dress. They talk about your hair, and how it looks in the sun. You have filled their imagination with fire, Heals Like A Willow, and they would feel themselves burn inside you."

Willow glanced at Richard, oblivious on his robe beside her. He was watching the dancers, face somber. She knew that look; he was wrestling with his soul again.

"He's kind of skinny," She Sews the Roses said, jerking

her head at Richard. "And he looks like he doesn't see much of this world."

Willow cocked her jaw. "He sees more than most. Do you always judge a man by his muscles?"

"Come, girl, be sensible. A man's a great deal like a horse, you know. You can just tell by looking at them: the shoulders; the line of the back; how hard their rumps are; the power in the legs; the size of their testicles—those things. This one, well, even if he's White, he still looks like he'd gaunt up and fall over the first time you needed him to do anything important. And what sort of children would his seed grow? Spindly-legged things, sickly whiners with hollow eyes. You know the kind."

Heedless of Willow's narrowing glare, She Sews the Roses spread her arms wide. "So, what *do* you see in him? Not wealth. He's not even a trader, just an *engagé*. Four Bears, now, he'd make you a rich woman. A favorite wife. Give you a place by his side and anything you wanted. You would sleep on a white buffalo robe . . . be looked up to by every person on the river."

Willow glanced over at Four Bears, who picked that moment to meet her eyes. They stared, measuring each other, probing and challenging. In the process, she read his soul, understanding all that drove him.

"I do not think so," Willow told She Sews the Roses. "I will stick with my skinny White man. And as to what I see in him, if you can't feel his *puha,* then you would never understand if I told you."

"Power? *Him?*" She Sews the Roses made a face. "Very well. But you're making a mistake."

"Am I?"

The elder wrung her hands, nodding seriously despite swaying to the beat of the drums. "A mistake, yes. Even if you don't go with Four Bears. You surely don't want to go back to the mountains, do you? Stay with us, girl. These people, they will make you one of them. It's a better life. A woman's worth more here. You'll have status, and a say in the council. You can own property, a house, fields, and corn. You can buy rights to Power—own part of the sacred bundles, even join the White Buffalo Cow Society."

"My place is with my people," Willow said, catching sight of Travis as he came strutting through the doorway. He was followed by a young woman who ducked away to an expectant young man. The two bent their heads together, whispering excitedly. Travis started toward them, a new pair of moccasins in his hand. He grinned crookedly, a sparkle in his eyes.

Richard watched with a wooden face. The hunter made his way through the dancers, doing a little jumping and yipping of his own. Grinning, he settled on his haunches and slapped the moccasins down beside Richard, crying, "Hyar's a gift, coon. Fresh made."

"And where did you get them?" Richard asked wearily.

"Why, from that lass's young buck, coon."

"Travis, I don't think I can—"

"It's Mandan custom." Travis glanced up, winked at Willow—and noticed She Sews the Roses. His expression froze, wariness cooling the twinkle in his eyes. With barely a hesitation, he added, "'Course, I got me Bear Power along with being a great warrior, so this coon gets a little more than a squeeze ter his pizzle."

Richard made a face and rubbed the bridge of his nose. "I'm glad for you—I really am."

Travis shot another glance at She Sews the Roses and added, "Yer just not catching on quick enough, Doodle. They's others a-sneaking in from the sides, and yer blinder than a fire-burned buffler bull."

"I'm what? What did you say?"

Travis met Willow's gaze and shook his head. "I said, ye don't know shit, Dick."

Richard nodded in slow agreement. "Well, for once I can't help but agree with you. I've got a funny feeling, Travis, like I'm on the verge of making . . ."

A young man leading a robe-covered young woman stopped before Richard, nodded, and spoke softly in his tongue, an expectant tone in his voice. The young woman stared self-consciously at the ground.

Travis translated. "Dick. He wants ter know if'n ye'll lay with his wife. He says it would be an honor to the both of them."

Willow watched Richard from the corner of her eye.

Richard swallowed hard as the white-tanned robe slipped open to expose the young woman's body. From the barely budded breasts and the smooth brown skin, Willow doubted she was more than a year beyond her first menstruation.

He took a deep breath, and made a futile gesture with his hand. "Travis, tell her . . . tell her that I can't—wounded."

Travis chuckled, but spoke solemnly in the Mandan tongue. The young man nodded, and clutched his wife's hand.

"All right, coon," Travis growled out of the side of his mouth. "Ye'd better pray fer 'em. And do it up right pert, hear?"

Richard winced, teeth gritted, as he sat up. Sweat began to bead on his face, from the heat in the lodge as well as the pain of his exertion.

"Dear Lord God!" he cried out. "Grant this young man and woman big medicine! Impart unto them the knowledge of Plato, Aristotle, and, yes, most of all, Saint Augustine. Let them know forbearance of the flesh! Render judgment unto them with the same authority and sanction as would be rendered by Saint Bernard of Clairvaux!"

"Who's Saint Bernard of Clairvaux?" Travis asked.

"Christian mystical philosopher. All of his life he looked

forward to climbing the ladder to Heaven and watching the damned sinners falling past him into the pit."

"A treasure of a man, I'm sure," Travis agreed.

"They made him a saint."

"That happened ter lots of coons. Think of old Saint Louis, now, he's some, he is. Got a whole damned city named fer him." Travis turned back to the waiting Mandan, speaking rapidly. The young man nodded, and with a flourish, removed the beautifully beaded robe the young woman wore. This he folded very carefully and laid it before Richard, who gave Travis a satisfied smile, a look of accomplishment in his eyes.

The youth turned and led the naked girl over to Green, who sat conversing with Four Bears.

Richard's grin faded as the trader glanced up, eyes gleaming, and rose to take the young woman's arm. Willow watched Richard's face fall as they walked past and the naked girl gave him an excited smile of gratitude.

"Are you sure about this one having Power?" She Sews The Roses whispered into Willow's ear. "Take my word for it, go to Four Bears. At least he's a man!"

◆

Far to the west, beyond the treeline at the river's edge, the stark white of roiling thunderheads contrasted with the hot

blue sky above and mocked the black depths below—now partially obscured by silver skirts of rain sheeting across the far horizons of grass.

Willow was familiar with such storms; in the blackness beneath those soft clouds, wind, hail, and violent rains hammered at unwary victims, filled the drainages, and flattened all but the most sturdy of shelters. Lightning carved the heavens in streaks as thunder blasted and tumbled away into the distance.

Today, because of the storms, the wind was right, and *Maria* sailed upstream before the rushing breeze. They were being drawn into the storm, and a premonition of danger lay curled within Willow's souls.

Richard sat hunched on the coiled painter, his back bare to allow the wound to breathe. She had checked it that morning, satisfied with the dark scab surrounded by crusted yellow. The White man's spirit water had worked again—despite Green's scowling reluctance to use it thus.

Whites were funny that way. They insisted on drinking it, which only made their souls burn and their thoughts turn foolish.

She stepped past Richard and leaned down, arms braced, to watch the keel slice the murky water in a hissing rush. *Maria* surged ahead like a living thing. Willow could sense the boat's soul, even though the Whites scoffed at the idea.

The wind blew her hair out in a fine mist of black strands. The sail groaned and popped, the wooden mast complaining. For once, the *engagés* rode atop the cargo box. Some slept, recovering from their "rest" among the Mandan, while others tended to their mending. Several gambling games were being played, accompanied by shouts and curses.

On shore, Travis and Baptiste would be trotting the horses through the rolling hills beyond the river's bluffs, out where they could spot trouble before running afoul of it. Too many enemies filled this country. In that sense, Green's advice had been correct.

So, you stayed, silly woman. Here you are, your souls hurting. Dreams of Richard filled her restless sleep, his smile shining for her, a dancing light in his brown eyes. Her body ached for his, longing to join with him as a man and woman should. She had come to love him, and condemned herself in the process. No matter how she sought to delude herself, he had committed himself to Boston, to his Laura, and to the notion that this world held no possibility for the two of them. Ache for him as she might in her dreams, he would never share her bed.

Would it have been better to have taken a horse, chanced the Sioux, Assiniboin, Crow, Ree, and Hidatsa? And beyond them lay the Cheyenne, the Atsina, Arapaho, and Blackfeet. Like hungry coyotes, they filled this lush grassland with its endless herds of buffalo, antelope, and elk. Here—at least in summertime—a person would be hard-pressed to starve to death. So much game, and prairie turnips and ground bean grew everywhere.

She looked to the west, past the storm, and in her mind's eye imagined herself floating, rising up past the riverbank that slipped so gracefully behind them. Out there, beyond the trees, over the endless rolling grass, the land would become broken, cut by steep drainages that carved sharply twisted channels into the pale clay. The bluestem grass would give way to patches of sagebrush, to isolated stands of limber pine and juniper. Out there the sky would lose this dull, lowland blue to become deeper, crystalline. In the distance, stark against infinity, her mountains waited. Her souls rushed toward those pine green slopes, where flinty granite underlay beds of quartzite and the softened curves of overhanging sandstone. A swelling joy filled her when she thought of those high peaks, of the rich aroma of pine and fir. She could hear the sibilant wind in swaying branches.

Eagle soared there, drifting out from the cliffs over dizzying heights.

That was her land, the home of her souls. There she would find herself again. Only in that high country could she hear *Tam Apo*'s echoed voice in the breeze, see His pulse in the rippling waters, and feel His strength in the defiant rock.

Soon, Heals Like A Willow. Soon.

One of the *engagés* on the cargo box laughed raucously. Her reverie snapped like a dry stick.

She turned, pulling her gleaming hair back from her cheeks, and walked over to settle against the cargo box across from Richard where he perched on the coiled painter. The heat from the planks massaged her tense back, and she leaned her head against the oak.

Richard glanced uneasily at her. "Travis says that Four Bears asked you to stay with him."

"Yes."

He fumbled with the scalps tied on his belt. The sun had turned his pale shoulders ruddy. "Did you think about staying?"

She tried to see into his lowered eyes. "I did. He offered me many things."

"Well, if he offered so much . . ."

"He didn't offer me his soul."

"I see." He pursed his lips, the frown deepening.

"Richard, what happened to you? Green has a word, he calls you 'brooding.' What does that mean?"

"It means absorbed to the point of distraction."

"I don't know those words." English was so hard. She felt lucky enough to have finally managed the "ch" in Richard's name.

"It means I don't know the answers any more. Not about life, about my father, or myself. Is it so wrong to believe in one man for one woman? Travis, Green, and the rest fornicate with any squaw that comes along! For God's sake, why?" He glared at her.

Uneasily, she answered, "If God did not make men to lie with women, why do you have a pizzle and I have a cunt?"

"*Where* did you hear that word?"

"That is what the *engagés* call my—"

"I—I know. Never mind, I . . . Willow, just promise me. Don't *ever* use that word. Not around civilized men."

She closed her eyes in disgust. "How can I understand your trouble when you won't even talk to me about it? Does this offend the Power of your damned philos'phy?"

He gave her a misery-laden stare, finally whispering, "No. I mean . . . it shouldn't." He paused, gesturing with his hands. "Something's happening to me, Willow."

"It's the Power in your soul, Richard. It looks for a way out."

"Power? That's magic . . . superstition. I don't believe in that kind of nonsense."

"You want everything to fit the way you believe. It's like seeing a fish and trying to make it into a bird. I can't understand you. What makes your way right, and everyone else's wrong?"

He gave her a hostile stare. "Four thousand years of rigorous philosophical dissection, debate, and discipline."

She took a breath to still her growing anger. "Different people have different truths. No one truth is better than the others. If you wish to know the Mandan, listen to their stories. In the Mandan village I heard the story of Black Wolf, one of the Mandan heroes from the beginning times. He went out and killed the monster Four Stripes. To do so the Old Ones turned him into a woman, and Black Wolf slept with Four Stripes to lull his suspicions. Afterwards, as Four Stripes slept, Black Wolf killed him. The Old Ones turned him into a man again, and he started home. On his way back to his people, the Sacred Grandmothers told him that a young woman should couple with a powerful man, and then when her husband lay with her, she would give that power to her man."

"Willow, you can't compare a story with truth. Something in the universe must be ultimate. Absolute. That's what I've lost."

It is hopeless. He cannot, will not, understand. She rolled the fringes on her sleeve between slim brown fingers. "You're wrong, Richard. Stories are full of truth. That's the Power they have. They are more than just the words. The stories live, and have Power all their own. They carry the souls, take them places and teach them things." She paused. "And what does the White man's God say? Are there no stories?"

"Of course we have stories. Adam and Eve. They lived in simple purity in the Garden of Eden. Eve ate an apple and obtained knowledge. In the process, she found out she was naked, and covered herself. When God saw her and Adam wearing clothes, he knew they'd eaten the forbidden fruit and cast them out of the garden. That's it."

"There must be another story. Does Eve never lie with Adam?"

"Well, yes, but the story doesn't exactly tell about it."

"Is she the only woman in your stories?"

"No, there's Mary, the mother of God. But she's a virgin. Jesus, her son, is born through immaculate . . . uh, by God's will. No man lies with her. Willow, believe me, there are no sexual unions in our stories. None. Even Mary Magdalene never lies with Jesus." Richard's frown deepened, and she could see his soul quickening, the gleam that thrilled her growing in his eyes. "Dear Lord God, there's no female element! That's one of the big differences."

"I don't understand."

He made a fist, thumping his knee. "No sexual stories. No female element to the stories. We don't talk about it . . . we never have. The celibacy of the priesthood, the virtues of the virgin marriage bed, original sin, all of it goes back to that epistemological framework." He gave her a quizzical look. "But what does it mean for us as a people?"

Willow stared out over the wind-rippled water. "It means you keep your women in houses like you do your God. Your Boston-God stories don't have women." She gestured around them. "I have heard Travis say this country is too dangerous for White women. You have been so blinded by your White God, you cannot join with a woman when you desire to. You are so trapped that you even hate your friends when they join with women. You have said you cannot take me back to Boston, that they will not understand."

"No, it's not—"

"I don't believe you, Richard." She cringed from the cold futility within her. "You claim to seek Power and knowledge. I have seen the thirst in your soul, and I have respected that, but now, I wonder if I was wrong."

"Willow, listen. Before I came here, everything was clear and concise. Right was right, and wrong was wrong. But everything I believed, it has all turned to shifting sand. I just have to find the way, is all."

It's hopeless, Willow. She steeled herself. "You've said that over and over. You will never find it, Richard. If someone tells you a new truth, you will call it a silly story. You deny the *puha* within you, and call it nonsense. You are like Coyote, who cast his eyes into a tree so he could see from the heights—but only blinded himself. I am sorry for you." She stood. Feeling absolutely wretched, she climbed onto the top of the cargo box. The *engagés* had been watching the exchange with amused eyes.

From behind her, Richard called, "Willow, please come back."

Too late, Richard. I've had enough. She ignored him as she stalked through the curious *engagés*. Her hand on her war club, she dared one to smirk, or make one of their pizzle-in-hand gestures. None did.

Green stood beside Henri at the steering oar; his face beamed with pleasure as the wind tugged at his baggy white shirt. At the sight of her smoldering glare, his smile disappeared.

"Green," she said calmly. "Tomorrow morning, I am taking my horse. I will be returning to my people."

"Now, Willow"—he raised weather-browned hands in mollification—"you know this country is crawling with hostile . . ."

"I am *leaving*." With that, she jumped down on the stern where Toussaint and de Clerk were playing eucher. Boiling with rage, she settled herself to watch the wake spreading out in a rippling V.

NINE

◆

The study of truth is partly hard and partly easy. A proof of this is the fact that no one man is able to grasp it adequately. However, not all men entirely fail. Each says something about the nature of the world, and, though individually he adds little or nothing to our understanding of it, but from the combination of all something considerable is accomplished. Thus, as truth seems to be like the door which, the proverb says, no one can fail to find, in that respect our study of it is simplified. But the fact that we can have some notion of it as a whole, but not of the particular part we want, shows it is difficult. Perhaps, too, the difficulty is of two sorts and its cause is not so much in the things themselves as within us. For as the eyes of bats are to the brightness of daylight, so is the reason within our soul to things that by nature are the clearest of all. . . .

—Aristotle, *Metaphysics*, Book II

Now, what's all this foolishness about?" Travis asked as he stepped out of the darkness into the glow of Willow's small fire. She'd built it out beyond the boatmen's camp and placed her bedding and packs under the spreading branches of a grizzled old bur oak.

She looked up at him, dark eyes gleaming in the firelight. Her slim fingers stroked a willow stick she'd been smoothing with a sandstone abrader. When finished, the straight white wood would make an excellent arrow shaft. "I am leaving in the morning, Travis."

He scratched his bearded cheeks, grunted, and swatted a mosquito. "Baptiste and me, we cut fresh sign out in the hills today. Thirty, maybe forty hosses ridden Injun-file. 'Course, a feller cain't tell much from tracks alone. Warn't no travois drags, Willow. All warriors."

She said nothing.

He added, "Reckon we had us this palaver a time or two before. Ye knows how the wind blows out hyar, and she's a mite dangerous . . . specially this time of year. It's war season."

She shot him a sidelong glance, and returned to her work. How pretty she looked with the firelight accenting her graceful cheeks and the softness of her lips. Her long black hair spilled down over her shoulders and breasts, so rich and glossy he longed to reach out and touch it.

Willow took a deep breath, tilted her head back, and exhaled wearily. "I cannot stay here any longer, Travis. I have only been fooling myself."

"Uh-huh." *All right, coon, how'n hell are ye gonna handle this?* He squatted down on his haunches, pulled out his pipe and makings, and tamped tobacco into the bowl.

"And the worst thing is, I don't know how it happened to me! I am *Dukurika*—a woman of the mountains. He's a skinny White man with hair on his face. His skin is like a dead man's . . . one who's been floating in the river. You've seen such a corpse? The skin is that color of white. So, in the name of *Tam Apo*, why do I want him to touch me? Why do I want him to share my blanket?" She clenched both fists. "*Why* does he fill my dreams at night?"

"Dreams, huh?" Travis used twigs to snake an ember from the fire and light his pipe. Injuns set a heap of store on dreams. Over the years, that had rubbed off on him—like his Immel and Jones dream that kept recurring night after night.

"Dreams—yes." Her slender hands absently caressed the smoothed wood. "I see him with me, walking in the mountains. We hold each other and look out from the high places. Together, we share the hunt, then laugh as we cut up the meat . . . enjoy that rich smell of a freshly killed elk.

"And at night, we lie side by side under a warm buffalo robe. The fire crackles and sends its sparks up to join the stars. The nights are glass-clear up there, not like these plains. You can see so many more of the star people, like white frost on the black sky. Richard and I are together beneath that sky and talk of a great many things: of God, and Power, and the curious things men think and say."

She shook her head. "But it will not be that way, Travis. Something is not right inside him. Maybe it's that Whites only have one soul? I don't know."

"Willow, keep in mind—"

"Yes, I know. He has grown stronger in the ways of a man, but he has lost the way of the soul. Do you understand?"

"Yep. I reckon."

"I would help him find it again, except he will not open himself to the search. He has his way—and will accept no other."

Travis sucked at his pipe. "I just saw him over to the boat. He's all-fired anxious ter talk to ye."

"I do not wish to talk to him." She looked up. "I have no

more words. My souls still ache from the death of my husband and son. I cannot ache for Richard, too. I do not have enough of myself to give away any more. Not like this, not day by day." She closed her eyes. "Among my people, we believe that unfulfilled dreams will cause the souls to sicken and die. It is happening to me, Travis."

"Aw, I'm sorry, child." Travis handed her his pipe while he considered options. Problem was, he didn't have a whole lot of sympathy for the knothead Doodle.

She puffed, blowing the smoke toward the oak branches overhead.

"Ye might want ter at least hear what he's got ter say. He seemed—"

"No."

From the way she said it, that seemed like the kit and kaboodle. Travis rubbed the smooth scar tissue on his nose with a nervous finger, squinting out at the darkness. Buffalo wolves howled an eerie duet out on the grassy hills. "I'm a curious coon. I heard tell that Green asked ye ter take up with him. Then Four Bears made ye an offer. Does it have ter be Richard? Most Injun women would jump at the chance to marry white."

"I'm not like most women, Travis. I want more than White man goods, robes, horses, and a share of a chief's status." She handed his pipe back gloomily. "In all of my life, I have known only two men I could share my souls with. One, I married. He's dead because I couldn't save him. And Richard will not share his soul with me because his God has blinded him."

"Huh?" Travis cocked his head. What in Tarnal Hell did *that* mean? "Ye lost me there, gal."

She studied him with those dark, depthless eyes. "You can know a people by their stories, Travis. I have learned this of you Whites: in all of your stories, there is no woman to make up half of the world. Richard told me of Adam and

Eve, of Mary. There is no woman in any of the stories—at least, none who is important. And none of the women lie with men. Among my people, Coyote lies with women all the time. He even carries a spare penis, just in case. The Pawnee, the Rees, the Mandan, all have stories about women and men, coupling, creating life and the world around them. Tell me, when your God creates the world, does he couple with a woman to do so?"

Travis rolled his pipestem in his fingers. This wasn't an angle on God that he'd ever thought about. "Reckon not."

"Are any of the heroes saved by a woman?"

"Nope."

"And there is no coupling?"

"Nope."

"This is not balanced, Travis. No wonder you Whites think you have only one soul."

"And just how many should we have?"

"My people believe two. The first is the *mugwa,* the life soul. The second is *navuzieip,* the free soul."

"Free soul?" He squinted at her. She wasn't gigging him, just for fun, was she? Making jokes to see how far he'd go?

"The soul that leaves your body and wanders when you dream."

"I guess I'd always figgered that was just me imagining." But the dream he'd had down by Atkinson still chilled his gizzard. Michael Immel and Robert Jones had come to him, warned him about trouble at the mouth of the Big Horn.

Willow's words drew him back to the here and now. "Mother Earth and Father Sky, each is half of Creation. Tell me, why would your God be male if there was no female? Why would he need a pizzle and balls? Wouldn't you think such a God would be neither? Like a rock?" She sighted down the straight arrow shaft, then glanced at him. "I think maybe you Whites don't know shit about God. I don't understand how you can be so clever with things like boats, and guns, and glass, but so blind and confused about God."

"Now, I don't hold with a lot of Bible doings, but we ain't confused," Travis growled irritably. "Not at all. God just, well, He is, that's all. And—and just 'cause ye think *we're* confused ain't no reason ter go running off to get *scalped!*"

She gave him an irritating, knowing smile. "Travis, I have learned what I came among you to learn. *Tam Apo,* Our Father, must be much like your God, but beneath him is *Tam Segobia,* Our Mother. He has Wolf and Coyote as helpers. Women fill our stories—maybe not as many as among the river peoples, where women own the houses and men belong to their mothers' clans, but they are there. And we have a voice in our councils.

"You Whites trap your women in houses to have your children. But I think I understand why now . . . and why Richard cannot share himself with me." She reached over and tossed a broken branch onto the fire. "I pity your people, Travis. They will never be whole."

He rubbed the tobacco-stained pipestem with a callused thumb. Just how did God expect him to answer that? "This child's been a heap of places, gal. Seen me a heap of sights. Some of what yer saying is fire in the pan; some's damp powder. Whites is folks like any others. Reckon they's some cruel—but so's Injuns, or this child ain't seen squat. Now, the good book our Lord gives us teaches folks to turn the other cheek, to show charity to the weak and hurt."

Her eyes flashed. "I think that is a lie. What did you do to the Shawnee? How do you treat your slaves? Even the belly-crawling Pawnee adopt a slave into a family. Do Whites? I've heard the stories Baptiste tells."

"Well, hell, whites is plumb nice compared ter Blackfeet, or Rees, or—"

"Good, bad, it does not matter. You don't understand what I am saying. Your souls are half empty."

He scowled at the fire, scratching for an answer and coming up completely blank.

She tucked her knees up and propped her chin on them to watch the fire. "Richard will always be White. I will always be Injun. He is a man. I am a woman—a thing to be kept."

"Maybe. Hell, I don't know what he's gonna be. Willow, he's come a long way from the skinny runt what François dumped on deck that night. He's come right about, he has. Taken coup, stoled hosses, larned a thing or two." *And why the hell am I defending him? He's been like ter drive me crazy since that Ree fight.*

"Those are warrior's skills, Travis. What of his soul?" She rocked back and forth, her delicate face framed by that gleaming raven hair.

"Soul? What in Hob do I know about souls?"

"Enough, Bear Man. You see more than you admit. He says he seeks to know the world; but he cannot until he looks within himself. Not just for courage, but for balance and understanding. His *puha* is struggling to come out, and he struggles just as hard to keep it trapped. I told him once that he couldn't 'think' his way to God. Maybe I was wrong. Maybe the White God can be known only by thoughts; but if that is so, it is a very different god from *Tam Apo,* who must be known here." She touched her chest.

Travis scratched his ear. As palaver went, this one was turning out poor beaver. "Ye ain't like any woman I ever knew, red or white. Reckon ye'd drive a coon plumb berserk."

"The way I did Packrat?" Willow raised an eyebrow and smiled grimly. "My father is a *puhagan.* I am his daughter. Among the *Dukurika* we keep the old ways—the ways from before the coming of the horses. My father taught me to ask hard questions. We are not like the *Agaiduka* and *Ku'chendikani,* who are starting to believe more like the Crow, Blackfeet, and Arapaho."

"Yer father, huh? Reckon he got a handful a-raising ye, girl."

"He did." She smiled wistfully. "During the late winter nights High Wolf, my father, told the old stories. The ones about the time after the Creation. Then we talked about what they meant. Why did Coyote do everything he could to pester Wolf? What did it mean when *Pachee Goyo* was carried away by Cannibal Owl? Why are *Nunumbi* and *Pandzoavits* magical, and most people are not?"

"Nunumbi? Pandzoavits?"

"Nunumbi are the little people, the ones who shoot magical arrows into people and cause sudden sharp pains, or trip them when they're walking in the forest. *Pandzoavits* are the rock ogres, with sticky hands covered with pine sap. When they catch lone travelers, they grab them and put them in baskets they carry on their backs. Then they run home to eat their catch." She smiled. "I was a full woman before I finally confronted my father. I told him I had never seen a *Nunumbi,* or a rock ogre, never felt their power, and didn't really believe in them any more."

"Uh-huh. And what did he say?"

"High Wolf nodded and smiled at me. That's when he told me that *Nunumbi* were real only so long as we believed in them. That was a very important lesson for me, Travis. I believe in the *Nunumbi* and *Pandzoavits,* and use power to guard against them; but unlike Richard, I believe in them because I *want* to."

"And that makes a difference? Wanting to?" He stared hollowly at the pipe, way out of his depth with such things.

"A heap of difference." She slapped at a mosquito that landed on her shin; the arrow shaft lay forgotten beside her. "Answer me this, Travis. Who needs who? If God did not believe in people, would people be like plants in darkness, and wither away and die? Or, if people did not believe in God, would God slowly waste into nothingness and die?"

Travis stared absently into the fire, trying to track his way around her slippery question. Finally he gave up. "Damned if I know, Willow."

She stretched then, her lithe body supple and provocative in the firelight. "Perhaps you should think about it, Bear Man. Then you would know why believing because you want to is so important."

"Tarnation! I'm the wrong coon fer telling this to. Go talk ter Dick about this hyar God, and such."

"I don't think his soul would hear the question, or feel the answer."

Travis knocked the dottle out of his pipe. "Just promise me ye won't ride off tomorrow."

"So that Green can have his Snake woman to help with the trade?"

"Nope. So I can get ye home safe. Reckon I'd not want ter dream about ye laying out there in the grass, scalped, wolf-chewed, and rotting in the sun."

"I will think on this. But I do not promise, Travis."

❖

The camp slept. A great horned owl's *hoo-hoo-hooo* carried on the night, water lapped at *Maria*'s hull, and night insects chirred and buzzed in the darkness. Richard lay on his stomach. He slept restlessly, his left leg drawn up, his right arm tucked close to his body. Though his wound might be healing, his soul ached. Perhaps he heard the yipping cackle of the coyotes on the near shore and the piercing rejoinder of the wolves to the south. Or was it just the dream . . . ?

I feel no fear, only a dull emptiness, like the hollow-stomached longing that comes from perpetual grief. As I walk up Park Street, and turn left onto Tremont, my steps echo. Boston is unusually quiet on this somber gray morning. The clouds hang low in the sky, brooding, and look ragged where wisps trail beneath.

The cobblestones are wet and grimy, gritty under the soles of my boots. Bits of trash soak in the puddled water.

Something is wrong. I glance anxiously at the shop windows. They gape back at me, and when I stop and peer inside, I see nothing. Only featureless gray. No familiar floor, ceiling, or walls—just a foggy emptiness.

The buildings are nothing but shells! When I tap my fingers on the wet brick, it sounds hollow. Rapping my knuckles on a stone wall, I get a wooden sound in return. I try a door this time, hammering on it with my fists. It's not right, somehow, and when I grip the doorknob, it doesn't turn, doesn't even rattle. I look closely and discover that the door isn't real, but painted onto the wall.

A suffocating anxiety filters through my chest. I back into the middle of the street and shout, "Hello!"

The call echoes into the blanket of silence.

I turn, running headlong to Hanover Street and round the corner. Everything seems familiar. I crisscross the street, racing from window to window. Each building is a sham—a false front beyond which lies that unsettling gray nothingness.

In the middle of the street, I cup hands to my mouth, hollering, "Is anyone here?"

Silence answers.

I cock my head. Even in its quietest moments, one can hear something in Boston: the breeze in the rafters; sea gulls; a slamming door; cart wheels on the paving. Now my ears fail to catch

the slightest whisper. Not the creak of a timber or the scurry of a mouse.

It isn't just the silence. Nothing moves but the wounded clouds drifting eastward. No pigeons, no birds, not even flies. I look up: no slips of smoke rise from the chimneys.

My heart begins to pound. Something is terribly wrong. I sense rising danger, brewing like a witch's cauldron. I break into a run, dodging left onto Union, panting as I fly down the silent street. I veer onto Charlestown Street, sprinting now, for something pursues me through the silent city.

Throwing a look over my shoulder, I see a darkness settling over the empty hulls of buildings. The miasma rolls toward me, devouring the city as it comes.

Dear Lord God, what had become of all the people? Will? Laura? Jeffry? Father? Are you gone? Dead?

I run faster. Fear prickles along my spine now, goading me to greater effort. It's coming . . . coming . . . I dash onto Causeway and run onto the Charles River Bridge. The planks boom beneath my boot heels.

In the middle of the bridge, I stop, for the Cambridge shore is murky and uncertain. I turn: All of Boston has been engulfed by the pall. The skyline can barely be discerned, the buildings no more than dark squares. No light burns in that sullen twilight; no sound is heard. It is as if the city never was.

Fear runs bright within me. I'm panicky, frantic to run, with nowhere to go. "What happened here? I don't understand!"

"What did you expect?" Professor Ames steps out of the gloom behind me. "You didn't think Boston was real, did you, Richard?"

"Not . . . real?"

Ames stares wistfully at the darkened city. The mild blue eyes have turned glassy in his ruddy face. He's a small man, frail-looking, with snowy hair, and as usual, dressed in black. "You still don't understand, do you?"

"I must find Will and Laura. My father's in there and he . . ." I bury my face in my hands, crushed by the realization of what I've done, how much I've lost. "He trusted me, sir. And I failed him. He'll never forgive me for this. . . . Never."

"It's not there, Richard," Ames says gently.

I look out between my fingers. The only thing that remains is a dark haze, like billowed smoke from a range fire.

"Not there?" I stagger forward, arms wide. Even the Charles River Bridge abutments have vanished. I stand on a bridge to nowhere.

"It never was." Ames's voice fades.

"But, sir! I was there . . . and so were you that last night at Will's, when Laura and I . . ." I turn back. Ames is gone.

My mind reels, like a drunken man's. I reach out and steady myself on the weathered wooden railing. All that remains is the bridge. The haze covering Boston swirls and darkens to sackcloth. When I look over into the water, it isn't the Charles that I see but the murky Missouri with its flotsam and foam.

My limbs are suddenly weak. *Boston, where is Boston? It couldn't just disappear like that.*

"It was there," I insist, looking back. The haze lifts and I catch glimpses of virgin forest. The treetops are barely visible in the darkness.

"I don't understand!" Where am I to go? What am I to do?

Harsh laughter makes me spin around. Lightning Raven, old One-Eye, the Sioux *wechashawakan,* sits on a buffalo robe, bathed in firelight. I am afraid of this old man. I first met him in my dreams, and then face to face in Wah-Menitu's village. He fixes me with the scarred socket of his empty eye. "It is all illusion, White Coyote. You—and your philosophy. None of it is real here. I watch you, and you become more and more like *Inktomi,* the Trickster. You fool yourself because you are a coward."

I back away. The bridge is gone, and the river runs just behind my heels. "No, I'm brave. I fought Trudeau, stole my horses back. I fought the Rees, and Packrat."

One-Eye's face twists with disgust—and fills the world. "Any man can fight and die, White Coyote. You are afraid to look at truth. Afraid of what you might discover." He drifts there in the air and as I watch he changes. His back arches, malformed and hairy. The sagging face is taking on a canine look, eyes, two of them now, yellowing, piercing me. The long lip lifts to expose wolfish teeth.

I back into the water, stepping down from the bank. The wolf leers down at me, death and violence in his eyes. Fear drives me out into the current. I stagger back and forth, arms flailing for balance.

I sense the wolf's intent—to tear my flesh from my bones. It will eat me alive. The current is tugging at me, wrapping around my legs and drawing me backwards into deeper water.

The wolf leaps—growling—and, with nowhere to go, I twist and dive into the black swirling water. Thrashing and kicking, I'm sucked down, ever deeper, my lungs fit to burst. I whimper fearfully as I'm whirled around and around.

I've got to find the way out . . . got to find . . .

Richard jolted awake, gasping for breath. Safe—he was safe on *Maria*'s deck. The fear slowly melted from his veins while a cool breeze caressed his skin. A gaudy sun had just cleared the eastern horizon to cast bloody light over the dark-shadowed land.

Boston an illusion? He rubbed a hand over his sweat-damp face. The dream remained so clear, as if lived rather than spun from phantasms. A Power dream, Willow would have told him.

Willow!—He had to see her, talk to her.

Am I a coward? Is that it?

Birds riddled the morning with intertwining songs, their music alive in the branches. Richard willed himself to sit up and stare out at the river; the water looked placid in the crimson light.

But no matter how smooth the surface, strong currents run beneath. A man could float along, mistaking the whirls and eddies for reality on life's journey to the sea of death. But dive down below and he would truly know the current's power as it jetted in endless passage.

Boston: a place of caged bears, all ignorant of the reality beyond the bars. What was it Professor Ames had once said? Something about a building, and walls . . . It hadn't made sense at the time, and Richard couldn't remember. Well, it would come back to him.

Boston—his world—where men constantly erected new bars to imprison themselves. They called the bars religion, philosophy, morality, or ethics, and the worst thing was that they never saw them for what they were: artifacts based on illusion. Not ultimate reality.

Richard moved slowly, deliberately, to remove his blanket. He gasped, not at the healing wound, but at the sunburn on his shoulders. The pain reassured him. That—unlike the city of his dreams—was palpable.

After all those months of patient lectures by Travis and Baptiste, he could finally understand what they were trying to tell him about freedom, and life.

Jaw clamped, Richard braced himself on the cargo box as he emptied his night water over the side. He'd lain on the deck for long enough.

One careful step after another, he made his way to the plank and tottered down to the camp. Smoke rose in blue twists from the *engagés'* breakfast fires. Men sat on rumpled blankets, smoking their long-stemmed pipes while they talked over the last of their watered-down coffee. Tin pots clanked as they were collected for the day.

Richard nodded to Toussaint and Simon as he passed their fire. Trudeau ignored him, as did de Clerk and the rest. At Travis's fire, the beds were already rolled, the saddles missing.

Richard studied the crushed grass, picking the trail through the bur oak and ash, to find the cavvy. Baptiste talked soothingly as he saddled the hammer-headed roan. Travis had picked up the white mare's front hoof, inspecting a cut on her fetlock.

"Good morning," Richard said.

"Yor up?" Baptiste asked. "I guess Willow's doctoring did you some good. Hell, I never seen a coon heal that fast from a wound like that."

"She's some, she is," Travis agreed, lowering the hoof and slapping the mare reassuringly. He straightened and studied Richard through neutral eyes.

"Where is she?" Richard looked around, expecting to see her ghost through the trees like a brown wraith, her bedroll under one arm, her packs secured by the other. "I really need to talk to her." Richard noticed that Willow's horse was missing.

"Too late, coon. She done lit out fer her people. Packed up afore dawn, saddled her little brown mare, and headed fer the mountains." Travis absently scratched the mare's ears. Baptiste had crossed his arms, head tilted. He watched Richard through hard black eyes.

Richard stared dumbly. "What? This is a joke, right? Another trick you're playing on me? Look, I've got to tell her something. It's important, Travis."

"Too late," Baptiste said gruffly. "She's done left, Dick. Ain't no trick to it. She pulled her stick."

"I don't . . . I mean, you didn't just *let* her ride off?"

"Wal, what did ye expect? That we'd tie her up and threaten to shoot her?" Travis demanded. "She's free, Dick. Ye freed her yerself back when ye raised the Pawnee."

"She can't leave. Not now. Not when I've—"

"She's *gone,* I said." Travis stepped closer, blue eyes cold as winter ice. "Because she wanted ye . . . and ye didn't want her. Not as a woman, anyway. Hell, I tried to talk her out of pulling her traps, spoke fer ye—Hob hisself knows why—but she'd made up her mind. And rightly so, I reckon."

"We've got to go after her." Richard eased his good shoulder against one of the trees to support the sudden weakness in his legs.

"Nope," Travis replied curtly. "Baptiste run a scout up the river last night. Atkinson and O'Fallon is about three days upriver. We gotta find a place ter cache *Maria*. By the time we get that done, Willow's gonna be long gone. She's gonna be riding careful, hiding tracks."

"But you could follow her, Travis. You're the best there is at working out tracks."

The scarred hunter gave him a grim smile. "Maybe. But we got the boat ter take care of. Dick, hear me, now. We're on the upper river. Ain't no friends out hyar. Understand? Assiniboin, Yanktoni, Atsina, Blackfeet, Cheyenne—any of 'em will take the boat."

"But you can't just leave Willow alone out there!"

"She's a growed woman," Baptiste said coldly. "She knows this country, Dick. She ain't no pilgrim."

Richard wrapped an arm around the tree, steadying himself with something stable in a world suddenly shaken. "What if they find her out there?"

"Then they'll rape her fer a while and lift her topknot after they's through." Travis spun on his heel, but not before Richard saw the strain on his face. "I ain't a gonna think about that, Dick. I got a boat ter get upriver. Now, come on, Baptiste, we ain't got all day."

Mute, Richard watched them pack, grab up their rifles, and climb into their saddles. Then they hazed the rest of the horses out of the little clearing. Travis hesitated at the break in the bur oak, touched the brim of his hat, and clucked his horse onward.

Richard rubbed the back of his neck, and made his way to Willow's camp. He bent down to run his fingers over the flattened grass where her bed had been. The fire still held warm embers, faint ribbons of smoke rising from the ashes.

A sickness lodged in the pit of his stomach. *My fault . . . all my fault.*

TEN

◆

Adam, though his rational faculties be supposed, at the very first, entirely perfect,
could not have inferred from the fluidity
and transparency of water that it
would suffocate him, or from the
light and warmth of fire that it
would consume him. No object
ever discovers, by the qualities
which appear to the senses, either the causes
which produced it, or the effects which will arise from it;
nor can our reason, unassisted by experience, ever draw
any inference concerning real existence and matter of
fact.

—David Hume, *An Enquiry Concerning
Human Understanding*

Travis lay in the grass beside Dave Green and Henri.
The booshway growled angrily under his breath as
he glared at the river beyond the mat of buffaloberry
branches. Henri had his pipe clamped between his teeth; the
bowl was stone-cold. Despite Green's growling, the patroon
remained calm, staring out at the river's main channel.

Travis gave Green a sidelong glance. The booshway wore
a baggy white stroud shirt, a felt hat pulled low on his blond
hair. His blocky face had a hard set, blue eyes narrow as he
glared at the world. His thick fists were clenched.

Travis worked his chew from one side of his mouth to the
other, and spat a brown streak with enough accuracy to
knock a grasshopper from a spike of bluestem. Dave was fit
to kill, all right.

The patch of buffaloberry where they lay concealed them from observation. They'd found the perfect place to hide the boat. Behind them, *Maria* was screened from view by a wall of young cottonwoods. They'd pulled her into an old loop of the river, cut off now, and mostly silted in. To the north, grassy bluffs—worn down by countless seasons of wind and storm—had turned tawny in the late August sun.

"We'll be fine," Travis said. "The boat's outa sight. Ain't nothing to give us away to Atkinson."

"It's not Atkinson and O'Fallon." Green shook his head slowly. "Though it'd be hell if they caught us up here without a permit."

"Willow?"

"I'm going to reach out with these hands"—Green's outstretched thick fingers curled—"and choke the life right out of that skinny little Doodle bastard!"

"Now, Dave"—Travis swatted at a big bottle fly—"she's free. Ye agreed to that way back this side of Fort Atkinson. Said she's a guest, remember?"

"Why didn't you stop her?" Green demanded, his square face reddening with anger. "You had the chance! Don't you know how important she is to us? Damn, man, she can bring in the Shoshoni! Think of the opportunities that squaw represented. And you . . . you just *let her go?*"

Henri's mustache twitched, but he kept his expression bland.

Travis's eyes followed the fluttering path of a little blue butterfly that wobbled past his nose. "She ain't just a squaw, Dave."

"Now, what in hell does that mean?"

Travis rolled his chew and shifted away from the stiff grass prickling his side. "Reckon she's a friend of mine."

"Then, why in hell did you just let your *friend*—and an opportunity that could save us years—ride off into the plains? Don't you—"

"Because I set store by friends, Dave," Travis replied coldly. "Or maybe ye've a short memory on that account?"

"Easy, my friends," Henri said, studying the river.

Green ground his teeth. "No. I haven't forgotten, Trav." Silence stretched. A flock of siskins twittered in the overhanging cottonwood branches, playing among the triangular leaves.

"So." Green relented. "She made a friend out of you?"

"Uh-huh." Travis squinted across the river. She'd be down there, someplace. Far to the south, cutting across country, keeping off the skyline, running shy of the waterholes and creeks to avoid human hunters. "Never met a woman like her afore. Seems ter me, Dave, that we otta cross our lucky stars that her type's as rare as it is. Too many Injun women like Willow, and we'd be in a fix fer sure up hyar."

Henri tapped wistfully at his cold pipe and added, "I know that one, she is like the fox, cunning and quick. And she fights like the panther when cornered. If anyone can cross the plains, it is *ma petite Willow*."

"Well, I sure never met a woman who could see as clearly as Willow did. That queer look she'd give a feller . . . I guess I believe her when she says she's looking straight into your soul." Green shifted, curious. "You ever try and take her? Offer to marry her?"

"Nope." Travis worked his chew and fingered his rifle.

"Why not? She was the match of Calf in the Moonlight, that's sure. Or did that warn you off?"

"Nope. First off, she and Dick was making eyes at each other. Another reason was she didn't give me no sign she's interested in the likes of me. Last of all, I don't reckon no coon with sense would go pushing himself off on her. She kilt the last red bastard did that."

"Hamilton killed him."

"He just finished the job she'd started. Mark me, Dave. She

had that Pawnee kid right where she wanted him. You told me yerself how he was plumb spooked at Fort Atkinson. Said he was crazy enough to try and ride off on a hobbled hoss. She done that to him. Claims she drove him insane—and this child believes it. Only coon hyar could have had her was Dick."

"Yep. And I'm going have his sorry hide just as soon as the damned army floats past. That white-arsed Doodle's going to wish he'd died clear back when he had the scours." Green clenched a gnarled fist to make his point.

"Leave him be, Dave."

"*Leave him be?* Not on your—"

"Leave him be." Travis poked Green with a hard finger.

"Damn you, Travis, sometimes I don't understand how your head works. Just let him alone? After he soured the deal with Willow? It was his stupid, bull-headed idiocy that drove her off. Hob take him! A woman like that . . . and he just ignored her!"

Travis spat one last time, then plucked the chewed quid from his mouth, studying the toothmarked leaves before flinging it out into the nodding sunflowers that grew to his left. "How come ye quit playing cards with me?"

"Got tired of getting skinned down to my bones. Tarnal Hell, if I played for money with you, you'd own this whole shitaree—boat, barrels, and muskets. I can't pull nothing over on you."

"Then trust me, Dave. I seen the look in Dick's eyes when he figgered out that Willow'd gone fer good. He ain't looked that bad since the night François dumped his sorry carcass on deck. Leave him be . . . in fact, be nice as Hob. Reckon he'll do just fine a-twisting his own tail. Hell, the way he blames hisself, if'n he was Christ, he'd be pounding the nails into the Cross."

Green considered, a grim smile curling his hard lips. He fingered his thick blond beard. "All right. I'll let him alone."

"Good."

"I don't know why I let you talk me into these things."

Henri chuckled to himself.

Travis pointed down at the bend of the river. Baptiste came toward them at a dead run, skirting wide of the spiky green rushes in the marsh bottom. "Lookee yonder. The way Baptiste's moving, Atkinson and his soldiers is just round the bend. Reckon I'm gonna Injun over and make sure the *engagés* stay put."

Green's fists clenched. "All right. Try not to shoot any if you can help it. Last thing we need is for the army to hear a shot."

Travis grinned, backing away. "Ye know me. If'n I'm ary a thing, it's careful!"

"Oui." Henri added. "And sneaky as a Comanche in a trader's horse herd."

Some long-gone storm had blown down a giant cottonwood. In subsequent years the bark had sloughed off to expose the smooth wood to sun and weather. Time had silvered the bare trunk, which now served as home for ants, spiders, and field mice, and made a perfect seat for Richard Hamilton as well.

He sat hunched in the midday sun, using a long stem of grass to slap aimlessly at bugs, grass spikes, or simply nothing as the mood struck him.

Maria lay grounded on the mud behind him while the *engagés* sat in clusters in the shade of the cottonwoods. The day of rest would have been a delightful respite, but for the muggy heat, the biting flies, and the sense of desolation that possessed him.

In the beginning, he had expected to see her come riding in, head high, raven braids bouncing as she pulled her mare

up. Then, ever so regal, she'd give them that knowing look and fall in on one side of the horse herd.

But the distant horizon had remained empty. Nor had she appeared out of the tree-filled bottoms with their brushy cover.

Face it, she's gone. The thought turned over and over in Richard's mind. Each time it did, the soul-sickness expanded, eating more of him.

Sure, he was supposed to think of Laura, of how they would marry eventually, but Laura lived in a different world, one Richard couldn't be sure existed any more. Here, on the river, he dreamed of Willow, and forbidden love.

How did you make such a mess of this?

He closed his eyes, remembering the first moment he saw her, sitting straight and proud on Packrat's horse. *I shot him dead to protect you, Willow. Blew his chest open.* She'd been hurt, and he'd held her, carried her, marveling at the softness of her body.

"The first time I ever held a woman." He slashed bitterly at a ladybug, missing the insect but knocking it off the half-eaten leaf it had been laboriously crossing.

How close he had come to surrendering to her that day above the Grand Detour! He'd been bathing in the clear water, enjoying the sunlight sparkling off the ripples and warming his bare skin. What horror he'd felt when he looked over to see her standing there like a goddess. He could recall every detail—how the sunlight had caressed her, the way her hair glinted. Yes, and the way the water had beaded like diamonds on her dark skin. Somehow, in the talk that followed, they'd drifted together, responding to the caress of the water, and each other.

Why didn't you do something? Slashing at the grass again, the stem broke. He rolled it between thumb and forefinger, scowling. "Because she was an Indian . . . and I was a fool."

"First his woman leaves him, and now he talks to himself," Trudeau's voice intruded.

Richard jumped to his feet, wincing at the dull ache it caused in his back. Trudeau stood several paces away, white shirt rippling in the breeze. Mockery filled those dark eyes. Off to one side stood Toussaint, arms crossed.

"Go away," Richard said wearily.

"Go away? Like your woman, eh?" Trudeau laughed, shook his head, and sauntered off toward the other *engagés*, his fingers tapping the grass spikes as he went.

Toussaint studied Richard with veiled eyes. "Trudeau, he's still bitter, Reeshaw," Toussaint made a Gallic shrug. "A man ees no more than he ees."

As the big *engagé* trailed off in Trudeau's wake, Richard plucked another grass stem, looking closely at the tiny veins in the rough green leaves. "A man is no more than he is. *Cogito, ergo sum.* God, does that mean I'm going to be a fool for the rest of my life?"

"What's that, coon?"

Richard shook himself, surprised that Travis had stopped behind him. "Is everyone sneaking up on me?"

"Nope, just walking normal like." Travis cocked his head, careful eyes on the *engagés*. "But ye was so all-fired interested in that stem of grass, I could'a lifted yer topknot clean, and ye'd never have known a thing till the breeze was blowing acrost yer skull."

"Did you come here specifically to harass me?"

"Nope. Come ter do a head count on the *engagés* . . . and it looks like they're all hyar."

"Green ordered Toussaint to keep track." Richard winced as he swiveled his shoulder, surprised at how much more he could move it today. "He's a strange man."

"Yep. Come from Montreal, way back when. Story has it that Toussaint come home early one night and caught his wife in bed with his best friend. Supposedly he kilt 'em both, throwed lamp oil on everything, and set the whole shitaree afire. Trouble was, he had two twin daughters, little babies in a crib. They burnt, too. Now, some folks might forgive a man fer burning his wife and her lover, but not them baby girls."

"Did he ever say why he burned the girls?"

"Not ter me, he didn't. I ain't never heard him talk about it. Story tells it that he burnt 'em because he warn't sure they's his daughters. But that's just story."

Richard rubbed the back of his neck, glancing skeptically at Toussaint. "I can't believe it. The man saved my life that time the bank caved in and pitched me into the river. I would have drowned but for him. And he always seems to be concerned with doing the right thing."

"Uh-huh. Wal, if'n yer gonna fall in the river and drown again, don't go sleeping with his wife first. He might not pull ye out next time."

"Just once I wish you'd—"

"Come on, coon." Travis turned on his heel, the Hawken balanced in his right hand. "I figger ye'll want ter see this."

Richard glanced warily over at Toussaint, who now lounged against a cottonwood, chin propped on his callused hand as he watched three-card monte being played on a blanket. Killed his wife? *A man ees no more than he ees?*

Richard shook himself and followed in Travis's tracks. They wound through the cottonwoods, then down toward the willows. Travis raised a hand for care, and led the way into a copse of cottonwood saplings just up the bank from the roiling water.

Richard crouched and followed Travis into the conceal-
ment of the trees. "What are we doing?"

"Atkinson and O'Fallon is coming. They're just yonder,
round that bend." Travis studied Richard from the corner of
his eye. "Ye thought much about them?"

Richard sighed. "It would be a fast and safe trip back to
Saint Louis, wouldn't it?"

"Yep."

"Wait a minute. Why are you bringing this up? I said I'd
stick with you until the mouth of the Yellowstone. We're not
there yet."

"Ye ever think about what happens when ye get there?"

"Yes. I take a horse and ride for Saint Louis."

"Uh-huh. So, tell me, Dick. What're the chances that
ye'll make it—a lone white man—two thousand miles
through the dead of winter, with the temperature at forty
below, snow drifted higher than an elk's ass, and ten thousand Injuns all fit ter lift yer outfit and hair first chance they
get?"

Richard exhaled wearily, dropping his head into his
hands. "I don't know. Damn, Travis, I'm not even sure I care
any more. But, I . . . Just a moment, this is lunacy. Why are
you doing this? What do you care? You're tempting me,
damn you. Why? What game are you playing?"

Travis fingered the scars running across his face as he
watched the river. "I ain't playing no game, Dick. I'm giving ye facts, is all. And I reckon I'm a mite curious. How are
ye gonna choose? Coming round that bend is General Atkinson, nine keelboats, and hundreds of soldiers. Ye'll be back
in Boston in time fer Christmas—and nary a chance of getting yer hair lifted on the way."

"And the other way?"

"Ye'll stick it out on the boat . . . as an *engagé*. Sweating
and pulling yer way to the Yellerstone. I reckon it'll be the
end of September by the time we get there. Probably be the

first of November by the time we make the mouth of the Big Horn. Ye won't have safe passage down the river fer another year—and then it won't be no nine keelboats full of soldiers."

"Salvation or Hell, is that what you're offering me? Who are you, Satan in the wilderness?"

Travis smiled grimly. "I been called worse."

"I don't get it. You've laid a trap in this, haven't you?"

"Nope. It ain't no skin off my arse no matter what ye choose."

"If Willow hadn't left, you wouldn't be doing this, would you?"

"I reckon not."

Richard rubbed his sweaty face. That's when he saw the coyote watching him intently from the thick grass. The yellow eyes seemed to bore into his, measuring and weighing. But he didn't have time for coyotes. "I don't understand."

"Call her a test, Dick. Philos'phers take them, don't they?"

"Yes." *A test? To see if I'm stupid enough to stay, or smart enough to go?* It had to be something deeper than that. Travis Hartman never did anything simple or superficial.

"Is it that you want me to go? That you're mad because Willow left? Look, I didn't force her to go, Travis."

"Nope. At least, not at gunpoint." The hunter cocked his head as if listening. "Tell me, Dick, do you love her?"

Images of Willow filled his mind, the firelight on her face at night, her slender hands so graceful, the endless depths of those large dark eyes that seemed to have looked into eternity. How whitely her teeth flashed when she smiled.

And Laura?

She's become a myth, Richard. As much an illusion as Boston. Face it, she's a dream.

Richard cleared his throat. "Yes."

Travis pulled his rifle up beside him, and chewed

thoughtfully at the fringes of his mustache. "And if'n ye could get her back, would ye?"

Richard nodded, unwilling to make the vocal commitment that his soul screamed.

"Wal, coon, she's upriver." Travis jerked a thumb. "That is, if'n she makes it safe back to her people. More than one man around hyar is ready ter choke ye dead fer making her leave. Me, I understand her reasons, and I figger I understand yers. Ye made that choice, and now, by God, ye'll live with it."

"Then, you're telling me this because you *want* me to leave?"

Travis's blue eyes were cool. "This hyar's yer Yellowstone, Dick. I'm just making ye choose early because it's the smartest thing. If'n ye want ter go home to Boston now, ye'd be best ter take Atkinson's boats. But, when ye makes that choice, ye'll live with it fer the rest of yer life."

Richard closed his eyes. "But if I go with you . . . there's a good chance I'll be killed up there." The *wechashawakan* had as much as promised it that night at Wah-Menitu's village. But he'd also promised that the answers lay upriver, and hollow emptiness back east.

"I reckon if'n I's a philos'pher, I'd take Atkinson's boats back."

"Just once I'd like to see you be wrong for a change."

"Last time I's wrong, I got half my guts carved out and had ter have yer likes sew me shut."

Richard grinned in spite of himself. "So, let's say I go with you. What are my chances of finding Willow?"

Travis shrugged. "Baptiste and me, we figger it's fifty-fifty that she makes it home safe. She ain't no pilgrim, that's certain. The way she had it figgered, she'd cut straight southwest to the Little Missouri, stick ter the uplands, sneak down ter water at night, and make about twenty-five miles a day. More'n that, she'll wear that little mare down."

"If no one catches her."

"There's always that."

The pesky coyote's stare still fixed on Richard. Didn't the creature have enough sense to steer shy of men?

"I'd have stopped her if I'd known. Travis, I would have thrown myself at her feet and begged forgiveness for all the stupid things I've said and done. God, I hate myself. What a hypocrite I've been. Talking about Truth—Truth from the narrowed blinders of a silly Bostonian. I've been wrong all along. Arrogant in my ignorance."

"Would ye fix it?" Travis reached into his possibles for his tobacco. He cut a chew off the twist and offered it to Richard.

"If I could." Richard studied the brown plug, and shook his head. "Everything we accept as true, it all comes from Greek, Roman, and Judaic foundations. Christian thoughts and dogma were built upon them and have shaped everything we believe. But it's only true in Boston. Not here. You tried to tell me." He swallowed hard. "Willow tried to tell me."

"She's a one fer that, she is. The night afore she left, she asked me about God. She asked, 'If God doesn't believe in us, will we die? Or, if we don't believe in God, will God die?' And she said it was really important to know what you want ter believe. Now, that took me some figgering, 'cause I reckoned that ye just believed what ye was supposed to. Hell, this child never wondered *why* he's supposed to."

"She confronted me with the same epistemological challenge."

"Huh? Epissed . . ."

"Epistemological. The study of how we know what we know."

"Ye didn't use that word on her, did ye?"

"Of course. I think I mentioned eschatology as well."

"Esskat . . . Shit! No wonder she left."

"But that's the root of—"

"Shut up, yonder's Atkinson."

Richard crouched lower behind the branches. The first keelboat had rounded the sinuous bend in the river. It was following the main channel as it came into view. The brown boat's reflection elongated on the glassy blue surface. A second boat rounded the curve, and then another, and another.

On they came, rushing headlong down the river. Driven by human-powered paddlewheels, they seemed to fly across the water. Blue-coated soldiers lounged on the decks and cargo boxes. Some relaxed on bales; others occupied themselves with card games, mending clothes, or cleaning equipment.

"Hell of a fleet, ain't it? Not even Manuel Lisa ever got so many boats upriver. And ain't them paddlewheels some?" Travis spat, then pointed. "Lookee thar! William Ashley, by God. And them coons in the buckskins, why, I seen them up ter the Platte last year. Tarnal Hell, look at them packs of beaver!"

Richard squinted at the brown bundles lined up along the cargo boxes. "That's beaver?"

"Uh-huh. And ye can bet they's more prime stuff cached in the cargo boxes. Hell, old Atkinson should have had lots of room by the time his soldiers ate their way upriver and he give away all his presents. Ashley's a rich man, coon. That's a lifetime's wealth right afore yer eyes." Travis paused. "Lessen, of course, he up and gives the like away to François and his boys."

Richard bit off a quick retort, and Travis chuckled. The boats were moving fast, water boiling at the bows. With all those soldiers, that much power, it would be a safe trip. And not all would be lost. Talking with Ashley and the others, Richard could learn enough about the fur trade to repay at least a little of what his father had lost.

"If I want to leave, I can just up and run out to the edge of the river?"

Travis shook his head. "Wait until tonight. Ye can take yer white mare and head downriver. I'd reckon ye'll make their camp by morning."

"They'd ask where I came from. I'd have to tell them something—and Green doesn't have a trading permit. I couldn't lie, Travis."

"Nope. But then I know ye, Dick. If'n ye give yer word that ye won't tell 'em nothing about us fer a couple of days, we'll be so far upriver they won't come after us. By the time we take fur ter Saint Loowee, it'll be blowed over. Hell, maybe ye could talk ter old Red-Hair Clark and smooth it out fer us?"

"My father has a great deal of influence. It wouldn't . . . my God, what am I saying?" He watched the boats shoot past. They had to be making close to six knots.

They watched in silence as the line of craft rounded the cottonwood-lined bend of the river and vanished as if no more than a mirage.

The swelling emptiness in Richard's chest expanded; he lowered his forehead onto his hands. For long seconds, he was content to hear the rustle of the leaves, the chatter of the birds, and the humming click of the insects.

Dear Lord God, what am I going to do? Which direction do I go from here? He tried to quiet his milling thoughts. All those arguments on ethics, on responsibility, on man in nature, seemed no help to him now. The answer, the thing he was looking for, lay just over the mind's horizon. There, in the blackness of imagination. If only he could reach out just a little further . . . stretch that last bit and lay ahold of . . .

"Damn it."

"They's past, coon," Travis said, laying a gentle hand on Richard's wounded shoulder. "Wal, it's yer decision ter make."

Richard lifted his head, blinking, more soul-sick than he'd ever felt. "I've made it."

"Do I need ter saddle yer hoss?"

"Nope. But I changed my mind about that chew. Cut me a piece. I think I need it."

Travis gave him a wry smile. "Glad ter have ye aboard, Dick."

"Yes, well—then why don't I feel so good about it?"

The hunter straightened, stepping out of the cottonwoods to stare after the army boats. "Because, coon, I knew ye wouldn't."

Richard glanced over at the tall grass. The coyote had vanished as if he'd never been.

◆

At the top of a rise, Willow pulled her horse up, watching her backtrail in the slanting light of sunset. The whole world might have turned to soft gold as the tawny grasses glowed in the yellow light. Undulations in the land created soft shadows and honeyed contours that grew ever fainter until they met the darkening blue of the northeastern sky. The heavens rose like a glassy dome, a fitting cap for the majesty of the vista.

Nowhere in that infinity of grass did she see more than scattered bands of buffalo and antelope. Her horse stamped, flicking ears and tail at the bothersome flies.

Willow reached out to pat the mare on the neck, whispering, "And to think I don't like horses."

An ear swiveled in her direction.

"You and me, we are going to be friends for a while. At least until we reach the mountains. After that, who knows? Perhaps I shall turn you loose in the meadows."

Willow clucked her mare forward, winding down from the high bluff into a hollow. Spikes of grass made a hissing sound as the mare broke through their virgin ranks. They pattered off the bottom of Willow's moccasins, seeds knocked from the bristling heads.

So much grass, ridge after ridge, as far as the eye could see.

Following the lay of the land, Willow crossed a divide and worked her way down into a shallow valley as the sun turned gaudily red, flattened on the dark silhouette of horizon, then sank behind the distant bluffs.

Just after sunset, she made camp in a patch of chokecherry and wild plum. A small fire, barely enough to see by, satisfied her needs. The night was pleasant, and she needed only to warm a tin cup of water for tea. The rest of her meal consisted of dried berries, pemmican she'd traded for among the Mandan, and slivers of jerked buffalo meat.

Unrolling her blanket, she leaned back against the saddle and watched the night sky darken. Frosty specks of starlight twinkled and grew ever brighter.

The air carried the scent of dry grass, brush, and leaves. Occasionally the breeze would tease her with smoke from her dying fire, now burned to faint red embers.

The mare crunched contentedly on grass, molars grinding loudly in the newly fallen silence. Somewhere in the distance, buffalo wolves howled into the gloom, to be answered a moment later by a band of coyotes, their yipping calls higher, mocking, the way Coyote had mocked Wolf since the beginning of time.

The familiar stories of her Shoshoni people brought her comfort. Coyote and Wolf, always in opposition. Wolf, ever so responsible, dedicated, and obsessed with duty. Forever crossed by Coyote, the Trickster, who sought shortcuts, gratification, and trouble.

She sipped her mint tea, and stared into the starry maze of night. "How did I act? Like Wolf, responsible, and prudent? Or have I tricked myself?"

As a child, she'd looked up at the night sky, conjuring patterns among the stars. And tonight, as she did so, she could see Richard's face, his eyes, nose, and mouth, shaded into reality by the longing in her souls and the dusting of starlight across the heavens.

He'd be in camp by now, staring into a fire as Travis and Baptiste smoked their long-stemmed pipes. The *engagés'* fires would be flickering in the background as soft French songs rose on the night.

What is he thinking? Am I in his thoughts the way he fills mine? She emptied the last of her tea, setting her cup to one side. Such a useful thing, a tin cup. Travis had given it to her.

You made your choice, Willow. You must live with it.

It hadn't been so hard. She'd simply saddled up and ridden out. The longing for Richard, and the companionship of Travis and Baptiste, had only begun to hurt. In the coming days that gnawing ache would try her souls.

She crossed her arms, seeing a star streak across the sky and vanish. "Yes, it will hurt. But only for a while." As the distance between them grew, so would the ache fade.

"In the end," she promised herself, "it will be much kinder for you than suffering each day—so close to him, and so far away."

She resettled herself under the blanket. "Good-bye, Richard. May *Tam Apo* watch over you, and help send you back to your Boston."

Then tears blurred her vision of the stars.

ELEVEN

◇

. . . Moral virtue is not implanted in us by nature; for nothing that derived from nature can be metamorphosed by habit. Thus a stone that naturally must fall downwards, cannot be habituated or taught to rise upwards, even if we tried to train it by throwing it up ten thousand times. Nor again can fire be trained to sink downwards, nor anything else that follows any single natural law be habituated or trained to follow another. It is neither by nature, then, nor in defiance of nature, that virtues are nourished within us. Nature gives us the capacity to receive them, and that capacity is perfected by habit.

—Aristotle, *Nicomachean Ethics*

The days of September wore away under enamel blue skies, warm winds, and amber sunlight. The land had changed, the last stands of green ash left behind them. Cottonwoods in solid ranks lined the floodplain now, groves of bur oak only dotting the higher drainages. The Missouri ran almost clear—a man could see the bottom as he wrestled the heavy cordelle through rush-and-cattail-clogged shallows.

They pulled across the mucky confluence of the Little Missouri, and passed the mouth of Little Muddy Creek. Several times, small bands of Assiniboin rode down from the uplands to trade. Each time, Green bartered trinkets, pow-

der, and ball for buffalo robes, thick moccasins, and sections of pemmican-filled buffalo gut.

"Laying in fer winter," Travis remarked when Richard asked about it.

The night air brought a new crispness, one that tingled the skin and quickened the heart. How different the chill was—not the sapping damp cold of the woodlands, but cold that gave a fellow a sudden slap.

Like an ox, Richard labored on the cordelle, sparing neither his body nor soul. He drove himself, heedless of his injured shoulder, and then harder and harder as he healed completely and the scab fell away from the puckered scar.

At first, Trudeau had snorted, commenting about a booshway Yankee who couldn't even keep a squaw. Richard ignored him, but as his body hardened, Trudeau fell silent.

I bear my own cross, Richard told himself, bitter at the irony, for his cross was made of bristly hemp, his Golgotha forever around the river's next bend.

He had the time to think now, for the endless toil was mindless. The river had finally washed away his foolishness. Time and again, his thoughts turned to Phillip. By now his father thought his only son dead.

First Mother, and now me. How deep is the wound in his soul?

Every ache, every blister and trickle of sweat that ran down his bent back, came in the penitent quest for self-forgiveness. He'd stagger forward, coaxing more out of his fatigue-numb flesh.

A philosopher? No, a fool. And an arrogant one at that! Muscles popping, he'd throw himself into the pole, trying to shove *Maria* upriver by sheer force of body and will. He welcomed the pain as the pole bruised his shoulder. *If I can chase down the Crow, I can endure this.*

He could envision his father, incomplete, and adrift. Like a dim reflection of his civilization, he had nothing but a shield of masculinity left.

Panting, he'd wipe stinging sweat from his eyes and glance over at Travis where he sat his horse at the edge of the cavvy, the Hawken resting crossways on the saddlebow. Over the distance, their eyes would meet. The flicker of understanding passing between them.

Then Richard would redouble his efforts, seeking to peel the cleats off the *passe avant* as he pushed the boat upriver. The other *engagés* might not have existed, phantoms among whom he worked.

Blind, everyone was blind. *But I have the first faint images of the vision.*

At night, he'd eat all he could hold, drink the last of the watery coffee, and seek his blankets. Then, despite the thick haze of exhaustion, the dreams would come. Fantastic images of Willow, her warm lips parting, dark eyes gleaming, soft strands of raven black hair curling around her perfect cheeks . . .

She danced in the sunlight, naked, full breasts swaying, water gleaming in silver droplets on her smooth brown skin. Around she spun, arms like wings as she rose and fell to the rhythm of French songs. Her dark eyes sparkled with a diamond intensity.

"I have the answer, Ritshard," her sensual voice told him. "It is here." And she pressed the hollow between her breasts. "The truth is here, Ritshard."

He reached for her—only to have her drift away like smoke on a soft morning breeze.

"Tell me! Please!" And he chased after her, nearly berserk with the need to hold her, to tell her it would all be fine in the end.

"I love you, Ritshard." Her distant voice caressed his soul. Then she faded like a chimera. Panic rose, timed to the beat of his heart, driven by a premonition. Subtle tentacles of horror tightened around him, invisible and shadowy.

He ran then. And ran, and ran, as he had in pursuit of the stolen horses; but the entire time, down in the root of his soul, no matter how hard he ran, he knew he was too late.

Finally, staggering with exhaustion, he topped one of the grassy knolls and found her.

She lay sprawled on her back in the grass, bloody sockets where those lustrous brown eyes had been. Her wealth of shining hair was gone, the skull caked with blackened blood. Her lips—dried by the hot wind—had pulled back from broken teeth. Maggots writhed in a gray-white ball where her tongue should have been.

Arrows pierced both of her breasts. Her nipples had been hacked off. The edges of the ragged wound in her belly had curled up and hardened, but he could see where they'd pulled her intestines out and strung them around for the coyotes and ravens.

My fault. The words would echo around his head. He bent

down to kiss her sun-dried skin. As his lips touched her, a shadow blotted out the world. Terrifying, it lowered itself over him, and a horrible chill settled into his soul until he could only bury his face against her wind-dried flesh . . .

Gasping, he awoke to stare around the silent camp. Any regret for his aching muscles, for the blisters and exhaustion, had vanished. And with sunrise, he rose again, ready to pull or push the boat onward, alone if necessary.

That night, he would dream it all again.

❖

Leading Richard's white mare, Travis rode the gray gelding down toward the line of *engagés* who cordelled *Maria* against the current. Like obstinate mules on a towline, they threaded through the marshy shallows, splashing and singing, as ragged-looking a crew as had ever ascended the river. At the end came Dick, back bent, head down, driven by that stubborn will.

Travis made a quick scout of the grassy flats leading up from the river. To the north, the bluff had been cut off sharp, and one day, some fool like Atkinson would build a fort on that level high ground. But, God willing, not for many years yet.

The wide floodplain to the south of the river rose in a sloping ridge. Here and there, cairns of white rock had been piled: ancient Injun signs that rose above the autumn yellow grass. Tufts of cloud sailed serenely from the west, schooners of white against the high blue.

Fat prairie dogs with sparkling eyes stood at the mounded

entrances to their holes. With each shrill bark, their tails flicked. The year had been a good one for prairie dogs, and if these critters were this fat, so were the buffalo.

A badger broke cover from one of the holes, its fur shaking in time to its waddling, bow-legged run. The blizzard of barks and squeaks went silent as the prairie dogs dived for safety.

Travis checked the pack behind his saddle, then clucked his horse to the edge of the flat beside the cordellers. He shifted, hearing the saddle leather complain, and called out, "Hyar! Dick!"

Richard left the line of curious cordellers and slogged through the rushes and tall grass. The Doodle had gone plumb to hell, ragged, dirty, face smudged, beard matted with filth. Sun-browned skin and hard muscle showed through rents in the shirt.

"Come on, Dick. Hyar's yer hoss. Climb up, coon."

Richard studied the white mare, noting the saddle with his rifle and possibles tied across the bows. "I've got work to do, Travis."

"Fer now, yer doing it with me."

Richard slid a muddy moccasin into the stirrup and swung onto the mare. Travis tossed him the lead rope before kicking his gelding around and into a trot for the high ridge.

"This wind, coon," Travis called over his shoulder, "it's mountain wind. Ain't a thing atween us and the Shining

Mountains. Take a sniff. Ye can smell it. This hyar be the last step. God's country starts at the mouth of the Yellerstone. Ye'll see. Wild, unkept. Full of bears and painters and buffler. Nothing soft about it, not like downriver."

"I didn't notice much that was soft downriver, Travis. In fact, some of the country was pretty hard."

"Huh! Ye'll see, Dick."

"My name's Richard."

"I think I heard that afore." Travis crested the rounded top of the ridge and pointed. "Thar she be, coon. Take a look."

At the base of the bluff, a sinuous ribbon of water wound its way out of the south to join the broad Missouri. Even from this distance, the water looked clear, inviting, somehow fresh and pristine. In the floodplain, the cottonwoods rustled with the wind, some of the leaves already turned bright yellow.

"The Yellowstone," Richard said reverently.

"I ain't been here since twenty-three. Last time I saw her, the ice was breaking and Perez, Sal Smith, ol' Jacques Lejeuness, and me was taking a pirogue full of fur south ter Saint Loowee." He gestured around. "'Course, all this was snow-covered, colder than a bat's ass. And this wind what feels so warm and dry today, she's a-blowing like the gates of Hell swung open, fit ter freeze a man's piss afore it hit the ground."

Richard slouched on the mare. "Did I ever tell you that you have a unique way with words?"

"Nope. C'mon." Travis booted his gelding and led the way down into the broad floodplain. Buffalo chips, bleached light gray, dotted the short grass that crackled dryly under the horses' hooves. Travis sniffed, detecting the moist smell of the Yellowstone.

"This hyar, she's a mite of a dangerous place." Travis glanced around. "A heap of coons has gone under hyarabouts. Kilt by Blackfeet, Sioux, Assiniboin, Atsina, and anybody else passing through. This country around the mouth of the Yellowstone, it's open ground, claimed by the River Crows, Blackfeet, and the Assiniboin, and even sometimes by the Hidatsa."

"You said Immel and Jones were killed on the Yellowstone." Richard's eyes had narrowed as they neared the outermost of the cottonwoods. "Was that around here?"

"Upstream a mite. Hell, lookee thar." Travis pointed to a big bundle resting in a cottonwood. Brown, a little longer than a man, it lay on a platform that had been laid across a crook in the branches.

"What is it, Travis?"

"Dead man wrapped in a buffalo robe. Tree burial."

Richard frowned, slowing his horse. "Whose?"

"Crow, most likely. Can't tell without dragging him down. He's gone beaver. Best leave him rest." Travis trotted his horse across an old river channel, hooves clattering in the rocks. "Death can come right quick in this country, Dick. A coon's got ter be on his uppers. Cain't take no chances, can't let yerself go—or the next thing, yer topknot's gonna be dangling from some Blackfoot coup stick."

"Are you trying to make a specific point?" Richard looked back over his shoulder at the lonesome corpse.

"Yep."

"Well, why don't you try saying it outright?"

They rode across the shallows and onto a gravel bar in the Yellowstone. Travis slid off his horse, tying the animal to a half-buried log that had drifted down to lodge here.

Richard stepped down and tied off his animal as Travis waded out into the river and drank deeply. He sucked down the cool water, happy with the familiar taste. Water trickling from his beard, he said, "Come on, Dick. Drink up. This hyar's mountain water."

Richard followed, mud washing from his worn moccasins and frayed hide pants. As he drank, Travis studied him, noting the dullness in the eyes, the smudged dirt, the stoop to the normally straight shoulders.

"All right, Dick. Peel yer clothes off'n that sorry carcass of yers."

Richard squinted at him. "What?"

"I said, peel, coon. Yer gonna wash up. Hell, ye smells like a hiverner, and yer all gone ter shit—and poor doings at that."

"I'm fine."

"The hell ye are! Yer crappy! Filthy, broke down like a runty camp dog. Ye ain't even wearing yer coups any more. Why? 'Cause yer all punky inside. It's eating ye, Dick. All that blame yer heaping on yerself. Well, by God and Hell, yer done with it hyar!"

"I said, I'm fine."

"Skin yerself, pilgrim." Travis gestured with his rifle.

Richard's fists knotted. "I'm going back to the boat."

"No, ye ain't." Travis balanced on his toes. "I brung ye hyar ter fix yerself. Yer carcass ain't a-going nowhar's until ye've made peace and cleaned up."

"You can't stop me."

"Wal, Doodle, it seems ye left yer rifle on yer saddle. I didn't." Travis cocked his gun, the click loud. "I can stop ye fer good, right hyar."

"Go ahead."

Travis shouldered his rifle, settling the sight blade on Richard's right eye. "Take a close look, coon." Despite the muted sound of the river, the click of the set trigger made Richard flinch. "Now, yer just a hair from dead. A mite of pressure from my finger, and old 'Meat-in-the-pot' hyar will raise ye certain. Take a look down that barrel, now. That's death, Dick."

Richard swallowed hard. "Travis? Why . . . why are you doing this?"

"Figgered to larn ye a lesson." And at that, he lowered the

rifle, pulling the trigger as he caught the cock with the crook of his thumb and set it at half-cock. "Yer fixing ter get yerself killed anyway. As yer friend, I could make it quicker than the Blackfoot would."

"You wouldn't have shot me."

"I don't point no rifle at no one lessen I'm ready ter kill him." Travis tilted his head. "Now, Dick, ye've had time to punish yerself. It's over, hyar and now. If'n it ain't, I'm gonna shoot ye dead and leave ye fer wolfmeat."

Richard sagged then, looking uncomfortable.

"Dick, I ain't got time fer this nonsense. We're on the Yellerstone now. Baptiste and me, we need another man ter help keep watch and guard the hosses. Look at ye! Yer trying right hard to ruin yerself, Dick, and I ain't gonna have it, that's all."

Richard lowered his head, water rippling around his ankles. "It's all gone hollow, Travis. I've been purging myself. That's all."

"I reckon a feller needs that on occasion. But time's come to ante up."

Richard paced back and forth, gesturing his futility. "Dear Lord God, Travis, I'm just beginning to understand how smart Willow is. She asked questions I've never heard before, challenged the very foundations of what I believe, what my people believe. But, do you know what? They'd throw her out of Boston! Call her a savage! Is that just? Is it ethical? Hell, to them she's nothing more than a greasy squaw!"

"You know she ain't. If'n they don't in Boston, I reckon that's their loss." Travis fingered the sight on his rifle. "But I never had no truck with them ignorant puff-and-struts."

"Everything they believe is wrong. All of it."

"Wal, ain't it all right fer some folks ter believe one way, and other folks ter believe another?"

"No! Don't you see? Not if you want to know *ultimate*

Truth, Travis! It's like . . . " Richard's brow furrowed, then his eyes lit. "Of course! That's the example Professor Ames used. Travis, think of a building. Our people see the north wall and we call it God. The Mandan see the south wall, and call it God. The Shoshoni see the east wall, and Rees the west. Each calls its wall 'God.' But which is the real God? None—they are only sides of God! What a philosopher wants to know is the whole of God—all the walls, the floors, the hallways and closets and roof. That's the ultimate Truth."

Travis cocked his head. "Maybe."

"I was taught to believe that the north wall was all there was. We've accepted that for over two thousand years. And we've made assumptions based on that acceptance. From each assumption, we've made *other* assumptions about right and wrong, good and evil, duty, honor, and sacrifice. Like weaving a tapestry of how the building should look, each thread elaborating the nature of God and world. Now, the whole tapestry has come unraveled. I don't know which assumptions are correct any more."

"So, why are ye pushing yerself so?"

"Because I'm ashamed of my hypocrisy. Willow must think I'm a complete idiot."

"Hell, she only stayed as long as she did because of ye, ye knothead!"

"And if she dies out there? Damn it, Travis, I have nightmares about it, of her lying dead, scalped, and rotting."

"She's a full-growed woman, coon. Snake Indian down ter the center of her bones. And, hell, even if they catch her, she'll make it through. She's got a heap of sense. Damn it, Dick, is it so hard fer ye to trust her?"

"I . . . hell, I don't know."

"Wal, I do. Now, listen. This country's hard. Sometimes folks die. That's life, boy. Real life, not the Boston-be-safe-in-a-cage kind. She knows what she's doing."

"If I could only apologize, tell her how much I love her."

"Do it when ye sees her in the mountains, coon."

"If I see her in the mountains."

"Wal, acting like ye are now, I ain't sure yer gonna live that long."

"Me? She's the one out alone."

"She's got sense. You don't. Now, skin yerself and start scrubbing."

"And if I don't?"

"Wal, any coon wants ter go moping about in this country's nigh dead anyway, so I ought just as well shoot ye hyar. First time yer out picking up firewood, a-feeling sorry fer yerself, some Blackfoot's gonna sneak up and kill ye anyway. Why, if'n yer as good as dead, I might as well save ye the trouble of waiting. And this way, there ain't no chance of somebody who's depending on ye being let down, neither."

Richard narrowed his eyes. "That's not reason enough to shoot me, Travis."

"Ain't it? I'll be honest with ye, Dick. *I'm damned tired of fooling with ye.* Hear? Look down south there, damn ye! Immel and Jones died just a mite yonder, where we're going. That's good enough fer this beaver. Now, if'n it ain't fer ye, well, I reckon we'd have ter figger which side of the building ye was seeing and which I was. Then we'd have a palaver over ethics—and in the end, I'd still shoot ye dead."

Then Travis smiled cynically and added: "Of course, there's the matter of the bet I made with Green and Baptiste."

"Bet? What bet?"

"I said I'd cure ye or kill ye—and bet a hun'ert prime plews on the outcome. Which, when a feller comes right down to it, makes all them walls yer talking about a mite frivolous."

"Maybe I'm making a career of being a fool."

"Wal, a coon's got ter do something with his life."

Richard kicked angrily at the water. Then he took a deep breath, pulled off the ragged remains of his shirt, stepped out of his moccasins and pants, and splashed into the water.

Willow followed a southwesterly course across hilly country cut by a cat's-cradle maze of drainages. The soil here came in many colors, yellow, bright red, and sometimes streaked in white, gray, and blue clay layers. Oaks crowded the bottoms while irregular patches of limber pine, juniper, and ponderosa timbered the higher slopes. Buffaloberry, serviceberry, and squaw currant matted the draws and covered cool streams. She knew where she was now, in the broken country just north of the Black Hills.

She traveled along the hillsides, sometimes leading the brown mare when the deer trails became too narrow. Off to the south, high-rising plumes of blue-brown smoke marked a fire racing across the grasslands. One set by lightning, or a human hand?

Let's just hope we don't meet them.

Nor were humans her only fear. A mountain lion had almost cost her her horse that morning. The lion had screamed less than a bow-shot above the trail she followed. Only by sheer willpower, and a little terror-mustered strength, had she been able to hold the mare. Her other great dread was bears. This was perfect bear country, the sleek beasts haunting the berry bushes with their ripened fall bounty. Each time they crossed a bear trail, the mare rolled her eyes and stamped. As long as Willow didn't surprise one, she and the horse had a chance to skirt wide and avoid a confrontation.

Willow ducked under the slanting branches of a giant

chokecherry, her mare bulling through with a crackle of branches and more than a little sidestepping.

"Don't you try that with me on your back," she chided, "or I'll cut your throat and eat you myself."

The mare huffed her sides, nostrils distended as she studied the slope below. Two gray wolves slipped through the tall dry grass and disappeared into the buffaloberry thickets.

Willow kept to the deer trail, moving slowly. Every so often she'd stop, generally in the shadow of a limber pine, to study both her backtrail and the nearest high points. Those hilltops worried her. There, high above the surrounding country, enemy scouts might lie in wait.

Warriors used such heights to keep an eye on the entire country. Like eagles, they watched for buffalo, elk, or antelope. To pass the time, men flaked their fine arrowheads from obsidian, chert, or quartzite. Sometimes a young woman would accompany her man, and while they talked, she'd work on weaving, making a basket or net, or perhaps painting designs on leather.

But more than game could be spotted. So could enemy warriors, loose horses—or a vulnerable woman traveling alone.

And if I'd been traveling this carefully, Packrat would never have captured me in the first place.

She tossed her braids back and stepped over a deadfall.

The trail skirted a patch of rosebushes, the spiny branches ripe with rosehips. Reaching out, Willow was able to pluck several and eat them. Since reaching the hills, she'd traveled on a full stomach—wild turkey one night, sharp-tailed grouse the next. Each day's forage provided chokecherries, wild plum, and the myriad of berries.

She rounded the side of the hill and stopped to stare out across the irregular bluffs. Far to the west, beyond the Powder River, high thunderheads obscured the horizon; but here, closer, was a landmark she recognized.

A half-day's ride to the south, a colossal pillar of naked gray stone rose from the rumpled land. Long grooves, like the grain of a tree, lined the sides leading up to the flat top. A dense forest of pines grew in the detritus at the base of the slope.

The giant monolith was called *We'shobengar,* a place of terrible Power. Among her people it was forbidden even to point at it, lest terrible *puha* be unleashed against the offender. Many peoples told the story of how a pretty girl was promised to Grizzly Bear in marriage. But when she grew into a young woman, her heart settled on a young man of her people. To avoid her fated marriage, she and the young man eloped.

When Grizzly Bear heard that his bride had fled, he pursued her in anger. Being a spirit animal possessed of great Power, he soon chased down the young couple. The girl and her lover took refuge at the top of the high pillar of rock, just out of Bear's reach. The giant grizzly scratched and scratched, cutting those long grooves in the sheer rock, but he could not reach the lovers.

The beautiful young woman and her handsome young lover were not allowed to escape, however. The giant grizzly moved into the rock, living there as he waited for his bride to try and climb down. In the end, only the vultures were happy, for the trapped lovers finally starved to death. And ever since, the spirit of the grizzly had lived inside the Bear Lodge, waiting through time for his wife to descend.

Willow massaged the back of her neck as she studied the tall pillar. *You see? Things could be worse, Willow. You could be trapped up there with Richard. The only way out to be eaten alive by the bear, or eaten dead by the buzzards.*

The southern flank of the hillside offered some protection for her movements. She studied the slope, picking the route with the most cover. From here, she would veer eastward, cross the head of the Little Missouri, then the Little Powder River, and finally the Powder River itself. After that, the Powder River Mountains lay only two hard days' ride to the west. If she placed herself correctly, she could slip right up Crazy Woman Creek on the old elk trail.

And then I will be home. Tam Apo, *guide me. I'm so close.* But then, because Coyote had fooled around with the beginning of the world, that's when unexpected disaster was most likely to strike.

She smiled wryly. "We'll just take our time, horse. Travel smart. That's the way to make it home."

The mare stamped, and ducked her head to rub her rope halter on a foreleg.

"Evening is coming. If we can cross this last creek and climb the other side of the valley, we can be out in the flats by nightfall. Then, if the moon holds, we can be far out into the sagebrush before it becomes too dark to travel."

Taking a deep breath, she gave the mare a jerk and started her careful descent of the hill.

Maybe it was only nerves, but she kept glancing at *We'shobengar,* unable to shake the feeling of eyes watching her every move.

Licking her lips, she patted the Pawnee war club at her side, and checked to make sure she could swing her bow down and that her quiver hung ready at hand.

Easy, Willow. You're just worried, stirred by We'shobengar's *dark Power, that's all. Relax, take your time, think. You'll make it.*

If only she hadn't thought about Coyote, and the tricks he played on people's hopes and fears.

TWELVE

◆

The causes and means by which any virtue is either produced or destroyed are the same; and equally so in any part. For it is by playing the harp that both good and bad harpists are produced; and the case of builders and others is similar, for it is by building well that they become good builders and by building badly that they become bad builders. If it were not so, there would be no need of anybody to teach them; they would all be born good or bad in their several crafts. The case of virtues is the same. It is by our actions and dealings between man and man that we become just or unjust. It is by our actions in the face of danger, and by our training ourselves to fear, or to courage, that we become either cowardly or courageous.

—Aristotle, *Nicomachean Ethics*

Phillip barely allowed himself to breathe. His heart was pounding painfully in his chest. *Dear Lord, pray that this man has answers.*

Blue smoke curled up from Charles Eckhart's cigar as he sat in a chair across from Phillip's cherrywood desk. The ship's clock tick-tocked the hour: well past six. Eckhart looked rumpled and travel-worn. He kept glancing around the office, at the Charleville musket, at the fireplace and globe, and the huge leatherbound Bible that lay open to Leviticus.

Through the French window behind Phillip, the faint glow of late afternoon sunlight slanted through the smoky haze that drifted up from Boston's endless chimneys. Out in the Commons, boys were playing and running.

Phillip nerved himself. "Thank you for coming so far, Mr. Eckhart. What . . . news?"

Eckhart puffed out a cloud of smoke and shook his head. "My regrets, sir, but I haven't anything pleasant to report. I enlisted numerous agents in Saint Louis, but we uncovered nothing. Several rumors came to our ears, one about a man named François who had recently arrived in Saint Louis, and flushly at that. He had been involved in nefarious dealings in Illinois and might have obtained ill-gotten gains there. Before we could approach the man, however, he was found floating in the river, his throat cut."

"Hardly conclusive," Phillip grumbled, watching Eckhart intently. He fought the urge to massage his tense chest.

"We agree, sir. It was, however, the most likely avenue of inquiry at the time. I mention it only to assure you, sir, that I followed out every possibility. My sources in Saint Louis included Mr. Blackman, of course, as well as General Clark, Colonel Benton, and Mr. Ferrar, all noteworthy gentlemen, and all most anxious to help ascertain your son's circumstances."

In the silence that followed, Phillip carefully reordered his desk, squaring the ledgers just so, placing the British officer's button in line with the inkwell and quills. Hope welled suddenly. "And the chance that he absconded?"

Eckhart puffed and exhaled, smoke rising in a plume. "My opinion—and the one I am submitting to the company, sir—is that he was the victim of foul play. Up until the time he stepped off the boat, he was a model courier. Suspicious of everyone, standoffish, and private. Of all the passengers, I made the greatest effort to gain his confidence, and he proved most disagreeable. Nor did his behavior in any way draw attention to the fact that he carried money. Rather, he acted the way a boorish scholar should."

"But something happened," Phillip insisted. "I want to know what."

"There was one incident." Eckhart studied the ash on his cigar. "Your son claimed that someone had left a human head in his room the night before we reached Saint Louis. I heard this from a fellow passenger, who'd heard it from a crewman on the *Virgil*. By the time my investigation led me to this information, the *Virgil* had departed from Saint Louis. Since that time, I have contacted the *Virgil*'s captain, and he confirms that a human head had indeed been left in Mr. Hamilton's quarters. At the time, he thought it a practical joke since the young man was so socially disagreeable—frontier humor being what it is. That may indeed be the case, or it might have something to do with your son's disappearance."

Phillip removed his glasses and took a deep breath. "And my son? What are the chances that he's alive?" There, it was out. Pay the devil his due, he'd finally have an answer.

Eckhart's gaze narrowed, cigar smoke rising like lazy serpents around his nose. "I can't tell you with certainty, sir. Man to man, however, the chances are that he's dead, buried, or sunk in the river. That someone, somehow, caught wind of that money and waylaid him."

My God, my God, what have I done? Oh, Richard. I'm so sorry. Phillip closed his eyes. Completely forgotten, the wire spectacles bent double in his knotted fist.

Following the Yellowstone south, the *Maria* might have entered another world. Beyond the cottonwoods, the broad floodplain stretched east and west to badlands of eroded clays, narrow channels, and soft soils that grew scabby little plants barely worthy of the name.

At night the *engagés* marveled at the petrified wood Travis and Baptiste brought in from their hunts. On one excursion they located the petrified bones of some large animal. Most were too big to carry, but one—Richard recognized it as a vertebra—would have dwarfed the biggest of horses. It, too, was solid stone.

"From before the Flood," Green whispered, shaking his head. "Damnation, all the times I been up and down through here, I've seen the petrified wood, but the animal bones? Tarnation, that runs a shiver down my backside."

That night the men burned the fires brighter than usual, and more than one slept on his rifle while dreams of monsters filled his head.

The Yellowstone was as stubbornly different from the Missouri as the Missouri had been from the Mississippi. In places, gravel banks and braided channels ran so shallow that *Maria* had to be grasshoppered across the shoals to deeper water. The crew would construct a huge A-frame of cottonwoods, and the frame was winched forward in one giant step—the boat hanging beneath—before the tackle was reset and the process repeated. On such days, all hands worked like dogs.

"By God, I'll be happy to be done with this," Travis growled, as he wiped a muddy sleeve over his muddier face. "She's nigh to two hundred miles from the mouth down ter the Big Horn. Hob's balls, I ain't never seen the river this bad afore."

Gravel bars weren't the worst. For the first time, Richard saw rapids. Here, the cordelle was run out, and *Maria* was drawn ahead with tackle and a makeshift capstan.

A sweating Toussaint told Richard: "And what you see here? Poof! This ees not whitewater, *mon ami*. For this, we would not have to portage even a canoe *d' maître*."

"Will there be that kind of water further up?"

"Somewhere, I'm sure. The *Roche Jaune,* she starts in the mountains, *oui?* Where there are mountains, you will find whitewater. But this boat, *Maria?* She will not go so far. She is made for calmer waters, not like the canoe."

One early October morning, Richard awoke to find a thin scale of ice on the top of his cup. Thick white frost lay on the grass, and the air had a glasslike clarity. As the breakfast fires crackled, he huddled in his blanket, puffed out his breath, and looked up at the cottonwood leaves. The number of yellow ones wobbling on the morning breeze surprised him.

"Geese'll be headed south," Travis remarked over his steaming coffee—if the thin brown liquid could be called such. "Surprised we ain't had snow."

"Snow?" Richard wondered.

"Yep. I seen snow up hyar first of September. She's holding back a mite this year."

"That's worrisome," Baptiste said, head thrown back to study the enamel sky. "Warmer the fall, the colder the winter. Mark my words, coons, we're gonna have us a hell of a cold one."

"Forty below," Travis muttered, then threw out the last of the grounds from their pan. "Tarnal Hell, I wisht like Hob

that old Dave would be a mite freer with the coffee on a morning like this."

"If'n he's much freer," Baptiste rejoined, "ye'll be without come the mouth of the Big Horn. Hell, only reason he brung any was just ter keep the *engagés* from slitting his throat and stealing his outfit."

True to Travis's words, the next day the first waves of geese, herons, loons, and pelicans cut the afternoon sky. Thereafter, endless honking, piping V's winged southward.

A relentless wind was blowing out of the west the day they finally reached the mouth of the Powder River. With savage fury it spattered the miserable line of *engagés* in cold rain. To the west, a sullen cloud bank darkened into blackness, and promised increased fury—one with teeth of snow. A blizzard of yellow cottonwood leaves fluttered past as the wind ripped the last of the glorious fall colors away. Naked now, the land turned brown and gray.

Richard hunched a shoulder to the brunt of the biting wind and slashing rain. Only ceaseless exertion countered the growing cold as they waded through opaque, chalky water at the Powder's confluence. Forlorn yellow leaves bobbed on the surface. Splashing chest-deep, the men cursed and ground their teeth, calling encouragement as their feet churned the soft mud under the main channel.

To the right, chop covered the Yellowstone, driving whitecaps onto the rounded cobbles in the low channel.

"Doesn't this wind ever let up?" Richard yelled, wiping at his wet face.

"*Non.*" Simon craned his neck to shout back along the cordelle. "Sometimes she get much worse, *oui?* Blows like this for days until you wish to cut off your ears just to still the howl."

"And tonight," de Clerk promised from behind, "you will discover a new meaning of cold, *mon ami.* Smell the wind. That fresh crispness, *oui,* that is snow. First it will rain—enough to soak us through. And then the snow comes. Wet, melting, and, oh, so miserable!"

"I can hardly wait." Richard clawed his way up the slippery far bank, cramped fingers around the gritty cordelle. Feet braced, he pulled with all his might as *Maria* steered wide around the shallow mudbars at the Powder's mouth. On deck, polers battled the wind, shoving the keelboat against the blast.

Soaked, cold, muddy, and wretched as he was, Richard hesitated long enough to stare up the Powder's mucky channel. The water looked solid, like paint, and the banks were covered with cottonwoods and willows. Nothing much marked it as special, but its headwaters formed in Willow's mountains.

Was she there, even now, walking along the streams that would eventually flow to this spot?

Please God, make it so.

De Clerk's predictions for the night's weather came true. The brunt of the storm bore down on them, driven by the west wind. In the light of a sputtering fire, Richard watched a slushy rain fall like flickering silver arrows. Behind a hastily constructed wall of brush, he huddled in his wet blanket like a sodden turtle. No songs rose to duel with the storm, no laughter, jokes, or jests. The other *engagés* crouched over their feeble fires, trying to protect their fragile source of heat.

"How do, coon?" Travis asked, as he appeared out of the inky night and hunkered down beside Richard. "How's life on the river?"

"Wet, cold, and wretched," Richard replied, prodding his smoking fire with a damp stick. Overhead, the wind roared through the trees, pelting them with half-frozen water.

"Reckon so, lad; but fer nights like this, ye'd not know ter appreciate them warm, sunny mornings when everything's fresh green and the meadowlarks is trilling."

"I'll try to remember that." Richard hugged himself, trying to keep some warmth in. "I've just been thinking, is all. Look at us. We're conquering the world, taking civilization around the earth. Isaac Newton has discovered how the universe works, exposed the hand of God in the clockwork precision of science with its mathematical perfection. A new freedom is blowing around the world; old orders are falling. Napoleon taught us that the age of despots is passed. So, if civilization has produced all of these good things, how can the philosophical framework be flawed?"

"Damned if I know."

"Damned if I do, either. And I'm not sure I ever will. The world's just so big, Travis."

"Seems ter me, ye've started to see the whole beaver. Remember when we talked about that?"

"I do, and it seems like a lifetime ago. I want to apologize for being such a boor. You've been right, Travis, about so many things." Richard glanced across at his friend. "Why on earth did you stick with me? It would have been easier to just let Green, or Trudeau, or the river kill me."

Travis wiped at the scarred ruin of his nose. "It was that day when Green pulled down on ye with that pistol. Ye looked right into that barrel, and there was fire in yer eyes. I just figgered I'd take the chance, and hell, once I did, I just couldn't let ye whip me and prove me wrong."

Richard shook his head. "You've the patience of a saint, Travis Hartman."

"Me? Ha! They's men out hyar what call me a devil. And some call me a bloody heller. Saint, now, that's some. Ye just needed out of the cage, Dick."

Richard stared up at the dripping black heavens. "I've still got a long way to go. It's like arguing with yourself. You can always win because you anticipate your own answers." He paused. "When we get to the mouth of the Big Horn, I'm going after her, Travis."

"Is that a fact?"

"I'm free, aren't I? I have to go and find her. There are things I have to tell her."

"And then what? Just talk about philos'phy and ride off when ye finally figger out ye can't pin God down like a butterfly on a board? Tell me, Dick, ye just going to ride in fer a nice chat and ride out of her life again?"

I'll cross that bridge when I reach it. Then he imagined his father's face, heartbroken with grief. "Travis, no matter what, I have to go back. I left some unfinished business in Boston. You understand that, don't you?"

"Be a man and don't go hurting her no more."

Richard nodded, rainwater trickling coldly down around his face. "Whatever happens between us, Willow and I will figure it out together."

"It won't be easy."

Richard turned his head toward the south, now obscured by blackness, storm, and cold. "No, it won't. But then, wasn't it you who told me that nothing in life is easy?"

When Heals Like A Willow saw the riders, she should have turned her mare's head west, hammered her in the ribs, and ridden as if the rock ogres were chasing her. Instead, she left her horse hobbled and sidelined in a steep-walled gully and crawled out to scout them. She lay in the bottom of a shallow drainage—little more than a depression screened by short sagebrush—and watched as the file of horsemen approached. Even if one had looked her way, he wouldn't have thought the scanty cover shielded so much as a jackrabbit.

The warriors passed silently, black silhouettes against the evening sky. They rode arrogantly, the way warriors did when they had nothing to fear. Willow knew that cut of clothing, those decorations and adornments: *Pa'kiani,* the dreaded Blackfeet.

They followed the ridgetop across the brittle caprock Willow had just crossed. Here the shale had been burned to a dull red color, no doubt from some antic of Coyote's just after the Creation. The land was covered with such outcrops of rock, interbedded with layers of coal in bands of gray, black, and bright orange-red. The stone was not without merit, for it could be chipped into useful—if soft—tools, and in this land chert, quartzite, and obsidian were scarce.

Willow emptied her mind so that no part of her *mugwa* would touch one of the Blackfeets' souls. Nevertheless, she tensed when, one by one, they crossed her route, oblivious to her previous passage.

Then she saw the hunched form tied to one of the last horses. The captive was followed by two young men, both hard-eyed, their hair blowing wildly in the west wind. Each carried a trade musket, butt-propped on his rawhide saddle, ready to be leveled and fired. One wore a red blanket tied loosely around his shoulders, the other a buffalo robe. Neither took his eyes from the captive. The prisoner bounced along, defeat reflected in his sloped shoulders and sagging back. Despite the biting wind, he wore only fringed buck-

skin pants of *Ku'chendikani* design. His hands and feet were expertly bound; his blood-matted hair whipped in the wind.

He turned his head then, squinting westward toward the distant Powder River mountains—and Willow jammed a fist into her mouth to stifle a sudden gasp.

She hardly recognized the battered and bruised face so similar to her dead husband's. White Hail's left eye had swollen shut, and the dark lump on the right side of his jaw implied it was broken. Bruises, or dried splotches of blood, mottled his cheeks, ribs, and shoulders.

Willow lowered her head to the dirt, breathing deeply as she struggled to quiet her panicked souls. So, the premonition hadn't been for her but for her brother-in-law, White Hail.

And what will you do now? He is surrounded by more than twenty warriors.

She lifted her head again, watching as they rode off into the twilight. The wind continued to pull at her, flapping her dress and tugging at her hair as she lay in the narrow drainage.

She shot a glance over her shoulder to the west. Darkness was coming soon, the distant mountains obscured by silver-wreathed gray clouds. The bite in the wind promised bitter temperatures.

Would the *Pa'kiani* ride on? Or would they find shelter in some nearby winding gully, or under the lee of a hill?

Willow rose carefully, scuttling forward across the crumbly dirt and chipped rock. She eased up to the ridgetop—careful not to skyline herself—and watched as the now shadowy figures turned off and rode down the lee side of the ridge.

It's impossible! I can't take him away from them.

The wind battered at her, trying to knock her off her feet. Willow used the last of the dying light to take her bearings. To the west, the land dropped away, cut by thousands of drainages that reminded her of a maze of roots all woven together from the stem of the Powder River. To the east, it opened into undulating hills capped by red humps of burned shale.

But to the northeast, a bluff slanted out at an angle. The *Pa'kiani* had just disappeared in that direction, and what better place for fleeing warriors? From the heights, they would be able to scout the country prior to leaving in the morning. The tilted caprock would provide some protection from the bitter wind, and the horses would find sufficient grass on the slope below the rocky point. Such places collected large snowdrifts in the winter, and consequently grew excellent grass in the spring as well as tall sagebrush for fires.

Willow chewed nervously at her lips. *A smart woman would ride off.* She hated the pang in her heart. White Hail had always been kind to her, his adoration and love shining in his mischievous eyes.

"He was foolish to ride off to find the Mandan," she told the wind. Red Calf would have been behind it, goading him to bring her trinkets with which to adorn herself. Women could be such fools.

Willow turned her steps toward where her horse was hobbled, and added, "Just as I'm foolish enough to go and try to save him. The *Pa'kiani* will no doubt kill us both in the end."

And if they do, the Pa'kiani *will leave my corpse lying around for the coyotes. Since my* mugwa *will be free to wreak havoc, I will find Red Calf, and make her suffer until she dies.*

Borne on the capricious wind, white flakes of snow drifted out of the black sky to settle on White Hail's clay-cold skin. The shivers wracked him; they antagonized his bruises and aches rather than warmed his battered body.

He lay bound, hands tied uncomfortably to his ankles. The clever *Pa'kiani* had trussed a stick between the knots so that he couldn't manage to wiggle his fingers close enough to untie them. Then they'd staked him to a sagebrush so that he couldn't chafe the thongs on the rocks.

White Hail shivered again, and wondered how long it would take him to die. He'd always been tough, capable of enduring cold and heat, privation and exertion. The *Pa'kiani* would make his death as painful and horrible as they could. For White Hail's part, he would have to use all of his resolution, every small grain of courage he could muster. Prisoner though he might be, he'd give them not one mouse hair of satisfaction.

The war between *Pa'kiani* and *Ku'chendikani* was a very old one. In the time of White Hail's grandfather, the Shoshoni had obtained horses from their *Yamparika* Comanche cousins and ridden out on a war of extermination. Like a huge pack of wolves, they'd swept up from the south, murdering *Pa'kiani,* chasing them ever northward, and collecting coup on the way.

The *Pa'kiani* had fled north in terror and defeat. But in the process, they had obtained horses of their own, and way up in the north, they had met the British traders who gave them a deadly new weapon. Armed with the White man's guns, they swept back south, defeating the Shoshoni in battle, overwhelming camps, murdering men, women, and children—invincible.

Almost too late, the Shoshoni had met the Americans, and now struggled to obtain guns of their own. At present, the powerful *Pa'kiani* were checked—barely—but the Shoshoni bands had been pressed back into the mountains, into remote strongholds where ambushes could blunt *Pa'kiani* superiority in firepower and numbers.

And I had to fall prey to these vermin. White Hail swallowed the grunt of pain his latest bout of shivering invoked. The snow was falling faster now, spinning down in fluffy flakes to melt and trickle down his numb skin.

What I'd give for a blanket. Tam Apo, *please, give me courage. Show me the way to die well, and give these* Pa'kiani *weasels nothing more than the coup they've already taken from me.*

White Hail shifted, stifling a groan. The snow fell so thickly he could barely see the sandstone cliff they'd camped beneath. A lookout huddled up there, keeping guard—as if he could see anything through the darkness and falling veils of snow. Two other youths slept by the horses, ready to spring to life and wake the rest of the warriors who lay wrapped in their blankets like logs among the sagebrush.

Even if I could get loose, how would I escape? The thought slipped around in White Hail's stumbling mind. The *Pa'kiani* slept on their weapons. The only way he could kill would be to bash his victim's brains out with a rock, and the sharp-eared *Pa'kiani* would hear that.

White Hail, accept it. You are dead. The spirits have turned away, brought you bad luck from the moment you began this crazy journey to the Mandan.

A terrible bout of shivers left him gasping for breath. He tried to swallow, but the grating ache in his jaw just hurt worse.

Would Red Calf miss him? She would give him three moons, then she would take the baby and look for another man to keep her.

Will you so much as shed a tear for me, Red Calf? Lying in the dark, shivering to death in agony, he could finally face the truth Heals Like A Willow had tried to tell him so many months ago. Red Calf would barely grieve. She had already cast her eye on Fast Black Horse, preferring to be his third wife rather than White Hail's first.

White Hail cocked his head. Had he heard something, or was his muzzy soul slipping loose from his body? A man imagined things when he was close upon death.

So many mistakes. White Hail tried to see through the twirling snowflakes and the black clouds, wondering if his brother were there, waiting for him.

Will you pray for me, Brother? Call my mugwa *to you? Please, Brother, I don't want my souls to roam around all alone, hated and feared, doing horrible things.*

"Too many mistakes," he whispered wearily, trying to shift his position. The action speared pain through his side. The *Pa'kiani* had taken him completely by surprise—caught him sound asleep just before dawn.

I didn't even lay a hand on a weapon. Which was why he was still alive. Instead, they'd jumped on him, muscled him down, and bound him. Then, for hours, they'd counted coup, beating him with clubs, willow sticks, and rocks, and burning him with hot sticks from his campfire. And in the end, they'd taken him along as a trophy on their ride north-ward. They would take him to one of their villages, beat him to death, scalp him, and feed his mutilated body to their dogs.

If I live long enough. He smiled, the movement of his lips tormenting his swollen jaw.

He couldn't defy the bone-chilling cold much longer. Each flake of snow that melted and trickled down his side drained off that much more of his heat. *Tam Apo* willing, he would be dead by morning. Either that, or so disoriented they would have to kill him.

Don't let me cry out. Don't let my mugwa *grow so tired I lose control of myself. Not in front of these spit-licking dogs.*

But it could happen that way. A man did foolish things in delirium. He wept, shamed himself, and whimpered.

Tam Apo, *help me.*

The wind gusted and twisted, snow now falling in wreaths. Good. If it kept up like this, he would be stone dead in the morning. The Blackfeet would kick him around, cut off his scalp and genitals, pull out his intestines, mutilate his body, and ride off. When they went, however, it would be without the satisfaction of hearing White Hail beg.

"Come on," he whispered to the storm. "Kill me."

"You can die later," a familiar voice—a woman's, barely audible over the wind—whispered. "For now, be very quiet or they will wake up and kill us both."

At the corner of his vision, a low, snow-mounded shape moved ever so slowly. White Hail squinted and blinked, then succumbed to the shivers again, half-wondering if the apparition would still be there when his vision cleared.

Yes, there. He scowled, watching as it hunched over his bound hands and feet. His legs had grown so numb he barely felt the thongs part.

"We must go slowly, *teci,* quietly," the voice told him in the language of the People. "Can you stand?"

White Hail stared, trying to comprehend. "Where are we going? Who are you?"

"Shhh!" Then a warm hand reached out, feeling his forehead, his chest, and arms. "You are very cold. You're not thinking clearly. Very well, White Hail. This is a test of your manhood. If you are a brave warrior, you will stand, and make no noise. If you are little more than food for *Pa'kiani* dogs, you can stay here and grovel at their feet like a maggot in rotten meat."

White Hail steeled himself, groaning in spite of his attempt at silence. His legs failed him at the last instant, but she caught him, supporting his weight.

"Easy . . . easy, White Hail," the woman whispered. Carefully they took a step, and then another, picking their way through the sleeping warriors as snow fell in skirts of white that obscured the world.

"Willow?" White Hail wondered. "Heals Like A Willow, am I dying? Is this my *mugwa* leaving my body?"

"Shut up!" she hissed.

He clamped his jaw—and regretted it instantly as pain seared the right side of his head. If anything, the ache cleared his thoughts enough that he could concentrate on keeping his feet. Heals Like A Willow! His befuddled mind struggled with the reality. But where had she come from? How had she found him?

Is this real, or a trick? A part of death I just don't understand?

They were climbing now, heading straight up toward the point. White Hail frowned, unease prickling somewhere deep in his thoughts. This was wrong, somehow, but he couldn't find his way through the veils of fog that filled his head.

Dangerous, so very dangerous, with the *Pa'kiani* sleeping all around them.

Now they were working their way up the steep slope, around boulders, one step at a time. They paused periodically when agony raced through his bruised ribs and aching joints.

They climbed higher, up where the wind whipped around, right up under the sandstone ledge.

"This way," Willow whispered. "I have a horse. We'll get you up on top, and . . . "

They were climbing over the last of the cracked sandstone now. Snow covered the rocks in a fluffy whiteness that illuminated the ground enough for him to see his dark legs against the snow. They had to crawl over the top, each movement a spear of agony, and then they were up, gasping, she from the exertion of supporting his weight, he from the horrible pain. The wind savaged him, beating his numb skin with snow—and immediately to his right, something, a snowy lump, moved as if alive.

And then White Hail remembered. They'd just crawled over the rim—right in front of the *Pa'kiani* guard who'd been placed on the high point. With a stifled cry, White Hail threw himself on the guard in a last desperate attempt to save them.

"Stop that!" she whispered. "He's already dead. I killed him first."

"Willow? Is it really you?"

"Yes, *teci;* now be quiet. Take his blanket and clothes. Then I'll see if I can steal you a horse."

As he prodded the corpse, she drifted away into the storm.

Willow. Here. Perhaps *Tam Apo* had heard after all.

THIRTEEN

❖

War itself requires no special motive but appears to be an integral part of human nature; it even passes for something noble, to which the love of glory impels men quite apart from any self-centered urges. Thus among the American savages just as much as among those of Europe during the age of chivalry, military valor is held to be of great worth in itself, not only during war (which is natural) but in order that there should continue to be war. Often war is waged only in order to demonstrate valor; thus an inner dignity is attributed to war itself, and even some philosophers have praised it as an ennoblement of humanity, forgetting the pronouncement of the Greek who said, "War is an evil inasmuch as it produces more wicked men than it takes away." So much for the measures nature takes to lead the human race, considered as a class of animals, for her own purposes.

—Immanuel Kant, *Perpetual Peace: A Philosophical Sketch*

The big coyote sat on a rocky knob and watched the six horses and three blanket-wrapped riders pass below. His buff-gray coat ruffled in the cool breeze; the bushy tail curled around his delicate feet. He might have been a king, so majestically did he perch on the height, surrounded by blue-green sagebrush with its waving spikes.

Richard couldn't take his eyes from the animal. He felt wary of that piercing yellow-eyed stare, those pricked ears, and the rapt attention with which the creature watched them file by.

Baptiste led the way, then Travis, and finally Richard. They traveled Indian-file, following a small creek up into the highlands south of the Yellowstone River. Each led a packhorse, the panniers piled high. Ropes tied in diamond hitches secured tarps, or manties, that protected the goods from rain and the rigors of travel.

Tall sagebrush, some as high as a horse, choked the narrow bottoms, and the white limbs of cottonwoods rose against the gray sky. The hills around them had a chapped look, prickly with scrubby sage, rocky outcrops, and waving spikes of tall grass.

Richard thumped his white mare in the ribs with moccasined heels and rode up beside Travis. "Did you see that coyote up there?"

Travis glanced sidelong at the skylined creature, and nodded. "Yep. Curious old coon, ain't he? Probably figgering he'll just Injun into camp tonight and chew every single bit of harness and rigging on these saddles into bits."

"They do that?"

"Yep. Sneaking thieves. I've heard tell they like the leather cause of the hoss sweat, the salt taste. That, and hell, coyotes is just ornery. They'll chew packs, steal food, anything they can get away with."

Richard couldn't shake his unease. Why did the creature watch them with such intensity, as if a spectator at a great event?

"I wish he'd go away," Richard declared.

Baptiste pulled his horse up, and turned in the saddle, head cocked. "Coyote makes powerful medicine fo' the folks out heah. They calls him the Trickster."

Travis hunched on his saddle, spat over the off-side, and squinted up at the coyote. "That true, ye flea-bit varmint? Ye a-waiting ter trick us? Wal, I'm telling ye, don't go ter no trouble, lessen we raise ye, hear? We ain't no Injun coons. We's white! And a heap more trouble than yer likes is fit fer."

Baptiste narrowed an eye. "Who's white?"

"We is," Travis insisted. "That's if'n I decides ter count yer mangy hide in with our august and noble company."

"August and noble? Where'd you heah that?"

"Why, I been a-listening ter Dick, hyar, and improving my elocution."

"It ain't working," Baptiste growled.

Richard ignored the banter and kept his attention on the coyote. He might have been stone, so still did he sit.

"Willow told me that among her people, Coyote caused all kinds of trouble at the beginning of the world." He fingered his rifle, oddly reassured by the smooth wood and cold steel.

"Yep," Baptiste agreed while the breeze flicked his long fringes. "Crow tell stories about him, too. They call him Old Man Coyote." Baptiste narrowed his eyes, turning his attention from the coyote to Richard, then back. "Raises yor hair, does he?"

Richard started to nod, then shook his head. "It's crazy. I'm sorry, just tired, that's all. Maybe it's the weather."

"No, tell us," Travis said softly, as his gelding dropped its head to crop.

"Nothing." Richard flushed, suddenly self-conscious. "It's irrational. I'm spooky, that's all." *Good God, I'm an educated man, and there's nothing up there but a hungry old coyote that's never seen a white man before.* "Come on, let's go."

Travis and Baptiste traded looks, then the black hunter kicked his animal around and jerked the packhorse in line. Travis followed as Richard dropped back to his place.

From his high rock, the coyote watched them go. His only movement was the flick of an ear, almost a parting gesture.

Richard clamped down on the stirring unease within. Since coming to this wild land, some part of him that he'd never known had come to life. Was it just intuition, or the stirring of his vivid dreams and the building sense of premonition? The tension kept him alert, his eyes scanning the sage-clad ridges to either side.

This trip had come on him suddenly. Baptiste had ridden in the night before, cold, wet, and mud-spattered, with the news that he'd spotted a Crow hunting party a day's ride to the south.

"About time," Green had cried, warming his hands on the crackling fire before his tent. "I've been half worried the Crow had left this country."

Baptiste had accepted a steaming tin cup from Henri, sipped the watery coffee, and told them, "Wal, Long Hair and his River Crows was palavering with Atkinson and O'Fallon. After they done broke up the council, Long Hair talked the clans into heading south to make their fall hunt on the Tongue. Soon's they lay in enough buffler, they's gonna head down to the mouth of the Powder fo' winter camp."

"You told them we were building a post at the mouth of the Big Horn?" Green rubbed his jaw nervously, an eyebrow raised.

"Yep. They said they's glad the white generals fulfilled their word so fast. I told 'em we'd be ready to trade just as soon as we could get a post up. Maybe another moon. Figgered it might be better to keep 'em away until we get buildings up."

Green frowned for a moment, then nodded. "Yes, I suppose you're right. They'd steal us blind."

"They's Crow." Travis chuckled.

"Since they be making a hunt," Baptiste continued, "I told 'em we might send a party to their village. Trade there. Dave, we're a gonna be needing robes, moccasins, and such right quick. Specially with this weather turning. That, or yor *engagés* is gonna freeze."

That same night they had filled the panniers with powder,

lead, skinning knives, glass beads, cloth, and other foofawraw. Then, in the blackness before dawn, Travis had toed Richard in the side, "C'mon, coon. They don't need yer stringy carcass on the cordelle today. Let's go meet the Crow."

So Richard had thrown back his frosty blankets and stumbled over to help load the recalcitrant horses. He'd picked up his rifle and possibles, and, at the last minute, tied his coups onto his belt. From the river, they had cut south, wound through the pine-covered hills with their outcrops of sandstone and shale, and found the drainage they now followed.

Richard pulled his blanket tighter about his shoulders. Glancing back, he could still see the coyote watching them from that solitary pinnacle.

Easing up beside Travis, he asked, "Tell me about the Crow. You said they'd rob us?"

Travis smiled grimly, the scars rearranging themselves on his face. "Given half a chance. I've lived with them." He paused wistfully. "They're related to the Hidatsa, and they know the benefits of having whites fer friends. Especially with the Blackfeet on one side, and the Sioux, Cheyenne, and Arapaho on the other."

"What sort of people are they?"

Travis stared off into the distance. "Wal, coon, they's unlike any ye've met. And, tell the truth, after yer reaction ter Mandan, I figgered I'd bring ye along just ter see yer philos'phy reaction ter Crow doings."

"Meaning you expect me to be appalled."

"Wal, they got their notions. Now, when it comes to laying with women, they don't hold back. They figger it's just plumb natural ter chase each other's wives."

"Surely there must be some sense of fidelity?"

"There is. Most Crows marry and stick ter it. Of course, they got themselves a kidnapping ceremony every year where they steal each other's women. But, Dick, ye got ter quit judging folks based on white ways. These Crow, I reckon they're the most friendly of folks. Give ye the shirt off'n their back."

"As well as their wives."

"Sometimes."

"Travis, what about the children? How do they feel, not knowing who their father is? What kind of life can they have, knowing they're most likely bastards?"

"Don't matter to 'em. Among Crow, thar ain't no such thing as a bastard. Children belong to the mother, to her clan. And there ain't no one loves children like the Crow. Hell, most Injuns out hyar, they go to war and kill their enemies—men, women, and children. Not the Crow, they kill the enemy warriors, take the women and kids, adopt them into the tribe, and make 'em Crow."

"Seems to me, they couldn't turn their backs on them."

Travis shrugged, careful eyes on the country. "I've met Blackfoot women who was taken over the dead bodies of their husbands who wouldn't go back ter the Blackfeet after living with Crow fer a couple of years. No, Crow are a heap different. Women own property, and even get adopted into the sacred societies with their men."

"But they're all thieves. What good are the fruits of labor if another can take them away? It flies in the face of every philosophical principle. From Aristotle to Hegel, it's become an established fact that property, and its protection, is a human fundamental."

Travis shrugged in response to Richard's lifted eyebrow. "Whose property? Among Crow, everything belongs to the clan. Take the medicine bundles, now. A man can buy the right to part of a bundle, and he takes care of it, but it still belongs to the clan. A man only owns his weapons, and of course, his hosses—at least till the Blackfoot steal 'em. When he kills meat, he can keep the best parts, but the rest belongs ter the clan. Ye see, they work together, feed each other, share things in a way we'd call stealing."

"I don't understand about the clans."

"Clans hold the people together. These are River Crow. Most of 'em is Whistling Water, Streaked Lodge, and one clan called the Piegan—but *don't* confuse them with the Blackfoot. The Kicked-in-the-belly, the Filth-eaters, and Sore-lips are mostly Mountain Crow, and live farther west. According ter Crow lights, people are like them clumps of driftwood that pile up along the river, all tangled together. And, since yer all so fired interested, no man will lay with a woman belonging to his clan. They figger that ter be incest."

"And Long Hair is the chief?"

"Yep. But not like among the Pawnee and Arikara. He ain't a chief because his pap was. Take old Long Hair—a character, he is—he ain't got no authority over another Crow. He can make decisions, all right, but the other Crow only obey if'n it suits them. They call him Long Hair because he carries his hair in a little box that he straps on like a pack. Says he'll have Power so long as he don't cut his hair. Most of the Mountain Crow, now, they follow old Rotten Belly. He's a quiet sort, hard to figger, but smart as all Hob. Story is Rotten Belly and Long Hair locked horns a while back and split the tribe."

"Sounds like anarchy."

"Huh?"

"Mass confusion."

"Nope. They trust a leader—or his medicine Power. The clans really have the authority. Them and the societies."

"And these societies, are they like those Black Mouths I met among the Mandan?"

"Wal, the warrior societies are like . . . like the Freemasons. All men of a certain age who patrol the camps. Every year a different society is given responsibility to oversee the hunts and keep order in camp. Let's see, there's the Half-

Shaved Heads, the Foxes, the Big Dogs, and Muddy Hand societies. Some societies, like the Hammer Society, is fer young men. Others, like the Raven Society, fer old men."

"It sounds worse than Boston." Richard thought back to the rigid social circles of his youth, to families like George Peterson's who would only receive people of a certain standing.

"Maybe. Then ye've got the sacred societies, like the Tobacco Society. Tobacco is a medicine plant ter the Crow. They think it was the first plant ter grow after the world was created. The Tobacco Society oversees the planting come spring and they're the keepers of the rituals. Takes years of study ter larn the songs and the dances, and the who-does-what."

"Then I guess pretty much everyone has to be in a society?"

"If they'll take ye. Some folks pay ter join societies that are responsible for things like the Bear Dance or the Horse Dance. All them societies got rules. They don't just run around like a bunch of crazy chickens."

"But which society controls the others?"

"None of 'em. Everyone's equal except for certain times and duties."

"It sounds crazy."

"To white notions, maybe, but it suits the Crow just fine. Never knew such a bunch of happy folks." Travis squinted up at the sage-covered hills. "They're free, Dick. They just do as God and the spirits tells 'em."

"And hope the Blackfeet don't scalp them."

"There's always that. But in this country, that's just the way it is. Red or white."

"Why, Travis? Peace would make everyone's life easier. Can't they all get together and sit down in council—Blackfeet, Sioux, Crow, and all the rest—and make a treaty that would let them live without constant war?"

"The traders would like that. But, nope, I don't reckon so.

Men make their name in war and hoss stealing. Thinking about it, they ain't that all-fired different from them kings back in Europe. Folks is too proud. Hosses is too tempting."

"But free? I wonder, Travis. How can you be free when you're probably going to die tomorrow?"

The hunter cast a sidelong glance. "Ain't that when a coon's about as free as he can get?"

Baptiste called over his shoulder, "If'n' you's to ask the Crow, they'd say it's just the way the world was made. Goes clear back to the Creation when old man Coyote was swimming around in all the water. He got a duck to bring up mud, and he made the world. Then, being Coyote, he called a meeting of all the animals and they got inta a hell of a squabble. Old man Coyote and his younger brother started stealing women, raiding, and so on. He taught such things to the Crow, and the world's been squabbling ever since."

Richard shook his head. "Coyote, again. It seems like he's always trouble."

"Yep." Travis tensed as four mule deer—does and fawns—broke from the trees and bounded gracefully up the slope. "That old coyote still bothering ye?"

"I feel . . . as if something's wrong. I don't know why."

"Uh-huh, wal, keep yer eyes peeled, coon. Willow said ye had Power, and in this country it pays ter heed hunches. Baptiste and me, we'll keep an eye skinned."

❖

They were called the Gourd Buttes for the plants that grew along their lower slopes. Visible all across the Powder River basin, they made an excellent guide for a traveler. Also, from those heights, a scout could see anyone passing, or locate the large herds of buffalo that roamed the basin's grasslands.

Willow passed far to the north, following drainages, staying low off the skyline. She caught occasional glimpses of the flat-topped buttes as she steered her course westward from the crossing of the Powder River. They had just topped the divide into the valley of the Crazy Woman. The snow which had blown down with such vengeance had now fallen victim to warm sunshine. The yellow or gray clays turned to mud from the melt; it balled on the horses' hooves.

Despite the warmth, that crisp undercurrent of fall lingered in the air, and strengthened with the night as the temperature fell below freezing. Ahead of them, the Powder River Mountains glowed whitely in the sunset. The glory of snow-capped peaks gave way to the cool pine-green of the steep slopes with their rocky uplifts.

Willow led the way down into a draw where a seep flowed out of a coal seam. The willows and cottonwoods that grew there stood bare over a carpet of brown leaves.

White Hail clung to his horse, a white-faced roan with a swayback and bowed legs; not the finest of the Blackfeet horses. In the tension and danger of the rescue, evidently quality hadn't been the highest of Willow's priorities.

She helped White Hail down and hobbled the animals, then began the task of snapping dead branches from the cottonwoods and inspecting the ground litter for dryness.

White Hail slumped with exhaustion. He'd taken a warm buffalo robe from the dead lookout, and now wore it

wrapped around his shoulders. The swelling on his jaw had dropped, but his mouth felt like a stranger's. The lower jaw no longer lined up with the upper, and missing teeth added to the strange feeling when he moved his tongue around. Scabs had formed on his burns and cuts, and the bruises on his ribs and shoulders had dulled into yellow and purple splotches. He hurt all over—both in body and souls.

"I still cannot believe it's you," he said thickly.

Willow frayed grass stems and tipped a bit of charred tinder into the starter. Her strike-a-light clicked when she struck flint to steel. Blowing the spark into flame, she fed twigs to the flicker of fire, and told him, "It's me, *teci*. But I'd rather bet on gaming pieces than the luck of being at the right place at the right time to rescue you again."

"Luck? Maybe my Power isn't broken. Maybe my Spirit Helper sent you my way. Nothing happens without reason." He swallowed painfully, crawling down to the seep. He scooped out leaves. When the water had pooled, he drank and resettled himself with his back against one of the cottonwoods. "I still don't know how you did it—got me away, I mean."

Willow wiped her hands on her dress, satisfied that the fire was started, and untied her pack from behind the saddle. "They did not expect trouble. Only a fool would be out in such a storm. The snow was falling so thick, and the guards were so cold, it was easy."

He glanced away, fingers tracing the lines of a stick he picked up. "How did you steal that horse? How did you sneak it past the guards?"

"I killed them." She opened her pack, pulling out her little metal pot and dipping it full of water from the hollow he'd dug. "I used that ax. Slipped up behind them and split their heads open. It didn't make as much noise as I thought it would."

He winced, raising fingers to his swollen jaw. "I wish

you'd told me that you'd already killed that guard on top of the hill. I looked pretty foolish wrestling with a dead man."

"Ummm, and the worst is, given your condition, he might have won." She shaved dried meat and berries into the water before putting it on to boil. "And then you wouldn't have that nice warm buffalo robe to wear."

In silence, they watched the last of the day turn to twilight.

As the light failed, a distant band of coyotes wailed. She asked, "White Hail, how did you happen to be out here? What were you doing?"

He tapped his stick on the leaves. "I was taking ten horses to trade with the Mandan for White man's things. Since the baby was born, Red Calf has been saying that she's no longer beautiful." He stared woodenly at the dirty leather covering his knee. "The birth was difficult. I waited the proper time, but when I joined her under the robes, she would not have me. Said she was not ready. I waited . . . and waited some more, but still she would not couple. Then, one day, I saw her with Fast Black Horse. She was admiring his warhorse, talking about how sleek and powerful it was. How it was a true stallion, capable of filling a mare."

"And what did Fast Black Horse say?"

"He said that such a horse was for only the finest of mares, for mares that would run free, full of spirit. It was the way he said it."

"Yes, I know," she replied wearily. "And you decided that by making a trip east, you could bring back riches and prove yourself worthy of her again. You are a fool, White Hail. She's not worth your life. I think your brother would tell you to go home and throw her things out of your lodge."

"But what of the child? My son is beautiful, Willow."

She stirred the fire and added more wood, then braced her arms on her knees. "For now, he needs her milk. Let him suck and grow. When he is ready to take a name, Red Calf will be with child again, and you can claim your son. Two Half Moons can watch over him while you're away hunting or stealing horses. She'll make him into a human being."

"She's old."

"A child will give her a reason to get older."

White Hail rubbed the back of his neck and made a face. "Why do you always have the answers, sister?"

"Because, unlike most, I think in, and out, and around problems." She gestured. "It isn't hard to do, brother."

He grunted in defeat, then asked, "Are you sure the Blackfeet will not track us?"

"By the time they could see well enough, another hand of snow would have covered our tracks. We kept to the ridges, and then dropped down into the valley bottoms on rock outcrops. Unless they want to waste a great deal of time circling, I don't think they'll follow. And, if they do, by the time they cut our trail, we'll be far ahead of them."

He twirled the stick in his fingers. "They'd been on a long raid . . . far to the south. They fought our *Yamparika* cousins, lost many men and horses. I think they'll keep going north. Their war leader, his Power is bad. I do not think he will lead another party of *Pa'kiani* warriors."

Willow shrugged. If the Blackfeet wanted to go south to fight with the feisty Comanche, it was better than having them raid the *Dukurika* or *Ku'chendikani*. "I would not guess what goes on in *Pa'kiani* souls, such as they may be."

White Hail glanced at her tin pot, at the knife and ax, and the Pawnee war club. Then his gaze strayed to the metal buckles on the saddle and the bow and quiver. "Enough about me, Heals Like A Willow. Tell me about these things you have. About the metal—and the Pawnee weapons. And, tell me, are those not scalps sewn to the seams of your dress?"

As the stew simmered, she told him of leaving the *Ku'chendikani* and how the Pawnee warrior Packrat took her prisoner, about her travels eastward, and her meeting the Whites.

"Ah! A White man saved you?" White Hail's eyes went large. "Did you glimpse his Power? Are they not as great as I have said?"

Sober-eyed, she cocked her head. "His name is Richard. I looked into his eyes . . . saw his soul."

"What is this tone in your voice, sister? I'm not used to hearing it. Tell me all about it."

She fiddled with the fire. "Another time. You need rest."

"You could tell me while I rest."

From the look in his eyes, he wouldn't relent. She sighed and began. He listened as the night fell cool and clear around them. She told of Travis, Green, the *engagés* and the *Maria*.

"This is ready to eat." She handed him the tin. "Do not chew. The bone in your jaw is not ready for that. It's bad enough that you talk. Just swallow the meat whole. I cut it into chunks small enough that you won't choke."

She continued her story as he sipped and watched her, alternately startled and awed by the things she described.

When he'd emptied the tin pot, Willow took it, refilled it with water, and made a stew for herself. As it cooked, White Hail stared thoughtfully at the patterns of twinkling stars glowing overhead.

"At least you understand their Power, *papinkwihi*. You see, I was right. They are magical."

"They are *men!*" she flared. "And I have come to know them for all that they are. White Hail, do not make yourself into a fool over them the way you have over Red Calf."

He stiffened, stung by her words.

She didn't relent. "There is no other way to say it. At least, not a way that you will take seriously. *Teci*, they are men, no better or worse than any others. They are bringing many things to our land. Some are good, others are bad. It is up to us to find a way to take what is good, and avoid what is bad."

"And if the People will not believe you?"

She shook her head, stirring the fire with her stick. "I don't know. I'm afraid that too many of our people think as you do, that the White men, and their goods, are Powerful and good. But tell me, White Hail, did you know that first the White trader comes with wonders, but when he finally leaves, there is only death?"

"I do not believe that."

"You may believe what you will."

"The traders want peace. I have heard them say so."

In English she remarked, "I didn't know you talked their tongue." At his puzzled look she repeated her question in Shoshoni.

"You have learned their language?" White Hail's amazement gave her ironic amusement.

"And more."

"And you still believe they are bad for us?" He shook his head. "Willow, what would you have us do? Go to war with them?"

Willow stared down into her stew, watching the steam rise. "No, Brother. For all the danger and death they bring to their friends, the vengeance they take on their enemies is even more horrible."

He frowned into the firelight.

She finished her stew, and began to repack.

"What are you doing?"

Willow rose and retied the pack to her saddle. "The Blackfeet are behind us somewhere. Who knows what other enemies might be out here? If we keep to the ridges, we can go that much farther before dawn. By this time tomorrow, I want to be at the base of the mountains. From there, we'll follow the foothills south, and then up the forks of the Powder River. We should find the *Dukurika* in the canyons on the other side of the mountains."

"The *Dukurika?*" He stood skeptically. "I'm not going up there."

"As you wish, *teci,*" she said. "You have a horse."

Through veiled eyes, he studied her. "Heals Like A Willow, you are a very different woman from the one I knew. No, I think I will ride along—and perhaps learn what has happened to you. You have told me many things, but I think there is a great deal more that you aren't telling me."

"Perhaps."

"Did one of the White men give you his Power? Is that what happened? Was it this Ritshard? Why are you so secretive?"

Did one of the White men give me his Power? How strange that you should ask that, White Hail.

"Richard gave me nothing." She bent down, unfastening the hobbles. "Come, I will help you onto your horse. We have a long way to ride tonight, so save your strength and stop asking questions."

"I can get on my own horse, *papinkwihi.* And I have a lot of questions to ask you."

"We will ride in silence," she ordered, heeled her mare around, and turned her back on the valley with its little seep and dying fire.

The River Crow had placed their village in the wide bottoms of the Tongue River. The cluster of parchment brown tipis blended with the grass and freshly fallen cottonwood leaves. Richard, Baptiste, and Travis inspected the village from a cobble-strewn flat on one of the sagebrush-dotted terraces, a good seventy feet above the floodplain.

A haze of smoke rose from the smokeholes to hang like blue mist among the winter-bare cottonwoods. Unlike the Sioux lodges, the Crow extended the poles almost twice the height of the intersection point, giving their lodges an hourglass look. From the pole tips, bits of colored cloth, horsetails, and other streamers hung like flags.

Out in the hills to the east, the horse herd grazed. So many animals! Richard couldn't count the number. The huge herd had to cover several square miles.

"My sweet Lord, I guess stealing horses does pay off."

"And they's the best," Baptiste agreed.

The day had warmed, bright and sunny. But here and there, on the north slopes of drainages, patches of snow still clung to the shadows.

"Right time of year to hunt," Baptiste remarked. "Meat will cure plumb fine fo' winter."

"Uh-huh, and ye'll do yer best ter eat 'em outa all they've kilt, too, won't ye?"

"Reckon so." Baptiste's white teeth flashed in his dark face. "Now, what say we goes on down and stir up the dogs some."

"Stir up the dogs?" Richard asked.

"Ye'll see," Travis rejoined.

Even as they rode down the loose slope, people were turning out to watch. So did an incredible number of dogs, who, upon catching sight of the strangers, charged forth barking and yipping.

Over the tumult, Richard could hear the camp crier calling out the arrival of the visitors.

What followed was a melee of shouted greetings, cacophonous dogs, and squealing children. Richard had all he could handle just controlling his excited horse and keeping a grip on his packhorse's lead rope.

They entered the camp like lords returning from the Crusades, winding through the village in a parade of women, children, and men. Before each lodge, a brightly painted shield, decorated with feathers and strips of fur, hung on a tripod.

Dismounting, Travis gave orders concerning the packs, each of which was immediately taken under guard by several young men bearing fur-covered sticks. When some inquisitive Crow came too close, he or she was first warned, and then whacked.

Travis explained: "Camp police from that society I told ye about."

Richard couldn't help but gawk. He was surrounded by brown faces; some were painted, and occasionally one was tattooed around the chin or on the forehead. Children were everywhere, apparently as wild as ferrets, for none was rebuked by their parents as they charged around, or mobbed the traders, pulling at clothing, laughing, and shoving.

Panic seized him as he looked around. A sea of Indians surrounded him. Everywhere he looked, impenetrable black eyes stared back. They shoved against him, tens of hands touching him, prodding, pulling at his possibles and groping his flesh. Coupled with the sense of foreboding came a sudden realization that there was no boat to run to, no armed *engagés* to protect him.

"I hope they're friendly. If something goes wrong, what happens to us?"

"They'll slit yor throat, plumb shoah, and you ain't a gonna have but a split second to worry about it!" Baptiste cried, and laughed in a way that sent shivers up Richard's back.

He was suddenly plagued by the way that coyote had watched so intently—like a witness from an Old Testament account.

FOURTEEN

Spirit is the *self* of the actual consciousness, to which spirit stands opposed, or rather which appears over against itself, as an objective actual world that has lost, however, all sense of strangeness for the self, just as the self has lost all sense of having a dependent or independent existence by itself, cut off and separated from that world.

—Georg Friedrich Wilhelm Hegel,
Phenomenology of Mind

At a shouted order, the din subsided and the crowding Crow parted for a burly warrior. He carried another of the staffs, this one curved over at the top to form a crook, like a shepherd's, from which dangled feathers and scalp locks. He wore fringed leggings and a breechclout. His numerous scars puckered his bare breast and shoulders. Richard had seen the like among the Mandan. More of the scarifying torture?

The warrior stopped at the edge of the crowd, his haughty face breaking into a smile as he recognized Travis and Baptiste. He'd plaited his hair into a single braid that hung down his back. The forelocks had been roached high and curled back above a smooth forehead. His black eyes sparkled, a smile coming to his lips.

"Travis!" he cried, and stepped forward, hugging the hunter with enough vigor to make Travis groan.

"Two White Elk!" Travis pounded the man on the back. "By God, coon, ye be a sight fer sore eyes."

"So're ye," the Crow responded. "My heart sings." And then he launched into a string of Crow talk, his hands flying in the sign language of the Plains.

"Reckon ye know Baptiste de Bourgmont." Travis turned to Richard. "This hyar be my friend, Dick Hamilton."

Two White Elk studied Richard thoughtfully, noted the coups on his belt, and wrapped Richard in his arms. Richard's ribs creaked and his breath tried to slip past resisting lips. The man smelled of smoke and grease, and kept chattering on in Crow.

"Two White Elk says yer most welcome," Travis translated.

"My pleasure," Richard managed to wheeze as Two White Elk turned him loose to crush Baptiste to his breast.

"Time to smoke and make palaver," Baptiste called as he produced a twist of tobacco.

The center of a flurry of activity, they were led through a maze of lodges to a tipi painted with antlered animals that Richard decided were elk. Tendrils of smoke still rose from white ash in a firepit in front of the lodge. Willow-frame backrests were produced, set around the firepit, and covered with soft buffalo robes. Travis settled himself in the first one, acting all the while like a lord among vassals.

A young woman appeared out of the crowd, a long beaded sack in her arms. This she ceremoniously handed to Two White Elk. Even as Richard seated himself, the soldiers were calling orders, gesturing with their sticks. The rest of the Crow settled themselves cross-legged around the margins.

From the corner of his eye, Richard saw their packs being brought and laid beside the elk lodge.

In a sudden stillness, Two White Elk withdrew a long pipe from the beaded bag. He cut tobacco from a twist, and tamped it into the bowl of the redstone pipe with a crooked finger. When he had finished, he raised the pipe and sang a prayer before offering it to the heavens, the earth, and the cardinal directions.

Lit with an ember from the fire, the calumet passed from hand to hand until the participants had smoked. Then Two White Elk stood, speaking eloquently.

"He's telling everyone about his coups, the hosses he's stole, and the other great deeds he's done," Baptiste explained. "Now he's telling everyone about Travis, and how he's a great warrior and friend of the Crow, and that we should be treated as honored guests."

Even as the speech continued, buffalo and mountain sheep-horn bowls filled with steaming meat were brought. To Richard's delight, each of the whites was offered his own steaming buffalo tongue on a wooden platter.

Baptiste indicated the roasted tongue. "Special honor."

"I'm all for that." Richard replied, stomach growling. The feast began in earnest, and he stuffed himself with the delicate tongue, hump roast, and pemmican.

Tea was brewed, a subtle flavor of mint and raspberry soothing to the taste. All the while people chattered amiably; children continued to scurry through the crowd like mice. The conversation between Travis and Two White Elk never let up. For the most part, they seemed oblivious of the others, like the best of friends.

"Where's Long Hair?" Richard asked.

"Out hunting buffler," Baptiste managed through a full mouth. "They killed a bunch a couple of days ago, and they's looking fo' another herd. If'n a rider comes in, this whole shitaree could be on the move in half an hour."

"They can take down the village in half an hour?"

"Yep. And if'n they's to get a good kill, they'll need to. Have to race the wolves fo' the meat."

Travis was talking seriously with Two White Elk, his hands adding to his stumbling speech.

Seeing Richard's interest, Baptiste added, "Crow ain't an

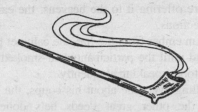

easy language ter larn. I can just pick up occasional words, and that's only 'cause I larned some Hidatsa. Crow split off from Hidatsa a time back."

"Two White Elk spoke English."

"Yep. But just what little he larned from Travis."

Richard watched the people, meeting their inquisitive stares, trying to fathom the things going on in their heads. Individual men and women kept coming up to talk to Travis. The hunter greeted many with hugs, calling them by name like old friends.

At last, the packs were brought forth, and Travis stood, raising his hands and calling out. When he had their attention, he made a short speech in the sibilant Crow tongue. Immediately, half of the circle of spectators vanished, hurrying off toward their lodges.

"Told 'em what we'd come to trade fo'," Baptiste said.

The Crow reappeared bearing robes, sections of buffalo gut stuffed with pemmican, and parfleches of jerked meat. Some of the women brought moccasins tied on strings like dried herrings.

"Come on," Baptiste said, rising. "Time to work. You and me, we unpacks and guard the goods. Don't let no Crow run off with nothing. Travis will call fo' what he needs as he needs it."

The soldiers kept the Crow in some semblance of order as they crowded around. As Richard had seen Green do so many times, Travis seated himself and took charge. Richard untied the manty and did as he was told, growling at the unruly children who tried to sneak little brown hands into the packs. A good-humored soldier helped to fend off the more obnoxious of the kids.

As the stock of powder, lead, cloth, beads, and needles shrank, another, larger stack of robes, moccasins, and other goods grew beside it.

When the sun finally slanted over the western horizon, Richard was more than ready for the trading to end. To his knowledge, only two bars of lead and four tin cups had mysteriously vanished from under his eyes. For the life of him, he couldn't tell who had pinched them.

As evening softened the camp, they tied their plunder together, lashing it tightly with sinew rope.

"Soldiers will guard it." Travis stretched his back, glancing at Two White Elk. "Come on, reckon it's time ter enjoy Two White Elk's lodge, have a smoke, and eat a little."

"We done good," Baptiste said, grinning at the plunder.

"How are we going to carry all that? We only brought three pack animals."

"Don't worry yor head none, Dick. Travis done traded old Two White Elk fo' more hosses. 'Sides, we're gonna need 'em afore spring." He slapped Richard on the back. "Come on, let's fill our bellies."

Richard and Baptiste saw to the final packs, making sure they were securely tied and under guard. The evening chill was settling as they pulled the lodge flap aside and stepped into the tipi.

Two White Elk called out the Crow welcome, *"Kahe!"* when Richard ducked through the door flap. Then he was shown to one of the seats in the rear behind the firepit. Two young women sat to one side, each nodding at him and giggling, talking about him in Crow. An older woman crouched behind them, head cocked to their talk as she watched Richard with curious eyes. Travis was already seated, talking and laughing with Two White Elk. Baptiste was also greeted with a *"Kahe!"* when he finally ducked through the flap.

The lodge was roomy, perhaps six paces across. The poles rose to the soot-blackened smokehole above, and a fire crackled in the central pit. A rawhide rope was tied off at the intersection of the poles and ran down to a peg driven into the ground behind the firepit. The rope anchored the lodge from blowing over in high winds. Amazed, Richard decided that no less than eighteen hides, artfully sewn together, made the cover. A liner had been tied a third of the way up the inside poles for insulation. It, too, was decorated with brightly painted buffalo, horses, and geometric figures. Bundled robes for bedding, and stacked parfleches, were tucked against the liner sides. The tripod and shield now stood inside the doorway.

The usual horn bowls were laid out, each brimming with its treat. "I'm not going to have to eat dog again, am I?"

"Nope." Travis grinned. "Crow don't eat dog."

"Good." Richard stared down into the bowls. "Uh, I'm not going to regret this later, am I?"

"According to Boston ways, maybe. But 'tain't nothing ye ain't already et."

A constant stream of visitors flowed through the lodge. Most settled around the sides to listen as Travis, Baptiste, and Two White Elk talked about old times.

How unlike the drawing rooms of Boston! Here, the camaraderie seemed palpable. Most of the conversation ended in uproarious laughter; Richard could only smile in ignorance. The women, unlike those of the Sioux, joined in, often interrupting, adding their comments. The only curiosity was the old woman who sat behind Two White Elk's wives. She talked to everyone, but never even deigned to notice Two White Elks—nor he her.

"What's in yor noodle, Doodle?" Baptiste asked once.

"I'm thinking that they don't seem like savages."

Baptiste nodded. "More like family."

"Yes."

"Now, ain't that an amazement." And Baptiste gave him a conspiratorial wink.

"What about the old woman?"

"Her? She's Two White Elk's mother-in-law. Them two girls in front is her daughters, Two White Elk's wives."

"They don't like each other?"

"They think each other's shining."

"But they don't talk."

"Nope. Among Crow, a man don't never talk to his maw-in-law—lessen he buys the right."

"That's crazy."

"Makes a heap of sense to this chile." He paused. "But then, I never had no maw-in-law."

Richard bit his lip. Damn slavery. To change the subject, he asked, "He married sisters?"

"Uh-huh. I reckon it's easier that way. A stronger bond atwixt families. The girls know each other. Ain't so much jealousy atween first and second wives."

"How perfectly . . . logical. I wonder why we didn't think of that?"

"Didn't have no Crow philos'phers, coon!"

The night wore on. His stomach full, warm in the fire's heat, Richard nodded off, soothed by the babble of voices. A life like this, it wouldn't be so bad, would it? As he dozed, uneasy fragments of dreams slipped around his head. In most of them, Laura Templeton was giving him a hard-eyed squint. She stood with her delicate hands braced on her hips, and the expression on her beautiful face boded no good.

A toe in the ribs brought him awake, yipping, "Laura, damn it! I didn't do anything." He stared owlishly about. Travis grinned down, the scars a demon's mask in the fire-light. "Didn't do what?"

"Nothing!"

"Ye gonna sleep thar, coon? Or would ye like some of these soft blankets that New Moon Rising's laid out fer ye?"

Richard jerked upright to see that the lodge had been transformed. Bedding now surrounded the walls, and a young woman watched him with curious eyes. She knelt on the buffalo robes she'd just unrolled. The thickly furred hide looked wondrously inviting.

Richard sighed. "I'll take those robes, all right. But I must go outside first."

"Yep. Me too." Travis led the way, ducking out into the cold night. Their breath clouded white as they walked out toward the edge of camp. The lodges looked magical, the thin hide glowing, lit from inside like giant lanterns.

Richard unlaced his pants and sighed as he relieved himself. "Such a pretty night."

Beside him, Travis grunted. "Uh, coon? That gal, New Moon Rising? She's fixing on warming yer robes fer ye."

"You mean with hot rocks? Like a fire brick wrapped up and put at the bottom of the bed?"

"I reckon with herself. She's fixing ter spend the night with ye."

Richard's urine stopped in midstream.

"Wal, I said I'd ask ye."

Richard puffed a frosty breath, and continued to empty his water. "Do I have a way out of this?"

"I figgered maybe fer just one night—and not really knowing her—ye might be considering a change. It wouldn't hurt nothing. She's not like Willow—I mean, no attachments or obligations or nothing."

"Travis, trust me on this, please?"

"I'll tell her it'd be bad fer yer medicine. But ye might give her something. I saved a couple hanks of beads and some other foofawraw in my possibles ter give Two White Elk and his family fer gifts."

"Thanks, Travis."

Richard laced his pants, and together they walked back. The rich smells of woodsmoke, cured leather, and horses filled the night air.

"Makes me feel right at home," Travis said wistfully.

"Baptiste said you lived with the Crow for two years."

"Yep."

"And . . . you took a wife?"

"Yep."

"Sounds like you don't want to talk about it."

"Nope."

Outside the lodge, Richard steeled himself, taking the string of beads Travis offered. He ducked inside where New Moon Rising still knelt on the robes. Two White Elk lay under the robes with one of his wives. Baptiste's curly hair was visible above his bedding—and so was a Crow woman's long shiny hair.

Richard swallowed, and approached New Moon Rising. She smiled up at him. An inquisitiveness filled her dark eyes, her lips parted to expose white teeth.

"I . . . I can't. Right now, it would be bad for my medicine. But, here, I offer these beads for your kind . . . um, offer."

Travis spoke gently, translating to Crow.

New Moon Rising nodded, the glow of expectation ebbing like a winter tide. Richard handed her the beads, and she touched him ever so briefly in the exchange. Then she stood, and without a word, slipped out.

The old woman tied the door flap closed behind the girl, and settled herself in the bed beside the entrance. Richard rubbed the back of his neck, growled to settle his churning emotions, and pulled the robes over him.

Meanwhile, Travis settled himself in the bed where Two White Elk's second wife lay, and began shucking off his clothing. Richard gaped, on the point of blurting out a protest, then forced his eyes closed as Travis tucked himself in.

It's Travis's business . . . and Two White Elk's. Go to sleep, Richard.

As the firelight flickered on the lodgepoles, a female giggle made Richard start. Then someone sighed with an import he had never heard before.

In desperation, he rolled himself over, used his fingers to plug his ears, and wished desperately that he could think of anything except Willow and how she'd looked that day on the river.

◆

Willow and White Hail climbed a long, rocky slope that led up into the Powder River Mountains.

The trail they followed was old, so old that the People's stories said it had been made just after the Creation. Among the *Dukurika*, it was known as the Ghost Way. Travelers passing this way placed a rock on each of the cairns that lined the route. To do so was to recognize the spirits who guarded the way. So many stones had been piled that the cairns had grown to the size of a small lodge. So many rocks, so many travelers. How many years had passed since the first stones were laid?

Willow paused to catch her breath and turned to look back

across the valley below them. The Red Wall—a long sandstone hogback that ran north-south at the base of the Powder River Mountains—rose to the east, and gleamed in ocher magnificence under the morning sun. Out beyond the Red Wall, sharp ridges dotted with pine and juniper gave way to the Powder River basin's distant buttes and drainage-cut ridges. There the Gourd Buttes rose like slumbering blue sentinels, the last bulwark before the horizon lost itself in the hazy distance.

Sagebrush and patches of scrubby mountain mahogany grew out of the slanting rock. Just to the north of their path, the sheer-walled canyon of the Middle Fork of the Powder River sliced deeply into the mountain's heart, exposing layers of sandstone, clinging pines, and fallen rock. In the tree-thick bottoms the river ran clear and cold, dashing white over boulders.

The bulk of Black Mountain jutted against the southern horizon, a huge hump of uplifted rock running east-west. She had passed below its heights as Packrat's captive. That road down the Platte had taken her to Richard—and to the lonely ache that rode in the depths of her souls.

"You look sad, sister." White Hail slipped down from his horse's back. Some of the strength had returned to his legs, but his jaw was healing crooked.

Willow shrugged and bent to pick up a stone the size of her fist. She took several steps uphill, and tossed the rock onto a cairn marking the Ghost Way. "My hurts are my own, White Hail."

"Come," he said, leading his horse up next to hers, "I can walk for a while. It will do this *Pa'kiani* beast good to rest." He raised an eyebrow. "If only you could have stolen that white gelding the war chief rode. Now *that* was a warhorse."

"Perhaps I should have left you with the *Pa'kiani*. You could complain to them." She started forward, leading her mare toward the next of the rockpiles, searching the ground for a suitable offering.

"Forgive me. Willow, what hurt are you hiding under this blanket of bitterness and anger?"

"What goes on within my souls doesn't concern you."

He sighed wearily as she located and tossed a rock high onto the next cairn. It clattered as it settled into place.

"Do you recall that once you called me your friend? No? I remember that day very well. I had come to ask you to be my wife. You said you could never marry me, but that I would be your *teci* forever."

"Yes, I remember."

"That man, the one you called brother, is speaking to you now." He studied her anxiously. "Or have the Whites witched you with their Power? Is that it? Some evil they shot into you like a *Nunumbi* arrow?"

She picked up another rock as they climbed, hefting it in her hand. Cold from the night before, it chilled her fingers. "Ease your worries, Brother. No evil White Power was shot into my soul." *No, indeed, I did this to myself.* And she tried to ignore Richard's soft brown eyes as they stared at her souls. If she allowed herself the freedom, she could sense Richard's gentle kindness. So close, so sweet and beckoning, that she wished nothing more than to let herself fall into that warmth and drown.

"I have seen such a look in your eyes before, Willow. The last time it was tainted with grief for my brother's death." White Hail led his horse around a patch of mountain mahogany and jerked at the lead rope to keep the swayback from stopping to crop grass. "Tell me, was it a man who did this to you? Was it this Ritshard who bruised your souls? Did you love him?"

She picked up another rock so he wouldn't see her face.

"I think it was him," White Hail continued neutrally.

Willow tossed the rock onto the next pile. "Shouldn't you save your breath for the climb?"

"Shouldn't you share some of the burden bearing down

on your souls? Perhaps both of us would climb with more energy."

She led her horse around the remains of a juniper. A lightning strike had blackened the branches and trunk.

"Are you afraid of me, *papinkwihi?*" White Hail asked. "Do you think I would judge you harshly? Or perhaps you distrust me so much that you think I would tell everyone your secret?"

"No, not that."

"Then tell me, Willow: will you keep this thing inside you until it festers and fills your *mugwa* with poison?"

The breeze had begun to tease fitfully as the morning warmed. A small herd of deer rose from their beds among the mountain mahogany and watched, ears wide, before they turned and bounded away.

Oh, Willow, what harm will it do? "Yes, I loved him."

White Hail climbed beside her, face tilted up to the morning. She watched him furtively, waiting for some reaction.

"Having a White man for a husband would not be such a bad thing. A woman could do much worse."

"It wasn't a matter of wealth, White Hail."

"He didn't want you?"

She closed her eyes for a moment, seeking some sense of inner peace that eluded her. When she looked out again, the world appeared just as callous. "He didn't want me."

"Another wife?" This time White Hail picked up the rock to toss onto the next cairn.

"Yes . . . another woman."

"He could have married you, too. As I've told you, being a second wife isn't so bad."

"He didn't *want* me for a wife, White Hail."

"Then he was a fool."

"He wanted something called Boston."

"Is that a kind of White man's Power?"

"No, it is a place far to the east where a great many White

men live. He is from there, and he wants to go back. He told me stories about it, about people living in lodges built on top of lodges, of giant boats that the wind blows back and forth across the ocean. The pathways between the houses are even covered with stone so one's feet don't get muddy." She shook her head. "I'm not sure I believe all the things I heard, but I don't think he lied, either."

"So, go with this Ritshard and see if it's true."

"He said his people would not like me, that I wasn't White. And, White Hail, the Whites, they own things—even their women. They put them inside their lodges and never let them out. That's why you have never seen a White woman. Why no one you know has ever seen a White woman. They even keep their god in a building. It's called church."

"Indeed! I never would have thought." He shook his head in wonderment. "How incredibly Powerful they must be if they can keep God in a building. This building, is it very big?"

"I saw buildings at Fort Atkinson. They are much bigger than the Mandan lodges—but big enough to hold God? Perhaps the White man's god is not very big."

"He must not be very Powerful." White Hail picked up another rock and gestured toward the sky with it. "*Tam Apo* needs all of the sky to hold him. *Tam Segobia,* Our Mother, fills the entire earth."

"The White men have no *Tam Segobia.* In the White stories, their god created the earth and all the animals. He created man, but only as the last thing did he create a woman—and then, she acted like Coyote, tricking their first man, Adam, into God's disfavor."

"That's what they believe?"

She picked her way carefully through a thick patch of sagebrush. "On my souls. I think that's why they distrust women so. I heard stories from the *engagés,* stories about something called original sin. Because a child is born from a woman's vagina, its soul is unclean."

White Hail reached up to rub his sore jaw. "I have seen the Whites among the Mandan. They seem to couple with a great many women. And among the *A'ni,* they have a reputation for all being 'young men,' meaning they take any chance they can get to couple with a woman."

"It is so," she agreed. "I saw them. Many would have coupled with me if I'd let them; but it is different. There was a Frenchman named Trudeau. He wanted to lie with me more than any of the others. The look he gave me was the one a warrior gives a captive woman. An enemy look. Do you understand what I mean?"

"Maybe." White Hail gave her a hard-eyed glance. "This Ritshard looked at you that way?"

She struggled for the right words. "No. He wanted me, White Hail. Not as a possession, or a conquest. But he feared me at the same time, as if . . . I were a trickster, like this Eve woman in their Creation story."

And, like a pattern in cat's cradle, a piece of the puzzle suddenly came clear. *Oh, poor Richard. Your people have misled you so completely.*

White Hail tossed a rock as they passed another cairn.

"How appropriate," Willow whispered. "This is a sacred trail, a way of climbing the mountains in search of Power. For myself, I am finally beginning to understand."

"That this Ritshard is a fool?" White Hail said sourly. "I need climb no mountains to know that, Sister."

"Not a fool, White Hail. If you had been born and immediately had one of your eyes covered, one of your ears plugged, one of your nostrils sealed with pine pitch, and one of your arms tied up, would you know the world the way you now do?"

"Of course not! Don't be silly."

"Richard is not a fool, *teci.* He searches like a *puhagan.*

I've seen the Power in his soul, but his White ways have crippled him. Not like I just said, but in his soul. I understood part of it, but not all. Not until just now."

"So . . . you would go back to him?"

"I can't, Brother. The day before I left, I explained the problem to him. If he is truly to become *puhagan,* he must free his soul from the entrapment it was born into."

"Do you think he will?"

Willow picked up another rock, hefting it in her hand as she continued to lead her horse up the long trail. She felt good today: lungs working just hard enough to breathe deeply but not pant; the exercise warming her sufficiently to balance the cool breeze; strength and agility filling her legs. With a perfect toss, her rock clattered into place near the top of the next cairn.

"I don't know. I think he will need to shed more of his old self first, much as the buffalo shed an old winter coat. Until he does, it will smother him."

They climbed in silence then, and Willow was more than aware of White Hail's periodic looks. Finally, he told her seriously, "I am going to kick Red Calf out of my lodge."

"That is the first sensible thing I've heard you say in a long time."

"I would like you to move into it when she is gone."

"Your sense was short-lived, brother."

He was watching her from the corner of his eye. "Are you waiting for this White man, this Ritshard, to come to his senses?"

"No," she lied. And then she told the truth: "He will not come for me. He must go back to Boston. It is a need deep within his soul. One that will never let him rest until he fulfills it."

"And what if I told you my souls yearned like that for you?"

"I'd say you had better go back to Red Calf. She'll only kill your body. In the end, I'll kill your souls."

After a pause he asked, "The way you talk . . . does this Ritshard only have *one* soul?"

"That is what the Whites believe. Everything is singular. One soul, one god, one truth, one right way. It's as if they see life with only one eye—despite having two in their heads."

"How strange . . . and frightening, too. I can't imagine. If the *navuzieip* and the *mugwa* were joined into one, how could they dream? I'd think they'd go crazy—like two people trying to talk out of one mouth."

"They *are* crazy, *teci*. Crazy like Coyote. Never pity them, but watch them constantly. Think of a rattlesnake in a bush. You can never trust it."

White Hail walked in thoughtful silence, and finally asked, "What will you do? You're a young woman, Willow. Are you going to keep all the men who desire you at an arm's length? My brother is dead. This White man is far away, and not coming to seek you out. Are you going to live alone?"

Her gaze followed an eagle that circled high overhead. "For now. I need to be alone in the high places, listen to the wind, watch winter come to cover *Tam Segobia,* and let my souls heal themselves."

❖

We're almost there! Dave Green had dreamed, hoped, and prayed for this day, and now, after nearly three thousand miles of winding, treacherous river, he was about to live it.

He could not have wished for a more perfect day: the sky was a throbbing blue vault overhead; the sun shone golden and warm on the tawny grasses. A mild breeze coasted softly down the valley of the Yellowstone, and the air smelled of river, juniper, and pine mixed with the pungency of sage. Flocks of gray-capped finches rose in a mob as the *Maria* passed the high bank where they'd been hunting for seeds.

"We should see it any time now," he muttered, pacing nervously. His heart was pounding as he shifted from foot to foot.

The *engagés* sang, voices spirited as they poled the keelboat against the current. Henri wore a constant smile that curled up his thick black mustache.

As they rounded a bend, he could see the familiar opening in the south bank. "There it is, boys! Feast your eyes!"

Ululating cheers broke out as the *engagés* looked up from their toil.

Made it! Made it, by God! Dave knotted a fist and shook it. Looking down at the current, he could see where the murky waters of the Big Horn ran parallel to the clear waters of the Yellowstone.

"Steer wide," Dave urged Henri. "There's probably mudbanks just out from the mouth."

"*Oui, bourgeois.*" Henri was chortling like a giddy boy, his white teeth shining.

"Take a good look, boys!" Green whooped. "That's the mouth of the Big Horn! Let's bring her in in style!"

With a shout, the *engagés* bent to their poles with renewed vigor. *Maria* shot ahead.

Green paced anxiously back and forth as he had during every tense moment on the journey up the river. The wild whoops had stopped, the *engagés* now calling encouragement to each other as they panted and set their poles into the main channel's gravelly bottom and shoved the boat forward.

"I have hoped that I would live to see this day. *Merci, mon Dieu,*" Henri said reverently as he caressed his steering oar and watched the wide mouth of the Big Horn. At the margins of its discharge, swirls and eddies marred the smooth surface.

"We all have, Henri." Green smacked a balled fist into his palm. "By the Blessed God in Heaven, I had my doubts. I guess even a fool gets a little luck every now and then."

"*Oui,* and only two men dead. We had a charmed voyage, Dave." And at that Henri crossed himself.

The Big Horn's broad swell of murky water silvered in the sun. Like a conquering hero, Green propped his fists on his hips to look up the meandering channel with its willow-lined banks giving way to cottonwoods and brush.

There is the doorway to my empire. Tan sandstone outcrops rose on either side of the wide valley, their slopes dotted with pine and juniper. His heart was swelling in his chest as he danced a happy jig and turned his attention back to the Yellowstone.

"It's not far now, boys," he called down to the sweating *engagés.* "Right up there, see? That high bank. That's the spot we've been waiting for!"

He strode to the front of the cargo box, barely able to contain himself as he studied the landing. The Yellowstone's sloping bank had grown over since the Missouri Fur Company had abandoned Fort Benton three years before. Where once the feet of Immel, Jones, and scurrilous old Bouché had walked, only tall yellow grass and rosebushes remained.

Green gave the signal, and Henri leaned into his oar, heeling the *Maria* up against the bank. Trudeau picked up

the painter, looping the coils around his shoulder. Taking a short run, he spanned the narrowing gap in à mighty leap. His moccasins made a hollow thud on the bank; he scrambled ashore, followed immediately by Toussaint. Together they lined out the painter, tying it off to a worn cottonwood that had served the same purpose since Manuel Lisa himself had chosen this spot for Fort Raymond, back in late fall of 1807. After being abandoned for years, Joshua Pilcher had rebuilt the post in 1821 and renamed it Fort Benton.

"Tie her fast now," Green barked. "Wouldn't want her to float clear back to Saint Louis without us!"

"Oui, bourgeois!" Toussaint laughed as someone tossed him the stern line.

Green studied the high brush with a narrowed eye. *I wish to hell Travis was here. It'd be just my luck that having come this far, there's a big band of Blackfeet the other side of the rise.*

Then he shouted for attention. "Now, let's not forget where we are, boys. Henri, break out the rifles. Trudeau, you set up guards and make a scout as soon as you get a musket. Keep an eye peeled out there!"

Able hands slid out the plank, settling it in place. Henri smacked the toil from his hands, sighed, and ducked down into the cargo box. One by one, he handed the muskets up to Green, who passed them to Etienne, and then on to the others.

"All right," Green said, as Henri handed him his old faithful Hawken. "Let's see what remains of Fort Benton. Now, I want a keen eye peeled, boys. At the first hint of Injun sign, sing out—and I don't want anyone to wander off. Keep within sight of your companions!"

Green led the scramble up the slope and onto the flats. How many years had it been since he'd stood here, a young *engagé*, so full of hopes and dreams?

Well, David, today you've come back. And it's yours, all

yours. He hefted his rifle and walked forward, past the weather-gray stumps with their ax marks. The grass rustled beneath his boots as he followed the familiar path. The place looked sadly desolate. Most of the palisade had fallen down, and the cabins were nothing more than burned-out shells.

Henri stopped beside him, peering around owlishly. "Some of the logs can be saved."

"Yep. We'll have to pack a bunch more in." Dave glanced up at the cobalt November sky and sniffed the warm breeze. "It's fine weather. But it won't last." He stepped over the fallen palisade and took stock. "I'd say build a blockhouse first. That will give us defense and shelter from the blizzards at the same time."

Toussaint came at a trot, the usual sad expression on his face. "*Bourgeois,* we 'ave found old firepits. The ashes, they are long cold, three, maybe four months. From zee rocks piled inside, they are *les Indiens.*"

"But nothing fresh?"

"*Non, bourgeois.* Trudeau, he see old platforms in zee trees to the west, but the bodies are no longer there. He thinks they are old."

"I wish Travis and Baptiste were here," Henri muttered. "I would sleep better."

"*Moi aussi,*" Toussaint agreed.

Green slapped them both on the back, and shook his head. "For the moment, Travis is better off where he is. And we're going to need those Crow supplies a heap more than three more rifles here. Toussaint, we've got three, maybe four hours of daylight left. Let's get camp set up. But first, I want some of these old palisades dragged up for a breastwork. Tonight, we'll have us one hell of a feast, two gills of whiskey per man, a little dancing and singing, and then, by God, tomorrow, we go to work on the post."

"*Oui!*" Toussaint's expression brightened; calling orders, he walked off toward *Maria.*

Green took a deep breath, inhaling the rich fragrance of the land. "God damn the naysayers, I'm here! At the mouth of the Big Horn—and before the rest of the insiders like Astor, Chouteau, Pilcher, and the others."

Henri slapped him on the back. "I'll go and see to the boat, Dave. There is much work to be done."

"Yes, a lot of work." *But for now, I've beaten the odds.* Green tightened his grip on his rifle. *And, as God is my witness, there's no one who can take it away from me now. If it comes to war, I won't be licked by man, beast, or weather!*

His steps light, buoyed with exuberance, he walked across the narrow neck of land and stared to the south. *Travis? No matter what I tell the rest, I wish you were here with me, old friend. You be careful down there. I just got a feeling, hear?*

FIFTEEN

So many things are now clear to us. Now let that honest fellow speak out, I will say, now let him answer my question. He does not believe in the beautiful by itself, he will have no perpetual model of perfect, unchangeable beauty, but he believes in a myriad of beautiful things. This is the sort of sight-fancier who will not brook being told that the beautiful is one, and the just is one, and so forth. Here, then, is my question: "My good man, of all these beautiful things, is there a solitary one which will not sometimes appear ugly? Of all these just things, will one never appear unjust? Of all these pious things, will one never appear unpious?"

—Plato, *The Republic*

Richard awakened to tickles and itches. Still mostly asleep, he reached up, scratched, and rolled over. A pinprick of pain made him scratch yet again. The annoyance awakened him enough that he recognized the sounds of the village—and remembered other sounds from the night before.

God would have spared Sodom and Gomorrah had he known about the Crow.

A tickle traced across his face, but this time his quick fingers captured the tiny creature. In the thin dawn light, Richard stared at a little black speck barely larger than a . . .

Dear Lord God, it's a louse! His stunned brain couldn't accept what he was seeing. Not until the scalp over his right ear began to tickle.

He crushed the little insect between the nails of his thumb and forefinger. His hair seemed to burn now, and tickles were born all over his flesh, along his legs, around his testicles, on the soft skin of his sides.

I can't believe this. Pulling back the covers, he noted that only the old woman was up, tending the fire as she boiled something that smelled delicious in a dented copper kettle.

Richard tiptoed to the doorway, slipped out into the chilly air, and greeted the crystal morning with less than abundant enthusiasm. His breath puffing, he shivered and followed the path down toward the slow current of the Tongue River.

Every man has his vulnerability, the thing, or circumstance, they can't abide. For some it might be leeches, for others, ticks or spiders. That day on the Tongue, Richard discovered that his was lice. Perhaps it was being raised on Beacon Street, but the very idea that he'd been infested with the filthy beasts just set his gut to crawling.

I've got to be rid of them . . . now! In a panic, he hurried across the frost-crusted grass.

Several young men were already splashing about in the water a hundred yards downstream as Richard scowled at the pink horizon. His breath whitened in the chill air. The ground under his feet had frozen hard. With deepening dread, he slipped out of his clothes.

He waded bravely into the shallows and gasped at the numbing cold. Sloshing out into deeper water, he dived in. At first the terrible cold shocked his nerves. Then it began to eat into his very core.

Holding his head underwater, he scrubbed his hair vigorously, rooting his scalp with frantic fingernails. Tarnal Hell, the critters couldn't take cold like this, could they? Surely it would stun them to death, drown them.

Soap, oh, Heavenly Father, what I'd give for a good bar of lye soap!

Lungs laboring, muscles knotted, flesh shivering and goosebumped, he got his feet under him and stood in the hip-deep water. Beneath his feet, the mud was gooey for the first couple of inches, but rounded river cobbles beneath provided solid footing.

To his surprise, the air felt even colder than the water.

"Another dousing won't hurt," he told himself firmly. "Right." Better to turn blue and die of pneumonia than to have lice. He dived in again, bubbles gurgling around his ears as he scratched and scrubbed.

When he could stand it no longer, he surfaced, teeth chattering. He barely noticed the rosette sky, the magnificent orb of the rising sun, or the dappled shadows on the sage-covered hills. Rubbing water droplets away, he blinked at his cold-pimpled skin, searching desperately for little scurrying beasts. He caught one down deep in the mat of his pubic hair, gleefully pinching the defiler between his nails. But, if there was one . . .

He ducked himself again, this time clawing at his crotch, scratching and flailing to dislodge any unwelcome invaders. The cold had become unbearable.

Enough. Richard, any more of this and you'll freeze to death.

He stood up, thigh-deep in the river, rubbed water from his eyes, and bent over despite wracking shivers to pick carefully through his pubic hair. *God damn! I've never been so cold in all my life!*

But, lice! Dear Jesus, a man had to draw the line somewhere. He'd curled over until he could see the underside of his cold-knotted scrotum and continued the hunt for tiny insect bodies, unaware at first that another body was in the water beside him.

Richard glanced sideways to find New Moon Rising—naked herself and dripping wet—bent over as he was, neck craned curiously to see what he'd been so intent on. In a straightforward tone, she asked him a question. Her mild brown eyes reflected frank curiosity.

For a moment, he stood as if rooted.

Nor was she the only one. The current had carried Richard fifty paces down from where he'd left his clothes, and five other young women were in the process of either disrobing or wading out to join him and New Moon Rising.

"Oh, good God!" Thrashing through the water, he stumbled and fell, flailing. He found his feet, coughing and sputtering. When he looked back, the young women were still standing there, silently watching him.

"Graybacks, huh?" Travis asked as their horses picked their way across a sage-covered bench and began to climb a long gentle ridge. The notion of Richard with lice pleased him immensely—but the tale wasn't half as entertaining as the stories the Crow girls were telling about him down at the river. It seemed they had trouble with the English word "Richard" so they were calling him "Looks for His Balls."

With a straight face, Travis said, "They can devil a man half to distraction, I'll tell ye."

"Don't I know it." Richard stared glumly at him, absently scratching his flank as he rode along.

"Looks like you needs 'nuther hand, Dick," Baptiste observed. "You got one fo' the reins, another to hang on to yor shooter, but one shy fo' the scratching, coon."

Travis chuckled, and fought the desire to do a little scratching of his own. "Yep. Why I reckon best medicine fer graybacks is ter boil these hyar clothes. They's a smudge can be made out of larkspur and fir sap. Ye can trade fer some when the Mountain Crow come in. Burn it and the soot'll kill the varmints. In summer, ye can burn it and the smoke'll keep the skeeters down."

"What about now, Travis?" Richard demanded. "I tried drowning and freezing them to death."

Travis could not help but smirk. "Hell, it might have worked, coon. But ye run outa that river so fast, and crawled right back inta them clothes of yern. Why, the onliest thing graybacks likes better than a man's hair is the seams in his duds."

Travis patted his Hawken and looked back over his shoulder at the pack string. He'd saved a trade rifle to barter with Two White Elk for the four additional packhorses that now followed them. The Crow nags, backs covered by their packs, were tail-hitched to the Pawnee horses. All in all, it was a damn fine trade. And if worse came to worst and they didn't get a good hunt before deep cold, they could eat the horses.

"What did Two White Elk tell you?" Richard asked suddenly. "You and he talked a lot."

"Oh, lots of things. About the Blackfoot, about what old

friends had counted coup, about who'd married who and who'd divorced who. Who'd been killed. That sort of thing."

"Travis . . . can I ask something personal?"

By God, hyar it comes! Travis raised an eyebrow and shot a knowing look across at Baptiste. The corner of the black hunter's lip curled in disgust.

"Ask what? About the phil'sophical importance of graybacks?"

"No. I mean . . . well, you and Two White Elk's wife. Isn't he your best friend?" Richard's face looked like a mask, as if he were trying desperately to act unconcerned.

"Son of a *bitch!*" Baptiste roared, slapping a hand on his thigh with enough fury to spook his horse into a quick sidestep. "I'm gonna wring his damn Doodle neck!"

Richard looked plumb panicked as he gave Baptiste the sort of glance a condemned man might.

Travis chuckled. "Relax, Dick. I bet that neck-chopper yonder that ye'd ask about it first chance ye got."

"But I . . ."

"Bet him twenty prime plews, I did. And by Hob's balls, Baptiste, they'd better be right prime."

"They'll be as prime as any upriver, you miserable duck-fucker."

"What's a duck-fucker?" Richard's nervous gaze slipped from Travis to Baptiste.

"Feller what cares fer chickens and the like on board

ship." Travis nodded at Baptiste. "That old slave there, he ain't about ter let me forget I's a sailor once before I got religion and skipped ship."

"Go on," Baptiste cried in disgust. "Answer his question. But, holy hinges of Hell, Dick, stop costing me money. Just fer once, can't ye let somethin' happen without asking questions about it?"

Richard looked sheepish, his fist knotted on the reins.

Travis glanced sideways at Richard. "Two White Elk, he's my brother, Dick. Crow do that. Adopt each other. Wal, Two White Elk and me . . . let's just say we got a heap in common. Things we share that are special to just us."

"I could tell."

In steely tones Travis said, "No, I don't think you could, Doodle. And right hyar and now, I ain't about ter discuss it with ye. Ye've not earned that right, and I ain't sure ye ever will."

Travis pounded heels into his horse's ribs and cantered on ahead, letting the crisp breeze chill the heat out of his anger.

He don't know no better, coon. It's different fer him, a Boston boy that never had to wipe the snot out of his own nose.

Travis sighed wearily, letting his horse slow and cool out as he neared the ridgetop. It didn't do for a man to charge headlong over a hill, not in this country. Even if an Eastern Doodle had driven him half to distraction.

Travis let his horse walk over the crest and gazed on the snow-capped peaks to the west. Yep, there they were, worthy of their name, gleaming in the light. The sight kindled something happy down inside him. Since ascending the Yellowstone, bits and pieces had been coming back to him. Fragments of memory that he'd pushed out of his head. Seeing Two White Elk had opened the gates, releasing the flood.

Now he looked out at the country, taking his time to inspect every ridge and gully, mindful of any irregularity. Dark clumps of buffalo spotted the breaks down into the Big Horn. That would bear remembering, depending on how long it took to reach the river's mouth, where, hopefully, they'd find Dave in the process of rebuilding Fort Benton.

If the weather held, the *engagés* could cobble together some sort of shelter, and he, Baptiste, and Richard could shoot enough meat to get them through the deep cold. A warm spell generally opened the country around the end of January or first of February. The chinooks would blow and give them another chance to hunt buffalo in addition to the deer, antelope, and small game that could be collected around the fort.

Travis sucked the sweet air into his lungs, savoring the odors of sage, earth, and grass. So fresh, why, nothing could compare. The spirit of the sky, soil, sun and stars, the rocks and plants, surrounded a man—the very essence of what it meant to be alive.

The hollow clopping of horses' hooves intruded, and Travis paid no heed as they rode up next to him. He simply raised an arm and pointed. "Yonder."

"What are they?" Richard asked. "Clouds?"

Baptiste chuckled, teeth flashing. "He do take all."

"The Shining Mountains, Dick. Part of 'em at least. We call 'em the Big Horns."

Richard fixed on the distant mountains like a pointer, his fingers tracing the curved cock on his rifle. "Willow's mountains? So high? Why are they white?"

"Ain't you never seen no mountains afore?" Baptiste asked.

"Well, some." Richard rubbed his jaw. "Around Pittsburgh and along the Ohio River."

"He ain't never seen mountains," Travis confirmed. "Not

shining ones, anyway. And yep, if'n Willow's alive, that's where she's headed. Hell, she otta be there by now."

"And this river running down the valley in front of yor nose"—Baptiste pointed—"is the Big Horn. And just yonder, to the north beyond them bluffs, is where we otta find Green and the boat."

Travis tarried, eyes on the distant mountains; the memories, so long suppressed, began to boil up inside him. For a brief instant he lived with Moonlight again. Once more he could enjoy her smile, the laughter in her eyes, the way she held him and teased him by plucking at the hair on his chest with her nimble brown fingers. She'd been so small and elfish, an imp of a thing with an insatiable appetite for fun. He closed his eyes. He could see her looking up at him after they'd made love. He'd place his hands just so, on each side of her head, marveling that such a tiny slip of a woman could wield such power over him.

They'd had two years together. Some of them right over yonder, at the foot of those mountains, and up in the gentle pine and fir slopes of the Pryors. A man could live like that . . . if only for a moment.

But I never knew those two years were going to have to last me all of my life.

"Travis?" Richard's voice cut through the dream.

"Huh?"

"That's the third time I asked you."

"Asked me what?"

Richard scratched under his arm, squinting curiously at him. "I thought you were the one who talked about being on your uppers, about not locking yourself in your head."

"Yep, wal, Travis, he's a fine one fo' giving advice," Baptiste said dryly. "But he ain't always a one to take it."

Travis gave Baptiste an evil scowl. "Ye got something ter say?"

"Just that we ain't getting no closer to camp a-sitting

up heah." Baptiste winked, and smiled. "Maybe Dick and me, we'll mosey on. Catch up with us when you will, coon."

Richard gave Travis a skeptical glance as the horses filed past, but for once he held his peace.

Travis had to rein in his horse, the animal anxious to follow the others. The breeze hissing through the short sage and grass seemed to carry her whisper to his lonely ears.

"Yep, wal, gal. I do shorely miss ye."

Impatient, the horse whinnied, shattering his tranquillity with the surety of an ax through river ice.

"All right, damn ye." Travis let the horse have its head, taking one last look at the Big Horns, so clear and clean in the distance.

❖

Generations of *Dukurika* had camped in the overhang high on the canyon wall. Sometime in the distant past, perhaps just after the Creation, the limestone beneath the sandstone caprock had been undercut, leaving a big hollow that ran back into the mountain. Since the overhang had a southern exposure, it received sunlight all year long. The rock was

warmed during the day, and radiated heat throughout the night. Because the camp was high on the hillside, it remained warm when the cold air settled in the canyon bottom. There the *Dukurika* cached their deep-frozen meat supplies.

The camp was protected from both the west and north winds. Water could be had by climbing down to the creek. Wood was plentiful, with juniper and limber pine on the slope below, and lodgepole and fir forests above.

Mountain sheep wintered on the slopes to the east, nibbling the bitterbrush and cinquefoil. Elk used the grassy flats below for winter range, and mule deer liked the brush-filled draws and pawed through snow for last season's forbs.

Willow had found High Wolf's band at the shelter, right where she'd expected. Early that afternoon, she had picketed the horses on the rim above, and led an uneasy White Hail down the precarious trail through the caprock. Nervous flutters had filled her stomach when she called out their arrival.

Young Felt the Fire had poked his head around a rock outcrop and asked who was there. At Willow's answer, he'd vanished, to be replaced an instant later by Eagle Trapper, who cried out in happy amazement, clapped his hands, and rushed out to hug her.

Somehow she had survived a blizzard of questions, hugs, jokes, and proddings. The dogs had barked, the children had squealed, and her parents had beamed. The telling of her adventures had lasted from the time she arrived, all through the afternoon and evening, and now extended into the night.

I am home.

After all the upset that began with the death of her husband and child, she was once again high in her beloved mountains. She sighed as she looked up at the night sky. In the high mountain blackness, the stars shone with a brilliance she'd missed out on the plains.

A roaring fire crackled lively sparks into the cold air and illuminated the sandstone cliff above the camp. A framework of poles and hides—enough to protect bedding and packs—had been built behind the drip line and across the rock overhang.

Willow stood before the fire, a soft, white mountain sheep robe over her shoulders.

One by one she studied the familiar faces cast in the flickering yellow light. This year's camp consisted of three extended families of High Wolf's small band.

High Wolf, her father, the band's headman and *puhagan*, perched on an angular slab of rock, his favorite dog, Star, at his feet. White Alder, her mother, sat cross-legged on an elk hide to High Wolf's left, a glossy bearskin robe over her shoulders. White Hail—an honored guest—sat at High Wolf's right, his *Pa'kiani* buffalo robe pulled tight against the night's chill. Rock Hare, Willow's brother, sat beside his wife, Red Squirrel, who suckled her infant son under a fox-hide cape. Marmot and Pika, their two boys, five and four years old, cuddled together under a soft bear robe and watched with gleaming eyes.

Next in the circle was Many Elk, High Wolf's longtime friend and companion. He had been like an uncle to Willow. His wife, Lodgepole, sat beside him, covered with a finely tanned sheep hide. Their son, Black Marten, and his wife, Sweet Grease, shared a buffalo robe with their three children.

Beside them, filling out the circle, were Eagle Trapper and Good Root, also old friends of High Wolf's. *Tam Apo* had smiled upon them, for their five children had all lived; the eldest, Felt the Fire, was ten, while little Flicker, the youngest, still nursed and slept in a fur-lined cradleboard.

The band's pack of dogs lay along the margins of the shelf that dropped off into the canyon.

In celebration of Willow's arrival, a feast of succulent sheep and baked ricegrass cakes had been prepared. The empty dishes—cut from the boss of a mountain sheep's horn—had been licked clean by the dogs and now lay empty before them.

Willow finally brought the long story of her adventures to a conclusion: "From the Spirit Trail, we crossed the mountains. The snow is still passable beneath the peaks. And here we are. I am home."

"These things you tell us"—High Wolf shook his head, fingers scratching Star's neck—"they seem almost impossible."

Willow's father was an old man. After forty-five winters, his hair remained thick but silver streaked the black; he braided it tightly into two queues that hung down either side of his broad face. A thin, straight nose ran from strong brows and accented his prominent cheekbones. Good-humored eyes looked out from deep sockets, the corners crinkled in crow's-feet from squinting across snow fields and into cold winds. His heavy jaw ended in a pointed chin that gave his face a triangular look.

He wore a finely crafted sheephide coat, the leather tanned maiden-soft, and tailored to his broad shoulders and muscular arms. Zigzags of lightning, Power lines of thunder, and images of wolf and mountain sheep had been painted on the white leather.

"Nevertheless, I tell you the truth," Willow replied.

"She does indeed," White Hail added. "Upon my soul, I swear it."

"I have heard of these White 'men,'" High Wolf said. "I have seen the things traded to us from the *Ku'chendikani* and the *A'ni*. I thought the White men were Powerful spirits who lived far to the east, though some have been reported to have passed through our land. But now you tell me they are men?"

Willow used her toe to nudge a juniper log further into the fire. "They are men, just like us. And like us, they are both good and bad. I'm afraid my words will not be believed, but I insist that we will come to grief if we treat them like spirits instead of like ordinary men. They have things we need—and many that we do not."

"Willow and I disagree on this," White Hail said. "The White men bring us great wealth. Wondrous weapons to destroy our enemies, and better axes and knives. The beads they bring are lustrous, and gleam in the sunlight. Their metal kettles never break. I've seen paints of unbelievable brightness and color, metal needles that never dull. So many things we need."

Willow shook her head. "They will make us no wealthier than our enemies, and the guns they trade, they trade to everyone. We will obtain nothing from the White men that every other people will not receive. The trap is that White Hail is partly right. We must have guns to balance the advantage given to the *Pa'kiani* and *A'ni.*"

Many Elk tugged at one of his long braids. "Why do we need guns? We are not warriors, Willow. The way it is now, when the *Pa'kiani* come, we simply disappear into the forest. We know the hidden ways and can vanish like mist. They travel on horses . . . and only on the main trails. The only thing to be gained by fighting is an opportunity to have a funeral for someone you love. Then a person must live in grief for the rest of his life. Winning a fight does not bring the dead one back."

White Hail stiffened slightly; but then, *Ku'chendikani* and *Dukurika* had never really understood each other's concepts of war. Among the Sheepeaters, honor came from the hunt, not from scalps and raids.

"The White men come for furs," Willow stated. "For now, that is all they want."

"Is that so bad?" High Wolf frowned as he stroked his dog. "If they come here, we can give them furs for their metal pots and knives and axes."

"The fewer things we trade them," Willow insisted, "the better off our people will be."

White Hail made a face—then relented under Willow's scowl.

Willow's mother was short and broad. Despite the eight children—only two had lived—that White Alder had borne High Wolf, the years had been kind to her. She still looked young enough to be Willow's older sister. Now she said, "These White men things you talk of, I have seen some. Like the iron knife you have, Willow. I would like an iron knife like that. I have seen those glass beads. Those are very good beads. If these few things are good, then perhaps many of their things are good."

"Mother, *Tam Apo* gave us everything we need. It's all here, in our mountains. As long as we avoid raiders and fighting, we need no guns. We kill enough in our sheep drives on the ridges. We know the ways of brother elk in the timber, and catch enough of his kin in our snares for food and hides. We do not need horses and guns to shoot buffalo when we can trap them in our surrounds and pens. While the Plains people must move constantly to feed their horses, we stay in one place and harvest roots, berries, and grass seeds in late summer. Our food can be cached for later use because we don't have to move it with us all the time."

"Yes, yes, we know these things," Eagle Trapper replied as he absently ruffled his son's hair. "We have argued it with our *Ku'chendikani* cousins for years. But what about these White men? If they can make such tools as your iron ax, what else can they make? You have told us about the big wooden lodge that floats, and the giant log lodges. I would like to see these things."

Her brother Rock Hare nodded. He'd looked skeptical as Willow related her story. "I, too, would like to see these things my sister claims. I have seen guns. For a long time I have wanted one. To know that the White men are bringing such things here, near our mountains, makes me think I might go down and get one from them."

Willow sighed wearily. Rock Hare was four years older than she, and had always seemed invincible, all-knowing, and capable. Now he acted pitifully innocent and vulnerable. When had that changed? "Why do you want a gun, Brother? What will it get you that your bow will not? Remember the winter of the big snow? We had crept up on six deer in the willows. You told me you would kill them all. And one by one you did, the only sound the twang of your bowstring, and your sharp arrows striking flesh. With a gun, Brother, you would have killed only one deer. At the bang, the others would have run."

He raised a mocking eyebrow. "I suppose you know *all* about guns, Sister?"

"I know of them. Travis persuaded me to shoot one when he was teaching Richard to shoot. I will stick to a bow, and kill silently. And, Brother, when I run out of arrows, I will make more. When you run out of powder for your gun, you must go to the White men and trade them as many hides as they ask for more powder."

"In saying this," White Hail agreed, "Willow is right. Only the White men can make gunpowder and bullets. I have seen *Ku'chendikani* trying to mix their own powder from bark, charcoal, fine-ground bone, all sorts of things. Nothing works. You *must* trade for them with the Whites."

"Are they all bad?" A pensive Eagle Trapper rested his knobby chin on balled fists. "Are none of their things good? If this is so, I think we should just avoid them altogether. But

I know the Whites have traded with the *Ku'chendikani*. Nothing terrible has happened to them."

Willow studied them, trying to read the effect of her words. "Many of the Whites' things are bad, yes, but not all. Let me tell you about their spirit water."

White Hail's eyes gleamed and he smiled wistfully.

Willow continued, "It has wonderful abilities. I poured some on a White man's wounds. They healed cleanly, without forming pus and hot flesh. But the White men do not use it for this. Instead, they drink it, and it makes their souls crazy. It turns a wise man into a fool."

"Then we would not want it," High Wolf agreed.

Willow shrugged. "Are you sure? Remember the time when Half Bear was hurt? The elk was supposed to be dead, but jumped up at the last instant and gored him. The wound angered, and grew hot, dripping and stinking from the evil that entered it. Half Bear's *mugwa* was driven from his body and he died horribly. I think I could have healed him with the spirit water."

"How?" High Wolf demanded, his *puhagan's* interest piqued. "What Power does it have?"

"I don't know. Maybe it drives the evil spirits from a wound the way it drives the good sense from a man's soul when he drinks it."

High Wolf stared thoughtfully at his dog. "Then that would be a good thing."

"My people," Willow pleaded, "you must be very careful with the White men. They are unbelievably clever. They aren't like us. They don't think the way we do. In the beginning, they give gifts: pots, iron needles, strike-a-lights, little things that amaze and delight.

"The first thing we, as *Dukurika*, will do is show these wonderful things to our friends. And, as is proper and polite, when our friends marvel, we will give the gift to them. And they to someone else, and so on. This is where the White man is so very clever, for in the trail of the gift, I will always want another strike-a-light or another mirror like the one I gave away. Like thirst in the alkali flats, the desire will grow. But the next time the White man comes, he will not give away the wonderful things. At that time he will say, 'Trade! I will give you a strike-a-light for a beaver hide.'

"And, my people, the thirst will have grown so powerful, you will take your hides down and give them all to the White men so that you have many strike-a-lights to give to all of your relatives."

"And the next time the White men come, all these people will trade." High Wolf nodded his understanding. "These White men are clever indeed."

Willow raised her hands. "Never underestimate them. Respect them, but never trust them. They act like Coyote in the beginning times. As long as you always understand that you are Wolf, and they are Coyote, you will do well with them."

Everyone around the circle was nodding thoughtfully, remembering the Creation and how Coyote always caused trouble. Everyone but Good Root, who watched her with suspicious eyes. She'd always been one of those aggravating sorts, a woman who used words like little splinters, never hurting her victim outright, but always sliding something irritating under the skin.

Men who act like Coyote? Richard's eyes watched from her memory. No, he'd never tried to trick her. He'd always been incomprehensibly honest—at the same time he tricked himself.

Was he on his way back to Boston, traveling downriver even as she stood here? *What will you think when you pass all those places we saw together, Richard? Will you remember me at the site of the Ree battle? At the Grand Detour? Or the camp where you shot Packrat?*

SIXTEEN

◈

But it is manifest that this imaginary right of slaying the defeated in no way results from the state of war. Men are not enemies by nature, if only for that reason that, living in their primitive independence, they have no mutual relationships sufficiently durable to constitute a state of peace, or a state of war. It is the relationship of things, and not of men, which constitutes war; and since the state of war cannot arise from simple personal relations, but only from real relations, private war—war between man and man—cannot exist either in the state of nature, where there is no settled ownership, or in the social state, where everything is under the authority of laws.

—Jean-Jacques Rousseau, *The Social Contract*

Richard rode last in line as they traveled north down the broad valley of the Big Horn. Travis was in the lead; he'd been unusually quiet since leaving the Crow village. Baptiste walked his gelding to one side of the pack string, his rifle cradled on the saddle before him, wary eyes missing nothing.

The Big Horn River flowed down through a broken brown land of jutting sandstone ridges, accented by the speckled slopes where limber pine, juniper, and ponderosas grew. Patches of sage mottled the hillsides and flats, contrasting to the autumn-tawny grasses that swayed with the perpetual wind.

The river itself wasn't much, at least, not to Richard's

eyes. After all the months on the Missouri, the terrible toil to reach this place, he'd expected something magnificent. Instead, he saw an unremarkable course of placid, silt-murky water that lazed indolently between cottonwood-rich banks. Greasewood patches interspersed with tall grasses and stands of sagebrush covered the broad floodplain. On the whole, the land appeared rocky and dry. The nights were clear and nippy, while the days warmed slowly as the sun climbed its winter arc across the sky. When the air warmed, however, the wind picked up, until by late afternoon it roared over the rocky outcrops, moaned in the trees, and hissed through the sage. Richard rode hunkered against the blast, eyes in a squint.

Even so, the land had an essence, a raw presence he couldn't define. Not the somber, threatening antiquity of the Eastern forests, but something primal that hearkened to a language of the bones as well as the senses.

How odd that the earth could speak in such different tongues. Rifle in one hand, lead rope in the other, Richard studied the notion. In Boston, he couldn't have conceived that the land lived, that it could be felt. Grass was grass, a tree a tree, and dirt . . . well, what could one say about dirt? Abstractions that defied any meaningful relationship beyond the dialectical "me—it."

And what would his friends at Fenno's say about this notion?

They'd laugh me out of the tavern. As he would have once done to any fool who made such a ludicrous postulation. *Yet here I am, suddenly aware of what cannot be.* Or what his people would not accept. *And does that go so far as to encompass a Crow man sharing his wife with his best friend?*

What was too much in this land of wild excess? Some dilemmas had a great many horns. His gaze roamed the endless sky. An eagle hovered in midair, suspended by the powerful currents that blew up the eastern bluffs. How magical: a floating dot of life against the infinity of blue.

He'd crossed a perceptual chasm: Boston on one side, the wilderness on the other. Each incomprehensible to the other. Boston—rational, ordered, so carefully compartmentalized and predictable; the wilderness—intuitive, and anarchic in its savagery and violence.

In Boston, a man could take his leisure in a lamplit drawing room, a fine glass of brandy at his side, and read Kant. Kant had meaning there, so safe and sound behind a fortification of brick, walnut paneling, and French windows.

But where did a man find a philosopher for the wilderness? Not even Thomas Hobbes wrote in a language eloquent enough for the serpentine grace of the river, the razor-clarity of the night sky, or the eider mantle of sage-rounded hills. Nor did he understand the visceral dialectic of man in the wilderness; not nasty, short, brutish, and mean, but defiant in victory or painfully broken in defeat—with all the vibrant stages in between.

Since I've come here, I've but barely begun to understand. Fear now cut as keenly as broken glass. Contentment was a coveted thing of brevity; but when he had it, it ran warm and full in his soul. Joy, sorrow, love, and hate, each had been honed until life hung upon their pointed spikes, pierced through.

How did a man communicate gut truths like those to Professor Ames, or Will Templeton, or George Peterson? One might as well explain "yellow" to a blind man or Mozart to the deaf.

If this new reality is only perception, how do you know it's true? He smiled grimly, avoiding the epistemological trap that would lead him to chase his tail around and around in endless circles.

The coyote gave him a start. The creature stood sky-lined on the ridge, quartered to the wind that whipped its tail and ruffled the long gray-brown fur. The ears were pricked, and even over the distance, Richard could feel those measuring yellow eyes.

What on earth would possess a coyote to—

A hollow boom rolled through the hills, like fading thunder across the sky. Even the earth seemed to shake.

"What the hell?" Baptiste pulled his horse up, listening as the sound rolled away.

Travis reined in. The pack string slowed, shook, and began to nibble what grass they could reach past their tail-hitches.

Richard cupped a hand to his ear, catching only the ripping of grass and the grinding of equine molars above the sounds of wind in the sage.

Finally Travis shrugged. "Wal, she's a funny country. A feller hears them booms every so often. And groans sometimes, too. Especially at night when yer laying with yer ear ter the ground. It's like the old earth is a-talking ter ye."

"I heard a boom like that," Baptiste agreed. "Down on the Cheyenne River, it was. Way out in the badlands. Just a big boom—and the sky so clear and hot."

"Hell, remember back in eighteen hun'ert and eleven? We's nigh ter Saint Loowee and the whole goddam ground bucked and reared. Earthquake, remember? Hellacious thing that was. Trees all knocked over, and the very sand underfoot a-welling up like water."

"I ain't nevah fo'getting that," Baptiste agreed fervently. "Heard they's places the Mississippi even ran backwards after that."

Richard nibbled at the corner of his lip. That sense of unease had begun to creep back into his soul. This time he didn't scoff, but pulled his mare up from her grazing and urged her alongside Travis.

The scarred hunter was searching the surrounding hills, careful blue eyes intent on the rimrock, on each patch of trees.

"Didn't sound like a shot," Richard said. "But . . . there's something—"

"Uh-huh."

"Aw, I reckon it's just the spirits," Baptiste said. "A feller hears funny sounds out heah."

Travis shot a quick glance at Richard. "Got an itch in yer gut?"

"Just a feeling, kind of like something's gone wrong."

"Willow said ye had the makings." Travis reached up to scratch his beard. "Baptiste, I'd say we're no more than six, maybe seven miles from the Yellowstone. Reckon we'd best trot these mangy hosses on down. Skin yer eyes, coons. Let's go fast, but let's be savvy. If'n thar be trouble, we'd best see it afore it breaks on us."

"You really think there's . . ."

But Travis had booted his bay gelding and was already trotting forward, grass and cottonwood leaves rustling under the hooves.

Richard circled around to come in behind the string with their bouncing packs. Baptiste rode past, eyes narrowed, mouth grim, rifle clutched in one powerful black hand. When Richard glanced back at the heights, he saw nothing more than sagebrush quivering in the wind. The coyote had vanished as if it had never been.

A tightness began to build in his chest as they trotted grimly onward. Travis rode like a hunting wolf, using the cottonwoods as cover, threading his way through thickets of willow and fording the shallows when oxbows of the Big Horn blocked their way.

If anything, the wind seemed colder as it rushed down

from the west. It moaned around the buff sandstone caprock and whispered secrets among the pines. The tall grass lashed at the soles of Richard's moccasins, and hissed around the fast-moving horse hooves. In his imagination, the whole world might have been calling a warning.

"Use your head," he muttered to himself. "Nothing's wrong." They'd reach the mouth of the Big Horn, and find Green and the *engagés* refurbishing the old Missouri Fur Company post. In the end, it would turn out that he'd done another silly thing in a long line of silly things.

Travis slowed as they broke out of the trees. He pointed at the squared headlands that opened into the distance. "Yonder's the mouth of the Big Horn."

"I ain't heard nothing else, Travis," Baptiste called, his rifle still at the ready. "Ain't seen no sign, neither."

"Nope." Travis didn't sound convinced.

For the fifth time, Richard checked the priming in his rifle, then patted his powder horn and bullet pouch. In the process, his hand brushed the scalps, and their silken touch sent a tingle along his backbone.

"How do you want to do this?" Baptiste asked. "Ride right down the middle of the valley, or choose one side?"

"Down the middle, I reckon." Travis squinted at the distant trees that marked the Yellowstone. "If'n she's trouble, we'll pitch in."

"From heah, we'd hear the shots," Baptiste replied. "Ain't nothing wrong, Travis. Yor hoodoo shy. Skittish as a one-eyed hoss."

"Maybe."

They started forward again, Richard's mouth dry. Even the burning itch of a louse bite over his left ear could be forgotten.

Travis used a gravel-bottomed ford to cross the Big Horn one last time. The horses splashed through belly-deep water, and buck-jumped up the far bank. Then Travis wound through the sage to a deeply rutted buffalo trail, leaning wide to study the ground. "They's been hyar," he muttered, voice hushed. "Reckon that's Toussaint's footprint—or this child ain't seen sign."

"How old?" Baptiste asked.

"Day . . . maybe two."

"Well, they made it safe this far."

"Uh-huh. On yer uppers, coons. Fort's just yonder." Travis kneed his horse forward, half-crouched, rifle ready.

Leaving the sage, they rode through a patch of chokecherry and serviceberry and into an abandoned camp. Green's tent stood amid smoldering firepits. Here and there, rolls of blankets and other packs lay, some kicked about.

Beyond the camp, part of a palisade had been constructed, the poles freshly hewn, scarred with yellow notches where the axes had cut.

Richard barely noticed. *Engagés* lay here and there, sprawled like rag dolls. Their colorful clothing was blood-splotched and torn, and flapped and rippled as the wind blew along dead flesh.

"Dear Lord God." Richard swallowed hard. He heard the metallic click as Baptiste cocked his rifle. The horses stamped, wanting to shy from the flapping clothing and the smell of blood and violence.

"Blackfoot," Travis announced in a flat voice. With his rifle, he pointed to a half-naked man pitched face-first in the grass. A bullet had blown a gaping hole through his back to expose bits of spine, ribs, and shoulder blade.

"They didn't pick him up?" Baptiste wondered, glancing around nervously.

They followed the route of the battle down from the camp, over the edge of the terrace, and onto the riverbank. There, the scene became macabre. The dead lay as they'd fallen, transfixed by arrows, bludgeoned, or shot, but

Richard saw the first piece: a head. The face had been peeled away; the neck was nothing more than stringy knots of tissue.

He'd seen the like once, decayed and worried by rooting pigs. And again, later, when François had left it in his room aboard the *Virgil*. Richard's stomach twisted at the thought.

"What the hell?" Travis pointed at a shattered arm, the flesh mutilated, as if wolf-chewed.

"God damn," Baptiste whispered, eyes fixed on a pair of legs that dangled from the spreading branch of a cottonwood. One of the legs hung oddly, as if the bone had been smashed; trails of intestine hung like a strand of gray rope from the remains of the hips.

"It's as if the hand of God ripped him in two and tossed him up there!" Travis shivered, his blue eyes oddly glazed.

Richard slipped off his horse, stepping carefully over one of the dead *engagés*. A bullet had caught the man in the groin, and he'd thrashed on the ground for a short time before a hatchet split his forehead open. The eyes blood-streaked, Louis de Clerk stared emptily at the sky, pupils still wide as if in disbelief.

Richard had to nerve himself to pick up a piece of wood. "Milled," he said, running his hands over the splintered piece. "Oak. I know the grain of it. I lay on it long enough while my back healed. This is oak, Travis. A piece of the boat."

Travis paled, clutching at his saddle for support.

Baptiste stepped down, ground-reining his horse as he inspected the brutalized remains of a dead Indian. "Sweet Jesus. This coon's full of splinters."

"Keg over there," Baptiste called, pointing at part of a smashed flour barrel. "What the hell happened? Damn it! *What the hell happened heah?*"

"Green blew up the boat," Travis said woodenly.

"Huh?" Richard turned, a shredded length of cloth in his hands. He stared at the frayed fabric, aware of the splinters, of the acrid smell of burned powder.

Travis rubbed his face, looking as old and tired as Job. "Blackfoot hit 'em by surprise. Probably snuck up on their bellies, crawling through the sagebrush. Everyone panicked, ran for the boat.

"Green got 'em lined out, but too late. Them's the red bastards ye see shot. When they swarmed the boat, Dave ducked below, probably hid down behind the powder with a strike-a-light. He waited till the Blackfoot was all aboard . . . and blew the whole damned shitaree."

"Sweet Jesus," Baptiste murmured, sinking to his knees. He just stared at the ground with an empty gaze.

Richard stepped over what looked like a bloody lump of heart and lungs. A jellied leg lay to one side, the thigh bone splintered like kindling. He stared down at the river, running placidly with its smooth-swirling water. Only the litter on the bank looked out of place.

"Damn it, Davey," Travis whispered, and slipped off his horse, stumbling, legs gone weak. Richard looked over to see tears, like tiny diamonds, on his cheeks.

None too steady, Richard climbed back up the bank, along the line of dead. There lay Toussaint, as if he'd slumped down and fallen over. No less than six arrow shafts stuck out of his big body, most broken off before he died. A rifle was still clutched in his hand, the stock shattered, but around the big boatman lay three Blackfeet, their heads crushed.

A soft groan, barely audible, came from the willows just west of camp. Richard approached on cat feet, recognizing the trail for what it was. A man had dragged himself along here, bleeding, mashing the grass flat.

At the edge of the willows, Richard crouched, rifle cocked. Every so cautiously, he stepped into the grove, following the wounded man's route.

He was lying on his stomach, young, little more than a boy. His right arm was a mangled mass of coagulated blood and broken bone, matted with dirt, leaves, and grass stems. A splinter of oak, like a stiletto, was driven into his lower back, and from the bloody smears, the boy had tried to pull it out.

The Blackfoot boy moaned again, glancing up. His black eyes might have been cast of glass. In that moment, Richard read the boy's soul: panic, shock—a terrible, naked disbelief.

Richard raised his rifle as he looked into those haunted eyes, and, as if in a dream, set the trigger and shot the boy through the head.

He never looked back as he turned and retraced his way to the clearing. He'd poured another charge and was seating his bullet on its patch when Travis came running up.

"Whar at, coon?"

"Just one," Richard said, awed by the control in his voice. "Back yonder."

"Might be more," Travis stared around anxiously, rifle clutched like a lover. His mouth was working in a slack-lipped way. Bright panic glittered in his eyes. "Might be . . . more."

"Travis?"

The hunter's hands were shaking, the eyes unfocused.

"*Travis!* Take a scout." Richard rammed the ball home. "Check for sign."

Travis nodded, shook his head, and took a deep breath. "Damn . . . damn . . ." And then he strode away, waving the all-clear to Baptiste who'd covered them from under the lip of the bluff.

Richard watched him disappear into the sagebrush, then carefully primed the pan and snapped the frisson closed. *What now? Oh, Lord God, what now?*

"Don't think about it," he told himself, willing his soul to be as empty as the Indian boy's had been.

Trudeau had died hard. He'd been shot in the back, low down above where the spine joined the hips. As he'd tried to crawl away, some warrior had driven an arrow through his back and pinned him to the ground before his scalp was cut off. Just enough strength had remained that he could claw at the grass, but not free himself. From the scraped soil, uprooted grass, and the dirt-packed fingernails, he'd hung on until just before their arrival.

"God damn!" Baptiste kept saying in a fragile voice as he walked from body to body. "God damn 'em all!"

Richard slowly shook his head as he looked over the camp. *This is like a dream, Richard. This can't happen.*

Travis emerged from the sagebrush, expression strained. "Got tracks. I make it four of them. Two is carrying one, and the fourth ain't no daisy. He's dragging a leg."

"Let's go get 'em." Baptiste turned for his horse.

Richard rubbed his face; how hot he felt! He made himself walk steadfastly as he caught up his horse and vaulted into the saddle.

They took the trail back toward the bluff, and located where no less than twenty horses had been held.

"Make it five," Travis said, indicating the ground. "Kid. Probably a horse guard on his first raid."

"Guess it's his last one," Baptiste said, a savage glitter in his eyes. His jaw muscles had bunched under that smooth ebony skin.

"I reckon so," Travis rasped. His knobby knuckles were moon white where they grasped his Hawken too tight.

❖

Travis stared into the flames of the Blackfeet campfire with unseeing eyes. He felt like a senseless husk—like an old log so rot-punky inside that he'd gone hollow. Nothing rose out of his soul. Not anger, or rage, or even grief.

The night pressed down on all sides, cold and silent but for the sounds of the river. Nothing stirred him, not when he looked at Baptiste's slack face, or at Richard's—their eyes fully as blank as his own. The three of them just crouched there, staring into the dancing flames, night-blind, and none caring a damn.

Travis glanced at the Blackfeet corpses still lying where they'd fallen. The panicked warriors had made no effort to hide their trail as they fled westward, scrambling their horses up over the bluffs, sliding them down steep hillsides, and galloping hard across the flats. Dashing pell-mell upstream for the fast-water ford that would let them cross the Yellowstone and escape northward into their territory.

The two wounded had slowed them, as had the riderless horses. In the end, no doubt refusing to believe in the existence of any pursuit, they'd camped in this sheltered cove, surrounded on three sides by rimrock.

I wouldn't have believed anyone would follow, either. Travis traced fingertips along the ridges of scar tissue on his face. The flames wavered and leaped, burning patterns on the back of his eyes.

Travis had placed Richard on the right and Baptiste on the left. Slowly, carefully, they'd crawled through the sagebrush, and there, hunched over the fire, the Blackfeet seemed as dull and spiritless as the hunters who surrounded them.

It was too easy. They's already beaten—Power broken. At the first shot, they could do nothing else but jump up . . . ready to die.

They'd barely fought, jabbing with their guns, slashing with bows, as three White rifles blasted the night. The wounded man hadn't even tried to stand, but lay like a wilted flower, accepting death. One of the boys, the horse guard most likely, had charged off in panic and run plumb into Richard.

Travis glanced over to where Hamilton, wrapped in his blanket, stared owl-eyed into the flames. *Was that really ye, Dick? I'd have never believed ye'd bash a boy's brains out like that. And nary a flicker of an eye.*

Nor had Richard stopped there. He'd come roaring in out of the night and beaten the wounded warrior to death with his rifle. Then, lips back, teeth clenched, he had whipped his knife out and bent down. The keen blade slid around the top of the skull, parting the connective tissue as Dick peeled the scalp off. Holding it high in the firelight, fist gripping the hank of hair midway, he'd watched it bob and sway in the breeze. Laughter had choked in his throat—the kind a crazy man made—and he'd turned back to the first Blackfoot and repeated the deed.

To look at him over the fire now, Richard appeared as hollow as Travis felt. A man with nothing left inside.

Travis rubbed his eyes, afterimages of the flickering fire

burning in his soul. *It warn't just Dick, coon. Ye were a mite berserk yerself. A calm—like ice in yer soul. Mindless, because God damn, it happened to ye again! Just like in the dream. They told ye, "Don't go ter the Yellowstone." They come to ye down just this side of Fort Atkinson and warned ye.*

He shivered and threw another piece of wood on the fire. It popped, sparks twirling up.

It had happened here, real close, probably within a rifle shot of where he now sat. Immel and Jones had been this close to Fort Benton when the Blackfeet ambushed them, killed them, cut their bodies to pieces, and left them for the wolves to scatter.

Travis glanced at the dead again. Maybe these were some of the same Blackfeet that had killed Immel and Jones. *Just like the seasons, it all comes around.* But he hadn't listened.

And what if he had? Would Green have believed a dream? Turned back on Travis's word? Not a chance in Hell.

Travis chewed at the callus on his blood-caked thumb. *Maybe some things are just fated to be, no matter what. Just like Calf in the Moonlight and me. Or Dick and Willow. Or Green and the Blackfoot.*

Baptiste had finally roused himself enough to kick dirt over the tacky stain where a Blackfoot had bled out, then unrolled his blankets. He didn't even look at Travis as he lay down and settled his blanket over him. Cradling his rifle to his side, he pulled his hat low over his eyes—a dark shadow of a man blending into the night. Of them all, Baptiste had been the most sane, thirsting for revenge, driven by anger and frustration.

But, Dick, now. He'd been different. Not a stitch of emotion, as if his soul had shut off. Just like back at camp where he'd shot that kid.

Never seen a coon so cool, Dick. Just like ye done killed

men all day long, part of a job, like hoeing weeds in a garden.

Images—like all the others that haunted him—came trooping out of his mind: Dave Green, the young *engagé*, pulling his first boat upriver for Manuel Lisa. Shivering out in the snow on the Little Missouri. Plotting, dreaming, seeing a future, like a mirage—shimmering, wavering, a vision of the mountains so far away. *But when the picture come clear, Davey, it wasn't like ye wanted.*

How sure Dave had been that night in Saint Louis. Half a world away, and not a year passed. But Dave Green would dream no more. How many pieces did that much powder blow a man into?

Toussaint, Trudeau, Henri, the others . . . gone. All gone. Travis sucked idly at his tongue, watching the fire leap and dance. *Manuel Lisa, Michael Immel, Robert Jones, William Issom, Andrew Brown . . . no, stop it. Damn, Travis, yer list could go on forever.*

So much death. He shook his head. *I know more dead men than live ones.*

He glanced up at the dancing stars, the Milky Way splotching the darkness like a pale band across the sky. "Was it so damn bad? Hell, all Dave wanted ter do was take a boat up and make a little trade. Son of a bitch, it just don't make sense."

"Never does," Richard said.

Travis looked across and met his eyes, gleaming like an animal's in the firelight. "Ye otta be asleep."

"You, too."

"Can't."

"Me neither." Richard rubbed his hands nervously and looked around at the dead Blackfeet, at the bloody curve of skull where his knife had cut the scalp away. He'd done it quick and clean, as if he'd been cutting off men's hair all his life.

Travis threw another piece of wood into the fire, noticing

that Baptiste's breathing had deepened. "Back at the boat . . . I mean . . . wal, the camp. Thanks fer keeping my head on, Dick."

"Keeping your head on?"

Travis pulled at his beard while the greedy flames licked up around the wood. "There's times a man goes plumb crazy. Loses all his sense. Reckon I's headed that way today. I'd a just wandered around, getting crazier and crazier till . . . Hell, who knows? Anyhow, thanks for telling me ter go cut fer sign."

Richard shivered, tucking his blanket tighter. "I told myself it was a dream. I knew it was a lie, but it was so easy to believe. Why is that?"

"How the hell should I know?"

"I'd just wake up, and the boat would be waiting for us." He puffed a frosty breath up toward the stars. "But it's not. And everyone's dead. Green. The *engagés*. So I killed them, Travis. The boy in the willows . . . the warriors here." He squinted quizzically. "I thought I'd pay 'em back, make it right. But . . . but, it's not right. Is it?"

"Maybe. I don't know."

"I keep trying to understand. What happened, Travis? Tell it to me. Make it rational. It is, isn't it? We're not just animals, are we? We *do* think. We do have reasons, don't we? This didn't just happen for nothing."

Travis took a deep breath. "I reckon we all had reasons. Green wanted ter trade . . . make his name on the river. To the Blackfoot, that boat was more wealth than they'd seen in years. The warriors who take a whole boat, why, they's gonna be sung about fer years. Marry who they want and become chiefs. That's reasonable, ain't it?"

"Yes."

"And Dave, he makes a mistake. Maybe he puts the wrong coon on guard. Maybe he figgers that he's safe, that no enemies will come until he's forted up. No matter, the Blackfoot hit the camp. Dave's a quick one. He sees it's all lost, so he ducks down below deck and waits. Maybe he's wounded, but he lets as many of them skunking Bug's Boys climb aboard as he can, and then he strikes his spark and boom! If'n Dave can't have it, ain't no Blackfoot gonna get rich off'n Dave Green's sweat and blood."

"But to blow it all up?"

"Ain't the first time." Travis scratched his chin, remembering the *Tonquin*. "It's a hunch, Dick. But I figger he's wounded, knowing he's gonna lose it all anyway. Folks get a mite crazy when a dream dies right in front of 'em."

"I guess."

"And then there's us. We come riding in, and it's all gone. Friends are dead. The boat's blown ter hell. Just dead men and splinters a-laying all around." He watched the firelight, trying to block other images: old friends gone to rot and bones, a pretty young Crow woman smiling up at him, reaching for him with soft, warm, and loving arms. That spark of life growing inside her womb . . .

I went crazy fer a long time, then. "I've done this before," Travis whispered. "But that time, there warn't no Dick to give me something ter do."

"Before?"

"When they killed my Calf in the Moonlight—my Crow wife. Cut the little baby out of her belly. I warn't there, Dick. Out hunting, ye see. Then—like t'day—I found her. I got real crazy that time. Did things . . . things I don't want ter remember."

For a long time they watched the fire leap and crackle, the sparks dancing upward and winking out like stars dying in the night sky.

"When dreams die," Richard said hoarsely. "We're good at that, aren't we? Killing dreams, I mean."

"Reckon so."

The weather had turned blustery and cold. Richard, Travis, and Baptiste had picked up what they could salvage from the campsite: axes, powder horns, rifles, and twists of tobacco. Bits and pieces of stuff were scattered along the shore, including strap iron that could be traded as raw material for arrowheads, some hanks of beads that hadn't broken, gun flints, two lead ingots, a couple of tins of tallow, and several slightly frayed bolts of cloth. All in all, they could make packs for only six additional horses.

Where disbelief had once driven him, now a terrible despair closed in around Richard's soul like a fog on Boston Harbor. He acted mechanically, picking up bits of this or pieces of that. Some stubborn remnant of conscience insisted that the dead should be buried, but Travis declared, "They's wolf meat now, Dick. Ye'd dig for days to cover 'em, and by Hob, the second ye's outa sight, the wolves would dig fer days to uncover 'em again. Best let nature have 'em, the way God intended."

So he'd let the corpses lie, and tried to ignore the ravens that landed on the bodies at every opportunity, and the coyotes that slunk back and forth in the night.

"Where to?" Baptiste asked as they mantied up the last of the packs.

"Downriver, I guess," Travis decided. "Go back and maybe winter with old James Kipp among the Mandan."

Baptiste leaned on his horse, arms hanging over the saddle. "Huh, wal, I reckon that Green told me ten percent. I's a partner, Travis. Reckon as surviving parties, half this plunder's mine."

Travis squinted, considered for a moment, and nodded. "Reckon so. Dave would have wanted it that way."

Baptiste stared up at the clouds, the cold wind tossing his long woolly black hair. "I been thinking I'd take my share and maybe mosey back to the River Crow. A night of soft woman next to this coon set right, it did." He paused. "Y'all could come along."

Travis glanced at Richard. "How about ye, Dick? Whar to?"

Richard fingered the reins he held, glancing idly around the desolate flat. Four ravens stood over a hole they'd pecked in Toussaint's belly. They were cawing outrage at a fifth over some raven insult.

"I think I'm going south."

"South?" Travis asked. "Going ter find Willow, are ye?"

Richard nodded. "I have to see her before I head back. And then, well, I remember something you told me a long time ago, Travis. That if I ever got lost, all I needed to do was follow the rivers east of the mountains and they'd take me to the Missouri. Well, the Platte heads just down south of Willow's mountains, doesn't it?"

"That's a heap of empty, hostile country." Baptiste looked dubious. "Dick, whyn't you come winter with the Crow? Hell, come spring we'll travel back to the Mandan with 'em. You can catch a boat downriver from there."

"That's a sight of sense." Travis looked unsettled himself.

"If I travel overland, I'll be in Saint Louis by spring," Richard insisted. "And, like you said, it's all empty country." He smiled sheepishly. "Besides, the sooner I get back, the sooner I can send a message to my father. Let him know I'm alive."

"Uh-huh—and François?"

"If he's still around, I guess I'll just have to settle up, now won't I?"

"Remember that's city." Baptiste pointed a finger. "Them white folk, they don't take to no murder, no matter how fitting!"

Richard shrugged. "Oh, I suppose I can figure a way without getting myself hung. Remember, I'm a gentleman."

"Yep, wal, don't use no ax on him."

"South ter the Snakes, and then east along the Platte," Travis mused. "Hmm. Mind the company, Dick?"

"What?" Richard turned to stare at Travis.

"You crazy?" Baptiste jerked a thumb over his shoulder. "They's a right warm Crow village four day's ride yonder, piled high with meat, surrounded by warriors, and chockful of women ready to hop inta yor blankets, and you wants to go riding off into the plains in winter?"

Travis scuffed his moccasin on the hard ground, watching as it scraped the grass away. "Wal, Baptiste, I'll tell ye. I'd consider it, but while ye was a-slipping yer pizzle inta that gal, Two White Elk and me got ter talking about old times. Calf in the Moonlight was Two White Elk's sister. Now, maybe I could find that again . . . and maybe I couldn't. He treated me like a brother. Even give me one of his wives—as a Crow does to blood kin. But, coon, my heart's been hurting since. Ye understand?"

Baptiste made a face. "Aw, hell, it ain't the fust time we've split up. Come on, then. I'll ride on down to the mouth of the Greasy Grass with y'all. See y'all that far at least."

"Done." Travis stepped into the stirrup and threw a leg over.

Richard frowned and mounted, taking only one look back at the Yellowstone and the broken dead who lay there.

SEVENTEEN

◆

> I am not permitted even to assume God, freedom, or immortality for the sake of the necessary practical employment of my reason, if I cannot deny speculative reason of its pretensions of transcendent insights, because reason, in order to arrive at these, must use principles which are intended originally for objects of possible experience only. If, in spite of this, these principles are applied to what cannot be an object of experience, it really changes this into an appearance, and thus renders all practical extension of pure reason impossible. I had therefore to deny knowledge in order to make room for faith.
>
> —Immanuel Kant, *Critique of Pure Reason*

Heals Like A Willow sat on a spire of rock that jutted up from the Powder River Mountains' western flank. From this aerie, she could see across the basins to the south and west. The Owl Creek Mountains, like a rocky hump, divided the basins. The river called *Pia'ogwe*, Big River, emerged from its sheer-walled canyon in the Owl Creek Mountains amid the blood-red ridges. Beside it was *Pa'gushowener*, the Hot-Water-Stand, the big hot springs Green had talked about.

Farther across the basin she could see *I'sawe,* the Coyote's Penis, the tall guardian peak that marked the beginning of the snow-capped basalt cliffs beyond. The Wind River Mountains stood like jagged teeth bared against the distant blue horizon.

Down in the broad basin to the south, Packrat had captured her en route to this high point. Her goal then had been to grieve for her husband and son. She could finally release the hurt. Not only could she ache over the loss of her husband and baby boy, but she could conjure Richard's gentle eyes, and what might have been between them. Past and future pain, all reconciled at once.

My souls are still wounded. Why hadn't scars formed? Would they ever?

Perhaps it was because she had failed to heal her husband and infant son. That was, after all, her Power.

I healed Travis, Richard, and the others. And, like a puhagan, *I used my Power to destroy Packrat's soul.* The way of Power was neutral, to be used for good or evil depending on the will of the user.

Willow tucked her sheephide coat tight. The chill wind blew bitterly across these heights.

She sensed him before she heard his careful approach. The way was treacherous, a difficult climb. A slip would mean broken bones at the very least.

She allowed the vista before her and the Power of the land to soothe her souls. How old had she been? Seven, perhaps eight summers the first time she'd climbed up here to see what it was like. Perhaps that was when Power first entered her souls and set her on the path she'd followed.

His clothing rasped on the rock, and he grunted as he pulled himself over the lip. She refused to look at him for the moment, allowing her dream soul to float on the distance.

He waited patiently.

Finally she said, "You're not as spry as you once were."

"No. And when it really gets cold, my joints ache."

She smiled and took her father's hand in hers, marveling at how warm he was. He wore his decorated sheephide coat, warm leather leggings, and a beaverhide hat from which his gray-streaked braids had escaped. "I think you need to sweat more. You know full well that the older you get, the more tiny evils slip into your bones. I think it's the small things, Father, that build up and lead to old age."

He settled himself beside her in the brunt of the wind. "You're cold, girl. About to freeze up here."

"My body, yes. But my souls feel a special warmth. I've missed this. *Tam Apo*'s presence is here, His breath on the wind, His soul in the sun. And what does *Tam Apo* cover? There, beneath His magnificence, is the whole of *Tam Segobia,* Our Mother. From here I can begin to understand Her Power, the beauty of Her soil so like skin, the plants like Her sleek hair, and Her bones in the very rock. The Power here, Father, is that the two halves of the world come together."

High Wolf glanced suspiciously at her from the corner of his eye. "Did I ever tell you that my children came out backward? The son whom I wanted to become *puhagan* is only interested in his family. The daughter whom I expected to fill my life with grandchildren is so tightly wrapped in Power that she even frightens me."

"Do not fear me, Father. I would never harm you."

He rested a hand on her shoulder. "No, girl. I know your heart . . . or at least I think I do. Sometimes, though, Power can do terrible things. *Pandzoavits,* the rock ogres, have been known to grant people Power, and it shrivels them like green grass in the heat of a fire."

"That is not my Power, Father."

"I know. But, Daughter, the lesson should never be forgotten."

"You've always been wise. And besides, I gave you a grandchild. His death still wounds my soul."

High Wolf's nostrils quivered as he scented the wind like a hunting wolf. "Snow is coming." After a pause, he asked, "What happened to your family, Heals Like A Willow? We heard very little about it. Only rumors that came up the trails during the trading season."

"They both came down with a fever, sweating and delirious. I did all I could, all I knew to do. I used the sage, phlox, and blazing star tea. I built a sweat lodge, and tried to sweat the spirit of the sickness from them. Their bowels loosened and ran like water. I sang for them, and the *Ku'chendikani puhagan* came and performed a sucking cure, removing *Nunumbi* poisons. Try as we might, their *navuzieip* drifted away, and their *mugwa* followed. All that was left for me was their corpses, Father."

She hesitated, then looked at High Wolf. "The one thing I didn't do . . . I didn't send my *mugwa* to bring them back from the Land of the Dead. That's why they died."

His gaze sharpened. "Nor should you have, Daughter. A woman—especially a young woman who bleeds every moon—does *not* send her soul anywhere."

Willow bit her lip, and jerked an uneasy nod.

High Wolf sighed. "I'm glad you did nothing foolish, *peti*. Willow, death comes and goes. No one knows the way of it. Your mother bore me eight children. I have you and Rock Hare—the rest are dead. One day, I will die, and sometime, so will you. Coyote decided that for us just after the Creation."

"Yes, I know," she said ironically.

The crow's-feet around his eyes tightened as he squinted into the distance. "What is this other sadness you carry within you, girl? You guard it very well, but I can sense it. I think White Hail knows, but he is honorable and will not say. An interesting man, this White Hail. Married to another, but in love with you, his brother's wife. It would be proper for you to marry, become a second wife for him."

"I can't marry him, Father. The mating wouldn't be right. Not for him or for me."

High Wolf grunted a simple assent, giving her a sidelong glance. "And this other sadness? You are very skillful at avoiding answers."

She sighed, rubbing her hands together inside her sheephide coat. "He was a White man, Father."

"Ah?"

"His name is Richard Hamilton, a man from a place called Boston."

"He is Powerful?"

"Yes, but not trained." She turned. "I looked into his soul, Father. Down deep inside, into the *mugwa*, and he looked back. Not in fear, but with curiosity. Do you know how many men can look into a woman's eye of the soul without fear?"

"Not many, I'll admit. Did he sicken? Go weak? Show signs of being a berdache?"

"No. He only grew stronger."

"Then what happened?"

So she told him, starting at the beginning where Richard shot Packrat, following all the way to the last discussion she had with him.

"The fact is, Father, that the Whites are a great deal like the *Ku'chendikani*. They have God—a father who created the earth. He did it alone without any mother like *Tam Segobia*. I might not have understood, but it was the same argument that I used to have with Slim Pole."

"And Ritshard did not respond as the *Ku'chendikani* do?

That *Tam Apo* has His own mysterious reasons for making the Creation as He did?"

"No." She frowned. "That is one of the things that attracted me to him. Ask a question, a serious question, and he loses himself in the search to answer it. Down in his *mugwa,* he has the roots of a great *puhagan.* But the White ways have blinded him, separated him from himself with something called 'reason.' The Whites believe they can 'think' their way to God." She waved out toward the spectacular vista. "They don't understand that God must be sought in the heart and souls."

High Wolf cocked his head, and Willow could read his expression well enough to know he was skeptical of her attraction.

"Father, you need not worry about me. He is far away, on the river north of the mountains. He will not be there long. His heart is telling him to go back to Boston."

"Once before," High Wolf reminded, "I was worried by a young man. That time, my daughter ran off to the *Ku'chendikani,* and my souls wept. I do not know Boston, but I fear it is farther away than the places *Ku'chendikani* travel."

"Yes, Father. A great deal farther." She placed her hand on his. "But you need not worry this time. Some mountains cannot be climbed. In this case, he is White and I am *Dukurika.* We are separated by a vast distance, greater than that between sky and earth."

High Wolf raised an eyebrow. "But, if you will remember, Daughter, in the *Dukurika* story, *Tam Apo* and *Tam Segobia* joined, and in their mating created the world."

Willow nodded, brushing a tear from her eye and blaming it on the bitter wind. "Yes, but you will also recall that they were torn apart, which is why today earth and sky are separate. And, if the story is true, they will be separate until the end of time."

◆

Richard, Baptiste, and Travis camped that night on a grassy flat where a small creek ran into the Big Horn. The packs were arranged in a circle around the fire, rude fortifications in the event of attack. The horses stood in a makeshift corral at the edge of the firelight, heads hanging. Holding eight horses was one thing; holding thirty was something else.

Richard sat hunched, a blanket over his shoulders as he ran a cleaning patch through his rifle. "I still have trouble believing it happened."

"Yep." Baptiste rubbed his hands together, the callused skin making a soft sawing sound. "But ol' God sure got Hisself a belly laugh outa us."

"God?" Richard wondered.

"Ain't He the one supposed to know if'n a sparrow fall?"

"Reckon so," Travis said tiredly. "Wal, if'n it was God, He played hell, all right."

They sat in silence, the only sounds those of the night and the fire. Richard loaded his Hawken and rammed a ball home. The wiping rod clicked as he ran it through the ferrules and into place. He just sat there, feeling the polished wood, pressing his thumb on the barrel keys and lock.

"It's like being cast loose." Richard stared vacantly. "The

boat was always waiting for you. When you reached the boat, there were men you knew. Food. Safety."

"Yep," Travis muttered. He lay back, staring up at the starry sky. In the far east, a half-moon glowed, a hazy ring around it.

Richard shook his head. "How funny. You know, I keep thinking it's all a mistake, that we're going to go back. Find *Maria* tied off on the bank, and Green, and Henri, surly old Trudeau, Toussaint and the rest, all acting just like nothing happened." He rubbed his fingers along the browned barrel. "But I know it's a lie. They're really dead."

When had the boat become so important? Once, he'd hated it—and the men who worked it. He scratched at a louse bite under his arm. Of all the anchors in his life, only Boston had meant as much to him as the *Maria*.

But I spent a lifetime in Boston.

"Wolfmeat, fer sure," Baptiste agreed, still rubbing his hands. "Wolfmeat . . . just like we'll be one day."

"Or worm meat," Travis added. "Depends on where ye goes under. Fer me, I'd a heap rather be wolfmeat than worm meat. Now, a feller dies back in the settlements, they dig a hole and cover his carcass up. Hell of a thing, being dumped down in the dark damp dirt to rot and feed worms. Not this coon. I want my bones scattered around in the grass and sunlight."

"Wal, you still get turned to shit one way or another, be it wolf or worm." Baptiste rubbed his hands harder, the muscles at the corner of his jaw jumping and wiggling.

"They took me prisoner," Richard said absently. "Carried me off and made me work like a convict at labor. So, why do I miss them so much?"

"Ye made a place, Dick." Travis slipped his pipe from his possibles. He shaved tobacco into the bowl, tamped it, and lit a stick in the fire to start it. He puffed and passed the pipe to Baptiste, who took a pull and passed it in turn to Richard.

"Made a place?" Richard watched the blue smoke curl upward before passing the pipe back to Travis.

"Reckon so." Travis puffed, then blew streams of smoke through his ruined nose. "Hell, remember that first day when Dave was gonna kill ye?"

Richard nodded.

"Wal, ye warn't worth shit then, Dick." Travis tapped his teeth with the long pipestem. "But I saw fire in yer eyes and give ye a chance. Tarnal Hell, coon, ye made ye a place. Worked up plumb from the bottom, ye did."

Was that it?

Baptiste said, "Feller's life changes when he finally becomes a man. Ain't no going back after that. Like dropping a glass bottle. It can't be undropped."

"I sure miss them." Richard reached for Travis's pipe and smoked the last out of the bowl before knocking out the dottle and reaching for his tobacco to refill it.

"Yep, wal, hyar's to ye, Dave." Travis raised his cup, though it held only tea made from rosehips they'd collected.

"To Dave," Baptiste assented, lifting his cup.

"To Dave, and all the rest," Richard amended, raising his own empty cup.

"Old Henri could sure make a tongue stew," Travis said wistfully. "And that cussed Simon? Damnation, that cornpone he cooked fer breakfast, that was some. It was."

"Warn't nobody could sing like Louis de Clerk." Baptiste smiled. "And that Etienne, why, he's a pulling fool on the cordelle. Never seen his like."

"Good men all around." Richard relit Travis's pipe and drew, the bowl glowing red. He puffed the smoke out and handed it to Baptiste.

"Remember when Jean-Paul snuck that snake inter Eppecartes's bed?"

Richard smiled, images flashing through his mind. "And old Toussaint? Remember him in the Ree fight?"

"He's some, he was. Took a heap of them Bug's Boys with him back on the Yellerstone, too," Baptiste reminded them. "I hope I go under like that, dragging a heap of 'em with me."

As they talked, Richard saw the men, one by one, their faces reflected in the fire, bits of laughter, a remark recalled. *I received something from each of them.*

He thought of Trudeau, back broken, pinned to the ground by a bloody arrow. How he'd hated Trudeau, the bully, the womanizer. And in the end, he'd fought him fist to fist, and won. *I couldn't hate him. Not after that.*

And Toussaint? To think of Toussaint was to remember muddy cold water, the collapsing bank, splashing and floundering, and Toussaint's strong arm clamping on from behind to tow Richard to shore. But he'd burned his wife and children? *A man is no more than he is.*

Then there was Green, indomitable, willing his boat ever onward. A tragic figure fit for Euripides. He'd built the dream, nurtured it, and turned it into reality despite insurmountable odds. Green had placed a fortune at risk, defied and defrauded the government, outfoxed the competition, the river, and the Indians to haul his boat all the way to the mouth of the Big Horn.

What thoughts passed through his head as he hid down there, wounded, maybe dying, in the hold? Did he hate the Blackfeet warriors leaping onto the deck? Or were his last thoughts on the gruesome irony of having come so far, made the final destination, only to lose it all?

"Damn," Travis said. "Damn it all."

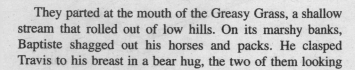

They parted at the mouth of the Greasy Grass, a shallow stream that rolled out of low hills. On its marshy banks, Baptiste shagged out his horses and packs. He clasped Travis to his breast in a bear hug, the two of them looking into each other's eyes, sharing a communication Richard suspected went clear to the quick of the soul.

"You all sure you don't need no more of these hosses?" Baptiste indicated the cavvy. Twenty-three animals milled, heads up, ears pricked as they watched the four animals Travis and Richard had led aside.

"Six is enough for us and our plunder," Travis told him, slapping his back. "Take 'em. Trade 'em ter the Crow. That many critters would just get in our way."

"Dick?" Baptiste stepped over, his rifle in the crook of his arm. He took Richard's hand in a powerful grip before drawing him into a hug. "Take care, coon."

"You, too. And, Baptiste, thanks for everything. All the things you taught me. I won't forget . . . ever."

"Watch old Travis for me." He paused, eyes questioning. "Hell, you could just ride over to the Crow for a spell. You don't gotta go chasing down after the Bad Lodges."

"The who?"

"The Snakes. Crow calls 'em Bad Lodges 'cause of the wickiups they make sometimes."

"I've got to go. It's something I must do for myself. For Willow."

"Wal, Dick, you's always welcome in my lodge."

"I don't suppose you'd ever call me Richard?"

"Reckon not."

"Somehow, I thought you'd say that. God go with you."

"Yep. You, too, Doodle." And at that Baptiste turned,

walked to his horse, and stepped lithely into the saddle. He touched the brim of his big black hat with a finger. "So long, coons. Watch yer topknots!"

Travis shouted, "Watch yers!"

Baptiste snaked up his lead rope and turned his horse, driving the cavvy toward the ridgeline that would take him east to the Tongue River divide. He'd laid claim to a powerful white gelding taken from the Blackfeet. His long fringes swayed with each of the horse's dancing steps.

"Just like that?" Richard asked, stunned by the quickness of it.

"Just like that," Travis agreed. "He'll be around. Seems I never could shake him fer long. Not since that night down ter Louisiana. By God, imagine that. Him a-hiding up in that tree just over my head while them slavers swarmed all over."

"I'll miss him."

They mounted up, fighting the horses, who wanted to follow their fellows. Richard kicked his mount ahead into the hill-cradled valley of the Greasy Grass. As they rode, he concentrated on any sign of disturbance. The enormity of their situation had finally come home to him.

We are alone out here, two thousand miles from Saint Louis. There is no one but us. Travis and me. No rescue, no reinforcements, only us.

Any mishap could spell disaster: a broken leg; a wound like that the Ree had given him; a disorienting fall; getting horse-kicked. Anything.

If I die out here, no one but God will ever know.

He glanced up at the faint white haze of high clouds that had blown in from the west. The air had a feel to it, an expectant stillness. "How far to Willow's people?"

Travis had been brooding, expression pinched, a bitterness in his blue eyes. "About a week or two. Depends. I ain't exactly sure. I been around them mountains, but never up inter 'em. I know they's only certain trails what go up. Willow said something ter me, once—that her folks generally wintered on the southwest side of the mountains. Now, we're on the northeast, so I guess we're just opposite of where we need ter be."

"So we should go right over the top?"

A ghost of a smile bent Travis's lips. "Reckon not. That's about as good a way as any ter freeze yer arse ter death. Up high, there, the snow's deep enough to bog a hoss. And a feller cain't make his way across the passes. Nope. I figger the best way is to circle around the base of the mountains and come up from the south, up through the hills."

"Hills? Don't all mountains have hills around them?"

"Not these. Ye'll see. 'Cept on the south, they's sheer rock walls that climb right up inta the sky. A coon's got ter know the trails. Trust me, I figger it's best to go around."

"It's going to be a cold trip, isn't it?"

"Reckon so." Travis grinned then, the first time since the disaster. "Ye'll be a hiverner by the time ye make her back ter Saint Loowee, Dick."

"We're in a fix, aren't we, Travis?" Richard glanced around at the hills. The north slopes were timbered in dark patches of ponderosa pine. On the flanks, tawny grass waved in the wind, speckled here and there with sagebrush. A sense of loneliness welled from the cold land, the wind, and the impotence within that tried to smother him.

"Huh? A fix? Hell, we're right chipper, Dick. We got two good mounts and four packhosses full of goods—and the right trade stuff ter boot. We got good Crow-tanned robes, pemmican and buffalo jerky, tobacco, more'n enough powder and lead, and a stack of guns. With them doings, we can nigh trade fer the moon. Nope, ye ain't in a fix until ye've lost yer possibles, and yer afoot in the snow. That's when it's Katy bar the door."

"What do you do then?"

"Then it's cat-scratch." Travis rubbed one of the scars on his cheek. "To tell the truth, Dick, ye do whatever ye can. Most of all, ye think! Use yer noodle. Most important thing is to stay warm and dry. Next most important thing is to keep yer belly full. Third, make ye a shelter. Anything to cut the wind and cold, even digging it outa the snow." He chuckled. "Larned that from a Cree, I did."

"What about frostbite?"

"That's a killer, Dick. I had an old Assiniboin tell me once that he lived by wrapping himself up so thick in hides that he flat couldn't freeze. But most of it is ter use yer smarts. Break yer knife? Use a sharp rock. I seen Injuns make cutting tools outa the damndest things. Figger this: rock cuts; bark and twigs make cord; wood burns; and hide and hair covers. Travel when ye can, and hole up when she's too damn stormy."

"What do you eat? I mean, if the ground is covered with snow?"

"Anything ye can," Travis said. "Meat's meat. Roschips, dried berries on branches, hell, I even heard tell of stripping pine bark and eating the inside."

"Well, let's not go quite that far, shall we?"

"Reckon I'd rather have fat cow any day."

EIGHTEEN

◇

It is therefore neither absurd nor reprehensible, neither against the dictates of true reason, for a man to use all his endeavours to preserve and defend his body and the members thereof from death and sorrows. But that which is not contrary to right reason, that all men account to be done justly and with the right. Neither by the word *right* is anything else signified, than the liberty which every man hath to make use of his natural faculties according to right reason. Therefore the first foundation of natural right is this, that *every man as much as in him lies endeavour to protect his life and members.*

—Thomas Hobbes, *Leviathan*

Light flakes of snow twisted and tumbled from the gray skies as Willow stopped on the rimrock above the camp, a tightly strapped bundle of firewood on her back. For long moments she looked out over the canyon, taking in the beauty. Snow dusted the dark green trees on the far side with a tracery of white. The wind had sifted snow into the crevices and cracks of the caprock, accenting the buff sandstone. From high up the canyon, a lone wolf howled—a reminder to the world of Wolf's frustration with Coyote during those early days of Creation.

She took a deep breath, drawing the familiar scent of rocks, juniper and pine, and moist earth into her lungs.

Home. The only place she'd ever truly belonged. As a child she'd scampered over the rocks, hidden in the hollows, and explored the meadows of these mountains. The plants that grew from this soil, the animals that lived here, all had fed her growing body. The solitude of the high points, the roar of wind through the trees, and the patter of rain on the rocks had filled her ears. She'd been charmed by the mixed colors of the earth, and the interplay of shadows in the distance. Here she had first heard the voices of *Tam Apo* and *Tam Segobia*.

She resettled the heavy firewood and picked her way along the narrow path that led down the base of the rimrock. The path wound about like an outrageous serpent's trail, climbing over spalled rock, dipping down around clumps of juniper. It finally ended at the rock overhang where High Wolf's band had made their isolated camp.

They didn't always live like this. In summer the *Dukurika* gathered in large groups. Memory of the great ceremonials brought a smile to her lips. As a child, the excitement had built with each step traveled toward the dance ground, until she thought her breast would burst open. What a magical time it was, filled with food, games, magic tricks, warm days of play and long summer nights before roaring fires. And so many people. The throng had seemed to be everyone in the whole world.

The most important dance was the "Stand Alone in Thirst Dance." For four days and nights the men danced, fasted, and waited for a vision. Some prayed for the gift of Power, or courage, or skill in the hunt. At the same time the dancers offered thanks to the spirits of the animals and plants that had fed them, and asked for continued grace from the spirits.

Before Willow's birth, the "Stand Alone in Thirst Dance" had been brought to the *Ku'chendikani* by Yellow Hand, the great *Yamparika puhagan*. High Wolf himself had danced to the sun twice.

When people weren't dancing, they were trading, or gambling. Young men found pretty girls to impress. When they impressed well enough, and when the families were in agreement, marriages were made. Or, if there were problems, a young man and woman eloped to make a life for themselves.

Willow smiled at the image of a young man dressed in finely tanned buckskin leggings. How broad and muscular his shoulders had been. The sunlight had glowed blue in his long black hair. He'd had a rainbow-colored abalone shell gorget at his throat. But the most important thing had been the depth reflected in his eyes.

He had taken her hand, saying in his *Ku'chendikani* accent, "I have heard of a Powerful young woman among the *Dukurika*. I had heard that she was the most beautiful woman anywhere, and that her name was Heals Like A Willow. I am hoping that you are she, for if any woman could be more beautiful than you, my eyes could not bear to look at her."

She had laughed at that, her heart dancing with his. "And if you have heard of Heals Like A Willow, Buffalo-eater, you know that I'm considered odd, dangerous, and most men will have nothing to do with me."

"I've heard such tales," he asserted, a smile on his lips. "But having looked into your eyes, I think they were the bitter declarations of men who were simply unworthy of your beauty and spirit."

I loved you from that moment on, husband. Who would have guessed they would have only a few glorious years?

Willow walked into camp. The dogs lay curled in furry balls, their tails smacking the cold ground as they watched her with kindly brown eyes.

"I miss you, husband." She rolled her shoulders where the load had stiffened them, and searched about for her ax. White Alder had admired it in *Dukurika* fashion, and Willow had graciously surrendered it. How did one say no to one's mother? From White Alder it had gone to Lodgepole, and then to Red Squirrel, and the last Willow had seen of it, Rock Hare was carrying it. The same had happened to all the rest of her belongings—all but the Pawnee bow, arrows, and war club.

Rock Hare was tall, lithe, and handsome. He wore a thick coat made of bearhide and sheepskin leggings that ran down over high moccasins. He sat with his back to the rock, a pile of juniper bark to one side. This he shredded, drawing the stiff bark over a stick to separate the fibers. After picking them apart, he placed the threads on his thigh, twisting them around and around into a firm strand. The next fibers he twisted the other way. When he had three strands, he braided them into the length of cord he was making.

"What are you doing?" Willow crouched next to him.

"Making another snare, Sister." He glanced at her. "This one shall catch the cottontail who has been making tracks down in the berry bushes in the canyon bottom."

"Where is the ax? I'm going to cut down some of those snags on the canyon rim. We could throw the trees over the edge; what doesn't snap when it hits the rocks, we can cut up with the ax."

"Good idea. I think the ax is next to my bed."

She stood, traced her way inside the shelter, and located the ax in the dim light. Not until she stepped outside did she notice the abused edge. Not just dulled, it had been bent and gouged.

"Rock Hare?" She stalked over to where he worked. "What did you do with this? How did this happen?" She thrust it toward him.

Nonplussed, Rock Hare studied the ax, and then her. "How did what happen?"

"This edge, you silly packrat! Look at it!"

He eyes lit then, and he smiled. "It's a wonderful thing I discovered about the ax. When you strike rocks with it, sparks fly! Eagle Trapper and I tried making fires by hitting different kinds of rock with the ax, but it didn't work. A strike-a-light is better."

The slow anger continued to build. "You will sharpen it again, Brother."

"All right. When I am done with my snare."

"Now, Brother."

Mild surprise showed in his eyes as he realized the extent of her anger. Scowling, he took the ax and studied the edge, a frown lining his forehead. "This is iron. A big piece. How can I sharpen it?"

"With blocks of sandstone, the same way you grind wood, antler, or slate."

He glanced suspiciously at her. "But this is iron. It's a lot harder than wood or antler."

"Then you had better get to work, because it will take you a long time."

"I don't have any sandstone blocks big enough for this. And I'm not sure what kind I'd need."

Willow narrowed her eyes to evil slits. "Then you had better go and find out, Brother. Sharpen the ax. We need it for cutting wood, and if you ever hit a rock with it again, I'll burn your bedding!"

He rubbed the back of his neck, watching her suspiciously. "You wouldn't dare."

"Wouldn't I? What kind of fool uses a valuable ax to hit rocks . . . and just to see *sparks!*"

"You don't tell people what to do in this camp, *Sister.*"

"When it concerns things like the ax, I do, *Brother.*"

"Well—go back to your *Kuchendikani,* or your White men, then. Order them about like children."

"Sharpen the ax and it will be forgotten, Rock Hare." She met the flash in his eyes, overcame it by force of will, and glared fire into his souls until he glanced away.

"All right. I'll sharpen the ax. Now, go away and leave me alone." He made a shooing gesture with his hand.

Willow took a deep breath and shook her head. "I'm sorry, *paci*. Perhaps it's my fault. I should have told you what to use an ax for. It has a special spirit, one that's used for chopping wood or bone. Not for rocks."

"I'll sharpen it." Rock Hare nodded curtly, as if to convince himself.

"All right. It's forgotten between us, then. I'm going for another load of firewood. With the storm coming, we'll need it. Do you remember how we'd make a big fire and tell the winter stories about Coyote and Wolf and the Bald One? We'll do that again, just like in the old days."

"Yes. It will be good." He smiled his relief that the ax affair was over.

Willow retraced her way to the path that led out onto the rimrock.

"He just didn't know," she told herself as she walked back into the trees. All the dead branches within reach had been broken off by previous hands. As a result, Willow had to extend her search. By the time she'd accumulated another load and followed the path back to camp, twilight had settled on the land.

High Wolf crouched over one of the fires, laughing and talking with Many Elk. Eagle Trapper and Black Marten were inspecting arrows, discussing which feathers needed replacing, while Felt the Fire led the children in a round of the string game.

Cat's cradle, Willow thought as she unloaded the wood from her tired shoulders and inspected the pile. The women had brought in enough to see them through several days.

Now, as the evening meal cooked, the women huddled over a game of four-stick-dice being played on a blanket.

From the intent expressions, a wager had been made, the stakes high. The dice—made of split willow stems, the pieces nearly finger-length—were tossed against a round rock placed on flat piece of rawhide. The score was determined by the number of dice that landed with the red-painted flat side up.

A cast was made, the dice clattered on the rock, and Good Root howled in misery as Lodgepole clapped her hands and yipped victory.

Counting heads, Willow turned to White Alder. "Mother, where is Rock Hare?"

Her mother looked up from the game with a frown. "He went with White Hail. They're down in the canyon somewhere. Rock Hare made a new snare. He took it down to set it."

"Did he sharpen the ax?"

"What?"

But Willow knew. She took a moment to calm herself, before hunting down the ax—right where Rock Hare left it, as dull and bent as when she'd given it to him.

"God damn you, Rock Hare."

"What was that?" Many Elk asked, as he studied the binding on one of his stone-tipped arrows.

"It's a White man's curse. Somehow, it fit."

"Who were you cursing?" Lodgepole gave her an uneasy glance as she reached for a beautiful white leather coat that Good Root reluctantly surrendered.

"No one, *pia*." Willow used the kin term for "Mother" to placate. "I was upset because Rock Hare didn't sharpen the ax."

"He's a man," Lodgepole replied, as she rose and tucked the coat over her arm.

Good Root muttered to herself as she stepped over to the hides, pegged and stretched for tanning. Her fingers probed the brain and urine mixture that coated the elk hide. Satisfied with the results, she pulled the pegs loose, then rolled it into a tight bundle.

"That's a good hide." Lodgepole studied the thick roll with calculating eyes. "Big bull. Had antlers like trees. But that hide, almost pure white. I've never seen such a white elk."

"And you'd like to gamble for it, wouldn't you?" Good Root gave her a lopsided squint. "Not likely. Not until your *puha* changes."

Willow hefted the ax, remembering the *Pa'kiani* skull she'd split with it. And now Rock Hare used it to smack rocks just to see the sparks fly?

"Willow?" Lodgepole laid a gentle hand on her arm. "I've seen that expression on your face before. Calm down."

"I told him I'd burn his bedding if he didn't sharpen this."

"Oh? And where would Red Squirrel and the baby sleep? Out in the snow with Rock Hare?" She made a chiding sound with her lips. "Willow, he's a man. God made them to be lazy in everything but hunting. Look around you, girl. Even *Tam Segobia* holds up the sky. If men didn't have women to look after them, you know they'd all die. Oh, sure, they'd hunt all the food they could eat—and then freeze to death in the first storm because they didn't have anything to wear!"

Willow ran gentle fingers over the ax head, remembering the river and the *engagés,* all so busily occupied. They'd worked like ants, toiling and sweating, pulling that huge boat against the current. No ax went dull in their camp. No rifle was left uncleaned.

"Willow?" Lodgepole asked. "Did you hear me?"

"Yes . . . I did. I was remembering the White men, is all."

"Do you want to talk about it, child? I can see the longing in your eyes."

"No, but thank you, Aunt. You wouldn't know what I was

saying. I think a person must stand between two worlds to see either clearly. Perhaps . . . perhaps that is what he needs."

"Who? Rock Hare?"

"It wouldn't hurt him to pull a boat for a while. But, no, I was thinking of another. One who seeks the ways of the *puhagan,* but has been kept from the way by a blindness worse than Rock Hare's."

"Rock Hare isn't blind. You're talking in riddles, Willow."

"No, Aunt. I'm speaking very clearly. Now, if you'll excuse me, I have to go and see if I can find the right size sandstone blocks to sharpen this ax before the snow covers everything and the light is gone."

❖

The cougar screamed in the middle of the night. Richard bolted upright, grabbing for his rifle with mittened hands. Travis growled like an animal, thrashing out of his blankets and leaping to his feet.

The horses blew and stamped, tossing their heads in panic. Richard heard the picket rope snap—and the horses bolted into the night. For what seemed an eternity, their pounding hooves faded into the darkness.

"Good God, Travis, what kind of beast screams like

that?" Richard grabbed up his rifle, earing the cock back as he peered anxiously beyond the circle of packs.

"Painter!" Travis cried as he danced around and swung his arms at the darkness. "Go on! Git outa hyar! Git, now!"

Richard swallowed hard, heart hammering as he waited for God knew what. His only security came from the rifle. But what help would that be? The cat, seeing so well in the darkness, could be upon him before he so much as raised the gun.

Still growling and muttering to himself, Travis stomped around cursing, then bent down and stirred the fire. He fed bits of frozen sagebrush to the glowing coals. The gusting wind ebbed and flowed, picking up now, whistling down from the heights to savage their lonely camp.

With the first feeble fingers of flame, Richard's panic finally drained away, but he didn't let loose of his Hawken.

"Damn cat," Travis cursed, leaving the fire to check the frayed picket rope. "Hell, they don't cotton much to hoss flesh, 'cept maybe the foals come spring."

Richard exhaled the last of his fear, and added, "That sound . . . horrible, like a scream from Hell."

"Yep. That's a cat all right." Travis returned to hunch over the fire. "Reckon we got a couple of hours afore daylight. Then we've got ter run down them fool hosses."

"The painter? He won't come back, will he? Try for us?"

"Painters ain't much on man flesh. Oh, they'll take ye, given half a chance, but not like a griz. Nope, painters prefer deer, rabbits, smaller stuff that don't fight back. 'Course, they'll take a dog, child, anything easy."

Richard rubbed his head and shivered against the cold invading all the places his blanket had been keeping warm. "We don't seem to have any luck at all, do we?"

"These is just runaways. 'T'ain't like they was stoled."

Richard shrugged into the buffalo coat he and Travis had sewn from the Crow hides they'd traded for, and pulled his hat from his possibles. And such a hat it was. Travis had cut a patch of hide in the shape of a simple cross, then sewed three of the seams together to make the body of the cap, and rolled the fourth piece into a furry bun for a bill. It didn't look like much, but the woolly buffalo fur was warm.

Another gust of wind blasted the camp, tearing flames right off the fire.

"Until I came to this country, I never knew the wind could blow with such fury."

Travis bent down to shave jerky into a tin pot. "Generally when she blows like this it means a change in the weather."

"Snow? You mean, more than we've had?"

"Yep. Best eat up, Dick. I reckon it'll be a long, cold day. Come daylight, we'll find the hosses and I reckon we'd best make tracks fer the Tongue River bottoms. Hole up down there until the storm breaks."

Another gust of wind howled through, spattering them with bits of blown sand and snow. "Willow's people, they wouldn't be camped out here? Along one of the rivers?"

"Not Sheepeaters. They's mountain folk. No, from what I know about Sheepeaters—and it ain't a whole lot—they'll stick ter the hills. That way, ain't no Blackfoot war party's gonna catch 'em. They tend ter country where most folks don't go."

Richard watched tendrils of steam blow away as the stew began to cook. "What about our packs, Travis?"

"Leave 'em sit. They'll be fine until we get the hosses. Hell, them mangy beasts won't be more than a mile or two. We'll come back and pack up.

"And hope the coyotes and wolves don't chew all the lacings to pieces."

"Yep. There's always that. Reckon we'll piss around 'em first. Mark the camp with man-scent ter keep 'em off."

"Mark it?"

"Wolves and coyotes, ye see, is respectful critters. Mostly. Until their stomachs gets the better part of their manners."

With the first haze of dawn, they peed a circle around their camp. Richard hung his possibles around his shoulder—making sure he had a full day's supply of jerky—and checked his Hawken before they started off. The horse tracks were easily visible through crusted patches of snow, and where the hooves had bruised dry grass or marred frozen dirt.

"Thar's that coon's sign." Travis pointed to a big cat track.

Richard placed his mittened hand alongside the track. "How big would you say?"

"Six, seven feet long. Maybe two hundred an' fifty pounds. He ain't a very big one."

"I don't know. I've seen a lot of cat feet in my day. They don't grow 'em like that in Boston."

"Do tell?"

The wind continued to pound them as they trotted across the rolling ridges and grass-filled draws where the horses had run in blind panic.

"Whoa up!" Travis called, slowing and bending to study the snow at the head of a deep gully. "What in Tarnal Hell? They split up hyar. Four's gone off ter the right, two's ter the left."

"Is that bad?"

Travis shrugged, staring down the valley. "Depends on how the draws run. You go left, I'll go right. They'll probably be bunched up at the first side canyon, looking at each other over the gully. That, or they found a place where the banks caved in and crossed so's ter tie up again."

Richard nodded, following along the left side, studying out the tracks. Little wisps of snow were blowing down out of the heavy sky, the wind biting at any bit of exposed flesh.

At the first side canyon, there were no horses. Richard could see where they'd stood, no doubt whinnying back and forth to their friends on the other side of the sheer-walled gully. The piles of horse manure were stone-cold to the touch, outsides frozen. Hours old.

"Which way'd they go?" Travis shouted.

"Up there!" Richard pointed to the east where the gully had to head.

"Mine went on south." Travis shot a nervous glance up at the scudding clouds. "Camp's up at the head of this draw. I'll meet ye thar."

Richard licked his lips, looking uncertainly up the winding drainage. "Are you sure?"

"Dick, we gotta catch these hosses afore it really starts ter snow. Watch yer backtrail. I'll see ye soon. They ain't gone that far. But if'n ye really gets lost, head on south. Make ye a camp on the Tongue River. North side. I'll find ye."

Richard shivered, then with a wave he turned to follow the horse tracks that headed up the side canyon. The snow was patchy here, most of it piled behind the sagebrush like white cones, and drifted along the north slopes.

The tracks changed from a trot to a full run. Probably panicked at being separated from their fellows. Richard pushed himself to a brisk walk to keep warm. For water, he scooped up the crusted snow, crunching ice crystals.

Near the head of the gully, the horses had bolted across the drainage and headed southward again. On the snowy slope, Richard saw yet another set of tracks, those of a big dog. And then another cut in, and another.

Wolf pack! He made a face and studied the snow that blew past, not in small flakes but big ones, and a lot of them. They were starting to stick in the hollows.

Richard cursed and charged up and out of the little valley, chasing the tracks. "Damn wolves! What are you doing? Just running the horses for the hell of it?"

A full-grown wolf couldn't take down an adult horse, could he? The tracks led across ridges and shallow gullies. Wolves would play with animals, run them just for the sake of running.

Except this didn't feel right. It had an ominous sense about it, as if the wolves had been working the horses with a purpose. He checked the Hawken's priming, ensuring it was still dry.

Snow began to clot the folds of his buffalo coat, and he had to keep the lock of his rifle dry. The trail drew him onward: a hoof scar here; a set of pockmarks in the old snow there; a bruised sagebrush. With an odd satisfaction, Richard trotted along, reading the sign with a sense of authority.

He crossed another of the ridges and descended into a broad valley, the treeline like a gray mat in the haze of blowing snow. They'd be down there, in the trees, out of the wind. By now, the wolves should have broken off to seek easier prey. Yes—the trees, that's where the horses were. They were Indian animals, used to camping on the rivers.

He could feel the leaden ache in his legs as he hurried down, and his breath was coming short. *Slow down. Catch your breath. Travis always said not to overheat and sweat in the cold.*

Snow fell across the valley in lacy veils that turned the entire world into a chiaroscuro of pale shadows. Snow crunched underfoot as Richard passed beneath ghostly branches.

Searching for fresh sign, he crisscrossed and found what looked like tracks, now no more than snow-filled dimples.

He glanced backward at his tracks through the trees. Should he go back?

Travis wouldn't. He'd see it through. Besides, the horses had to be somewhere close.

Richard wavered, listening, the silence so complete he could hear the rustle of snow crystals falling. The wind had dropped to a mere breeze.

I should go back. But what if the horses were just a short ways away? Travis would chide him for getting so close and turning back.

He pushed onward, soon realizing the dimples weren't horse tracks. A wolf yipped off to his right, and Richard turned, heading into the wind. He'd not gone far before he saw the wolves, five of them occupied with a bloody pile of . . .

"You sons of bitches!" He leveled the Hawken, eared the cock back, set the trigger, and shot the big gray wolf that stood atop his favorite white mare. At the report, the wolves jumped. The big gray yelped, whipped around to bite at his side—and staggered sideways, stiff-legged, to fall and thrash in the snow.

The other wolves vanished, slipping away soundlessly into the trees.

As Richard reloaded, he could see them, watching from cover. He approached the dead horse warily and studied the torn carcass. The ground here was mucky, an old beaver dam that had silted in and frozen. The horse had been driven into the soft soil where it bogged, unable to kick, and the wolves had ripped its belly open.

Richard rubbed his wet face and groaned, then glanced at the dead wolf. "Damn you. Maybe you took my horse, but I killed you and I'll take coup, you bastard."

Richard narrowed an eye, appraising the thick pelt. Images of a warm wolf coat filled his mind. Loath to leave it, he still had to find the other wayward horse. It wouldn't take that long, and the loss of a horse deserved some recompense. He pulled his knife, flopped the wolf onto its back, and slit the belly open.

The task of skinning took longer than he anticipated. As snow fell, he pulled the last of the hide loose and rolled it into a thick bundle. Using tendons cut from the wolf, he tied it tightly and threw it over his shoulder.

With a last shake of the head, he sadly inspected his mare. "Goodbye girl. Damn, this country's sure hard on folks I love. It breaks my heart, but if God's just, your soul now runs with the wind and dances among the stars. I'm sorry I didn't get here sooner."

The big flakes of snow melted as they landed on the wolf's pink carcass. He gave it a kick and started back through the trees. If he kept the wind to his left, which should be west, it would guide him back to the north.

The world had turned to snow, and the wolf had been a big animal. How long had it taken to skin him? His tracks were nothing more than dimples.

Richard stared around in the haze, trying to pick his direction. Then the wind changed; fine snow filtered down in swirls. Which way? *One way's as good as the next.*

He started forward, beating snow from his coat and rifle as his feet crunched in the new-fallen blanket. No matter how far he walked, it seemed that he never broke out of the trees.

I'm headed up or downstream. I've got to go right or left to find the slope.

He'd walked under the black lump in the tree before he recognized it; a shiver traced down his back. Burials. One, two, three . . . Jesus, at least ten that he could see through the falling white veils. Each of the corpses had been wrapped in a robe now mounded with snow. The subtle stench of death carried down to Richard's nostrils.

He turned, uneasy at the number of them he'd walked so carelessly beneath. "Good God." His heart thudded as he carefully backtracked until he'd passed beyond them.

Chewing his lip, he cut right, away from the burial ground. Whose? Blackfeet? Crow? Arapaho? Would any of them show much mercy to a lone White man walking among their ghosts?

"I'm sorry," he called to the silent dead. "I didn't mean to disturb you."

And then he fled, charging headlong through the trees. Frantic only to escape, to put as much distance between himself and the silent corpses as he could.

Crossing a low spot, he slipped and tumbled. He stared anxiously at the ice he'd exposed, and realized he was on a frozen pond.

Dear God, if you fall through, you'll freeze! Treading carefully, he could hear the ice crackle underfoot. Grasping willows, he pulled himself up on firm ground, and charged onward, half expecting the sound of ghosts in pursuit.

"Silly," he gasped under his breath. "You're being foolish. They're dead, Richard. Just like passing through a cemetery."

But the dead in a cemetery are safely underground. You don't have to smell them, see their bodies!

He nodded to himself. "Right . . . and maybe the folks that stuck them up there heard the shot when you killed the wolf. So, fearing the dead might be irrational, but their living relatives might just find a dead horse and a lone White man's tracks mighty interesting."

That thought inspired him to hurry through the falling snow. His belly rumbled, and every so often he'd cup up a snowball to chew for water. Was it his imagination, or was the light dimming?

That was when he came to the river: cool dark water

interspersed with patches of snow-covered ice. But which river was it? The Tongue?

"Well, for God's sake, don't cross it."

And with that, he continued onward, seeking a way through the trees, and from there, into the uplands that would take him back to camp.

The sky grew ever darker.

NINETEEN

◇

As men, therefore, are so slightly acquainted with nature, and cannot agree about the meaning of the word *law*, it would be very difficult for them to agree on a good definition of natural law. Accordingly, all those definitions we encounter in books, besides lacking uniformity, err from being derived from several kinds of knowledge which men do not naturally possess, and from advantages they cannot comprehend, as long as they remain in a state of nature.

—Jean Jacques Rousseau, *Discourse on the Origin and Foundation of Inequality Among Mankind*

Travis spent three days in complete misery while the storm blew itself out. Most of the time he huddled under his blanket, nursing the small sagebrush fire for warmth. Occasionally, when the wind lulled, he'd shake the snow off his blankets and check the horses. They were picketed with their tails to the brunt of the storm—and looked just as miserable as he felt.

"That'll teach ye ter go a-tearing off when a painter

screams." He'd look off to the south, hoping to see a half-frozen Richard staggering toward camp.

Then the storm would pick up and he'd return to his blanket, and memories of other storms he'd waited out like this. The one that ran through his head most often was the time with Dave Green so long ago on the Little Missouri.

"Huh, funny how things go around, ain't it?" he'd ask the spectral images that surrounded him in his blanket shelter. Wasn't it curious that each of the faces he saw in the embers of his fire belonged to a dead man? But look as he might, he didn't see Richard's there.

"Poor damned Doodle." Travis shifted, feeling the weight of the snow. He'd propped up the blanket with his ramrod, and now lifted a corner to make sure he wasn't buried so deep he'd suffocate.

So, where had Richard gone? Travis had found five of their six animals just before the heavy snow began to fall. The only missing animal was Richard's white mare—and Travis had half expected to find that the mare, with Richard on her, had beaten him back to camp.

"Wal, coon. Hyar's ter hoping yer a-waiting down ter the Tongue."

Aye, but can that poor Doodle survive the likes of this? The unspoken question rolled around in Travis's uneasy soul.

On the fourth day, the cold awakened him. He poked up through his snowy warren and stared around in the predawn pink. Overhead the sky was vividly clear, the air so sharp it prickled the nostrils with each inhalation.

"Deep cold," Travis whispered, looking at the hunched horses. They stood together in a clump, shivering with their heads down. They'd eaten the grass down to dirt, and tramped the manure-filled snow.

"C'mon, coons," Travis told them. "Let's get the packs on

yer cussed backs and make our way down ter the Tongue. See if'n by some chance of fate old Dick's still alive and waiting fer us."

He kicked the packs from the snow, rolled his ice-stiff blanket, and chewed a thick stick of jerky as he packed the horses, careful to knock as much ice as he could from their backs before seating the load.

A finger after sunup, he swung into the saddle and squinted around. The land looked soft and virginal under the endless white undulations. Sculpted drifts feathered off in intricate patterns.

Travis kicked his reluctant gelding into a trot along the ridge, the rest of the horses following. The air was so still, the land so quiet; the cold seemed to throb with a vibrancy that defied the senses. It bit into the very soul with needle teeth.

"Deep cold, fer sure," Travis murmured, his breath floating off in lacy white. His beard had already frosted and was now icing. "Wal, this coon figgers we'd better find us a hole. How about it, you hosses? Ye ready fer grass?"

He glanced at the distant Big Horn Mountains, etched so clearly against the enamel blue sky that they made the eyes ache.

Travis let the gelding warm to its own pace as they headed down into the valley of the Tongue. Here and there, they had to buck drifts, but keeping to the high ground they made good time.

By midmorning, he had reached the river. He set up camp beside the main channel, where the current ran free of ice, and unpacked. From the fallen cottonwoods, he cobbled together a makeshift corral and turned the packhorses in.

After collecting wood, laying a fire, and forting up the packs, he stepped into the stirrup and urged his reluctant gelding out of camp.

The big bay whinnied, his cries echoed by the pack string

as Travis trotted downstream, cutting for sign. Where the river looped, he encountered what looked to be an Arapaho burial ground. Hunched over the saddle, blowing into his mittens to warm them, Travis counted nearly thirty corpses wedged in the forks of high branches.

He rode wide, following the river, seeing where snow had blown across the ice in a solid sheet. A mile beyond, he heard the ravens cawing and coyotes yipping.

The scavengers fled at his approach. In the trampled snow he recognized the chewed remains of a frozen horse: Dick's white mare. And just off to the side? That ravaged chunk of meat, just about man-sized? Travis made a face.

The gelding stamped, more than a little spooked by his stable mate's bloody body and the smell of the predators that feasted there.

"Wolf, by God!" Travis identified the carcass. "And not a scrap of hair on it." The ribs had been chewed open, the gut cavity cleaned out. But why would the coyotes have chewed out the ribs like that?

"Bullet hole?" Travis stepped down and started to lead the blowing gelding forward, only to have the animal pitch a fit. "Hyar, now! Don't ye go a-getting spooky with me, damn yer eyes. Whoa, now. What in hell?" Travis checked the footing and nodded at the boggy trap. "Wal, ye've a sight more sense than old Dick's mare had." After tying off the horse, Travis walked out to the wolf carcass.

He pried the frozen wolf loose from the ice. "Sure enough. Look't that. Somebody shot his lights out slick and skinned the hide off."

Travis backed away, patting his trembling horse on the neck. "What do ye think? Like maybe old Dick tracked his hoss down hyar? Ketched that wolf chewing on her and raised him?"

Travis cocked his head, watching his frosted breath rising

in the still air. "Wal, I'd make it about ten below, and nigh ter midday. Damnation, Dick, with the snow, I ain't even sure I can find yer carcass, unless the ravens and coyotes raise enough Cain ter signal me."

He slapped his horse and stepped into the saddle. "C'mon, hoss. We'd best get back. If'n by some tarnal luck Dick's alive, maybe so he'll see the fire and come a-running."

With that, Travis reined his gelding around and headed back upriver. With each step, the snow groaned under the gelding's hooves.

It's damn cold. What are the chances he's still alive? Travis shook his head, heart sinking in his breast.

❖

Richard awakened, shivering, momentarily disoriented as he stared around the dark hole. He'd been dreaming about his father. Phillip Hamilton had been sitting at his cherrywood desk, head in hands. Those old shoulders had convulsed as the old man cried.

Crying for me. I'm not dead, Father. But the dream had left a hole in Richard's soul. *I never understood, Father. We're two of a kind, you and me. Forever frightened of each other.*

He sighed and shivered, blinking. Daylight could be seen where the sandstone overhang wasn't covered by snow. Coal, that's what he huddled against, and memory of his horrible ordeal returned.

He'd climbed into the uplands as the darkness closed in. Knowing that if he stopped he'd freeze, he'd continued uphill because camp had to be someplace near the divide between the Tongue and Greasy Grass.

The storm had never relented, and Richard had run out of ridge to climb. Every direction led down . . . but down toward what?

In desperation, he'd chosen a way with the wind to his back, and finally, after wallowing through drifts, had found this hole and the undercut coal seam.

For three miserable days now he'd hidden here, curled into a ball, wrapped in everything he owned. He sat up, restricted by the hard wolf hide. He'd tied it on with the hair-side in; now it had frozen around him like a knight's cuirass.

His stomach growled its hunger. He'd made a day's supply of jerky last four, and his belly hadn't been fooled. *Damn it, why didn't I take a haunch off that wolf?*

Well, no matter, he'd head on south to the Tongue, and Travis would find him. Then he could stuff himself with pemmican and meat. Richard stood, willing circulation into his legs. He picked up his rifle and slung his possibles around his shoulders. Ice clattered from the folds of his clothing.

"By God," he said aloud, shivering. "I'm alive." His toes still wiggled, so his feet weren't frostbitten.

With that, he broke through the cornice of snow, and bulled his way through the drift that had filled the little drainage channel where he'd taken refuge.

The midmorning brightness of sun on snow blinded him. Shading his eyes with a mittened hand, he squinted around to find the most likely way out of the narrow gully.

The cold began to bite through his hides. Puffing out a breath, he watched it rise, and rise, and rise, then dissipate slowly in the still air. The inside of his nose prickled as if the little hairs were frozen. His beard had iced like a confectioner's Saint Nicholas. "Blessed God, just how cold is it?"

Step by step, he packed a trail and climbed to the top, pulling his way up the last hill by tugging on sagebrush.

Snow groaned under his moccasin-wrapped feet as he crested the drifted knoll and looked out in amazement.

In all his life, he'd never seen air so clear. In every direction, the land was sculpted, each fold of the ground outlined in stark white contrast to the crystalline dome of the sky. But such snow! It glowed, as if possessed by an unearthly tint of blue. Against that splendor, the majesty of the Big Horns rose in the west—magnificent slabs of tilted rock laced with woven white and spotted dark green with timber that gave way to an ivory magnificence of high peaks.

God lives here. Richard wiped at his frozen beard, stunned by the sight. Then the bitter cold, and the growling of his stomach, turned his thoughts to other things.

In all the world, the only sound is my stomach gurgling! Now, what, Dr. Hegel, would you make of that? He studied the route he would take, following the windward side of the ridges downward toward the south. The Tongue had to be there, somewhere.

"Why didn't I just stay there when I had the chance?" he muttered as he started to plod south. "Because I got spooked by a bunch of dead Indians, that's why."

And you thought you were good enough to find camp again. He snorted, hating to make such an admission, even in the privacy of his own mind.

He'd made barely an hour's progress when he spotted the antelope, perhaps forty of them feeding along a wind-blown ridge.

Make it right, Richard. You'll get one shot, and if you miss . . . In this cold, you'll be dead before morning if you don't put something in your stomach.

He checked the priming in his rifle and shook his gun to make sure the fire channel was clear. Then he chipped the ice out of the muzzle with his ramrod.

Ever so carefully, he began his sneak, cutting below the ridge to get downwind, first wading, then wallowing, and finally practically swimming through the deep drift in the lee of the ridge.

Heart pounding, he crawled toward the ridge crest, aware that the sun was slanting against him, glaring off the snow. Antelope had unbelievably good vision, and moved at even the slightest show of a head, shoulder, or buttocks.

His elbows for levers, Richard pulled himself over the snow-blocked grass, wincing as prickly pear lanced through the leather of his buffalo coat.

He stopped, judging the amount of time he'd traveled. A full hand's breadth from the slant of the sun.

Now what? Think, Richard. Did they move on? God help me, I can't make a mistake. Not now.

His stomach made a noise like a dying man's groan. Tarnal Hell, even the antelope had to have heard that! The cold, a palpable presence, leeched his flesh, sucking his strength, devouring the sap of his soul.

If I raise my head, I could ruin everything. But what if they're not here?

Richard fought down a shiver that wasn't nearly as terrifying as the numbness creeping into his feet.

Slowly. Be careful. Don't do anything stupid. He eased his head up the slightest bit, squinting into the glare, and saw nothing. Just as slowly, he let himself sink down to earth and levered himself forward again. As he moved, the quivering of his arms surprised him. He'd cradled the gun in his elbows as he crawled, and now realized that it too was shivering in time to the rest of his body.

You're tired, Richard. You haven't eaten. If you don't shoot an antelope, it's over.

He swallowed hard, wondering how death would steal over his clay-cold body. When a man froze, did he know the precise moment when the soul left the body? Blasphemous Hell, what if he was just as cold in death as in life? He couldn't bear it.

He carefully lifted his head and saw—nothing!

They're gone, Richard. You don't have much time. He pulled himself forward. *This is the last chance.*

Raising his wobbling head, he carefully peeked over the ridge, disappointment rising. *Dear Lord God, they couldn't have winded me and run clear . . .* The barest flick of an ear caught his attention. The scrubby sagebrush had masked the antelopes' position.

Richard's heart began to pound, blood racing through his stiffening limbs. *There . . . right there! Don't make a mess of this, Richard.*

He tensed his muscles, trying to make heat to battle the numbness. Filling his lungs, he carefully pulled himself another elbow length forward.

Careful . . . careful . . . He moved with deliberate slowness, knowing the cold had stolen most of his control.

A doe stepped into full view, her head down as she nibbled the spikes off a sagebrush. Richard barely allowed himself to breathe, afraid she might hear his pounding heart.

She took another step, and Richard could see the frosty breath around her black nose.

At that moment, his stomach growled angrily, and time stood still as the doe raised her head.

Do I rise up? Take the shot? Another voice cautioned, *For God's sake, no! If you bumble because of the cold, she'll be gone!*

Unsure, he waited, trying not to breathe, but just as suddenly starved for air.

Please, Mother. Just one shot. I need you! After what seemed an eternity, the doe dropped her head to browse.

Richard eased the rifle into place, sliding his cheek against the ice-cold stock. And, to his horror, couldn't control his wobbling muscles.

In one desperate instant, he tensed his entire body, saw the front sight steady in the buckhorn, and triggered the gun.

The pan flashed, eternity hung on an instant, then the rifle boomed fire and smoke.

Richard rolled on his side and sucked in cold air like a drowning man. He could hear the clatter of hooves as the herd raced away. Had he hit?

If I didn't, how am I going to stand it?

On weak limbs, he pulled himself up, used the rifle as a prop, and climbed to his feet. He tottered forward, vaguely aware that the cold had sapped still more of his strength.

He found the place where her feet had torn the snow. A clump of stiff antelope hair lay to one side. Had he just grazed her?

"No. Please! Tell me I hit her."

He staggered on, following the tracks, and, yes, there was a spot of bright red blood in the snow. Then another and another, until the gushing spray of crimson was impossible to miss.

She lay piled up in the deep snow at the bottom of the ridge. Richard dropped to his knees, reaching out with his snow-packed mittens to rub her bristly hair. "Bless you, Mother. Thank you so much." He swallowed hard, a terrible understanding dawning within him. Throwing his head back, he called out to the setting sun, "*Tam Apo!* Take the soul of this antelope, and grant her eternal peace. This beautiful creature gave her life that I might live. With all my heart, I thank her for the gift she has given me. Please, bless her. And tell her that I, Richard Hamilton, thank and respect her."

Then, shivering and weak, he slipped his knife from its sheath and cut open the white belly. The hot blood steamed with a sweet musk that fed his soul. Hands aquiver, Richard cut loose the liver and leaned back.

As the sun burned eerily bright in the frozen land, he ate, heedless of the hot red liquid that dribbled down and froze on his beard.

TWENTY

But as long as we remain ignorant of the constitution of natural man, it will be futile for us to attempt to determine what law he received, or what law best suits him. All we can clearly determine in regard to that law is that in order for it to be law, he to whom it obliges must manage to submit to it willfully and knowingly, but also that, for it to be natural, it must speak immediately by the voice of nature.

—Jean-Jacques Rousseau, *Discourse on the Origin and Foundation of Inequality Among Mankind*

Water Deer and Gray Moth arrived at High Wolf's camp two days after the storm. They had braved the deep cold to make the long hike from their band's camp in the foothills to the north.

Both men were tightly bundled, puffing frosty breath, with round snowshoes tied onto their packs, clumps of ice still caught in the thong webbing.

High Wolf greeted them, smoked their tobacco in his tubular steatite pipe, and waited curiously as the formalities for visitors were conducted.

White Alder set food before them. Both men wolfed it down, an indication that they'd eaten little if anything on the journey. Water Deer in turn offered three squirrels, with apologies that their haste, along with the brutal cold, had limited their ability to hunt.

Now Many Elk, White Alder, and Lodgepole huddled around, eager to hear what had brought the men to their camp.

As Willow sat to one side, sewing a pair of moccasins, she, too, studied them. Water Deer was young, lean, with a guileless face. He wore sheephide, tanned to a light brown and painted with red and black circles. His mittens were stained, and his thick moccasins had a scuffed look. Gray Moth, on the other hand, was chubby, dressed in a worn coat from which loose sheep hair filtered like snow, indicating it was nearly worn out on the inside. His mittens had holes, and his moccasins had been wrapped with rabbit fur, the pelts tied on.

While Water Deer glanced enthusiastically at Willow, Gray Moth sat with pursed lips, definitely uneasy as he stared into the fire.

"You see," Water Deer began, as he toasted his hands and shot another glance at Willow where she sat wrapped in warm furs by the cook fire, "we are great hunters. At our camp, we have meat stacked like firewood. So much we can barely stumble over it. Meat becomes a problem for us, especially since the territory where we dig roots in spring produces in plenty. Isn't that right, Gray Moth? Why, there's times the roots grow so big, and so closely together, they practically pop out of the ground. A woman barely needs to dig them. They almost jump out into her hand. And that's a fact!"

High Wolf now studied the men with new interest. One of his eyebrows had lifted slightly, amusement in the pattern of his crow's-feet.

"But the greatest of our hunters is Gray Moth," Water Deer patted his companion on the back. Gray Moth smiled self-consciously, glancing furtively at High Wolf and Many Elk, who'd taken seats across from them.

"Indeed," Water Deer cried, "there is no one who can sneak like Gray Moth. He is silent as the night breeze. I've seen him ghost up to elk, close enough to touch them. He organizes our spring hunt, and through his skill, we have so much to eat that most of our food is freely given to the coyotes. You know, just to keep it from piling up before Gray Moth brings in more."

"And how is White Rock?" High Wolf asked. "I saw him last summer at the gathering. We talked for quite a while. He was looking healthy."

"Oh, yes." Water Deer waved it away. "As healthy as a bull buffalo. But you know White Rock. I don't think there's another like him among all the People . . . except maybe you, High Wolf. No one is wiser than White Rock. He knows the ways of the mountains, where the fattest game can be found. Take our camp, for example, always warm, sweet water running from a spring. And I think I told you about the root grounds. Biscuit-root the size of a man's head grows there."

High Wolf's lips bent into a crooked smile, and he glanced speculatively at Willow.

Water Deer continued to tell of all the wonderful things at White Rock's camp.

Willow added wood to the fire, then stared out over the canyon. Snow mantled the trees on the far side, contrasting with the cool green of the forest. In the trees, nutcrackers cawed, flitting from branch to branch, while, closer, the chickadees twittered. Sound carried in the deep cold. With her iron needle, she poked another hole in the sole leather and pulled the thread through.

"Things are good indeed," Water Deer continued. "Except for one bit of misfortune."

People shifted, waiting politely.

Willow cocked her head.

Water Deer stared sadly into the fire. "The tragedy is all of ours, of course, but more of Gray Moth's than anyone else's."

"I had heard his wife was ailing," High Wolf stated, as if suddenly remembering.

"We don't know what it was." Water Deer spread his hands. "A pain in her side. Over time, it just seemed to get worse. White Rock sang over her, and we administered the usual cures. She sweated, and followed all the rituals. But . . ."

High Wolf's expression turned sympathetic. "Ah, we sorrow to hear of your loss, Gray Moth."

The chubby hunter nodded, and cast a nervous glance at Willow. "I've been terribly sad." Then he lowered his eyes.

"Yes," Water Deer continued, "sad indeed. And Gray Moth, with his beautiful children. It was hardest on them. Such bright and wonderful children. Two boys—and a little girl. How lucky we are that the baby has passed beyond suckling. I don't think there are more obedient children in all the world. Just mention that something needs to be done, and they are already running to do it. In all my life, I don't think I've ever seen children so ready and willing to please."

"They must be special children," Many Elk said neutrally, casting a glance at his own grandchildren clustered under a buffalo robe, kicking and giggling.

"Special," Water Deer agreed. "I couldn't think of a better word to describe them." He glanced cautiously at Willow. "Such children would bring pride to any woman. And Gray Moth could sire many more."

Gray Moth gave the fire a fleeting smile, and rubbed his plump hands anxiously.

"So many gifts, Gray Moth," High Wolf said gently. "But to lose a wife, that is difficult for all. Our hearts are heavy for you."

"It is hard," Gray Moth agreed.

"Well," High Wolf added, "here you may forget your woes for a while. Some of our young men—Rock Hare, Black Marten, and White Hail—have gone to see where the deer are feeding. And, as you can see, we have more than enough to feed you for as long as you would care to stay with us."

"Perhaps you need help bringing in meat?" Water Deer asked. "Gray Moth is a hard worker. Why, there are times we must almost tie him up to keep him from working so hard." Water Deer gave his friend a solicitous glance. "In the White Rock band, we feel honored to have such a one as he. It isn't often that a band can manage to keep a man like Gray Moth—not when so many others offer him and his children a place at their fire."

"White Rock is lucky indeed." High Wolf nodded soberly.

"Enough of us." Water Deer poked at the fire with a stick. "Tell us of your camp, High Wolf. Is all going well?"

"Very well, but perhaps not with the wondrous fortune White Rock seems to enjoy."

Appearing nonchalant, Water Deer said, "We have heard that your daughter has returned."

"Indeed she has, and from a remarkable journey." High Wolf shot Willow a suggestive glance.

Willow set her moccasins aside and crossed to the fire, where she crouched beside Many Elk. "I have recently returned."

"Ah." Water Deer smiled brightly, eyes keen. "We have heard that you, too, have lost loved ones to the Land of the Dead."

"My husband and son," she said. "Last winter."

Water Deer's expression turned appropriately gloomy. "Our hearts are heavy." He paused. "We are all lucky that some *Ku'chendikani* didn't snatch you up with hollow promises of horses and a fine lodge."

"One is here," Willow replied offhandedly, "trying to do exactly that, though he no longer makes such open attempts."

"Indeed?" Water Deer asked, and even Gray Moth looked up, slightly startled.

"Oh, yes," Willow said solemnly. "Now he seeks to impress me by showing what a good hunter he is, and how hard he can work. He doesn't make any declarations, but he hints at how good life would be if I went with him. You should hear him. The way he tells it, his camp has more meat than any other."

Water Deer shrugged. "You know how *Ku'chendikani* are. They tell the most outlandish stories."

"They do." Willow used a stick to poke at the fire. "Fortunately, I know him rather well. My husband was his brother, and I lived in his camp, so I know when I hear something that isn't quite right. It would be a little more difficult if I didn't know the people who told me stories."

"It would, wouldn't it?" Water Deer watched her warily. "It's a good thing that here, among the *Dukurika,* we don't tell wild stories."

"A very good thing." Willow frowned at the fire. "A woman who hadn't grown up in these mountains, and didn't know the root grounds, one who hadn't talked much to people from different bands, would be at a disadvantage."

Water Deer reached up under his hat to scratch his head. "How lucky we are to meet up with such a wise woman."

"Some call me wise," Willow agreed. "Others call me trouble. They say I ask too many questions about too many things. That a woman's duty is to her family. I have trouble with that because sometimes Power calls me. When that happens, I must allow my *navuzieip* to do as it must. Some do not always understand that."

"This Power," Water Deer mused, expressionless, "it is unusual in a woman. Some have talked about it and believe it comes to you because High Wolf is such a Powerful *puhagan.* Some would believe this was a bad thing. White Rock, however, is not one of them, nor are any of the people in his band. We would be honored if a woman with such Power were to come among us. Unlike so many, we do not fear Power and ability, but would value such counsel at our fires."

"Indeed? Then White Rock's band demonstrates a most unusual wisdom." Willow glanced at High Wolf, who sat pensively.

Water Deer rubbed his hands together. "It is said that you have traveled among the White men and brought many fine things to High Wolf's camp. It is said that you have obtained the White man's Power."

Willow briefly met Water Deer's sharp eyes. "Such talk shows that *Dukurika* are as prone to wild tales as the *Ku'chendikani*. If true stories were told, they would say that I recommend that our people have as little to do as possible with the White men."

"Why would that be?" The slightest of frowns marred Water Deer's straight forehead.

"The White men have a great many wonderful things, Water Deer. But to know them is to discover that they have a great deal in common with Coyote in the beginning times. Like Coyote, they promise many marvelous things, but underneath the promises, they want something entirely different. And just like Coyote, they usually end up tricking themselves and destroying the thing they really want."

"Are they evil sprits, then? Is that what you are trying to tell us?"

"They are not spirits. Not gifted with Power as we know it. They have no concept of *puha*. They are no more evil than Coyote was. No, Water Deer, they are tricksters, very clever, seeking trade to make themselves rich and powerful. But they always end up making a mess of things. And like Coyote, they never learn from their mistakes."

Water Deer sighed, looking muddled. Gray Moth continued to stare at the fire, a terrible weariness in the set of his mouth.

Water Deer collected himself, buoyed by some inner resolution. "High Wolf is lucky indeed to have such a daughter as you, Willow. I can see now, more than ever before, just how wise you really are. I must confess, I had not expected the stories to be true. How lucky Gray Moth and I are that White Rock suggested we come hunting in this direction."

"The trouble with hunting is that you don't always bring home game," Willow remarked.

Water Deer and Gray Moth left the next morning, plodding north up the trail that led out of the canyon. Throughout their visit, Willow was polite and explicit in her descriptions of the White men.

White Hail settled next to her that evening as she kept an eye on the ricegrass cakes and biscuit-root cooking on the fire. The children were racing around, playing hide-and-seek in the rocks as they pelted each other with snowballs. White Alder, Good Root, and Red Squirrel played the hand game, their counters resting between two logs. Good Root sang and rocked as she passed the little polished bone back and forth, using sleights to keep its location secret. At last she stopped and held out her hands.

White Alder chose Good Root's right hand, which to her dismay was empty. Red Squirrel chuckled as a counter was passed to her pile. The fine white coat had changed hands two times since the night Good Root had lost it to Lodgepole. If Red Squirrel's luck held, it would pass to her later in the evening.

Willow glanced at White Hail. The *Pa'kiani* had marked him for life—his once handsome face would be forever off-center because of his crooked jaw. He was a patient man, trying to wear her down with his amiable presence.

The pressure to marry had been subtle. High Wolf had

kept his counsel, his face pensive. White Alder had made several comments about women and men, and how *Tam Apo* and *Tam Segobia* each acted as half of a whole.

"Gray Moth and Water Deer, they were only the first," White Hail said neutrally. "I think it will be a busy winter at High Wolf's camp."

Assured that the cakes were browning evenly, Willow took out the ax and the piece of sandstone she'd found to whet it. "Then I suppose High Wolf had better hope his hunters bring in more game than usual. I don't think three squirrels are going to help much."

"You don't look happy, Willow." White Hail pursed his lips for a moment. "Coming home wasn't what you expected, was it?"

The stone rang on the steel as she thought. "I don't know what I expected. In some ways, yes. I've been happy here. In others, no."

"Have you considered why?"

She gestured out to the world beyond the canyon. "My life changed out there. I have a feeling, White Hail. A sense of a coming storm. It's not something you can smell, like snow in the wind, but a different sense, like the one on a golden fall day that tells you that a difficult and bitter winter lies just over the northern horizon. I look around, and see my people basking in the sunshine and warmth, not realizing the leaves are beginning to change color."

"When winter comes, it makes no difference how mild you wish the weather to be. It will be as it will. A person must face it, no matter what."

"And tell me, White Hail, when did sense creep into your soul?"

He chuckled. "When the *Pa'kiani* beat it into me. No matter how I believed in my *puha,* and my skill, they caught me anyway. All the lies I told myself were stripped away like bark from a pine, and only the soft yellow wood underneath was left. From that time, I have known the color of my wood."

"Does that mean that no strength is left in your trunk?"

He watched her hands as she honed the ax. "My branches still reach for the sky, but I understand that a bolt of lightning can splinter even the tallest and strongest of trees."

"Now that is wisdom worthy of your brother."

His laughter was hollow. "Does that mean I might be worthy of my brother's wife?"

"We have had this conversation before."

"Does the White man, Ritshard, still fill your dreams?"

She ground the sandstone harder on the edge.

"Careful," he noted wryly, "if you slip, you'll cut yourself."

If I slip . . . Perhaps, White Hail, I already have.

❖

Travis scouted for four days' travel in either direction of his camp on the Tongue. Enduring the horrible cold, he rode up to the narrow valley where the river disgorged from the Big Horns, and then down, past the Arapaho burial ground, almost to the Crow village. In that time, he watched carefully for the slightest trace of fire, listened for the distant crack of a rifle shot, and cut for tracks in the snow.

In all that empty whiteness, no trace of Richard could be found. He stared out over the drifted slopes, stippled with gnarly sage. The broken and rounded land was packed with blue-shadowed banks of wind-deposited white, and the deep cold grew ever more bitter.

He hated this kind of cold; it played hell with the mass of scars crisscrossing his face. The sting worked in around the puckered flesh like little needles prickling him to the bone. His ruined nose took it the worst. He wished for his old wool muffler, but it had been aboard *Maria*—blown to hell along with the boat.

It had been eight days since they'd been separated. In despair, Travis finally rode into his camp, built a fire, and stripped the saddle from his gelding. He'd hung the packs in the trees to keep them intact, away from the doings of coyotes, wolves, and porcupines. He kicked at the hoof-packed snow; the packhorses had eaten their pasture down to dirt.

"It's piss-poor bull, old coon," he told his gelding, running gentle hands down the horse's snow-barked canon bones. "All we've done is run yer fat off, and froze fer nothing." He made a face, patting the horse gently, and muttered, "Damnation, Dick."

The horse flicked a frosted ear in reply, no doubt happy to be corralled with his mates again.

Travis knocked the patchy ice from his clothing and settled himself by the fire. He built a smoke and puffed thoughtfully as he extended his hands to the leaping flames. "Wal, Dick, ye were some, ye was. Made it a sight further than I'd a thought fer a fool-headed Doodle."

He puffed out a weary exhale to watch the delicate patterns of frost rise on the frigid air. How intricately beautiful—yet so deadly. This was killing cold, the kind that snapped trees and crackled ice. An unprotected man would be wolfmeat in an hour, froze solid in two.

So, what now, coon? Give Dick up fer dead? As he sat, he watched a flock of rosy finches flutter past. How, he wondered, could such little birds stand such bitter air.

Baptiste was no more than six days north, camped with the Crow. *But do I want to go back there? The only thing waiting for me in Two White Elk's lodge is memories of Moonlight. Her soft smile, the light in her eyes.*

He grunted disgustedly and extended his chin toward the fire, letting the packed ice in his beard melt. *Face it, coon, all ye got is memories. Too damned many of them.*

As the water dripped from his beard, he puffed his pipe empty. Like the cold, heat played tricks with his face, slivers of fire running along the scars. In the corral, the horses stomped, heads down, ice glittering on their backs.

Willow would want to know what had happened to the expedition, and most particularly to Dick. What would her reaction be? The stoic acceptance an Indian showed toward an outsider's death, or the gnashing and wailing for a loved one?

"The first, I'd bet. With a deep sadness." She'd loved Richard, loved him in a way the poor Doodle had never been able to comprehend.

"More's the pity, Dick. Unlike ye, I got ter love a woman with all my heart once. Hell, ye stupid fool, ye done froze ter death, and missed it all."

But then, life was full of that, wasn't it? Getting so close, and missing it all. *I never used to feel that way. What happened, Travis Hartman, that ye stopped traveling just for the going? When did it start being so damned all-fired important to* get *somewhere?*

He made a thick stew, melting snow on the shaved jerky, adding rosehips and slices of pemmican. Then he chopped tobacco from a twist into his pipe.

As the stew boiled, he watched the evening descend in awesome pinks that shaded first into lavender and then into deep blue. The colors reflected off the snow, glowed in an unearthly way in the trees, and left the distant Big Horns luminous.

How silent the land was, but with a kind of clarity that conjured awe instead of loneliness.

Travis snaked his boiling stew from the fire, steam so thick it might have been smoke. Sipping gingerly at the corner of the pot, he savored the taste. An owl finally broke the silence when it hooted in the trees.

Wiping the drops from his mustache, he nodded to himself. "Ferget trying to get someplace, ye ignorant coon. Cast it all loose, and let it float. Green was looking forward, and look what it got him. Me, I'm starting to look backward too much." He belched, drank the rest of his stew, and cast a glance at the horses standing in the icy gloom. "Reckon tomorrow we'll pack up and go see the Crow. Ye knot-headed hosses would like that. Ye can frisk with their hoss herds, and I won't have ter take care of ye. Then, come spring, I reckon we'll load up and mosey down Willow's way. It won't hurt her any more ter larn about Dick then as now."

The decision made, he pulled his knife and chopped more tobacco. Out in the hills coyotes howled.

Richard wallowed through a drift, his antelope-hide pack dragging across the snow behind him. Step by weary step he tramped upward. He was puffing like a steamboat when he finally crested the ridge. On the north side stood a patch of grimly frozen pines. He trudged on, following the ridge to its highest pinnacle.

Gasping and wheezing, he unslung his pack with its frozen meat, and walked out onto the bare rock.

The view was magnificent. To the west, so clear and perfect he might have been able to reach out and touch them, the Big Horns rose in sheer-walled splendor.

He turned slowly, shading his eyes against the glare off the snow. Before him spread a winter-blanched world of ridge and swale, drainages tracing like God's fingers through the rolling hills.

He studied each of the flat valleys and the canted slopes sprinkled with sage and occasional pines. In places, bold lines of rock thrust through the snow to mark tilted slabs of earth. To the southeast, flat-topped buttes stood like wary sentinels in the open basin.

Streams meandered through the gentle valley, the bottoms gray-fuzzed with naked cottonwoods. But which was the Tongue? And where, in all this endless distance, could he expect to find Travis?

He shook his head. "I'd have seen a river, wouldn't I? The Tongue's not just some stream you can leap over. I saw it! In the storm, I saw it!"

He rubbed a frozen mitten over his eyes, squinting against the glare. "I turned, climbed out of the valley."

Unless I crossed the Tongue.

"How?" The river he'd seen was open water.

He slumped then, studying the Big Horns. They were so close now, almost to his right. "I've been walking south for days. Like it or not, I've crossed the Tongue somehow . . . some way."

He'd slipped on ice—thought it was a frozen pond. Damnation, it could have been the river. He'd been crossing streams every day since, searching out the places where they were frozen across.

He looked back to the north. "Travis? Are you back there? What do I do now? Backtrack? And if you've given me up for dead, what then? On the horses, you could be halfway back to the Mandan by now."

He was alone.

"Oh, wonderful, Richard. For the first time in your life, you can pick any direction you want—and you don't know where in hell it will take you." Or worse, what—or who—he'd find when he got there. Two White Elk would be one thing; a party of Rees, Pawnee, or Blackfeet something entirely different.

He turned again to the Big Horns, studying the snowy slopes. The south side, Travis had said. Richard studied the slope of the mountains, the way they rose from the south like a humped whale's back. How on earth could he find Willow's village in that maze of steep canyons, unscalable heights, and deep snow?

The faintest of breezes began to prickle on the exposed skin of his face. So far, the air had been still as death. Each night he found enough shelter so that by hovering over a fire, eating, dozing, and exercising, he could keep frostbite at bay.

The wind puffed a little harder, unnoticeable on a summer's day, but here, with the bone-numbing cold, the air felt like fire.

Off to the south he could see several herds of buffalo—little more than black specks on the snow. Shooting one meant fresh meat, and his outermost moccasins were wearing thin.

"Come on, Richard. You've got to get off this point." The

closest shelter was down there, to the south. And if he followed the base of the Big Horns, wood, game, and the other things he needed to survive would be plentiful.

Stepping off the point, he glanced uneasily at the tall mountains. *Willow? Where are you?*

What if he managed to survive, alone, lost, without a horse? Suppose he managed to locate Willow's people. Blessed God, they wouldn't just shoot him dead. Would they?

Aching despair began to chew on his soul again. No matter which direction he chose, it could only end in disaster.

As the afternoon sun dipped toward the southwest, God smiled upon him. He'd been crossing buffalo tracks, and here and there a frozen pile of manure. Nevertheless, it was a surprise when a yearling bull walked out from behind the shoulder of a low ridge. Richard stopped short, carefully lifted his rifle, and eased back the cock.

The animal seemed to gleam in the sunlight, the head and lower body midnight black, the hump and shoulders almost blond. Billows of frosted breath blew out to each side with his puffing exhales.

Nestling the Hawken's butt into his shoulder, Richard set the trigger, aimed for the vital spot just behind the point of the elbow, and shot.

Through the smoke, he saw the bull hunch. Then the animal leaped straight into the air, kicking its back legs with the speed of a rattlesnake. The bull spun, charging away, only to crash to earth in a pall of flying snow.

Richard blinked, swallowing hard. As the snow settled around the thrashing animal, he uncapped his horn, pouring in another charge. When he pulled off his mitten to pluck a bullet from his pouch, the bitter air stung his flesh. Seating the ball on a patch, he rammed the load home, and replaced his mitten before tilting the rifle to prime the pan.

Rifle ready, he approached cautiously, vaguely aware of the blood-spattered snow. The wound in the buffalo's side steamed, blood droplets already freezing on the long black hair. The bull stared vacantly, the eyes glassy in death.

"I'm sorry." Then he raised his face to the heavens and shouted his prayer for the animal's soul. The last of his words disappeared into the crystalline silence. He patted the thick fur. How warm it would be!

Richard glanced up at the slanting sun. Before he finished the tedious job of skinning, it would be dark. He started twisting sagebrush from the frozen soil, and kicked snow aside before laying his fire.

Only when he had a small blaze going did he pull his skinning knife from its belt sheath and begin slitting the thick hide. As the sun dropped into the southwest, Richard peeled back the skin, and steam rose from the fat-mottled flesh. The smell of buffalo filled his lungs, twining with his soul.

Cutting loose choice parts, he propped them over the coals to roast. By full dark, blood-smeared and tired, he had cut the animal apart. Grunting with effort, he tugged the hide to one side. An inch thick through the middle of the cape, it weighed twice what he did.

From the west, the wind continued to rise, wisps of snow like ethereal serpents slithering over the ground.

Richard stopped periodically to eat, kick through the snow, and twist sagebrush free to feed his fire. In the faltering heat of the coals, he dried his blood-saturated mittens.

Now what? He had meat without end, but here, in the open, the wind rising, no shelter presented itself. Turning to the hide, he realized the outside had already frosted. With frantic haste he tugged it out flat, then folded it double, hair-side in. The edges where he'd hacked off the legs were already frozen stiff. Another gust of wind roared out of the darkness, pelting him with snow and searing his face. Richard hurried to crawl inside until the hide lay on him like a heavy blanket.

"Dear Lord God," he whispered, tucking himself deeper into the soft curly hair. He pulled himself into a fetal ball and hugged himself. The pungent smell of buffalo closed around him.

The wind had begun to gust, driving the terrible cold until it cut like a saber blade. He couldn't afford a mistake. As he lay shivering inside the hide, his thoughts turned to Boston. Laura's face had a soft glow, her blue eyes twinkling like stars. He imagined reaching up to remove one of her hairpins so that her soft blond hair spilled over his hands like warm gold. In dancing lamplight, he sipped strong ale, and laughed with Will Templeton and Professor Ames. Once again he walked the cobblestone streets, greeting every cheery face with a warm salutation.

In the dream, he pictured himself, Jeffry, and Father. Together, they'd sit beside a warm fire. Yes, like a real family should.

That dream of his father crying had touched a fragile spot in his soul. That could be fixed, couldn't it? That chasm that had grown between them wasn't totally insurmountable.

Baptiste had once told him, *"White folks think everybody has a pap, just like a right hand."*

"I'll make it right. I swear. All I have to do is make my way home."

Home! He could hear the songs of the shipwrights as they walked up from the harbor. He longed for the seamen, the laborers who lived on Fish Street, the riggers, the caulkers. Once, he'd dismissed them as inconsequential—if he gave them any thought at all. Now, after the river and the *engagés*, he shared a kinship with them.

How fondly he remembered the river now, the warm

nights around cheerful fires, Travis's scarred face aglow in flickering yellow light as he smoked his pipe. He could hear the songs rising from the throats of the *engagés*. Across the fire, Baptiste's sleek ebony skin had a satin gleam and his straight white teeth flashed in a quick smile. Green stood there, thumbs stuck in his belt, worry battling with his eternal optimism.

But more than any other, Willow stared out at him, that soft, knowing light in her depthless eyes.

If I could just do it all over again. Willow . . . Willow . . . I love you so much.

Her lips parted, as if speaking to him, but the words never came. He started awake, listening, expecting to hear her, but only the wind—howling like a thousand lost souls—filled the night.

Before anything else, he had to settle accounts with two people: his father and Willow. And, God willing, he'd make it right with both of them.

He dozed then. It wasn't until he tried to straighten his legs that he realized something had gone wrong. He kicked out, struggling, only to sag in weary exhaustion.

"Of all the—I'm *trapped* in here!" He tried again, pressing up and out. Over an inch thick in places and full of moisture and blood, the hide had sagged and molded around every contour of his body. Then, in the subzero temperatures, it had frozen solid and clamped him like a vise.

TWENTY-ONE

❖

... I conceive that in all deliberations, that is to say, in all alternate successions of contrary appetites, the last is that which we call WILL, and is immediately before the doing of the action, or next before the doing of it becomes impossible. All other appetites to do, and to quit, that come upon a man during his deliberations, are called intentions and inclinations, but not wills, there being but one will, which also in this case may be called the last will, though the intentions change often.

—Thomas Hobbes, *Leviathan*

Willow sat bolt upright in her robes. Beyond the protection of the rock overhang, the wind whistled through the rocks and whimpered in the branches of the trees. Over the deep breathing of the sleepers, she could hear the blowing snow patter on the leather shelter wall.

Richard? His image sifted through her thoughts, unsettling her even more than the dreams that had haunted her sleep.

Willing her souls to silence, she closed her eyes, stilling everything, seeking . . . and finding nothing.

He called to me. She settled into the soft bedding again, and listened to the gusting night wind. Where was he? At the mouth of the Big Horn? By now, Richard, Travis, and the rest should be building their post, perhaps with the *Maria* frozen into the ice. Or would they have drawn the boat up on shore?

She snuggled deeper into the warm hides, a smooth otter pelt against her cheek. In her imagination, his brown eyes softened, that faint quirk of a smile on his lips. She could imagine his hand, reaching out to her with such gentleness.

Oh, Willow, how did he charm you so? She tucked a fist under her chin, trying to understand. Everything about Richard was a contradiction. That incredible gentleness with which he looked at her; the terrible violence with which he'd fought Trudeau. A warrior who had taken trophies in battle, stolen horses, and fought with great courage; he had marveled at the colors in a sunset, or would mourn a wounded songbird. He had fearlessly looked into the eye of her soul and remained unaffected by her Power. But his desire to join with her under the robes had terrified him.

Richard, my Richard, you were always afraid of the wrong things, the inconsequential things. The terrible longing ached inside her chest.

She took a deep breath of the cold night air. A smart woman would take her time, find herself a good man, and resume her life. She would have children, raise them correctly, and praise her man for his hunting talent and all the other skills he excelled at. She would keep the fires warm and the food cooked, and finally smile with relief when her children turned into adults and moved off to start lodges and families of their own. *Tam Apo* had made the world that way. Such things were expected of a smart woman.

It's not a bad life, she reminded herself sternly. *I had started just such a life with my husband.*

Why did she resist doing it again?

"Because if my husband was stupid enough to dull an ax on a rock, I'd break a club over his head," she whispered.

The Whites had changed her opinions, showed her different strengths, and, at the same time, different weaknesses. She still couldn't understand how they could put God into a building. And the way they thought of women disturbed her deeply.

The truth is, Willow, that you've stepped between peoples, and now, neither one satisfies you. And the final question remained: *What do you really want?*

She tossed and turned, gnawing at the answer, and finding none. But in the process of shuffling longing against reality, she understood that when the winter broke, she would travel to the mouth of the Big Horn.

It's only to go and see them, she insisted to herself. *I'm curious, is all. I just want to know how they are doing. See what they've built.*

As the long hours of night passed, she began planning her route, and what she would take.

The wind howled throughout the endless night, and Richard alternately slept and struggled within his death trap. The warmth of his body should have been sufficient to loosen the hide, shouldn't it? But the relentless cold had frozen the thick skin into something like iron.

If only I hadn't tucked myself in so tightly. He tried once again to draw his arm back so he could reach his belt knife. No amount of straining helped. The wet green hide, covered with stringy tissue and bits of muscle, cocooned him like an iron maiden.

Another gust of wind stirred the air. He shifted as much as he could in the glovelike tightness and stared past the frost-matted buffalo hair above his head. A faint light was visible. Morning had come. Trembling with effort, he gasped and relaxed.

What if it shrinks? I'm going to be squeezed to death. The image of rawhide, sewn wet around a cracked rifle stock and allowed to shrink dry, reminded him of just how strong even thin hide could be. He'd seen Indian hammers held together the same way.

Panic lent him renewed energy as he pushed down with his legs. Despite his wiry strength, he made the barest of progress as he wedged his feet down.

Panting, he strained to reach his hip, fingers brushing the knife handle ever so briefly. He just couldn't get his arm back far enough, despite cramping his muscles.

Closing his eyes, he sucked deep breaths to fight the sick feeling in his gut. If only there were a way to get some leverage! Out of the question since he lay curled on his side like a baby.

Worse, his bladder began to nag at him. His urine would only add to the trouble, spreading out, chilling and leeching warmth from his tired body.

I won't have time to be squeezed to death. As I get hungry, I won't make heat. The cold will get me first.

If only the buffalo wool didn't insulate so well. But then he'd have frozen to death.

Think, Richard. Use your noodle. Where's the way out?

"If it had snowed hard last night, or if that airhole had been downwind, the snow would have covered it and I'd be dead already. God, what a fool I've been."

As the light grew brighter, Richard continued to twist and push, and finally drifted off to sleep, defeated.

Curious fragments of dreams tortured him. Images of his father mixed with those of Travis, Dave Green, and Baptiste. Out of the twisted collage, he could hear the old Sioux *wechashawakan* laughing at him. Woven in were images of dead men, their bodies blasted apart. The listless eyes of the Blackfoot boy stared at him, uncomprehending, soul-dead before Richard's rifle shot blew the brain out of his head. In the background, Laura was sobbing, the dull ache of her grief almost palpable.

Sound, coupled with curious vibrations, brought him awake. His heart, already pounding from the dream, beat harder. There, that sound! He could feel a sensation, like scratching, through the hide at his back.

And then, something puffed—an animal's exhalation. Listening carefully, he could hear soft feet on the snow. The sniffing sound came again.

Craning his neck, he could just see the black tip of a nose at the airhole. Then came the sound of scratching again, like a dog's.

Wolves!

"Get away!"

Silence.

A shadow moved across the airhole. Richard twisted, surprised that he could move further than before. Flopping and jerking like a fish on the bank, he forced his left hand around to his hip, fingers slipping off the wooden knife handle. Just a little more. He grunted with effort, body trembling. Ignoring a painful cramp, he got a tenuous grasp on the knife handle. He exhaled, driving all the air from his lungs, and wrapped fingers around the handle. With a mighty jerk, he pulled the knife partway from the sheath.

One more time. He gulped air, charged his lungs, and exhaled until he wheezed. He jerked again. A little further. *That's it. Come on!*

He wrenched the blade free, and gasped in relief. *Careful now, don't cut yourself.* He wiggled, changing his grip on the knife, slipping it up along his body. The blade had bent, and God alone knew what he'd done to the sheath. Well, at least he hadn't cut his hip open in the process.

He had to hold it by the curved blade—cramped as he was—and work the tip into the thick hair above his shoulder. Using it like a drill, he twisted the point back and forth. Hair rasped and gave, the hide making a hollow sound. In sudden victory, he slid the blade through and into the air beyond. Changing his grip to the handle, he sawed. Ice-stiff, the hide resisted. Richard worked diligently.

As the slit lengthened, he pressed upward, levering himself around, and managed to get a better grip on the knife. His fingers cramped and ached; his bladder shot pains through his pelvis.

Come on. Almost there. His slit was nearly a foot long now, and the hide had some resilience. If only he weren't running out of room. The further he got from his original hole, the more the hide restricted his movements, and the slower his progress, until his cuts were mere jiggles of the blade.

He backed the blade through the clinging skin, twisted it around, and began cutting upward, working within inches of his chin.

Stopping to rest, he cocked his head. The wolves were silent. Had they gone, or were they watching—waiting?

He flexed his fingers, and resumed working until he once again ran out of space.

How far had he cut? Two feet?

Richard shifted around as far as possible, braced his shoulder, and pushed. Light filled his trap. Laughter bubbled up with excitement, and he pushed again, seeing a good four inches of gap. He pulled his feet up, got the leverage, and shoved with all his might. With a knee for a brace, he grabbed the knife, sawing desperately until he could wiggle around and pry the hide apart with his hands.

Like a worm from a nut, he poked his head out and twisted, half sprawling atop his death trap.

He staggered to his feet and stared around. The wolves

were there, fifteen of them, no more than thirty yards away and watching with wary amber eyes. The buffalo had been gnawed to bloody bones. They'd ransacked his meat pack, chewed the antelope hide to ribbons, and the gut pile was gone.

Richard attended to his bladder, laughing and chortling to himself as he stared up at the slanting sun so low in the southwest. He'd been trapped in there for almost an entire day! The wind had brought warmth, enough so that the sun's heat could soften the bloody skin atop the hide. Not much, but just enough.

And but for the wolves, I would have slept through it, missed my opportunity.

Richard relaced his pants and picked up his rifle and possibles. He stared at the buffalo hide where the snow had drifted around it. It looked like a pastry dough folded in half, hardly the terrible trap that he'd just escaped. But if the wind hadn't come, and the cold hadn't broken . . . He shivered at the thought.

"By God, I'll never do that again." He turned to the wolves, who'd backed ever farther away. "Sorry, coons. I'm not your meat this time—but it looks like you've had a fill of mine." Then he bowed to them. "Thank you for waking me up. I owe you my life."

From their expressive eyes and cocked heads, he could almost believe they understood him. Then one, a small gray one, wheeled and trotted over the rise, bushy tail bobbing. One by one, the others followed, some casting final glances back at him.

Richard stepped across to the carcass, and used his bent knife to chisel meat scraps from the bones. Measuring the length of afternoon light, he went about the task of twisting up sagebrush, and dipped into his little tin of charred grass. With the strike-a-light, he started a fire and collected snow in the tin cup.

The idea of eating meat with wolf spit on it caused only a moment's hesitation before he chopped it up and put it in his pot to boil.

As darkness fell, he pried the slit hide apart with his rifle barrel and crawled into his cocoon. This time he'd sleep warm, and be able to escape the next morning.

◈

"What's you brooding so, fo', Travis? It ain't like you." Baptiste inspected him with curious eyes, the long stem of his pipe clamped in his teeth.

They slouched against the willow backrests in Two White Elk's lodge, a crackling fire in the hearth. Two White Elk's wives were playing a game of tickle with the children. The old woman sat in her place before the lodge door, studiously sewing a pair of moccasins and humming a song under her breath.

"Wal, who else would it be like? If'n I'm a-doing it, it otta be like me." Travis snorted, his cold pipe cradled in his hands. He rolled the stem back and forth in his fingers, staring into the stained bowl, then relented. "I keep wondering, is all. Hell, I shoulda sent Dick back on Atkinson's boats. That coon'd be ter Saint Loowee by now."

Baptiste stretched a buckskin-clad leg toward the fire and shrugged. "Cain't tell. A man does what he does. So, why're you stuck on Dick when you could be crucifying yourself fo' all the rest, too?"

"The rest of us, we knew what we was signing on fer. They's old hands, every one of 'em. Dick, why he was just a Doodle, and it was plain dumb luck got him inta this fix."

Baptiste leaned back on the robe-covered backrest and sucked on his pipe, then let two streamers of blue smoke

twine out of his nostrils. "You give him a chance, Travis. Let him choose. He figgered to stick it out with us. And by that time, he know'd the risks. Reckon if'n he's gone beaver, he done made that choice hisself."

"Hell! I made it fer him. Sure, I told him ter go, and then I looked him in the eye with that look I got, the one that says, If'n ye don't choose right, yer shit. And Dick never wanted no one to think he's shit."

"And what makes you think he's gone beaver? Hell, maybe he holed up somewhere and rode her out."

Travis pinned Baptiste with a hard eye.

"All right." Baptiste scratched his ear. "Believe what you wants. But figger this. He might have been a pilgrim to start with, but he had some fine larning on the way upriver. Now, shore 'nuff, that coon had some queer ideas, but he had a plumb smart head on his shoulders. He larned quick, he did. Took to it like a fish to water when he warn't locked up in nonsense thoughts."

"Yep. That he did. I just wish ter hell I'd sent him back on Atkinson's boats."

"You couldn't, and you knows it. Travis, life gives men a chance if'n they'll take it. I took it, and so far I'm prime beaver. Dick took it, and he made his own way. So far as I recollect, ain't nobody told him it would be poseys and fat cow. Ain't nothing fo' certain, Travis. Not fo' you, me, nor any other coon. So Dick's gone under? By God, Travis, he lived afore he did."

"That he did."

"Ain't that what it's all about?"

"Yep."

"And yor going up to find Willow come spring?"

"Uh-huh."

"Wal, I reckon I might's well ride along. Keep you from moping when yor eyes otta be peeled."

"Did I ever tell ye that yer a sassy nigger?"

"Reckon so." Baptiste paused. "I got other news."

"What might that be?"

"Ashley's gonna have him a rendezvous."

"A what?"

"A rendezvous. Remember all them packs of beaver he took downriver?"

"I ain't likely ter fergit."

Baptiste leaned forward, a keen light in his eye. He tapped the buffalo robe with his finger to make his point. "Wal, he's a gonna use all that beaver to buy supplies. Powder, shot, foofawraw, traps, all the things a coon needs."

"That ain't news, Baptiste."

"Depends on how you reads sign. He ain't taking it to no post. He ain't putting it on no boat. Instead, he's outfitting a brigade. Gonna bring it all on hossback to someplace down on the Green River, or some such. He's got trappers out all over the mountains a-trapping plews. They's all coming together next summer fo' a rendezvous, and Ashley's gonna trade fo' fur. Like bringing a whole post *to* the mountains, coon. And this child's gonna be there with a load of fur. No boats, no river . . . and no Saint Loowee. Just trade at the Rendezvous, and Ashley worries 'bout getting the shitaree back."

"It'll never work."

"I figger it will, and I'm fixing to ride down there and see fo' myself. So, let's go see Willow and her kin, trade what we can in the meantime fo' plews, and give it a throw."

"Yer sassy all right!" But deep down, he could see how the whole thing might work. Assuming Ashley made it across fifteen hundred miles of hostile plains.

"Shit! I ain't nothing you didn't teach me to be. And God alone knows what you taught Dick." Baptiste gave him a smile. "So I ain't burying him till I knows better."

"But I'll say ye ain't betting on seeing him again either, lessen it's as a pile of bones."

❖

High Wolf's people held the *Ap'ene Kar,* the midwinter Father Dance, on the flat caprock above the camp. Here, on the edge of the canyon wall, the horizon was visible, as well as the entire vault of the sky.

Wood had been carried in, the firepit cleaned out, and a new fire laid. Beside it, the sacred cedar tree had been placed. Rock Hare, Many Elk, and High Wolf had gone out four days before, ritually scouted, and finally "killed" the tree. Then they'd offered prayers to the tree's soul, chopped it down, and dragged it to the dance ring where, propped on all sides, it now stood.

The people had tramped the snow flat, and the few scrubby sagebrush that might impede the dance had been twisted out. Then, just as the sun slid behind the western horizon, the fire had been lit.

Now the people stood in a circle around the roaring fire. They were dressed warmly in sheephide coats, thick moccasins, and warm buffalo- or elk-hide robes. Excitement gleamed in the eyes of the children, and men and women held

hands. The last glow of sunset had left the western horizon. Stars packed the crystal-cold night sky. All eyes had turned to the horizon where a new glow could be seen across the ragged snow-mantled peaks.

As the first sliver of moon cleared the peaks, Eagle Trapper thumped a long drumstick on the big round drum. The instrument was as wide as a man's arm, the head stretched tightly over the wooden cylinder and bound with rawhide strips. The resonant bass carried in the night, echoing from the canyon below. Even the stars seemed to dance to the beat. The dark trees absorbed the rhythm as it mingled with their snow-packed branches.

With the first throbbing beats of the drum, fires of memory stirred in Willow's souls. Excitement tingled within her. How long had it been since she'd danced the *Ap'ene Kar?* The bonfire devoured thick sections of pine that popped and showered sparks into the frigid night.

Each day during the last moon, High Wolf had climbed to the high places to watch the sun rise across the peaks, and marked off another notch on a slim section of elk antler he carried. Over the years, he had learned which peaks were illuminated on which days. So he counted his notches to be sure of the days in case clouds obscured the horizon on this, the most holy of days.

High Wolf always held the *Ap'ene Kar* on the winter sol-

stice. Some *puhagans* held the Father Dance during full
moon, but High Wolf's vision had told him to hold it during
the longest night of the year.

Willow stood in the circle with the rest, swaying in time
with the music as Eagle Trapper beat the drum and sang the
greeting song. From the shadowed depths of the forest came
High Wolf, dressed in his finest clothing, his face painted in
white and black streaks. He carried sage bundles in his
hands, and shook them, like rattles, in time to the drum.
With each shake he sent the plant's healing Power in all
directions. The people parted and he walked into the center
of the dance ring. There, he lifted his head to the cold night
sky. For a moment, he seemed to reflect on the cold heavens.
Then he opened his mouth and began to sing the familiar old
songs.

Willow and the rest closed the ring, men alternating with
women. Her feet seemed to move of their own accord to the
rhythm of the song. Around her, the people lifted their faces,
sang and danced in the shuffling step of the Father Dance.
Across the ring, Red Squirrel was holding little Pika's hand
as the child frowned and tried to imitate his mother's dance
step.

That was how I learned. Willow smiled at the thought,
remembering White Alder's gentle hands on her shoulders.
It seemed like forever since that day. Willow sang louder,
her heart at peace—as if time had ceased for this one glorious moment.

In the beginning times, Coyote had been instrumental in
the first Father Dance. He and the Hoodwinked Dancers had
used it to banish disease and bring good health.

Tonight, it would do that for her people, and—High Wolf
said—for the new year that would begin tomorrow at dawn.
As the dancers circled in their shuffling step, High Wolf
danced out from the center to shake his sage bundles at each
person in turn, bathing them with the sacred essence. Wil-

low's heart thrilled when her turn came. How long had it been since High Wolf had purified her and driven away the little evils that clung to her?

Too long. For that brief moment, Willow surrendered herself to the swaying beat of the drum, her souls twining up into the night sky as if to join the very stars. A lightness filled her breast, as if her own fire burned there and drove away the darkness.

High Wolf stopped the greeting song with a high yip. For a long moment the mountains were bathed in silence. Then Eagle Trapper hammered the drum, and High Wolf began the Water Song. As his lilting voice rose and fell, the dancers picked up the beat and resumed their endless circling.

Willow might have left her body, floating in the cold air, seeing the world through happy eyes. *Home . . . I'm home again. The world is set right once more.*

She hadn't realized how much she'd needed this healing, how parts of her souls had become disjointed. In a world turned strange and uncertain, she could forget her worries and follow the familiar patterns of a life nearly forgotten.

I am one with my people. For the dance went back to the beginning of time. She stood now as each of her ancestors had once stood. In her *mugwa*'s eye, she could see them, feel them, dancing as she danced. The continuity reassured her. Time might not have been. No past or future, only the eternal now of the dance, of her souls swaying with the music.

One by one, they sang and danced the Water Songs, and High Wolf told the stories about Coyote after the Creation. How he found the first women, desired them, and how he had to break the teeth out of their vaginas before he could copulate with them to create people.

For once, Willow didn't smile at the story. Was that why Richard feared laying with her?

Even in the silliest of stories, you will find truth if you look hard enough. She shook her head. *So, where does the truth hide in Richard's stories about Adam, Eve, and Mary?*

High Wolf paused beside her, staring at her from the corners of his eyes. "Such a look, *peti*. Tell me, which demon are you wrestling with this time? And on a night of healing, too."

She lifted an eyebrow. "I'm sorry, Father. I was thinking about stories, and how, even if you don't believe they happened the way they were told, they still teach you things. Even now, at my age, I find something new in them."

He gestured for her to accompany him and walked away from the circle of rapt listeners. Many Elk had taken the place beside the fire and the sacred cedar tree, and was now telling the story about Cottontail Rabbit shooting the sun. In the leaping firelight, the faces of the children beamed with excitement, while the adults smiled knowingly at each other.

High Wolf led her to the edge of the canyon, and stopped, staring over the chasm to the southern horizon, masked as it was by a black picket of conifers. "Willow, tell me what a person is."

She tugged her buffalo robe tight against the chill, and followed his gaze across the distance. "A person? Um . . . a human. Two-legged. A man."

"Not a woman?"

"Maybe a woman."

"Not a child?"

"Maybe."

"An elder?"

"Yes, of course."

"An infant?"

She shrugged. "Sometimes . . . after it's lived long enough to gain a *mugwa*."

"Then, all these things—infant, child, youngster, man, woman, elder—are persons?"

"Of course. What's the meaning of this?"

"To teach you something, *peti*. That everything changes."

"I see."

"Do you?"

She exhaled wearily, watching her white breath rise. "Our perception of truth, of life, of the world itself, changes as we do, *appi*."

"Nothing is fixed, Willow. Not the stars, the sun, the mountains, or the very rock in *Tam Segobia*'s breast. Tell me, did you expect to find everything pegged in place, unchanging?"

"No, never, but I know someone who does."

"Then he is a fool."

"No, Father. Not a fool. He's just been taught wrong, that's all. Like a child who has been told all of his life that water runs uphill, he can't quite allow himself to believe what he sees with his own eyes. When I left, it was driving him mad."

"The measure of anyone, Willow, is how they adjust to the changes in the world. How about you, Daughter? Have you learned to live with the changes?"

She took a deep breath, searching her souls. "I don't know, Father. Sometimes, like tonight, I am so happy to be home, sharing with my people. Then, at other times, I want to beat Rock Hare over the head with a stick, or slap Lodgepole for some of the stupid things she says about White men, or *Ku'chendikani*. She's stupid, Father, like a grouse who thinks she's seen through a hawk's eyes."

He nodded thoughtfully, eyes still on the sky. "The girl who left here five summers ago to marry a *Ku'chendikani* was very different from the woman who has returned to me. You are still my *peti,* Willow. But now, I sometimes wonder who and what you are. I look at you, and sometimes, as tonight at the dance, I see the girl I knew. And other times, like now, I hear a stranger talking with my daughter's voice."

"I've changed, Father."

"And I must try to adapt. But so must you, Willow. You fit here, among our people—but at the same time, you do not. What are you going to do, Willow? What are your plans?"

She lowered her head, shrugging her frustration. "I don't know, *appi.* I only know that I've changed. You're right about that. Sometimes . . . it's as if I were a leaf on the wind. Blowing, swirling, tossed here and there—and never knowing where I'm going to land."

High Wolf pursed his lips, eyes narrowed in the darkness. "I would not say such things aloud, girl. Those are not words to reassure those who already wonder at your strangeness."

"Am I strange, Father?"

He nodded. "I think you are a leaf on the wind—and it's blowing in a terrible storm. I just hope that it is not going to harm my people."

The joy, sparked within her during the Father Dance, had faded, like the last embers of a dying fire. Each time she reached out to grasp a piece of her past, it seemed to dissolve like mud held underwater in a tightly gripped fist.

And soon, Willow, there will be nothing left to squeeze.

TWENTY-TWO

◆

Nature is to be viewed as a system of stages, in which one stage necessarily arises from the other and is the truth closest to the other from which it results, though not in such a way that the one would naturally generate the other, but rather in the inner idea which constitutes the domain of nature. It has been an awkward concept in older as well as more recent philosophies of nature to see the progression and transition of one natural form and sphere into another as an external, actual process which is generally relegated to the darkness of the past.

This externality is precisely characteristic of nature: differences are allowed to disintegrate and to appear as existences indifferent to each other; and the dialectical concept, which leads the stages further, is the interior which emerges only in the spirit.

—Georg Friedrich Wilhelm Hegel,
The Philosophy of Nature

How great is the gulf between man and beast? When the extraneous trappings are stripped away, how different is the human being from his kin in the animal world? Is it a matter of size, or fur, or the shape of a foot? To those who know the rudiments of survival in a state of nature, they might say that the difference lies in dreams.

Richard huddled in a mat of moldy brown cottonwood, currant, and willow leaves that had blown into this protected warren last fall. His knees tucked tightly to his chest. He slept like a rabbit in a hole, just another creature hidden in the thermal shelter of the snow-cloaked brush under the embankment. Dried threads of last year's grass waved before his face, swaying with each breath. Muted sounds died in his throat. His closed eyes darted under their lids, seeing the dream with such clarity . . .

I have transcended myself, floating in the air like some sprite, looking down on my flesh from above. I should be awed by this experience, but for the moment, I am too concerned with what I see. How pitiful I look now, how empty and sodden.

My body is sprawled on its back in the snow, my skin alabaster pale and slightly blue. I look into my eyes, frozen open with milky gray exposed behind wide pupils. My limbs jut out like boards and my fingers clutch at nothingness, flesh puffy white. My mouth hangs open—stopped in mid-scream. I peer inside, and see ice around the stiff tongue, crystals sparkling on my teeth, all illuminated by the snow filling the throat.

Could this frozen meat really be me? I pull back, refusing to accept what my swimming senses tell me is true.

I must see this as something else, not really Richard Hamilton. I can't help but stare at this abandoned corpse as if it were a stranger's. The oak-hard flesh has taken on a pearlescent hue that contrasts with the frosted nipples. Crystalline ice glints in the curly chest hair, like little diamonds in the blue light.

He's cold, so damnably cold! I can imagine the bones inside, frost-cracked and splintered, with pink marrow puffed out. His heart must have stopped in midbeat, the blood solidified as it jetted. Cold . . . cold . . . forever.

I am fascinated by the gruesome expression of death, and the corpse's stark contrast to the purity of the snow. *Richard . . . Richard Hamilton . . . how did you come to this? Is this all that's left of life? Why, Richard? What's the purpose?*

At that moment I sense the change. I glance around, seeing nothing but hazy white fog around me. The cold presses down like a weight, bitter and powerful.

The silence is broken by the faintest groaning sound—like ice being crushed between molars. Fear tickles within me, for the sound comes from the hollow just below the ribs. I see movement, and a crack ruptures the bluish-white skin. It opens slowly, pulling the stomach apart, running down toward the ice-encrusted navel and widening to expose an inky blackness.

I try to back away from the midnight eternity, wishing only to turn and flee. Instead, like a fly trapped in honey, I can only stare at the gaping tear in the corpse's belly. That is when I discern the faintest of white sparks—a tiny twinkling that becomes a minute star gleaming in the blackness.

With unexpected suddenness, the star splinters, glasslike shards of light exploding in all directions, and there, in its place, a slender stem of green rises out of the darkness. The shoot grows with slim grace, a single spear of verdant life that ascends from my dead body's gaping black gut to unfold tendrils. From them leaves uncurl, vibrantly alive. At the tip, a bulb forms, swells, and finally bursts forth in a bloodred rose that pulses with color and fragrance . . .

Richard jerked awake in his leaf-filled hollow under the bank. Afterimages of the dream burned in his memory—as intense as if he'd really seen it. How macabre! He snorted in irritation and threw his stiff hide to one side. Powdery snow cascaded from the branches and onto his warm flesh.

Gasping, he ducked out from under the overhanging brush and into the creek bottom. From a leaden sky, snow fell in tiny crystals, adding to the endless white.

"God help me." Richard rubbed his face with blood-stiff

mittens and shook his head. The warm spell had lasted no more than three days. Time enough for him to travel southward to this tree-sheltered valley with its plentiful supply of wood. The day before he'd shot another buffalo, a young cow, and skinned it for the hide. He'd managed to cobble together a warmer outfit.

As his dream self had just done, he glanced down. His living body was encased in wrappings. Cut so carefully, each piece had been tied on—hair-side in—like a medieval knight's armor. He'd crafted thicker moccasins from the heavy hide that covered the buffalo's forehead, and stuffed them with more buffalo hair for warmth. He'd added another layer to the hat Travis had made for him.

"I look like an overstuffed doll." Bits of dried and frozen flesh still clung to the hide, having resisted his attempts to scrape it clean.

He kicked his sleeping robe out of the leaf mat he'd piled atop it, and considered the thing. In the beginning, he'd worn it, hair-side in, like a cloak, and, green hide as it was, it had frozen into his general shape, conforming to his head and shoulders. The result was something like wearing a part-time tent—heavy, immobilizing, but warm.

In the ash of last night's fire, he found embers and stoked them to life. On the flames, he cooked a mixture of liver, heart, and backstrap for breakfast. Snow obscured the mountains to the west, but he knew pretty much where he was. The highest peaks were behind him now. But progress had slowed. As he traveled south, the terrain grew ever rougher.

"I'm all right," he told himself. "So long as I have a rifle, a knife, and can make fire, I'm all right." His lips pursed as he watched the meat cooking.

Travel had become a ritual. Walk too fast, and the cold air burned his lungs, or he started to sweat. Go too slow, and the chill ate into him. Each night he found a sheltered spot to make camp, start his fire, dry his moccasins, and cook his meat. He'd char grass stems to replace the ones in his tinderbox, and eat his meal. Shelters were cobbled together from brush, or dug into the leaf mat under fallen trees—anything that broke the wind and provided a little extra warmth.

Sleep itself had become an art. Some inner sense woke him if his feet became too cold, and he'd stamp them back to life. God preserve him if they froze. He'd heard enough stories in New England about blackened flesh and amputation.

"Just be careful," he told himself over and over. "Don't take any chances. You're still alive. Though no one would believe it. Hell, I don't myself."

The important things were fire, knife, and rifle. With those, he was beginning to believe he could survive anything.

He broke camp, walked over to the stream, and studied it. Most of the channel was frozen over, snow glaring on the ice.

"Take no chances." He repeated the phrase—his mantra of survival—as he turned westward, seeking a safe ford. If he got wet now, in cold like this, he could freeze before he could make a fire.

By midday he had found his crossing—a place where a gravel bar had braided the channel—and crossed the shallows without mishap. But which river? The Powder?

The clouds were breaking overhead as he trudged up out of the valley. The eternal Big Horns lay to his right. A giant slab, like one of God's shoulders, rose into the cloud-shrouded heights, and behind it, the mountain's slope lessened.

"Travis said the slope wasn't as bad the further south you went." Well, he'd have to go a way farther before he could scale the likes of that.

Richard followed the ridges; there the climb was easier, and the snow not as deep.

Snow had become as normal to him as sunlight or wind. He lived in a world of powdery white, wary of its glare at midday, frightened of its hidden danger. At times the wind kicked up, and the world vanished in a hurricane haze that staggered him. It blew fine granules of snow into every nook and cranny, seeking to rob him of warmth and life.

On sunny days he cast a shadow that brought insane laughter bubbling into his throat. What he saw resembled no human shape, but something headless and monstrously humpbacked, wrapped in stiff hides and tied together with brittle tendons and stripped ligament.

"'Just like ourselves,' Socrates said, 'For, first of all tell me this: What do you think such people would have seen of themselves and each other except their shadows?'" Richard finally understood, too, the incredible richness of Plato's Allegory of the Cave.

And what sort of being is this monster cast upon the snow? He'd look at his shadow and ask, "What is your nature, dark being? A repository of the highest human thoughts, or a terrible beast that slays to eat, gorging himself on raw flesh and hot blood? A killer who stalks the wilderness?"

Then he'd bark an insane laugh, crying out, "By God, *both!*" And in that lay the ultimate irony. "What," he'd croak, "is the measure of man?" And "Know thyself!" More maniacal laughter would follow.

One hill led to another, each a little steeper than the last. On the heights, he'd brace himself against the cutting wind and study the route ahead. Sometimes he had to work over sections of rimrock—chipped and worn from time—before picking his way around tumbled boulders that had fallen from above.

The slopes were brush-covered, and occasionally, he jumped herds of deer that bounded off, only to stop and stare at him, their huge ears spread wide.

"Where am I going?" he asked himself. "Boston. That's where. Home." Wasn't it odd that the house on Beacon Street conjured only the most contented of memories?

If I were there now, I would sit by the fire and have Jeffry bring me a hot pot of tea. I'd stretch out in the big chair, roast my feet, and sip tea as I read. I'd be so warm. So wonderfully warm.

Phillip's fleshy face, the bulbous nose and sagging jowls, filled his mind. His father's hawkish gray eyes looked at him, curiously wounded.

"Don't never go agin' yer pap," Baptiste spoke from the past. *"Don't matter what's ahind you. I reckon it can be patched. If'n not, I reckon I'll trade you, 'cause you got a pap and I don't."*

"Can we do that, Father?" Richard asked Phillip's spectral image. He placed Phillip in a chair across the fire, and the old man frowned as he fingered his watch chain. *"Perhaps, Richard. I should never have sent you west, risked your life that way."*

"And had you never sent me, I would never have known what an arrogant fool I was, Father."

"We have both been fools, Son. You in your way, and I in mine."

"I never understood, Father. How lonely you've been. Blaming yourself for Mother's death. Never able to free yourself of the guilt." Richard blinked against the glare on the snow. What a terrible weight a woman could place upon a man's soul. And if he arrived at the *Dukurika* camp, and Willow wasn't waiting? "If she, too, lies dead out here someplace, can I ever forgive myself?" He shook his head. "Oh, Father, I do understand. God help me, give me another chance. Make Willow be waiting for me, alive, healthy. Let me see her again. With all my soul, I beg you."

Frowning with concentration, he pictured her face: There was her wry smile; her long black hair; and the sparkle in her eyes. Closing his eyes, he sniffed at the cold air, seeking her scent. He remembered the way she'd felt in his arms that day he'd killed Packrat. Her breast had brushed his arm so softly and caused a quaking of his soul.

"Remember how she pressed against me when we lay side by side in the water at the Grand Detour?" How he'd thrilled as his penis slipped along the curve of her hip. "Why didn't I mate with you when I had the chance, Willow?"

And if he found her again? *I'll wrap you in my arms and drown myself in you, Willow. I'll lie under the robes beside you, and hug you close. I'll look into your eyes forever, and marvel at their secrets.*

He dared not anticipate the other images—fleeting sensations of the soul as he kissed her, ran his hands over her full breasts, and shivered as her warm skin touched his. When he had such thoughts, especially at night, his erection no longer embarrassed him.

And why is that? Tell me, Richard. What's changed in you, in your principles?

"Reality," he'd whisper. "Somewhere along the way, the blinders fell off and I became a man."

And if you lie with her? How will you live the rest of your life? With Willow?

"No. I don't belong here. My place—my world—is in Boston."

And if you return and marry Laura? Will you look into her blue eyes and tell your wife that you've had carnal intercourse with an Indian woman? Or will you live with a secret?

"I don't know."

Then why is it suddenly morally acceptable to fuck Heals Like A Willow?

"It's not fucking. One doesn't 'fuck' the woman one loves."

Ah. Love, you say? Tell me, philosopher, what is love? Eros? Agape? Or Philos?

He balled a fist, looking at his inquisitive shadow. "Oh, don't try and twist me up in all the philosophical investigations of love! I know the arguments from Abelard to Zeno, just as surely as you do."

But what is it that you feel for Willow?

"Something of the soul, a sharing, a longing for her to be close, to share my life, to share hers."

But only for the moment.

"You know reality as well as I do, shadow."

Then you have fallen into the trap of utilitarian ethics. Since when did you become a follower of Bentham? Pleasure is good? What happened to your loyalty to the idealist ethics that you embraced from Kant, Fichte, and Hegel? You are no better than Menon trying to argue virtue with Socrates.

"Damn you! The problem with you—and all your book-bound philosophers—is that you are safe, surrounded by your cities, and laws, and constables." Richard squinted up at the pale white sun that hung low in the west. "Life is more elemental here, shadow monster. You seek Truth?"

Why else do I examine you?

"Truth, my friend, is food, shelter, warmth, companionship, and living to see another sunset. There, damn you. How much more elemental can you get? That's Truth."

You disappoint me, Richard. You used to be better than this.

"You can argue abstracts all you want over ale with other philosophers in safe, cozy Boston. This is the wilderness. The rules are different here."

What did you just say?

"I said the rules are different. We've forgotten what it means to be alive in the real world! Don't you see? Boston, America, Europe, the whole of it is removed from nature, living within the artificial security of the state and all its conventions and institutions. I am a man in love with a woman! What could be more right than that?"

And he paused, reaching the crest of a tilted slope and staring out over a sheer red cliff that dropped nearly two hundred feet to the gentle valley below. It extended north-south, as far as he could see. In the glaring light of sunset, the crimson sandstone blazed like blood.

In the distance, the cliff continued like a monstrous, crested wave of stone—a giant breaker turned to crimson rock. Nowhere did he see a trail down that sheer wall.

"Dear Lord God," he whispered, as if the sight and declaration were both gifts from the divine.

He took a deep breath, studying the land. Far to the south, he could see the dark bulk of yet another mountain, separated from him by an endless sea of choppy ridges. Across the valley, to the west, the sloping flank of the Big Horns rose to meet the afternoon sky. Juniper and pine dotted the long incline, mottled here and there by patches of gray brush and the infinite speckling of sagebrush. Turning, he looked to the north, where a thick bank of gray clouds masked the high peaks. Wispy stringers, the kind made by falling snow, feathered out from the bottom of the storm front.

He'd been so lost in his argument with himself, he'd failed to pay attention to the time, to the building storm in the north. Night would fall soon, and that brooding cloud-bank would roar down from the peaks.

"I think, Richard, that we'd better leave ethical dilemmas for the future and worry about getting off this ridge."

He turned southward, scrambling along the rocky crest of

the cliff. Was it better to drop back down the eastern side to the sage-filled valley? But the wind was coming from the north. He'd find no adequate shelter there, not from a storm like this one fixed to be.

The sun had slanted behind the mountain, casting rays of yellow across the sky in contrast to the blue and purple shadows that loomed ever longer. The bloodred of the sandstone slowly dulled to maroon.

He'd followed the ridge's spine before he found the cleft: A crack as wide as his shoulders had split the forbidding rock like God's meat cleaver. Dirt, tumbled rock, and snow filled the slanting bottom. It appeared to offer a way down the red wall—or did it? What if he made it halfway down and it narrowed?

Richard growled to himself, plagued by indecision. "I can't afford a mistake . . . but then, I can't stay up here."

The light continued to fade as the storm dropped down from the peaks.

"God help me." He lowered himself into the crack, trying to brace himself against the sides. His frozen buffalo-hide cape cramped his movements. He took a moment to shrug out of it and pitch it headlong down the gloomy fissure.

He was being swallowed by solid rock as he dropped into the darkness. Under his feet, stones slipped atop the frozen dirt. The walls narrowed, close as a coffin. *Blessed God, if this leaves me stranded on the cliff, I'm dead.*

With cold stones rasping his shoulders, he shimmied down the precarious slope. The next thing to go were his mittens. He tossed them down the chute. "I'll pick them up at the bottom," he promised. "Better to take the chance of losing one than to fall and break a leg." The Hawken had turned into an impediment.

If only he could pitch the rifle as well. Keeping a grip on the cold Hawken numbed his fingers and slowed his descent. Feeling with his feet, he placed each step carefully on the tumbled rock wedged in the bottom. If only he could use both hands.

"Don't slip, Richard." *And be careful.* He was deep into the crack now, and wedged his elbows to look back. A tightness formed in his throat. The earth had closed around him, cold and unforgiving as a tomb. He closed his eyes, gut sinking. *I've made a terrible mistake!*

If only he didn't have to hang on to the rifle. Bracing himself, he lifted the heavy Hawken and slid it down the back of his shirt, thrusting the muzzle past his belt. The barrel burned cold against his hot skin, and the butt rested along the side of his head, but his hands were free.

Step by careful step, he lowered himself, unwilling to look down. He tested each handhold, cursing the hard wrappings of hide that hindered his movements. Feeling his way through the thick layers of moccasin he prayed each step would hold.

No doubt of it, the crack was narrowing. How far had he come? Fifty feet, seventy? Looking out, he could see the dusky sky growing darker by the second. The rock bore in on him like jaws, crushing his spirit with its ponderous weight.

Swallowing hard against the dryness in his throat, he eased himself down, blocked his foot on a wedged rock, and shifted his weight onto it. Below him, pebbles rattled for what seemed an eternity.

What if this ends in a straight drop? Don't . . . don't think it.

His possibles rasped with each movement. Wind-blown snow had collected here, adding to the treacherous footing. Craning his neck, he could look down between his legs. Perhaps twenty feet below him in the gloom, the crack opened out. But from there it was still a long way to the valley floor, and growing darker by the moment.

He wiped at the fear-sweat that had begun to dampen his face. He took another purchase, only to have his foot slip.

Jamming his arms out, he clawed at the snow, and saved himself at the last minute. The rifle butt hammered the side of his head hard. Clinging to the rock, he trembled, panting.

You've got to move! But terror had locked his muscles. *Come on.* Trapped! Dear God, I'm trapped in the middle of the earth!

The ache in his cold hands finally overcame claustrophobia. Mustering courage, he tried again, kicking a foothold into the snow before slowly shifting his weight. Crabbing around, he lowered himself. His hands throbbed as he clutched the snow. His fingers were turning numb.

"You've got to go, coon. Lose the feeling in your fingers, and you'll slip for sure." Hitching his possibles around, he backed down, and thunked his temple painfully with the gunstock.

Why'd I do this? Better to have taken my chances on top.

Panicked, his clothing scraping the rock on either side, he scrambled another body-length down. The awkward rifle was pulling his shirt out so that cold air stole his warmth. What a terrible place to die, wedged here in cold, eternal shadow.

You're a fool, Richard. A damned fool! He climbed over a rock that choked the crevice, then stole a glance over his shoulder. The crack ended just under his feet—and his heart sank. Runoff from the crevice had worn a narrow channel into bedrock the width of his hand, but to either side the anticipated ledge was nothing more than a bulge in the cliff. Richard carefully rolled over, only to have the rifle butt smack him painfully in the face.

He pulled the gun from his sagging shirt, puffing with exertion, and leaned over to look down. The drop was at least fifteen feet before the ground began to slope. His cape hung in a juniper tree that clung to the scree. Wedging his elbows, he peered into the evening gloom. The first snowflakes came twisting out of the gray sky.

What now? He shivered from the cold, scared stiff by his predicament.

"You can do this, Richard." *Fifteen feet isn't so bad.* And the slope would give. He picked a place that didn't look as if it had too many rocks. He closed his eyes, unable to will himself to jump. His guts had that watery feel, and every nerve prickled. All he had to do was step out, and fall—but some stubborn instinct deep in his brain panicked and refused.

Richard, you must. He resettled his possibles, gripped his rifle tight . . . and jumped. For a split second, his stomach rose and tingled. Air rushed past him.

The impact stunned him, and he rolled. End over end, he tumbled down the frozen scree. Lights flashed in his eyes when he hit his head. With each thumping jolt, his breath huffed. A small juniper stopped him, and for a second he gasped, dazed, aware of the pain that shot up his legs. He lay there, terrified of what he'd done to himself. Then, choking with fear, he felt his ankles, moved his feet. Hands, arms, everything all right. Nothing broken.

He practically cried from relief, picking himself up to make sure he could walk despite the aches. The strap on his possibles had broken, and he limped back up the slope to pick up the spilled strike-a-light, tinder tin, awls, and other necessities. He'd lost his rifle when he hit, and found it half-buried in snow. He grabbed it up, and started to run his fingers over the wood when his heart stopped in his chest. For the moment, all he could do was stare. The cock, made from cast iron, had been snapped off clean above the mounting screw, the metal edge pale and jagged.

He dropped to his knees, searching the scuffed snow with trembling fingers until he found the piece, flint still cradled in the leather-lined jaws.

Fear gave way to futile anger, and then to the horrible realization: The broken piece couldn't be fixed.

In mute defeat, he stood there as the snow settled soundlessly around him.

TWENTY-THREE

◈

> Now then, I want to give the proof at once to you as my judges, why I think it likely that one who has spent his life in philosophy should be confident when he is going to die.... The fact is, those who undertake philosophy correctly are simply and solely practicing dying, practicing death, all the time, but nobody sees it. If this is true, then it would surely be unreasonable that they should earnestly do this and nothing else all their lives, yet when death comes they should object to what they had been so earnestly practicing.
>
> —Plato, *Phaedo*

Breath puffing, Willow ran forward, feinted, and jammed her hip into Red Squirrel's with enough momentum to throw Red Squirrel off balance. In that instant, Willow caught the double-ball with her shinny stick and batted it in White Alder's direction.

With a growl, Red Squirrel launched herself at White Alder, her shinny stick held out like a baton.

They played on the snow-covered flats above camp, just back from the rimrock. The game was double-ball shinny, played on a field marked out over the distance of a bow-shot. The ball was sewn out of leather, stuffed with buffalo hair, and looked something like two wasp wings tied in the center. To win, one group of women had to fling the double-ball across the opponent's goal line.

Good Root had stolen the double-ball away from White Alder. Willow dashed forward. Snow flew as she blocked Lodgepole, twisted away, and scrimmaged with Good Root for the double-ball. Willow managed to snag it, and started forward, only to have Red Squirrel butt her from one side. As Willow staggered, Red Squirrel whooped and flicked the double-ball off Willow's stick to Good Root.

Huffing and gasping, the women ran in pursuit. Despite her aching lungs, Willow thrilled with the competition. It had been years since she'd played, but many of her old skills weren't forgotten. She caught up with Good Root, used a side-armed strike, and knocked the double-ball from Good Root's stick.

Sweet Grease cut in, snagged the ball with her stick, and flipped it across the trampled snow back to White Alder, regaining the ground they'd just lost to Good Root.

Willow sprinted back the way she'd come, angling to one side and shouting to her mother. White Alder saw, made the pass, and Willow artfully caught the ball. From some last reserves, she tucked a shoulder, bulled Red Squirrel out of the way, and sent the double-ball bouncing across the boundary.

Yipping like coyote pups, her team came together—jumping, ripping the air with their shinny sticks, and pounding each other on the back. Lodgepole, Red Squirrel, Good Root, and their girls muttered among themselves, as they bent over and panted for breath.

"Good game," White Alder wheezed. Then she too bent over, panting for breath.

Willow grinned at her teammates, flushed with excitement. She wiped the sweat from her forehead, and sucked air into her starved lungs.

"You haven't lost any speed," Sweet Grease told her, patting Willow's shoulder. "We haven't beaten Lodgepole in how long? Three winters?"

"Three at least," White Alder agreed, straightening and flipping one of her braids over her shoulder. "It feels . . . well, real good. Good indeed, after all these years of listening to those old grouse clucking to each other." White Alder winked. "Good to have you back, *peti.*"

Willow nodded, and started toward the sweat lodge, plodding through the deep snow on trembling legs. In the chill air, she'd begun to cool down just as they reached the domed lodge back within the trees. There, a fire burned like a sooty eye in the packed snow. Hot stones were piled in the middle of the blaze. The little girls, too young to play with the adults, had kept the fire hot.

"That Willow," Lodgepole grumbled as she walked up, "she's half wildcat."

"All wildcat," Red Squirrel complained as she pulled her dress over her head. Steam curled up from her sweaty skin. She winced, and massaged her left breast. She glanced at Willow, and grinned. "That was a hard elbow you hit me with. If Rock Hare gets too friendly tonight, I might just make him sleep in the snow."

"He doesn't need to play with your breasts to do what he's going to want to do," Sweet Grease said as she pulled her own dress off. "But then, given where I'm going to have bruises tomorrow, Black Marten might just have to sleep in the snow with Rock Hare."

Willow chuckled as she shucked out of her own dress and ducked into the dark interior of the sweat lodge. The winning team got the rear of the lodge; the losers had to tend the hot rocks and steam.

Willow sat cross-legged beside her mother as the glowing rocks were carried in on smoking branches. Good Root recited the prayer for health, called for the blessing of the steam, and closed the flap to seal them into the darkness. Water trickled musically, then steam exploded in a violent hissing.

Willow closed her eyes, sighing as the steam clouded around her, soothing her tired muscles and aches, cleansing her body and souls. White Alder began to sing the sweat-lodge song, and one by one the women joined her, offering thanks to Power for the healing steam. When the song finished, they sat in silence until White Alder said, "Them two men from Black Storm's camp finally left today."

"Good," Red Squirrel muttered. "They were nothing more than walking appetites. It seems we've had to feed half the men in the mountains this winter."

"They always bring something with them," Sweet Grease reminded.

Willow ground her teeth, grateful for the darkness. The pressure had been growing. Nothing overt, just the ever more pointed references about the suitors who came, looked her over, and made their oblique offers. She let each one know that she wasn't interested.

Why, Willow? She clamped her eyes shut, fists knotted at her sides as the sweat beaded and rolled down her skin.

"That Three Moons," Lodgepole said, referring to one of the men who'd left that morning. "If I were younger, why, I don't think I'd complain if he crawled into my robes some night. Quite the handsome sort, and did you see that smile? And the way his eyes twinkled when he told a joke?"

"I did." Good Root sighed. "And besides that, I caught a glimpse of him one morning. His *we'an* would take a two-handed hold."

"Is that all that you look for in a man?" White Alder growled.

Lodgepole chuckled. "Of course it is. Why do you think they called her Good Root? She's wanted one all of her life—and ended up married to Eagle Trapper!"

"His root is just fine," Good Root snapped back. "Five children prove it!"

Willow cocked her jaw, grateful for the lull as more water was sprinkled on the rocks. The curling steam thickened around her, stifling and hot. Water was trickling down her face, dripping from her nose, salty on her lips.

He *was* a handsome man. No, more than that, Three Moons would be the answer to any *Dukurika* woman's dreams. Tall and attractive, broad of shoulder and strong of arm, he'd been more than genial, he'd delighted everyone. His smile brought warmth, and the amiable gleam in his eyes had promised things most men would never have thought of: attention, helpfulness, and tender hugs on difficult days. Even White Hail had warmed to him, and they'd become fast friends. Willow had been surprised to discover that White Hail had told Three Moons stories about her husband, about the sort of man he'd been.

Three Moons's charm had even conquered High Wolf. More than once they'd sat up late at night discussing the stars, and the ways of animals, Three Moons asking the old *puhagan* serious questions.

Would it have hurt to have been polite to him? Willow wrinkled her nose, letting her shoulders sag.

"Enough," Lodgepole finally stated, and threw the flap back. "I'm going to rub myself dry and go see what those lazy men have come back with. No doubt they've killed something big and want to brag about it."

"They don't want to brag about it to us," Red Squirrel declared as she slipped out into the afternoon. "They just want us to cook it for them."

"Sure they do," Good Root agreed as she ducked outside. "But they want us to praise them and their skill at the same time. It makes them feel better. And for some reason, men need all the praise they can get."

One by one the women stepped outside to scrub their hot skin with crusted snow. Sweet Grease settled the flap after she left. Only White Alder and Willow remained in the hot darkness. White Alder leaned forward and sprinkled more water on the hot rocks. As the steam worked its magic on their sweltering bodies, the voices of the others became ever fainter as they walked back to camp.

"I need a little longer in the steam," White Alder said. "It's good for my bones. My joints and muscles don't hurt as bad the next day."

"You amaze me," Willow said gently. "My mother, and you look and act more like an older sister."

"Huh! Well, you should feel me on the inside, girl."

"I did, once, long ago. I can't remember what it was like."

"Being in the womb? I don't think anyone does. It must be pleasant. I think that's why childbirth is always so difficult. Who wants to leave that nice warm place and come outside into the cold?"

Willow rubbed her hands over her arms to slick the water off. "Is that what people think I'm doing? Staying in the womb? Do they think I don't want to come out?"

"You tell me, girl. What do you want, Willow? I have to admit, I think I fell in love with Three Moons myself. At least a little. And I thought no man would touch my soul while your father was around."

"I liked him, Mother. He'd have made a wonderful husband."

"But not for you?"

She shook her head, and realized her mother couldn't see her in the darkness.

Perhaps White Alder didn't need to. She said, "You have not slept well these last days. Last night, I listened to you.

You were talking in a language I have never heard. None of the words made sense."

In English, Willow said: "Did the words I spoke sound like this? Is this the tongue you heard me speak?"

"What was that?"

"Did I sound like that in my sleep?"

"Maybe. I think so. Maybe not. It's all grouse squawking to me."

"Richard. I expect I was talking to him."

"Ritshard. You said that word. He's the White man, isn't he?" After a long silence, White Alder asked, "What happened to you, girl? Can I help you heal this thing inside you? Can your father?"

"No, Mother. It's not a thing to be healed. A *puhagan* can't blow it away with his fan, or suck it out with a hollow tube."

"Your father says you've been between worlds." In the darkness, Willow could feel her mother lean close, her voice a mere whisper. "He says that Power is growing inside you."

"Why do you lower your voice?"

"Because not all people have your father's tolerance. Is that what it is, Willow?"

"I don't know, Mother. Can't I just be left alone?"

White Alder leaned back to her place, silent again. At last she said, "You're a grown woman, Willow. I think you know how people are by now. What do you think? Will they leave you alone? You, a strong, healthy young woman?"

Willow clamped her eyes shut. *You've got to make a decision. Soon. Would life with Three Moons be so bad?*

If only Richard didn't haunt her dreams. She could see him so clearly, hear him as if he were just beyond the dream soul's reach.

"It's the future that bothers me, Mother. But, yes, I'll make my decision soon. One way . . . or another."

The morning dawned brittle with cold. Richard awoke, horrible dreams spinning away in his mind. He uncurled from his robe and looked out at the world from under the base of a spreading juniper tree. He'd taken refuge there, sheltered from the wind and blowing snow by the shaggy branches.

He turned his attention to the cliff he'd fallen down the night before. Snow made patterns, delicate as lace, on the shadowed red rock. Eight inches of white covered the ground, creating a wilderness of beauty. Hard to think that death stalked those frigid blue shadows.

Still unwilling to believe his disaster, Richard picked up the frosted rifle. He closed his eyes, wishing with all his might—and opened them. The snapped metal still mocked him with its gleaming gray.

Every time he looked at the broken gun, his stomach turned.

He unwrapped himself from the frozen folds of his buffalo robe and winced at bruises suffered in the fall. He shook the powdery snow from his robe and shivered as white breath curled around him. His legs were tender, strained from their hard landing. He had a scab on the side of his head from the fall.

Heavy, deafening silence pressed down, unmarred by so much as a whisper of breeze or the flutter of a leaf. Nothing moved in this world of white. The land seemed to be wait-ing, watching.

Cold, desperately cold.

Richard slung his possibles over his shoulder—the strap knotted where it had broken—and tried to pull his frozen robe tighter. He pulled a piece of meat from his pack, shaved some with his bent knife, and popped it into his mouth. Chewing the tough stuff aggravated the bruise on his head. His rifle leaned against a branch. Leave it behind?

No, he resolved. *Maybe somewhere, somehow, I can fix it. With what, fool?*

Nevertheless, he hefted the Hawken, feeling its weight. He'd clubbed men to death with it. Perhaps he could . . . He snorted at his ridiculous thoughts. As if a buffalo was going to walk up and let him club it to death!

Snow crunched under his moccasins as he turned, looked back at the red wall's sheer heights, amazed he'd survived the descent. If, in reality, he had. Breaking the rifle might have killed him as dead as a broken neck.

He rubbed frost from his frozen beard and looked up at the mountains. Where did he go to find Willow? Damnation, her people could be anywhere.

Well, let's head south a little farther, and skirt the worst of the terrain. He limped steadfastly forward, snow protest-ing underfoot. He was a mote—a single brown speck in an eternity of white. When he looked back, only footprints remained as mute evidence of his passing.

Alone. He clamped his jaw. Nothing could prepare a man for this feeling of futility. *Don't give in to it, Richard. If you do, you'll sink down in the snow and die here.*

The Hawken felt heavier, dead weight. Tears came to his snow-burned eyes. The rifle had come to be more than a piece of machinery, more like a friend who had buoyed, comforted, and fed him.

He clung to the cold steel and endured the relentless reality of punching one step after another through the dragging snow.

One step after another. The massive weight of the wilderness bore down on him, fit to smother his fragile spark of life.

At midday, he cut deer tracks, stared absently at them, and plodded onward. Here a mouse had dotted the white as it scurried from one protective patch of sage to another. Later he saw where a coyote had trotted across the wide valley, but no sound broke the oppressive silence.

That night, Richard camped in a hollow created by an outcrop of rocks. After kicking the snow out of it, he built a small fire and squatted over it, nursing the flames with bits of sagebrush. As he dried his moccasins, he worshiped the fire. Extending his hands to the heat, he closed his eyes and let the warm smoke rise around him to bathe his face. If he lost his strike-a-light, he'd have nothing. Reaching into his meat pack, his fingers groped around the bottom.

Frowning, he lifted the pack and looked inside. Only bloody leather remained. *When did I eat it all? No, there's got to be more.* The slow realization dawned that he'd eaten all day as he walked. Pulling a piece of meat, slicing it, and chewing to keep his strength up, to keep his belly full.

"Richard, you didn't think." Instead, he'd drowned in self-pity over the broken gun.

Mistakes, too many mistakes. A smart man wouldn't have tried to descend the red wall. He'd have taken a chance on the storm, then gone around, looked for a safe way.

Too late . . . too late for everything.

Hollow-eyed, he stared at the glowing embers. *What now,*

Richard? He swallowed hard and took a deep breath before answering, "Can't give up. I'll make do."

No, you won't. You'll die out here. Die . . . all alone. He jammed a balled fist into his mouth and clamped his eyes shut, desperate to keep from sobbing.

That night, horrible dreams haunted his sleep:

Willow lay dead, scalped and gutted. Maggots wiggled in the wounds that mutilated her body. When he touched her, the skin broke like a bruised tomato's, and putrid fluid ran out to stain the grass.

Phillip Hamilton knelt in his office, back bowed as he wept for his dead son. Guilt, so much guilt for one old man to bear. Finally he looked up, unseeing, into Richard's eyes and lifted that long-forgotten pistol to his temple.

"No! Father, no! I'm alive! You hear—alive!"

No shot accompanied the discharge of the pistol. Only a curl of flame and smoke that destroyed the image.

From the angry mists, a face formed: old One-Eye, the Sioux *wechashawakan.* He was watching Richard through that gaping socket where his right eye had been.

Wolves and coyotes circled in the darkness, watching, waiting, while the old Sioux medicine man laughed . . .

"I do not know if you will live, White man, but you will find your answers out here in the snow."

Richard cried out, "Tell me!"

But the image of the old medicine man blurred into a huge wolf, black as midnight. *"The answers are in this world, and the next—if you are brave enough to seek them."*

"I am," Richard cried. "I won't give up. I won't!"

He started awake just before dawn. In the distance, the wolves were howling, their unearthly cries twining with his dreams until that world and this were indistinct.

He shivered in the cold, his thoughts in a Gordian knot. How did a man tell the difference between dream and reality? And, if he couldn't, did it really matter in the end? Was one reality more important than the other?

Richard shivered and stirred the embers in his fire. For long moments, he huddled over the flames, head cradled in his hands. The dreams had grown so powerful, the images frighteningly real. "Am I losing my sanity?"

His forced laughter sounded oddly harsh to his ears. Then, shaking it off, he scooped a handful of snow, picked up his possibles, and started along the slope. He climbed as he went, seeking a high point to look for . . . what? Game? Smoke from someone's fire?

"I won't give up. I won't." One step after another. One, two, one, two . . . He dropped into the litany, plagued only by guilt and his nagging belly. Thoughts of tender roast beef, of steaming turkey, freshly baked bread, of chocolate and mint, swirled like fog through his mind.

"A chicken," he mused. "Roasted in a big pan, basted with butter, with onions and leeks, and lots of salt and pepper."

At midday the sun still hung low in the south, no matter how hard he wished it to rise higher and warmer. Step by step, he slogged through the snow; each swing of his feet nibbled at his reserves.

Food. I must find food.

He plucked leaves from sagebrush, and chewed them, then made a face as his mouth filled with the bitter flavor. Within minutes his head began to ache, and he spat to clear his mouth. He'd heard somewhere that headache was the first sign of poisoning. Who'd told him that? Henri, Baptiste?

Rosehips? He squinted across the sage-studded hills, seeing nothing that resembled brush. When he crossed the drainages—mocked by rabbit tracks—the serviceberry bushes and chokecherry stems were bare.

Food, I'll die without it.

But where would he find it? How long could he continue?

That night he used a fallen cottonwood in a brushy creek bottom for shelter; its branches fed his fire. Hollow-eyed, he watched the flames, and relived that last meal in Boston. *I skipped breakfast. Told Father that the sooner it was over, the better. I didn't eat. If I could just lick that plate now, I'd be eternally grateful.*

Phillip had watched him with grim eyes.

If I could do it again, Father, it would be so different.

The next morning he started out, shivering and lightheaded. One step after another, he pushed on doggedly, slipping back and forth from a snow-cold waste to a hot plain where he followed Travis Hartman's wavering form in pursuit of horses.

Blinking, he found himself sprawled face-down in the snow, shivering. Had he fallen? Sitting up, he gazed around, trying to determine where he was. Flickers of light, like dancing sparks, filled his eyes.

Lightheaded . . . I'm dizzy. "Come on, Richard. Stand up. Let's go." He struggled to his feet, using the rifle barrel for a support. Another racking attack of shivers left him shaken and wobbly—and completely frightened by his weakness. He wiggled his toes. They felt cold, nothing like the misty warmth he'd heard tell of.

"Dear Lord God, don't let my feet freeze." He steeled his resolve and walked on, setting a distant knob as his pilot. He frowned, aware of the way the world turned watery. He couldn't think.

He squeezed his eyes shut for a moment and took stock.

He was traversing a long slope, sage-dotted, and rising up to the west. He'd climbed high enough to have a good view of the land. To the east, endless ridges of bent and folded rock dropped away to the hazy Powder River basin. Southward lay the distant black peaks of yet another mountain range. The sky was so clear, azure to the north, unmarred by clouds. All about him, diamond sparkles reflected the weak winter sunlight.

He shifted the Hawken, hearing gurgling noises from his hunger-cramped stomach. He'd been climbing for two days now, crabbing his way along the slopes. Just how high were these long hills?

Richard sighed, feeling slightly faint and nauseous. Resolutely, he tramped forward, watching his feet drive through the white crust to leave sharp-edged holes.

Food, Richard. You must eat, or die. In the distance a herd of antelope watched, ears pricked. Finally a nervous doe flashed her rump patch and they vanished, spurts of snow flying from their feet.

The sun was dipping low in the southwest, evening close, and the night's unbearable cold with it. *Tomorrow, I won't wake up. Too many of my reserves are gone.*

He'd walked past the dead elk. Then stopped to stare at it. It had been an old bull. The guts had been eaten out by the wolves and coyotes; strips of hide hung from gnawed bones. White smears of raven droppings streaked the antlers. It stank to high heaven.

"Meat's meat, coon," Travis's voice reminded sardonically. Moose or mouse? Wasn't that what Travis had said?

No, not carrion. Richard pinched his nose at the smell, and started on, making three steps . . . four . . . then he halted, blinking hard against the sensation of floating. *"Meat's meat, coon."*

"How do I want to die? It won't be hard. I'll just lay down in the robe. Close my eyes. I've been shivering for months now. And then a person gets to feeling warm . . . warm and sleepy."

Willow's face hovered in the wavering afternoon light. Such a beautiful woman, her eyes glowing, her smile lighting for him. How terrible never to see her again.

He hung his head, turned around, and walked back to the elk. "Meat's meat," he muttered hoarsely to himself. "Come spring breakup, Mandan eat drowned buffalo that float downriver under the ice. Eat it with spoons."

He used the rifle barrel to beat snow off the bones, and pulled his knife, looking for whatever the scavengers might have left. Around the putrid carcass, the trampled snow was covered with a powdering of loose hair ripped from what was left of the hide.

He screwed up his face and shook his head. "I can't do this. I can't." He started to turn away when the voice said, *You'll live, Richard.*

He swallowed hard, the empty knot of his stomach, the weak shivers in his limbs, reminding him of his weakness.

He took a deep breath and studied the knife in his hand. The blade was irrevocably bent. In weary defeat, he dropped to his knees in the snow and began hacking strips from the exposed pelvis and back ribs.

Next, he cut the ligaments around the joints and twisted the big leg bones loose before finally severing the tendons. One by one he laid them on the hard-packed snow, and with the rifle barrel, cracked them open.

Splintered bones all around him, Richard ate. He started slowly, placing a lump of marrow far back on his tongue, choking it down fast. Then another.

As to the taste, well, he'd eaten cheeses that smelled worse, and maybe tasted almost the same. Yes, that was it. People paid handsomely to provide a taste like this for the finest social gatherings.

He ate more, filling his mind with Boston, hearing the sounds of a minuet being played in the background.

From the skull he extracted the brains; and the tongue—surrounded by bone—hadn't been eaten. He didn't think as he chiseled his way through the frozen hide, more clumps of hair coming off in patches to blow about. The neck meat was still there, and he hacked it from the vertebrae and thick waxy tendons.

He looked up suddenly, wary of the coming night. He stood, his pack full again. Strength and warmth returned as the cheese-tasting marrow began to digest.

"I'll live," he vowed. "For one more day, I'll live." Now all that remained was to find a sheltered spot. Start a fire, and boil the prizes he'd chopped off the dead elk.

TWENTY-FOUR

Certainly the older accepted teleological perspective provided the basis for the relation to the concept, and in the same way, the relation to the spirit, but it focused only on the external purposes and observed the spirit as if it were intertwined with finite and natural purposes. Because of the vapidity of such discrete purposes, purposes for which natural things were shown to be useful, the teleological perspective has been discredited for demonstrating the wisdom of God. The idea that natural things are useful carries the implicit truth that these things are not in and for themselves an absolute goal; nevertheless it cannot determine whether such things are defective and inadequate. For this determination it must be postulated that the immanent moment of its idea, which brings about its transiency and transition into another existence, produces at the same time a transformation into a higher concept.

—Georg Friedrich Wilhelm Hegel,
The Philosophy of Nature

The dream was so vivid that Heals Like A Willow jerked upright from her robes, gasping. She placed a hand to her throat, and stared around in the shelter's darkness. Only small patches of starlight could be seen through the gaps where the leather didn't fit tightly.

Willow swallowed hard, whispering, "Richard? Where are you?"

"What is this?" High Wolf asked from the darkness. "Is everything all right?"

"Someone cried out," White Alder growled, sitting up.

Willow sighed. "Go back to sleep. It was only me. I had a dream, that's all."

People settled into their bedding, mumbling to themselves. In the darkness, Willow could feel their unease. She was making them as uncomfortable as they were making her.

Willow pulled her loose hair around, twisting it into a rope before rubbing the sleep from her eyes. She slipped a sheephide cape over herself and tucked it tightly around her shoulders before she stood and stepped out through the flap.

The night air made her skin prickle as she watched the twinkling stars. A shiver unrelated to the cold ran through her.

She heard the flap pulled back again as High Wolf ducked out to stand beside her. He wore his coat, and had a cape over his shoulders. He, too, stared up at the stars. With each exhale, his frosty breath puffed like a buffalo bull's.

"I'm all right," Willow said gently. "Go back to sleep."

"Dreams are strange things, Daughter. The *puha* flows inside you. I think you know this."

"I know," she said wearily. "It's all right, *appi*. It wasn't a Power dream. Just a . . . well, about the White man."

"Ritshard."

She nodded.

"He has *puha* flowing within him?"

"He has something," she admitted. "I told you about looking into the eye of his soul."

"When these things happen, souls join. You were aware of this?"

She kicked at the snow. "I was proud, Father. I had destroyed the Pawnee, broken his will to live. To use Power that way, it just came upon me. I was worried about the White men, not sure what to think, and I didn't trust them. I thought I would show Richard my Power, make him and the rest of the White men wary so they wouldn't hurt me. And, in my pride, I looked into the eye of his soul."

"And he looked back." High Wolf scratched the back of his neck. "Most men would fear a woman seeing into their soul."

"He didn't."

"And you didn't fear when he looked into yours?"

"No, Father. But something changed. I started to love him. I understood from the beginning that he and I were different. I was wary, careful, but he filled my heart. When I couldn't stand it any longer, I left."

"I see. And what are these dreams?"

She closed her eyes. "I hear his voice calling to me, telling me things I can't quite understand. I see him, cold and alone out in the snow. I sense his fear, his hunger, how desperate he is."

"He is calling you. These things happen, but mostly to men." He glanced at her from the corner of his eye, then at the shelter, lowering his voice. "It would make many people nervous to hear such things from a woman's lips."

"And you?"

He shook his head slowly. "I know your heart, Heals Like A Willow. *Puha* can be used for anything you wish. You used it against the Pawnee, but he should have expected you to protect yourself. I don't worry about you. I know the shape and color of your souls, and I trust the way you use *puha*—although I don't tell everyone about it. People talk, and the next thing you know, someone is shouting, 'Witchcraft!' You are not a witch, Daughter. You don't yearn for the things a witch does."

"What about the dreams, Father?"

"What else do you see in the dreams?"

"That he needs me desperately."

"He is with his boat, up where the *Pia'ogwe* empties into the *Gete'ogwe*—"

"No. Father, my *navuzieip* has traveled to him and seen him. He is alone—in the snow. I see red sandstone . . . a rim . . ." She frowned. "Like the Red Wall. Something terrible happened at the Red Wall."

"You're sure? Could it be *Ainkahonobita ogwebi,* the Red Canyon?"

She shook her head. "No, *appi.* It is the Red Wall. I was just there with White Hail. I know the place." She shook her head in confusion. "Or did I dream it because I was just there? What is true and what is a trick?"

"Dreams are strange that way. They *can* trick you, Willow. You have to ask yourself, was it a Power dream? Did you really see the place?"

She nodded. "Yes. And more. I saw Richard dying. I saw

him freezing to death, and his *mugwa* had come loose, already on its way to the Land of the Dead."

"Then he is dead?"

"No. Because my *navuzieip* was there, Father. Trying to save him. That was when I awakened everyone in the tent. It terrified me because I knew his soul was gone—just like my husband's was. And I couldn't save him. I had to just sit there in the snow, and hold him while he died in my arms. Powerless . . . so horribly powerless. I couldn't stand that again, *appi*."

He cleared his throat, staring at the stars. Willow listened to the distant hooting of a great horned owl, followed by the faint ululations of a tribe of coyotes high on the rim.

"You could go after him," High Wolf finally said. "If you are a true *puhagan*, you could send your own soul to the Land of the Dead to bring this Ritshard back."

"And if I am not a true *puhagan*, Father? What then? You know what will happen to me."

He sucked his lips. "It is not something to undertake lightly, Heals Like A Willow. If you are not *puhagan*, your *mugwa* will not return from the Land of the Dead. *Peti*, you'll be as dead as the White man. The journey to the Land of the Dead is full of traps." He glanced nervously at the shelter behind him. "I will tell you what I know, though, Wolf help me, I may be telling you how to destroy yourself."

"I am listening, *appi*." She faced him bravely, ready to hear what no woman her age should know.

The wind came from the west: a terrible wind, the likes of which Richard had never imagined. By itself, it would have been miserable, ripping the slightest warmth away, chilling the skin until it iced, freezing tears on eyelashes. But this wind scoured the ground of snow and drove it head-long. Howling wreaths of white roared across the land, turning the very air opaque.

Richard huddled in the lee of a sandstone outcrop, his buffalo robe pulled tight, and waited in dumb misery as the wind screamed like banshees and the world disappeared into a racing wall of solid white. Through the gap in his robe, he could see swirling dervishes, ripples and eddies in the air.

It's like a river . . . a river of snow.

He tucked himself tighter into his robe, huddled down as far as he could behind the rocks, and watched the fine crystals settle around him like baker's flour. Here, at least, he was out of the main blast. Travel was unthinkable. A man wouldn't be able to see five feet in front of him. The universe had suddenly gone colorless, worse than any of the fogs he'd ever seen in Boston.

He shook his head, dog-weary and cold. Perdition might have been this way: torn by winds so violent only the devil could have conjured them; bone-splitting cold, so intense that a man's spit crackled when it hit the ground; scrubby trees, rock formations spawned of a demon's dreams, and prickly pear to plague every step. Starvation and disaster loomed on every hand.

He bowed his head. *I was a gentleman.* Or had that just been an oddly alien dream?

What are you now, Richard?

In numb misery he shivered and hugged himself. "I'm nothing. I'm no different than a vulture . . . or even a worm. I've lived off rotten meat—a scavenger of corrupted flesh." He snorted his derision. "And I was a gentleman?"

Another howling gust tore past, and more twirls of snow dusted down to cake him.

"I tried so hard to keep something of myself. I tried to cling to something from the past, some bit of who I was."

He'd tried, and failed. Everything was stripped clean, like the scavenged bones he gnawed with his teeth. All that Richard Hamilton had been was gone. Only a little thread of life remained.

The worst part is, you're losing that as well.

He shifted, working his toes from habit rather than worry about frostbite. It was too late for his face; his cheeks were peeling, and the skin on his nose had turned black. The single most damning sign of doom was his stamina. Where once he'd been able to walk all day, now he could only take one hundred steps, maybe less, before he had to stop and rest.

The snow and cold had sapped his warmth, his endurance, and was playing with his very sanity.

That morning, before the wind rose, he'd found another carcass, a buffalo—not so long dead as the elk, but rancid nevertheless. And from it he'd plundered bones, withered hump meat, and scraps from the neck. The scavengers didn't seem as drawn to the neck meat. Like men, they knew the best parts were the guts, rich in energy and nutrients.

I'm losing, Willow. Bit by bit, I'm feeling my life slip away. A man can't live on bones. He just can't.

The wind howled, deafening, like the laughter of God.

A pink morning sky shadowed silhouettes of pine and fir that surrounded the little meadow. The vigorous winds had died during the night, and in their wake, the air had turned from frigid to medium cold.

White Hail lifted Willow's pack and gave her an inquiring glance as he walked to her horse. The half-cocked jaw gave him a permanently skeptical look. That gleam of wild youth was gone from his eyes, replaced by sober reflection. The finely tailored sheephide clothing he now wore was decorated with *Dukurika* patterns. He helped Heals Like A Willow center her pack on the brown mare's rump. As she tied the straps, he worked the flat of his hand under the leather to ensure that nothing would gouge the horse's kidneys.

The horses had spent their time here, on this little meadow in the timber. Aspen poles had been lashed across trees to block the trails leading in and out of the clearing. A spring that fed summer's lush grass also provided winter water for the horses. It had trickled across the flats in scalloped ice sheets. What had once been a pristine meadow had now been trampled with horse tracks and dotted by black mounds of manure.

As they packed the horses, White Hail said, "A man with any sense would knock you alongside the head, tie you up, and call in the *puhagan* to drive the insanity out of your souls. Only when you came to your senses would a wise man let you loose."

Willow's deft fingers tied the last of the knots. "If a man was really wise, he'd leave me alone. If he was a little less wise, he'd sneak up behind me, because if I have any warning, I'll fight like a cornered bobcat. Ask the Arikara. Now, if he'd tied me up, he'd be a fool to let me loose because I'd kill him the instant he did. So a wise man wouldn't try any such thing."

"Willow, I wasn't—"

"And to discuss your final point, you may call the *puhagan*. Among the *Dukurika* there is none so widely acclaimed as High Wolf . . . who, you will remember, is the man who carried my pack up here."

White Hail huffed his weary resignation. "Sometimes I wonder what my brother saw in you."

"Haven't I warned you, White Hail?"

"Time after time. The fact is, I'm starting to believe you." He grunted, checking knots. "Half the time I think you're more like a man than a woman."

"Don't be silly, *teci*."

"The only person silly is you, *papinkwihi*, chasing out after a White man who called from your dreams. He's supposed to be north of the mountains on the river, yet you say he's south. How do you expect to find him even if he is?"

"I'll know."

"Willow, it's the middle of the winter. Yes, it's warmed up, for now. It always does. Usually just before a terrible storm blows in. We could have another bitterly cold spell." He glanced up at the bright morning sky, hands raised. "Why am I telling her this? She knows how foolish she's being."

Willow turned, glaring hotly. "You *don't* need to come. Go back to the camp and stay warm. Rock Hare and Eagle Trapper are going hunting tomorrow, they'd like your company. Well enough, I might add, that they keep hinting I ought to marry you and keep you here."

"Well, why don't you? And forget this crazy trip out into the cold. The White man will take care of himself. They have their own Power."

"Ah! Now you're as much an expert on White men as Lodgepole is?" Willow scrambled up on her mare, grabbing up the reins as the animal sidestepped and tossed her head, clearly irritated at the idea of going anywhere. White Hail growled to himself, then pulled himself onto his *Pa'kiani* mount. He checked his pack one last time and kicked his horse around.

He threw a glance over his shoulder, and sighed as the trees closed in behind him to block the little meadow from view. He had to admit, life among the *Dukurika* had its advantages. If only Willow weren't so headstrong.

"Well," he told himself, "we'll go ride around, sleep in the snow, and suffer wind chill for a couple of weeks. After that, maybe she'll give up this madness and decide that I'm the right man for her. By spring, she'll have forgotten she ever knew a White man."

Indeed, it might just work out that way.

❖

On the heels of the vicious winds had come warm weather. "Warm," Richard discovered, was a truly relative term. That bone-brutal cold might have been blown eastward, but come nighttime a man had better have a warm fire and a shelter of some sort.

Another danger came with warm weather. On the southern exposures, the snow softened into daytime slush. His moccasins became soaked, chilling his feet; the untanned leather he had tied on like patchwork shrank and hardened each time it was dried over the fire.

The gnawing ache in his belly remained constant. Day by

day, he limped onward, not traveling so much as searching for food.

With building excitement he found a rabbit's hole. After trimming a juniper stick, he waited half of the day crouched in the soggy snow over the cottontail's hole, knowing the rabbit had to come out sometime.

The world had funneled into this one spot on earth. His mind went blank, concentration centered on the reality of his prey. Nothing existed but the eternal now. A strange peace filled him. The universe contained only himself and the rabbit. As he tightened his grip on the stick, his teetering imagination played and replayed the way he'd strike—and when he did, the triumph would shake the world.

You'll get one chance, Richard.

When it happened, he almost missed it. It took a moment to realize that the rabbit's nose had appeared, wrinkling and twitching. The cottontail hopped a body-length from the hole.

Now! His muscles had grown so slack and cold that he wobbled as he struck. The blow glanced off the rabbit's back. But it stunned the animal enough that he could leap on it. He'd never known that a rabbit could scream until the moment when he grabbed its head and twisted to break its neck.

Fingers clumsy and shaking, he slit the soft white belly open, heedless that it still quivered, and licked up the blood. He swallowed the liver, heart, and kidneys on the spot—strength, enough to get him back to his little camp, stoke his fire, and roast the rest. The stomach and intestines, along with the lungs, he chopped up and boiled with twig ends he'd seen deer eating. It made a thin and bitter stew.

That night, surrounded by lonely darkness, he gazed

vacantly at his fire, chewing slowly to savor every bite of the tender meat. His stomach was full for the first time in three days.

The fire popped and spat. Canted from sticks, his moccasin outers hung, steaming. The rabbit hide was propped in the smoke to dry and be stuffed inside his left moccasin as a liner. Richard cocked his head, staring up at the clear night with its quarter moon. Coyotes yipped in chorus to the distant howl of the buffalo wolves.

"You've got nothing on me, coyotes," he whispered softly. "I got the rabbit today. Maybe tomorrow I can be like wolf and bring down an elk." With his teeth, he cracked the last of the rabbit bones to suck the marrow.

He flipped the bone splinters into the coals and lost himself in the flames. Faces formed in the leaping light: Professor Ames, George Peterson, Thomas Hanson, and Will Templeton.

"Remember . . . remember those times? Do you, old friends? The wonderful ale. Lamb chops . . . roast joints of beef. Fish chowders and hot biscuits, freshly baked, steaming with melted butter. And the conversations—remember them? Anselm and Aquinas, Plato and Epictetus. Locke, Hume, and Fichte. Descartes, Voltaire, and Rousseau. What is the nature of man? Of ethics and morality? Of the individual in the state? Is existence phenomenology, or is phenomenology existence?"

He chuckled. "I killed a rabbit today. Thus, today, existence is rabbit. Three days ago, it was a dead buffalo. I didn't get much from it. Coyotes were there first, and then the ravens. That day, existence was buffalo bones, and what I could scrape out of them. Marrow mostly. You see, it's a funny thing, but that's all that's left when the coyotes and wolves get there first. They chew the ends off the ribs . . . things they can break. But I'm a man. I have a rifle barrel, and I can break the bones. I . . . am a man . . . human. I have a rifle."

He rubbed his painfully frostbitten nose. Pulling off his filthy mittens, he reshuffled his robes, digging deep along his side to scratch a sudden burning itch. In the process, he couldn't help but smell himself. Yep. Bad, all right. Funny how a person could take his own stink when another's would make him want to throw up.

"Do you remember"—he followed up another itch— "hot, steaming baths poured into the wash tub? Remember those?" He grinned as he recalled the whitewashed wooden walls, the warm Franklin stove with its kettles blowing pale steam from the spouts, and Jeffry, so stiff and proper as he poured the water by lamplight and lectured on the way a gentleman should dress.

"You've no idea what I'd give for a bath like that." Richard pulled his hides closed, scowling in irritation. *Hell, I know better than to scratch an itch. Scratch one, and another starts. Scratch it, and the next thing you know, you're scratching like a street cur. One scratch into a universe of scratching—what a teleology!*

He squinted up at the stars, forgetting the burning itches that now peppered his skin. "Damn lice." Every now and then he caught one in his beard and pinched it to death. "It'll warm up sometime. I'll find water. Take a bath then."

I won't quit. I'll survive this, Willow. I promise. And to hell with you, Coyote!

For a moment, he thought he heard voices—and was on the verge of standing to stare into the darkness when they vanished. "Philosophy lecture," he added, suddenly placing the sound. "A year ago fall . . . on Enlightenment." He smiled and tossed a stick onto the embers. "The real is the rational."

"Can you prove that, Mr. Hamilton?" Professor Ames asked, a slight frown on his forehead, glasses pinched to his nose.

"I . . . I don't know, sir. I could once . . . a long time ago."

He stopped, staring owlishly around. *You're seeing things.* Dear Lord God. *And on a full stomach, too.*

He rubbed his cold face, then stretched his hands out to the flickering fire. "Take hold of yourself, Richard. You must, for if you don't, you'll go crazy and die out here."

But why is that so bad? Can you prove *to me that death is that terrible? The cold would be gone. The fear of frostbite, the hunger . . . none of it would concern you.*

"I can't die. Can't. Willow's here, somewhere. And then I've got to get back to Boston. Remember? Find Willow—and go back to Boston."

You have no evidence that death is such a bad thing, Richard. Just a loosening of the soul, and then all this misery will be over. Do you hear? It will all be over. Over . . . forever.

"It would, wouldn't it?" He nodded to himself and picked up his broken rifle, tucking it to his chest. Eyes vacant, he rocked it back and forth, as a mother would her baby.

TWENTY-FIVE

❖

My memory of past errors and perplexities, makes me diffident for the future. The wretched condition, weakness, and disorder of the faculties, I must employ in my enquiries, increase my apprehensions. And the impossibility of amending or correcting these faculties, reduces me almost to despair, and makes me resolve to perish on the barren rock, on which I am at present, rather than venture myself upon that boundless ocean, which runs out into immensity. This sudden view of my danger strikes me with melancholy; and as 'tis usual for that passion, above all others, to indulge itself; I cannot forebear feeding my despair, with all those desponding reflections. . . .

—David Hume, *A Treatise of Human Nature*

Meat Pole and his small band traditionally camped below a sandstone rim on the southern slope of the Powder River Mountains. There, surrounded by giant boulders cracked off the rim, and sheltered by pines and juniper, they were protected from the prevailing winds. From the heights, they could watch the surrounding mountain slopes for elk, sheep, and deer.

A small seep provided enough water for their needs. In the dry sand, and in the gaps under the rock, they stored their winter food in steatite bowls and crude clay pots. Winter meat was cached in the shadows of the rock, where it stayed frozen until needed. Sloping shelters of hide and brush kept their bedding dry.

Willow and White Hail had arrived just before dark. They'd picketed the horses in a hollow under the rim where the animals could paw for grass.

Meat Pole had greeted them cordially. In the wavering yellow light of the fire, his people sat wrapped in their fine robes, excited by the prospect of stories and news of other bands.

Willow remembered Meat Pole from years past, but when had he aged so? And how long had it been since she had last seen him? Four years, five? Perhaps it had been the summer she met her husband. *Or is it just that I have changed so much?*

Meat Pole was the band's leader, or *tekwhani*. Short, squat, and thickset, he looked to be about four tens of years in age. His broad face, prominent cheekbones, and square jaw were classically *Dukurika*. He wore a hide cape made from the shoulders of the white bear, and the claws hung over his chest in a long necklace.

His people wore fine, tailored hides, tanned as soft as a baby's cheek, and decorated with colored quillwork, bone beads, and strips of silken fur taken from otter, fox, and marten.

The band consisted of four men, five women, and a cluster of children. The dog pack slept in curled balls of fur around the camp's periphery.

From the feast they'd been given, Willow decided that Meat Pole's band was faring well through this colder-than-normal winter. Willow and White Hail finally finished their share of the roasted mountain sheep, biscuit-root, and serviceberry pemmican. Each portion had been served in dishes crafted from sheep-horn bosses. They sat beside Meat Pole, in the place of honor. Immediately behind them, the sandstone rim reflected the fire's heat and light. Just over her shoulder she could see the painted figures of mountain sheep, wolves, and elk. The paintings had been done in charcoal, blood, and fat. Some had faded, especially the yellow, red, and purple colors created from flower petals.

Meat Pole leaned back and belched after he lay his horn bowl down for one of the dogs to lick clean. "Thanks to the animals, our bellies are full." He smiled happily and glanced at Willow. "We have heard rumors that you just returned to High Wolf's band."

Willow licked her fingers clean and wiped the grease from her lips with a sleeve. "That is true. And it's quite a story."

"You will make us very happy if you tell it from the beginning to the end."

When Willow had related her journey east, and answered the many questions about the White men, White Hail told of his rescue from the *Pa'kiani* and the trip to High Wolf's camp. Then they had to answer questions about High Wolf, and his band.

Finally Meat Pole lifted an eyebrow, asking, "What brings you here in the middle of winter, Heals Like a Willow? This is not the time to travel. Snow is deep, and hard on horses. It is a time for snowshoes."

At last! Willow crossed her arms, tucking her hands into the folds of her coat. "I have come looking for someone."

Meat Pole nodded, cocked his head, and said, "Ask. Perhaps we know this person?"

She smiled briefly. "I doubt it, honored *Tekwahni*. I am looking for a White man who is lost somewhere around here."

Willow held her breath, hardly daring to hope. People whispered back and forth, glancing curiously at her.

"I have not heard of a White man." Meat Pole paused thoughtfully. "He has a horse? Would we have heard his thunder-weapon? I have heard that White men only hunt with guns."

"I don't know if he has a horse. I would think he had a gun."

Meat Pole frowned, then looked at young Spotted Falcon, who sat beside his wife, Green Shoot, a woman of Willow's age. "The only unusual thing we know of is what Spotted Falcon saw several days ago."

Was this finally it? Willow turned her attention to the young man.

Spotted Falcon shifted uncomfortably. "I was hunting to the south, along the long ridges. The elk winter there, and sometimes the buffalo. We did not need meat, but I thought I would go see anyway. You know how it is."

"And what did you see?" White Hail asked, nodding solicitously.

Spotted Falcon glanced away, obviously uneasy. "They were tracks . . . and I only saw them from a distance. From a higher ridge. To have gone down, I would have had to cross a deep drift, and then climb it again on the way back."

Willow shot a glance at the piled snowshoes that leaned against the rocks beside the dog travois frames. A drift would not have slowed Spotted Falcon in the slightest. "Tell me about these tracks."

He scratched his ear, thought for a moment, and said, "Well, they looked like a man's tracks. You know how a man's tracks are different from an animal's?"

"I do." A *Dukurika* hunter like Spotted Falcon would have no trouble reading tracks, even from a distance.

"The strange thing is"—Spotted Falcon now tugged on his ear—"the tracks didn't go in a straight line. You know how a man walks? He goes in a mostly straight line. Men usually know where they are going and walk with a purpose."

"And these tracks didn't?"

"They wandered in and out and around. This . . . this

frightened me. That country down there, *Pandzoavits* lives down there, somewhere. The way these tracks looked . . ."

"I see. You are a wise man." Willow glanced at White Hail, reading his veiled expression. Her excitement was building. Could it be? "But a lost man might make such tracks?"

Spotted Falcon shot a quick glance at Meat Pole and shrugged. "He might. If he wasn't well, or was hurt, he might."

Willow bit her lip, frowning, remembering the visions her *navuzieip* had seen. Richard had called to her in desperation.

"Perhaps tomorrow," she declared, "we will ride down there, look and see."

"And if it was *Pandzoavits?*" Meat Pole asked.

Willow lifted an eyebrow, and looked at White Hail. "This *Ku'chendikani* warrior has obsidian-tipped arrows. He claims to be a great warrior. I'll distract *Pandzoavits,* and White Hail can shoot him in the anus with one of his arrows."

Chuckles broke out among Meat Pole's people. Everyone knew that the anus was the only vulnerable spot on a rock ogre's body.

White Hail only gave her a wooden look.

"You had better be quick, Heals Like A Willow," Meat Pole said. "If *Pandzoavits* catches you with his sticky hands, he'll turn and run. Even a great warrior like White Hail might not get a shot."

White Hail stroked his chin and arched an eyebrow. *"Tekwhani,* I know Heals Like A Willow. I think a rock ogre would have his hands full. He could try and eat her, but I have come to find out that Willow doesn't digest well."

It was only later, when Willow had retired to her blankets,

that White Hail came to crouch over her. He asked, "Do you think these tracks are Ritshard's?"

"I don't know. Maybe. If they are, we will need to hurry."

White Hail bowed his head for a moment. "You know, it's cold tonight."

"Yes, it is."

"I could make you warmer. These people"—he jerked his head toward the shelters—"they think we're together."

She sighed wearily. "What speaks for you, White Hail? Your *we'an,* or your pride?"

"Just once, can't you and I—"

"White Hail, go find your robes and *sleep.*"

He stood slowly. "You will fill my dreams anyway. Is that so different from filling my bed?"

"I can't control your *navuzieip.* If you long for me that desperately, I think it would be best for you to return to Red Calf and soothe your needs." But her last words were wasted on his retreating back.

Richard fell face-first into the snow. Had he tripped over a malicious sagebrush, or just collapsed? He lay for a moment, outstretched, aware of the cold soaking into his body. His arms trembled as he pushed up and sat back, on his knees.

Little yellow lights danced through his vision like fireflies as he looked out over the humped side of the mountain. The slope was dotted here and there by junipers and textured by sagebrush. Rocks, blown smooth by the wind and baked hard and dark by the sun, thrust roughly through the snow.

To the south, past the guardian ranks of ridges, stretched a broad, snowy basin, hilly in places, lumped here and there by tree-cloaked hills. In the west, ragged snow-capped mountains, like teeth in a dog's jaw, jutted into the morning sky. He could make out the intricate details of canyons, rocky slopes, and patches of timber. So clear, yet so distant.

How beautiful it was, mountain and basin softened by pastel blues and pinks cast by the low sun. The land dreamed, spinning images that he could but barely catch. *I can hear it, now. The clutter is gone. All of the thoughts drained away. I've lost so much of me that I'm empty. Only the land is left. It fills the universe.*

He used his Hawken as a crutch, pulled himself stubbornly to his feet, and teetered there on the awkward tripod.

Weak. When did I get so weak? Since the rabbit, he'd had nothing but boiled twigs and stripped pine bark to eat. Three days? Frowning, he couldn't remember.

Why do you try, Richard? The struggle is pointless. You've nowhere to go. For days you've been wandering around these foothills. Sometimes east, sometimes west, afraid to climb because you know the snow is deeper up there and you haven't the strength to wade through it.

"I just need food," he insisted dully. "If I could kill something . . ."

Like the deer this morning? The ones who stopped to stare—fearless of the man with the broken rifle?

"Not them . . . maybe some others."

Throw your rifle away, Richard. It's just weight, sapping your energy. And you have so little to spare.

"No. I can't. So long as I have a rifle I'm a man. Do you hear me? *A man!*"

He staggered, mouth hanging open. Reaching up with a trembling hand, he rubbed his face, barely aware of the flaking skin, the hollow cheeks and sunken eyes. "A man," he rasped in final defiance, and grunted as he wobbled onward, the rifle acting as his trusty support.

Vision had become a tricky thing, wavering, shifting, sometimes glassy. At midday like this, colors, mostly red or yellow, flickered at the edge of his sight. Sometimes people hid in them. Professor Ames, Laura, or Will Templeton. Often it was his father, trying desperately to tell him something.

Willow came to him frequently, usually in dreams. Like a succubus, she'd wrap herself around him, incredibly warm and soft. He'd bask in her glory, drawing strength from her body and soul. Rising, they would dance around and around in the streets of Boston while smiling people clapped and quartets played the latest compositions from Vienna, Berlin, Salzburg, and Paris.

"Dance, Willow!" he cried hoarsely as he wove awkwardly through the sage. "Dance with me tonight."

He fell again, and struggled to rise.

Where are you going, Richard?

Damn that voice! It spoke out of the very air. More than once he had caught himself blinking up into the sky, trying to catch the culprit.

"I'm going . . . that's all. Going to Willow—as if it's any concern of yours." He began to shiver again, waiting until the spell passed before chancing the next step.

"Damn the shakes. They take so much out of a man."

You're losing, Richard. The race is nearly run. Stop, now. Rest a while.

He managed to make it to a rock outcrop on the spine of a wind-blown ridge, and settled there. In the sunlight, his back propped against the lichen-covered stone, he stared dully down the long slope of the hillside he'd been traversing. A golden eagle hung on the air currents, washed by the wind. How stately, majestic in the ease with which it flew, barely moving a wing.

When I die, I'm going to fly like that. Sail on the winds, eastward, ever eastward, across the Missouri, then across the Mississippi, and over the forests and up the clear Ohio. Then I'll soar north along the Allegheny and eastwards, over the granite-domed mountains, across the Berkshires, and into Boston. There, you will find me, Father. A huge, dark hunter, perched spectrally on your window.

He hung his head, half in dream. The chilled breeze bobbed the sparse grasses poking through the crusted snow. The sun's warmth caressed him, stroking the weariness within his starved muscles, sending him deeper into the dream, into Willow's arms to twirl around and around. They skipped off rocks and sage. Spiraled over endless heights like the eagle as they embraced each other and rose through the clouds.

Richard stared into her eyes, falling into their depths the way a pebble sinks into a bottomless pool. Her soul wrapped around his, soothing and healing. *Willow . . . oh, Willow, how I've come to love you.*

He jerked upright, blinking, surprised at how little

remained of the day. Cold was creeping into the air, its defiant tendrils ignoring the sun's slanting rays.

Fire. I've got to make fire. He tried to stand, and couldn't. Instead, he crawled out like a baby to strip branches from the sagebrush. When he pulled his tinder from its tin and tried to hold his strike-a-light, his arms trembled. It took many tries before he struck a spark, and bent down to blow it to life.

One by one, he fed grass stems, then sagebrush twigs until his fire crackled. Ritually, he charred tinder for his strike-a-light and packed it safely in his tin box.

With resignation, he pulled his knife and began slicing up the empty hide bag he'd used to pack his meat. If nothing else, the caked blood would give him something, and the hide—gluey when boiled—might stick his soul to his body for one more day.

And if you do not find food tomorrow? What then? Eat the rest of your clothing?

As he placed his pitiful stew on the flames to boil, he nodded acceptance.

Let yourself go, Richard. As it is, you can barely walk. But dead, your soul will soar free.

How good it sounded. Free! Able to sail up to God, and demand answers for all the myriad questions that plagued him. A solution to the doubts that infested his mind.

You don't need to linger, Richard. Just take the tip of the knife and open a vein. It won't hurt.

He made a face, trying to focus his blurry eyes. Pulling back the edge of his mitten, he looked at his wrist, grimy with dirt and old blood. The knife lay cool and heavy in his right hand. It felt oddly vivid in contrast to the rest of the world, which had grown so hazy.

It wouldn't hurt. Not like the beatings he'd taken. Hard to think that up until François waylaid him, a barked shin or pinched finger was the worst pain he'd ever experienced.

He took one last rubbery gaze around his little camp—a feeble way of saying goodbye to the things that made up his world. The possibles, the broken Hawken, his smelly, stiff buffalo robe.

He shook his head and squinted. A pair of eyes gleamed in the darkness, reflecting the fire's glow.

"What do you want, Coyote? Ready to take my carcass? Huh? Is that it?"

Coyote the Trickster. The cavorting counterpart to Wolf just after the Creation. Willow had told him the stories. The *wechashawakan* had tried to warn him that night in Wah-Menitu's village. And now the beast waited for him to kill himself. Later, after the fire burned out, Coyote would slip in, his pointed nose quivering as it smelled the blood. Tentatively, he would lick at the frozen edges of the pool, and then deal with the problem of ripping away all those pieces of rock-hard hide tied to Richard's cold body.

"But you ain't getting much, you son of a bitch. My belly's all gone gaunt. Not a lick of fat left for you. Tricked again, Coyote."

Tricked . . . by what? "What was I going to do?"

Going to open a vein, the voice reminded.

Richard nodded absently, the knife forgotten in his hand. He frowned and looked down into the fire. Curls of smoke rose in the playful light.

An image formed in the embers: a face. Whose? The lines solidified into familiar features. Tonight, Travis

watched him from the coals of the fire, all those hideous scars crisscrossing his cheeks and nose. "Travis wouldn't open a vein. He'd just be a tough. Make do. Hell, he'd slither out there and kill that damned coyote. 'Meat's meat,' he'd say."

Richard glanced down at the knife, slowly shook his head, and struggled to slip it back into its sheath. Damn! If he could just control his muscles. Anything but the trembling. He hated the loss of memory, and the weird hallucinations.

"Yer doing fine," Travis insisted from somewhere. "Buck up yer grit, and see to 'er, coon."

"Yes . . . see to her." He stared dully into the flames, then remembered to pull his pot away from the heat. The hide soup was half boiled away. For the moment, he'd just let it cool, and then go get more snow to melt into it.

He fell asleep before he remembered.

The next day, he didn't attempt to travel. Instead, he tottered out for more sagebrush, levering the plants from the ground with his rifle barrel since he didn't have the strength to twist them off their roots. For breakfast he ate the last of his hide bag.

He was blessed by another sunny day.

As it warmed up, Richard sat with his back against the rocks, blinking, trying to remember where he was. How could Professor Ames have found him? He looked up at the white-haired professor, and they talked for a while. But Richard couldn't quite remember about what. And when he turned to ask, the professor was gone, only rocks sitting where he'd been but a moment before.

You're losing your mind, Richard.

No, not losing it. It just floated, hovering there in the silvered air, seeing all around. He smiled at the sensation, distantly aware of his cracked lips.

Night was coming. This time, he didn't care . . .

"I have to admit," Heals Like A Willow said as she rode along, "I don't know why you insisted on coming. You're making your *mugwa* crazy."

White Hail chuckled in his maddening way. "Someone with sense had to accompany you. It's the middle of winter. A time for sitting by fires and telling stories." He gestured toward the west and the hazy cloudbank hanging over the Wind River Mountains. "You saw the sunset last night. Orange and pink over the peaks. You tell me it isn't going to snow. And I don't need to be a *puhagan* to know the signs."

The horses bucked deep drifts on the northern side of the ridge before cresting out onto a knob. In places angular rock had been exposed by the wind and amber clumps of needle-andthread, wheatgrass, and threadleaf sedge thrust through the crusted snow. From this high point, they could see across the basin to the south, past *Ki'nyatiwener,* the Hawk-Stand Rock, to *Wongo'yigwindo'yap,* the Pine-Stand Mountains. To the west, most of the view was blocked by the bulk of *Tunangarit,* the mountain known as Thundersitter. Willow pulled her mare up, shielding her face from the wind, searching the rolling hills below.

They'd followed the winter trails: ancestral routes that wound along the ridgetops. Willow had listened to her heart, steering by some faint urge that brought her this way. White Hail decried it all as foolishness, but something in her souls pinched at the idea of going any other direction.

The information gleaned at Meat Pole's camp was the only hint, tenuous as it was, that Richard might be in the area. So they'd come south as Spotted Falcon directed, and now Willow scanned the country below, looking for anything out of the ordinary. The rolling hills dropped away in a series of rocky humps as the mountains sloped down toward the Wind River Basin. Out to the west, beyond Thundersitter, the clouds had a soft, hazy look, the kind that fooled like Coyote, for the haze was that of wind-packed snow blowing down around the peaks.

"I don't think we want to be out in the open tonight," White Hail told her, attention on the western sky.

"No," she said. "I think not."

"We could turn around, try and make it back to Meat Pole's camp."

Willow tightened her blanket, squinting against the gusts as she searched. "I suppose we could. I'd rather make camp down lower, maybe in that valley down there to the right. Wood would be plentiful, and we'd have shelter from the wind."

He added, "We wouldn't have to leave until spring."

Willow met his level stare. "Why are you tormenting yourself, White Hail? You didn't have to come to High Wolf's camp in the first place. You didn't have to stay there with your heart in your throat every time a man came and asked to marry me. You didn't have to come on this trip. And if I find Richard, it will only sicken your souls. I have done nothing to encourage you."

"No. You've been honest." He gave her that familiar grin. "But I have hope."

"Go home to your wife and child."

"Red Calf is no wife." He glanced away. "I have come to understand that. I'm not very smart when it comes to women."

"No, you're not. You're better at stealing horses and getting caught by Blackfeet."

"And you, Willow?" A gust of wind flattened his sheephide coat against his shoulders. "You're good at getting caught by Pawnee, and involving yourself with silly White men, and the even sillier idea that there's one out here—let alone the one you really want to find. Face it, he's up at the mouth of the *Pia'ogwe*. This is crazy! Some evil spirit's dream that has . . . Willow? Are you listening to a single word I'm saying?"

She canted her head to keep the wind from tearing her eyes. What *was* that? Blinking, she could see dark dots moving against the snow: wolves padded around a rockpile on a lower ridge to the southwest. Something about the way they acted—hanging back. Why?

"Willow," White Hail insisted, "when that storm arrives, it's going to get colder than a rock ogre's heart. Come on, let's find a . . . Where are you going?"

"This way. Are you coming?" What would keep a group of wolves so interested, but at such a distance? Were it prey, they'd close in, bring the beast to bay, and kill it. No, this had to be something different, and Willow had always had an affinity for Wolf, the most sacred of *Dukurika* spirit animals.

"Willow? *Tam Apo,* but you're stubborn! *Willow!"*

Richard floated, savoring the warmth. Visions spun around him, Harvard trees lush with spring leaves, and the brick buildings looking so rosy in the sunlight. He strolled along familiar shady walks. Professor Ames walked beside him, casting curious glances his way.

"So, Richard, did you find the answers you were searching for?"

"Some, sir, but not all. It took a long time to discover the errors in our philosophical framework."

"Errors, Richard. Indeed?"

"Yes, sir. Philosophers, especially those in our modern

era, are incredibly vain. We are forever flawed by our own arrogance."

"Arrogance?"

"A form of the same arrogance that I left Boston with, sir: the notion that we have a unique understanding of truth. Which is not to say that our philosophy is meaningless, only that we have but a part of the whole. Human nature, it's so varied, forever depending upon the initial assumptions we make about life. Our philosophy is the product of Greek, Roman, and Hebrew thought, modified in the crucible of the Middle Ages, and recast by the Renaissance and Enlightenment. There is a great deal more to investigate, but none of us is willing to explore the alternatives. Our rationality has become a prison, as much a syllogism as Plato penned in the Dialogues of Ion."

"But, Richard, philosophy is a means of liberation."

"Are you free, sir?"

"I am. I have the ability to think, to investigate."

"That is the trap; for, you see, sir, you can only investigate within the framework of your experience, what you've been taught. I am seeking to find a different framework."

"Indeed. And have you discovered such a framework?"

"In part, sir. So much of what we believe has become cluttered with elegantly formulated arguments and proofs. Before I could see clearly, I had to strip away all the illusions and diversions. They all sound so logical in Boston, London, or Berlin. But, sir, Truth isn't found in elaborate philosophical constructions; it's in the essential fundamentals of life. We are all animals beneath our dress, manners, and the conventions of society."

"Animals, Richard, really? From Aristotle on, great minds have argued that humans are distinct from the animal world, that our values, abilities, perhaps even the divine spark of creation have placed us above the base realities of animal existence."

"Before anything else, sir, we need food, water, shelter, to protect ourselves from beasts, and to mate. Those five facts are the foundation of human reality. Society has placed us in a cage of our own construction, and from it we look out of windows, catching but the briefest glimpses of nature. And then we retreat to our warm drawing rooms and lecture halls to debate that momentary glimpse, fooling ourselves all the while that we see from above, like God, and know Truth."

"Your thesis will not find a warm reception among your peers, Richard. How do you expect to prove such assertions?"

"They can only be experienced, sir. You see, that's the flaw in enlightened reason. It becomes a mental exercise, totally logical—a sophisticated syllogism: 'Socrates is a man. A man has two legs. My cat is named Socrates. Therefore, my cat has two legs.'"

"The logical flaws in a syllogism will always be detected by a critical examination, Richard."

"Will they? Doesn't finding the flaw in that example hinge on knowing both men and cats? Professor, let me postulate an axiom: Nature cannot be fooled by logical architecture, no matter how grand its construction."

"So, you have Truth, and it consists of man being an animal?"

"No, sir. I have only discovered the foundation from

which to work. Something is missing—the final nail that will pin it all together. Human nature is so complex."

"Yes, so complex . . ." Ames began to laugh, and slowly faded into a gray mist.

Dear Professor Ames, more like a father than a teacher. If only his own father had had that gentle look, that warmth of personality. But Phillip Hamilton had been forever cold, unforgiving, and strict.

Richard cried out into the haze, "Father, why couldn't you have smiled at me? Why couldn't you have shared part of yourself with me? What did I ever do to hurt you?"

The disembodied voice, backed by the ticking of a ship's clock, sounded sad and weary. "I wanted you to be a man. I failed, boy. Despite your self-proclaimed philosophy, don't you understand the suffocating guilt? It devours us, boy, it's been eating at you and me until we have nothing left to share with each other except misery."

Guilt? Dear God, what a horrible monster that was, forever lurking in the human heart. He could sense it, black and terrible, a miasma rising in his breast. Oh, he knew it all right, had seen it in his dreams devouring Boston, and settling over Willow's dead body. *It came from me, from inside.*

"I'm so sorry, Father." An ache filled his chest. "I understand now. For I have my own guilt, Father. My own needs for atonement."

"Richard?" Phillip's voice barked, "What have you done now? Where is the money, Richard? Have you failed me again?"

The old fear didn't rise to choke him. "Yes, Father. I failed you."

His father responded evenly. "Please, see that you don't again."

What curious irony. "I won't, Father. I'm dying. I can't

fail you again." And what sorrow that brought. So many things left to do, so many mistakes to correct—and no time left. "But it's all right, Father. I forgive you for trying too hard. Do you hear me? I *forgive* you!" He sank down onto his knees then, head bowed. "But, sir, can you ever forgive me?"

The sensation was so gentle that he never knew when he floated away, lost in the warm gray haze. Fragments of memory flitted through his mind on siskin wings, echoes of the boasts he'd made that night in Will Templeton's parlor. Oh, he'd conquered the wild frontier and its wilder men, hadn't he? Like a vulture, he'd lived on carrion, and chewed bitter twigs. He'd killed, taken scalps—and worn them with the pride of a savage.

Eyes watched him. Familiar eyes—Will Templeton's, Thomas Hanson's, Peterson's, Fenno's, and the rest. For a short eternity, Laura's blue eyes withered his soul, her disapproval nearly palpable. *Oh, Laura, I'm sorry—sorry for the life that we'll never have together.*

The eyes changed—a reconciliation of opposites. Now Trudeau watched him. Why Trudeau? He used women, took them against their will. What did he have in common with Laura?

Richard squeezed the image from his mind, only to hear Toussaint repeat, *A man ees what he ees.*

From the watery darkness came a new image. That of a terrible pistol pointed at him. A firm hand curled around the grip, and behind the black maw of the muzzle, Dave Green's implacable face loomed.

"Dear God, Dave. Don't shoot! I'm not the same man I was then. I've changed. Grown. But now it's too late."

And in the distance, François laughed, chortling, "Animal! that's all you are . . . an animal like the rest of us, *oui?*"

The cloudy gray swirled, and Willow reached out of the mist, her arms open for his embrace.

Richard whispered miserably, "If only I could go back, be everything you thought I could."

Her voice, like fingers on velvet, said, "You have followed your own path. You could do no less."

"But where has it led me, Willow?"

"To the final truth."

The final truth—the last fading moments of life, and a crushing loneliness. Shouldn't there be more? A rising fanfare of trumpets, a swelling of light and brilliance?

"Reckon that's all there is," Travis called from somewhere distant. "Ye done fine, coon. Now, let go and cross the next divide. Almost there. Just a little farther. C'mon, Dick. Ye can do it."

And the terrible gray cold closed around him.

TWENTY-SIX

Thus if I make the assertion that the quality of space and time, according to which, as a condition of their existence I accept both external objects and my own soul, lies in my manner of intuition and not in these objects by themselves, I do not mean to state that such bodies only seem to exist externally to me, or that my soul only seems to be apparent in my self-consciousness. It would be my own fault if I changed that which ought to count as appearance into mere illusion.

This cannot occur, however, according to our principle of the ideality of all sensible intuitions.

—Immanuel Kant, *Critique of Pure Reason*

Willow dismounted, watching the wolves. They hesitated uneasily, then trotted away over the crest of the ridge, paws swishing in the freezing snow. The rock outcrop stood like a rock ogre's cairn, the snow curiously trampled.

White Hail slid off his horse, inspecting the tracks. "It looks like a man has been crawling here. See, that's a print from a mitten. And here, this sagebrush has been shredded."

Willow hurried toward the rocks, leading her mare. Here and there, she could pick out a footprint in the trampled snow, a pockmark, as if from a stick, and mitten prints.

The rocks jutted from the top of the ridge, lonely sentinels overlooking the rough country to the south. She tied her horse to a thick sage and stepped around the canted stone.

Richard lay propped against a sandstone boulder, eyes closed. His body was wrapped in so many frozen hides, he looked more like a winter-story monster than a man. She crouched beside him, ignoring the stale smells of sweat, smoke, and dried blood. His eyes were sunken, cheeks hollow and peeling. Frostbite had blackened his nose, and filth matted his beard. Beside him lay his possibles, the familiar Hawken, mud-spattered and tarnished. Nothing but charcoal and ashes remained in the cold firepit.

"Richard?" She touched his cold face, and his eyes barely flickered. "Richard! It's Willow!"

"You came all this way for . . . for *that?*" White Hail asked from behind her.

"Build a fire," she ordered. "He's almost dead."

"Looks like he hasn't eaten in days." White Hail studied Richard skeptically. "I think we're too late."

"A fire, White Hail. Now! And after that, I need you to

take the horses and ride down to the valley. Cut me sticks. Long ones, for a sweat lodge."

White Hail placed a hand on her shoulder, his gaze penetrating her panic. "Willow, no matter what, we *must* move off this point. Are you listening? Look out at that storm, and *think,* Willow."

She knotted her fists, studied the dark wall of clouds to the west, and nodded miserably. White Hail muttered under his breath as he walked to her horse and led it over.

"Richard?" Willow cradled his face in her hands. "You must be brave. *Live* for me!" And her souls froze. Hadn't she said those words before? Over her husband and son, and with the same impassioned pleading?

I couldn't save them. I didn't have the Power. Not again. Heart skipping, she took a deep breath. *"Tam Apo,* do you hear me? I can't bear it."

White Hail collected Richard's possibles and tied them onto his horse, including the broken rifle.

"Help me wrap him," Willow said, spreading her blanket beside Richard. With White Hail's help, they laid him in soft hides and folded them around his body.

"We'll have to lash him crosswise, like packing a deer," White Hail said. When they lifted him to her mare, Willow was shocked to find how light he was.

"Cling to life, Richard. It's not long now. We'll have you warm and fed." Then Willow took the reins and led her horse down off the point, headed to the drainage White Hail had spotted from above. The storm was closer now, roaring down upon them.

Desperation built with each step as Willow watched her moccasins punch through the crusted snow. With each frantic look back to Richard's bobbing body, she prayed that his *mugwa* would cling to this world.

A half-hand's time had passed by the time they reached

the snowy bottoms. The few solitary cottonwoods that stood in the rounded valley had a pathetic look. Serviceberry, chokecherry, and juniper poked up through the snow.

"White Hail, build a fire. Hurry!" Willow stepped back and began pulling at the knots while White Hail kicked a hole in the deep snow.

Willow tossed the lashing aside, and slid Richard down onto the trampled snow. Her frantic fingers pulled the robe aside and her heart sank. His half-lidded eyes were vacant, his face slack. To her relief, his erratic breathing rasped shallowly.

White Hail was muttering to himself as he stripped bark from the junipers, and built a fire in the hollow he'd kicked in the snow.

Willow stared into Richard's slack face, fear twining through her souls. "Richard, it's Willow. Come back to me." A painful knot began to swell under her tongue, and tears traced down her cheeks to chill in the cold.

By some bizarre trick of the light, her husband's face superimposed itself on Richard's. Her fingers had rested as futilely on his cold skin. How could it happen again?

Richard mumbled something, the words disjointed, the ramblings a body made when the *mugwa* had come free.

She closed her eyes, steeling herself. If his soul had fled the body, only one way remained to save him. *I can't. I don't have the Power to go among the Dead to find his soul. Why didn't I bring High Wolf with me? He could do this, send his soul in search of Richard's.*

When she shivered and looked around, White Hail had the fire crackling. Together, they carried Richard over to it. Then White Hail placed Willow's pack beside her, asking, "How is he?"

"His *mugwa* is gone."

White Hail shrugged. "Then we can do nothing. You'd need a *puhagan* to save him."

"I know." She knotted her fists, eyes closed. What happened to an *omaihen* woman, a forbidden woman, who sent her soul into the afterlife? Would the angry spirits really trap her soul there?

"You tried, Willow," White Hail soothed. "It's not your fault."

How will I live with myself if I fail again? She looked down into his face. *For the rest of my life, I'll hate myself if I don't at least try.* A new fear was born within as she said: "I'm not finished, White Hail. I need poles, something to make a sweat lodge. Take my ax and see if you can find chokecherry stems long enough."

White Hail took her hand, staring into her eyes. "Willow, if he's lost his soul, there's *nothing* you can do."

"I can go after it."

White Hail's eyes widened. "Go after it? You're a woman! Only a *puhagan* can send his soul out to find another. Don't you understand?"

"I don't have *time* to find a *puhagan!* This thing will be done now! I will make the journey after his soul, White Hail. High Wolf told me the way."

For what seemed like an eternity, their eyes locked, wills battling. And in the end, he relented. "Very well, but you'll probably kill us all."

"Then you can leave as soon as you fetch me the poles. Now, go. Hurry! We've wasted enough time as it is."

Growling to himself, White Hail took her ax and stalked off toward the chokecherry bushes as the wind bore the first flakes of snow.

Willow looked up at the threatening sky and struggled to smother her own rising fear. White Hail's words burned within her: "*You're a woman! Only a* puhagan *can send his soul out to find another.*" Under her breath, she whispered, "I'm forbidden to do this . . . *omaihen—omaihen . . .*"

To even consider such a thing was madness. Only the

most powerful *puhagan*—and all of them men—could send their souls to the Land of the Dead. But High Wolf had told her what would happen and how to find her way. He'd also told her about the spirits guarding the way—terrible creatures that tested the soul-traveler. Those who failed were destroyed in the most hideous of ways.

Yet like the summer moths that flew into crackling fires, she was being drawn, seeing the path she would take. One by one she recalled the things High Wolf had told her. If she could free her soul, it must find the tunnel between the worlds. There in the darkness, monsters would lurk, ready to leap upon her soul if her courage faltered. She would emerge on a mountaintop, and then follow dark paths down into the valley. The whole time she would be stalked by Water Babies, *Nunumbi,* and *Pandzoavits*.

If she made it to the bottom of the mountain, she must find Richard's soul. Here, too, she could fail, for not all souls wanted to return to the living, and the pain, cold, and suffering that living entailed.

She closed her eyes, anxiety rising bright within. On the river, Richard had chosen Boston—and that White woman—over her. Why did she think he would be any different in the Land of the Dead?

Because he's here. Not with Travis and Green at the confluence of the Pia'ogwe *and* Gete'ogwe. He had come seeking her, in the dead of winter. She had to know why.

Whether his *mugwa* accompanied her or stayed with the Dead, she'd still have to find her way back up the mountain trails to the peak, relocate the tunnel, and retrace her way back to her own body.

Branches cracked as White Hail bulled into the bush. The chopping echoed hollowly around the valley.

Am I strong enough? How did one measure such a thing? Driving the thought from her heart, she set about collecting snow in Richard's tin cup, then placed it at the fire's edge to melt. Turning to her pack, she undid the straps and pulled out her blanket and robe. With Richard's bent knife, she cut the strands of tendon he'd used to tie the green hides to his body.

First, she checked his feet: cold as clay, but to her relief, unfrozen. Snow was falling faster. She added pieces of sage to the fire. With his rifle, she battered rocks from the frosted ground and tumbled them into the blaze to heat. Next, she began kicking the snow away where they'd build the sweat lodge.

Her nose crinkled at the smell as she cut the last of the hides away and placed a hand on Richard's chest. Cold, so cold, but his heart still beat, slow and irregular.

White Hail plodded into camp, long branches trailing behind him in the snow. He shook his head as he looked at Richard, but began the task of wedging the butts into the ground and bending the poles into a low arch. They built the lodge right over his body. Willow used Richard's thongs to tie the saplings into a low dome-shaped framework. One by one they settled their hide robes over them.

"I hope you know what you're doing," White Hail said, as they inspected the low dome of the sweat lodge.

Willow shook snow out of her hair. "If I don't, you can have my horse and Richard's rifle. The cock is broken, but you can get another one."

"Thank you," White Hail told her dryly. "If I live long enough."

Willow rubbed her face, and took a deep breath. With a sagebrush stem, she rolled a hot rock onto one of Richard's frozen hides. Ignoring the smell of burning leather, she ducked into the shelter and dropped the hot rock next to Richard. Snowflakes sizzled as she carried the rocks one by one into the darkness, creating a glowing pile.

"You know what to do?" She took one last look at White Hail.

"I do." He sounded as if his *mugwa* were at risk, too. And perhaps it was, being this close to something so dangerous. "I'll keep melting water, bring you hot stones when you call, and, in the meantime, make us some sort of wickiup." He glanced around in the gloom. Snow was falling in white curtains now, night approaching. "At least we're not up on the point."

Willow ducked into the lodge, settled the robe in place, and pulled the last of Richard's clothing off. She slipped out of her robe, cape, dress, and moccasins.

She shivered in the cold, and pulled the blanket back. "I'm ready for the water now."

"*Tam Apo* guide you." White Hail handed her the tin of water. "I have loved you for a long time, Willow. I will always love you."

She hesitated, seeing the conviction in his dark eyes; but words had been exhausted between them long ago.

With finality, she ducked into the blackness and resettled the robe. She filled her lungs and sprinkled water on the glowing rocks. Steam hissed and exploded to fill the interior, hot enough to scald.

She clenched her fists, the steam's Power prickling on her skin, in her lungs. It bathed her with its cleansing tendrils, twining around her. Then she lowered herself onto Richard's cold body, hugging him tightly.

Richard, how cold you are. The chill sucked warmth from her breasts, her stomach, her thighs, as she pressed herself against him.

She closed her eyes and began to sing, calling upon Wolf and the Spirit Powers to help her. The magnitude of what she was attempting awed her. So many strands of her life had come undone. Worry about White men had been gnawing at her. Her dissatisfaction with her own people, with *Dukurika* men who would chip an ax on rock to see sparks, chafed her.

Perhaps, by doing this crazy thing, she could weave them together again, find the balance in her world.

And if I do not succeed, I shall die, which is a resolution in itself.

She sang and prayed, souls rising to the challenge. Outside, White Hail's voice rose in song, adding his support to her call to Power.

The hot steam burned into her, stifling, unbearable. Sweat beaded to run down onto Richard's body. *You can stand it, Willow.* Her lungs sucked for cool air as her flesh crawled and squirmed. Only Richard was cool . . . cool . . . her senses swam, the darkness going gray.

She reached out with her life soul, searching, seeking, loosening herself from her body.

There, in the rippling mists of death, lay what she sought, be it success—or oblivion.

❖

Overhead, cottonwoods reflected the firelight, their triangular leaves bathed in the golden glow. Richard leaned closer to his fire, naked heat eating into his chest and arms. Around him other fires popped and burned, smoke mingling with the warm air, redolent with the scents of corn and boiling pork, the pots watched carefully by the *engagés*. Jokes were called back and forth, and Toussaint's rich baritone filled the night with song. The breeze carried the river's musky smells to Richard's fire.

Green sat before his tent, a bowl of stew on his lap as he listened to Henri; the patroon waved his arms in Gallic emphasis as he predicted the next day's travel.

Richard sighed, a terrible weariness like lead in his limbs. How good to be in camp again—cold, snow, wind, and hunger nothing more than a dream. Tomorrow, just after sunrise, they would line out the cordelle and resume the endless struggle to pull the boat upriver.

Richard listened to the boatmen's song, and leaned back from the fire to pull his pipe from his possibles. He tamped tobacco into the stained bowl, and lit a twig. As he drew, he watched the yellow fire drawn downward and filled his lungs with rich blue smoke.

Why had he never sensed this peace on the river before? How could he have been so obsessed with Boston, and home, and all the other trivialities? What a fool he'd been about Laura. She'd never shown the slightest interest in him until he'd become involved in his father's business. How charming she'd been that last night in Boston—and Will had been her accomplice.

Do I blame her? No, after all, she was doing what they all expected her to do: marry for wealth and station. He smiled crookedly, having never really considered himself a prize before. Poor Laura. For the rest of her life, she would be nothing more than a reflection of her husband.

Willow, however, had been free. Ah, to see her flashing black eyes, see her raven hair gleaming in the sunlight. Within her Shoshoni heart burned a spirit fit for a man. Her supple body had awakened his male instincts, brought him to the verge of bursting the bonds he'd tied himself with.

He'd made so many mistakes in his arrogance. By now Phillip knew about the money. Richard could see the old man in his office, hands clasped on the polished desk. The color would have drained from his cheeks, and he would have shaken his head before bowing his head and closing his eyes.

Did you think I'd stolen it, Father? Took it and ran off? At the thought, Richard winced. *I was a fool, Father. I just wish . . . well, that I could have seen as clearly then as I do now.*

So many regrets for such a short life. But here, on the river, they were only melancholy reminders of the past. Come morning, he would rise again, and with the others, face the Missouri and its current. Looking over his shoulder, he could see *Maria* tied by her painter, awaiting the dawn.

Why did I ever want to go back? He puzzled on that for a moment, then let it go. Better the freedom of the river where life was only work, the capriciousness of current, sawyer, mud, and mosquitoes.

He barely heard the cry—ever so faint in the tranquil night. He cocked his head, listening. There, just at the edge of hearing. A woman's voice . . . Willow's, calling his name over and over.

"Here, Willow!" He stood up, fire-blinded to the darkness. How many times had Travis reproved him for such stupidity?

She stopped at the edge of the dark-shadowed trees beyond camp, staring at him with frightened eyes. Yes, as beautiful as ever—but naked.

"Willow? What's wrong?" Suddenly worried, he stepped away from the fire's warm security, desperately reluctant to leave that sphere of light. Behind him, the *engagés* had also stood, their songs forgotten.

She looked terrified, legs braced, shoulders hunched,

ready to bolt. Firelight cast her perfect body in a bronze glow. Her lips moved, mouthing inaudible words, black hair shimmering around her like a shroud.

Trudeau had come to stand beside him, a feral gleam in his eyes. "She was always a beauty, *non?*"

"Shut up, damn it! Something's wrong."

"*Oui,*" Trudeau agreed. "And now, perhaps, I 'ave her forever, eh?"

"Forever? What are you talking about?"

"She needs but step into zee camp. Then you will see, *mon ami.*"

Unnerved, Richard took another reluctant step. "Willow? What are you doing out there? Where are your clothes?"

Her chest heaved, breasts rising as she gasped for breath. "Richard?" she whispered hoarsely. "Come to me. Please? Away from the camp."

"Away? That's crazy! Here, let me get you a robe, and then come in by the fire where it's warm."

"No!" She shivered, then tensed as if poised to flee. "Bring nothing, Richard. Just come to me. *Please?* If you love me, come to me. Richard, you must. I can't get back without you."

"Get back? I don't understand."

She reached out to him, imploring. "Richard, if you love me, if you ever loved me, *help me!*"

He took another step, fear ballooning inside him. "Willow, I can't. I belong here."

Her throat worked, head shaking. "No . . . I mean . . . You can stay if you want. But I came for you, to take you back with me. Richard, *please!*"

He pointed back at Trudeau, at the crackling fires, and Dave Green, who'd come to stand behind him. "This is the camp, Willow."

Her face contorted and her fists knotted. "They're all

dead, Richard. You're in the Land of the Dead! You know that, don't you?"

Dead? He turned, seeing humor in Trudeau's eyes. Toussaint lifted his eyebrows, shrugging. A knowing twinkle glimmered in Green's eyes.

Willow reached out to him, her arms trembling. "Richard, please. This is so difficult—more dangerous than I ever guessed. If we're to get back, we must go together. I need your help to retrace the way. Oh, please, don't you understand? I *can't* get back alone. I need the threads of your soul to weave the way."

Dead? He rubbed the back of his neck, trying to comprehend.

"Do you love me, Richard? At least tell me that. If I'm to lose my soul here, in the blackness, I must know if you ever really loved me."

His chest heaved, and he nodded. "*Yes.* With all my heart. I never knew how much."

"Then come. Take my hand. At least we can be together here"—she shot a frightened glance into the black forest—"or wherever we end up."

He took another step toward her, fear rising. *Dear Lord, what's happening?*

"Trust me, Richard." She reached out to him. Her hair had begun to float like black mist around her naked shoulders.

With each step he took, the terror rose within him. He, too, was trembling; it was like walking out in front of an enemy's rifle. If he took another step, the fear would choke him to death. *Turn around! Run to the safety of the fire, now, before it's too late!*

Tears streaked down Willow's cheeks. Her lips were working, but he could not hear her words. He shook his head, on the verge of sobbing. Behind lay safety, the warm fire. He'd do anything for that security. He started to turn back—and saw the look in her eyes: pained disbelief surrendering to abject terror.

I can't let her down again.

With the last of his courage, Richard reached out and entwined his fingers with hers.

Willow pulled him to her, choking on tears, hugging him with a fierce desperation. For a long time they held each other, souls mingling. The terror that had threatened to overwhelm him receded. But what danger lurked around them in those dark trees?

He used his thumb to brush strands of raven black hair from her brow. "I don't understand any of this. What's happening? Can't we go back to the fire?"

"If we do, we'll die, just as they did." She pushed back, running her fingers across his face the way someone would to convince himself it were real. "We're not safe yet. Together, we can do this. Hold on to me, Richard. Under no circumstances should you let go of my hand, do you understand? For no reason—no matter what."

"I won't let go."

"Promise."

"I promise."

And hand-in-hand they turned, walking into the terrible darkness and cold.

◈

Through the long night, White Hail waited and sang. His robes were part of the sweat lodge, and he had only his coat between him and the storm. But one thing he had plenty of was fire. He stomped out another hollow in the snow and built a second blaze. When the chill ate into him, he huddled between the fires and melted the snow from his coat. When he became too hot, he ranged out into the night in search of sagebrush, cottonwood, and juniper. By the armload, he packed it back. Some went to feed the fires, while the rest of it he wove into a rude wickiup just large enough to provide him some shelter. When he completed that, he packed the back of it with snow to seal it against the wind.

His thoughts centered on the sweat lodge, and the battle Willow waged within it.

Between wood trips, White Hail pulled glowing rocks from the fire and bore them into the sweat lodge. As snowflakes landed on the rocks, they sizzled and vanished in tiny puffs. Inside, he'd glance at Willow's dark form where she lay unmoving on the smelly White man. Her skin was clammy to the touch, as cold as the man's. From time to time she'd whimper, and her breathing had dropped to a grating rasp.

"Help her, *Tam Apo*," White Hail whispered fervently, and then he'd pour water over the glowing red eye of rock. As the searing steam hissed and billowed, he'd recover the cool rocks, back out, and secure the flap to seal the hot Power within. He'd drop his rocks back in the fire to reheat, and scoop up more snow to melt in the tin cup.

As the long night wore on, he continued to sing his prayers to *Tam Apo*, lifting his head to the falling snow. They'd hear in the Spirit World, wouldn't they? They'd send her back, understanding that it was desperation that had goaded her to do this *omaihen* thing. Wouldn't they?

Oh, Willow, only you could be so brave. Try as he might, he couldn't understand what would motivate her to risk her souls in such a dangerous quest. What if something went wrong? Power had its dark side, and Heals Like A Willow might come back changed, her *mugwa* twisted by *Pandzoavits.* Witchcraft! The very thought of it chilled his bones worse than the storm.

Oh, Brother, if you could see your wife now, what would you think? He glanced again at the sweat lodge. It might have been some giant black turtle crouched in the snow.

White Hail shook his head. He could *feel* Power loose on the night, smell it in snow-laden wind. *No matter how this ends, my world will never be the same again.* He poked at the flames with a stick, stirring the coals and watching the falling flakes melting away in the smoke. *If Willow survives, she will have proved herself a most Powerful* puhagan. *If she comes back possessed by evil Power, she'll be a very dangerous witch. But if she dies, no one will ever trust me again. I'm tainted by association.*

That was when he began to understand that he couldn't win. Even in the best case, if Willow survived unscathed, she'd never be the exciting young woman who had married White Hail's brother. When he looked into her eyes, he'd see terrible *puha* looking back.

Face it, White Hail, the Willow you once loved is gone. He could no more bring her back than he could the snowflakes that melted in his fire.

By that time, the fires were down to coals. He slapped his knees, stood, and marched out once again to see what he could scrounge for fuel. Willow would need more hot rocks and steam.

When the first tints of dawn finally cast their gray light through the clouds, White Hail removed jerky, pemmican, and dried berries from the packs. Willow would be desperately hungry when she returned from the Land of the Dead. She *would* return. She had to.

A wretched headache stabbed like an antler tine behind Willow's eyes. She blinked awake to blurry darkness. It felt as though sand grated under her eyelids. She drew a deep breath—and the steam nearly suffocated her. Thoughts faded as soon as they formed, like water poured on sand.

I am . . . where? The familiar sound of wind on hide coverings told her she was in a lodge. Curse the headache! It interfered with her thinking. She shifted, startled to find another human body beneath hers. She reached up to touch the face—and encountered a beard.

Richard! She was lying naked atop Richard, sweat beading and trickling down her sides. In the moist air, his smell nearly gagged her—and her stomach was already upset. Images came whirling out of her *mugwa* like snowflakes from a winter sky: dark caves; eerie trails winding through black timber; shapes darting away from the edge of her vision; the boatmen's camp in the Land of the Dead. A shiver ran down her back at the memory of the soul-wrenching terror.

Lost . . . in the Land of the Dead. I was holding Richard's

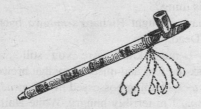

hand, lost in the forest. . . . Yes! And then she'd collapsed, sobbing hysterically as Richard asked what was wrong. She'd cried, *"I can't find the way!"* That was the last thing she could remember.

But here she was, back in the sweat lodge. Alive. Vague memories stirred: she and Richard being chased through the black forest by shadowy monsters. Real, or imagined? Some parts of her memory were missing—rubbed out like drawings on loose dirt. She could recall the mountain peak . . . Wolf . . . the frigid sucking away of her soul, then voices. Richard and Wolf, arguing over her. Their words had drifted off, like strands of mist in the branches.

She tried to move, only to have Richard's arms tighten around her. "Are you all right?" she asked.

"Are you?"

"Yes. Just terribly tired—and what a headache!"

"Me, too. Weak. Haven't eaten. Dear Lord God, such a dream. So vivid, I can recall every detail. But . . . I'm not still dreaming, am I? I mean, you're here? Alive?"

She sighed, sinking down on him. "I came to find you. Heard you calling to my souls."

"You *heard* me? Willow, I don't—"

"Richard, be quiet. The questions can wait until we heal you." She raised her voice. "White Hail?"

"Willow! Are you all right?" The flap rose, light spilling in with blinding glare. His cock-jawed expression added to the nervousness in his eyes. Snow was caked on the shoulders of his coat. "You're alive? Willow? Have you . . . have you done this thing?"

"Yes. I have brought Richard's *mugwa* back from the Land of the Dead."

"Willow, I must know. Are you still . . . you?" He couldn't mask the fear and uncertainty that brewed within.

"I'm me, *teci*. Nothing possessed my *mugwa*." *At least, I don't think so.* "I'm terribly hungry, White Hail. We could use food, and fire, and something to wrap around Richard besides frozen hides."

White Hail's expression tightened as he inspected the White man. "Food is ready. I'll see what I can do for the *Taipo*." The flap settled back in place.

"Who's that?" Richard asked warily.

"My husband's brother."

"Husband?" He stiffened suddenly. "You—you're married? When?"

"My dead husband's brother," she corrected, reaching up to press his nose with a finger. "I'm married to no one."

He smiled then, sighing. "I'm glad. I came to tell you. I was wrong, Willow. About so many things. I wanted to tell you that day you left." He searched her eyes in the dimness. "Can you forgive me for being a damned idiot?"

"Yes." And her heart soared as she ran fingers down the side of his sunken face.

"I love you, Willow. I came to tell you that I love you with all of my soul. I couldn't die until you'd heard me say that."

"I've heard you, Richard."

He shook his head, tightening his hold on her. "For now, I'm happy to be alive, to have you . . . if you'll have me. The future will take care of itself."

"I will have you, Richard. For as long as I can."

"Thank God," he whispered softly.

White Hail ducked into the lodge, two steaming tins in his hands. "I've made stew," he said, setting the tins down. His hard black eyes fixed on Richard, on his arms about Willow. "But you should know that we don't have much food left." He pointed at the damp robes above. "That's all we have for clothing. You used our robes to cover the lodge. If you're going to dress your *Taipo*, it will have to be with what he was wearing."

TWENTY-SEVEN

◇

Courage then, as has been stated, is the usual condition with regard to things that cause confidence or fear in the circumstances described. A man chooses action, or endures pain, because it is honorable to do so, or because the opposite course is disgraceful. But to die to escape from poverty, or love, or anything painful, is the act not of a courageous person but of a coward. For it is weakness to fly from troubles; nor does the suicide face death because it is noble, but because it is a refuge from evil. . . .

—Aristotle, *Nicomachean Ethics*

The Shoshoni warrior, White Hail, rode first, his horse breaking trail through the deep snow. Lead rope in hand, Willow followed on foot, breath puffing whitely as she slogged along in White Hail's trail. Richard clung weakly to Willow's mare. He still teetered on the edge of exhaustion and shivered continually.

They climbed higher, following the windblown ridgeline toward a low saddle in the mountain wall. The northern slopes were timbered with dark green pine and gray-stemmed brush, while juniper clung to the rocky soil on the southern exposures. Wind had sculpted the drifts into scallops, angles, and cornices. Ripples of white undulated around the sagebrush. The world looked as if God had frosted it like a cake—the job so perfect as to be the envy of any Bostonian confectioner.

Richard barely noticed the country, his concentration

dedicated to keeping his seat. The mare swayed with each step, often sliding in the deep snow. Sometimes she'd stumble, step in a hidden hole, and pitch sideways to recover. Through it all, Richard had to cling like a tick to a tail. Still lightheaded from starvation, yet the question plagued him: How had Willow found him—and odder yet, how could they have shared a dream in such intimate detail?

That experience *had* to be a dream. Any other explanation defied rationality.

As if I've been rational during the last year. The cold wind made his eyes water, and he blinked to clear them. Well, what was one more problem to solve? God had been giving him more than his share recently.

He squinted against the wind that tugged relentlessly at him and sought to break his hold on the mare. It whipped Richard's beard and the hair that straggled from the confines of his hat.

Each time the Shoshoni warrior looked back, his flint black eyes betrayed a steely resentment.

Why does he hate me so? What have I ever done to him? But when they stopped to let Willow rest, Richard finally saw the worried longing in the warrior's eyes as he watched Willow.

So, he loves her, and she loves me. Richard closed his eyes, taking stock of himself—and not finding much. His muscles quaked from the effort to hold on to the horse. The odor creeping up from his patchwork of frozen hides offended his own nose. No wonder White Hail looked at him like some sort of bug. Willow seemed completely unconcerned. She walked back, smiling at him and patting his hand. "Are you all right?"

"Tired," he told her, grinning wryly. "If any Pawnee warriors show up, well, I'm not worth a shit."

Her grin met his, and her eyes sparkled like stars. When

he looked back at White Hail, the warrior's face was expressionless, but dark fires burned behind his eyes.

Late that afternoon; they crested the low saddle and dropped down into a valley on the northern side of the pass. Fir, lodgepole, and limber pine darkened the slopes; the skirts of the trees were deep in soft-mounded snow. North and west, in the distance, rugged ridges crowded upon each other like concertina folds. Deep drifts lay under each rocky prominence. Far out over the grim basin, torn shreds of cloud drifted westward toward the Big Horns.

Willow spoke to the warrior before wading back to Richard. "Let me help you down. We will camp here."

"Sorry. I guess I'm off my uppers, as Travis would say."

She caught him as he tumbled down, searching his eyes with hers. Pulling a hand from her mitten, she felt his cheek, pinching his skin. "Have you been dizzy? Seen—how would you say?—sparks behind your eyes?"

"Yes. Starved, I think. Still a little numb from exhaustion. I'm trying to understand what happened. This Land of the Dead business."

"We'll talk about that later. Come, you're shivering. We'll get a fire started. Sit there, on that log. It won't be long."

"I can do something, get firewood or . . ."

She pointed a mittened finger. "Sit there, Richard."

Richard shuffled to the log, secretly grateful since his feet barely supported him. Had he ever felt this tired? From the core of his bones out to his hair, every part of him was dead-weary. He dusted off the snow and sat. The warrior gave him a wary look before slipping into the soft shadows under the trees. Sticks snapped as White Hail broke squaw wood. Meanwhile, Willow attended to picketing the horses, stripping off saddles, and making camp under the low-hanging branches of a huge fir tree.

When she came for him, he'd begun to shiver, blinking at the black dots that formed before his eyes. Willow practically carried him into the branch-screened bower.

White Hail had started a fire in a hollow scooped in the duff. He glanced up from the spindle of flame, distaste in the set of his mouth.

Willow guided Richard to a nest of blankets and robes beside the fire. The warrior said something, and Willow answered.

"I guess White Hail would rather not have found me." Richard leaned his head back, neck muscles flaccid. "I didn't spoil his journey with you, did I?"

"What he wants or doesn't want is his concern." She glanced across at Richard. "Is it that obvious?"

He smiled. "Maybe I got used to men looking at you that way on the river."

"White Hail is my *teci*, my husband's brother. When my husband died, White Hail wanted to marry me. I'm smarter than he is, and told him no." She shrugged. "That was another time, another place." She studied him with worried eyes. "Richard, we haven't spoken. What happened? Why are you here? Why were the *engagés,* and Henri, and Dave Green all in the Land of the Dead?"

How can she have been there, too? He took a deep breath. "Blackfeet. A war party came up from the south, ambushed the camp on the Big Horn. Overran it. Green waited until they swarmed the boat, then set off the powder."

"And Travis and Baptiste?" she asked, voice neutral. But Richard saw her fist clench.

White Hail ducked out to scoop snow into the tin pots. He set them on the fire and began shaving dried meat, pemmican, and something that looked like hardtack into the melting snow.

"Alive. At least, I think so. Baptiste went to join the Crow; Travis and I started south to find you. We were separated back at the beginning of the deep cold. I did all right until I broke my gun. I fell off this cliff. A red sandstone ridge sharp as a knife—just east of the mountains."

"The Red Wall," she whispered. "That's where I dreamed you called to me."

"I did . . . in my dreams." Richard stared down at his hands. Once they'd been strong, callused and hard from the cordelle. Now he opened and closed his thin fingers, a bone-deep weakness within them. "Willow, you talk about the camp I saw in my delirium. Green, Henri, the *engagés* . . . I dreamed that I was there. Was I babbling? Out of my head? How much did I tell you?"

She leaned toward him, eyes luminous in the firelight. "You said nothing to me. You were dying, Richard. I sent my soul to find you, bring your *mugwa* back to your body. A *puhagan* can do these things. I had to take the chance, even though a woman isn't supposed to. I am *omaihen*."

At the word, White Hail froze in place, a pot half raised.

Willow spoke in *Dukurika,* her words a staccato. White Hail answered in kind. It ended when Willow made the familiar hand sign for enough.

"What was all that?" Richard asked softly. White Hail studiously returned to his chores, as if it took all of his effort to make those routine tasks appear effortless.

"I told him I needed your help to return from the Land of the Dead. Richard, do not mention this among the *Dukurika*. White Hail will keep his tongue, for he owes me his life. From now on, he will fear your Power. We would never have made it back without your *puha*. We did this thing together."

"This is crazy, Willow." He lowered his head into his hands. "But I'm not up to arguing with you right now. There must be some logical explanation for what happened."

When he finally looked up, her dark eyes were slightly

hostile. "You have not changed, have you? Everything must still fit into your box."

He swallowed hard, hating White Hail's presence, irritated with himself. He gave her a sheepish smile. "I'm sorry. When inquiry fails, only faith is left." *Faith?* The Shoshoni notion of two souls was difficult enough to comprehend. He glanced at her, stung by the old hurt in her eyes. Damn it, did he always have to let her down?

"Old habits die hard, Willow. Suppose you wanted to think like a White man, how long would it take to ignore your Shoshoni instincts?" Richard took the steaming tin Willow passed him. "That's more than my share."

Willow shrugged. "White Hail and I need less. We still have two days' travel to reach *Pa'gushowener.* Until then, you need the food, Richard. Gather your strength. Who knows, maybe we'll kill something on the way."

He pursed his lips, staring down into the steaming tin. His belly won out over ethical concerns. By the time he'd emptied the tin, his stomach was aching. Despite the discomfort, he craved more.

When supper was finished, Willow repacked the tins and slipped out into the night. Richard stared at the fire for a while, then looked up at White Hail, saying, "She's an incredible woman, isn't she?"

The warrior met his English query with silence, no hint of expression in his gleaming eyes. He was a handsome young man, his brown skin smooth over prominent cheeks, his nose long and straight. The crooked set of his jaw pursed his lips into a perpetual expression of mild skepticism.

When Willow returned, she lifted an eyebrow. "You will need to drain your pizzle, Richard. I don't want to get up in the middle of the night with you."

"Drain my . . . ? Oh, yes, I suppose." He eyed the hand she reached down to him. "What are you doing? I *don't* need help."

"You can barely walk. Do you want me to have to pick you up when you collapse in the snow?"

He vented an exasperated sigh, and let her help him to his feet. Together they walked out into the night, and he had to admit his wobbly legs would have failed him but for her support.

He endured, despite chafing embarrassment. Upon their return to the camp, Willow spread out the robes, eased him down, and slid in next to him.

Richard tried to close his eyes, to make himself drift off, but his mind resisted stubbornly. Had she saved his life? Hell, yes! So what difference did it make to him if she'd done it through her body heat, or through some mystical twining of souls?

I am alive. That's all that matters.

But it's the method of your salvation that cannot be explained with any satisfaction, the little internal voice insisted.

Her head rested in the hollow of his shoulder, her body warmth joining his. When he inhaled, the familiar scent of her hair mixed with the pungent smell of fir needles and smoke; it brought a smile to his lips.

He remembered the way she'd looked that day at the Grand Detour, how her body had felt as it slid against his. He tightened his hold on her, feeling her snuggle closer to him.

Go to hell! he told the little voice inside, and only then did he drift off into fitful dreams.

◆

"Have you considered strangling him?" Willow asked White Hail dryly as they walked side by side through the snow. Sun-warmed and water-rotten, it soaked their moccasins.

They led the horses west down a long valley that would lead them to the very banks of the *Pia'ogwe.* To their left, immediately south, rose the slope of the mountain called *Tunangarit,* Thundersitter. To their right, the valley was hemmed by a bloodred sandstone ridge that jutted up in sheer cliffs. In places melted snow had trickled down the red rock, looking for all the world like dark sweat.

"Strangle him? What are you talking about?" White Hail gave her a hesitant look. He'd almost glanced back at Richard, but caught himself in time.

"Strangling would be best," she said. "You'd have to do it when I wasn't looking, of course. Any other way of killing him would look too much like murder."

White Hail scowled at her, then smiled sheepishly. To avoid her gaze, he looked out at the ragged sandstone ridge. "Woman, you've always been a step ahead of me, knowing the twists in my trail before I did. I can't understand what my brother saw in you."

"Go home, White Hail. When have I been wrong? About Red Calf? About the *Pa'kiani?* About finding Richard? About bringing back his soul? And now I see you becoming more bitter than gall drippings. If you persist, that bitterness will consume you, a festering evil beyond your control. Do you want that, White Hail? Is that the sort of man you would become?"

He paused thoughtfully. "No, Willow. I would rather be the sort of man I once was. What's happened to me? Why do I feel poisoned?"

"It's me, White Hail. The effect I have on you—just as I foretold so long ago when you came to ask me to marry you. *Teci*, I am going to ask you to do something for me, for both of us."

He sighed then. "Yes?"

"Leave. Jump up on your horse, and ride off to find the *Ku'chendikani*. Throw Red Calf out of your lodge, take care of Two Half Moons, and concentrate on hunting. If you wish wealth, hunt beaver for their hides, and trade them when the Whites arrive. There is no rule that says you cannot be brave and wise at the same time."

He considered her suspiciously. "And what will you and the White man do out here all alone?"

"I am taking him to the hot springs at *Pa'gushowener*. High Wolf will take his camp there after the equinox. He always does. He says the hot water helps him to restore his Power."

White Hail gestured his incomprehension. "Why alone, Willow? What if the *Pa'kiani* come? Or the *A'ni*, or some other enemy?"

She reached out, laying a hand on White Hail's shoulder. "I want time alone with him. My *navuzieip* has dreamed it,

White Hail—now I want to live it. I'll tell you another reason I want you to leave, Brother. He will be my husband. I don't think you will sleep well knowing we are joined under the robes just across from you."

White Hail snorted: "If his *we'an* is as weak as the rest of him, I don't have much to worry about."

"I'll wager his *we'an* is healthier than you think."

White Hail fingered the knife at his belt and slowly shook his head. "That night you went after the *Taipo*'s soul, I knew that my life was changing forever. I knew that you would come back changed if you even survived. You have great *puha*. Greater than most *puhagans,* since you can see into souls and travel to the Land of the Dead. For once, Willow, I will do as you say." A crooked smile bent his lips. "And, somehow, I think we will still be friends after this. But as to the White man . . ." his nose wrinkled. "He still stinks."

"*Tam Apo* go with you," Willow called as White Hail swung up onto his horse. He never looked back as he kicked the *Pa'kiani* gelding into a trot, hooves snowballing.

"What's happening?" Richard asked from where he rode on her mare.

"White Hail is going home to throw out his wife and live with his aunt for a while." She walked back, taking his hand. "I told him that you will be my husband."

"Husband?" His soft brown gaze probed hers. "I would like that, Willow. But do you understand how difficult this will be for us? The uncertainties?"

She squeezed his hand. "Richard, nothing in life is certain. You should know that by now."

His smile warmed. "Yes, I know. However, I think we have something special, you and I."

Richard rode stubbornly, his fingers woven into the brown mare's mane. A terrible fatigue sapped the last of his energy. His stomach knotted with a perpetually ravenous appetite. Willow had fed him all she could spare from her scanty rations, but eat as he might, he remained desperate for yet another bite.

Memories of long-ago meals, untouched food left on plates, tortured him. How fine life had been in Boston, food no farther away than the bell cord, or the nearest tavern. *I'll never think of food the same way. These days will always haunt me.* Even as he thought of it, the musty taste of rotten buffalo lingered on his tongue.

From Sally's magnificent culinary creations in Boston to scavenging rotten meat in the Big Horns was more than the distance between places. *Who am I now? What am I?*

"I'm alive, that's what."

Willow had been pushing herself, walking at a brisk pace as she traveled the sage-dotted ridgetops. Travel was easier since the snow had blown from the rocky crests. Now the ridges led down into the wide valley of the *Pia'ogwe,* the Shoshoni's Big River. To the south, the Owl Creek Mountains sloped up in a smooth incline, as if God had tilted the plain to form a ramp up to the sky. There, the peak Willow called Thundersitter dominated the southern horizon. To the west of it, the *Pia'ogwe* had cut a sheer-walled gorge through the tilted rock. White limestone lipped the edges—a layer of fat in a gargantuan wound.

At the base of the mountain, the red sandstone ridges huddled in on each other like horseshoe crabs on a beach. Those formations gave way to broken country stretching northward into the snow-shadowed basin. There, brown stone thrust out over yellow, white, and blue clays; the entire landscape, painted by the whim of nature, contrasted to the enamel blue of endless sky and sun-polished snow fields.

Willow turned north as they crested a ridge and dropped

into the *Pia'ogwe*'s broad floodplain. The cottonwoods were bare and gray, branches lonely for summer.

Richard glanced curiously at the clear river; bits of ice floated on its dark surface. It was hard to believe that these clear waters would become the same chalk-muddy Big Horn he'd ridden beside with Baptiste and Travis.

Two round-humped hills marked Willow's destination, and even in the afternoon sun, Richard could see the steam rising whitely from the crinkled earth at the bottom of the hills.

"That's *Pa'gushowener?* What's that mean?" he asked.

"It means 'Hot-Water-Stand.' It's a sacred place for us. You and I will camp beside the springs and heal you."

When she led him over the last rise, Richard could only gape. Scalloped formations of rock nestled beneath the rounded red and white hills. Each travertine formation pooled with clear, steaming water through which could be seen beds of orange, red, green, and blue. Only fairy tales could conjure an image like this, yet here it was before his eyes.

"It's magical!"

Willow stopped short, staring at one of the cottonwoods by the river. A large buck deer—tied off by the antlers—hung from a thick branch. The arrow transfixing its breast gleamed in the sunlight.

"What is it? An offering?" Richard glanced around, his

starvation-numbed mind suddenly aware of potential ambush.

"White Hail," Willow told him as a wry smile crossed her lips. "That's his arrow. These tracks, fresh . . . and made by his horse. See, there's the chip out of the left front hoof. Yes, Richard. It is an offering: food. Let me help you down. We'll camp here for the night. Then, tomorrow, we'll find a better place, build a shelter, and fort up."

"Fort up? As in 'prepare for a fight'?" He glanced back at the Hawken tied onto the pack. "My rifle's broken, Willow."

She gave him a thoughtful, sloe-eyed look. "But isn't 'fort up' the word Whites use for a permanent camp? Or should I have said 'build a post'?"

" 'Fort up' will be fine."

She took his hands, steadying him as he dismounted. She held him, staring into his eyes. "I've dreamed of having you here, Richard." She reached up, touching her lips to his, and he kissed her, ever so gently.

"For now, I want you to start healing yourself. Go and lie in the hot pool. I'll see to the horse, set up camp, and make a fire. Go on!" She waved him away.

Richard walked wearily to the edge of the nearest pool and stared at his reflection. More of a silhouette, really; he looked like something out of German mythology. He touched a finger to water as warm as any Jeffry had poured in the bath on Beacon Street.

Stripping out of his crusty hides, he shivered in the cold air, then waded into the warm water. The heat, enough to make him gasp, tingled his feet and toes. A wallow had been scraped into the crusty bottom near the edge of the pool. Not only was the water cooler, but the spot overlooked the river. The clear, ice-cold waters of the *Pia'ogwe* weren't twenty feet below. Richard settled himself, lying back to bask.

Even before he ducked his head, sweat beaded to roll

down his face. Eyes almost at water level, his imagination found faces and images in the patterns of steam. *Puha*, right here, before him.

Water. The age-old symbol of rebirth. What will you become this time, Richard? Still a philosopher? Or something else? Cupping his hands, he poured water over his head, then used his fingers and the flaky grit from the bottom to scrub himself clean before moving to clear water where he rinsed.

I could stay here forever, floating in the mist. That triggered his memory. *What really happened? Did I go to the Spirit World, the Land of the Dead, as Willow insists?*

He splashed in the heat, muscles and bones growing lax. "Damn it, it's not rational."

Or is it that you just won't admit what happened? Is that it, Richard? More of your arrogant American certainty that if it isn't scientific, not in a book, it can't be real?

"That's not it at all. Prove to me, rationally, empirically, that my soul—"

One of your souls.

"All right, prove to me that *one* of my souls went beyond the veil, into the afterlife. Whatever that is. And Willow's soul came to get mine. Good Lord, this isn't the Middle Ages!"

Ah, but something happened to you. Perhaps as it did to Augustine in the desert? To Aquinas, to Meister Eckhardt? To any of the great mystics? Something, Richard. They weren't all crazy.

"Maybe they were."

You're desperate to clutch any straw that might offer an alternative to a phenomenon you can't rationalize.

"Everything in the universe has an—".

"What are you doing?" Willow asked from behind him.

"Arguing with myself about the 'Land of the Dead.' Half of me says it was real, the other half is still skeptical."

"At least half of you is learning." She appeared out of the mist, wading in the knee-deep water. Tendrils of steam curled around her sleek brown legs, wound around her flat muscular belly, and spun illusions over her full breasts. Her long black hair was pulled back over her shoulder and hung down below her rump. It swung with each step, swirling the mist.

Precious Lord God, she looks like a goddess.

She approached gracefully, hips swaying, arms balancing precisely. Reading his expression, she flashed him a smile, challenge in her dark eyes.

"Are you going to run away again?"

"Just stand there, Willow. Yes, like that, with the steam rising around you. I want to memorize the way you look, plant it deep inside my soul, in that place of treasured memories. Blessed God but you're beautiful."

She lifted her chin, a sudden glint in her eye, then, quick as lightning, shifted and kicked water all over him. Before he could recover, she belly-flopped beside him, shrieking delight. She twisted like an otter, black hair wrapping around her, and surfaced beside him.

"That's the only way to do it," she told him. "Just dive in and feel the heat prickle all over your body. Hiyyaa! I'm alive, Richard. Every nerve—singing with the Power of the water."

"What a wonderful phrase." He splashed her back.

She studied him curiously, half seated, half floating. Her toes stuck out like dots in the twilight. "Is it so hard to believe in the Land of the Dead? Where do your souls go when you die? Somewhere?"

He frowned, lips pinched. "I don't know. No one does. I keep searching for an explanation."

She bobbed toward him, taking his hand and searching his eyes. "Can't some things just *be?* It happened, didn't it?"

"That's what perplexes me. How do I prove it? This could

be one of the most important discoveries of science, but I must have proof. Not for myself, but for others."

"Other Whites, you mean."

"Yes, other Whites."

"Richard, listen to me. Hear my words. Read my soul." She came close, her body sliding smoothly against his until he could feel her heart beating—sense that joining he'd felt in the Land of the Dead. "The *puha* will defy you if you seek to measure it. You can't *think* your way to it the way you try to do with God. You can't put it in a box. The only proof you have is that you are alive. You may believe or disbelieve, that is your choice. But if you believe, it is only because you *want* to, do you understand?"

With the barest hint of a nod, he surrendered and pulled her closer until his lips could brush hers. "We call it faith, Willow. That's the nail I've been missing—the thing to tie it all together. It took a very brave woman to come after my soul in the afterworld. Thank you for saving my life."

"We did it together," she reminded him soberly, and ran her long fingers down the side of his body. "I could never have returned without your help."

He slipped his arms around her and drew her onto him. Her breasts lay warm on his chest. "You and I, Heals Like A Willow, we're going to do a great many things together. You just wait until I get my strength back."

She smiled, relaxing against him. "I'm not a patient woman, Richard."

TWENTY-EIGHT

◈

The dialectic by which the object, as implicitly null, suspends itself, is the action of the self-assured living thing, which in this process against an inorganic nature thus retains, develops, and objectifies itself.

The living individual, which in its first process is as subject and concept, through its second has assimilated its external objectivity.

It is now, therefore, implicitly a genus, with substantial generality. The judgment of this concept is the relation of the subject to another subject, the sexual difference.

—Georg Friedrich Wilhelm Hegel, *Encyclopedia of the Philosophical Sciences in Outline*

The night wind blew in fits and starts, sometimes the barest of breezes, sometimes gusting hard enough to flatten the fire and tear sparks away into the night.

Willow had built a brush lean-to between the boles of two large cottonwoods. It would serve more as a windbreak than anything else. Tomorrow she would build a true wickiup out of brush and poles. To do so she would need willow, sagebrush, and bundles of grass.

The bank here was as high as a tall man above the river's edge, and Willow had placed their camp several paces back from the edge. As a result, they could see the moonlight reflected on the swirling water when the wind wasn't driving rippling waves across it.

Willow smiled as she watched Richard eat. Why was it that seeing a man eat reassured a woman? Was it some sense that *Tam Segobia* had placed in a woman's *mugwa?* Richard sat propped against the saddle. With greasy fingers, he plucked strands of meat from the ravaged deer haunch, chewing with studied enjoyment. He'd been nibbling like this for hours, ever since emerging from the spring.

She returned to scraping bits of tissue and muscle from the deer hide. In the morning, she'd finish slicing the deer's carcass into strips thin enough to smoke and dry.

I've dreamed of this moment. She stole another glance. His hair shone in the firelight; how soft his beard looked now that it was clean. A fish splashed in the river below their camp.

Tam Apo, was it so much to ask after this last year? Stringy connective tissue bunched on the pale hide. Using a hafted chert scraper, she hacked it loose, balled it, and tossed it over the bank into the river. She worked her fatigued fingers and stood up, amused with herself. "I'm tired. I'm going to wash my hands and sleep."

He grinned up at her. "It's been a long day. And, to tell you the truth, I haven't felt this good for . . . well . . . I guess I've *never* felt this good."

She took his greasy hand, and together they walked to the edge of the hot pool. "I think that hide will make you a good shirt, much better than those pieces you've been tying on like some stunted *Pandzoavits.*"

"They kept me alive. I was scared to death of frostbite."

She shook the water from her hands as they walked back to the fire. "You did very well, Richard. I'm proud of you. I'm not sure that even Travis could have done so well."

"Well, you know how these philosophers are."

She chuckled, hugged him, and laid out the robes before unlacing her moccasins. She wrinkled her nose. "We're clean, but the robes still have a smell."

"The sky's clear," he noted. "It's going to be cold tonight. I guess we'll just have to lie in the water again tomorrow." He paused, eyes shining. "I can't stop thinking about you. About the way you looked in the pool this afternoon."

She slipped her dress over her head, the wind chilling her warm skin. "Come to me, Richard."

A faint smile crooked his lips as he peeled his clothing away. Then he slipped in beside her, wrapping his arms around her and pulling her close.

For the moment, she closed her eyes, savoring the feel of his skin against hers, of his rapid heartbeat. As they warmed the robes, she ran her hand along his side to the curve of his buttock. Massaging the skin, she enjoyed the tension her fingers invoked. He sighed, his penis hardening against her hip.

"Willow?" he said, voice husky, "I've never done this before."

"I think I can lead you through it. And Richard, I'll take a great deal of pleasure in teaching you." She rolled onto her back, drew him onto her.

"I won't hurt you, will I?"

She laughed, arms around him in a fierce hug. His breath was warm on the curve of her neck. Her own heart racing, she pulled her knees up and reached down to guide him. He made a strangled sound as his rigid penis slid inside her. Her hips strained to meet his; then she locked her muscles to savor their union.

"Dear Lord God," he whispered, daring to look down at her. Her souls thrilled at the worship in his eyes. She moved slowly, using her muscles and the slightest of undulations.

Now we have shared souls, hearts, and bodies, Richard. Tam Apo *willing, we always will.*

So, that was what it was all about? Richard half-floated in the hot water. He lay on his back, only his face exposed to the air. Streamers of mist drifted in front of his nose, and water lapped at his cheeks. The breeze carried across the river from the southwest to ripple the surface of his bathing pond. The pale morning sky was frosted with horsetail filaments of cloud that diluted the hazy sunlight.

Eyes closed, he lay there, buoyed in body and soul. Ravens cawed as they flapped overhead. He and Willow had made love off and on throughout the night, and again as the morning broke.

They'd come here, bathed, and she'd ordered him to remain while she went about the preparation of food, and started construction of a wickiup. Weak as he was, he'd barely resisted, preferring to soak and relive every moment of their night together. Nothing had prepared him for this sense of elation.

Like any young man, he'd grown up with the urges and the attraction. He'd expected the physical sensations, but in imagination, the act had been somehow mechanical, the only passion animalistically physical. The *engagés* rutting with the Ree women and the Omaha squaw, and Travis dallying with the Sioux squaw had reinforced that idea. Copulation had come to seem nothing more than animalistic grunting.

He'd never considered that sexual joinings could come in two sorts: the sating of desire, and those of mutual intimacy. *Poor Travis, he has only the former.* Surely it hadn't always been that way. He had loved Calf in the Moonlight, married her. He must have felt this swelling joy.

An unexpected contentment ran down to the root of Richard's soul. And for that, he was glad that he'd turned down New Moon Rising's offer to warm his robes that night in the Crow village.

How much better that it was Willow. That first time, she had anticipated his quick ejaculation. *I would have thought that was all there was to it. Enter, explode, and wait until later to do it all again.*

But then Willow's fingers had stroked him to renewed vigor. She'd soothed, taught, and explained what made a woman happy. Under her guidance, he'd explored her breasts, run his hands over her stomach and the firm curves of hip and buttocks. One by one she taught him the secrets of her body and that joining could be done in more than one way.

During their fourth coupling she, too, had stiffened and cried out. Her reaction was stunning. Why had no one told him that a woman reached that pinnacle of ecstasy?

With Laura, his attempts would have been fumbling, shy, and nowhere as satisfying. Laura. He pursed his lips. Once, guilt would have tortured him. Now, he could barely remember her except as a dream.

He searched himself for regrets, and found none. *I would live last night over again, exactly the same way, with the same passion and reverence.*

He had joined his life to a woman beneath contempt in the eyes of Bostonian society. He'd forsaken his vow of a virgin bride. How many men had slid themselves into her body before him? Two that he knew of. Definitely her husband—and that same vagina had passed their child into the world. And Packrat—how many times had he mounted her and sated himself inside her? She'd as much as told him that *Dukurika* placed no emphasis on virginity; in *Tam Apo*'s eyes, men and women were supposed to copulate.

He smiled wearily, stretching out his arms and legs and arching his back to float free of the bottom. Travis had once asked, "What in Tarnal Hell are ye in love with? The woman? Or what's atwixt her legs?"

Oh, Travis, how right you were. Some whim of the mind conjured the serene eyes of Mother Mary, who stared down at him from his right. And from the left watched the haggard eyes of the fallen Magdalene. The two Marys of Christian civilization, eternally unrecognized as an elemental duality, a dialectical abstraction taken to obsessive extremes: the pristine Madonna or the gutter whore, and no common ground between.

Dear God, how we've deluded ourselves. How many people have been crippled by that myth? One for sure: Richard John Charles Hamilton. He cocked his head, surprised that he no longer cared, slightly puzzled by the lack of concern.

What if, by chance, he returned to Boston? Married Laura?

What if I do? First, I have to live that long. Second, Willow and I will have come to some bad end. And, should those criteria be fulfilled and I return to Boston, then I will determine the course of action appropriate to the circumstances.

What if he had impregnated Willow with his seed?

Then I will deal with it. He paused. *I will live here, now, taking all that I can from this fragile existence.*

Life was too much of an uncertain thing, as ephemeral as clouds on a hot day. If Willow were to have his child, he would take responsibility for it. Travis had been right, no one could escape responsibility.

Again, his reaction surprised him. The usual trepidation no longer plagued him. Why?

And the answer flowed easily from within. *Because I will deal with the eventualities. Because I can.*

But if I die tomorrow, or the day after, I can say that I have lived, loved.

Indeed he had. Her gasps of pleasure echoed in his ears. He could conjure the feel of her body out of the warm water, firm and soft, conforming to him. Man and woman, a sum of parts that made a balanced whole. The magic dazzled, profound in its simplicity.

He opened his eyes to the world, possessed of a new excitement. *In the shadow of death, I finally understand.* To reach this place, he'd had to lose everything—be stripped of the clutter of preconception imposed by his society. *I had to lose myself to find myself.*

"I have become Wolf," he whispered to an imaginary Sioux *wechashawakan* hovering in the trailers of steam. And a smile crossed his lips.

❖

As days passed into weeks, Richard regained his strength. Life at *Pa'gushowener* had a fairy-tale quality. Occasional storms roared down out of the north and left wind-drifted snow in their wakes. Then the skies would turn blue and cloudless and the slow melt would begin. The nights brought a clear cold, ameliorated by their cheery fire, the sagebrush shelter, and two bodies snuggled together under the robes.

During the day they walked the hills, collecting juniper bark to be shredded and twisted into netting. With sinew cord, they set snares for rabbits. With the Pawnee bow and arrows, they hunted the brush along the river for ducks. Willow taught Richard the proper way to net fish, and how to weave a fish trap from sticks and bait it. Together they built an antelope trap in an arroyo, using juniper and sagebrush for wing walls. Willow taught him different ways to sneak

up on buffalo, and how killing with a bow differed from using a rifle.

Richard struggled with the rudiments of the Shoshoni language, and spent his evenings listening to the winter stories about the Creation, about Wolf and Trickster Coyote, who traveled the land with his two penises. He heard about the *Pandzoavits,* the rock ogres, about Cannibal Owl, Water Babies, and the *Nunumbi.* She told him the stories about *Pachee Goyo,* the Bald One, who hunted the Water Buffalo that lived under Bull Lake. *Pachee Goyo* was abducted by Cannibal Owl but managed to escape when he killed Cannibal Owl with sharp flakes of obsidian.

Each night, they soaked in the hot springs, holding hands and talking of the day's adventures before retiring to the little shelter for supper and trysting under the robes.

Then came the evening when Richard and Willow returned from one of their hunts, the brown mare packed with sage grouse they'd killed with throwing sticks.

She held his hand as they walked, and thought back to the days on the river. "You know, Richard, even in my dreams I wasn't this happy."

"It's like the perfect paradise," he admitted, a pensive look on his face.

She gave him a sidelong inspection. *Richard has changed.* He'd made peace with the endless questions that had plagued him on the river. This new Richard was reserved, quietly contemplative. The burning in his soul had quenched, replaced by a deeper introspection.

But then, he's not the only one who's changed. She looked out at the world with a stranger's eyes. Little more than a year had passed since she wedged the body of her first husband and her son into the crack in the sandstone. Since then, she'd glimpsed four different worlds: Pawnee, White, Shoshoni, and the Land of the Dead. *Like Richard, I, too, have lost my innocence.*

She noticed the tension in his face. "What are you thinking when you look like that?"

"Look like what?"

"Like that. With that ghost of a frown. I see a distance in your eyes. As if you don't see this world for the moment."

"I was thinking about my father. About Boston."

Dread spread through her. "Boston. If I could pierce it with an arrow, kill it, I would."

His frown deepened. "How do I explain this? My father sent me off to Saint Louis with a great deal of wealth. I was robbed, lost every penny of it. Then, to save my life, I signed on with the *Maria*. So, here I am, Willow, living in a kind of paradise I'd never dreamed. But my father lost thirty thousand dollars because I was a fool." He pursed his lips, then added: "It's funny, but I never understood him until recently. I imagine him sitting behind his desk, looking miserable because he thinks I'm dead—or worse, that I've betrayed him and taken the money for myself. He never forgave himself for my mother's death, and he'll never forgive himself for sending me to Saint Louis."

"Your words frighten me."

"You?" he asked, arching an eyebrow. "Heals Like A Willow, who drove Packrat insane? The woman who killed so many Rees, and saved my life? The woman who crossed the wilderness, rescued White Hail from the Blackfeet, and dared to search the Land of the Dead for my soul? Is that the same Willow who now says she's frightened?"

"Don't joke. I'm afraid you will go to Boston and never come back." *That you will stay with this yellow-haired Laura you used to dream about.*

"I haven't left yet."

"No, you haven't. But you're a man, Richard. Men always leave."

He glanced suspiciously at her. "But they come back, don't they?"

"Will you? Have you asked yourself that question? Where do you belong—here with me? Or in your Boston with its philosophy, and God in buildings, and women in houses with their children?"

"Willow, it's as if I was reborn when I awoke after the Land of the Dead. I don't fully understand this new life— where I'm going."

"But the old life still intrudes?"

"He's still my father, Willow. He thinks I'm dead. Thinks he sent me to that death. You lost a son. How much worse would it have been if you'd sent him out to his death? I think you understand the Power of guilt."

She nodded reluctantly. The mare stopped to rub her head on a propped foreleg. "Richard, do you *want* to go back?"

But he didn't have time to answer the question, for as they topped the ridge that led down to their wickiup, Willow spied two men sitting at the fire.

Richard reached out to stop her. "We'll talk of that later. Recognize them?"

From their sheephide coats they were *Dukurika*. She cupped hands around her mouth, shouting, "Who's there?"

The men stood, craning their necks. One shouted back, "Rock Hare and Eagle Trapper! Is that you, Sister? I know that horse! But who walks beside you?"

"His name is Richard!"

"Where is White Hail?"

"Back with the *Ku'chendikani*."

Willow strode forward until they were close enough for her to recognize them. Rock Hare had that superior air about him: the proud male in all of his magnificence. Eagle Trapper watched curiously as she and Richard picketed the horse and unslung the heavy pack full of grouse.

"Who are they?" Richard asked in English. "The Shoshoni was so fast, I missed most of it."

She pointed, saying slowly in Shoshoni, "Rock Hare, my brother. Eagle Trapper, my friend."

Richard stepped forward, extended a hand, and in passable Shoshoni said, "My heart is happy to meet you."

"He speaks like a human!" Eagle Trapper was staring as if seeing a new kind of animal. "He is dressed like a human!"

"But he has skin like a corpse. And the hair—all over his face! Like a dog. Hyyyah! What they say about them is true."

"What's happening?" Richard asked, hand still held out.

"They've never seen a White man before." Willow stepped forward to take Rock Hare's hand and place it in Richard's. She told him, "Shake hands. It's a White man form of greeting. Just do it. I'll explain later."

Rock Hare shook hands, but his heart wasn't in it.

Eagle Trapper adamantly crossed his arms. "I do not shake hands with a man who looks like a corpse."

In English, Willow said, "Richard, Eagle Trapper is frightened of you."

"And of his Power," Eagle Trapper added. "We have heard rumors. Stories that come from the *Ku'chendikani*. It is said that you have become a witch."

"What?" Willow's heart skipped, unsure if this was some sort of joke.

Rock Hare glanced around nervously, as if trying to see everything but his sister and the White man. "Well, it's a rumor, Willow. The story came to us that you had sent your *mugwa* into the Land of the Dead to find this White man. That you brought him back from the Dead, and in the process, angered the Spirit World with your pollution. It is said your *puha* has turned evil now."

She locked her knees to keep from staggering. An electric fear tightened in her chest.

White Hail might have been jealous of Richard, but he wouldn't have turned on her. She couldn't believe that. The only person he would have told would have been Two Half Moons, and Willow trusted her implicitly. But somehow, someone had found out. Who? *Red Calf!* Somehow, some way, she'd managed to learn the story and work her poison.

"What's wrong?" Richard asked.

"The *Ku'chendikani,* White Hail's people, are saying that by going after your soul in the Land of the Dead, I've become a witch."

Richard cried, "That's ridiculous!"

Rock Hare asked uneasily. "Is it true, Sister?"

"No," she said unevenly. "What . . . what does Father think?"

"He doesn't know what to think. He'll arrive tomorrow. We came ahead to scout the way. We didn't expect to find you here. We thought you'd run off to the *Ku'chendikani,* or the White men, or some such thing."

"I'm *no* witch," Willow insisted, "but that doesn't mean I'm not shaken to be accused of being one. Well, I can't fix that tonight. Come, help us pluck these birds. Then we can go and soak while they cook."

But try as she might, she couldn't dismiss the brewing worry; a cold wind of premonition blew around her souls.

TWENTY-NINE

If then the means by which the soul discovers truth, and generally discerns things unchanging or even those things variable about truth, are science, prudence, wisdom and intuitive reason, and if no one of the first three—prudence, science, and wisdom—is a means of grasping primary principles, our only possible conclusion is that they are determined by intuitive reason.

—Aristotle, *Nicomachean Ethics*

The wind came from the west, roaring down across the ragged plains from where the Big Horns thrust up like a humped giant against the horizon. It howled over the broken hills, around the lonely sandstone outcrops, shivered the sage, and whistled over the tilted shale beds of the Powder River basin. Heedless of the wind's cold caress, the land lay dormant under the frozen spell, numbed by ice, and gnarled as the bent sage that trapped snow in pimpled drifts.

The long column of people and horses looked like some mythical serpent winding through the snow-crusted valley, crossing the drainage, and winding through the drifted sage before climbing the other side.

"Never seen a winter like this," Travis growled wearily as he slumped on his horse. The melancholy had settled on him, and the relentless cold just pressed it down tighter around his soul.

"Nope," Baptiste agreed.

They were both warmly dressed in heavy hunting shirts and hairy buffalo coats. Fur hats covered their heads, and mittens protected their hands. Their legs were encased in thick leggings made from elk hide with rabbit fur sewn on the inside.

They rode side by side on mud-spattered horses, rifles resting on saddlebows. Ahead of them, Two White Elk joked with Lightning Bull, both of them bragging about the hunt they'd just finished. Behind them rode a knot of happy and tired warriors, blood-splotched and mud-smeared. Still farther behind came the women leading packhorses. The animals slipped and slid in the hoof-churned mud and snow, piled high with chunks of freshly butchered meat.

A week ago, the weather had warmed above freezing during the day—just enough of a break in the deadly cold that the Crow had taken the opportunity to hunt. A band of winter-thin bison had moved into the Tongue River bottoms to avoid the deep snow on the ridges.

"Hell of a winter," Baptiste observed, as his little buckskin slipped and scrambled up the snow-packed trail beaten through the leeside drift. They followed the other warriors out onto a windswept ridgetop studded with scabby-looking sage and red shale. The wind worried their fur hats and hide fringes as the horses clopped across the flat ridgetop, thankful for solid footing.

"Worst in memory," Travis agreed. "Whoa up a minute." He pulled his horse out of line and walked it to the side. There he squinted into the gale and studied the Big Horn Mountains, so majestically white against the clear sky.

"Yep, bad, all right." Baptiste slouched over his rifle, eyes slitted against the cold wind. "What's wrong, coon? You been too damned quiet and mopey. Even Two White Elk is getting fidgety, a-giving you that worried look. It's Moonlight, ain't it? She been a-prying at your soul, now ain't she? And Dick, too. You ain't figgered him fo' dead yet."

"Yep, I reckon ye read the spots on the cards, all right." Travis sighed. "Hell, every time I turn around, I expect ter see Calf in the Moonlight come walkin' around a lodge. I keep listening fer her voice, seeing her face in every young woman's. And, when I ain't doing that, I'm wondering about old Dick."

"He's dead, Travis. Sho' 'nuff, you know how damn cold it got. Then the wind blowing the drifts around. Even if'n he'd a had a hoss, he'd a been lost and froze."

The cold wind made Travis's eyes water, and he blinked. "I gotta look, is all."

"Fo' what? Bones?"

The Crow continued to pass, still laughing and talking, every last one happy about the fresh meat. During the relentless cold, people had reached deeply into their parfleches for pemmican and jerky. Folks ate more when it grew cold enough to make trees pop, and spit crackle when it hit the ground. Nearly a quarter of the horses had died, some frozen solid on their feet. The worst of winter was past now. The thawing winds of March had come, and buffalo had been killed. Within weeks, all that would remain of the kill would be splintered bone—and that thrown out only after it was boiled for marrow butter.

"You been itching," Baptiste said. "I can see it in yor eyes."

"Reckon so." Travis cocked his jaw. "We got all the beaver we can trade fer hyar. We're just wasting time, eating their food."

"We done repaid that debt today." Baptiste jerked a thumb at the meat-laden packhorses that scrambled up through the beaten-down drift to clop across the ridgetop on shaking legs. "Ain't no red bastard heah shot more buff than you and me."

"That's a fact."

"So, why is you figgering to pull yor stick, fo' God's sake? You got a nice warm lodge to live in, and young New Moon Rising a warming yor robes. Tarnal Hell, any damned fool knows that spring's the most miserable time fo' travel. The snow's melting, mud up to an elk's arse everywhere. Hellacious storms come a-rolling in and pile up—and then it rains on the whole shitaree and makes what's plain torment into pure misery. A feller can't keep his powder dry, and . . . and there ain't no place, for God's sake, where a coon can throw out his bed and be dry! Ain't nothing so horrible as spring travel!"

"Reckon so." Travis snorted. The last of the packhorses had passed, the Crow women leading them only mildly interested in the whites as they stared off to the west.

"Then why, in sweet Jesus' name, would you be wanting to ride out in all that slop?"

Travis growled nervously to himself, then said, "Aw hell, I reckon yer right, Baptiste. I'll give it another couple of weeks, and I'm pulling my stick. Ride or stay, it's yer decision, coon."

Baptiste slapped Travis on the shoulder. "I'll ride with you, old beaver. Head down to Rendezvous with you. But I just ain't a-going slopping through no mud. I done enough of that in Louisiana. I didn't like it there, and I'll tell you, coon, that mud whar a heap site warmer than this heah mud."

"Reckon so, but this mud don't have no snakes nor 'gaters slithering through it."

"Maybe, but Louisiana mud ain't sticky like this mud. Why, I seen it suck a hoss's hoof clean off'n the bone. Left that po' hoss a-stumping around with the damnedest gait you ever seen."

"So, are we gonna sit up hyar, freezing our pizzles off, a-lying about mud, or are we gonna go back and fill our gizzards with hot hump steak?"

Baptiste twisted his lips in disgust, spat downwind, and reined his horse around. "And I thought you was the one talking 'bout riding off all hellbent to slip and slide and sleep in the mud. Now yor talking 'bout hot food. You takes all, you do, Travis."

Travis shot one last look back at the Big Horns to the south, the peaks so white in the distance. "I reckon I do. Now, come on, let's catch them Injuns afore they eat all that meat." He let his horse follow the beaten track. The gelding slid down the pockmarked slope on braced legs.

I'm a-coming, Dick. And if'n I find yer bones . . . well, I guess I could scatter a little tobacco over 'em at least.

Loud whoops shattered the quiet night air as Richard walked along the curving edge of the steam-cloaked pool. The sound of violent splashing worthy of Perry on Lake Erie carried across the water; waves chopped at the shoreline of the hot pool. The high-pitched laughter belonged to Rock Hare, the deeper bellow to Eagle Trapper. Both *Dukurika* hunters were obscured by the thick plume of steam that rose in the moonlight.

Richard found Willow on the far side of the pools. She was standing on the bank overlooking the river. The *Pia'ogwe* had cut down through solid rock here, and below the jagged cliffs the swirling black waters were moon-bathed in silver.

She'd wrapped her mountain sheep cape tightly about her shoulders, head back as she watched the starred heavens. With her long black hair streaming down and the gentle curves of her heart-shaped face caressed by the moonlight, she seemed like an exquisite sculpture, the sort Michelangelo would have crafted.

He walked up behind her, lacing his arms around her waist. His frosted breath hung in the stone-cold air. "I thought the pools were sacred. Listen to them; the splashes sound like cannon balls."

"The pools *are* sacred," she answered absently. "Is that any reason people can't enjoy themselves? That's another difference between my people and yours. To White men the sacred must be deadly serious, never room for laughter, jokes, or humor."

"It would be unthinkable," Richard agreed. "God—and holy things—are for serious contemplation."

She pointed across the distance. "You've seen the mountain we call Coyote's Penis? The story is that just after the Creation, Coyote was wandering around the land to see what he could see. One time, Coyote was sneaking along the Big River, and he saw Wolf's daughter bathing on the other side. Being Wolf's daughter, she didn't like Coyote, wanted nothing to do with him. But he'd always desired her, and seeing her there in the water, he wanted her more than ever. He sent his penis swimming across the river to mate with her. Just as his penis was about to slide inside her, Trout rushed up from the bottom of the river. Thinking he saw a big worm, he bit Coyote's penis clean in two."

"That makes me cringe just to think of it."

"Oh, yes, and Coyote screamed in the most hideous fashion, for it hurts to have one's penis bitten off. Anyway, Wolf's daughter waded across the river to see what had happened, and found Coyote thrashing around in the brush, holding his bloody stump. The pain had dulled his wits so much that he told her how he'd tried to trick her, and how Trout had mistaken his penis for a worm and bitten it in two.

"Wolf's daughter immediately ran home and told Wolf what Coyote had tried to do. Wolf was infuriated! He called to Bald Eagle, who was fishing on the river, and told him:

'Coyote tried to sneak his penis into my daughter, and Trout mistook it for a worm and bit it off. Go and see if you can find it floating in the river.'

"Bald Eagle owed Wolf a favor and flew down the river, looking for the penis. There it was, floating along, looking pathetic and limp, so Bald Eagle swooped down and grabbed it out of the water. He carried it high up on top of the mountain and left it there where Coyote couldn't reach it. It was so high up that it turned to stone, and you can still see it there today."

Richard gave her a quizzical glance. "You're right, a White man would never tell a story like that."

"But my people do. The lesson it teaches is that a man should be careful about letting his lust overwhelm his sense. But the other thing is, like all Coyote stories, it's funny. *Tam Apo* made people to laugh as well as cry. Often a joke can teach a holy truth better than a somber story. Someday I'll tell you about how Coyote faked his death, then disguised himself so he could marry his daughters and lie with them, and how they baked his penis in the fire when they discovered what he'd done to them."

He thought back to Wolf, nodding slowly. "Coyote. The root of all evil and mayhem. What does that say about the nature of the universe?"

"According to the stories my people tell, it wavers between Wolf's kindness and sense, and Coyote's cunning and trouble. One must always challenge the other."

He tightened his grip on her. "Then the transcendental dialectic is the only constant."

"What are these words?"

"It means the inevitable conflict of ideas coming from a common source. Good versus evil, or, in the Shoshoni case, Wolf versus Coyote."

"We call it 'opposites crossed.' That's just how the world was made."

Wild laughter exploded behind them; a body thudded into the water with a cascade of droplets hissing like rain.

"Willow, why are you out here? I thought you'd come back to the fire after we left the water."

She turned and looked up at him, moonlight revealing the desperation in her eyes. "Do you know what it means when Rock Hare says that people are calling me a witch?"

"I don't believe in witches. Rational people don't."

"My people do. What was the argument you made the other day when we were fleshing the buffalo hide? That human understanding is always colored by individual perception? My people perceive witches. They *want* to believe in them. Therefore, they do."

"But what people want to believe doesn't create truth."

"It doesn't have to, Richard. Your people don't believe a joke can teach a sacred truth. But it can."

"All right. Is witchcraft as serious a charge as say . . . a charge of murder would be among my people?"

She considered, finally shrugging. "I don't know your people that well. What if someone among your people accused someone else of having incest with their children? The children might deny it, but the suspicion has been planted. No one will look at those people the same way again. They've become *omaihen,* no matter what they protest."

"And you think that will happen to you?"

"It has happened," Willow whispered softly. "I'm sure it's a woman named Red Calf. She's White Hail's wife, the one he was going to throw away. I'm sure it's her. She tried to call me a witch after my husband died. People will remember. If White Hail cast her out, and if he told of me sending my soul to find yours in the Land of the Dead, it will confirm people's suspicions."

"Wait. Didn't you tell me that *puhagan* go after souls all the time, that your father, High Wolf, has sent his soul to the Land of the Dead?"

"He's a man, Richard. For a woman to become a true *puhagan* is *omaihen*, forbidden."

"I'm sorry, Willow. What should I have done? What can we do?"

"Nothing. What is done is done." She stared out over the river, where moonlight shone on the icy water. In the distance the buttes and hills rose in ghostly luminescence that contrasted with patches of shadow. She raised her hands, irritated. "And maybe it's true. Remember, I killed Packrat's soul. Drove him mad. I can't forget that. I have great *puha*, Richard. I can kill with it."

"I don't believe in witches."

"No, but Packrat did. My people do. Tell me, if a person believes, is that not his individual truth? Just as I called up the *Dukurika* version of the Land of the Dead?"

"Some would make that argument. But, Willow, you've always been a little hazy on how you drove Packrat mad."

"I was his captive. I didn't tell him when I began to bleed. Once, when he took me, he looked down and found his penis covered with woman's blood. I broke his Power, killed his soul."

He flinched. *She was a captive, Richard. Captors treat slaves however they will. And she paid him back for it the only way she could.* He calmly said, "I didn't know that menstrual blood was that dangerous."

She laughed nervously. "Oh, Richard, I don't know what to do. And it's not just the talk of being a witch. It's as if I came home to people who had changed—and all the while it was I who was different."

"Different how?"

"Oh, one day Rock Hare took the ax. He beat the edge off my ax. How? By hitting rocks with it to see the sparks fly. And then he wouldn't sharpen it. Instead, he went off to hunt. Then came all the unmarried men, coming to look me over, to see if they wanted to marry me. Why? They wanted the—how do you say?—prestige. Some thought I had a way with the Whites, special access to trade. If I'd wanted that, I could have married Dave Green and saved myself the hard work expected of an Indian wife.

"I'm not sure you will understand my feelings, but it was as if I didn't belong any more. My people, they didn't believe the stories I told about *Maria,* about the *engagés,* about killing the Rees. None of it. They listened politely, but I could see it in their eyes. They thought they were all just marvelous stories that I'd made up."

He nuzzled her neck, savoring the sulfur smell the water had left in her hair. "You've seen beyond the horizon, Willow. They're still innocent. You're not. Like Adam and Eve in our stories, you've bitten the apple, seen beyond the Garden of Paradise."

"Where do I go? Where do I belong, Richard? For the first time, I think I understand the Shoshoni women among the Mandan. I was very upset when they didn't want to return to their relatives. But now I see through their eyes. Unlike them, I have no place. Not among the *Dukurika,* not among the *Ku'chendikani,* not among the Whites, or Mandan. I've become like a tree that's fallen into the river. The current of life carries me along, but I can't find the right soil for my roots."

"We'll find it."

"We?" She turned, trying to read his expression in the moonlight. "You're going back to Boston, Richard."

"Willow, I never said a thing about—"

"You don't need to."

"I haven't made that decision."

She reached up to run a gentle finger along his cheek. "But you will, Richard. You don't know it yet, but you'll go in the end."

"That's silly."

"Say what you will. I'm cold and tired. Come, take my

hand. I want to go back to camp. Then I want you to hold me all night long."

"Afraid you'll dream about being a witch?"

Her head bowed. "Yes. And I want to enjoy you all I can. Maybe tomorrow, maybe the day after, I will begin my bleeding."

"I'm not worried about it. I can still sleep with you, can't I, even if we don't couple?"

That familiar wry smile curled her lips. "Oh yes, I know. You're a great *puhagan,* without fear of pollution from anything so threatening as a lowly female's blood. Aren't you even a little afraid of me?"

"So much so that I'll just have to hold you even more tightly." He kissed the top of her head.

She gave him a saucy smile, took his hand, and led him back along the curving edge of the pond.

◆

When High Wolf arrived the following day, White Rock's band accompanied him, bringing nearly forty people and almost a hundred dogs to the flats around the steaming *Pa'-gushowener.*

Willow and Richard walked through High Wolf's camp as the people unloaded the dog travois and began building wickiups from poles, hide, sagebrush, and grass. To Willow's dismay, people greeted her with uncharacteristic reserve, watching uneasily from the corners of their eyes. She noticed that children were being kept at a conspicuous distance. Their reaction to Richard was one of wide-eyed amazement, and, in a manner most rude for *Dukurika,* they pointed at him behind his back.

They don't trust me—my own relatives! Stunned and

injured, she could imagine the whispered conversations passing from lip to lip.

Richard watched with open delight, oblivious to the stares, as brush lodges were constructed on the grassy slope south of the hot pools. "Why don't they have tipis like the Crow and Sioux?"

"To haul such big tipis, you must have horses. White Hail's *Ku'chendikani* live in tipis," Willow told him, hiding the turmoil inside. "Sometimes we use small tipis that the dogs can haul. But why haul a lodge around when you can build one out of what's handy at the next camp?"

"A horse can haul more than a dog can. Think about how much more work they can do." He hooked a thumb back at their horse picketed on grass beside the river.

When they passed old woman Yellow Tooth, she wouldn't meet Willow's eyes. "Horses need a great deal of grass, Richard. Those cakes you like so much? They are made from grass seeds we gather in late summer. Horses would eat that grass. In spring, we dig the roots of the desert parsley, and eat the leaves. Horses trample those plants. A horse can't walk through the dense timber where we hunt. Have you ever seen a horse jump from rock to rock on a mountainside? No? Well, a dog can, and my people often cross steep mountain valleys, and climb up and down cliffs. Horses are animals for wide plains and open trails, not for the places the *Dukurika* live."

"I guess I didn't think about that."

Willow's heart leaped when she saw High Wolf. Would he, too, turn his back on her? He looked fit and hale. His white-tanned sheephide coat accented his broad shoulders. High moccasins rose to his knees, topped by bands of wolf fur, and the sun glinted in the silver threads in his long braided hair. High Wolf was carrying armloads of sagebrush to White Alder, who wove the branches around the outside of a dome-shaped willow-pole framework.

Willow walked forward. "Greetings, Father." She hated the reserve in her voice, and the fluttering of her heart. Her nerves tingled anxiously. *If he doesn't acknowledge me, what will I do?*

High Wolf dropped his load of sagebrush and turned toward her, smacking his hands. He cocked his head, inspecting her with those familiar bright eyes, then carefully studied Richard from head to foot, before saying, "So, this is a White man? Look at all that hair! And such a thin face—and those pale eyes! Can he really see through them?"

"Richard, this is High Wolf, my father."

Richard smiled, stepping forward and offering his hand. In carefully practiced Shoshoni, he said, "Greetings, High Wolf. I am called Richard Hamilton."

High Wolf contemplated the outstretched hand for a moment, then took it in a limp grip. He glanced at Willow. "This is a White man's thing?"

"An offer of friendship," she said, as High Wolf withdrew his hand and inspected it curiously to see if there had been any change.

White Alder took a hesitant step forward, her body canted to the side, expression wary, as if approaching some exotic animal she couldn't be too sure of. "Willow? This is the White man? The one in your dreams?"

"He is. Richard, this is my mother, White Alder."

By now Richard had sensed the tension, giving her an

uneasy glance as he offered his hand. Although White Alder had seen him shake High Wolf's, she held back. "Is he dangerous?"

"No." Richard replied. "I am happy to meet Willow's mother. I am Richard Hamilton—um, of Boston, madam. I assure you, I am a . . . a gentleman."

"He is a noted warrior," Willow supplied since her mother had no idea of the meaning of "Boston," "madam," or "gentleman."

In English, Richard asked, "Do they know we're lovers? Will that be a problem?"

"No," she replied tersely. Leave it to Richard to worry about trivia when witch talk was in the air. Then, trying to mask her desperation, Willow said too quickly, "Father, I know you are busy, but could I . . . ?"

"Yes, yes." He turned to White Alder. "I think I must go and talk to our daughter. I will be back to help you as soon as I can."

White Alder's reserved gaze went from Richard to Willow. "Go, husband. Find out what all this foolishness is."

As they walked toward Willow's camp, Richard added nervously, "He's going to see only one bed."

"Richard, you are my husband. This is about witchcraft. And *puha,* and *omaihen.*"

"Yes, yes, I know. But you're still their daughter. And I'm essentially a stranger who's sharing your robes. I'd think they'd be a little more concerned about that."

"Why should they? Unless, of course, we're both witches."

"Both?" He raised an eyebrow. "Me—a witch? How irrational can you get?"

High Wolf feigned indifference as he walked, his curious study of Richard conducted as surreptitiously as possible.

At their camp, High Wolf ceremoniously seated himself cross-legged before the smoldering fire, took a deep breath, and propped his arms on his knees. "I have heard that White Hail went back to his people."

"He did."

"So, Daughter, what have you gotten yourself into this time?"

"You remember the dreams I was having in camp?" At her father's nod, Willow seated herself between him and Richard. She told of her travels with White Hail, of seeing the wolves and finding Richard. She related the steps she'd taken to save him, including sending her soul into the Land of the Dead; how she'd talked Richard into coming back to the living, and their journey.

When she finished, High Wolf leaned his head back and pulled his tubular stone pipe from the badger hide pouch at his side. Tamping the bowl with kinnikinnick, he used a twig to fish around in the fire for an ember, and lit it. After making his offerings, and singing a prayer, he puffed and passed the pipe to Willow, who repeated the ritual, then handed the pipe to Richard.

High Wolf watched, expression pensive. When the pipe was returned to him, he studied the curls of smoke rising from the stained end of the steatite tube. "I always knew you had great *puha,* and it frightened me. Daughter, you've always been different, a little odd, but that was all right because I'd looked into your souls and seen all that you were.

"I am relieved by some parts of your story, and even more disturbed by others. I am relieved that you escaped the Land of the Dead despite being *omaihen,* for that tells me that you have not been overcome by a *puha* too powerful for you to use wisely. Instead, it was this White man who saved you, and his *puha* must be very Powerful if he could help you find the way back. I am glad that you survived. I never thought that you were evil, Daughter."

"And what disturbs you?"

High Wolf puffed on his pipe and blew smoke into the air with solemnity. "What I see for you in this world, Willow. Now I know what happened—and that you have a Power greater than any woman I have ever known. I do not believe you would misuse such great Power, but they"—he indicated the *Dukurika* camp—"do not know. The rumors have already frightened them. Many are thinking of leaving . . . of going as far from you as they can."

Willow had been translating for Richard, filling in the words he didn't know. As she spoke, her guts knotted and cramped.

"I will speak for you. But many will suspect my words since you are my daughter. They might stay if I ask them to, but if anyone grows sick, or has bad luck, they will blame you. I think you know that, don't you?"

She nodded, a hand held to her sour stomach. "I feared as much, but I hoped that . . . that . . ."

"Yes, I know." He gave her the old familiar smile that had soothed her over the years. "I'm sorry, Daughter. It's not me, but the people who will fear you. You know people as well as I do. What they fear, they hate. What they hate, they finally destroy."

Willow drooped, soul-weary. "What should I do?"

High Wolf pursed his weathered brown lips. "Does this White man have a place? Will you go with him?"

Willow nodded. "I will." *But for how long?*

High Wolf scratched his ear. "I always knew you would be trouble. You asked too many questions. You wanted too many answers for things that must remain mysterious. That was the *puha*. Had you been a man, you would have been the greatest *puhagan* ever. But now, I see you here, full of Power, with the haze of the Spirit World around you so strong that any normal person should fear you."

"But you don't?"

"No. We've seen the truth in each other's souls." He indicated Richard. "Are all White men as Powerful as he?"

"No." She took Richard's hand. "He is like me, Father. Among his own people, he asks the kind of questions that I do. It is only recently that he has begun to understand his *puha*."

High Wolf nodded respectfully to Richard. "Take care of my daughter. She will need all of your skill and Power."

"I will," Richard replied, catching most of the meaning.

Will you? Willow questioned, looking into his soft brown eyes. *How can you, with Boston always calling?*

High Wolf sighed, slapping hands to his legs. "And that is that. If you decide to leave, I would go soon. Maybe even tomorrow morning. For now, I must go and help your mother. Explain what has happened. And perhaps we will come to your camp tonight. You can feed us, I hope? That dried buffalo meat back there—it's not for coyotes, is it?"

"No, Father." She patted his arm. "I think I could feed you with it."

He stood then, looking around, the sun glinting in his gray-streaked hair. Despite the slight stoop to his back, he looked weathered and powerful, the sort of elder anyone would look up to. "I think you should eat that horse. Dogs would serve you better. One of my bitches will whelp soon. I could give you some pups. They'll be good dogs. A person shouldn't live without dogs. It's not natural, or healthy."

Willow stood. "I think we'll keep our horse for a while. But if we need dogs, I know where to find the very best."

Richard arose and stood before High Wolf, offering his hand again. "You are welcome here any time, sir. My . . . uh, our camp is always yours."

High Wolf shook the hand, and for a long moment, stared into Richard's eyes, both of them locked, measuring. In the end, High Wolf nodded ever so slightly. "You are a good man. Not everyone has Wolf as a guardian spirit. He chooses carefully . . . as does my daughter."

Then he turned, walking purposefully back toward the *Dukurika* camp.

"Quite a man," Richard mused. "So stately and possessed. I think I could come to like him a great deal."

"And he you," she said sadly. "But I don't think you'll get the chance, Richard. He's right. We must leave. Tomorrow, before trouble starts."

"Go where?" Richard wondered.

She sniffed the west wind, blowing mildly on this warm day. "I know a place. Tonight we will feed my parents, and tomorrow we will cross the river and go to *Ainkahonobita*, Red Canyon Spring. It's just west—a half-day's journey."

"And after that?"

Suddenly desolate, she pulled him to her, hugging him close in an attempt to draw on his strength. "I don't know, Richard. For once in my life, I just don't know."

"I won't leave you, Willow. I promise you that. We'll find a way, somehow. You have my word."

And she did feel better—even if she knew he was lying to her, and himself.

THIRTY

The essence of the spirit is therefore free-dom—the absolute and negative identifica-tion of the concept with itself. It can remove itself, therefore, from everything external, and from its own externality as well as from its very being, and thus bear infinite pain, the negation of its immediate individuality; in other words, it can be identi-cal to itself in this negativity. This possibility is the self contained being within itself, its simple concept, or absolute generality by itself.

—Georg Friedrich Wilhelm Hegel,
The Philosophy of Spirit

The Owl Creek Mountains ran east-west, separating the Warm Wind Valley and the *Pia'ogwe*'s basin. *Ainkahonobita,* Red Canyon, lay in the foothills on the north slope of the Owl Creeks. Bright red sandstone rose in sheer cliffs that walled the northern side of the canyon, while to the south, the mountains drained into a creek that cut eastward toward the *Pia'ogwe*.

Ainkahonobita was an oasis. Its tall red cliffs caught the full measure of winter sun, and the surrounding heights pro-tected it from the prevailing westerly winds so that the canyon remained warm and sheltered. The spring to which Willow had led Richard wasn't hot, but ran warm enough that the water didn't freeze, and green grass and rushes grew there throughout the winter.

The slopes were timbered in pine and juniper, firewood abundant in every direction. Here, too, the buffalo, antelope, elk, and deer came to drink. Sheer-walled side canyons acted as natural corrals for their horse, and forage was plentiful on the sun-melted slopes.

Willow's inclination had been to build a wickiup, but Richard insisted they elaborate. The construction took three days. They picked a place with southern exposure where the juniper-dotted ground sloped beneath the sandstone uplift. With digging sticks they excavated a waist-deep hollow in a space sheltered by the trees. The damp red dirt was piled to the sides. Then, on a much smaller scale than that used by the river tribes, four limber pine supporting posts were tamped into place in the lodge bottom, and stringers were run across the top to form a hollow square. With Willow's ax they trimmed juniper rafters to the right size, and laid stringers from the rafters to the ground. The whole was covered with rabbitbrush, hides, and sage, then overlaid with dirt.

"It looks like home." Richard had his arm around Willow's shoulders as they stood admiring their primitive house.

"So much work!" Willow rubbed the blisters on her hands. "You White men, always doing more than you need to."

"It will be warm, dry, and comfortable. You'll see."

As the cold spring storms roared down from the northwest and dropped successive snows, they remained snug in their haven, feasting on smoked meat and talking. By day, they explored the crimson sandstone that thrust up in layers around the valley; the color contrasted to the bright green of juniper and pine and with the enamel blue of sky.

One particularly warm day they took the worn game trail that followed a circuitous route to the canyon rim. Bright sunlight brought the colors out of the stone, glared off the patches of unmelted snow, and promised spring.

"I've never seen such a beautiful place," Richard

declared as he climbed to stand on a spur of rock high on the canyon wall. Before him the cliff dropped away in a sheer fall that dizzied the senses. From the edge, he had an eagle's view of the layered sandstone beds, straight down to the broken red rubble sloping away from the base of the cliff. He could see for miles up and down the rugged canyon and out over the mountains beyond. "It's as if God lives here."

"God lives everywhere." Willow put her arm about his waist, long black hair teased by the gusty breeze. "It's only you Whites who have put him inside a building. You'll never be the same, Richard. Your souls *feel* now."

"I suppose. How odd. It's as if half of myself lay dormant until you brought me back from the Land of the Dead." He traced a finger along her cheek. "You made me whole."

She slipped around to draw him tightly against her. "Make love to me, Richard."

"Here? It's cold. The wind's blowing. Dear Lord God, we can be seen for miles!"

Her fingers began unlacing his buckskin pants. "We're dangerous spirits, remember? Filled with terrible Power. We'll blind anyone who watches except *Tam Apo* and *Tam Segobia*—and they made us to couple anyway."

He couldn't pretend to ignore his erection when her fingers found it. She'd stripped his coat and shirt off, dropping them in a pile before she drew her dress over her head. She stood naked, feet spread, head back proudly, hands raised to the sun. The chill hardened her nipples, and her sleek black hair curled around her narrow waist and muscular rump.

My God, she's beautiful.

She was laughing, white teeth shining between those full lips as he lowered her to the weathered rock.

Perhaps it was the sunshine, the invigorating chill in the pine-laden air, the dizzying heights upon which they lay, or the smile of God, but the climax consumed Richard's entire body, his cries mingling with Willow's. Spent and shivering, he looked down into her glowing eyes and kissed her.

I'm free! Free as I never shall be again. In all the world, nothing matters except man and woman, love, and sunshine, and the good earth. Thank you, God. Thank you for this single moment. I am alive!

❖

The nightmare was so vivid that Phillip bolted upright in bed. He gasped for air. Twinges of pain darted through his chest, and a curious numbness tingled in his left arm. Sweat beaded on his doughy skin, and he could feel each laboring beat of his heart as it hammered at his breast bone.

"Dear God . . . dear, dear God!" He blinked anxiously around the dark room, cocking his head. In the silence, he could hear the *tick-tock* of the ship's clock in his office next door, and the pop of a log in the bedroom fireplace.

The constriction in his chest was ebbing now, but his frantic fingers continued to wad his nightshirt, crumpling it against his breast.

The dream: so vivid. He swallowed hard. He'd been standing on a dark and muddy shore. At his feet, murky water lapped the bank, the surface smooth and oily. Huge trees grew at his back, the branches overhead stretching out over the black water. What a dismal place. It stirred primeval roots of fear.

Phillip had turned this way and that, seeking the way to safety. With the brooding forest behind, muddy swamp to either side, and Stygian water before him, he could see no route of escape.

Something moved on one of the branches. He looked up, and made out the somber silhouette of a vulture. The carrion bird craned its neck, hopping out on a limb that hung low over the water.

A pale thing bobbed there. A bit of white flotsam that barely broke the surface.

Phillip squinted. Some sort of fish?

The vulture flapped scabby wings, and stalked lower on the branch. There it balanced precariously directly over the flotsam and pecked at its barely exposed target. No, not a fish, but some loathsome *thing*!

As the vulture's beak worried its prey, the white thing bobbed, sending slow ripples to wash at Phillip's feet.

But the vulture's actions were its own undoing, for the questing beak imparted motion, and the thing drifted silently in Phillip's direction.

How slowly it came, like a man-sized snow lump submerged in the water. Phillip bent down, a curiosity as terrible as Oedipus's driving him.

Only when it lodged in the mud at his feet did the current finally spin it, turn it, so that Phillip could see Richard's water-blanched face. The eyes were staring sightlessly into the murk, the fine brown hair wavering like moss. His tender throat had been slit wide.

The pain had pierced Phillip's chest then, heart hammering as he tried to back away. The vulture gave an angry, croaking cry, and Phillip had stumbled backward, brought up short by the thick bole of a tree.

He'd fallen to his knees in the mud, hands clasped as he looked up into the sullen sky. There, out of the mist, her face had formed: the delicate cheeks, high brow, and perfect jaw framed by lustrous hair; her curved lips and delicate nose; and her large brown eyes. Normally soft and loving, they were hard now, implacable with rage and loathing.

Such a terrible dream. Phillip climbed out of bed, pulling his nightshirt straight. The floor creaked as he padded to the door, and then out into the hallway. The chill in the dark house dried his sweat and made him shiver as he tottered down the hallway. The hinges creaked when he opened the latch on Richard's door. And the floor groaned as he walked over to the bed, reaching down to feel the cold, smooth covers.

"I'm sorry, Richard. My fault. All my fault." The sodden misery in his chest had eaten his insides, devoured all that had remained of him after Caroline's death.

What's left for me? He blinked in the darkness. How many times had he walked in here since Eckhart's visit just to feel the fabric? As if the mere touch could bring his son back?

"You're a fool, Phillip Hamilton. Everything you've fought, schemed, and struggled for has come to naught." He cocked his head, aching at the emptiness in his soul. "What was it all for, anyway?"

He had no answer. Hollow. Empty. Silent inside. And oh, so tired.

Turning back from the bed, he could make out the dark frame for the doorway against the pale plaster walls. He felt his way back into the hall. Accompanied by the squeaking floor and the ticking of the clock, he made his way to his office, crossed to his desk, and opened a drawer.

The pistol fit his hand like an old friend, the smooth wood polished and cool in his hot hand. His finger found the trigger as he stepped out into the hallway and hitched his way down the stairs and through the French doors into the dining room.

He took a long splinter from the tin over the hearth, and lit it in the dimly glowing coals. One by one, he lit the wicks on the whale-oil lamps, and adjusted the flames. That done, he walked around the table and stared up at her portrait.

"Caroline, you were there, watching me." He'd never forget that loathing in her eyes. How she must despise him for wasting her only son that way. How she must hate him for everything—for the neglect during her pregnancy, for his absence during Richard's birth, and most especially for having to face death alone.

"You know about me, don't you?" He pulled out one of the chairs, and lowered himself. "About everything I've done. I'm sorry, Caroline. Sorry for all of it. Sorry for being unfaithful to you, for sneaking out in the night to all those women. But I was lonely after you died . . . and weak. So pitifully weak. You could forgive me for the frailties of the flesh, couldn't you?"

He glanced down at the pistol in his hands, then back up at the portrait. "It's Richard that you can't forgive. Well, I can't either. I tried, Caroline. I really did. I . . . I thought the risk . . . well, I was wrong again."

He crooked his thumb around the cock, listening to it click crisply, the sound loud in the quiet house. Her brown eyes were boring into his, reading every miserable flaw in his soul.

"Well, you can see that I've nothing to live for any more, beloved wife. Without you, without Richard, there's nothing left. It was for the future, you see. I did it all for the future. And I . . . I tried, waiting, praying for a miracle . . . that Richard was alive."

Her face had turned silver as the tears welled in his eyes. "The dream, Caroline. I can't stand the dream any more."

He sniffed, and tried to swallow the painful cramp in his throat. His hand was shaking as he lifted the pistol.

Dear God, this is hard . . . harder than I thought. Why was he so afraid? It would bring peace, wouldn't it? The pain would be gone. All he'd have to do was explain himself to God, and then accept his punishment for all the things . . .

Suddenly the pistol was twisted out of his grip. Phillip jumped, startled half out of his skin. Sputtering, he jerked around, staring up wide-eyed as Jeffry carefully lowered the hammer to half-cock.

"Dear God! Jeffry? What are you doing up?"

Jeffry raised his eyes to the ceiling. "The floorboards, sir. You've grown moody over the last months. I keep track of which rooms you enter. I've noticed the pistol lying on your desk more often recently, noticed it was polished, loaded, and primed. You've always come down to speak with Mrs. Hamilton in the night, but only recently have you spent so much time in Master Richard's room."

Phillip sagged in the chair. Had he ever felt this listless and tired? "Why didn't you let me shoot?"

"Because in the afterlife, sir, you would have asked me why I didn't stop you."

"Afterlife? Do think there's a heaven, or a hell?"

"Yes, sir. All men have souls," He indicated the portrait. "Just as Mrs. Hamilton did, and Richard, and my Betsy. Sir, you'll have plenty of time with Master Richard, Mrs. Hamilton, and God when you do finally die. In the meantime, here,

in this life, you have work to do. God will call you when He's ready."

Phillip stared numbly at the carpet beneath his feet. "You can't stop me, you know. Not every time."

"No, sir." Jeffry patted him on the shoulder. "I can't. I pray, however, that in the future I won't need to."

❖

Their bodies were locked together, lax in the honeyed afterglow of passionate union. The doorway hanging was hooked back, allowing a shaft of moonlight to silver the inside of their shelter. With a delicate fingertip, Richard traced the hollow curve of Willow's cheek. She sighed in contentment.

He whispered, "Never, in all of my dreams, did I understand it would be like this."

She patted his cold shoulders, and pulled the heavy buffalo robe up to cover them. "The world was made in a very clever way. A man's *we'an* fits a woman's *ta'ih* just so, and the pleasure makes us want to fit them together as often as we can." She grinned at him, teeth shining in the darkness. "Did you know that just after the Creation, Coyote was wandering around and saw a pretty girl? He tricked her into carrying him across a river, but as she swam along, he kept trying to slip down so he could poke his *we'an* into her.

"She realized what he was doing, of course, and threw him off in the water. She was so mad, she stomped all the way home. What she didn't know was that Coyote had climbed out of the river and raced like a streak to her house.

"Coyote found the pretty girl's mother there, and tricked her into letting him inside their lodge. But even though he tried to disguise himself, Mother knew he was Coyote, and up to no good."

"And when the pretty girl arrived?"

Willow stared up into his eyes as she ran her fingers around his ears. "Well, she was still storm-mad, and told her mother all about Coyote trying to mate her in the river. 'Hush!' her mother said. 'Coyote's inside the lodge waiting for you, but he thinks he's disguised. He doesn't know about women, about how we take care of ourselves. Just let him try and slip his *we'an* into one of us. We'll show him.' "

"What does that mean, that he didn't know about women?"

Willow's grin widened. "Here's what happened: They finally went to sleep that night, and Coyote sneaked up next to the pretty girl. He reached down between her legs to find her *ta'ih,* but something snapped at him."

"What?"

"Oh, yes. You see, during the Creation, women were made with sharp teeth in their *ta'ih.* This was a real problem for Coyote because if he stuck himself in there, he was going to get his *we'an* bitten off."

"He has a real problem with that, doesn't he?"

She lifted an eyebrow. "Most men do. But Coyote never gives up. He sneaked back outside and looked around until he found a *tsokkainompeh,* you know, the grinding stone. And with it, he tiptoed back into the lodge. He thrust it into her as if it were his *we'an.* This time, when the girl's *ta'ih* bit at him, the teeth shattered on the stone."

"So he got her?"

"He got her. And, being Coyote, he used the rock to break the teeth out of Mother's *ta'ih,* and got her, too."

"Quite a fellow, this Coyote. He reminds me of Thomas Hanson. The rumor was that he'd stick himself into any woman who came along." Richard screwed up his face. "But teeth? That's a little ridiculous."

"Is it? I drove Packrat mad with woman's blood. Teeth come in many forms, Richard. But just so you won't worry. I happen to like your *we'an* right where it is." And she squeezed him with her vaginal muscles.

"So . . . what happened to Coyote?"

"He stayed there with the girl and her mother, until he drove them half mad with his demands and lazy tricks. One time they sent him for water, but Coyote spent the day playing. When he came back, the women had left, taking their children with them. From them are descended all the people on earth."

"Great! People are descended from *Coyote*?"

"Knowing people, do you doubt it?"

He watched the moonlight trace the delicate arch of her cheeks. "Willow, what if you conceive?"

"I don't know this word. Conceive?"

"What if, like Coyote, I give you a child?"

Her dark eyes seemed to expand, sucking him into their depths. "Then I shall bear it, Richard. I am strong and healthy. I bore my first without trouble. The first is generally the most difficult."

"I don't mean that, Willow, I'm talking about raising the boy, providing for him. What kind of life will he have?"

She frowned for the first time, and gently pushed him off to one side so she could see his face in the moonlight. "What are you saying, Richard?"

"I'm saying that if I make you pregnant, we're going to have to figure out how to raise the child. I can't be Coyote. Do you understand? I don't want you to think that I'm going to run off like the Trickster, but, at the same time, I don't know where I'm going, what I'm going to be."

She sighed. "Boston again?"

"I don't know. Maybe. I'm torn, Willow. Half of me belongs back there. Half of me belongs here."

She laid her warm hand on his cool cheek. "Richard, until I returned to High Wolf's camp, I couldn't have understood. But you've stepped between worlds. Perhaps you could live in both?"

"Both?"

"If you must go back to Boston, go. Marry this Laura if it will help you in that world. She can bear your children in her house in Boston, and I will bear your children here."

The simplicity with which she spoke confused him for a moment. It wasn't a joke. She was serious. He muttered, "Sometimes I'm still not prepared for Indian logic."

"It's not a problem, Richard." She read his unease. "Unlike Whites, I don't have to be a prize. I am not a 'lady.' I can provide for our children while you are away."

"Yes, I know you can. But, Willow, you'd accept me having another wife?"

"White Hail wanted me to be his second wife. Fast Black Horse wanted me to be his third. Had my husband lived, he would have brought a second wife to our lodge. Among my people, this is a normal thing. I didn't realize it would upset you so."

"Between two worlds," he whispered, and chuckled. "It has possibilities—but Laura would have a fit if she ever found out."

"If she ever found out? I don't understand."

"No, forget it. I'm playing Coyote with myself." He paused, juggling these new ideas in his mind. What of jealousy? Just how differently *did* white and Shoshoni minds think? "You don't want two husbands, do you?"

She laughed. "Do I look *crazy*? You're trouble enough.

I've heard of women taking two husbands—mostly among tribes where the women own the children. Among my people and yours where descent is from the man, how would a woman tell which man was the father of which child? I think it would cause too many problems. Especially with incest and inheritance."

"Is mating always so practical?"

"Of course not. We're talking about people, aren't we? I almost went crazy when all those *Dukurika* men came to marry me. I almost said yes when my souls were screaming no. Anything to be done with it." She snuggled against him. "Are you still convinced that I can't go with you?"

"Yes," he replied sadly. "Willow, please trust me about this. My people are unforgiving about some things, and intolerant of anything they can't understand."

"I trust you."

"You do?"

"Yes—but mostly because Travis, Green, and Baptiste told me the same thing." She gouged him in the ribs to make him squirm. "But in the meantime, Richard, your life is not the only one that has turned onto an unknown path. My future is as uncertain as yours. If some *puhagan* or *tekwhani* finally decides I really am a witch, they might hunt me down."

"And if they do?"

"They'll kill me, Richard. It's the only way to get rid of a witch who doesn't ask to be cured."

Long after she'd fallen asleep, he stared up at the dark rafters, trying to see into the future. What did a white philosopher do with an Indian wife and a half-breed family? He and Willow had tied their lives into a Gordian knot that he couldn't quite decide how to cut.

Willow in the West, and Laura in the East? Now, wouldn't that be something? But how could he make it work? *Sure, and you're Coyote all right. If Laura found out, her* ta'hi

*would have teeth, indeed. And in Boston you'll never find a
grinding stone within easy reach!*

Travis checked the knots on his diamond hitch. Everything looked tight. The packs were loaded just so, balanced,
padded to protect the horses' backs, and mantied.

He looked up at the sky, squinting into the bright sun. The
day was cold, cloudless, and breezy, the sort of deceptive
weather that promised spring, then slapped a coon down
with a hellacious blizzard.

Baptiste walked up, a braided leather rope coiled over his
shoulder. Behind him, Two White Elk carefully inspected
the horses, bending down every now and then to lift a hoof
or feel a pastern.

"'Bout ready?" Baptiste asked. He'd pulled his wide-
brimmed hat down low. His mane of thick black hair was
tied in a tail behind his neck. During the winter he'd traded
for a white coat with longer fringes than before.

"Reckon." Travis cocked his jaw, looking westward
toward the Big Horns.

Two White Elk stopped before him, searching his eyes.
"You do not need to do this. My lodge is always yours,
Travis. You are my brother. Forever. What's mine is yours."

"Likewise, coon." Travis grinned, fingering his scars nervously. Two White Elk's wives had come, each bearing a pack which they tied behind the saddles of Travis's and Baptiste's horses.

Two White Elk patted his shoulder. "I have talked to New Moon Rising's people. If you were to stay, she would make you a lodge. For a couple of horses, she would be your wife. Her family would be honored. So would she."

"Aw, she's just a kid. You know—and I know—that she's not . . ."

"Not my sister?" Two White Elk grinned weakly. "Brother, she's long dead. Her spirit is gone from this world. We were close. I know how she thought, what she would say to this grief of yours."

"She'd tell this child he's a double-dyed fool," Travis snorted. "Hell, I reckon I know that. And, my brother, I needed this winter with ye. I just didn't know it. It ain't yer sister's ghost what's got me set ter go. It's the going, hoss. I lost that a while back. Wal, this hyar winter with ye put me right with my wife's death. Now I got ter see ter Dick, bury him. Ye savvy? Might be I'll be back next winter, and see ter New Moon Rising. If'n she's still a-waiting, maybe I'll tie a hoss ter her lodge, send her folks some foofaw-raw."

"And this Bad-Lodge woman?"

"Willow?" Travis took up his reins, running them through his fingers as he thought. "It's me that's got ter tell her about Dick. It ain't right her thinking him a fool and dupe. She needs ter know about Green and the boat. It's just something I gotta do, Brother. Understand?"

Two White Elk's lips twitched. "White man's honor. I understand, Travis. But ride carefully. The Blackfeet have been bad the last couple of years. It wouldn't do to send your scalp home on one of their coup sticks."

Travis stepped into Two White Elk's arms, hugging him

fiercely. "Thanks, old friend. I'll be seeing ye. Go in Power." Then Travis turned to Two White Elk's wives, hugging each one, kissing their foreheads as he thanked them for their hospitality. Walking to his horse, he vaulted into the saddle and took his Hawken when Two White Elk handed it up.

"So long, coon!" Travis waved as he kicked the gelding around. He looked back as Baptiste lined out the pack string. Two White Elk stood watching, a wife under either arm. Behind him, the conical lodges of the River Crow gleamed in the sunlight.

For a time Travis rode in silence, chewing fretfully at his lip.

"You all right?" Baptiste asked, dropping back.

"Yep. Plumb chipper." Travis cocked his head, looking sideways at Baptiste. "I can let her go now."

"Who?"

"Moonlight. I guess I been running from her ghost all along." He shrugged. "Wal, what the hell, let's see what comes of the Snakes."

"Willow and ye?"

Travis frowned. "She don't need the likes of me pestering her. Besides, I'd remind her of Dick. And she sure never warmed ter me like that on the river. Reckon I'm her friend, that's all."

"Sometimes, them kind of wives is the best," Baptiste remarked. He narrowed his eyes as they crested the first ridge. In the distance, the Big Horns beckoned. "Just where at was you expecting to find Willow's band?"

"Beats Hob outa me. Ye and me, we're just gonna have ter shag up thar, and skin that beaver when we catch it."

"And hope we don't get no arrow shot through our lights in the process."

"Yep. There's always that. Shit, ye ain't figgering on dying old, are ye?"

The fourth moon—the moon of spring—had grown full and bright in the night sky. The world came alive again. The rich red soils of *Ainkahonobita* greened with spring grass. Phlox was blooming in star-shaped flowers of white and blue. Biscuit-root had leafed out in yellow-clustered flowers that signaled their root's freshness. Larkspur raised green-tufted heads above the bloodred dirt. The ragged cry of the red-tailed hawk sounded high above the twitter of grackles, finches, and siskins. Flickers called mating warbles to each other. In the brush, the rufous towhee skittered beneath the branches in search of hatchling bugs.

Willow had taken Richard root gathering that day, showing him how to lever biscuit-root from the damp soil with a juniper digging stick. She taught him the difference between wild onion and death camas. Under her tutelage he learned to sing the sacred song before eating the first flowers of the shooting star—a plant with the power to grant visions and to cure illness. From the spring-fed creek, she plucked the first mint leaves for tea. Together they boiled shoots of larkspur into a potent brew to kill lice and ticks in their clothing.

As evening extended fingers of shadow across the ocher cliffs, Willow bent over her *potton,* the grinding stone she'd made of hard sandstone. Richard sat beside the fire, watching dinner boil. First they'd dug a pit, lined it with hide, and filled it with water. Biscuit-root leaves,

mint, and small onion bulbs were added. Finally they'd lowered a buffalo tongue ceremoniously into the water. River cobbles had been placed in a hot fire, and when dropped into the water, steam exploded. One by one, Richard fished the rocks out, reheated them, and dropped them in again. The delightful aroma of cooking tongue and greens filled the cool air.

Willow tightened her grip on the *tsokkainompeh,* the hand-sized grinding stone, and used it to pulverize the roots against the *potton.* She ground them until she had a mush that she could flatten into patties to roast over the coals.

Richard was smiling to himself, eyes on the redtails as they circled in the late evening light, feet lowered in mating displays.

"Now, why would you be smiling?" Willow asked, her grinding stones making a hollow *kok-rock-kok* sound. She wiped some of the thick root paste from one finger.

"Just thinking that this is a slice of Heaven," he told her. "I never knew that such a place could exist."

"Ah! Thinking again? That's only half of the way to truth, Richard."

"I suppose." He used wooden tongs crafted from limber pine branches to fish one of the hot rocks from the fire. "You know, they'd never believe this in Boston."

"I know." She hammered the root paste with renewed vigor. Boston—always Boston. But the evening softness, with its shadows and colors, the birdsong, and the gurgling from the spring-fed creek soothed her.

Perhaps Boston would remain forever over the horizon—the sort of a place a person always talked about going to, but never really meant to.

She glanced at the dugout shelter they'd made of juniper and pine logs. It was something new, half Indian, half White, more than a wickiup but less than a house. The place even had a pole doorway hung on rawhide hinges. Inside lay their bedding of freshly tanned buffalo hides atop mounded straw.

I could stay here forever, loving him. Tam Apo, *can't you make the world leave us alone? Is that too much to ask?* As if in answer, a chorus of coyotes began yipping high up in the rocks, mocking her.

The wary manner in which Richard rose brought her to her feet; she followed his gaze down the canyon. Three horsemen were filing through the tall sagebrush. All carried rifles over their saddlebows.

"Visitors?" Richard wondered. "Friends or enemies?"

Willow shaded her eyes. "Two White men and an Indian."

"And how would you know that from this distance?"

"Two riders have stirrups," she answered. "Indians don't use them."

Richard ducked inside the shelter, retrieving their bows and quivers. "I don't know what good these will do against good rifles. Let's hope we don't have to use them. Willow, before they get here, slip over the edge of the bank."

She nodded, heart skipping, and hurried into the screen of juniper, then circled to the side. Water that drained off one of the sandstone ridges had cut a narrow channel alongside their camp, and here she secreted herself, using one of the junipers for cover. From this ambush she could probably take one, or maybe two. And if not, she could wound the horses, affecting the riders' control.

Who are they? Why are they here? Red Canyon was a favorite stopping place for travelers on the trail southward over the mountains. That none of the *Ku'chendikani* had ridden through made her suspect that stories about her and Richard had circulated among the bands—further proof of her spiritual alienation from her people. The thought tightened the fist of worry in her stomach.

She took a deep breath and checked her arrows. Each was tipped by a chert point carefully flaked to an edge sharp enough to sever a hair. Fletching made from sage-grouse feathers had been painstakingly tied to the shafts at an angle to impart spin that stabilized the arrow in flight With her Pawnee bow, she'd been able to drive such an arrow into a buffalo's chest until the point lodged in the far ribs. And it wasn't as if these strangers would kill any harder than Ree warriors.

The horsemen rode straight up the canyon, their rifles at rest, and pulled up before Richard, who stood before the steaming stew.

"How!" the first called, pulling his horse up and taking stock of their camp. He wore fringed buckskins, had a dark brown beard, amused eyes, and a pug nose. Built like a bear, with broad shoulders and thickly muscled legs, he looked as if he could crush rocks with his bare hands. Atop his head sat a felt hat adorned with an eagle feather.

The second White man was thin—barely more than a boy—with the reedy look of wiry strength. Long blond hair flowed out from under a wolfhide hat. His sparse beard scarcely hid his pointed chin. He, too, wore finely crafted buckskin decorated in Pawnee patterns. Unlike his bluff companion, he glanced this way and that with faded blue eyes, then studied Richard with evident disdain.

The Indian was *Ku'chendikani,* his legs bent around the barrel of a ratty paint horse. He looked vaguely familiar to Willow, with a weasel-thin face and hooked nose. His hands knotted on the reins, and his nervous black eyes searched the camp warily, as if looking for . . .

Me? Willow wondered as the lead White raised his hands, making the sign for peace. Next his fingers traced out, "We come looking for a White man."

THIRTY-ONE

I am ready to melt you and weld you together, so that you two may be made one, and as one you may join together as long as you live, and when you die, you may die together instead of apart, and be yonder in the House of Hades joined. Think of this as your passion, and if it will satisfy you to get this. If such a thing were offered we know that not a single one would object, or be found to wish anything else; he would simply believe he had heard that which he has so long desired, to be melted and united together with his beloved, and to become one from two. For the reason is that this is our ancient natural shape, when we were one whole; and so the desire for the whole and the pursuit of it is named Love.

—Plato, *Symposium*

Richard cocked his head as the bearded rider's hands made signs. "I'm sorry. I guess I've never learned sign talk."

"Hell!" the white roared, slapping his thigh. His horse started and pranced. "I mistook ye fer Injun."

"Richard Hamilton, sir. At your service."

The burly white laughed, kicked a leg over his saddle, and slid neatly off his horse. "Name's Fletch. Short fer Fletcher. And this hyar's Jonas Hayworth. That sneaky Injun yonder is Yeller Beaver. We're with Jed Smith's brigade. Over trapping the Green mostly, but we heard they's a white man hyar. And Yeller Beaver, he taken on an itch ta show us whar ye be."

Richard fingered the cool wood of his bow, frowning. "And why would you seek me out?"

"Wal, coon. Ain't that many white men out hyar. We run inter Jed Smith and Moses Harris. They's coming ahead of Gen'ral Ashley and the caravan. Smith figgered ye might have a way with the Snakes, since the story is yer living with one. He figgered it'd be worth our ride over ta see if'n ye could shanty some Snakes inter Rendezvous ta trade beaver. Figgered if'n ye'd have a mind, he might make ye an offer, buy yer plews, and see if'n ye'd represent the company with yer Snake friends."

"Represent the company? What company?"

"Ashley and Smith. Uh . . . ye've heard of us?"

Richard nodded, lowering his bow. "I have. Well, if it's trade you've come to talk, I take it you didn't come for war."

"Huh? War? Now, what kind of talk's that among white men?"

Richard gestured around. "Living out here alone, well, a man prepares for anything, and, to be honest, you might say I've been up the creek and over the mountain." He raised his voice. "Come on in, Willow, they're friendly."

Willow sighed, hating the premonition of trouble that crawled around her chest like a spider. She stepped out from behind the juniper, and watched Yellow Beaver's interest sharpen. The White men's expressions changed as well. Jonas Hayworth let out a low whistle and said, "By God, what a purty woman. Hell, most Injuns is uglier than sin plastered over."

"Shut up," Fletch growled. Then added, "Got ta excuse Jonas. He's raised without no upbringing."

Richard fixed Jonas with a hard stare. "I'll let it pass—this time. But if he wants to keep his hair, he'll treat my wife like a lady."

Fletch studied Richard with a keen eye and nodded. To

Jonas, he said, "Pilgrim, if'n I read sign, ye'd better keep a civil tongue in yer head or ye'll be wolfmeat."

Willow walked up to stand beside Richard. Suddenly Yellow Beaver seemed interested in everything but her. The White men she understood: Fletch was a bluff, hearty trader. Young Jonas wanted to prove himself a man, and lacked any good sense about how to do it. But Yellow Beaver, what was his purpose here?

"Supper is almost ready, gentlemen," Richard said pleasantly. "Would you join us?"

"Reckon so," Fletch replied, taking in the sloping sandstone that rose behind their shelter, and the high white limestone cliffs west of the red caprock. "Right fine place ye got ta hole up hyar. Right fine indeed. She's some, she is. Purty as a picture—and they's a sight of purty country out hyar." Then he added, "Jonas, see ta the hosses."

Tin cups magically appeared as the men settled around the fire and evening deepened. Richard scooped the cups full while Willow took her place beside him, every nerve taut.

"You say you've been trapping?" Richard asked as they ate. "You haven't run into another white man? Travis Hartman?"

"Hartman?" Fletch asked, wiping droplets from his mustache. "Nope. Ain't seen him, but I've heard tell of him. Bear-scarred, ain't he? One of Lisa's men. Old-timer. He out hyar, too?"

"We were separated last winter." Richard paused. "I've been hoping he made it back to the Crow. Baptiste de Bourgmont was going to winter with them."

"Huh. I heard tell they's a black man wintered with the Crow. Ain't no telling fer sure, though. Could'a been Ed Rose. He's tight with Crow. I ain't been up with the Crows since last fall with Ashley—and nip and tuck it was. Them thieving skunks damn near robbed us blind, but Gen'ral Ashley, he seed his way through. Then we met up with Atkinson and O'Fallon, and the Gen'ral floated on downriver. Rest of the boys wintered down ta Willow Valley."

Willow studiously ignored Jonas's stare. He seemed entranced by her, sipping his stew, chewing, blue eyes never wavering. In contrast, Yellow Beaver never looked up, eating halfheartedly as if his stomach were bothering him. Why?

"We saw you." Richard said. "I was on a boat, the *Maria*. Dave Green was booshway. We were hidden off in a side channel when you passed."

Fletch raised an eyebrow. "A boat, ye say?"

"Green wanted to open trade with the Crow. He started a post at the mouth of the Big Horn. Blackfeet overran him, and he blew up the boat and as many Blackfeet as he could."

"Bug's Boys! Huh! And old Dave Green gone under? Well, Tarnal Hell, them's poor doings. Sorry ta hear it." Fletch considered. "And ye made do by yerself?" He glanced at Willow. "And right fine ye did, too."

"What of this rendezvous you mentioned?" Richard raised an eyebrow.

Willow finally had enough of Jonas's devouring stare. She met his eyes, called upon her *puha,* and aimed it like an arrow. To her satisfaction, Jonas swallowed hard and looked away. He flushed and scratched the back of his neck, as if suddenly uncomfortable.

Fletch continued talking like a man who couldn't get enough of it. "We got a caravan coming up the trail. She otta be down ta Willow Valley come June. Powder, shot, foofawraw, everything a coon needs. Ashley figgers he can supply his brigades out hyar, and trade fer plews with Injuns and free trappers alike. Then he caravans the plews back ta Saint Loowee."

"And takes a hell of a profit, I'd suppose?"

"I reckon, but fer most of us coons, why, we're fer the mountains, and hooraw ta that!"

Willow glanced at Richard, reading his intense expression. Her cold intuition, so often forgotten in the warmth of his arms, flowed again. *Now he will be thinking of Boston more than ever.* Better to immerse herself in the inevitable. "This caravan," she said, "it would be a safe way to travel back to Saint Louis. From there, you could return to Boston."

The trappers stared at her, surprised by her English.

Richard nodded, fingering his chin. "Fletch, do you suppose I could arrange passage? They'd value another rifle, wouldn't they?"

"Reckon so." Fletch glanced uneasily at Willow, catching the subtle undercurrents of the conversation. "Though God knows why ye'd want ta go back. If this ain't Heaven right hyar, this child don't know sign."

Willow gave him a surreptitious smile, then looked at Yellow Beaver. In Shoshoni, she asked, "Why did you come here?"

Yellow Beaver avoided her eyes. "I came to see you, *Puhagan.* You, and your Powerful White man."

"And why would you do that?"

"I have heard stories. I thought I would come to see if they were true."

"What stories?"

Yellow Beaver's eyes flickered, then he dropped them. "We will talk later, *Puhagan.*"

Richard had understood most of the exchange. He studiously ignored Yellow Beaver, perhaps because his mind was on the whites' caravan.

"How'd ye make do without a rifle?" Fletch was asking.

"Broke the cock in a fall," Richard answered absentmindedly. "The bow has filled in."

"A Hawken's gun?" Fletch asked.

"Yes."

"We got parts. Ye still got the gun?"

"Parts?" Richard straightened. "With you?"

"Nope. But if some of the boys don't have one down ter Willow Valley, they'll be some a-coming with the caravan. Might take a bit of filing ta make 'er fit, but we can make her a daisy again."

Richard took a deep breath. "I'll admit, I've felt half naked without it. Having a broken gun is like having a friend with amputated legs."

"That's some, it is," Fletch agreed. "Wal, if'n yer of an interest, Rendezvous will be in the Willow Valley as soon as the caravan arrives. Maybe a month or so. Just about travel time ta get there."

"Willow Valley?" Richard shook his head. "I don't know that place."

Fletch took a stick to sketch in the dirt. "Hyar we be." He poked a hole. "This hyar's Wind River, what the Snakes call Big River." He sketched in a line. "Hyar's the Wind River Mountains. West of them is the Green River. West of them is the Bear River draining inta Bear Lake. Ye follers that south inta Willow Valley." Fletch gave him a level glance. "Yer welcome ta travel with us, if'n ye'd like. We could use another gun."

Richard studied the map, that pensive look of opportunity in his eyes. "So could I, but it would need a working lock."

He wanted to go, as plain as the sun in the sky; and with it, a conflict raged, his soul torn to stay with her. *Oh, Richard, why did these men have to come here?*

The talk continued, stories about beaver, about Indians and cold snows, but not until long after dark did Yellow Beaver catch Willow to one side.

"I have come here, *Puhagan,* to pay you to use your *puha.*"

Willow stopped short. He still refused to look at her, to meet her eyes. "What would you have me use *puha* for?"

He scuffed the grass with a moccasined toe. "It is said that you can do many things with *puha*. That you have traveled to the Land of the Dead in spite of being a young woman. It is said that you returned from there. This is true?"

"And if it is?"

"Then I would give you ten horses, ten buffalo hides, and anything else you wanted if you used your *puha* for me."

"And what would you have me do?"

"There is a man, his name is Slim Pole. I think you know him?"

"I do."

Yellow Beaver untied a little pouch from his belt, fingering it ever so carefully. "He is a very powerful man, and he does not like me. I wish to marry his granddaughter, but he has said no. When he speaks, people listen. This bag contains some of his hair, a bit of hide with his blood on it, and a bit of fingernail. It was all I could get. With it, you could use your *puha* to kill him."

Willow shivered, knotting her fists. Slim Pole? He'd never approved of her, but he'd been honest, and wise. A good man, and a *puhagan* who served his people well. With great deliberation, she said, "I am no *witch,* Yellow Beaver. You will leave this place. And you will never tell anyone why you have come here. Do you understand?"

He shrugged, crestfallen. "Perhaps if I made it twenty horses?"

"I said *no!*" She started to stalk off, then turned. "Wait. Who told you I was a witch?"

"A friend. Her name is Red Calf. She said you witched White Hail, hardened his heart against her so that he threw her out of his lodge. She had crept close to White Hail's lodge the night he threw her out. She heard the whole story when White Hail told it to Two Half Moons."

"Just *leave*! And tell people I am no witch." But as she walked unsteadily back toward her shelter, the relentless truth spread within her. Yellow Beaver would only be the first to seek her out. The charge had been made. Come what may, she would always be a witch to her people.

For hours she lay awake in the robes beside Richard, listening to the night sounds of owls hooting, the wailing chorus of the coyotes, and the burble of the creek. Outside, one of the White men, Fletch most likely, was snoring in his blankets by the fire.

Richard kept shifting and resettling himself.

"Are you awake?" she asked finally.

"Yes."

"This thing, this . . ."

"Rendezvous."

"Yes. I think we should go, Richard." A heaviness, like a terrible weight, pressed down on her heart. "It is a way for you to return to your Boston."

He remained silent for a long time. She could feel him turning the thought over and over in his soul. At last he asked, "What about you? About us?"

"Richard, you must go. It is within you. A thing you must do."

"You were upset when you came to bed. I heard Yellow Beaver call you *puhagan*. What did he want?"

"Nothing," she lied. "Go to sleep, Richard. Tomorrow we will load the horse and start for this Rendezvous."

"I can hear the sadness in your voice. Why are you telling me to do this?"

"Because you are a warrior, Richard. And your *mugwa* will slowly sicken if you do not go back to Boston and settle this longing within you." *And I must risk the chance that you will never come back to me.*

How had they accumulated so many things? Richard stared skeptically at the pack as he threw his diamond hitch over the buffalo-hide manty. *And we made most of it with our bare hands. The rope we twisted from juniper, the hides we scraped and tanned.* Willow's fleshing tool was made from the hock joint of a mule deer. They'd sharpened the digging stick with quartzite flakes from the quarry high on the ridge, and hardened the tip in the fire. Together they'd dug the biscuit-root that filled the net bags. Willow's agile fingers had woven the baskets. He'd made the stone hammer, using sharpened rabbit bones to sew green rawhide over the willow-stick handle before it dried tight.

Of his outfit, only his possibles and the broken rifle remained from the White world.

Beside him, Willow laced on her heavy travel moccasins, made from a buffalo he'd killed and prayed over.

The land provides.

Fletch and Jonas were already saddled up, their outfits little more than the blanket rolls behind their saddles and possibles hanging from their shoulders.

"Reckon we'll have ta steal ye some hosses," Fletch decided. "The two of ye walking, why we might be up and died of old age afore we get there."

"You could ride on." Richard looked up from his knots. "We'll follow behind."

Fletch had watched them pack, respect in his eyes. "Oh, I reckon we'll mosey along with ye. From the looks of things, Hamilton, there's a trick or two ye might be teaching us."

Me teach you? That thought surprised him. For so long he'd been a student of the frontier. That a seasoned hiverner like Fletch would look to him brought a certain amount of amazement.

He took a long moment and looked around. So many memories were here. The shelter with its pole doorway had kept them warm in the worst of storms. The sloping ridges of red sandstone had awed him with their beauty, the shadows they cast forever changing with the light. He'd climbed to those spectacular high points with Willow, the two of them exploring, laughing, sharing their souls. Here they'd worked, played, and loved. The canyon had cradled them within its rocky womb, and now he was about to leave. To what end?

"Ready?" Willow asked, sensing, as always, his mood.

"Reckon so," he drawled in Travis's twang. "But my heart's a mite sad."

She smiled, patting his arm, and took up the lead rope. Without a word, she tugged to start the mare and followed in the wake of the trappers' horses.

"We'll come back here someday," Richard promised as he walked beside her. But his memory played with images of Boston, of his friends there, and shaded walks at the university. Most of all, he remembered every line in his father's face, right down to the red veins in his nose.

Those terrible gray eyes had grown mild, warm and loving.

He thinks I'm dead by now. And the thought gouged him deeply. *Poor old fellow, all he ever wanted was a son to be proud of.*

Richard glanced down at himself, at the buckskin pants, the long fringes cut by Willow's careful hands, at the buffalo-hide jacket with its flowing fringe and the porcupine quills Willow had flattened and worked into intricate designs. Beneath lay his buckskin hunting shirt, with its brightly painted patterns. *I do look like an Indian.* Phillip Hamilton would still disapprove.

So, here I am. Richard John Charles Hamilton, squaw man, educated savage. His coups, saved for so long in his possibles, had been sewn on the front of his jacket. Pawnee, Ree, and Blackfeet scalps.

I'm sorry, Father, but I'll not take them off for you. Nor for any man. And how would Professor Ames interpret that?

"A man is only what he is," he muttered.

He glanced at Willow. Her smooth brow was lined with worry. What had happened between her and Yellow Beaver? Something about witchcraft, he supposed, for the *Ku'chendikani* had been gone before first light.

A squaw man? Charges of witchcraft? Once again, he'd dredged up the notion of taking Willow to Boston with him, but they'd crucify her. A white man married white; that, or he was the kind of human trash that decent people didn't associate with.

And how dare they think that about his Willow? She'd saved his life on the Missouri when the Rees would have killed him. She had healed the wound in his back when a white woman would have fainted at the sight of it. His Willow had crossed wilderness in the dead of winter and risked her soul to save him. How dare anyone condemn his precious woman who defied her people in the search for truth, and made sweet love on high rock pinnacles?

But destroy her they would—heedless of the beauty of her soul or the courage in her breast.

So, who's civilized and who's a savage?

Something was skewed, turned at angles to itself. The civilized concept of justice galled the very notions it espoused, coming as it did from a Christian society.

No, what they needed in philosophy lectures was a Travis Hartman to debate ethics——as if they'd understand the scope of Hartman's perceptivity when it came to human nature. With that thought came the sudden illumination that most knowledge was predicated upon experience. Perhaps all of it.

He vented a bitter laugh, causing Willow to give him one of her knowing, sidelong glances. In response to her unasked question, he said, "I sure hope Travis is at Rendezvous. I miss that old coon. And Baptiste, too, ever so sure of himself and life and truth."

"You are back to worrying about Truth?"

"No. I was just wishing I could sit around a fire and talk to them one more time. I guess I'm a lot smarter now than I ever was."

Her smile was fleeting. "Travis would be proud of you."

"I hope so." *At least someone would be proud of me.* It prickled deeply within him that he wasn't so sure he could be proud of himself any more.

Travis crept carefully along. The slightest misstep meant that he'd fall to his death hundreds of feet below. The scary trail followed an undercut hollow beneath thick sandstone

caprock. The overhang stuck out over the high valley, enough of it cracked and sagging that Travis's heart had a case of the grips. The wind roared in the conifers just above the rim, and tore through the brush clinging to the canyon below.

Tarnal Hell, what sort of damn fool situation did I get myself into? He stopped, one hand braced on the rockface, his moccasins precarious on the angular rocks tumbled from the rim. He'd followed a trail marked by scuffed moccasin tracks down under the rock wall. What had started out looking like a game trail had ended up in a jumble of boulders that almost blocked the narrow ledge over a sheer precipice. From where he balanced, he could spit nearly one hundred feet down. He placed each foot with care to keep from falling, or from starting a landslide that would pitch him into the depths. Now, he paused, hefting the rifle in his free hand. From the rock he stood on, he'd have to leap half a body-length to the next. *And if ye miss . . . ye'll bust a leg sure, coon.*

A feller could talk all he wanted about being a good hunter, but tracking down the *Dukurika* had challenged all of his and Baptiste's skills—and the closest they'd come was smoking fires and empty camps. The Sheepeaters had an uncanny sense, knowing by instinct that Travis and Baptiste were in the mountains.

But that had been the way of it. Living in the mountains, in terrain that a Natchez Trace Bald-knobber would salivate over, the Sheepeaters just melted away. In a sense it was more frustrating than being shot at.

"By damn," Travis muttered, looking up at the overhanging rock. "A Sheepeater would only need to roll a couple of rocks down, and this child would be wolfmeat."

He took a deep breath, steadied himself, and leaped. Windmilling, and using his rifle to balance, he caught himself short of disaster on the other side. And what if they hadn't come this way? What if they'd left a false trail and skipped off to the side just to sucker him into this dead end?

He hopped to the next rock, and then the next. If he fell, he'd break his neck. *And that'd serve ye right fer being a fool!*

With his next leap, he came to a resumption of the trail: a narrow path that followed the edge of the rock before the slope fell away over the cliff below. There, to his relief, were more of the scuffed moccasin tracks—none more than an hour old.

Travis ghosted along, silent as death, head cocked, listening. The caprock bulged out here, and he stopped in mid-step, hearing the cadence of human voices. Someone laughed, a child from the sound of it.

Travis nerved himself and eased around the corner. They didn't see him at first, preoccupied with cutting up a grouse. Four of them sat under a rock overhang: a man, woman, and two kids. They were dressed in the most beautiful of white-tanned hides, all painted with colorful designs, fur-lined and tailored. The workmanship looked as fine as any Travis had ever seen. Five dogs were watching the grouse plucking with avid interest.

The chubby man had a bland face, almond eyes, and a thatch of braided black hair. As he pulled feathers from the grouse's breast, he chided one of the children. The kids were laughing, white teeth flashing, and the young woman with them was smiling, a sparkle of enjoyment animating her brown features.

They had set up camp in a big hole in the side of the cliff, rainproof, sheltered from the wind, dry and cozy. Firewood was piled to one side, and from the soot-stained soil the place saw frequent use.

"Excuse me," Travis said gently in his limited Shoshoni. "I am a friend. I apologize for interrupting, but I need to find a *Dukurika* woman."

They froze, the way deer did in that panicked instant just after being shot at. Then the dogs exploded in a frenzy of barking.

Travis laid his rifle to the side and raised his hands. The Sheepeaters stared at him in horror. The dogs charged back and forth, barking and growling with teeth bared. One, a big black-and-gray animal, kept leaping at him, snapping his teeth.

"I mean no harm. Do you understand?" *Hell, I hope that's what I'm saying. Even if I remember the words, my accent might be so bad I'm telling 'em I'll eat 'em fer supper!* He used his hands in sign language, repeating his words in case they couldn't hear him over the barking dogs.

"I'm Travis Hartman. I'm a friend of Heals Like A Willow. She's a woman of High Wolf's band. I've come to look for her."

That didn't cause them the slightest relaxation. The round-faced man began whispering to himself.

Travis desperately wished he had his rifle in hand in case he had to whack the dog before it took his kneecap off. "Do you know Heals Like A Willow?"

The man swallowed hard and glanced around as if seeking an escape. He contemplated the lip of the overhang—as if considering throwing himself over—then licked his lips. The woman was whispering frantically, pulling the owl-eyed children behind her.

"I know her," the man said, voice trembling, hands forming the signs. "She is not here. I have nothing to do with her."

"Do you know where I can find her?" The dogs were milling and growling now, hair standing on their backs.

"She is at *Ainkahonobita,* the Red Canyon. Please, do not harm us, spirit. My wife and I are good. My children are good. We pray, we . . . "

"Easy. Easy, there, hoss," Travis soothed. He signed, "I am no spirit. I am Travis Hartman. A white man. Who are you?"

Flashing hands accompanied the words, "I am Gray Moth, a man of White Rock's band."

"You seem uneasy about Heals Like A Willow. Is she all right?"

Gray Moth looked scared half to death. In the end, all he could do was shrug.

"Is there a white man with Heals Like A Willow?"

Gray Moth nodded, looking even more uneasy.

Travis knotted his fists and shook them in the sudden exultation—and the frightened *Dukurika* nearly darted to suicide over the ledge. The dogs began to bark and snap again. Damn them; if the mutts attacked, they could drive him right over the edge.

"It's all right," Travis crooned. "I will not hurt you, you are good people, a good father and mother for such beautiful children."

At that, Gray Moth seemed to sweat relief.

"Where would I find Heals Like A Willow and the white man?"

"*Ainkahonobita,*" Gray Moth said again and signed, "Red Canyon."

Travis frowned. "I do not know this place."

The man and woman looked at each other, slightly perplexed, as if they misunderstood, or might be entering some sort of trap. The man signed: "Spirits know everything."

Travis shook his head and sighed. "I am a man, Gray Moth, just like you. *Newe,* a man. *Newe,* ain't that the word?"

From the slight glazing of Gray Moth's eyes, he didn't believe it for a moment.

Travis signed, "Please, just tell me where to find Red Canyon."

"West, across the Big River, at the foot of the Owl Creek Mountains. You will find red stone ridges. The witch and her White-man-spirit are living there, at the spring. No one goes there now."

"Witch?" Travis cocked his head. "Heals Like A Willow is a witch?"

Gray Moth nodded fervently.

Travis made a face, grunted, and said, "Thank you for your help, Gray Moth." He fished into his possibles for a twist of tobacco. "This is for you, for your help. May *Tam Apo* bless you with health and good hunting. Thank you. Travis Hartman is now your friend."

And with that, he picked up his rifle and eased back around the corner. Hurrying along the trail, he grimaced at the sight of the tumbled boulders. He glanced back at the way he'd come, half expecting Gray Moth to lean around the corner with his bow. The big dog was watching him, lips still curled in a snarl. The spot between Travis's shoulder blades prickled, anticipating an arrow's cutting bite. Heart in throat, he took the dizzying leaps.

"And those kids jump this?"

He trotted along the game trail, climbed up the narrow crack in the rock to the top of the rim, and met Baptiste, rifle in hand, keeping guard. "Anything?" Baptiste asked.

"Yep. Willow's at a place called Red Canyon, west of the mountains. I caught a bunch of 'em. Pap, Maw, two kids, and a dog pack. Scairt holy hell outn 'em. But they fessed up. Told me where to go—and hyar's the best. She's with a white man!"

Baptiste scratched his black chin. "I'll be damned. Do you suppose?"

"Beats hell outa me. I'm just a-hoping. But, c'mon, coon, let's make tracks. I ain't sure I trust old Gray Moth."

"And why's that?"

"When I mentioned Heals Like A Willow, he damned near shit hisself inside out. I finally got it outa him that she's a witch."

"What? A *witch*? Willow?"

"How the hell do I know? But if the Sheepeaters think that, and I told 'em we're her friends, we might just want ter pound hooves off'n this hyar mountain. Folks think funny thoughts when it comes ter witches."

Baptiste rocked his jaw back and forth skeptically, then shrugged. "Yep, let's pull our sticks." He walked to his horse, untying the reins. "Witch, huh? Wal, I reckon everybody's got to do something with their lives—and she never was the sort to sit at home in the lodge."

"Do tell?"

THIRTY-TWO

❖

And, in fact, we discover that the more a cultivated reason deliberately devotes itself to the enjoyment of life and happiness, the more a man falls short of true contentment. From this fact there arises in many persons, if only they are honest enough to admit it, a certain amount of misology: hatred of reason. This is particularly pertinent for those who are most experienced in its use. After cataloguing all the advantages which they draw—I will not say from the invention of the arts of common luxury—from the sciences (which in the end seem to them no more than a luxury of the understanding), they nevertheless discover that they have actually placed more trouble on their shoulders instead of gaining in happiness; in the end they envy, rather than despise, the common lot of men who are better guided by plain natural instinct, and who do not permit their reason much influence on their conduct.

—Immanuel Kant, *Foundations of the Metaphysics of Morals*

To the West, the Wind River Mountains rose into the spring-blue sky like ragged white teeth. At their feet, grassy bluffs stretched toward the river until they dulled into the baser greens of sage flats. Small herds of buffalo, like dark dots, accented the tan and white speckles of antelope that grazed in their midst.

Despite the clear day, a cold wind blew down from the mountains. Willow and Richard walked briskly to keep the chill at bay. Fletch and Jonas rode to one side, their rifles ready. Their route south followed the floodplain on the west side of the *Pia'ogwe*. They passed through stands of cottonwoods, their branches heavy with catkins and full buds. The entire bottomland had been grazed, old piles of horse manure turning gray in the sun.

"*Ku'chendikani,*" Willow explained. "These are their winter grounds."

"Friends of yers?" Fletch asked, an anxious set to his face.

"White Hail's people," Willow told Richard. To Fletch, she said, "Yes, friends."

I hope, Richard added mentally as he walked with his bow in one hand, his lead rope in the other. The furtive shape of a cottontail rabbit hid in the shadow of a sagebrush. No patch of brush or pile of deadfall escaped his scrutiny.

Fletch seemed just as keen, but young Jonas watched the

hawks in the sky, or worse, rode with his eyes in an unfocused stare that irritated Richard.

He's going to be wolfmeat if he doesn't mend his ways. At the thought, Richard smiled grimly.

"What is it?" Willow asked.

"I'm wondering why Travis never strangled me. The man has the patience of a saint."

Willow arched an eyebrow wryly. "He wasn't the only one."

Richard grinned at her. How beautiful she was, her black hair shining. He wanted to reach out and caress the smooth curve of her cheek. As if reading his thoughts, her dark eyes sparkled, and she lifted a perfect brow in silent question.

If we just weren't with these two hunters, I'd—

"Know them folks?" Fletch asked, pulling up his horse. The first of the scouts came riding out of the trees, whooping and kicking their horses. The young warriors clutched bows and arrows, gaily painted shields on their arms.

Richard shaded his eyes. Six, seven, nine, the warriors galloped toward them. "Willow? Do you know them? Are we in trouble?"

"*Ku'chendikani,*" she told him. "Slim Pole's band uses this country for the most part. I used to live in his village."

"Hot damn!" Jonas whooped as he clutched his rifle. "Fer a second there, I's figgering to shit myself inside out."

"Slim Pole?" Richard asked. "That's White Hail's village? The one he went back to?"

Willow nodded, face bleak.

"Reckon we need ta fort up?" Fletch checked the priming in his rifle as the scouts raced toward them. "Uh . . . they's friendly, right? I mean, Snakes and whites, we mostly get along. But they's some, like Mauvais Gouche, and that Iron Wrist, they's just as likely ta fight as look at ye."

"They'll be friendly." In Shoshoni, she told Richard, "I will do my best, husband. If there is trouble, it will be over me." Willow strode forward, raising her hands before her.

Richard called, "Is there anything I should do?"

She shot him a quick smile. "Just be rational."

As the warriors drew near, they suddenly crisscrossed in the maneuver that would have drawn cheers from any cavalry drill team. Dirt flew under racing hooves as the horses wheeled, cut at angles, and circled the party.

A tall warrior, older than the rest, rode up on his powerful warhorse. Richard took his measure. This man had a special grace, a keen glint in those black eyes. He wore his forelocks roached high over his forehead; a weasel-tail tie confined the rest of his long hair. A battered trade rifle was clutched in his hand.

"That's Fast Black Horse," Willow called back.

Richard studied the man with renewed interest. Fast Black Horse, the man who had wanted Willow for a third wife. That's where he'd heard of him before. Hostility bristled at the back of Richard's neck.

Good Lord, man, it was before your time. She didn't even know you then.

Willow stopped short of Fast Black Horse's prancing dapple gray stallion. He gave her a fierce scowl, until his eyes widened with recognition.

"Hello, warrior," Willow said evenly, and rested the tip of her bow on the ground before her. "Are you still interested in taking me for a wife?"

Richard narrowed his eyes to a predatory stare. She didn't have to bring it up, did she? It took all of his concentration to follow their Shoshoni, and the *Ku'chendikani* dialect was just different enough to challenge his ears.

Fast Black Horse used his heels to back his mount away, clearly wary. "A great many stories are told about you, Heals Like A Willow." He gestured with the rifle. "And now, here you come, followed by White men. Perhaps the stories are true?"

"I haven't heard the stories, so I can't tell you which are true, and which aren't."

Fast Black Horse turned and barked a quick order; a warrior broke ranks, racing his pony back toward the village. Then he gave her a flat stare. "What are you doing here? Have you come to work evil among us?"

"No, warrior. We are only passing through, traveling westward to the White man's gathering. We mean you no harm and no trouble."

Fast Black Horse kept his distance, watching her with hard eyes. "I have heard that you are a witch. That you went to the Land of the Dead, and *Pandzoavits* gave you rock ogre Power. That you couldn't control it and it made you warped and evil."

She crossed her arms. "Who says this? White Hail?"

"White Hail says little. His blood has become like water. But my wife would know these things. She has told me all about you, and the mistake I made in wanting to marry you."

"Ah, let me guess. You took Red Calf after White Hail threw her out. My sympathy, Fast Black Horse. You deserve better than her."

"A woman should know when to curb her tongue."

"So I have heard many times. But saying such things must not bother you, warrior, or you wouldn't have taken Red Calf into your lodge. Not only will she never curb her tongue, but she uses it to speak foolishness and lies."

Oblivious to the nature of the conversation, Fletch called out, "Will they trade fer a hoss?"

Willow translated, "The White man wants to trade for a horse. Do you think that would be possible?"

Fast Black Horse glanced around suspiciously. "Who would want to trade with a witch?"

"As *Tam Apo* is my witness, I am no witch." She raised

her voice so that the milling warriors could hear. "I am *no* witch!"

As far as Richard could see, no one looked convinced.

The rider dispatched to the village returned at a hard gallop, laid out over the neck of his pony as if one with the animal. He pulled up, sliding his bay on its hocks in the green grass. "Slim Pole would see Heals Like A Willow! He is preparing himself, and asks that Heals Like A Willow camp in the flats across the river from the village. No one is to see her until Slim Pole can talk to her. The Yellow Noses are to guard Willow's camp and make sure this is so."

Willow sighed and slapped hands to her sides in futility. "And how long is that supposed to take?"

Fast Black Horse chewed his lip for a moment, and studied her narrowly. "That will be up to Slim Pole—and what the spirits tell him."

Willow marched back to Richard, Fletch, and Jonas. "We are to camp on the flats across the river from the village. Slim Pole, the *puhagan* here, wants to see me."

"Poohuggun?" Fletch made a face. "What's that?"

"Medicine man," Richard supplied. To Willow, he asked, "Trouble?"

She took a deep breath and said, "I don't know."

"Camp?" Jonas asked incredulously. "It ain't nigh ta midday! Reckon we could make miles yet. And who's these red niggers, a telling a white man what ta do? We're Americans, God damn it!"

"Shut up, kid," Fletch growled. "Don't mind him. He didn't get no ejication in his upbringing." He looked at Richard. "What do ye think, Hamilton? Buck the banshee and pull our sticks, or see her through?"

Richard turned to Willow. "What do you think?"

"I think we should see Slim Pole," she said. "He's a wise man. He might stop this witching talk once and for all."

"Witch talk?" Fletch asked, perplexed.

"They think Willow's a witch." Richard was watching the sullen Fast Black Horse on the dapple gelding. "Or didn't you know that's why Yellow Beaver guided you to us?" His glance shifted to Willow. "That's what he wanted, wasn't it?"

"Yes," she said uneasily. "He wanted me to use *puha* to kill Slim Pole."

Richard cursed, then looked up at Fletch. "I think the best thing is to make camp. It will only cost a day or two, and if we can wrangle a horse out of it, so much the better."

"And if they don't cotton ta us?" Jonas asked, his thumb on the cock of his rifle.

"Then at least you'll be forted up," Willow replied. "Or would you rather build a post?"

"What's that mean?" Jonas demanded,

"It means, shut up," Fletch muttered. "Damn, boy, ye don't know shit!"

❖

The horses cropped at the first spring grass while they waited under the spreading limbs of cottonwoods. The sap-heavy branches waved in the afternoon breeze. Birdsong rose and fell as the finches and juncos fluttered about. A mourning dove cooed in the distance. White masses of cloud formed around the Wind River peaks and sailed out to dissipate over the basin before they reached the eastern horizon.

All of Willow's attempts to prepare for the meeting ended in a rising anxiety. *What do I say? How do I answer him? Slim Pole never approved of me.* Like it or not, charges of witchcraft often hinged more on people's likes than on any evidence of witching.

"A witch, huh?" Fletch asked, rubbing his bearded jaw. "Naw, she looks too good ta be a witch."

Jonas grinned nervously from where he sat leaned against a cottonwood trunk and continued to whip the moldy leaf mat with a grass stem.

"It's a long story," Richard told them. "It seems that women shouldn't involve themselves in healing."

"Healing, huh?" Fletch studied Willow with thoughtful eyes. "Think ye could fix my back? I get a twinge of an occasion."

"I'll take a look when we have time." *If I live through this.*

Willow fingered her chin. What would she do if Slim Pole declared her a witch? She glanced surreptitiously at Richard. He'd fight for her, take on Slim Pole's village—and die in the process.

So, what do I do? The only answer would be to accept whatever punishment Slim Pole decreed. For the first time, she regretted teaching Richard Shoshoni. He'd follow the conversation, understand enough to know what Slim Pole would do to her.

"Richard," she said softly, "I want you to do me a favor."

He nodded, taking her hand. "Anything."

"Let me talk to Slim Pole alone. And afterwards, promise me that you'll do anything I tell you to. It may be more involved than a simple meeting. Do you understand? I may have to stay here for a while in order to bring an end to all this."

He studied her uneasily. "Is it that serious?"

"I have let it go too far as it is. I can't afford to ignore it any longer." *And I don't dare tell you the rest.*

But as he looked into her eyes, she could feel him follow the tracks of her fear down into her souls. "I don't believe it. We're in the year eighteen twenty-six . . . and someone is going to accuse you of witchcraft? No, this has gone far enough."

She put a hand on his sleeve. "Yes, it has. But *I* must settle it—in my way. Do you understand? It's not a White matter. Anything you try will only make matters worse. You must trust me now and do as I say. Will you?"

He nodded reluctantly. "If you think it best. I love you a great deal, Willow."

"Now, you must have faith in me." She took his hand, touching it to her lips. "Because I love you with all of my souls. And I'll do what I must do. For you, for me, for us. Do you understand?"

"I do." He smiled then, reassuring her.

"Hyar comes," Fletch called, rising, his rifle in hand. He stared down toward the crossing.

Slim Pole rode at the head of a group of warriors. Willow could see that his pony was wet up to the chest from fording the river. Slim Pole wore his hair in two braids confined by weasel hide—protection against evil, as were the eagle feathers stuck through the beaver-hide hat he wore. A long, fringed hunting shirt hung from his thin shoulders, the front and back decorated with quillwork. Water had darkened his moccasins and leggings.

Willow stood as the old *puhagan* pulled up and slipped off his horse. How curious: that face no longer cowed her the way it once had. She could sense his Power now, measure its limits. It was as if she saw him through different eyes. *Have I changed so much? Or is it him?*

She gave Richard a last glance, an attempt to enforce her

will that he stay out of it. Then she squared her shoulders and walked forward to greet Slim Pole.

"Hello, *Puhagan*. It's been a long time."

"Heals Like A Willow, you are looking well." He probed her with his old brown eyes. "My vision hasn't improved any since our last meeting, but I can see your *puha*."

"Might we walk, you and I?" She thought of Richard. "It might avoid complications."

Slim Pole considered, thin brown lips pressed together, his weathered face wooden. "For what purpose?"

She lowered her voice. "My companions do not understand our ways, *Puhagan*."

He blinked, squinting in Richard's direction. "A pace or two," he consented. "But not out of sight of my warriors."

His words stung. "Then you believe the stories? You believe I am a witch?"

He lifted his hands in supplication. "If there is trouble, you always seem to be in the middle of it. Why is this, Willow? I suppose now you are going to tell me with great energy and enthusiasm that you are no witch?"

She sighed wearily. "I'm tired of saying that, Slim Pole. I don't feel like a witch. I'll tell you what I've done, and where I've been. Then you judge. Maybe I am a witch . . . and if so, I don't know what to do about it. I don't feel evil, if that's important. I haven't shot magic into any of our people to harm them. And you must know this: Yellow Beaver rode over to *Ainkahonobita* offering horses and anything I wanted if only I'd kill you." She gave him a level stare. "I'd keep an eye on him, if I were you. He's no good."

Slim Pole stopped short, staring at her. "No, he's no good. How many horses did he offer?"

"Twenty, and all the buffalo robes and meat, and, who knows, maybe even the moon and stars had I asked."

Slim Pole chuckled. "Perhaps you should have taken the price. Then we would know for certain if you are a witch."

"He carried a little bag,—hair, blood, a bit of fingernail. You might want to get that back."

"I will see to it." He paused. "Why do you tell me this? As proof you are no witch?"

"No. Well, perhaps. But mostly because I think you are a good man, Slim Pole. You lead your people well. And no matter what you decide today, I will bear you no ill will."

"You seem older, Willow. Almost a different person. What happened to you after you left? The stories say that you were taken by a Pawnee and carried far to the east, to the river there."

"I was. That story you may believe." She frowned. "Slim Pole, I have seen beyond the horizon. I traveled with the Whites, and now that I have returned, none of my people believe the things I try to tell them. They do not have room enough in their heads to understand about the giant boats and the White man's huge lodges."

"You saw these things in the Spirit World?"

"No, in *this* world. Things made by men." She stopped, puzzled. "But then, it's as incomprehensible for them as it is for me when Richard tells of ships, and boats that run with fires in their bellies."

"Boats with fire in their bellies?" Slim Pole's lips quirked at the notion.

Willow rubbed the back of her neck, shaking her head. "You must hear me, *Puhagan*. Listen to my words, and make them part of your soul. Great changes are coming to our People. They lie there, just over the horizon to the east. The Whites are coming here, to our mountains. And when they arrive, nothing will ever be the same again."

Slim Pole squinted eastward, deepening the wrinkles in his face. "Should we prepare to fight?"

"Can you stop the wind? Still the change of the seasons? No, *Puhagan*. This will not be a war of arrows and bullets. I've come to know the Whites. Heard their stories of war. They are like ants. Kick the anthill, and ever more come boiling out to fight. They will fight the way they work, with a single-minded determination we can't comprehend. For the sake of the People, Slim Pole, you must counsel them to bend with this coming wind of change. If they do not, the Whites will overwhelm them as a tornado does a tall pine. All that will be left will be a broken stump."

"Perhaps the Whites have done something to you, Willow. Is that it? Have they shot their Power into you, that you say these things? Are they like *Nunumbi*? Do they wield great Power?"

She shook her head. "Not like that. Their Power is called rationalism. With it, they capture souls, and lock them away like mice in pots." She quirked her lips. "I still have my souls, Slim Pole, so they did not work their magic on me."

His faded stare fixed on her. "When I look into your eyes, I see that you still have your souls. So . . . the stories say you were in the Land of the Dead?"

She steeled herself. "Yes, *Puhagan*. I found the way, and passed the guardians. But you should know that I would not have come back except for Richard. I would have become lost in the dark forest had he not sensed the right way."

He narrowed his eyes. "And which way was that?"

"Into the thickest tangle of the trees."

"You *have* been there." Slim Pole cocked his head. "Then that story is true. Did *Pandzoavits* give you Power?"

"None of the spirits gave me Power, Slim Pole." *I gave it to myself. And learned it from Richard.* But aloud she said, "Perhaps it came from the journey, from the Pawnee I fought, or the Rees I killed. Perhaps it came from the river, or the mountains. My Power is different, Slim Pole. It comes from visions and dreams from far away."

"Such things can be very dangerous. *Pachee Goyo* discovered this when returning from Cannibal Owl's island. Remember all of the odd creatures he encountered on the way?"

"I do. And like the Bald One, I have returned safely through those lands," Willow countered. "Slim Pole, I will tell you this: I am no longer of the People. I have become someone different. Not *Dukurika,* or *Ku'chendikani,* or White man. I have something of each people within me—but I am no danger to the People."

"Can you prove that?"

"How can I?" She pulled her hair around and twisted it into a thick braid, walking slowly beside the *puhagan.* "I can tell you over and over, but a witch would lie. You could look into the eye of my soul, but a witch would use just such a trick to capture your soul. Am I missing anything?"

"I could kill you, and burn your body so the ghost couldn't come back and haunt us."

"That wasn't what I had in mind."

"But what do I do with you, Willow? I have heard you speak, listened to the truth in your voice. You *are* something different. But what? I think you are too Powerful to roam loose and commit any mayhem you choose. I have told you before, spirit power is not meant for young women."

"I am nothing more than *Tam Apo* made me." On sudden inspiration, she stopped. "We think too much like Coyote, and not enough like Wolf. Humans always look for tricks when Power is involved."

"With good reason, girl."

When Willow pulled her knife, Slim Pole stepped back warily. Deftly she rolled up her sleeve to cut a small piece of skin from the inside of her elbow. Heedless of the stinging pain, she handed it to Slim Pole.

He stared thoughtfully at it, refusing to take the severed flesh. "What is that?"

"Proof," she said, holding it out to him. "The only thing I can offer. A piece of myself. Take it. Do with it what you will. Would a witch offer you a piece of herself?"

His eyes narrowed. "Perhaps you seek to distract me with some trick." He shook his head, answering himself with: "It's a piece of herself, a handle on her *mugwa*. A witch wouldn't dare offer such a prize to an adversary."

His hand trembled as he reached out and took the slip of bloody skin on his palm. "If you are a witch, Willow, you're the most foolish one who has ever lived."

"Foolish witches don't live long." She ignored the trickles of blood running down her arm.

"And what will you do now? Follow your White men? Go back to the mountains?" He paused. "I don't want you in my village."

She laughed bitterly. "None of the People want me, *Puhagan*. I will not be returning to your village, or any other for that matter. Like the Bald One, I still must search to find my place. And like him, I still have several challenges to face."

Slim Pole tightened his fist on the bit of skin. "You don't seem nervous for a woman who has just given a *puhagan* a piece of herself."

"I have nothing to fear from you, Slim Pole. You are Wolf, not Coyote. A man of honor and integrity. I have always respected your wisdom."

He looked away to the west, toward the mountains his failing vision could no longer see. The breeze teased loose strands of white hair that had pulled free of his beaver hat. Afternoon light played on the delicate brown skin of his wrinkled face. "I think I will tell my people to let you and your White men go. If you stayed away from my

Ku'chendikani for a long time, I might be tempted to think I'd made the right decision."

"I will do my best."

As the old man turned, Willow added, "*Puhagan,* I told you the truth about the Whites, about their boats and ways."

He glanced back, looking frail and old. "I heard your words. I cannot see over the horizon where you have looked. I can only hope such things are in a place I will never go." And with that, he walked carefully toward where Fast Black Horse and the warriors waited.

Pensive, heart heavy, Willow walked out of the trees. Slim Pole was talking to Fast Black Horse, his old hands moving like brown birds to accent his words. The warriors clustered, to listen intently.

Richard and the Whites waited among the trees, anxious attention on the Indians. Willow gave Richard a smile and walked over to where they waited. The horses still cropped contentedly, but Fletch and Jonas held their rifles ready. She took Richard's hands in hers and met his worried brown eyes.

"It's all right. Slim Pole and I talked. He will not call me a witch, but my *puha* worries him. It is something he doesn't understand."

"Then you're free?" Richard asked.

She hesitated, and shook her head. "No, Richard. My people will never trust me again. I am different, changed. Like a white rock among black stones, I no longer have a place."

"Then, what will we do?"

She exhaled wearily. "I don't know. I'm still a tree lost in the river."

"You're bleeding."

She glanced down and shrugged. "I gave Slim Pole a piece of skin. Nothing else would have convinced him."

"Reckon we'd best pull our sticks." Fletch cast uneasy glances at the warriors. "I'd hate like hell to have them change their minds."

"It's me they'd want," Willow told him. "Had anything gone wrong, I would have offered myself to them. You would have been free to go."

"Willow!" Richard cried.

"I told you to trust me," she reminded. "You do not know these people or their ways."

"Maybe not." Richard didn't look convinced as he turned to the packs. "Jonas, give me a hand loading the mare."

At that moment, an old woman appeared from the crossing, her dress wet to the waist. She hobbled through the warriors, leading a string of three horses.

"Wait." Willow reached out and caught Richard's sleeve. Then she hurried forward, a warmth stirring the empty feeling inside.

The sun glinted in Two Half Moons's silver-shot hair as she padded through the grass in soggy moccasins. She stopped before Willow, her lively old eyes gleaming like pebbles of obsidian. A young sorrel gelding, a bay mare, and a dappled gray were tethered together at the end of the lead rope.

"So," Two Half Moons said. "In trouble again, Heals Like A Willow? Look at you! Can this be the same woman I found freezing on the ridgetop? Now I can only wonder about what you have become."

Willow took the old woman in her arms, holding her close the way she would something delicate and precious. She could feel her aunt's bones through the thin doehide dress. "Hello, *napia*."

The reedy arms tightened, the old hands patting Willow fondly. Then she pushed back, inspecting Willow with pensive eyes. "You still look sad, girl. But now I see a strength in you that defies anything I have seen in a woman before. Can these stories White Hail tells me be true?"

"That depends on the stories."

"You have gone to a distant land and, like *Pachee Goyo,* you've come back changed. I think White Hail is right. You have found great *puha.*"

"White Hail is well?"

"He is. He has changed, too, Willow. Become a thoughtful and sober man where once there was only a wild youth. For the first time, people come ask his opinion about things. He has told me all about his adventures with you. About the things you told him, and the White man you saved in the Land of the Dead. Something in his souls changed. This is good. One day, I think he will become a great leader."

One of the horses, the young sorrel gelding, tossed his head and pawed at the grass, jerking at the lead rope the old woman held.

Willow smiled. "Tell him I am glad."

Two Half Moons glanced suspiciously at the Whites. Her skeptical expression deepened the wrinkles in her brown face. "They are ugly men, girl. What do you see in them? This Power that the Whites are said to have?"

"They are just men, Aunt. Come, I would have you meet them."

"No." Two Half Moons shook her head. "I have no need of their kind. It was you I came to see. To tell you that no matter what is said, you still have a place in my lodge."

"And you in mine."

"Here, take this. That ornery sorrel will pull me over if you don't. Then it will take all day to get me picked up again." Two Half Moons offered the lead rope to Willow. The braided leather was the same color as the old woman's age-knotted hand. "People in the village are saying that you wished to trade for horses. I have brought you three. They are a gift."

"I cannot take such a—"

"Hush, girl. You will need them. When you no longer do, bring them back to me."

"Aunt, I can't."

"Still arguing! And after you ignored my warnings the last time. Look where that got you! Listen to your elder for once. Take the horses." She made the sign for finality. "Willow, I am old. Pains come in the night, and my legs have lost the strength they once had. I think this might be my last summer."

Willow's heart felt ready to burst. She studied Two Half Moons's face, trying to memorize every wrinkle. "I hear your words, *napia,* but I don't believe them. You are good for a great many summers yet."

The thin brown lips bent in a wry smile. "Do not try to fool me about life, Willow. I've lived too much of it for silly talk and lies. Coyote made sure we die when our time comes. I have cheated death many times. This time, I will not. And, to be honest, I am tired of the aches and hurts. The winters are colder, the summers too hot."

"Isn't White Hail caring for you?"

"White Hail takes good care of me, and he's been talking to young Split Antelope. I think she will come to the lodge soon. She is a lot like you, that girl. She will be what she wants to be. I think his lodge will have more children soon."

"All the more reason for you to live. *Napia,* those children will need you. Someone must see that they are raised properly." *As I wanted you to help raise my son.*

Two Half Moons made a gesture with her birdlike hand. "My world was different, Willow. I see changes coming— like your White men, here. They have been all over the

country, you know. And I have heard more are coming. The
Pa'kiani are growing stronger, and the wind tells me that my
time is over."

"Wasn't it you who once brought me down from the
mountain? Perhaps you need me to do that for you."

Two Half Moons smiled to expose toothless pink gums.
"When I brought you down from the rim that day, you were
empty. When my *mugwa* leaves to travel to the Land of the
Dead, it will be full. But, tell me, you've been to the Land of
the Dead. Is it like the stories say?"

"Yes, Aunt." Willow jerked the pliable lead rope when the
sorrel pulled against it.

She nodded with a weary contentment. "Then I shall see
many old friends. The hunting will be good, and there will
be no talk of changes. I can gamble at the hand game, tease
the children, and tell your husband what has become of you.
I look forward to seeing him again."

The dapple gray mare stamped at the season's first flies,
and the bay shook her head.

Two Half Moons scowled at Willow's expression. "Oh,
stop that! You look as if the sun had just gone black. The
world is the way it is, girl, and nothing can stop the turning
of the seasons. Now, I will wish you well and leave."

"Are you sure you won't stay? Eat with us? Maybe spend
some time talking about better things?"

Two Half Moons cocked an eyebrow. "Last time, it was
me pleading with you. Why should I do what you
wouldn't that day I put the pack on your shoulders? No,
girl. I want it this way. To say goodbye and go back to my
lodge."

"I—I understand."

"Ah, good. You're showing sense for once. Now, take
the horses, and go to this meeting of White men that people are talking about." She reached out, laying a frail
hand on Willow's shoulder. "Be all that you can, girl.

That is all I have to say." With that, she patted Willow's arm one last time, love swelling in her old eyes. Then she turned and walked back toward the river without a backward glance.

"Who was that?" Richard asked as Willow led the horses back to the camp.

"A very dear old friend." She lowered her head, her heart like a stone. *I am slowly losing everything I love. My people, Two Half Moons . . . and finally, Richard.*

"You look so sad," Richard said, taking her arm.

"The sun just turned black," she whispered.

"What was that?"

"Nothing." She stiffened her resolve. "Come, let's pack these horses. We can go far before night falls."

THIRTY-THREE

◆

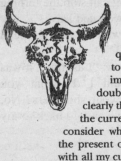

For example, let the question be: May I, when in distress, make a promise without the intention to keep it? I easily distinguish between the two meanings which the question can have, viz., whether it is prudent to make a false promise, or whether it is implicit to duty. The former can, without doubt, often be the case; however, I see most clearly that it is not sufficient merely to escape from the current difficulties by this means, but that I must consider whether much greater inconveniences than the present one may not later arise from this lie. Even with all my cunning, the consequences cannot be so easily anticipated.

—Immanuel Kant, *Foundations of the Metaphysics of Morals*

Rain fell from the solid bank of oppressive clouds. They hung so low they devoured the high ridges of Red Canyon. At the wispy fringes of gray, the ghosts of limber pine and juniper lurked, appeared, and were engulfed by the mist.

"We missed 'em," Travis declared sourly as he sat his horse and stared up at the water-slick layers of canted sandstone. The shelter, its doorway black and vacant, seemed to stare forlornly at them, echoes of loneliness in the cant of the logs.

"Well, hell," Baptiste muttered. He cocked his head so the rain dripped off the brim of his black felt hat. He glanced around at the spring-fed creek and the cropped grass. Here and there piles of horse dung were dark and unbleached by the sun. "We're close ahind 'em, Travis. The grass is still mashed flat. I'd say they's only a couple of days ahead of us."

"Reckon we'll make a camp of it hyar." Travis wiped water from his ruined face. His leather clothing was soaked, and his skin chafed. "This child's about half-froze fer a hot fire and a drying. Reckon that shelter looks plumb chipper fer an old beaver like me."

Baptiste gathered a handful of fringes and wrung them out. "Yer not the only one, coon." He worked his mouth distastefully. "I done started to think I's back in Louisiana."

"Then camp it is. Hell, this hyar little canyon makes a right fine hole. Old Dick done hisself slick, I tell ye. Yes, sir, slicker'n Hob."

Baptiste dismounted and took a halfhearted step, as if testing his land legs. That, or the cold water had picked a new path to run down inside his leathers. "Reckon she'll be a mite tough to sniff out their tracks after this rain."

"Maybe so." Travis swung a leg over his saddle and dropped to the ground. He shifted his rifle from one hand to the other, working fingers that had stiffened around the cold gun. "But, then, I figger ter be a fair sniffer when it comes ter tracks. Tarnal Hell." He winced. "My arse aches, I'm telling ye, hoss. Got prickles in my hind end like ants."

"Yor getting old, coon." Baptiste gave him a big grin. "Now, haul yo' rickety bones inside that shelter and clear out the buzzworms whilst I see to the hosses."

Travis hunched down at the doorway, studying the inside. The place looked neat and trim. Several hides still lay on the floor. Travis scented the air for some trace of Richard or Willow. Only the tang of smoke, juniper, and old leather rewarded him.

"Hell, Dick. I don't know whar yer off ter this time. Tarnation, Doodle, ain't I never gonna catch up with ye?"

◆

The journey to Willow Valley would remain with Richard forever. He marveled at the expanses and colors of the Green River basin. They trotted their horses through undulating waves of sea green sagebrush. Paintbrush bloomed red and yellow. Purple dagger-pod vied with clumps of sagebrush violets. Sun yellow daisies and buckwheats splotched the stands of tall grass in color. And in the distance, mountain ranges capped with pristine snow rose above turquoise sage flats. The hills consisted of banded clays, many eroded like the cathedrals of old. Herds of antelope coursed like schools of fish through the verdant grasslands. Bands of humped buffalo grazed the lush grass, clumps of shed fur hanging like moss from their sleek hides. Tan calves bounced behind the protective screen of cows who snorted at the sight of the riders, lifted their tails, and finally wheeled to dash away in a clicking of hooves.

They rode through it all: four people alone in the majesty of the wilderness.

On the banks of the swollen Green River, Willow and Richard crafted a bull boat out of willow stems, and covered it with hide. As Fletch and Jonas swam the horses across, Willow and Richard paddled their possessions to the west bank.

They climbed the long ridges to the west, winding through sagebrush and patchy stands of mountain mahogany. In the hollows, freshly budded aspens quivered in the breeze. The land might have been painted by the hand of God: thick-leafed balsam displayed a wealth of nodding yellow flowers as they passed. Larkspur bloomed so blue it hurt the eyes, and daisies painted patterns of soft purple, white, and yellow. Stands of lupine created a tapestry of sky blue accented by the yellows of desert parsley and red spots of biscuit-root. Onions lifted crowned flowers everywhere.

On the highest ridges, Richard was surprised to find oyster shells eroding out of the limestone beds.

"What does it mean?" he asked, looking back across the basin to the east as he fingered the shells. "How could they be here?"

"What are they?" Willow gave him a curious look. "Rock is rock, isn't it?"

"These are oysters, shells, like the ones the Shoshoni

trade for. A creature that only lives in the sea," he answered. "How did they get here? We're a good half mile higher than the basin—and thousands of miles from the ocean."

"*Tam Apo* works in mysterious ways." Willow shrugged. "In some of our legends the world was once covered with water. That was before Coyote and Wolf. A long, long time ago."

"Noah and the Flood," Fletch replied in awed tones. He picked up an oyster shell. "Hard ta figger. I ate oysters in Virginny as a kid. And hyar they be. Hell, I wonder if'n Salt Lake ain't part of the ocean maybe."

The following morning a spring storm rolled in and they rode in the rain. They crossed a misty divide and dropped down through valleys lush with cottonwoods and willows, the streams thick in beaver.

"Wisht ta hell we could trap some," Jonas lamented. "We'd make nigh a hundred in a week."

"Ain't got traps," Fletch growled.

In the marshy flats below the mountains, chirring red-winged and yellow-headed blackbirds perched on new shoots of cattails. When they paused, Willow waded out to dig some of the cattail from the muck, later making sweet cakes from the starchy roots. Nor did the delights of the wilderness stop there. Biscuit-root, onions, parsley, sego lily, bladderwort, and blazing star added taste to the meat they shot.

"Tarnal Hell," Fletch exclaimed. "A white man'd starve ta death atop all these greens, and right smart they is, too!"

Jonas nodded as he fished another of the biscuit-root cakes from the roasting stones in their fire.

They skirted the curiously green waters of Bear Lake, and climbed southward into Willow Valley. Sheer mountain walls rose on either side, the heights clad in velvet forests of pine and fir. The air seemed to have taken on a crystal purity.

For all of that, a knot had formed in Richard's belly. That

night, lying under the robes, he stared up at the myriad of stars. How clear they were in the cool black sky.

A terrible decision is coming. How will you choose? He chewed on the nagging problem of Boston, and his father. *How can I give this up? Dear Lord God, I have everything here. Freedom, Willow, and a wonderful life spreading out before me.* Assuming, that was, that some Blackfoot didn't lift his hair.

And, at the same time, the terrible weight of responsibility pulled relentlessly at him. *No, I've got to go back. If only for a week. I have to see Father. Tell him what happened. Maybe make peace. Then I can come back.*

"You are worried." Willow propped herself on her elbow beside him. With a slim hand she pulled back her hair. Despite the darkness, he could feel her sober stare.

"I don't know what to do." He sighed wearily. "I don't want to go back."

"Then don't go."

He reached out to finger her glossy hair. "He's my father, Willow. I owe him something. It's a matter of responsibility. Do you understand? My father gave me great wealth—and I lost it. Think of it like a thousand horses, and I was to drive them to the Missouri. But when I got there, they were stolen. By now, my father thinks I'm dead, and no word of his wealth—or his son—has come back to him."

He could barely make out her pursed lips as she watched him. "Was it your fault?"

"Yes." He pinched the bridge of his nose. "I was a fool, Willow. I never believed the world was real. Thirty thousand dollars. Think of it. More money than most people make in a lifetime. What could my father have been thinking when he sent such a foolish boy on so important a journey? Why didn't he hire a real man to make the trip?"

"Eventually every father must let his son become a man."

"And a son owes something to his father. Willow, look at

me, living in a paradise. Here I am, as happy as I've ever been, and he's back in Boston grieving. I have a duty to him, to myself."

"I don't know this word."

"Duty: an honorable responsibility. That's what I'm struggling with now. It's one thing to read about duty and discuss it in class as if it were an idea; and it is yet another to accept real responsibility . . . where fortunes, or even lives, can be won or lost. What a weight Dave Green took on when he risked everything with *Maria*. Looking back, I wonder why he didn't shoot me that day on the river."

"You have told me that Travis saved you. Maybe he understood what your father did."

Richard's thoughts went back to that night in Boston. To the dinner table, and Jeffry serving up one of Sally's masterpieces. Phillip's stern eyes burned in Richard's memory. "Did he? I wonder. Knowing what I know now, *I* wouldn't have sent me."

He frowned up into the sky. Responsibility—what an awesome thing. *So what will you do now? You have two responsibilities: one to your father in Boston, and another to Willow. How can you meet both?*

The world had laid an ethical trap for him, and now he was caught, damned either way. Two people, in two different worlds, depended on him. He could not take Willow to Boston, and he could not bring Phillip Hamilton to the mountains. Oh, he could send a letter, but his conscience demanded that he see his father face to face. Anything else would be a dereliction.

Willow asked, "What would you have become if you hadn't come here? Who would you be, Richard?"

"A silly student carried away with dreams about Truth and the nature of mankind."

"Would you have liked who you became?"

The distant yipping of coyotes carried on the night. "As I am now? No. I'd have despised that man, so pompous with his conceptions of life and nature. And he would have despised me, called me an animal and brute. So here I am, a savage who wears men's hair as a badge. And what has happened to my belief in rationality? Where did it go? Why was it such a flawed concept? Men aren't rational. They steal each other's horses, kill each other. No, not rational at all. Just—chaotic."

"I think *all* men are rational," she challenged. "Each does what he thinks is best. *Dukurika* avoid fights with others, and hide in the forest when danger is close. That's rational. According to the *Ku'chendikani,* a rational man steals as many horses as he can, because by doing so, he makes his people stronger. His children will have full bellies. His prowess as a warrior enables his people to keep their enemies at bay."

"That's not rational. That's pragmatic."

"I don't know that word."

"Pragmatic. It means doing what makes the most sense at the moment."

"Isn't that rational, Richard?"

"You're setting me up for epistemological tail-chasing." He paused. "Tell me, do you think Green was rational when he blew up *Maria*?"

"As he saw it, yes. You told me the *Pa'kiani* would have taken everything."

Richard squirmed uneasily under the blanket and raised up to see that the horses were still standing at their pickets. He listened intently to the soft whispers of the night, until satisfied that all was well with the camp. "Does that mean that everything depends upon an individual's perception?"

"We are all like Coyote," she replied. "A man can't know

more than what he sees. We make decisions, like Coyote when he went to steal Sage Grouse's eggs. He wanted to eat the eggs, but when he found Sage Grouse's nest, all the eggs had hatched into chicks. He was so mad he kicked dirt all over the chicks and urinated on them. To him it seemed right because he was hungry. Then he killed the chicks. And forever since, Sage Grouse goes out of her way to fly up and scare Coyote.

"The point of the story is that Coyote was doing what he was supposed to. Trying to fill his belly. And he's been suffering ever since because Sage Grouse always tries to ruin Coyote's plans."

"Maybe that's why I have to go back." He shook his head. "I don't want to be like Coyote, Willow."

"You can't fix what is already done."

"No. But Coyote would shirk his duty, wouldn't he?"

"Yes."

"Would Wolf?"

"No."

"A Sioux *wechashawakan* said that I came up the river as a dog, but that I would turn into either a coyote or a wolf. I am no longer Coyote. I can't shirk this duty."

She bit her lip, then grasped his hand. "You have already been Coyote, Richard. You said you would stay with me. Let me go with you to this Boston."

He closed his eyes, rubbing his thumb on her hand. "Do you remember when Slim Pole came to see you? You asked me to trust you? *If* I decide to go back, I'll need you to trust me. Going to Boston would break your soul, Willow."

"It didn't break yours."

"I was born to it—like a Pawnee chief—by station and birth. I wasn't Indian." He vented a dry laugh. "How funny. Back on the river, dreams of Boston kept me alive. I walked the streets, longed for it with all of my soul. And now, as we get closer to this rendezvous, the more I dread leaving you, leaving the mountains. To hell with duty."

"Then you must go."

At the despair in her voice, he said, "I haven't decided."

"Richard, listen to me. This duty, this worry about your father. If you do not go, you will never know if it was right or wrong. No matter what you once were, you are a warrior now. A man. A part of you will never be complete unless you go to this Boston."

She snuggled into the hollow of his arm, and he tightened his hold on her. The stars slowly slipped across the silent sky, but no answer came to him.

❖

As they rode south along the Little Bear River, Willow cast surreptitious glances at Richard. He'd withdrawn into himself, struggling with his soul. He rode head down, a frown lining his brow.

Fletch and Jonas noted his preoccupation, and directed more of their talk to her, asking about the plants, about the game, and different tribes of Indians. She told them what she knew about the beaver streams, and about *Tssa'shogup*: the land to the west and south.

Richard barely noticed the green meadows of tall grass that rippled like waves on a lake. His eyes were blind to the majestic mountains that rose to either side. He had removed himself from this world in an attempt to find the answer that she already knew.

She studied him from the corner of her eye. *What will I do when he leaves? Could Boston be such a terrible place? Would it be as bad as Richard says?*

Puffs of cloud drifted eastward across the sky. Along the

river, cottonwoods had leafed out and the land breathed and flexed itself for summer. In the backwaters, ducks guarded nests full of young. Willow's heart had always lifted in spring, enjoying the rebirth of *Tam Segobia*. This year, she entered a summer of dread.

Richard would go, and her love with him, heading for a place she could neither comprehend nor understand. *And then what will you do, Willow? Where will you go? Unlike Richard, who has two places, you have none.* She was still a tree adrift in the current—and one by one, her roots were being broken off.

She saw them first: Riders in the distance like dots on the grass. Five of them, leading more horses packed with meat. Even before Fletch whooped, she'd identified them as Whites by the way they sat their horses.

"Let's go!" Jonas crowed. They kicked their animals to a run, pounding across the grass. Fletch raised his rifle, firing a shot into the air. Willow tucked against her mare's neck, racing with the rest toward the Whites who'd pulled up to watch.

When they were within shouting distance, four of the five riders trotted to meet them. The remaining man held the packhorses as they whinnied and jostled.

To Willow's surprise, four of the strangers were Indian, but of a people she'd never seen before. In some ways, they reminded her of Pawnee with their shaved heads, but the decorations on their buckskins were unlike anything she'd seen.

The White man was small, whip-thin, with long brown

hair and beard. She instantly liked his soft brown eyes. He sat his horse as if part of the animal, a use-polished Hawken across the saddle. His buckskins were shiny with fat and blood, half the fringe missing.

"Fletch!" the hunter cried. "Hell, coon. I figgered you for dead! And who's this with you?"

"Jonas Hayworth." Fletch pointed. "And this hyar's Richard Hamilton, and the squaw's Willow. Hell, Tylor, it'd take a heap of grizzlies and a passel of Injuns to raise this child." The two rode close to clasp hands.

Jonas had a silly, uncomfortable grin on his face as he shook Tylor's hand. Richard rode close and shook hands, saying, "Richard Hamilton, sir. I'm pleased to meet you."

A curious light shone in Tylor's sharp eyes. "John Tylor, at your service. I assure you, sir, the pleasure is mine."

Richard straightened. "Indeed. And where are you from?"

Tylor's eyes veiled. "The East. A long time ago." He turned to Fletch. "Is the caravan coming?"

"Hell, we thought they'd a beat us hyar." Fletch scratched his ear. "And who're these coons?"

Tylor looked back at the Indians. "Iroquois. They, er, joined us. Nor'westers originally. Some of Ogden's brigade who decided to cast their lot with Americans rather than British. Not an unseemly choice, given their history. Meet Smokes His Pipe, Fights the Huron, and Calumet. Tall Fire's back there holding the horses."

The Iroquois nodded, taking their measure with hard black eyes. Willow bristled as they stared at her with open interest. Instinctively, she pulled her mare closer to Richard's mount.

"How far ta camp?" Fletch asked. "What's news?"

Tylor had heeled his horse around, resuming his inter-rupted travel. "About three miles. We just went out after meat. Most of the boys are waiting, gambling away their winter hunt. By now, each man jack of them has won and lost a fortune five or six times. A band of Snakes are camped with us."

The Iroquois snagged up the lead ropes from Tall Fire, and fell in behind.

"Hawyooo!" Fletch whooped. "We're damn near there! Hot damn, coons, she's a long way from Saint Loowee!"

"When would you expect the caravan?" Tylor glanced over. "Moses Harris and Jed Smith came in a couple of weeks ago. They said General Ashley was on the Platte."

"That's where Jonas and me left him." Fletch pointed to Richard. "Heard tell of a white man living with the Snakes up on the Wind River. Jonas and me went ta see, and Hob take us, we found old Richard, hyar."

"Indeed?" Tylor asked, speculative eyes on Richard.

"It's a long story." Richard continued to give Tylor a thoughtful study.

Willow placed her horse on Richard's far side, doing her best to ignore the rapacious glances of the Iroquois. Hadn't they brought any women with them?

I wouldn't trust them any further than Coyote! Maybe they, too, carried two penises.

"I don't suppose you've had word of a Travis Hartman?" Richard asked.

"Hartman?" Tylor lifted an eyebrow. "No. Last I heard he was on the Missouri, hunting for one of the Company posts."

As she glanced at the Iroquois, Willow stiffened, a crawling sensation in her gut. Mean lust reflected in their eyes—and even Trudeau hadn't sent such a cold shiver down her back. In Shoshoni, she asked: "Who are these Iroquois?"

To her surprise, Tylor answered in her tongue, "Indians from far to the east. They live in the forests of northern New York. Many have joined the Canadians."

"They have no women?" Willow asked. "From their looks, their blankets have been empty for many moons."

Smokes His Pipe laughed. "I speak your tongue. Perhaps you come to my bed, eh?"

Richard answered with frost in his voice, but smiled in a disarming way. "My wife's bed is full enough with me in it."

Tylor chuckled and gestured for the Iroquois to back down. "Coons, I think the woman is spoken for. And I think you'd best look elsewhere unless you're anxious to find the Village of Souls."

The Iroquois grinned at each other, but the Coyote look still filled their eyes.

John Tylor gave Richard a surreptitious study. "Tell me your story, Mr. Hamilton."

As Richard talked, Willow did her best to ignore the Iroquois. The grass had been grazed off here, old piles of horse droppings already sun-bleached. By the time they reached the camp, Richard had outlined his adventures.

The camp sat in the flats under the trees, a series of tents, tipis, and shelters dotting the flattened grass. In the distance a horse herd grazed under the watchful eyes of Indian guards.

Men gathered as they rode in, all calling questions about the caravan. Mixed among them were Shoshoni peoples that Willow assumed were *Agaiduka,* the Salmon-eaters who lived west of the mountains.

"Ho! Fletch!" a buckskin clad man called. "Welcome to Rendezvous, coon!"

"Indeed," John Tylor agreed. "Welcome to Rendezvous. Mr. Hamilton, my camp is over there to the west. On the small rise by the creek. If you'd like, you and your wife may establish yourselves there. It may be days yet before the caravan arrives, and Mr. Smith, our booshway, is out on an exploration. I would appreciate your company in the meantime."

"Thank you," Richard responded, inclining his head. "We accept your hospitality."

"Tarnal Hell," Fletch cried. "Somebody fetch this coon a cock fer his rifle. And a file." The burly trapper winked. "We'll fix ye up, Hamilton. Make a white man outa ye again."

Make a White man out of him, Willow thought to herself, glancing around at the hairy men in their grease-stained leathers. One or two were accompanied by bead-covered *Agaiduka* women. Most of the rest were staring at her, sizing her up with hungry eyes that seemed to look right through her dress. Some were shuffling, pushing each other to get a better look.

Richard, I don't like this place. If only we could go back to Ainkahonobita *and act as if Fletch had never ridden into camp. I would give my* mugwa *for that.*

John Tylor had laid out a neat and spare camp. His little lodge was made of cured buffalo hides tied over a pole A-frame. Richard sat with Willow at his side as the first bowl of tobacco he'd had in months sent ribbons of blue smoke into the cool air. A haunch of elk meat roasted on the evening fire.

A brilliant sunset illuminated the mountains east of them with an ethereal glow, and cast the western peaks in dark shadow.

Tylor studied Richard thoughtfully. Finally he asked, "What brought you to Rendezvous, Mr. Hamilton? Just the need of a cock for your rifle?"

"I have a choice to make. My father thinks I'm dead. He entrusted me with a small fortune. I lost it all when a boatman called François robbed me. I think he deserves to know

what happened." Richard frowned at the fire while meat sizzled; burning wood popped sparks and flared with dripping
grease. Colors waned as the evening sky dimmed; orange-
streaked clouds turned rose, and then maroon, before fading
into deep purple. The night calls of the robins joined with
those of the nighthawks, and the bedding finches. Out in the
distance, coyotes raised their pointed noses in jocular chorus.

The trappers camped just beyond them sang "Yankee
Doodle" and followed with various drinking songs around
their evening fires. The *Agaiduka* sang their own songs
about Coyote, Cottontail, and Chicken Hawk. As the singing
rose on the night, trappers hooked arms and danced, stomp-
ing around in moccasined feet.

Tylor pulled thoughtfully on his pipe, a vacant look in
his brown eyes. "You said you came upriver with a boat.
You're a learned man, Mr. Hamilton. Not the sort one
expects to find in the West. There's more than you told me
on the ride in."

"Yes, I suppose there is." Richard gave up his pipe, and
used a file to square out the rough hole in the new cock for
his Hawken. As he filed, he told about François, and Travis,
and Dave Green.

Willow sat close beside him, her shoulder touching his,
as if she savored even the slightest contact. Behind them,
they'd built a shelter from one of the buffalo hides and
spread their sleeping robes on the sweet-smelling grass
within.

Tylor listened carefully as Richard talked, his soft eyes thoughtful. Every now and then he nodded. The fragrant tobacco in his long-stemmed pipe added to the aromas of woodsmoke and cooking meat.

"And now," Richard concluded, "I'm here. I'm told I can accompany the caravan when it returns to Saint Louis."

Tylor considered him for a moment, then glanced at Willow. "From the tone of your voice, I'm not sure that you really want to go, Mr. Hamilton."

Richard inspected the curved metal of the cock and wiped silver filings from his hands. "I don't, Mr. Tylor. But I have a duty to my father. One I never understood when I set out on this adventure." He glanced at Willow, who was trying to hide the sadness in her eyes.

Tylor watched the curls of smoke rise from his pipe bowl. "Duty can become a terrible tyrant, indeed. And God knows, finding one's way through the maze of life is mostly the chore of sorting out what you owe to whom." Tylor glanced at Willow. "Obligations have a habit of sneaking up on us, entwining themselves with our lives. What with them and dreams and ambitions, it's a wonder that any of us remain sane. I don't envy you your choice. But, if I might ask, what are your plans if you stay in the mountains? How will you employ yourself, and is that what you want out of life?"

Richard glanced at Willow, meeting her liquid gaze. "I hadn't thought that far ahead."

What do *you want, Richard?* he asked himself. *You can't have the parlors of Boston with refined discussions and fine brandy and have* Ainkahonobita *at the same time.*

Willow said, "We can live well. *Tam Segobia* provides all that we need. We can find food, make clothing, and have a house anywhere. If Richard stays, he will not starve, Mr. Tylor. He is a hunter and a warrior."

"Indeed, Willow, I can see that." Tylor glanced at Richard

and lifted an eyebrow. "You know, some of the trappers in our party have taken wives among the *Agaiduka*. It wouldn't be a bad life. A living can be made here."

Richard smiled self-consciously. The file whispered as it shaved metal from the cock. Did he have to do anything? Willow was right. The land provided. But what about security? Who was to say that the Blackfeet wouldn't ride into Red Canyon and kill them both?

Richard drew breath. "It seems that as Hobbes noted, life is a compromise. Within society, a given amount of security is granted in exchange for compliance to the social contract. If our civilization has done anything worthwhile, it is that. But it takes so much from us by our agreement to conform to its ways. If I go back, I can't take Willow with me. You know how they'd treat us, Mr. Tylor. A white man doesn't marry an Indian—not in a city like Boston. And Willow would die there, from disease, from confinement, or from the acid in people's looks and actions."

"Indeed she would," Tylor agreed.

"I am willing to take my chances, despite what Richard tells me. I know Boston would be hard for me. But I—"

"No. Your courage isn't at issue, Willow. You don't have to put your hand in fire to know it's painful. Boston would be like that for you, for me." Richard gave her a reassuring smile. "How can I leave you? It's not just a matter of what I'll do. What about you? You can't go back to your people. You've said over and over that you don't fit. Not even High Wolf can make a place for you."

Willow shrugged. "I will make do, Richard. I always have. If you go, I will be waiting for you when you return."

"You are a brave woman," Tylor told her. "Some men would give anything for a woman like you." And he glanced away, not quite managing to hide the sudden pain in his eyes.

Richard quickly said, "That makes my choice a great deal more difficult."

"Loyalty, in wives or friends, is the rarest of virtues, Mr. Hamilton." Tylor knocked the dottle from his pipe. "Before you make your final decision, I suggest that you weigh that fact very carefully." He paused, staring absently into the distance. "Sometimes a man never knows what he has until he's lost it."

Richard took Willow's hand. An awkward silence followed. What had the man lost that hurt him so? A woman; position? What drove a gentleman like Tylor into the wilderness?

"I know what I have." Richard tightened his grip on Willow's hand.

Willow's smile was fleeting as she wound her fingers into his.

Tylor stood suddenly. "If you would excuse me for a moment, I'll take a quick look at the horses, and then we'll eat."

Richard watched him walk quietly away. "A most interesting man." In the dusk, he could see Tylor by the horses, head back as he looked up at the sky's evening glow.

"I like him, Richard." Willow gazed at the fire. "Perhaps you can be thankful. Unlike Tylor, you can go back."

"You think he can't? Do you know something about him that I don't?"

"I can see it in his soul. A thing beyond words."

"I'm sorry we hurt him. When he returns, we'll ask to hear his story."

"You may ask, but I don't think he will tell."

Richard took a deep breath and watched the sparks twirling up into the night. "No, I suppose he won't." He paused. "I'm stuck, Willow. I'll worry about you the whole time if I go. If I stay, I'll worry about Father. Given a choice between worries, I'll stay here."

"Is that easier?"

"It is. My father knew the risks when he sent me west. And I can write him a letter explaining what happened to me. Send him my apology. At least he'll know I'm alive. That's the lesser of the evils."

"But you would rather tell him face to face, wouldn't you?"

Richard stared at the cock, warm from his touch and the rasping file. "I owe it to him. The things I have to say to him should be said man to man."

She lifted an eyebrow and shrugged. "Then you should go, Richard. What if he dies? What if you never have the chance? Your soul will ache forever, knowing that you could have gone."

"And if something should happen while I was in the East? What then? What if you were killed? What if I could have made the difference?"

"You are trying to guess the future." She lifted his hand, brushing it against her lips. "I took a risk, too. I took it when I fell in love with you. I knew then that you would go back to your Boston. Half of my soul tells me that you will not return. The other half insists that you will."

"Where do you get the strength to tell me to go?"

"My people are different from yours. Every time a man leaves his lodge, a woman knows there is a chance that he will not return, whether it is to fight *Pa'kiani* or to hunt buffalo. Nothing is given to us forever, Richard. I have lost one husband, and a precious child. My people are lost to me—even the camp of my father. I will never see Two Half Moons again. My old world is dead. I have survived these things. If you never come back, I will survive that, too."

But would she? The fire popped and flared as grease dripped into the flames.

THIRTY-FOUR

◈

By our continual and earnest pursuit of a character, a name, a reputation in the world, we bring our own deportment and conduct frequently in review, and consider how they appear in the eyes of those who approach and regard us. This constant habit of surveying ourselves, as it were, in reflection, keeps alive all the sentiments of right and wrong, and begets, in noble natures, a certain reverence for themselves as well as others, which is the surest guardian of virtue.

—David Hume: *An Enquiry Concerning the Principles of Morals*

Travis and Baptiste had crossed the divide into the Bear River Valley, and were following the ridges down toward the river when they found William Ashley's caravan.

The supply train—a long line of pack animals and men—was crossing the sage flats beside a small creek. The animals were tail-hitched in groups of five, each string led by a man on foot. They proceeded at a fast walk, trampling the sage and grass into a churned trail.

Travis raised his rifle and fired it into the air. His horse pranced sideways, startled by the shot. For a moment, Travis had his hands full with the animal. In the valley below, the outriders stopped and turned their horses to look up the cobble-strewn ridge.

"Thought fo' a second that ragtail you ride was gonna pitch you on yo' head," Baptiste jested.

"Huh! Not this old Pawnee nag. She's the best out of old Half Man's string."

"Could have traded fo' one of Two White Elk's good hosses."

"Me and this old wolf bait knows one another."

"I reckon . . . a knothead fo' a knothead."

Travis kneed his horse down the steep slope. Hooves slipping on the rounded rocks, the animal uprooted sage and sent cascades of dirt flying. Their pack animals followed, nostrils wide and ears pricked. The packs rocked, but stayed, a test to Travis's genius at hitches.

Ahead of them, the caravan of horses and mules had come to a stop, the weary animals hanging their heads while the riders walked their horses out to meet the newcomers.

"Ashley, by God!" Baptiste whooped. "And a fair sight if'n I do say so!"

"Better hope they ain't none of 'em from Louisiana, hoss, or they'll raise yer fuzzy hair fer the bounty."

"Ain't no white nigger born can raise hair off'n Baptiste de Bourgmont!"

Travis loped his horse across the blue-green sage, Hawken held to one side, the wind whipping his beard and hair. Closing on the riders, he pulled his animal up and brought it to a stand, blowing and sweat-streaked.

Travis relaxed into his favorite slouch and studied the buckskin-clad men. "How do? I reckon this hyar's Ashley's caravan fer Rendezvous."

"Ye reckon right, stranger," one of the young men said as he stared wide-eyed at Travis's scars. "And who might ye be?"

"Travis Hartman, and this hyar wolfmeat with me is Baptiste de Bourgmont. Come down from the Crow country, we did."

"Name's Bill Smith, and this long-legged coon's Cub Davis." The young man wore a felt hat that barely contained his long black hair. Cub Davis didn't hardly look old enough to be off the teat—until a man looked into his dark eyes and saw the soul-gaunting of hard travel.

"Reckon ye wouldn't mind if'n we rode along with ye?" Travis asked. "We figgered ter head fer Willow Valley." He jerked a thumb at their loaded packhorses. "Got plews ter trade."

"Best rustle on up yonder," Smith gestured toward the column's van where a knot of riders had pulled up to look back. "The General's up there with Campbell and the others. Reckon he'll make ye right welcome."

As Travis prodded his horse forward, he heard Smith whisper, "What on earth happened to that face of his?" So he rode with his head tilted up, letting the sun bathe the scars.

Trotting past the line of animals and men, he couldn't help but wonder at the amount of goods they carried. Tins of whiskey, powder kegs, boxes, and bales were outlined under the manties. The lot of it couldn't have been loaded into *Maria*. No wonder the critters looked worn. But, then, so did the hollow-eyed men who watched him pass. Like their animals, they were dusty, mud-spattered, and hard used.

"Looks like a tough trip," Baptiste noted in a low voice. "These coons ain't green no more."

"Come on, men!" a hale voice shouted from ahead. "Let's go! Move out by the mess!" The speaker was a patrician-looking fellow who waved his hat as he shouted orders. He rode a big bay horse—a quality animal that didn't look nearly as ragged as the rest of the cavvy.

Reining out from the main party, he gave curt orders and turned his gelding to meet Travis and Baptiste. He pulled his sun-bleached and water-stained hat down over curly brown hair. His buckskin jacket was finely tailored, but showed the strain of wind, rain, and weather.

Travis pulled up in front of him and met those sharp eyes with his own, measuring, and liking what he saw. "Gen'ral Ashley. How do. I'm Travis Hartman, and my partner hyar's Baptiste de Bourgmont."

"Got plews to trade," Baptiste added and stuck out his hand to shake.

When Travis followed suit, he found the general's grip firm, a match for that penetrating stare. "Hartman and de Bourgmont. Your reputations have preceded you. Mr. Hartman, I'd have recognized you from the scars. You've both reputations as good men, solid and reliable. That said, you are more than welcome to accompany us." He studied them thoughtfully as they walked their horses alongside the moving train.

The rest of Ashley's crew had fallen in, watching curiously. How young they seemed to Travis's veteran eyes. Mere youths. Here and there, old canvas clothing, mostly turned to rags, hung on their lean frames. Some had crudely tailored hide shirts or breeches, the leather rough-tanned at best. Their moccasins were even cruder, as if they'd been making clothes on the trail. All but one, and he rode along in worn broadcloth.

"Where are you from?" Ashley asked. He cast appraising eyes on their pack string with the bundled plews.

"Wintered with the Crow," Baptiste replied. "Heard tell from Long Hair's camp that you was holding a trade fair, so we come to see."

Ashley lifted an eyebrow. "Ah, the Crow. Still thieves, I presume?"

"Hell, Crows is always that." Travis laughed.

"And you got away with your outfits? You're doing better than my brigade did last fall."

"Wal," Travis said carefully, "Baptiste and me, we got kin among 'em. 'Course, that didn't stop 'em from lifting our hosses down below the Cannonball last summer. Had a right pert chase ter get 'em back."

Ashley gave Baptiste a long look. "I suppose you're a friend of Mister Rose's?"

Baptiste's expression turned sour. "Reckon not, General. Him and me's been crosswise since the start. I reckon if'n I had to put it to words, I'd say we didn't agree with each other."

Ashley's smile broadened. "In that case, you're more than welcome in my camp. And forgive me for any suspicion, it's just that Negroes and Crow—well, enough said."

Baptiste quirked his lips. "I see a couple of niggers riding with ye."

"Indeed." Ashley's expression was veiled. "Riding yonder is Jim Beckwourth. But if I might offer a word or two of advice, take what he tells you with a grain of salt."

"Or a whole sack," the thin man in broadcloth said. He had ridden his pinto bone-pile alongside. The tired horse bobbed its head with each step. "I'm Robert Campbell, clerk for this expedition. If you need anything, powder, tobacco, or such for your outfit, I'm the man to see."

"I see you've had good trapping," Ashley noted, eyeing the packs again.

"Traded mostly," Travis told him. Then he related the story of Dave Green and the *Maria*. "What we saved from the wreck gave us an outfit. Come midwinter, the Crows was right fond ter trade. We got beaver, Crow-tanned buffalo robes—some of 'em's line blankets—fox pelts, and mink. Prime, all of it."

"I don't suppose any of that beaver bears my mark? Perhaps part of the packs I couldn't recover after the Crow stole them last year?"

"Reckon so." Travis lifted a questioning eyebrow. "We traded fer what we could get. If we hadn't a got 'em, ol' Jim Kipp or Josh Pilcher would'a."

Ashley waved it away. "Well, Mr. Hartman, since you didn't steal them in the first place, I'll give you fair price for my plews: three dollars a pound. I suppose it's better to buy them back than to have Missouri Fur profit from them."

"I reckon we figgered it the same," Baptiste replied. "Why, some plews gets traded around worse'n hosses these days."

"That they do," Ashley agreed. "And people, too, I might add." He studied them thoughtfully. "You both started with Lisa, didn't you?"

"Yep." Travis pulled the stopper from his powder horn and began reloading his rifle with practiced efficiency. "I come upriver back in eleven." He short-seated a ball. "Seen the tough years after eighteen and twelve. Wintered with the Sioux when that British coon, Dickson, was trying ter turn 'em against us. I reckon I been over the mountain and down the creek a time or two. Same with Baptiste hyar. What I don't know, he does."

"Perhaps I could make you an offer. Look around. Most of these young men could benefit from your experience. They're tough and able, ready to take on the wilderness. But they could use a knowing hand to teach them the ways of the land and Indians."

"Uh-huh? And what would y'all have in mind?" Baptiste cocked his head.

"Trapping parties, Mr. de Bourgmont. My brigades move into a river valley, then split up into little groups. Instead of trading with the Indians for the plews, we trap them ourselves. To do so, I need men who know the country and how to survive in it. I'll outfit you, supply you with everything you need. In return, you receive a percentage on the plews you bring in and reduced rates in trade for luxuries and foofawraw."

Travis glanced at Baptiste, who grunted uneasily and said, "Funny thing how a man's life changes. Last summer,

I's hunting fo' the Company. Green comes along, and I's a partner in *Maria*. The Blackfoot blows up the boat, and I got me my own outfit from what's left of the wreck. I don't know, Gen'ral. What's in them packs yonder, why, half o' it's mine. I just ain't sure I want to go back to working fo' somebody."

"That's prime, that is," Travis agreed. "Fat cow, if'n I do say so. Hell, Gen'ral, I reckon I got the bug ter be free fer a while. Reckon I might just foller whar my stick floats fer a change."

"Fair enough," Ashley agreed genially. "In that case, I can offer you my services. I'll trade with anyone, and save you the hazards of the journey to take your catch to market. Consider this: In the past, furs had to be taken to posts. On the way, theft, raiding, weather, and every other disaster could befall a party—as it did to mine among the Rees back in twenty-three. A man spent most of his time carrying furs to market and obtaining supplies. But now, gentlemen, you can trap and trade the year through. Concentrate your efforts on what you do best, and bring your harvest to Rendezvous. You need never leave the mountains again."

"Huh," Travis said. "Then this hyar's gonna happen again next year, and the year after that?"

"Absolutely." Ashley slapped his thigh. "I call your kind Free Trappers, and unlike the companies on the river, welcome your business. Why should the fur hunter go to a post? Bring the post to the fur hunter. Far more efficient, wouldn't you agree?"

Travis looked at Baptiste and shook his head, grinning. "Old Manuel Lisa would be a-spinning, wouldn't he?"

Baptiste scratched his neck. "Reckon so. 'Course, Gen'ral, he'd a beat you heah by a month and done had yor trade."

Ashley raised an eyebrow. "Perhaps. But not even he

could have anticipated this last winter." He gestured toward the men. "The snows caught us near the Pawnee villages. Even the old women among them hadn't ever seen snow so deep. Things got so bad we had to mount a relief expedition for our relief expedition."

"Yer men look a mite worn, all right," Travis observed. "But they march like an army."

"Thank you, sir." Ashley inclined his head at the compliment. "Discipline on the trail is the only means of survival out here. Some chafe and rebel. Nearly forty men deserted, but these, the ones who stuck it out, they're men, sir. And with them, I shall conquer the mountains."

"You just might at that," Baptiste agreed. "Reckon the Shining Mountains ain't never gonna be the same."

"Nope," Travis replied thoughtfully, remembering his dream out on the prairie north of Fort Atkinson. Lisa had come to him and told that the river was dying, and that the mountains would follow. "Old Lisa was right. Ain't none of it gonna be left. All gone dead, just like the river."

"What's that?" Ashley asked.

"Ruminating, Gen'ral. Just ruminating."

❖

Riders from the caravan began to trickle into camp, and excitement grew among the trappers waiting for Rendezvous. At the current rate of travel, talk said, Ashley and the supplies would arrive the following evening.

Richard's anxiety grew as the inevitable decision loomed. He sat that night, smoking his pipe and cleaning his neglected rifle. With the new cock, she shot again, and just as straight as before despite her rust pits and nicks.

If only his own life could be as easily fixed. He sighed as Willow came to crouch beside him. She fed wood into the fire where a pot boiled. Dinner would consist of buffalo, yampa root, sego lily, wild onion, and spicy beeplant flowers for seasoning.

"What's the word in the *Agaiduka* camp?" Richard asked as he watched her pull back a shining strand of black hair with a slim hand. How beautiful she was, and the brave expression she'd adopted made his heart ache. Did it have to be so hard on her?

Willow shrugged, checking the stew with her knife. She gave critical inspection to the starchy water steaming on the blade. "These Fish-eaters, they are a different people. The same, you know, but different." She said neutrally, "I could stay with them while you are gone."

"Yep." Richard lifted an eyebrow. "I guess you could. If I didn't know you better, I'd never guess that you were lying."

"Oh, Richard. It will be all right. None of them have ever heard anything about me. They don't know any of the stories the *Ku'chendikani*—"

"They'll hear," he answered, steepling his fingers before his chin. "It's inevitable, Willow. People—red or white—tell stories, especially about things as interesting as witchcraft."

John Tylor appeared in the company of two trappers. One was a young man with red-brown hair and serious blue eyes. He walked with an athletic grace, his slim build belying a wiry strength. His reddish beard had started to fill in over a pointed chin. The second man was older, perhaps thirty-five, with a keen gaze that took a man's measure at a glance. The breast of his fringed buckskin shirt was decorated with elaborate beadwork done in a fleur-de-lis pattern. The man's haunted amber eyes spoke of terrible secrets.

"Mr. Hamilton, I would like you to meet two of my asso-

ciates." Tylor indicated the young man. "Captain Thomas Fitzpatrick, one of General Ashley's most able brigade leaders."

"My pleasure," Fitzpatrick said with a faint Irish brogue.

"And Mr. Weberly Catton," Tylor continued.

"Mr. Catton," Richard took the older man's hand in a firm grip. "The pleasure is mine. And this is my wife, Heals Like A Willow."

"Pleasure, ma'am," Fitzpatrick said agreeably as they seated themselves. Catton nodded pleasantly at Willow as he settled himself beside Fitzpatrick.

Tylor squinted into the boiling pot. "I hope the two of you don't mind, but I took the liberty of inviting Messrs. Fitzpatrick and Catton to dine with us. I believe we have enough to go around."

"We do." Willow, too, watched Catton with a certain fascination. The man drew attention like a magnet. Something in his manner set him apart, an indefinable suggestion of tragedy, and greatness.

He has a puha *all his own,* Richard decided, hardly aware that he now accepted such irrational intuitions without qualm.

Tylor broke out his pipe and shaved tobacco into the bowl from the remains of a twist. "Thank God, caravan's coming," he groused. "This is my last carrot of tobacco. Lord knows, I've stretched it enough with red willow and kinnikinnick as it is."

"Aye, caravan's coming," Fitzpatrick said with a smile. "I can tell ye for a fact, John, there's tobacco a-plenty for all."

The magically ubiquitous tin cups appeared in eager hands as Willow ladled out steaming stew. Tylor laid his pipe aside and ate with the rest.

Fitzpatrick smiled at Willow as he sipped the steaming broth. He glanced at Tylor. "If she can cook like this, I want her."

"Want her?" Richard asked warily. Dear God, they didn't think he'd sell her, did they? "Mr. Fitzpatrick, my wife isn't—"

"I believe I've stepped ahead of meself"—Fitzpatrick chuckled in embarrassment—"or at least, ahead of John Tylor." He wiped his mouth with a leather sleeve. " 'Tis me understanding that ye might stay in the mountains with us, Mr. Hamilton. As one of Ashley and Smith's captains, I come to see if ye'd consider j'ining the Company."

Tylor sipped at his stew and added, "I realize you haven't made any decision yet, Richard. I thought, however, that I'd offer you some alternatives. Please, we're not trying to press you into anything unsuitable to your situation. But there are choices available." He smiled. "And we'd like you to know that you have a place here. With us."

"And you've choices beside the Company." Catton's cool gaze shifted from Willow to Richard. "Myself, I have a lovely wife in Missouri. We love each other a great deal, and she's borne me two wonderful sons. I believe John's purpose in asking me here is that I have experience with the benefits and tribulations of living between the frontier and the wilderness. It can be done."

Richard met Willow's inquiring eyes, then said, "Very well. Let's talk about these choices."

Fitzpatrick took another tin of stew, saying, "We're trapping in small bands, and I'd have no objection to yer wife and ye traveling wi' us. I think it's the way o' the future, Mr. Hamilton. The advantage being that ye'd have the protection of a large party when it comes to Blackfoot and Bannock raiders. In the meantime, a man can make himself a fine life oot hyar."

"I see," Richard said guardedly.

"Mr. Tylor wanted me t' meet the two of ye, get to know ye, and let ye form yer own opinion of me. I don't think a man should jump blind into a situation afore seeing as many sides of it as he can—though I myself be a bad one fer doing just that." He laughed, blue eyes shining. "Times are changing for fur hunters. Ye seem like a good man, Mr. Hamilton. If'n ye decide t' stay, the two of ye have a place in me party."

"And you, Mr. Catton?" Willow asked.

Catton studied his stew for a moment, then glanced up with that unsettling amber gaze. "My wife is one of the bravest women alive. For various reasons I am forced to leave Laura in the settlements. Living in such circumstances can be extraordinarily difficult. We manage, but then, Laura is a unique woman."

Willow hesitated, then asked, "Can you not overcome your White ways? A woman doesn't *need* to live in a building. If Indian women can stand the wilderness, can't an American woman?"

Catton smiled thinly. "I was raised among the Iroquois, ma'am. Not all of my ways are White." He gave her a quizzical study. "Laura has traveled the west with me. But she comes from a respected Kentucky family. She stays in Missouri because that is what is best for us. As I said, I have a variety of reasons for living as I do. My point in being here is to say that it can be done."

"In other words," Richard said, "I could travel back

and forth. But, Mr. Catton, a wife in a settlement is in a different situation from a Shoshoni woman living in the wilderness. Your wife has a militia to protect her and her property. The institutions of civilization provide security."

Catton nodded. "That is true. But believe me, not all dangers come from savages and wild animals."

Richard laughed ironically. "Yes, I know. The streets of Saint Louis are filled with threat enough."

Catton stared absently at the fire. "Safety is only an illusion—be one a king or Digger Indian. That reality eludes most people. One can be blinded by walls, streets, and an abstract promise of social contract."

"Your Iroquois gave you a most interesting education," Richard observed.

Catton studied him thoughtfully. "If a man lives at all, Mr. Hamilton, he cannot help but be exposed to certain fundamental truths. *Tawiskaron* lurks in every shadow."

"Who?"

"*Tawiskaron.* A Huron equivalent to Cain. The chaos that mingles itself with the good things in life."

"Coyote," Willow supplied.

"Aye, the Devil," Fitzpatrick said absently. "Even hyar, in this beautiful land."

As the fire popped, Richard turned the options over in his mind. Would it be so bad to stay? He could post a letter with the caravan and accompany Fitzpatrick. Traveling with a fur brigade would allow him to stay with Willow, provide a place for both of them. A few of the trappers here already had Indian wives. What would it be like, just traveling around the wilderness? He could trap, hunt, and Willow would be with him.

"I'll give it some thought." He glanced at Catton, and then at Tylor. Two of a kind, each burdened by some terrible secret that neither was keen on discussing. What had driven them here?

The talk turned to beaver, the coming caravan, and the fierce winter just passed. For the most part Richard and Willow sat silently, listening to the talk of Hudson's Bay trappers, Blackfeet depredations, and the recently negotiated peace with the *Agaiduka* Snakes who now camped with them.

When Richard finally walked out into the night, Tylor followed him.

"I hope I didn't make you uncomfortable, Mr. Hamilton. I didn't wish to intrude into your affairs, but I wanted you to know that other solutions to your problem might exist."

"You didn't intrude."

Tylor crossed his arms. "Mr. Hamilton, I want you to think very carefully about this. If I could, I would save you from making a terrible mistake."

"And that would be?" Richard looked up. The air was so clear that the myriad of stars seemed like a gray haze. Until he'd come to the West, he'd never seen the whole immensity of the night sky.

"I don't usually tell people this." Tylor hesitated. "I left a woman once. At the time, I was carried away with ideas of duty, a misplaced loyalty, and blind ambition. I was gone from my home for more than a year. She was beautiful, vivacious, and attractive. When I returned, all was in ruins. Everything."

"I'm sorry to hear that. And I will keep your confidence."

"Thank you." He paused. "I often wonder what would have happened had I stayed where I belonged and acted the way a proper husband should. As it was, she turned to one of my enemies. Betrayed me and my plots. I hated her once; but time has ameliorated that. With the years has come understanding. If I could offer a bit of advice, Mr. Hamil-

ton: Don't awaken some morning, years from now, suffering from the realization that you let something beautiful
slip through your fingers. I can tell you, you'll never
recover it."

At that, he turned and walked away into the night.

❖

In the bright midday sun, Richard scowled at the yellowed
paper. On John Tylor's advice, he'd gone to a young man
named James Clyman, who kept a journal. After Richard
explained his need, Clyman had parted with a clean sheet
from his precious book, and loaned a quill and ink bottle.

With birds singing in the cottonwoods, and the excited
shouts of mountain men and Indians for a background,
Richard labored over the words, scratching out text in the
dirt beside him with a stick. Despite all the papers he'd writ-
ten on philosophy, this was by far the most difficult screed
he'd ever attempted.

He frowned and resettled his back against the cottonwood log. He had so much to tell his father, and so little
space to write it all. How did one apologize for being a fool,
for losing a fortune, and at the same time justify the decision
to remain in the wilderness with an Indian wife to a man like
Phillip Hamilton? How did he put all of that on a single
sheet of paper?

After hours of labor, he had managed to write:

June 1826 Willow Valley
    Dear Father:
    I am alive.

And there it ended. He plowed the dark soil beside him with flowery prose, direct statements, and intricate arguments, only to wipe them clean and start again.

This is insane! But the compact eloquence he desired eluded him.

Willow hummed the Cottontail song as she walked up from the creek with a load of firewood over her shoulder. The collection of sticks and branches was bound, Indian-fashion, by a single cord. The load clattered as she dropped it and smacked her hands authoritatively. She glanced around the camp, satisfied that all was in order, and lifted an eyebrow as she noted his pinched expression.

"You have finished?" She walked over to inspect his paper.

He sighed, placing the sheet to one side and weighting it with a stone so the breeze wouldn't whisk it away. "No. The words escape me." He rubbed his forehead and stared at his fingers, now damp with sweat. *Come on, Richard. You can do this. They're just words on paper.*

She settled beside him and frowned curiously at his most recent scratchings in the dirt. "I think you are making the wrong decision, Richard."

He'd told her last night, holding her closely after they'd made love. *I'm not going.* The words had brought relief, and a terrible sense of injustice.

"Are you that anxious to be rid of me?" With a finger he replaced long strands of her black hair that the breeze had teased.

"No, Richard. I want you with me forever." She kissed

him tenderly. "I would never part with you—but I think you will regret staying here."

"I don't know what I'll regret any more." He balled up a lump of dirt and tossed it away. "Tylor's a cunning fellow. He knew that I'd be sorely tempted by Fitzpatrick's offer. It solves so many problems for us. We'd have a place, Willow. Traveling with a band of trappers would be like traveling with *Maria*. We'd have the safety of numbers. We could build a lodge, have our own home. Think of it as a new society for you, one where no one would care if the *Ku'chendikani* called you a witch. Whites and Indians, living together. Fitzpatrick offers us everything."

She ran her fingers down the side of his face. "And what of your father? What of your Boston?"

The dream image where his father looked at him so sadly filled his mind. To blank it out, he looked up at the mountains that rose like a wall to the east. "Willow, in life, we all must make choices. If I've learned anything, it's that the world isn't perfect. Oh, sure, I'll regret that I never told my father the things I want to tell him. At least, not man to man. But I'm not the first man to have regrets. I doubt I'll be the last."

"Did John Tylor tell you that?"

"He told me I'd be a fool to leave you." *And, God knows, I would be.* But that wasn't the issue, was it?

She glanced away. Four riders were racing horses across the open grasslands between them and the Indian camp. The riders hooted and whooped, quirting their horses. A large white stallion took the lead to cries of encouragement from a group of onlookers who waved their favorites forward.

"Look closely, Richard." She sighed. "Look into Tylor's eyes and see the regrets that linger in his soul. Would he go back if he could?"

Richard tapped his stick on the dirt. Yes, he'd seen that longing in Tylor's brown eyes. "I think he would."

"I think he left the Whites because he had no choice. You have a choice, Richard. In the end, it will make it worse for you."

"But what if I go, and when I come back, you're not here?" *How could I endure that? I'd blame myself for the rest of my life—worse than I blame myself for letting Father down now.*

"Then Coyote will have acted. What if you stay, and something happens anyway? What if your father dies in the meantime? Then it will be too late."

"What if, what if!" He chuckled ironically. "This is pointless, arguing in circles."

"Travis would tell you to go."

He hung his head. "Would he?"

"I think so."

Richard sighed. "I wonder. I sure miss him."

"Me, too."

"If I stay, we could go look for him."

"He would have gone back to the river, Richard. And from there maybe to Saint Louis."

He searched her eyes, so large and dark, looking for an answer. "You're just telling me that."

"Maybe."

"Ah, Willow, how I love you."

Her smile warmed him. "Perhaps as much as I love you, my man."

How was he supposed to turn his back on her? How could a man walk away from a woman like Willow? He'd have to be a worse fool than Coyote.

To the north, popping sounded—rifles being fired into the air—and faint cries carried on the wind. The horse racers stopped short, all heads turned toward the north.

Richard climbed to his feet, staring off up the valley. Joyous shouts broke out from the surrounding camps: "Caravan's a-coming! Caravan! Rendezvous!" Men leaped to their horses, flying northward in a rush of pounding hooves. "Caravan! Rendezvous! Hyar's to the mountains, boys!" Another staccato of shots filled the air.

Richard took Willow's hand and exhaled. "Well, I guess the time's come—one way or another."

THIRTY-FIVE

If the object of our moral purpose is that which, being within our power, is the object of our desire after deliberation, it follows that moral purpose is a deliberate desire for something in our power; for at first we deliberate on a thing and, after reaching a decision about it, we desire it in accordance with out deliberation.

—Aristotle, *Nicomachean Ethics*

During the first night after the arrival of the caravan, the revelry never let up. Loud screams punctuated by gunshots might have led one to believe he heard a massacre rather than a gleeful celebration. Giant bonfires illuminated the camps, and around them, black silhouettes of trappers could be seen dancing and cavorting.

Willow lay with her head pillowed on Richard's chest and listened to his deep breathing and the rhythmic thumping of his heart. The insects made their nocturnal whizzing and clickings despite the human uproar.

Would it be so bad to go off with Tom Fitzpatrick? The notion stuck to her with the persistence of warm pitch. *I would have a place, a people.* Living with the trappers wasn't such an alien idea after a summer with Green and the *engagés*. And other trappers already had *Agaiduka* wives. How curious it was—this need to belong. Rejection by her people had cut so deeply; that wound might never heal.

With the trappers she wouldn't have to worry about some frightened Shoshoni sneaking up behind her with a war club, and organized punishment for witchcraft was painful at best: A witch was tortured first, beaten and burned in an attempt to drive the evil away. If that didn't work, a hideous death followed.

Willow, be honest with yourself. Eventually, someone will die in strange circumstances. When that happens, the family will blame you. She was so weary of the ways of people.

How wonderful it would be to ride off with the trappers. She and Richard, together for always. Images mingled in her dream soul: They walked hand-in-hand through a warm spring morning; sat side-by-side before a crackling fire; laughed at stories while the firelight played on the tan walls of a tipi; lay together, naked bodies moving as they made love.

Her fists knotted in a vain attempt to strangle her frustration. If only she could draw all of him inside her, make him a part of her. But the womb only worked one way. In the beginning times, Coyote had seen to that.

I can keep him. The notion drew her on, teased the aching part of her souls. *All I need to do is plead with him to stay—and he will.*

Such ideas came upon a person in the depths of the night when the hours were the longest.

You lie to yourself, Willow. He must go. And you know it.

If only he didn't have to go right now. If, perhaps, he might go next year.

What a fool I am. She could feel the pulsing of her own

heart, matching his in its misery. *It must be now. I'll never be strong enough to let him go again.*

Into the aching loneliness of love came a naked grief. It devoured her, sucking away her souls, crushing her with its bruising weight until tears ran hot from her eyes. Thus she passed the night, drifting in soul-pain, her grief wetting his rising and falling chest.

Morning sunlight shot golden rays across Willow Valley. Richard took a moment to enjoy the view. He gazed up at the snow-capped peaks to the east, wondering at the steep slopes that rose so precipitously from the flats. Such contrast—the soft green of the valley, forgiving, fruitful, and lush, gave way so quickly to the vertical wall of gnarled stone that thrust up to tear at the sky with jagged summits.

He settled himself before the fire and used his knife to spear one of the long strips of meat they'd been roasting for breakfast. He blew to cool it, wincing as the smoke turned in his direction and finally drove him to his feet.

Willow squatted opposite him, a vacant expression on her delicate face, eyes puffy and lifeless. Richard watched her warily as she chewed, a piece of meat clutched in greasy fingers. Something had cracked her defiant courage.

Richard washed the last of the smoke-flavored elk down with water from his tin cup. Wiping his greasy hands on his pants, he stared pensively at the ash-white wood burning in the firepit.

"How about walking down to the traders?" he asked. "Tylor said they'd be set up by this morning. Let's go see."

She smiled up at him, the effort forced, as if only raw will animated her full lips.

Hand-in-hand, they strolled across the flower-sprinkled grass toward the distant knot of lodges and tents that marked Ashley's camp. She remained silent, even distant.

"Are you all right?" he asked. *Come on, Willow, tell me what's wrong.*

She nodded, eyes downcast.

"Bad dreams?" he suggested. "Want to talk about them?"

"No, Richard. I just . . . I'll be fine. I'm tired this morning, that's all. I didn't sleep well."

"Me neither," he admitted, trying to break through this new awkwardness. "I had horrible dreams. I was standing in my father's office. He was lying on the floor, gasping, dying. He kept reaching out to me, but I couldn't move, couldn't call out. I was paralyzed, my arms and legs too heavy to lift. As if—well, I'd been turned to stone." He forced a chuckle. "Imagine, me, a rock ogre? What do you think? Am I one handsome *Pandzoavits?*"

Her smile faded too quickly. "You wouldn't have dreamed such a thing if you hadn't decided to stay, Richard. Your soul is telling you to go to your father, now." She glanced off at the mountains. "If you don't, you will live that dream for the rest of your life. It isn't wise to ignore your *navuzieip.*"

"Why are you so insistent?"

"Because I must be. How can you live if your souls are sick? I know these things, Richard."

"And if leaving makes your souls sick?"

"I will heal them. Besides, it's only for a short time. You *will* come back." She sounded as if she was trying to convince herself.

They walked in awkward silence, approaching the shouting men who stood around the tents. Like the trade around *Maria,* this, too, consisted of utter disorder, men yelling and gesturing as they crowded around. Necks craned as men tried to see over their companions' shoulders. Some sat atop horses for a better view, and called out information to the fellows on the fringe.

Richard spotted Web Catton at the periphery and turned in his direction. Catton leaned on his rifle, an amused look on his sun-browned face. The beaded fleur-de-lis on his chest sparkled in the morning sunlight.

"Quite a mess." Richard pointed at the mob.

With forced gaiety, Willow said, "They remind me of children when the first fat is fried from the fall buffalo hunt."

Catton chuckled. "Reckon they do. 'Course, there's ways to get what you want without fooling with that mess. In fact, here he comes now."

A tall young man walked out from behind the tents, passed the armed guards who watched over the piled packs of trade goods, and headed toward them. He carried a large tin cup, balancing it, his tongue out the side of his mouth as he concentrated.

"Took you long enough, Jim," Catton announced.

"Reckon so, Web. Tarnal Hell, that's a damn riot yonder." The strapping young man handed Catton the cup and glanced curiously at Willow and Richard. Thoughtful brown eyes, a long nose, and broad mouth dominated his thin face. In spite of unruly brown locks and obvious youth, he had a seasoned look. "Reckon I don't know ye. Come with the caravan, did ye?"

"No, arrived from the north. I'm Richard Hamilton, and this is my wife, Heals Like A Willow."

He bobbed his head as if uncertain as to the social graces. "'Bliged, I reckon. Ma'am. I'm Jim Bridger, uh, one of Gen'ral Ashley's captains. Been out with Jed Smith scouting west and south for the last month."

"And, let me guess," Catton said wryly as he sipped at the liquid in the cup, "you found salt, sand, and desert." His face twisted bitterly. From the drink, or his description of the land, Richard couldn't tell.

"Reckon so," Bridger agreed. "Got my fill of that country, I'll tell ye. 'Course, Jedediah, he figgers ta go back after Rendyvous breaks up. Figgers there's got ta be a way down ta the ocean, and maybe beaver on the other side of the desert."

Catton shrugged, took another sip, and passed the cup to Richard. The clear liquid was straight alcohol, and Richard supposed his own expression mirrored Catton's.

Willow barely sipped, wrinkling her nose. In Shoshoni she muttered, "For outside the body only," and passed the cup to Bridger.

"What happens next?" Richard asked, as Bridger took a big swig from the tin and passed it back to Catton.

"Most everybody gets drunk as the whiskey is poured." Catton grinned at Bridger. "Me, I didn't want to fight all the elbows, so I sent Bridger into that mess for me."

The tall young man grinned, scuffing the ground with his moccasin toe. "Wal, ye see, ain't so many around as can say they done favors for Web Catton." He gave Richard a conspiratorial glance. "Reckon ye'd be plumb smart ta listen ta anything old Web tells ye. He done wrassled bears and treed painters out hyar when the rest of us was sucking a teat—and that's fat cow."

With a nod to Catton and Willow, Bridger turned, padding back past the guards to disappear among the packs.

"Good lad," Catton said, "He's got a way about him. I figger he'll make a right fair trapper if he lives long enough. Too bad that Hugh Glass hangs like a shadow over him."

"Hugh Glass . . . the man who got bear-chewed." Richard recalled the story. "Took him months to crawl into Fort Atkinson."

"That's him." Catton indicated the direction Bridger had gone. "Young Jim and old Fitzhugh were supposed to stay with Glass until he died. Problem was, Glass wasn't dead when they left." He shook his head. "Be a hell of a thing if that's all Bridger was ever remembered for." Catton offered his cup again.

"No. Thank you, Mr. Catton. I think we'll walk around, see the sights."

"You won't get close to the trade, not today. Them coons will be mobbing them kegs until they drink her dry, or pass out. Whatever comes first."

As they walked off, Richard wondered, "So, that's it? Just liquor?"

Willow shrugged as she watched the milling trappers and their Indian cohorts. Men would slip out of the crowd, tilting battered tin cups to their lips before they hollered to friends. Immediately they'd be mobbed by backslapping bear huggers until the tin was empty, then another hardy would take the tin and dive back into the writhing mass for a refill.

Richard caught the barest glimpse of a familiar black face in the seething mass of humans, but he couldn't be sure. A handful of Negroes were in the crowd, but he had yet to find Baptiste among them. "Come on. I thought I saw . . . "

"Saw who?"

"Well, maybe Baptiste."

Richard towed Willow behind him as he ducked past drinkers, periodically jumping up in an attempt to see, wishing he were taller.

Richard caught a glimpse of the black man again, and shoved to reach him, calling, "Baptiste!"

The man turned, his face unfamiliar. "Sorry," Richard wilted. "I thought you were someone else."

"Yassuh, dat happens. I's Peter Ranne, of Jed Smith's party, suh." The black smiled, nodding. "Shoa pleased to meet you."

"Richard Hamilton—and this is Willow, my wife."

"Pleased, ma'am," Ranne replied. But by then the shoving had become unbearable and Richard slipped back toward the fringes.

"Sorry," Richard told Willow as they broke free from the fringe of drinkers. He shrugged, relieved by Willow's understanding nod. "I'm trying too hard, I guess." He looked around. "Desperation. It's running through me like creek water."

She patted his hand. "I know, Richard. Let's leave this place. Some man in there grabbed me. I was packed in so tightly I couldn't pull my knife and cut him."

Richard took her arm in his and had just turned back toward camp when a burly man pushed his way out of the press and called out, "Hey, squaw!"

"I think he is the one who grabbed me." Willow dropped a hand to her knife, glaring at the man.

The trapper tottered forward, a tin cup in one grimy hand. His wispy mustache was wet, and spilled drink had dampened the thin red beard growing from his blocky jaw. His glazed blue eyes were fixed on Willow. "Hey! Squaw!" Thrusting out a fist, he offered several hanks of glass beads: yellow, blue, and red. "You take these, huh? You know, 'Fuck me'? You know them words?"

Richard pulled Willow behind him before she could strike. His voice dropped to a sibilant threat. "Get away from her. You leave Willow alone, or by damn, you'll—"

The trapper stopped short, blinking in confusion. "Who the hell are you?"

"Her husband, sir. And you'll offer an apology to my wife."

"Wife?" the big man laughed, taking another drink from his tin. "What white man's got an Injun wife? Hell, mister, if I can have her for a couple of hours, why, I'll give ye a hoss. Yep, a hoss! Ain't seed such a purty woman among these hyar Snakes. I reckon she'd put a hell of a squeeze on a man's pizzle. How 'bout that, coon?"

For a moment, Richard wasn't sure he understood; then something let loose within him. The frustration and anger, the indecision and reeling sense of loss were swept away on a tide of single-minded rage. The burly round-faced trapper filled Richard's world as he coiled and struck.

His first blow bent the man double, then he skipped in to hammer an elbow to the side of the neck. With a quick pivot, Richard back-heeled the man and threw him down. He was ready to drive a knee into his victim's stomach, when two trappers grabbed him from the side and flung him away.

Richard staggered to catch his balance. A ring had formed around them, men shouting and cheering, waving fists and dancing from foot to foot. Willow circled warily, body in a crouch, her gleaming knife tucked in, ready to strike.

The two men who'd thrown Richard off checked their companion. He moaned on the ground amid a scatter of broken beads and spilled whiskey. One, black-haired and wiry, rose and dusted off his hands, flexing his fingers. "Reckon that flat warn't called fer, coon. Ye'd have kilt him. I saw it in yer eyes, ye Injun-loving white nigger."

"Come on," Richard rasped. "Both of you, damn it! I'll whip you both, hear?"

The black-haired man indicated Willow. "She ain't gonna stick me! That ain't fair!"

To the delight of the assembled trappers, Willow hissed, "Come die!"

"Oh, Gawd," the downed man moaned. "I feel plumb awful." And he rolled on his side to vomit.

"Ain't gonna be no cutting hyar," a familiar voice called from behind Richard. "C'mon, coons, back ter drinking and fun. This squaw's off limits! Go, boys. Hyar's fer the mountains!"

Like a tribe of banshees, a series of wild shrieks and war whoops split the air as the trappers turned back to the trade tent. The downed man was picked up by his two friends, clapped on the back, and led off.

Richard took a deep breath, and turned, grinning. Travis Hartman watched him with twinkling blue eyes. The hunter's ruined face was one of the most beautiful sights Richard had ever seen. He leaped, hugging Travis as if to crush the life out of him. Willow had vaulted onto the both of them, shrieking. Round and round they went, like some huge awkward three-headed dancing bear.

"Yer some, Dick," Travis declared, "Hell, I figgered ye'd jist up and philos'phy him half ter death. But ye give him what fer, knuckle and skull, instead. What'd Willow feed ye all winter ter put the bark on ye so?"

"Blessed Lord God! What a relief! Travis, I thought you were dead!"

"Easy, coon. Don't bust me ribs!"

"What happened to you? Where did you go? Where's Baptiste? Where have you been all winter? How'd you get here?"

"Whoa up, lad! One thing at a time."

"We've missed you, Travis!" Willow was crying, as she clung to him.

Richard kept grinning like an idiot, checking the hideous scars to ensure that no new ones had appeared. The blue eyes still had the devilish gleam that laughed and warned at the same time.

"My God," Richard repeated, "it's so good to see you! You wouldn't believe the things I've been through."

Travis chuckled, gaze drifting from Richard to Willow. "Wal, I reckon at least the two of ye finally got the robes straightened out. 'Wife,' ye said, just afore ye lit inter that poor pilgrim!"

Richard lifted an eyebrow. "What of it?"

For the barest second, Travis gave him an iced look that chilled the guts. Then he grinned and bent over to kiss Willow on the cheek. "Fat cow, coon, that's what!"

Willow was prodding Travis in the ribs, laughing, saying,

"Where have you been, Bear Man? I feel fat on your ribs. Have you taken up with some woman?"

"Me? Hell, no. Wal, at least, not fer permanent. Them Crow, they fed me right pert, they did." He winked at her. "'Course, once a coon crawls under the robes, they try and work it outa ye, too!"

"Hah!" Willow challenged, slapping him on the shoulder. "An *A'ni* woman couldn't tire a dead man. You need a real woman, Travis."

Travis glanced at Richard. "And what if them coons would a tried ye, just now?"

Richard gave him a crooked smile. "I'd a whipped 'em both, damn it. Hell, Travis, what do you think? I'm some kind of Doodle that don't know shit?"

His arm still around Willow's shoulder, the scarred hunter threw his head back and laughed until the tears came.

◆

Travis puffed at his pipe, savoring the tobacco he'd traded for that afternoon: not quite Saint Louis fresh, but close enough by mountain standards. He cocked his head at a shouting match a couple of camps down the way. Someone else broke out into guffaws, and the babble of talking men was everywhere. Hard as it might be to believe, the second night of Rendezvous was even louder than the first. Travis sat in Richard's camp with his back to the log and listened as Richard told him of his winter adventure.

Baptiste sat cross-legged, nursing a whiskey head, slitted eyes watching the coals burn down in the fire. Willow and Richard were seated the way lovers ought to be, their shoulders touching, hands held in every spare moment.

Hard to believe that ol' Dick's the same coon what François sold me fer a penny in Saint Loowee. Travis took

this new Richard's measure: broad-shouldered, firm of eye, and easy in his movements. His nose and cheeks were mottled from frostbite, but those scars were easier to bear than Travis's. Something in Richard's core had toughened, and from the tale he'd just told, it wasn't any wonder.

"So, we ended up here," Richard finished, thoughtful eyes on Travis. "And I guess here is where I'll stay. Maybe join Tom Fitzpatrick's party and go fur hunting. We've talked about it. He's more than willing to have Willow along."

"Uh-huh." Travis knocked the dottle out of his pipe and shaved more tobacco into the bowl. He fired it with a twig and puffed blue smoke like a chimney. "If'n ye decide ter do that, Dick, latch onto Tylor, hyar, or ol' Catton if'n he's gonna winter over. Them coons can teach ye things this child ain't larned yet."

"I doubt that, Travis." Richard cocked his head. "They are interesting men. Real mysterious, both of them."

"I reckon," Travis said as he propped his arm on a knee. Willow was too sober, worrying herself about something. "They don't talk much, leastways, not about themselves. Tylor, hell, he come upriver with Lisa back in eighteen eleven. Then, when he got upriver, old Manuel give him a hoss and let him go. Disappeared inta the wilderness fer nigh onto two years. From time ter time he'd fetch up at a post, spend most of the winter a-yarning, resupply, and light out again fer who knows where. Thing is, Tylor always has his books. I remember a time or two where he'd send a paper downriver on a pirogue ter Lisa, and all it'd have on it was the names of books. And sure enough, next summer, they'd be packed away until the expedition met up with Tylor somewhere. One thing's plumb prime about him: he's a gentleman, he is—and his word's good."

"And Catton?" Willow asked.

"He's an odd coon, I'll tell ye." Travis considered his pipestem, then broke a piece off and flipped it into the fire. "There, that's a mite sweeter smoke. Where was I? Oh, Web Catton. Wal, I don't know a heap about him, neither. Reckon we shared a camp hyar and there over the years. He's married to a right fine gal back in America. A plumb proper lady, she is. Comes from the Bragg family of Kentucky. Real white-china folk with lots of land, hosses, and slaves and such. Old Web, he's white, I figger, but he's Injun-raised. Iroquois, I recall—and never a squeak of how that come about. Anyhow, he met this Laura Bragg, married her, and had a real tussle with her paw. Kilt him dead with a sword in a duel, he did.

"Web, he's a mite like Tylor. Travels the wilderness when and where he pleases. He's made peace with most of the Injuns, especially down south around Santy Fe."

Richard was fingering his chin, vacant stare on the fire. "What drove them out here?"

"How in hell should I know? Maybe they let some ornery coon run off with their pap's money?" At Richard's sour scowl, he added: "One thing's sure, neither one talks about it."

"And some folks shouldn't otta ask," Baptiste reminded darkly. "Folks has got their reasons fo' leaving the States."

Richard nodded soberly. "Yes, they do."

"Now, then," Travis asked, "are ye sure ye wants ter string along with Ashley's brigade? Hell, Dick, me and Baptiste would be right tickled ter have the two of ye join up with us."

Willow straightened, lifting an eyebrow. A spark of hope kindled in her dark eyes.

"And we don't care that Willow's no witch," Baptiste added. "And if'n she were, I'd figger she could cure this heah whiskey head right quick." He gave Willow a pleading look.

"Spirit water is for the outside," she said bluntly.

Baptiste groaned and carefully lowered his head to his knees.

"You and Baptiste have an outfit, Travis," Richard reminded.

"And you and Willow have the perfect place ter winter," Travis responded. "We seen that Red Canyon. Them springs is some, they is. And from there, a feller can trap the Big Horns, Owl Creeks, and west clean up inta the Yellowstone high country. Hell, Dick, throw in with us." Travis grinned. "Truth of it is, we got ter missing yer company. And Baptiste and me ain't doing so good on our writing no more."

"You don't need me to teach you writing."

"Wal, who's gonna philos'phy us half ter death? A coon never knows in this country. We might get surrounded by Blackfoots and need ye to give 'em a batch of Rousseau, or some such thing."

Without raising his head, Baptiste added, "Ain't no

campfire quite right 'thout ass-spitology and he-pissed-'em whatever it was."

"Eschatology and epistemology." Richard's face softened as he looked at Willow. "I could go back to *Ainkahonobita*. Couldn't you?"

She gave Richard that familiar probing gaze. "What of your father, Richard?"

"My father." Richard slumped, expression glum. "I'll write the letter, I promise."

Willow turned to Travis. "Will you tell him? He has been worried about me. You and Baptiste are here, Travis. I can go with you while Richard returns home. I know where streams of beaver can be found. I can take you there, and next year we can meet Richard someplace."

Travis sucked at his pipe. Tarnation! A year alone out in the wilderness with Willow? She might be his good friend, but damn it, pretty as she was, she'd drive him half berserk. He glanced at Richard. How torn he was. Willow was giving him a pleading look, tearing her heart out while she begged him to go.

By God, she loved him so much. It brought an ache to Travis's soul. He'd seen a look like that once, that pleading love in Moonlight's soft gaze. *Damn, it ain't many men have women like her and Willow.*

Aw, ter hell with it! If having Willow around brought on dreams of soft warm bodies, he'd just shinny over ter the River Crow and buy hisself a wife.

"Go, Dick." The words came to Travis's lips. "Do what ye must. Baptiste and me, we'll see ter Willow. My word on it."

Richard nodded, a distant look in his pained eyes. He said nothing, but rose and walked away from the camp, head down, shoulders sagging.

Willow struggled to keep from clinging to Richard as the long days of summer began. Together they watched the races, and shouted for their favorites. They attended the shooting matches, making private wagers over who would win. They went dancing with the Shoshonis in their camp. They shouted encouragement to the mountain men who wrestled with each other, screaming and yelling, their bodies thumping on the hard-tramped grass.

Rendezvous was like nothing she or Richard had ever seen. Games of euchre, monte, and poker were played on blankets, and every possession under the sun was wagered, lost, and won again. *Agaiduka* men hired out their women for powder, beads, shot, and whiskey. Brawls broke out, blows landed, then peace was made between the bloody, bruised antagonists.

Arm-in-arm, they watched it all, living as if each moment was forever. At night they sat around the fires, listening to tales of bears, Indian fights, and beaver. Outright lies mingled with hilarity as one man or another tried to outyarn his comrades. Interlocked in the tales were nuggets of information on rivers, the land, mountain passes, and places to camp.

And when the stories were finished, Richard and Willow twined their bodies together under the robes. They joined themselves with fierce passion one time, and tender caress the next. Each bout of lovemaking was driven by a subtle desperation, as passionate as if the last on earth.

But all things finally end.

The alcohol had been drunk. General Ashley's packs, once full of coffee, bolts of cloth, powder, and lead, now held beaver plews, a hundred to a pack. The summer sun burned down hot and brassy; the solstice passed.

Word passed from man to man that Ashley and Smith had sold out to a new firm, Smith, Jackson, & Sublette, and that the General was packing to leave.

"I will miss you with all of my souls, Richard." Willow ran her hands down the sides of his face as they lay entwined in the blankets that last night.

"And I you," he told her.

She smoothed the brown curls around his ears. "Richard, you've told me about Boston, and your father, and his business. I don't understand all of this, but I know what I learned from Green. If you have to stay for a while, I will understand."

"Willow, I'm not going to—"

"Hush. Hear me, husband. Listen to my words."

"All right."

"You might not be able to come back as soon as you plan. What if your father is sick? What if he needs you?"

"He might just throw me out on my ear."

"And maybe you can fix things between you. If it takes a while, I will wait. And Richard, if it is necessary, and if you still wish to, marry this Laura. I'm not a White woman. My people take second wives all the time. I will understand."

"She won't."

"That is up to her. But if you need her for the White world, marry her."

"Willow, that's completely—"

"Richard, I will wait for you. I have nothing else."

"How precious you are," he whispered. "I'm coming straight back to you."

"Yes, I know. But this is Coyote's world. What we plan doesn't always happen. Things go wrong."

"What if I get killed on the way?"

She considered. "If you are not back in two years, then I will know that your Boston has won . . . or you're dead."

"I don't kill so easily."

Neither does your Boston, Richard. She closed her eyes as he kissed her neck, nuzzling the hollow of her throat. She tightened her hold on him, straining, as if by sheer strength she could impress him upon her soft flesh. "Come back to me. Please, Richard." Tam Apo, *let my* puha *be more powerful than his Boston.*

◆

The dawn came too soon. Richard climbed out of their blankets as gray light outlined the high mountains to the east. While Willow attended to nature, he opened his pack and placed each article with great precision: pemmican, jerky, some of Willow's biscuit-root cakes. A spare elk-hide jacket she'd made for him, and three pairs of moccasins. He wanted to take everything, his digging stick, bow, arrows, net bags—all things he shared with Willow. But that was foolishness.

He stuck with necessities, then seated himself and poked at the fire as she prepared their final meal.

Richard watched her from the corner of his eye. *How carefully we move, so painfully aware of each other.*

Travis and Baptiste appeared out of the gloom. Robins and finches were greeting the morning, and the insects had begun to stir. John Tylor, his body still rolled in a brown blanket, called out, "Take care, Richard. Give my regards to the East."

"I will. And thank you for your friendship, John."

"Hyar, Dick," Travis said, handing Richard a small cylinder wrapped in buckskin.

"What's this?" Richard hefted it, surprised how heavy it was.

"Twenty-dollar gold pieces, coon. Ten of 'em. I done sewed 'em inta that hide and let her shrink down tight. Kept 'em in the bottom of my possibles."

"What's it for?" Richard looked perplexed.

"How ye figgering to get boat fare to Boston, coon?"

Travis lifted a grizzled eyebrow. "I been saving it in case trouble come along. Pay me back when ye can."

Richard shook his head, handing it back. "I can't take this, Travis. I'll make do."

"Nope." Travis stood firm. "We're partners now, Dick. Have been fer a spell. And, wal, ye'd do 'er fer me." He grinned. "'Course, it ain't thirty thousand, but I reckon ye'll keep it this time."

Richard took Travis's hand in a firm shake. "Thanks, Travis."

"Reckon it's my pleasure, Dick."

Baptiste appeared, leading Richard's horse, the animal saddled and ready. "Heah you be, coon. Fat and sleek." Baptiste offered his hand. "Take care, Dick. Come back to us safe and healthy."

Richard took his hand, then hugged him close. "You, too. And watch your topknot."

"Ain't no red Injun getting my wool."

Finally, Richard turned to Willow. Her eyes were shining, saying more than words. "I love you, Willow."

"And I you, my warrior." She hugged him one last time, tracing his face with her fingertips. "Go, Richard. I will wait for you."

He kissed her then, holding her until she finally pushed back. To his surprise, a tear had escaped her swimming vision and tickled its way down her cheek. He wiped it

away with his thumb. God in Heaven, how could he leave?

Richard turned quickly and stepped into the saddle. Travis handed up his rifle.

"Mind yer hair, Dick. Ashley's a-waiting on ye."

"Mind yours," he rejoined. He reined the horse around, walking the animal northward toward Ashley's camp. He kept looking back, waving. Willow stood there, chin up, back straight, the first rays of morning sunlight gleaming in her long black hair.

Damnation, he could just turn around. *I don't have to do this.*

But despite the wrenching in his soul, he finally turned his head toward the north. While, inside, a voice kept telling him, *This is a mistake—a horrible mistake.*

She stood in silence, watching him, barely aware that Travis had placed a reassuring arm around her shoulders. Baptiste sighed, watching with sad eyes. One by one, she returned Richard's waves, each more distant than the last.

"Yes . . . you'll be back, my man." She placed a hand to her stomach, pressing to still the terrible ache.

THIRTY-SIX

◆

> I am first affrighted and confounded with that forlorn solitude, in which I am plac'd with my philosophy, and fancy myself some strange uncouth monster, who not being able to mingle and unite in society, has been expell'd all human commerce, and left utterly abandon'd and disconsolate. Fain would I run into the crowd for shelter and warmth; but cannot prevail with myself to mix with such deformity. I call upon others to join me, in order to make a company apart; but no one will hearken to me. Every one keeps to a distance, and dreads that storm, which beats upon me from every side.

> —David Hume, *A Treatise of Human Nature*

Richard sat up late that first night, and watched the fire burn down to red embers. Around him, the men in his mess snored and wheezed, rolled in their blankets. The hum of mosquitoes and night insects mingled with the far-off cries of the coyotes and wolves.

He looked eastward at the dim black shadows of the mountains, but felt no relief.

Willow was a day's ride south. He could be there by morning, enfold himself in her arms, and spend the rest of his life there.

He closed his eyes, recreating her face, every detail of her hair, eyes, and smile. *Dear Lord God, this is going to be horrible.*

"It's not forever," he whispered under his breath. And tried to turn his thoughts to Phillip, to what it must feel like to be a lonely old man leaving nothing behind him.

Reckon I'm glad yor going, Baptiste had told him. *You fix things with yor pap. It be the right thing. And don't you fret none fo' Willow. Travis and me, we'll keep her plumb safe. You got my word, Dick.*

How his world had changed. He'd entrusted the love of his life to an ax-murdering escaped slave and an uncouth ruffian. And each would hold that trust inviolate. To the death, if necessary.

And I thought I understood ethics?

He stood then, walking out to the edge of the camp where Ashley's pickets watched the darkness. The night was star-filled, clear, and cool. Was Willow staring up at the stars right now? He could feel the longing in her heart.

"I could be there by morning."

But, he had come to understand, there were times when a man had to do unpleasant things. It wouldn't take long. Race to Boston, tell his father what had happened, and race back. He could be back in *Ainkahonobita* within ten months.

Wasn't that what he'd told himself the last time?

Two years. That's how long she'd said she would wait.

High in the sky, a shooting star streaked the darkness, and just beyond the fringe of sagebrush a coyote racked the night with a mocking howl.

◈

"I reckon they's done crossed the Green by now," Baptiste said as they rode out of Willow Valley.

"Yep." Travis had a chew juicing and spat. He glanced at Willow. "How ye doing, gal?"

"Sad, Travis. The same as yesterday, and the day before." She took a moment to look back. If she never returned to Willow Valley, it would be fine with her.

"Why'd you let him go?" Baptiste asked gently. "You coulda throw'd a fit and kept him heah. He'd a stayed if'n you'd asked him."

She'd been asking herself that same question over and over. "He's a warrior, Baptiste. He must return to his father, settle this thing between them. He must choose between me and Boston."

"And if it's Boston?" Travis asked, grabbing at a pesky fly.

She twisted her mare's mane in her fingers. "A woman must let a warrior face his challenges. Do you think life is ever safe? Too much of Coyote is in the world."

"He'll come back." Travis gave Baptiste a crafty squint. "Reckon I'll bet ye a pack of plews."

Baptiste narrowed an eye and rocked his jaw back and forth. "Travis Hartman, yor a black-hearted son of a bitch."

"Ye gonna take her?"

"Hell no!"

Richard called the mare Pia, the Shoshoni word for mother. She was really Willow's, a gift from Two Half Moons. But over the long months, Richard had come to think of her as his own. And, unlike his stiff-gaited old white mare, this dapple gray could move like the wind.

An early October frost lay on the ground. He watched the horse's ears swiveling as he walked her down the rutted wagon road. To either side, farms had been hacked out of the trees. The crops were in, the fields gleaned of their produce. Each squat cabin had a plume of blue smoke rising from the clay-coated chimney. Sometimes a buckskin-clad farmer

would wave, and more than one had offered his hospitality, corn, and pork in return for tales of the West.

And what tales I can tell.

Just like his horse. Funny how things went round. The animal had come from Willow's first husband's family—actually from White Hail's herd—then it had gone to Two Half Moons, and then to Willow. *Now, here we are, halfway across the world, and both longing for* Ainkahonobita.

The first July days with Ashley's caravan had been long, hot, and dusty. But then Richard had worked his way into Ashley's circle. On many a night they'd sat at the fire, discussing philosophy, the role of the state, and government. Ashley had the politician's bug.

"I'll tell you, Hamilton," he'd said one night, "my future is in government. Missouri may not look like much now, but we're building. I can see the day when Saint Louis will be the largest city in the country—bigger than New York, Philadelphia, or any of the other cities. Even bigger than your Boston."

"And why is that, sir?"

"Because of the location, Hamilton. Saint Louis controls the rivers."

Well it might, some day in the distant future, but as Richard rode past the outlying plantations, he had trouble making the outskirts of Saint Louis appear anything like those of Boston.

He reined Pia to one side to allow a squeaky wagon to pass, then trotted her on toward Saint Louis. He broke out of the last of the trees to encounter cleared land, most of it littered with stumps and piles of burned logs. Fences were going up here and there. In the distance he could see the two-story houses of the city's wealthier citizens.

Ashley was one of those now. He'd floated down to Saint Louis by boat with his bales of fur. Richard, hating to part with Pia, had ridden in, making no more than twenty miles a day.

He'd paralleled the route he'd poled and cordelled up with the *Maria*. Along the way, the ghosts of Trudeau, Toussaint, Green, and Henri had called to him.

"But here I am," he told Pia's patient ears. "Saint Louis again."

They clopped through the outskirts, and into the heart of the city, following Ashley's instructions. He found the street that would take him to Ashley's office—and then turned toward the river.

He knew the place by the signpost over the door: "The Green Tree Tavern." He stepped down and tied Pia off. He hesitated at the door and took a deep breath.

Are you ready for this, Richard? No, probably not. But all those long days on the trail, he'd promised himself to see this through. He'd studied on it, and decided to do it the way Travis Hartman would have. Nerving himself, he entered the grimy interior.

It took a moment for his eyes to adjust. Boatmen sat at the tables dressed in white cotton shirts, belted at the waist with bright red sashes. He walked to the first and rested the butt of his rifle on the stained hardwood floor.

The three boatmen looked him up and down, no expression on their faces. In French, Richard said, "I'm looking for a man. A cutthroat and thief. He's big. Blue eyes. His name is François. He used to run with a man named August. Do you know him?"

Glances were exchanged, and one man shrugged. "Why would you want him?"

"I've come to discuss a little business with him."

"You are too late." The second man watched Richard through half-lidded eyes.

"He's dead," said the third. "Found floating in the river with his throat slit." He ran a callused and dirty finger across his throat.

"And August?" Richard asked.

"Shot . . . when?" The first frowned. "Over a year ago. I think at the same time François was killed, *oui?*"

The second nodded. "Just before. François shot him. This I know for a fact. They argued over a woman." He glanced sidelong at Richard. "It was Lizette, you know. The whore. That's who they fought over. François had money—a lot of it. And Lizette had François."

"She killed François," the first said. "Cut his throat and rolled him into the river. You know how I know? Because he had a ribbon tied on his penis. That was her sign."

"And where is she?" Richard arched an eyebrow.

"Who knows? Some say New Orleans. But I have been there and heard no word of her. She is the kind of woman who is talked about. No, I think the ones who say Paris are right. You want my guess, *mon ami,* she killed François and August, took their money, and poof! She is gone."

"A smart one, that," the third man agreed. "But if François is no longer of help, perhaps . . . "

Richard sighed wearily. "Sorry, boys. *Merci beaucoup.*" He plucked up his rifle and headed for the door. Outside, in the fading twilight, he glanced down at the river, visible through a gap in the buildings.

"Ah, hell, it was worth a try." But then justice had always been a thing for the gods.

He untied Pia's reins and stepped into the high Shoshoni saddle. As he rode away, the three boatmen stepped out to stand before the Green Tree, the question lingering in their eyes.

◈

The sun hadn't cleared the summits surrounding *Ainka-honobita* when Willow stepped out of the shelter. She placed a hand to her stomach as her careful gaze surveyed the surroundings. Wisps of smoke still rose from the firepit. The woodpile looked like a gray jumble in the dawn. The junipers and limber pine stood like silent sentinels against the fading night.

Travis's and Baptiste's bedrolls had already been rolled. They had risen even earlier, taken their rifles, and were hunting the juniper breaks beneath the rimrock in hopes of killing meat.

Reassured, she made her way on careful feet to the draw and followed the trail down to the rocky bottom. To still the queasy tickles in her stomach, she sucked in the chilly air. Eyes closed, she propped one hand on a cottonwood trunk and fought the growing nausea.

Willow bent double. In a violent fit, her stomach pumped the last remains of last night's supper onto the tumbled red rocks. She spit, and wiped off her mouth. Sure that it was over, she straightened to catch her breath.

The chill braced her, cold air soothing her hot throat. High overhead a flock of blue herons fluted calls as they winged south across a golden sky. Two Half Moons had once told her that the second time wasn't as bad as the first. Grimacing at the taste of bile in her mouth, Willow wasn't sure.

Feeling better, she kicked loose soil over the damp stains and squatted to relieve herself. By the time she climbed out

of the wash, strength had returned to her legs. The rapidity of her recovery always surprised her.

She crossed the camp to the spring and drank deeply before rising. She'd plucked several pieces of wood from the pile when Travis stepped out from behind one of the junipers. He fixed her with a hard stare and came striding across the beaten grass. His Hawken hung from one hand, the tight grip purposeful.

"Good morning," she said.

He stopped before the fire, a sour look on his scarred face. "Been sick, ain't ye?"

She bent down to hide her face and stirred the fire for hot coals. Prodding them into a mound, she placed her firewood atop them and blew them to life. As the first flames leaped up, she said, "Something I ate."

"Not fer two mornings, Willow." He squatted down to her level, refusing to be put off. "Ye've missed yer bleeding, too, ain't ye? It's nigh on two months now since Dick left, and yer putting on fat, gal."

She bit her lip, flashing him a hot glance. For a long moment their eyes held, and she nodded in defeat. It wasn't as if she'd hide her condition for much longer.

Travis lowered his eyes to watch the fire. At last he reached up and scratched his ear. "Baptiste, he done noticed first. He's a keen old coon, he is. Wal, I reckon it ain't that much of a surprise."

"I'll be fine, Travis. I've done this before, you know."

"Yep." Then he grinned. "Why, Tarnal Hell, gal, this means this child'll be an uncle! Figger that fer beaver."

"Uncle Travis?" She lifted an inquisitive eyebrow. "And Uncle Baptiste?" Then she laughed.

Travis fingered the cock on his rifle as he looked up at the brightening sky. Nutcrackers were squawking in the trees, their raucous cries drowning the trill of a chickadee. "What about Dick? He otta know."

She shrugged. "He will find out when he finds out, Travis. What can we do? Nothing, and even if I could send word, I wouldn't. He has to make choices without my interference."

"Interference? Waugh! They's a child involved, Willow. Dick's got a right ter know. It's his kit, ain't it?"

"If the child is born, and lives, it will call him *appi*."

Travis was pulling on his beard now, frown lines wrinkling his scars. "Reckon I could go ter Boston and tell his sorry arse he's a pap. Painter crap! This coon don't hanker fer them doings. Not by a damn sight."

"Travis, if he comes, he'll know soon enough. The child won't be old enough to know a father until two years have passed anyway. And what if you ride off and tell Richard, and then you come back and the baby is dead? You know that happens. My first died like that."

"Yer fibbing ter yerself, ain't ye? Think, Willow. Ye knows Dick, how his head works. Hell, if'n anything happened, why he'd skewer hisself with guilt till Christ hisself couldn't fergive him." Travis lowered his voice. "'Sides, girl, they's more to it. He told ye about his pap, didn't he? 'Bout how the old man was gone when his wife died? And how he never could face Dick again? Ye want that?"

Willow sighed wearily. "I'm no White lady." She smacked her hips. "See? Like a good mare, I can drop a child without dying. *Dukurika* women are like that. And this stomach? It's strong . . ." *When it's not throwing up.* "It can push a child out, and I can still cook supper that evening. Or breakfast the next morning, if the child comes at night."

Travis suddenly rubbed his face, an odd fear in his eyes. "Nope, this coon's a gonna go fetch Dick from Boston."

"Travis, what is it? You tell me."

He started to stand, but she grabbed a handful of his shirt, twisting him back to face her.

The muscles in his face twitched and made the scars seem to writhe. "Aw, it's nothing. Seeing inter the past is all. Seeing . . . "

"What? This is Willow you are talking to."

His lips parted, the pain in his soul open to her. "I had a wife once. Crow she was."

"I know this."

"Uh-huh, but what ye don't know is that she's kilt by the Blackfeet. Pregnant. When they caught her, she couldn't run. Not heavy like that."

Willow released him and shrugged. "These things happen, Travis. Coyote made the world that way."

"I warn't thar, Willow. I's out hunting with Two White Elk. Warn't a damn thing I . . . I warn't thar, is all."

She nodded then. "Ah, so now, Dick must be. This is not a thing I can talk you out of, is it?"

He gave her a weak smile. "Nope. I reckon not. Not this time."

"But you don't want to go. I can see it in your soul, Travis."

"There's things a coon's gotta do, Willow. Just like Dick's a-doing now. Now, I ain't gonna lie and tell ye I'm just chipper ter go and . . . and . . . Hell, I *hate* the East."

She laughed, kicked at the dirt, and gave him a sidelong glance. "No wonder you come here to find Injun women. Without them, you White men will all die."

"I don't see whar yer stick floats."

"If you must do this thing"—she gave him a smug look— "I know a way to tell Richard without you going to the cities, Travis. You know it, too."

"I do?"

"Come, we will find the things we need."

William Simon was more scared than he'd ever been in all of his life. He hadn't come that far, he just knew it. But no matter which way he looked, all he could see were trees. Under his feet the carpet of leaves crackled and felt spongy, but study as he might, he could see no imprint of his small boots to tell him which way he'd come.

In the streets of his native Philadelphia safety lay in any direction, no farther than the closest door. He need only cry out for help. But here, lost in the forest, he felt as if something was watching him, stalking in those shadows.

"I gotta get back," he mumbled to himself as a tear streaked down from one eye. He sniffed, trying to be brave, and shouted, "Mama! Father!" He'd shouted before, but the endless trees seemed to swallow his words.

He ran, panicked. They had so little time at wood stops, and he'd just walked into the forest to see. That's all. He'd dreamed of the forests, of Indians, and hunting, just like the frontiersmen.

The *Sultana* would be leaving any minute now—and it would do so without Willy Simon.

I'm lost! Oh, please God, don't let me die here! "Mama, Papa—help me!" As he charged through the trees, he tripped, falling into the leaf mat.

In the distance, he heard the shrill steamboat whistle.

"They're leaving," he mewed piteously. Which way had the whistle been? Sound changed here in the forest, and he'd crossed a couple of small ridges.

Breath tearing in his throat, he ran for all he was worth, and heard the whistle again, but which way was it?

"Mama! Father! Help!" A vine slapped him across the face, and he splashed through a shallow stream. Shivering from fear and exertion, he blinked down at the water. Had he crossed it before?

He couldn't remember. "Help me!" Then he prayed out

loud, "God, don't let them leave without me. If You do this one thing, I'll be good, I promise! I'll never be bad again!"

"That's always a good policy," an amused voice answered.

Willy nearly fell over from fear. There, standing up the slope from him, was an Indian!

"Don't kill me—I'm only ten! I'm lost! Help! *Father!*"

"Whoa now." The man stepped out further, and Willy could see that while he wore buckskins, he was a white man with a beard, and a big rifle. "You're fine, Willy. I've come to find you."

"The boat's going to go, and I'm going to die here! I want my mama and papa."

"The *Sultana*'s not going to leave without you. Your folks told the captain you were missing and there's men combing these woods for you."

Willy felt a little better. The whistle sounded again, and the man cocked his head. "Sound plays tricks on you down in this little valley, doesn't it?"

"Yes, sir."

"Come on. It's this way." The man gave him a smile and started up the hillside.

Willy gulped, took his chance, and charged after him. "You're sure that's the way?"

"I am. Willy, remember, you can always follow the streams if you get lost. They'll take you back to the river."

"How do you know that?" Willy was eyeing the big rifle. It was scarred, the kind of rifle that had seen a lot of Indian battles.

"A man told me once, just like I'm telling you."

"Then, why aren't we following that stream back there?" He pointed at the brook they had just crossed.

"Because this way we cut the corner off the angle. Think. If you crossed all the streams, and water was running to the left, which way would you be from the boat?"

Willy put it together in his head. "Downstream. West. Because we're on the north bank."

"You've got it."

Willy trotted to keep up with the big man's steps. He got a closer look at the worn leather clothes. The buckskin was black and shiny, and bits of hair had been sewn into the seams. Colored quillwork made designs on the sleeves and chest. Here and there, a tear had been stitched with thongs from the long fringes.

Willy said, "I'll bet you don't get scared in the forest."

The man smiled. "Were you scared?"

"Yes, sir. I could feel eyes on me, like animals or monsters that would get me." He winced. "That must sound pretty silly to you."

"No, not silly at all." He winked at Willy. "You know why? Here, stand still for just a moment. There, now. Listen. Feel with your soul. Do you know what that is?"

Willy did, uneasy at the lurking presence. "I feel it. No, sir. I don't know what it is, like a haunt!"

"You're from a city, aren't you?"

"Yes, sir. Philadelphia."

"It's the land, Willy. It has power, a soul all of its own. That's what you're feeling." He glanced around, brown eyes serene. "I was just like you, once. The first time I felt the way you do now—that *things* were watching me. But do you know what?"

"No, sir."

"The land becomes your friend when it knows you." And he smiled.

"Willy!" Father's voice shouted from somewhere in the trees.

"I've got him!" the man called back.

"Father!" Willy's heart felt like it would burst from his chest. He charged headlong, arms out, never so happy in all his life. His father's strong arms plucked him up and hugged him to that familiar cloth-covered chest.

"The lad's all right," the stranger said. "Just lost his way."

"I, uh . . . thank you, sir," his father said uneasily.

As Willy was lowered to his feet, he noticed the strained expression on his father's face as he took in the bearded man's dirt-streaked leather clothing, and the battered rifle. Next to his father's fine suit, the stranger looked wild and unkempt, the kind of man Father would never acknowledge on the streets of Philadelphia.

"My pleasure. Richard Hamilton, sir. At your service." The dirty man offered his hand.

For once Father didn't shake, but clung to Willy's shoulders with both hands. "John Simon. Thank you. Thank you again, Mr. Hamilton. Come, Willy. We're late. Holding up the captain. Come on. Let's hurry." And his father dragged him off so fast that Willy had to run to keep up.

Willy threw a quick glance over his shoulder; the wild man followed behind, an ironic smile on his lips.

Men greeted them at the plank, most making jokes about his getting lost, or captured by Indians, or eaten by a bear. But his father laughed them off as they boarded and he pulled Willy toward the stairway. "Quite an adventure, eh, son?"

"Yes, sir. Who was that man?"

"Some frontier ruffian. He's riding down on the lower deck. Rabble, son. A fur hunter from out west, they say. But, son, you must always remember that you are a gentleman."

"Yes, sir." Willy glanced back down the stairs just as the wild man waved goodbye to him. Later, in their stateroom, he watched the forest pass slowly by as the *Sultana* steamed up the Ohio for Pittsburgh.

The soul of the land. That's what I felt out there. How brave Mr. Hamilton must be. But Father is right. A gentleman should only associate with other gentlemen.

Veils of misty rain marked the river with interlocking ringlets that danced on the waves. Richard leaned on the rail just below the driver as it rose and fell, in the endless cycle of powering the huge paddlewheel. Each revolution was accompanied by clanking and rattling and the endless *shish-shish-shish* of the paddles biting into the river. To block the noise, Richard imagined a perpetual waterfall, droplets cascading down just for him.

The dark, forested bank slid past, scarred here and there by farms. The water swirled and sucked from the bow wake and the ripples generated by the hull. This was the Ohio, the water dark by its very clarity. A tame river, soothing to the soul.

How unlike the Missouri, which always waited to kill the unwary. Only on rare occasions did the silent and deadly embarras come corkscrewing down the current. Here, the sawyers and planters were marked, mostly unchanging.

An irregular patch of cleared land was momentarily visible through falling curtains of rain. In the center of the newly cleared field, a pall of blue smoke issued from a smoldering pile of burned limbs. The farmers set fire to the litter created by their clearing. For days, the smell and haze of smoke never dissipated.

What of the forest's spirit? He shifted, a lonely sadness within. *We're killing it. Breaking the Power of the land.*

Richard twisted his head to see the gallery above him. No one stood out in the rain today. They were all huddled around the warm stoves inside. He could imagine the cigar and pipe smoke, the clatter of pasteboards at the card tables. The talk would be of business, politics, and market prices.

Here, on the cargo deck with the other cheap fares,

Richard lived under his blanket shelter. He'd come down-river in the *Virgil,* a gentleman with a stateroom, a grip full of a fortune of banknotes and a satchel of philosophy books. Now, a year later, he was going upriver as a laborer, work-ing off his passage as a deckhand, loading firewood and freight, doing menial chores on the boat.

He thought back to the Richard Hamilton who'd once traveled down this river, so certain of his own invincible truth. *Was that really me?*

He'd understood John Simon's reluctance to shake his hand that day the boy had gotten lost. *I'd have done the same thing, once.*

That led him to think about François. Blessed God, how ironic fate was. *It was he, not I, who ended up in the river with his throat cut.* Coyote pranced in the most curious of places.

A glass bottle floated past, bobbing in the *Sultana*'s wake, only to be scuttled by the thrashing paddlewheel.

Fate brought people, events, and goals relentlessly back to their starting points. Damp and cold, he squinted out at the drizzle. On the *Virgil,* he'd longed for Boston. Now, on the *Sultana,* his heart ached for Willow and *Ainkahonobita.* He shrank from the inevitable arrival at his destination.

No matter how many times he played out the meeting with his father, it was like an actor on a stage, the lines rehearsed. The real meeting would be so different. *How will he react?* Richard winced at the thought of those gray eyes, and his father's unforgiving face.

Father, for God's sake, let's make this pleasant. Coyote would grant him that, wouldn't he? *The difference is that this time, I will understand you, Father. This time, I don't have anything to prove to you.*

A flight of ducks darted past, swinging wide of the *Sultana.*

The future would always have to be faced; and face it he

would. If he reached Boston, he and his father would either repair their differences or they wouldn't. He would see Will Templeton, and Professor Ames. They would ask him what had happened, why he had changed so.

And what can I tell them? Nothing—at least, nothing they could understand. Anything he said would be illogical without the rational foofawraw to back it up.

As the rain fell, Richard stared down into the water, heart heavy with longing for Willow. Since he'd left her, he'd had no one to talk to. No one who understood his heart.

He absently fingered the hard roll of gold coins sewn into his jacket seam. The circles of fate. Once again he carried another man's money. The accumulated savings of Travis Hartman's hard life: in its own way, another fortune.

But, Travis, I'm going to hand it right back to you one day. I swear that before God. And he smiled wryly at the rain. This was a very different Richard Hamilton to whom Travis had entrusted his gold.

He always felt a warmth when he pictured the expression on Travis's face as he handed that roll of coins back. An offer given, a debt repaid, and a man's proof that he could face the world on his own merits.

That narrowing of Travis's hard blue eyes could speak more eloquently than Shakespeare's sonnets.

Life's circles: always ironic, always humbling. He reached up to flick a bead of water from the brim of his worn felt hat. The last time he'd passed these shores, he'd been dreamy-eyed with infatuation for Laura Templeton. Giddy fantasies had filled his head, visions spun of himself and Laura, hand-in-hand, gazing rapturously into each other's eyes.

Now, whenever he closed his eyes, he was with Willow— seeing the gleam in her dark eyes, feeling her touch, hearing her words. Sometimes they talked under the night sky. Other times their bodies locked together in that ultimate piercing unity of man and woman. However she appeared, she dominated his heart, body, and soul with a captor's totality.

It won't be long, Willow. I'm coming back—just as soon as I can. But then, he'd promised that to Laura the last time he'd traveled this river. Circles. Forever haunting. Endlessly mocking.

THIRTY-SEVEN

❖

Art goes yet further, imitating the rational and most excellent work of nature, *man.* For by art is created that great LEVIATHAN called COMMONWEALTH, or STATE, in Latin CIVITAS, which is but an artificial man; though of greater stature and strength than the natural, for whose protection and defense it was intended.

—Thomas Hobbes, *Leviathan*

Travis pulled his hat off and stared up at the morning sky. A light breeze was blowing from the west, as if urging him eastward. It whispered in the dry grass, rustled the yellow-brown leaves. The distant chirp of a horned lark was the only other sound. The soul of the land soothed, the aches of the body nettled. From long habit, his gaze went first to the horses who watched him with half-lidded eyes as they stood, heads down, and hobbled over close-cropped grass.

He threw the blanket back, grunted as he climbed stiffly to his feet, and stretched to loosen the weary ache of muscles, bones, and joints pushed too far.

To still the gnawing ache in his belly, he chewed a strip of jerky, then rolled up his blanket. The saddle leather was cold against his fingers as he threw it onto the dapple gelding and tightened the surcingle.

He walked off several paces to attend to nature, knowing full well that the gelding had swelled his chest against the cinch. Finished, he casually cinched up the slack, and stepped into the saddle. The lead ropes in hand, he resumed his race to the east, walking the horses into a trot, and holding the pace.

As he limbered to the saddle, the pains stitched through his body. *Getting too old fer this, hoss.*

Hell, how did age creep up on a man so? Time was, he could have ridden like this for days, and nary a complaint once his body warmed to the strain. But this time the ache hadn't left his bones and stringy muscles.

As the sun climbed the sky, he maintained the distance-eating pace, stubborn will overcoming the resistance of his flesh.

Today, like the day before, and the day before that, he'd switch off one horse for another. The trick was to balance the horses, and himself: endurance against time and distance. Changing off three mounts was about the best a man could do; more horses meant more cussed trouble to keep the cavvy together.

And it's still a gamble, coon. He kept throwing glances back, forever expecting to see riders racing up his backtrail. The rifle in his hand reassured him. A lone man with three horses made an all-fired tempting target.

Travis kept to the uplands, paralleling the Platte. When possible, he trailed through the hollows, off the skyline. Miles passed with the hours, an endless race across waving grass, crumbly stone, and dark patches of prickly pear. Hooves pounded across bleached buffalo chips, and crushed an occasional dry bone.

Why in hell are you doing this? The question rolled around in his fatigued mind. The answer haunting him: *For Moonlight. For me.* And damn it, just because it could be done and it otta be done.

Wasn't that what a man was made for? Doing things? Accepting challenges?

If'n not, he repeated over and over, *ye might just as well be dead.*

Down in the root of his soul, he could see Willow's face. Well, by God, if she could be so damned brave about bearing a child by herself, he could see to it that Dick got word.

If I could just see his face when he hears. Travis chuckled. Yep, that would be some, it would. The Doodle would get that stunned look, as if the world had just come unstuck again and turned upside down. Old Dick, just like always, would torture hisself right miserable.

And when ye hears, coon. Ye'll come. I know ye will, 'cause yer more a man than ye ever knew ye was. And Boston could just damned well rot itself.

Filling his lungs, Travis was on the point of howling. Then he topped the ridge. Looking back, he could see them, a line of riders following his tracks.

He pushed his horses across the ridge and into the swale on the other side.

Wal, coon, what're ye a gonna do now? Fort up and wait it out, or take a chance on losing them red bastards?

From the angle of the sun, he had about three hours to darkness. If he could outrace them into the night, he just might be able to lose their sorry carcasses.

"Ho, Hamilton! Time to get off! We're here," the wagon driver called.

Richard blinked and yawned. He peered owlishly out at the foggy gray morning. The wagon had ceased to rumble, bang, and lurch. Boston, at last.

He unrolled from his blanket and sat up on the unforgiving crates. The cries of gulls, the salty smell of the harbor, brought a deep contentment to his soul. He quickly rolled his blanket, grabbed up his rifle and possibles, and stretched.

When he jumped stiffly to the cobblestones, he needed a steadying hand on the wagon box while his legs firmed up. The wagonmaster had climbed down, and stood with his fingers shoved in his belt as he looked at the gray wooden doors of the warehouse. "Ain't that just fine," he muttered. "Locked. And all that worry and fuss about making time!"

Richard rubbed his neck to kill the ache. "Well, Mr. Jones, thank you for the ride. I do appreciate your kindness."

Jones cocked his head. "Pleasure's mine, Mr. Hamilton. You more than repaid me with all them stories about the western lands." He paused. "You gonna walk through the city—looking like that?"

Richard glanced down at his buckskins, black and shiny with dirt. Some of the fringe was gone, and holes gaped here and there. "It's all I own."

"God keep you, sir."

"And you, Mr. Jones." Richard hefted his rifle, hung his possibles on his shoulder, and slung his blanket on his back. Then he walked out into the morning fog. He could see the masts and spars of the ships. Jones hauled freight from Boston to Rhode Island, making a trip a week down south to Providence where Richard had managed to find passage from New York.

His moccasined feet scuffing the damp cobblestones amused him. "I left in a carriage and returned in a freight wagon." He shook his head, stepping out onto Sea Street, took that west to Essex Street, and then turned onto Boylston.

Little had changed during his absence. Mystification

filled him. *How can I be so different—and Boston remain so carelessly eternal?* He quoted to himself: "What a vanity is man's that he expects the world to notice his achievements, and to marvel at them, when in reality, the world, if it so much as pays the slightest attention, will only yawn, and then with but the briefest of enthusiasm."

His nose wrinkled at the acrid smells—smoke, urine, manure, rot, fish—borne on the early morning air. He grimaced at puddles of water, and the greasy scum that coated the cobblestones. He cringed at the filthy dampness soaking into the soles of his moccasins.

Cats slipped away into shadows, and the rats scurried into drainpipes and holes under foundations. Pigeons clucked and cooed from the rooftops, flapping as they sailed down to inspect the streets for garbage.

Richard passed shop windows, staring at the goods displayed. In the dawn twilight, Boston was just stirring, flexing its muscles for the day ahead. In a few hours, these streets would be crowded, the shops open for business. The several people he'd passed had gaped at him, as if seeing some sort of freak.

Never mind. You're home.

He rounded a familiar corner, and the Commons stretched before him. The trees were leaf-bare for winter, but the grass hadn't surrendered entirely. It still held a shade of green.

"What in hell?" a passing man asked, taking in Richard's skin clothes, the rifle, and his beard. "It's Daniel Boone!"

Richard glared, but managed to throttle the desire to feed the bastard the butt of his rifle. He hurried on self-consciously, stung by the derision.

He stepped out onto the Commons. Here he'd played as a boy, chasing bushy-tailed squirrels, running to and fro in the attempt to catch fall leaves as they fell. Here he'd made his first snowball—and thrown it at Jeffry.

He could see the house now, and slowed, a sudden constriction in his throat. He took a deep breath. Torn, he walked toward his home, his father, his past, and his future.

The first knock had been timid, and Jeffry barely heard it. He'd just stepped out of the kitchen and into the hallway when the knocker hammered more insistently.

"I'm coming," Jeffry growled, as he hurried past the hall chair and checked himself in the mirror. Early as it was, it wouldn't do to appear disheveled. The door knocker clanked again, demanding this time. Jeffry pulled himself straight and opened the door.

A vagabond stood on the step, his back to the door. Jeffry's nose wrinkled at the odor. And then, to his horror, he noticed the heavy-barreled rifle resting butt down by the intruder's leg. Beyond him, three or four of the neighbors had gathered, staring, some pointing.

"Looks like an Indian," Jeffry heard a man say to his companion.

William Pembroke, an associate of Master Hamilton's, had come to a stop, surprise on his face. Pembroke dealt in cotton and textiles. "I say," Pembroke called out, "you there. That's Phillip Hamilton's house. Have you business there?"

The vagabond rested his nervous hands on the muzzle of his rifle and called back, "Indeed I do, Mr. Pembroke. But none that concerns you, sir. If you have nothing better to do than stand about the streets gawking, I'd suggest that you'd be better employed counting cotton bales in your warehouse."

At the ragamuffin's voice, Jeffry froze, a hand half lifted.

Laughter broke out, and Pembroke reddened. Calls of "Who is that?" went back and forth.

No, it couldn't be! Jeffry cleared his throat. "May I help you, sir?"

The vagabond turned, bearded, dirty, with long greasy hair hanging over his leather collar. Jeffry's hand went to his throat.

"Jeffry? It's me. I—I'm home. Is Father . . . "

"Richard?" he asked in a hoarse whisper.

"Yes! Jeffry, I'm Richard. Richard Hamilton!"

"You? You're . . . dead." Jeffry's mouth dropped open—a slow shake of the head expressing his disbelief. He collected his swimming senses, swallowed hard, and glanced at the knot of watchers. "Come in, quickly, sir. But I don't . . . I mean. Why on earth are you dressed like . . . like *that!*"

Richard stepped inside, looking grateful when the heavy door clicked shut behind him. He sighed wearily. "Thank God." He leaned the rifle in the corner and dropped his blanket and a heavy hide bag on the tall-backed hall chair. "It's a long story. Tell me, how is Father? He's all right, isn't he?"

Jeffry's instinct was to dance and shout. "His health is fair, Master Richard, although his soul has withered over the last year since he received word of your death."

Richard glanced around, as if cataloguing the familiar artifacts of the hall. "I'm sorry, Jeffry. There was no way to send a message. I would have if I could." He placed his hands on Jeffry's shoulders. "My God, but you're a sight for sore eyes."

"And you, too, Master Richard." Jeffry's nose wiggled. "As soon as I inform Master Phillip of your return, I'll heat water for a bath, sir."

"Jeffry." Richard studied him from the corner of his eye. "What will . . . ? I mean, how . . . ? He hasn't disowned me, or anything, has he?"

Jeffry allowed the faintest quirk of the lips. "Oh no, Master Richard. Quite the contrary. In fact, well, he might even forgive the way you're dressed—um, assuming, you *meant* to arrive this way."

"I had no choice. I need to tell my father—explain to him, if you will."

Jeffry's eyebrow arched. "Master Richard. Please, sir—" But how could he give advice? *Don't hurt him again, Richard. Not after what he's been through. Just once, be kind to him.* With cold formality, he said, "I will tell him you're—"

"Jeffry?" Phillip called from above, and a band like iron clamped on Jeffry's heart. "Who was that pounding on the door at this time of morning?" And Phillip hitched his way out onto the landing at the top of the stairs. He peered down, squinting. "Who is that? Who's there?"

Before Jeffry could get his breath, Richard called out, "It's me, Father. It's Richard."

"Richard?" Phillip's fleshy face faded from florid to gray. "Richard? My . . . Richard?"

He grabbed for the banister. Jeffry started forward, but Richard beat him to the stairs, taking them three at a time. On the landing, he reached out, taking Phillip by the shoulders. "It's me, Father. Alive and well. I've been on the frontier. Gone places, and seen things."

"The frontier." Phillip's mouth worked, his gray eyes seeming to lose focus. "Dear Lord God, boy, it's you! Alive!"

And for the first time in more years than Jeffry could

remember, Richard took his father in his arms and hugged him. For long moments they stood, unwilling to relinquish their hold. Jeffry climbed partway up the steps, hesitating.

Finally, Richard pushed back, and Phillip fingered his buckskin jacket. "You smell of woodsmoke and sweat. And what's this . . . this long black hair? Some kind of animal?"

"They call it . . . a fetish." Richard took a deep breath. "Father, come, let's go into your office. I have some things to tell you, and, well, they're not pleasant."

Jeffry turned. They would want coffee, and he'd tell Sally to make enough breakfast for two. Richard, home. *Thank you, Lord, for such a miracle.*

But who was this strange Richard, so smelly and ragged, somehow wild? And so oddly sure of himself?

Phillip felt better once he'd seated himself behind the cherrywood desk. The thumping of his heart eased slightly. Was this lean man really his son? He looked like Richard, talked with his voice, but everything else about him was wrong. Right down to the filthy leather clothing.

But it is Richard, and he's alive! And for that, Phillip could only praise God. He scratched his fleshy nose to hide the fact that a tear was trickling down his face.

For the moment, all he could do was stare. *When did my son become this man?* Muscles packed his shoulders, and the almost predatory way he stood before the desk set Phillip back. Richard's face, despite being browned by the weather, had a mottled look. His expression had been honed. Even the wild cut of his clothing seemed to fit him now.

Richard was looking him straight in the eyes when he said, "I was robbed in Saint Louis. It was my fault. I'd had words with a man named François. He and several boatmen

jumped me while I was walking through Saint Louis."
Richard squared his shoulders. "The fact is, it was my fault,
sir. I'm sorry. So sorry. I came to apologize." He hesitated.
"It seems that I've let you down a great many times over the
years."

Phillip fiddled with the articles on his desk, and ended up
twirling the officer's brass button. *My God, how do I tell him
all the things I want to? What can I say?* "You're alive,
Richard. That's all that matters."

"But, *thirty* thousand dollars!" He spread his arms wide.
"Father, how can I ever pay that back?"

Phillip braced his arms on the desk. "Oh, dear me,
Richard. Do you think I'm a fool? I insured it, of course.
And, beyond that, I sent along an agent, a man named Eck-
hart, to watch after you."

"Eckhart? Charles Eckhart." Richard lifted an eyebrow.
"With the cigars and the card games?"

"Yes, the Virginian. You don't think I'd send you off
alone and helpless, do you? He told me you acted very
responsibly, didn't socialize, didn't do anything to jeopar-
dize the banknotes. He said that you were a model courier
for the money, close-mouthed and discreet. He lost you at
the landing, waiting by your luggage, but you never arrived
at the carriage hired to take you to the hotel."

"I . . . I wanted to walk. All that time on the boat . . . "

"The money was insured, Richard."

"Thank God!" Richard seemed to relax as he gripped the
handle of his knife with a brown hand. "Upon reaching Saint
Louis, I scoured the place, looking for any sign of François.
General Ashley used his offices, as did General William
Clark, but all we could discover was that several days after
Maria left upriver, François was found floating in the river.
It seems he'd shot August the night before in an argument
over a woman, a Creole of rather dim reputation. The facts
of François's death are rather peculiar. He was found naked,

his throat cut, and, well, a red ribbon was tied around his penis. The rumor is that this er . . . courtesan had the quirk of tying up her business with a bow."

"And the woman?"

"Disappeared completely the day after François's death. Rumor says she booked passage on a boat to New Orleans, and then to Paris."

Phillip scowled. "And if you'd caught this François?"

Richard's lips thinned. "I'd hoped to beat the hell out of him and dump him on General Clark's steps—alive or dead."

Phillip gasped, then shut his mouth with an audible click. Was this Richard talking? "I see. Enough of this for now. What's happened to you? Where have you been? Why are you dressed in such outlandish clothing?"

"It's a long story, Father."

Jeffry knocked, waited for Phillip's call, and entered with a tray holding a steaming pot and two cups. "Master Phillip, I would imagine Master Richard is famished, sir. I have informed Sally to set another place."

"By all means," Phillip was sniffing, struggling to keep tears at bay. "Come, son. Let's eat. You can tell me your story over breakfast."

"Should I clean up first?"

"Oh, dear Lord, no. That can wait. Yes, let's eat. There shall be time enough now for many things, my boy. Today, Richard, I am a young man again. And life has meaning once more. Yes, indeed, young as sprat, I tell you."

Richard took his father's arm, steadying him as they descended the steps together.

Richard studied his father as the fire popped in the tile-lined hearth in the parlor. Phillip stared down at the amber reflections in his brandy as he swirled it. Behind him, row upon row of books made a suitable backdrop. He'd dreamed this in the snow, and now, here it was, almost as he'd imagined. Richard chafed in his broadcloth suit and sipped from his own snifter as he sought to place this world against the one that existed so far to the west.

The week had fled on frantic wings. Time was so different here. The flames danced on oak logs. Somewhere, Willow was watching fire, too.

Blessed God, how I wish I could talk to her. She'd love to hear how this has turned out.

Each night of the week they had sat by the fire, sipping brandy. Phillip—and Jeffry invited in—had listened, rapt, as Richard talked, his eyes half-glazed with memories. In the mornings, they sat at the table over tea, eggs, and bacon, Richard telling his father of the Indians, and the river. They talked in the office, in the drawing room, and in the carriage.

Phillip had gasped at the scar on Richard's back; and Richard knew he'd come to suspect the long black patches of hair sewn into the buckskin jacket, but couldn't quite bring himself to ask. Nor was that the only secret between them. About some subjects, Richard couldn't talk.

"I don't know what went wrong," Phillip said suddenly. "Between you and me." He swirled his brandy. "It was as if a distance was forever between us. I couldn't . . . " He frowned, lost for words.

"I know, Father," Richard said. "In the last two years, I've come to understand. About you and me—and Mother. I was as blind as you were. I didn't help matters any, bullheaded as I was. I got straightened out on the river, I'm afraid."

A faint smile bent Phillip's lips. "And I, by reports of your death. I want you to know, Richard, that I'm very proud of you."

Richard chuckled. "Risks must be taken." And a melancholy pang lanced his chest. *But we're still living in differ-*

ent worlds. My truths are beyond your comprehension. The thoughts of Willow, of her body intertwined with his on a rocky spire, sent honeyed sensations through his heart. *I'm married to a savage, Father. If you knew that, it would break your heart.* "But for the sense of courage and honor you'd taught me, I'd have died on the river. I learned more from you than I ever knew, or could admit."

Phillip's face twitched as he battled to keep his expression neutral. "What about the West? What would you advise? Surely some aspect of the fur trade should prove profitable over the next ten years?"

Richard fingered his beard; not for love nor money would he cut it. "Fifty percent of the fur trade is capital, Father. Another fifty percent is the caliber of the people you employ. The final fifty percent is sheer blind luck."

"That's one hundred and fifty percent, Richard."

"Yes, sir. And men who don't understand those mathematics are headed for disaster. Dave Green did everything perfectly—and in the end he blew up his own boat. Had the Blackfeet come a week later, we'd have fought them off and Green would now have a foothold in the Crow and Snake trade."

"Could this be done again? With you and this Travis Hartman as booshways?"

"I wouldn't want to try it. I've gained an understanding of my capabilities. I don't think I'd make a good trader. I don't have the patience to stay at a post."

"I was thinking more in terms of administration, Richard. Overseeing the stocking of those posts, and the factors we'd employ. It would mean traveling back and forth from Boston to Saint Louis, and then into the wilderness."

Richard smiled. "A partner in the fur business?"

Phillip put down his snifter and rubbed his eyes. "I'm no longer young, Richard. Someone must take over the business. What you learn in the fur trade will prepare you to take my seat when my health. . . . What's the matter? Not philosophy, again?"

Richard bit his lip, then took a deep breath.

"Tell me, son," Phillip asked gently. "Are you in some sort of trouble? I have means of dealing with such things, settling any ruffled legal feathers."

Richard laughed, amused. "No, nothing like that. I broke no laws, committed no offenses." He cocked his head, as if amused by his own words. "Or, perhaps I have, in the eyes of some."

"Is this the big dark secret you've been so careful to avoid?"

Richard gave him a level stare. "Father, I have my—"

"Richard, please!" Phillip slapped the arm of his chair. "Just once, I would like to be your father. In all ways. Do you understand? We've a second chance here. Is it so impossible for us to trust each other?"

Richard steepled his fingers, eyes level. His heart skipped, nerves prickling. *Tell him, Richard. Eventually he'll have to know why you're returning.* "Very well, I'll tell you, sir. I have a wife."

"A wife? But, why didn't you say so before?"

"Because she's *Dukurika*, Father. Shoshoni, Snake Indian."

Phillip leaned back, struggling to understand. "You mean, you . . . "

"I do. I can't bring her here. Not to Boston. Men like your friend Pembroke would delight in the torment they could dish out over such an irresistible bit of gossip."

"But, a *savage*, Richard?"

He gauged Phillip's level of incredulity, and chuckled. "No more than I, Father. I've spared you many of the details of my survival in the wilderness. Do you seriously want honesty? Very well, that's what I'll give you. Morality is dictated by time, place, and necessity. Do I love her? Yes, with all my heart. As much as you loved Mother."

"Richard, surely—"

"Wait, Father. I can hear your protestations: It's undoubtedly something that will pass; a young man's first infatuation; the sort of fling a young man needs before the responsibilities of marriage preoccupy him. Were she a courtesan, I might agree, sir. But she's not. She's Heals Like A Willow. The woman who cut the arrow out of my back, who kept me from freezing to death, and helped me discover who I am."

"Richard, you're a young man of standing, worth nearly five hundred thousand dollars!" Phillip placed a hand to his heart.

Richard shook his head slowly. "Father, dear Father, I could try to explain from now until Hell freezes over, and you would never understand." He glanced toward the door. Jeffry stood there, silent, a stricken look on his face. "Jeffry, you might. You know what it's like to see from different eyes."

"Yes, sir," Jeffry replied mildly.

"What's this?" Phillip wondered.

Richard sipped his brandy. "Think about it, Father. Could you tell Pembroke that your slave is your best friend? The two of you don't fool me, not any longer. You play the roles so well, but you're just like Baptiste and Travis. Well, Father, I can't play the game."

"So you'll go back to your *Indian* wife?"

Richard nodded, gaze unwavering.

"Richard, you must think this—"

"No, Father. My choice is *made*. That's all there is to it."

Phillip sighed, and Jeffry stepped forward to refill his glass. In the strained silence, the fire crackled. Phillip's face was a mask, frown lines cut deeply into his forehead. Then he said, "It is not unheard of. More than one prominent man has had a white wife—and a woman of standing, I might add—in the settlements, and an Indian squaw out beyond the frontier."

"Yes, sir. But it would not be right for me."

Phillip shrugged, eyes narrowing. Richard could hear the thoughts behind that shrewd face: *The boy is young yet. And besides, time will do more to overcome Richard's notions than any argument.*

Ah, Father, plot and scheme as you like. This time, I've lived that other life. And I accept it with humility.

Phillip glanced at Jeffry. "By the way, Richard, I have received word that your young friend, Will Templeton, is planning a reception for you."

Richard cocked his head. "I wasn't aware that he knew I'd returned."

"Oh, Richard, all of Boston knows."

THIRTY-EIGHT

The most perfect philosophy of the natural kind only staves off our ignorance a little longer: as perhaps the most perfect philosophy of the moral or metaphysical kind serves only to discover larger portions of it. Thus observation of human blindness and weakness is the result of all philosophy, and meets us at every turn, in spite of our endeavours to elude or avoid it.

—David Hume, *Skeptical Doubts*

Autumn leaves had fallen from the oak, hickory, and beech trees to form brown drifts around the corners of the buildings. The day was warm enough, sunny, with a hint of November breeze blowing across the Charles River from Boston and into Harvard.

Richard and Professor Ames strolled past the chapel, the soles of their shoes tapping on the stone walk. Two years might have been yesterday as far as Ames was concerned. He still wore his black frock coat and slim trousers. His white head had lost no more hair, and the thoughtful expression remained as Richard related his experiences.

Richard clasped his hands behind him as he looked up at the pale autumn sky. How he missed the bright blue of the high mountain West. Was Willow looking up at it, even now? Wondering where he was?

"A most extraordinary adventure, Richard." Ames glanced at him with questioning eyes.

"And very difficult for me, Professor. I kept trying to fit everything into a rational framework. I was an enlightened man, sir. But one by one, the arguments proved hollow in the end."

"Indeed, Richard?" Ames raised an eyebrow.

Richard knew that look. "Sir, would you say I was an intelligent and competent student?"

"You've a keen mind, Richard. One of the best I've ever had the pleasure to instruct."

"Thank you, sir. Given that, I can't *tell* you why the arguments are flawed, because in some situations, they aren't. For example, Immanuel Kant creates a rational argument for Truth as it exists within his university in Prussia. When we read and debate his ideas, we do so within the framework of our own intellectual experience. We share social, intellectual, and historical bonds with Europe."

"Generally speaking, we do."

"Sir, knowledge is experience. You've read the same books that Kant has, so your knowledge comes from the same roots as Kant's. Therefore, you both perceive a similar framework for Truth derived from a Northern European perspective that traces its origins back through the Reformation to the Roman Church, to the Greeks and Hebrews before them."

"That is civilization, Richard."

"From our perspective, sir. I was cast out into the wilderness looking for ultimate Truth. My experiences have taught me that while it may exist in some abstract, we've leagues to go to reach even a fundamental understanding of what it might be."

"Richard, two thousand years of critical philosophical examination have led us to our current state of knowledge. Do you discard that?"

"No, sir. Not completely. Experience is necessary for knowledge, but not sufficient. Philosophers write from the culmination of their experience, but for no man can it be sufficient to find Truth."

"And why is that, Richard?"

"The world is too immense, too diverse. Once we saw God as a paternal Creator. Now we think of Him as a sort of watchmaker who's invented a perfect machine. The notion works well for the rational mind. But, sir, I experienced things out there that are not rational, not mechanistic."

"Then what is God, Richard?"

"In all honesty, I have no idea. Perhaps, as Spinoza proposes, we are indeed nothing more than modalities. I can tell you that one truth I've experienced is that each of us must find his own way to whatever element of truth he discovers—and in your analogy of the building, it won't even be a wall that we see, but most likely, only an individual brick in that wall. If we're lucky."

Ames raised a white eyebrow. "You've become a pessimist, Richard."

"Quite the contrary, sir. The difference is that I've seen through other eyes, glimpsed different sides of the building. I'm smart enough to begin to recognize just how big the building is, and how limited my experience has been."

Ames walked in silence, head bowed. "You seem very sure of yourself, Richard."

"I'm only sure about my own ignorance, sir, and how little I understand about God, nature, and reality. You could create clever arguments that could destroy every observation I've made. But, if you did, it would be through syllogistic tail-chasing, because I've been there and you haven't."

"For instance?"

"For instance, I can tell you that you can think about God, but you can never think your way *to* God. Or that people may believe in concepts, things, or phantoms because they *want* to believe in them. Or that a perfect argument for, or against, something cannot be constructed because the initial conditions are constantly changing."

"Your universe sounds like chaos, Richard."

"It is, sir. I fought that acceptance until the very end. It was only after the last of the veils of illusion had been ripped away that I could truly see how ridiculous I'd been. How arrogant I was in my knowledge of that one brick in that one wall."

"Tell me what you saw, Richard."

He shook his head slowly. "I can't, sir. No more than you can tell me the smell of cinnamon, or the color of violet. Imagine yourself in intense cold, starving in the snow. Now, describe the odor of hot antelope blood. Impossible, you say? Indeed. Some things can only be experienced, not communicated. But, once experienced, they are nevertheless known."

"Hence experience is necessary, but not sufficient for knowledge." Ames grasped his lapels, his face a study. They were approaching the library now, passing occasional students. "Tell me some of these things you experienced."

"As a people, we're as deficient as any other, Professor. Our perceptions of the universe are only male, when half of the world is female. You are familiar with Latin and Greek that have male, female, and neuter cases. Did you know some people speak in languages that deal with the animate and inanimate? What does that say about the human mind's ability to perceive?"

"And Rousseau?"

"Dear Lord God, Rousseau! He wrote a fantasy, sir. I've seen man in a state of nature, or at least as close as you can get. There is no innocent Eden out there among the savages. I doubt there ever was. Anywhere. He just rewrote one of our fundamental myths. Once you see past the differences in primitive society, people are the same everywhere. No better and no worse. We all want the same things—health, a mate, shelter, food and water, and to understand the universe."

"But we are civilized, Richard. And they are not. Civilization does better the human condition."

Richard clasped his hands behind his back. "In some ways. We have our books. Our provisions for the common defense. On the other hand, we have insulated ourselves from reality. We're killing the soul of the land, removing ourselves from God, and veiling ourselves with illusions about life until we're half blind to truth. Tell me, did God never laugh?"

"God, laugh? No, not to my knowledge."

"Then why does laughter exist in the universe? Humor plays an important part in Indian religion."

"Humor isn't suited to the sacred."

"Why not? Be careful, here, sir. You'll fall into a syllogistical trap if you don't think this through. Is it because humor *can't* teach a sacred truth, or because our theology is flawed? An artifact of omission due to historical processes?"

"I see," Ames mumbled absently, his mind gnawing on the problem.

Richard shot Ames a look from the corner of his eye. "I was told by a frontiersman that people in Boston were like caged bears. It's true, sir. We only know the reality of our cage. We perform our tricks, and we're fed, sheltered, and cared for. We've given up our freedom in return for security, you see."

"I don't understand the cage, Richard. I'm free here, able to go where I want, think what I want, write what I want. Isn't that freedom?"

"As you know it, yes. I'm going back, Professor." Richard tilted his head. "I suppose of all people you might be able to understand. If I'm so free here, why can't I bring my wife to Boston? Or one of my best friends?"

"I don't know, Richard. Why can't you?"

"Because my wife is an Indian, sir. And the friend to whom I refer is an escaped Negro slave."

Ames studied him through wide eyes. "You? Married to an Indian? A savage?"

"A savage. Illiterate, unschooled in the Classics, but she and I have argued endlessly, night on end, about the nature of God, and why the universe was created the way it was. She stunned me the other day, proposed that nothing could have existed until God split into two to create duality. Only when the Godhead had broken into male and female could it begin to define itself. It has interesting possibilities, since only in duality can identity be measured against something else."

"What you are saying is heresy. It wasn't so long ago that people were burned for such crimes."

"Yes, sir. But you're not one of those people. You once said in a lecture that the search for Truth will take you into dangerous country. It does. In ways you can't imagine. It's a damning thing to say, but Harvard isn't ready for my ideas yet. It may never be."

Ames paced for a while, hands clasped behind his back. "A savage, you say?"

"Yes, sir. My wife and I would not be received in any decent home in Boston. Therefore, I will ask you to keep this between you and me. Rather than be branded a freak or a madman, rather than be scorned and spit on in the street,

I'll return to my wilderness and the ability to associate with whom I choose."

"You don't sound like a madman, Richard." Ames puckered his lips, then said, "What you tell me is provocative, dangerous."

"Most people don't like dangerous ideas."

"But I do. That's what led me to philosophy in the first place. These ideas of yours must be fleshed out, placed into an orderly whole. It is the nature of philosophy to question, and you've unique insights I'd like to see developed, Richard."

"It would take a lifetime."

"That's how long it takes most philosophers." Ames gave him a sidelong glance. "You seem terribly confident, Richard. What if I can disprove everything you say with a logical argument?"

"What if you can, sir? In the final analysis, I know what I know, and it's based on what I've experienced. There are two sorts of people with whom you can never win an argument: those who base their belief on absolute faith, and those who know something by experience."

Ames was still frowning, his lower lip stuck out in a way that Richard had rarely seen, and then only when Ames was particularly engrossed in an idea. "I'm serious, Richard. I think you have something unique and wonderful. An insight into life and philosophy that will challenge and inspire students for generations to come. Philosophy isn't stagnant, Richard, and I think it could use a gadfly like you." He lowered his voice. "If you're willing to pay the price."

"I'll see, sir. Like I said, I have—"

"If you develop these ideas, organize them, I would recommend a lecturer's position for you. Of course, in the beginning you'd have to be careful. Challenging rather than offending. I'd begin by picking at the flaws in the epistemological framework. Omit any references to God for now—

Harvard being what it is. In a few years, once you were established, you could advance your more radical arguments." Ames watched him with steely eyes. "I believe you know how important such an offer is to a student, Richard."

Lecturer? His heart skipped, an excitement brewing in the depths of his soul. Everything he'd ever wanted, just handed to him?

"You would be taking a risk by recommending me, sir."

Ames shrugged. "Cultivating dangerous ideas takes risk. I'm an old man. They can't hurt me. Can I be any less courageous than Socrates was?"

"That's within you, sir. But remember, they executed Socrates for speaking his mind."

❖

Heals Like A Willow dropped her pack of wood and straightened slowly, awkward with her swollen belly. She winced and placed a hand on a nearby juniper for support. The red rocks of *Ainkahonobita* were maroon in the predawn light. A thick layer of frost had coated the brown grass.

Overhead two falcons soared through the chilly morning sky, twisting and turning before swooping low over the grassy flats under the canyon rim.

The rich odors of juniper, pine, and sage filled her nostrils as she drew the cold air into her lungs. The child sapped her reserves, and she had to rest more often.

"Y'all all right, Willow?" Baptiste asked as he rounded the corner of the shelter. His black face was pinched with worry.

"Yes, fine. I just needed to catch my breath."

Baptiste lifted the bundle of wood by its leather strap. "You carry all that? In yor condition? Come on, now, inside where it's warm. I got a stew on. Rabbit, just like you wanted." He glanced down at her belly. "He kicking in there yet?"

"No. It's early for that still. In a couple of months. Travis is still asleep?"

"Yep. I don't know how that coon did it. Crossing all that country. Dodging them Pawnee and all. Reckon he's about as crafty as an eagle."

Willow stopped short, breathing deeply. Baptiste rocked from foot to foot, his dark eyes narrowed with worry.

"It is all right," she told him, amused by his concern. "I would think you were my mother. You should be off with the Crows, not wasting your time here."

"No, ma'am. Not with you in this condition. I don't know much about it, but Baptiste'll stay with you. And Travis, too. Leastways, till Dick comes back."

She glanced away, hoping her eyes wouldn't betray her.

"He'll come," Baptiste said gently. "He'd a never left if'n he knew he'd planted a child in you. Dick's a man, gal. And don't you never ferget it."

She nodded, starting for the shelter again. "And this paper?"

"Travis done delivered it. It'll be a-heading right down the river slick, I tell you."

"He should never have ridden off like that. I must have been hydrophobied to think of such a thing. Fort Atkinson is too far for a man to ride alone."

"Dick's gotta know. And, hell, Travis probably enjoyed the ride. He snuck through Pawnee country like a snake through the grass. Them coons is still chasing around trying to find his sign."

But she knew how risky the trip had been, and what a toll it had taken on Travis. He'd ridden in two days ago, his three horses worn down to bones, and Travis himself looking little better, with hollow eyes. He'd slept like a rock since his return.

"Dick will come," Willow told herself. And to her child, she added, *He's like Wolf, little one. You will be proud of your father.*

Richard stood with his back to the piano, a glass of fine brandy in his hand. Almost two years had passed since the last time he was in Will Templeton's parlor. Around him, the room was crowded with old friends, but they seemed so young, so innocent.

He'd come to Will's house, uncertain, half anxious, half dreading. So much had changed since the last time he'd stood in this parlor. Right here he'd bragged to them, desperate to hide his dismay at being forced to take his father's money west. Here, his infatuation for Laura Templeton had been born from a touch of her slim hand, and a promise in those startling blue eyes.

She watched him now, from an overstuffed chaise on the opposite side of the room. Unspoken questions reflected in her charming eyes, inquiry in the tilt of her pink lips. Her hair was curled, bedecked with ribbons, and a pale blue velvet dress caressed her delicate body.

Why do I still find her enchanting? Richard gave her a quick smile, and continued telling the company his story about being lost, starving, and seeing visions of Professor

Ames. "I clung to the rifle, you see. That was all that made me human after the last veils of illusion were torn away by hunger and pure animal survival. For the first time, I could see myself clearly. All that I'd been, all that I could be." He turned the glass. "We spend a great deal of time fooling ourselves about what's real, what's important."

Will, attentive as ever, said, "There's more, I dare say. You're not telling us everything, Richard."

No, indeed I'm not. The West was so far from here—from the garlanded wallpaper, the gleaming crystal goblets and finely upholstered chairs. Soft rugs cushioned his feet from the hardwood floors, the wood polished to perfection. The dark furniture gleamed, and the bright damask upholstery looked French, imported, no doubt.

George Peterson and Thomas Hanson sat watching him curiously. Somehow, word of the lecturer's position had already spread. Behind his handsome face, Hanson's resentment festered.

Richard lowered his gaze to his brandy and nodded. "You've always known me too well, Will."

"Then tell us!" Templeton cried.

"I can't. Not in words. Until you live it, feel it in the gut, you can't comprehend. Until you've stood on the same mountain I have, you have no comparison with which to measure yourself."

"You expect me to sit here, accept your declarations on face value? An appeal to authority is worthless, Richard! Come on. You've had Professor Ames in a tizzy since he talked to you. He's been hammering on and on about epistemology and the assumptions we make about ourselves. What have you discovered?"

"That you have to be very careful about how you know what you know, and what you accept on face value. That's why I can't tell you, Will. As philosophers, we do entirely too much tail-chasing in the epistemological rafters, and not enough inspection of the stones from which we build the foundation."

"This is nothing more than . . . than rubbish!" Hanson stood and stretched, a smirk on his handsome face. "Wasn't it you who stood there once and bragged about taming the wilderness? The 'real' is the 'rational'? I don't know what happened to you, Richard. But if you call this philosophy, you're a fool."

"The only fool, Tom, is one who proclaims knowledge when he has none."

"And now you do?"

"Now I know how little I really know. My blinders have come off. How about yours?"

Hanson stepped close, his slitted eyes inches from Richard's. Richard smiled then, letting his gaze bore into Hanson's. "Don't even think it, Tom. You're not up to my kind of trouble."

Hanson broke then, dropping his eyes and stepped away. "I think I'm going for a walk. Laura, would you care to accompany me?"

"Thank you, Tom. But I think I'll stay for the moment."

"Laura?" Hanson's voice raised the slightest bit.

"You heard her." Richard cocked an eyebrow. Hanson fidgeted for the moment, then slipped out the doorway. Richard watched him go. "I'm sorry, Will."

Templeton took a deep breath, leaning back in his chair. "Richard, in your travels, you have changed. I thought for a moment Tom and you . . . well, what would have happened if he'd pushed it?"

"Nothing, Will. It wouldn't have been worth disrupting a charming evening."

"You've grown wise, Richard, and that is a gift rarer than knowledge."

"Indeed? I don't feel very wise. If anything, I'm more adrift than ever."

Peterson asked, "Tell us one of these truths, Richard. You seem so sure of yourself."

He rocked his brandy back and forth, watching the patterns of light. "If there is anything common to the condition of mankind beyond the obvious physical needs, I'd have to say it is responsibility." He glanced at Will. "I tried so hard to make the world fit what I had learned. I looked for rationality—and found it; but at cross-purposes with itself. And Truth? What is true for us, here, in Boston, is incomprehensible beyond the artificial construct of our society. What is rationally moral to us is immoral to others."

"I've never really thought about it in those terms." Will laced his hands over his knee. "And, while I can't agree, I'm loath to disagree because I don't understand exactly what you are saying."

Richard sighed. "You have to step outside of your reality, Will. Let me elaborate in a very personal way. As a philosopher, I ask you to listen, to think, and to make no judgments until you consider carefully what I have to say. This"—he gestured around the room—"all of it, is illusion. Our civilization has generated its own artificial reality."

Will frowned. "I think I understand."

"Do you? I have argued every nuance of philosophy with men you'd consider illiterate. And, if you'd believe it, with an Indian woman, too. We have debated morality, human responsibility, duty and honor. We have discussed the place of man in the state, the nature of integrity, and the condition of the soul in all its variations."

"Variations?"

"It is an argument a little too sophisticated for most Americans. Those discussions caused me to revise my notions of society and civilization completely. As a result, I have been exposed to flaws in our logic that I never would have suspected. Isn't it curious? Most people in our fair city would say that a savage woman isn't ready for our society.

The irony for me is that Boston isn't sophisticated enough to understand her. So, tell me, Will? How did we become so blind?"

Peterson shifted uncomfortably. "Are we blind, Richard?"

Richard glanced up, meeting Laura's eyes. She'd been sitting demurely, watching every move he made. She cocked her head inquisitively, measuring him, waiting.

"We are. The problem is epistemological. While men like Hume have questioned the mechanics of epistemology, no one has seriously questioned the effect it has upon us as a society. We believe the way we do because we have always believed that way." His gaze bored into Laura's, seeing the excitement in her eyes.

Peterson frowned. "Give me an example."

"Would you publicly debate a woman on the role of man in the state?"

"Of course not! That's preposterous. A woman doesn't have the faculty of mind to comprehend even the basics of the question."

"Ah! Is it because she doesn't have the ability, or is it that she's never been taught?"

"She doesn't have the ability."

"I can only retreat to my first position. There are things I can't tell you because you don't have a framework for understanding them. And here the debate must end, because I have had such a discussion with a woman and you have not. To take it any further will end in frustration for both of us, for we have no common experience upon which to examine the question. Think of it as a frontier too far."

Peterson gave him a sour look.

"George," Richard raised his hands, "I am not trying to irritate you. Only to illustrate my dilemma. Philosophy, when pursued diligently and fearlessly, is the most dangerous of businesses. If Socrates was put to death for being a gadfly, what would my society do to me? I ask the most dangerous of questions. I challenge the roots of our mythology. And worse, I don't do it abstractly. I've seen beyond the horizon, but no one wants to accept what I have to tell them. We believe what we believe because we want to. It's comfortable, familiar. And no one wants to think that it could all be wrong since what little we know looks right."

"So, what will you do next, Richard?" Will asked. "I understand that your father has offered you a position in his firm. You are to be in charge of his western operations."

Richard took a deep breath and drained his glass. "I don't know." Laura's attention had wavered during the philosophical discussion, but now she straightened. If anything, she'd grown more beautiful during the last couple of years. Her pale skin had a radiant flush, and her smile charmed.

"Well, enough of this," Will said, aware that Richard had locked eyes with his sister. "Come, George, let's see if Jonas has managed to browbeat the servants into setting the table." He glanced at Laura, and then Richard. "We'll be right back."

Richard had to admit, it was smoothly done. He doubted that Peterson even knew he was supposed to beat a hasty retreat.

They'd barely left the room when Laura said, "It must be very rewarding, Mr. Hamilton. How splendid to have been offered a lecturer's position at the university, and a position with your father's firm."

He smiled. "I suppose it is, Miss Templeton."

"I kept all of your letters, read them over and over. When you stopped writing, I was dismayed. When word came that you were missing, well, it nearly broke my heart."

"I thought of you a great deal. I'm sorry if I caused you any distress. At times, your memory kept me alive, gave me something to cling to."

She flashed him a radiant smile. "Thank you, Mr. Hamilton. That's one of the most flattering things I've ever heard, and from the direct way you said it, I think you really mean it."

He met her challenging gaze and said, "I suppose I've lost the ability to dissemble. I should have gone a little easier on Thomas. Forgive me. I was a bit boorish."

"I'm not used to seeing him back down. It's not in his character. He believes himself the most dashing man alive. He thinks he's won me. Does that interest you, Mr. Hamilton?"

"I think you could do better than Thomas Hanson. He wouldn't make much of a husband. But that's just my opinion. Outspoken lout that I am now."

"I see." She blushed and smiled at him self-consciously. "I think the West sounds very exciting. Tell me, what is Saint Louis like? What do the ladies wear?"

"Oh, about the same as they wear here."

"Fine dresses from Paris and London?"

"Yes, indeed. Saint Louis is far from isolated. The steamboats tie Saint Louis to New Orleans, and from there, to the world."

"It sounds like a very interesting place. Will you go there for your father?"

"I would have to. The fur trade can't be run from a distance. The competition is of a fierce nature, and the demand for goods changes constantly."

She tilted her head. "I remember the last night you were here, so shy and self-conscious. You almost threw up after you kissed my hand. You're so different now. You're like no one I've ever met. Dangerous somehow, exciting."

"I've never thought myself exciting or particularly dangerous."

"You don't see yourself as I do, from the outside. You're like a wolf, sir, trying to associate with a pack of hounds. You smile at them, but all the time, you're masking your teeth. And when you met the pack leader, you needed but snarl to send him slinking away with his tail between his legs."

"That doesn't sound particularly flattering, Miss Templeton."

She stood amidst a whisper of velvet and walked up to him, her blue eyes penetrating. "Perhaps some women would prefer a wolf to a dog."

"Spending time around a wolf can make you a little uncomfortable. A dog is a good deal more predictable and safe." She stood so close he could smell the gentle scent of lilac as he looked down into her eyes, reading her soul. Like Willow, she looked back fearlessly, telling him so many things. Her lips parted to expose delicate white teeth, and the pulse at her neck betrayed her excitement.

"I'd thought you'd already be married."

"I've been looking for the right man."

Richard, you've got to tell her. You owe it to her. "Laura, you'd better know. I have a wife already."

Her eyes narrowed, head tilting so the lamplight glistened in her blond locks. "In Saint Louis?"

"In the mountains. Far to the west."

"I've heard there are no women beyond a few settlements outside of Saint Louis."

He shrugged, watching her put the pieces together.

Laura said, "She's Indian, isn't she? Not a proper wife at all."

"As you can see, you couldn't really have much interest in a man like me. I wouldn't be a suitable choice for a lady like yourself."

She took a deep breath, swelling her ivory bosom, and paced thoughtfully toward the piano. She turned back, watching him through half-lidded eyes. "And to think I only found your letters forward and bold. Are you this honest with all the women you meet?"

He gave her a wry grin. "It's a fault I've developed. I just thought I'd avoid any misunderstandings before they'd—"

"I'm still interested, Mr. Hamilton."

"Miss Templeton, I'm not the pampered rich boy who left here two years ago. Not the boy who wrote you all those silly letters on the river. I've killed men. Fought with my bare hands. Lived like an animal. I'm married to an Indian woman whom I love. She'll probably bear my children when I get back to the mountains. And I *will* go back."

"You *are* a gentleman, aren't you? Honorable to the core."

Richard shifted, suddenly uncertain. Who was this Laura Templeton? What game was she playing? "I must admit, I didn't anticipate your reaction. I'm telling you the truth. I'm going back to Willow."

"You'll go back as your father's partner, Mr. Hamilton." She stared thoughtfully at the rug, then raised her eyes. "Very well, let's be honest. Marriage doesn't always have to do with love. Sometimes it's a partnership. I'm not a fool, Mr. Hamilton. I trust you, and Will trusts you, so I'll tell the truth, too. We put on a pretty good show here. But this is Boston. My father is a ship's captain. My mother was an indentured woman. Despite all of my brother's friends, I've turned nineteen and never fallen in love. The way you talk, I'd think you, of all people, could understand a pragmatic woman. I'll go to Saint Louis with you."

"How do you know what kind of man I am?"

She stepped close again and took his hands. "By looking into your eyes, by the things you just told me. You're honest, Mr. Hamilton. And I can see the interest in your eyes. You're tempted, aren't you?"

Tempted? He looked into her blue eyes, aware of her beauty and the challenge she radiated. "I'm not an oak tree, Miss Templeton. Just frail flesh and blood."

She smiled at that, a delicate eyebrow arching. "That makes two of us, sir."

"Yet you'd know I was with another woman."

"Most men are. Even my father. I suppose that's the price

a woman pays when she marries a wolf. But at least I'd marry a rich one."

At that Will arrived, leaning in the door. "Come, all. Supper is ready, and what a feast it is!"

THIRTY-NINE

❖

Very well, so far we are agreed, Glaucon. The state which is to be arranged in the best possible way must have women in common, children in common, and education in common. So also, its practices must be common to all, both in war and in peace. Kings among them must be those who have shown themselves best both in philosophy and warfare.

—Plato, *The Republic*

Richard was in his father's office, compiling lists of trade goods, things in constant demand on the frontier. As he finished list after list, Phillip would take them, squint through his glasses, and periodically grunt a question.

"Tin cones, Richard? What are these?" Phillip asked.

"Just what it sounds like. Tin rolled into a narrow cone. They hang them on moccasins like little bells, or they can be used for horsehair tassels."

"I see. Made locally in Saint Louis, I suppose? Labor and materials would be cheaper here. Perhaps some sort of machine could stamp them out?"

Richard nodded, rubbing his forehead. His mind was awhirl with so many things: trade, a lecturer's position, Laura Templeton—and Willow. So much to consider. Too much, really.

Jeffry stepped into the office, an eyebrow raised. "Master Richard, sir, a note has been delivered."

Richard opened the small white envelope, reading:

> I'll be walking in the Commons at 2:00.
> Laura

Richard glanced at the clock. The time was a quarter till.

Phillip was watching with mild curiosity. Richard chewed his lip, then said, "I think I'd better attend to this. It won't take long."

He nodded to Jeffry, tucked the note into his pocket, and headed down the steps for his hat and coat. The afternoon was chilly, a breeze rolling in off the harbor. Richard's boots clicked across the cobblestones and onto the browning grass.

He walked with his hands jammed into his pockets, the tall beaver hat pulled low on his head. How did he sort this all out? With so many directions, how did he choose?

"Mr. Hamilton?"

He glanced up as a carriage pulled even with him. When it stopped, Laura stepped out. She was dressed in a light pink satin dress that billowed under a gray wool coat. Richard recognized the carriage driver as the Templetons' house servant. He would watch from a discreet distance as they walked.

Richard bowed as Laura curtsied. "Miss Templeton. Good afternoon."

They fell in step, walking side-by-side. Richard gave her a curious sidelong glance.

"I wanted to talk," she said. "I wanted to elaborate on some of the things I said last night."

"It did seem a bit risky for a lady."

She chuckled. "Oh, Mr. Hamilton, you'll keep my confidence as I will keep yours." She gave him a sly glance. "So, what are you going to do? Become a professor? Go to Saint Louis for your father? Run off to the mountains? What?"

He watched the leaves crush under his boots as they walked. "I don't know yet. It's all happening so quickly. Everything I ever dreamed has come true. All I have to do is reach out and take it."

"You told me you dreamed about me."

"I did." He studied her for a moment, dropping all pretense. "Why, Laura? What's this all about?"

For a moment, their eyes met, hers challenging. "It's about escape, Mr. Hamilton. Two years ago, just after you left for the West, my mother died. I took over the running of the house. At the same time, Will took over my father's financial affairs. Will isn't a businessman. He's a philosopher at heart, interested in ideas, not figures."

"I see."

"Will and I have always talked. I began to advise him on business decisions. I discovered that I have a head for it. That year was busy, needless to say. When I should have been looking for a boy to marry, I was involved in tariffs, debits and credits. I doubled my father's profits in the last two years. About a month ago, he discovered that I, not Will, have been making many of the buying decisions. Since it's improper for a lady, I no longer have that privilege."

Richard puffed out a breath, seeing the faint white haze on the air. It brought memories of snow, of cold mountains and hunger. "And now?"

"In the parlor last night, you said that Boston was a big cage. I don't mind marriage, but I want more. I thought if anyone would understand, you would."

"To be a partner?" Willow's words echoed from the past.

She gave him a level-headed stare. "Yes. I can do it, Mr. Hamilton. I want the chance. Is Saint Louis such a place?"

"All this, just from last night?"

"I liked the way you looked at me. Challenging, as if asking what I was worth to myself. Would you accept a woman as a partner?"

"I already have. Her name is Heals Like A Willow."

"Will you bring her to Saint Louis?"

"No. Saint Louis isn't that much different from Boston, at least, among the upper classes. And Willow wouldn't like Saint Louis. The Power is wrong there."

"Power?"

"Spirit, if you will. The soul of the place."

"You wouldn't have to come back, Richard. You could stay out there, with her. You could tell me what goods are in demand, and I could forward your orders to your father here. You'd be free."

"What on earth makes you think you could live that way?"

"I'd be doing what I want to do."

"And when you get lonely? If you took a lover, someone would find out. They always do. The scandal would ruin you."

"I don't know." Then she put her hand on his arm. "Mr. Hamilton, I want the chance to do something with my life besides be a gentleman's wife, bear children, and keep a house. I'm willing to take risks."

It was in her eyes, something unquenchable, and a burning spirit that touched him. "Let me give it some thought."

The note would never qualify as great literature of the Western world. In roughly formed block letters, it stated:

DICK:

WILLOW is pregnant. Cum kwik. Yer kid xpected maybe April. WER camped at Red Canyon til rondeeyvu. Cum kwik. Willow KIN make a coon krazy. All well.

TRAVIS

"Dear Lord God," Richard whispered as he stared at the rough paper. "How on earth did he ever get it here?"

Phillip sat behind the cherrywood desk, staring up at him over the nose-pinch glasses. The ship's clock tick-tocked on the mantel. In the corner, the old Charleville musket stood in mute testament to another age.

"I've got to go." Richard tapped the paper with his finger as he paced. "That settles it."

"Go? Back to the wilderness?"

Richard lifted an eyebrow at his father's disapproval. "She's going to have my baby, Father. I *need* to be there, for both of them."

Phillip rubbed his face, rearranging the fleshy jowls. "Richard, I have tried to understand. I really have. But I—"

"You don't need to understand." Richard leaned over the desk. "You must only accept. Our worlds have always been different. I suppose they always will be."

"Richard, your place is here. This is your world." Phillip gestured out through the window at the Commons. "You belong here, among educated Americans. This Indian woman, I assume she's a good woman, but you have a future here. You can send her support, an allowance to raise the child. But, Richard, find yourself a white wife, one who can keep your house, provide me with grandchildren."

"Laura Templeton?"

"Discreet inquiries have been made. Her family is not opposed to such a union. She is a beautiful young woman, Richard. I hear that the two of you get along famously."

"Indeed? 'Famously'? Yes, Father, she's beautiful."

"A woman doesn't need brains, Richard."

"I suppose they don't. Not here. But Miss Templeton, it seems, has them anyway."

"Then marry her and stay! Or take her to Saint Louis and establish my office there."

Richard stopped short, half frantic, but the pieces began to fall into place. "How much are you willing to invest in this office in Saint Louis?"

"How much would you need?"

"Five thousand."

"I'll give you ten."

"I don't need ten. Five will be more than enough for what I have in mind. Father, I want total freedom to do this my way. Hire my people. Call it a . . . a challenge. You wouldn't want me to take over the company without having proved myself. All right. This is my chance to do it."

"And the Indian woman?"

"I'll deal with her in my own way."

"But, Richard. . . . All right. Yes." Phillip placed his hands flat on the desk. "Very well, I suppose you're a man now. I'll admit, I had a few . . . er, relationships before I met your mother. It's to be expected. This will pass."

"Perhaps, sir."

Phillip laughed ironically as he reached back and pulled the bell cord. "I heard an old saying once: 'I am a soldier in order that my son can be a farmer, in order that his son can be a poet.' Well, so be it. I was a soldier so that my son could be a merchant. Instead, I got a philosopher with queer ideas. But more than that, I fought so that I, and my kind, would be subservient to no one. In that, I can take some solace, even if it didn't work out as I dreamed."

"No, sir, life rarely does. The five thousand will allow for the establishment of a Saint Louis office and capital enough for an initial investment in trade goods. I think, working with my agent, I can double it within two years."

"Now you're talking like a businessman. You have a plan, I take it?"

Richard gave him a crooked grin. "Yes, I think I do."

Phillip reached into the desk drawer as Jeffry entered. "Richard needs to return west with as great a haste as possible. Could you pack his things?"

"Yes, sir." Jeffry bowed and left.

Richard stared thoughtfully at the door. "You should free him, you know."

Phillip cocked an eyebrow. "Richard, it's in my will. And Richard, if I should die before he does, don't make him miserable. Don't tell him, 'Go be free,' and cast him out on the street."

"No matter what, he can live here until he dies, or he decides to leave on his own. I give you my word, sir. Oh, and Father, one last thing."

"And that is?"

"Uh, that pistol. You don't suppose I could take it with me this time, do you?"

"A caller, Miss." Jonas handed Laura a card imprinted with Richard Hamilton's name. She put her needlework to one side and rose, checked her hair in the mirror, straightened her collar, and went down the stairs.

Richard was looking out the window at the misty rain falling on the street. His cloak draped his shoulders and he held his hat in one hand.

"Mr. Hamilton? You look as if you're in a hurry."

He turned, that daring smile on his lips, and kissed the back of her hand when she offered it. Then he looked significantly at Jonas.

Laura nodded at Jonas, knowing he'd go no farther than the hallway.

Richard stepped close. "I have to go. I just received a note from Travis. Willow's pregnant. I must leave as soon as I can. It's a long journey and I may not make it as it is."

She studied him, trying to read that glint in his eyes. "I see. Well, I wish you a safe and speedy journey, sir."

"Thank you." He paused, curiosity in the slight arch of eyebrow and the set of his lips. "Tell me, how serious were you when you told me you wanted more?"

She steeled herself, fists knotted. "Very."

He handed her a brown paper packet tied with string. She hefted the brick-sized bundle in her hands, light for its size. "And this is?"

"Those are banknotes. Two thousand, five hundred dollars' worth. Half of my father's investment in the Saint Louis trade. I'm taking the other half with me for initial expenses. Your travel to Saint Louis shouldn't cost more than two hundred dollars. That's standard fare for a lady to take a steamer to New York, a coach to Pittsburgh, and a steamboat to Saint Louis. You will travel as my fiancée. It will give you greater latitude in your dealings with men along the way and in Saint Louis."

"Mr. Hamilton, I—"

"When you arrive in Saint Louis, contact General

William Ashley. The General will tell you where your office will be. By the time you arrive, he'll also have found suitable quarters for a lady. He will give you an envelope from me containing a list of goods to procure. That you will transmit to my father here in Boston. After that, we've two years to double the investment."

"But, how are we . . . I mean, goodness, my head is spinning!"

"I'll send you reports from the interior, as well as things for the trade that will give us an edge on the competition. In the meantime, you'll run the Saint Louis office."

Laura took a deep breath, suddenly unsteady. She blinked, clutching the packet to her breast. "And I will marry you there? In Saint Louis?"

"Only if it's necessary to keep the business solvent. I'm a pragmatic man, Laura. Know in advance, however, it will be a marriage in name only."

"Why, Mr. Hamilton? Why are you doing this?"

"Something I saw in your eyes the other day. Let's just say I want to see the bear outside the cage."

"I don't understand."

"One day, perhaps you will. Now, I must be going. I'm leaving for New York tomorrow morning at first light. On the way I'll organize as much as I can so you won't be completely lost upon your arrival in Saint Louis."

"Wait! My God, Richard. How do you know I won't just—well, not appear?"

For a long moment his brown eyes burned into her soul, sending a thrill through her blood. "Won't you?" And then he stuck out his hand. "To Hamilton & Templeton."

"To Hamilton & Templeton." She shook, straightening, chin up. "I'll see you in Saint Louis, Mr. Hamilton."

Phillip stood on the top step, Jeffry behind him. The carriage clattered off into the morning fog that drifted across the Commons to obscure Beacon Street. His stiff leg ached, and his soul weighed heavily. Damn it, the frontier was so far away, and dangerous. *If I just had more time to talk him out of this foolishness! What would his mother say? Dallying with an Indian woman! Isn't his own kind good enough for him?*

The mist closed behind the carriage, until only the clopping hooves could be heard on the cobblestones.

"If I'd only had more time," he repeated aloud.

"Time, sir?" Jeffry asked.

"With Richard. He's got to come to his senses, that's all."

Jeffry nodded, expression stony. "Yes, sir."

"Does he do things like this just to torture me? Is that it?"

"No, sir."

"What is it, then?"

"You know, sir. He's your son. Like you, he's fighting another kind of revolution. The problem is, no one is on his side."

And were it I, a young man with a wife about to bear a child? How many times had he wished he could have changed the past? Been there at her side? He swallowed hard, Caroline's eyes softening in the shadowy sconces of his memory. The best a father could hope for was that his son wouldn't duplicate his mistakes.

"Another kind of revolution. Huh! Well, I pray to God that he makes it safely." *Go with my blessing, boy. Don't live your life as I have.*

"He will, sir. He's got the fight in him. Just like his father. That comes out in the blood, sir."

Phillip nodded wearily, hitching around on his bad leg. He paused as Jeffry opened the door. "Then why do I feel so damned old?"

"Perhaps you're not looking hard enough for Master Richard's frontier, sir."

Richard himself had said it was too far—even for a man like Ames to see. *So, why should I be different?*

"Oh, I'll find it. After all, I've got the sprat involved in the trade, haven't I? And he's become quite a man. The sort for an old man to be proud of." And at that, Phillip limped into the house, toward a satisfaction he couldn't completely comprehend.

EPILOGUE

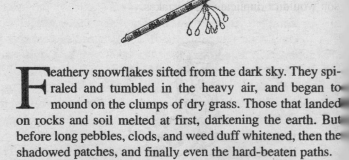

Feathery snowflakes sifted from the dark sky. They spiraled and tumbled in the heavy air, and began to mound on the clumps of dry grass. Those that landed on rocks and soil melted at first, darkening the earth. But before long pebbles, clods, and weed duff whitened, then the shadowed patches, and finally even the hard-beaten paths.

Willow had seen many spring storms like this. She walked slowly, heedless of the flakes that landed so gently on her robe-covered head. When she stepped on the cropped grass, the thin crust of snow groaned, moisture soaking into her moccasins.

The baby had been upset, kicking and squirming within her belly. Since sleep was an impossibility, Willow had climbed to her feet, massaged the small of her back, and draped a robe about her before ducking into the night. She prowled through snow-frosted junipers and hesitated to look eastward down the canyon.

How many times had she stopped here on moonlit nights? On clear days and cloudy? She knew each crevice in the high red rock wall. The patterns of sage on the amber grass had impressed her souls, until even now, in the darkness of this spring storm, she could see them so clearly.

Where are you, Richard? Flakes tumbled before her, their hiss on the ground barely audible. From old habit her hands went to her protruding belly. The child kicked, pressing perilously on her bladder.

"Soon, little one. Is that what you're trying to tell me? Is that why you won't let me sleep tonight?" She took a deep breath, ambling down into the canyon.

To one side she heard the warning cough of a mule deer, followed by the chunk of hooves as the herd bounded away. The sound of their passing was finally eaten by the silence of the night, the snow, and the comforting rock walls.

Until now, the pregnancy had been easy, almost second nature. She'd gone on about her tasks despite Travis's and Baptiste's constant harping. In self-defense she'd finally lit into Baptiste, scolding him unmercifully. To her dismay, he'd stiffened, wide-eyed, and avoided her for the rest of the day. The following morning when she'd gone to apologize, his bed had been missing, his horse and outfit gone.

"He went fer the Crow," Travis had replied laconically.

"I drove him away, didn't I?" And a horrible guilt had hollowed her souls.

"After a fashion, I reckon." Then Travis had turned into the wary male: he who dared not speak lest he say the wrong thing.

Contrite, Willow had reined in her surging emotions, attended to chores, and allowed Travis to handle those jobs he felt compelled to undertake on her behalf. At the same time, Travis had built a third lodge out of juniper, rock, sage, and earth.

A month later, in the middle of the deep cold, Baptiste had ridden in with two *A'ni* women: New Moon Rising and Makes Antelope. New Moon Rising had moved into Travis's bed, while Makes Antelope and Baptiste took up the new lodge.

Relations with Willow had been cool at first, but over the last weeks an equilibrium had been achieved.

"Tarnation, gal," Baptiste had said. "You ain't figgering on Travis and me birthin' no baby! Why, I done brung these heah gals fo' you. They got a sense fo' such doings."

"And your blankets are warmer now," she'd told him wryly. "They've a sense for those doings as well, I'd wager."

Baptiste gave her a wide grin.

Who am I to deny them the chance to be men? But the arrival of the Crow women had irrevocably shifted the tenuous balance in Willow's life. Where once she, Travis, and Baptiste had stood like a tripod, now she felt odd, uncomfortable, as if intruding on their affairs.

It's just the baby, Willow. Soon it will be over. A woman with a child in a cradleboard isn't as dependent as one with an infant in her belly.

The silence of the night pressed around her, cloaking her in the solitude of snow. The ache in her lower back was nagging again, and pains picked at her pelvis.

The faintest of breezes stirred the flakes into a slow

dance. What a cold, wet night. How good to have a snug shelter so close by. Spring was a miserable time for travel. Richard would probably arrive with the summer caravan. As Travis explained it, by the time the note made it to Boston— *if* it made it to Boston—and Richard traveled to Saint Louis, the caravan would be leaving for Rendezvous.

And he will come to me there. She smiled into the storm, picturing Richard's face as he met her, and this child. What a joyous day that would be.

The wind tugged at her. She started to turn, ready to retrace her way to the shelter. But the baby thrashed within her, causing her to gasp and suck shallow breaths as she cradled her belly.

"Easy, little one. You'll have plenty of time to use your legs and arms once you're born. There's no need to wear them out now." What she really needed was to go back to the fire and warm up.

She took a step and the child kicked again. Frowning, Willow gritted her teeth and stopped. What could possess the child to . . .

The muffled clink of metal carried through the curtains of snow.

Willow cocked her head, staring off into the snow-grayed darkness of the canyon bottom. In the time she'd stood there, a finger's depth had covered the ground.

Willow, it's just your imagination. No one would travel in weather like this. She turned once more, only to have the baby squirm uncomfortably. "Enough," she growled, starting resolutely up the trail. Her baby thumped her with enough vigor to make her draw breath.

She massaged her belly to still the child. "It's snowing out here. And I'm getting cold. We must go back to . . ."

She heard it again, a muffled *thump!* down in the valley. Willow turned, staring into the storm-blurred night until her eyes ached.

They might have materialized out of nothingness, little more than a moving shadow that appeared and blended back into the darkness and snow, a phantom in motion with the storm.

Real, or dream? Willow blinked hard, vaguely aware that her baby had gone still as the night. A swirling wall of white engulfed the apparition.

Just your imagination, Willow. A quirk of pregnancy. She took a deep breath. Foolishness! She wanted him so badly that she was spinning his image out of the night.

She turned—but when the horse snuffled, she froze, heart leaping in her breast.

Careful, Willow. You don't know who this is. Perhaps some Pa'kiani *riding through with murder on his mind.*

She stepped closer to one of the junipers, blending her form into the tree's.

Like *Pandzoavits* from mist, snow-caked and hunched, he rode out of the night. Pia plodded in a stumbling walk, head down, her gait that of a horse nearing exhaustion. A second animal followed on a lead, also white-backed and weary.

He was almost abreast of her when she said, "Richard?"

He pulled up, snow clinging to every fold of the robe he'd wrapped around him. In the darkness, his frosted beard was all she could see of his face.

"What are you doing out here?" he asked. "It's the middle of the night."

"The baby wouldn't let me sleep. It knew you were coming."

"Then I'm not too late?"

"No, husband."

He almost collapsed when he stepped down out of the saddle. She caught him, the two of them teetering together for a moment, and then his arms went around her.

"Blessed God, Willow, I've missed you!"

"And I you, my warrior!"

"Are you all right? Is everything all right? The child . . . ?"

"We are all fine. The baby can come any time now."

Bone-deep weariness echoed in his hollow chuckle. "Well, by God, I beat old Coyote this time, didn't I?"

"I think you've become Wolf, Richard. Now, come. Let me warm you, feed you, and make you a bed."

"Wind's blowing a mile a minute out in the flats. I'm half froze, Willow. But this time, you won't have to go clear to the Land of the Dead to find me."

"Only as far as Boston?"

He laughed again, tightening his hold on her. "I think Boston's dead—just the same as Cannibal Owl was for the Bald One. It's all worked out, Willow. I fixed everything—made peace. Now I can stay home."

This time, the child didn't kick as they turned toward their lodge.

Richard smacked his fist into his palm as he paced back and forth. This was miserable, just waiting and waiting. Behind him the fire popped and spat. Lazy snowflakes drifted insolently down. The clouds masked the red stone of *Ainkahonobita* and hid the sentinel pines that guarded the heights.

"Easy, coon." Travis sat on a log before the fire. "Could be worse. These Snakes, they make the man grunt and groan when the child's born. They claim it makes the birthing easier, shared, ye see."

"I'm not Shoshoni."

"Reckon even a blind buffler could see that." Travis ran a patch down the Hawken barrel as he cleaned his rifle. "How ye feeling?"

"About got my land legs back. I think Pia's going to be all right. By the time we got here, I was half afraid I'd broken her down."

"Naw, she's a tough one, she is. She's coming round." Travis glanced at the lodge.

Willow gave a muffled gasp. New Moon Rising and Makes Antelope spoke in low voices.

"That was sure a shock to ride in here and find three lodges," Richard admitted.

"Baptiste and me, we just got lonely." Travis scowled at a powder-stained patch. "And, wal, truth be told, it was getting ter be plumb hell a-watching Willow all the time. A beaver's got needs."

"That he does." Richard paced some more, arms crossed. His frosty breath rose in the cold air.

Baptiste appeared out of the trees leading a horse packed with firewood. He walked the animal up to the fire and untied each load. Then he pulled the halter from the animal and slapped it on the rump. "There, reckon that'll keep the fires going fo' a day or two." He walked up to the firepit and extended his hands. "What's the word on Willow?"

"Still waiting," Richard said.

"Birthing takes a while." Travis shifted. " 'Course, any coon what goes inter business with a woman fer a partner, why, hell, he'd best be waiting fer Christmas come July."

"She'll make it," Richard said absently. Then he turned a narrowed eye on Travis. "I'll bet you. Five packs of prime plews."

"I'd like some of that." Baptiste's face lit up. "Ain't no woman gonna make it in no business."

Travis squinted skeptically at Richard. "Naw, I ain't having none of it. Not with Dick looking that a-way."

◆

Willow lay back on the blankets and let the sweat dry on her hot flesh. She blinked her eyes in the darkness and let her thoughts float. Childbirth was that way. The terrible wrenching pain, the feeling as if one's guts were being pulled from the body, and finally, after the delivery, the foggy feeling as the body forgot the agony.

Perhaps *Tam Segobia* had made the world that way, so a woman would forget, lest she refuse to undergo such a horrible ordeal again.

New Moon Rising knelt beside her, wiping the blood and fluid from the squalling infant. The baby was changing color from blue to pink, a sign of health. New Moon Rising's hands were quick and sure, her care of the baby one less thing for Willow to worry about. She might have been *A'ni*, but at least she was a woman. *I'm still* Dukurika *down in my souls. I couldn't have stood to have Richard, Travis, or Baptiste here.*

Willow cramped again as the afterbirth passed. Makes Antelope had placed a hide to catch it, and now carefully folded the hide, binding it tightly with thongs. Willow would have to bury it with appropriate ceremony. That would be later. For now she was happy to let her weary body rest.

To Willow's relief, New Moon Rising had followed instructions, dipping the child *Dukurika*-fashion in warm water to clean it. Now she finished rubbing the baby clean, and bent down, chattering in her *A'ni* tongue. Willow smiled, and took her child. So, she'd borne a girl.

She pulled the blanket back, and nestled the little round head against her breast. As the tiny mouth found her nipple and began sucking, Willow closed her eyes, savoring the sensations that stimulated her milk.

For the moment, she could float in this sense of euphoria. Her daughter was born. Richard had returned from Boston. She'd won. *Tam Apo* had smiled on her.

She would see Richard soon, in spite of the *Dukurika*

warning about seeing a husband too soon after a birth. Together, they would raise this new daughter. Their girl would learn the ways of the *Dukurika* and of the Whites. Born into two worlds, she would be the first of a new tribe.

In the distance, she could hear the wavering howl as a wolf cried its Power into the spring storm.

◈

Richard stood on one of the worn sandstone boulders and watched evening come to *Ainkahonobita*. The sky was touched with hints of salmon pink that reflected on the melting snow. The junipers and pines stood in stark contrast to the pristine white. The air had warmed, promising a turn in the weather. Spring was like that, cold and snowy one day, warm and pleasant the next.

He recognized Willow's dainty step, but remained as he was, staring up at the sky while she stopped beside him and twined her arm with his.

"How's little Caroline?" he asked

"Little White Alder," she corrected gently, and poked him in the ribs. Then she said, "You have that look in your eyes."

"Just thinking about how I got here. My father sending me West, the trouble I got into with François, getting sold onto the boat. And you, your husband and son dying, your being captured by Packrat and taken East. So many little things, all leading to Caroline being born."

"*Tam Apo* made the world to work like that." She shrugged. "This bothers you?"

"I'm still looking for purpose, I guess. It all seems like chaos. François, August, Trudeau, and Dave Green, all of them dead. Yet here I stand, with you. Who would have thought that I, the least suited of all to survive, would have lived through it?"

"Perhaps it was you, Richard. You've never known the strength of your *puha*. You came looking for Wolf, and you found him. The others, they looked for what they wanted . . . and could not reach out with their souls to grasp it."

"Or they just didn't have the luck." He smiled weakly. "Luck and chaos are twins, you know."

"And what does that mean?"

"It means we had better live our lives with all the passion we can. If there is a truth, it's that this, like all things, will pass. The Blackfeet could come tomorrow, or the small pox, or a bad fall from a horse. Assuming there is an ultimate truth, it is that all is chaos."

"Only half," she corrected, placing soft fingers to his lips. "For everything Coyote did wrong, Wolf did something right. The world is made that way. Now, come with me. Those pesky *A'ni* women have been roasting hump meat all day. I think it's ready to come out of the pit."

He nodded, and together they turned, picking their way through the rocks toward home—for however long it would exist.

Selected Bibliography

Baldwin, Leland D.
The Keelboat Age on Western Waters. 1941. Reprint. Pittsburgh: University of Pittsburgh Press, 1980.

Billon, Frederic L.
Annals of Saint Louis in Its Territorial Days from 1804 to 1821. 1888. Reprint. New York: Arno Press & *The New York Times,* 1971.

Bradbury, John
Travels in the Interior of America in the Years 1809, 1810, and 1811. 1819. Reprint. 1904, Thwaits edition. Lincoln, NE: Bison Books, University of Nebraska Press, 1986.

Bowers, Alfred W.
Mandan Social and Ceremonial Organization. Chicago: University of Chicago Press, 1950.

Brown, Joseph Epes
The Sacred Pipe: Black Elk's Account of the Seven Rites of the Oglala Sioux. Norman, OK: University of Oklahoma Press, 1953.

Clokey, Richard M.
William H. Ashley: Enterprise and Politics in the Trans-Mississippi West. Norman, OK: University of Oklahoma Press, 1980.

Denig, Edwin Thompson
Five Indian Tribes of the Upper Missouri. Norman, OK: University of Oklahoma Press, 1961.

Dominguez, Steve

"Tukudeka Subsistence: Observations for a Preliminary Model." Unpublished manuscript, 1981.

Dorsey, George A.

The Mythology of the Wichita. Norman, OK: University of Oklahoma Press, 1995.

Fletcher, Alice C., and Francis La Flesche

The Omaha Tribe. Vols. I and II. Reprint. 1906, Bureau of American Ethnology Report. Lincoln, NE: Bison Books, University of Nebraska Press, 1992.

Frazer, Robert W.

Forts of the West. Norman, OK: University of Oklahoma Press, 1965.

Frey, Rodney

The World of the Crow: As Driftwood Lodges. Norman, OK: University of Oklahoma Press, 1987.

Gale, John

The Missouri Expedition 1818–1820: The Journal of Surgeon John Gale. Norman, OK: University of Oklahoma Press, 1960.

Garrard, Lewis H.

Wah-to-yah and the Taos Trail. Norman, OK: University of Oklahoma Press, 1955.

Gilmore, Melvin R.

Uses of Plants by the Indians of the Missouri River Region. Lincoln, NE: University of Nebraska Press, 1977.

Gowans, Fred R.

Rocky Mountain Rendezvous. Provo, UT: Brigham Young University Press, 1975.

Hafen, Leor R.

Broken Hand: The Life of Thomas Fitzpatrick. Reprint. 1931. Lincoln, NE: Bison Books, University of Nebraska Press, 1973.

Hultkrantz, Ake

The Religions of the American Indians, trans. Monica Setterwall. Berkeley: University of California Press, 1967.

Native Religions of North America. San Francisco: Harper & Row, 1987.

Shamanic Healing and Ritual Drama. New York: Crossroad Publishing Company, 1992.

Hunt, David C., et al.

Karl Bodmer's America. Lincoln, NE: The Josyln Art Museum and University of Nebraska Press, 1984.

Hyde, George E.

The Pawnee Indians. Norman, OK: University of Oklahoma Press, 1951.

Klein, Laura F., and Lillian A. Ackerman, eds.

Women and Power in Native North America. Lincoln, NE: University of Oklahoma Press, 1995.

Larson, Mary Lou, and Marcel Kornfeld

"Betwixt and Between the Basin and the Plains: The Limits of Numic Expansion," in *Across the West.* David B. Madson and David Rhode, eds. Salt Lake City: University of Utah Press, 1994.

Lauer, Quentin

Phenomenology: Its Genesis and Prospect. 1958. Reprint. New York: Harper Torchbooks, 1965.

Lavender, David

The Fist in the Wilderness. Albuquerque, NM: University of New Mexico Press, 1964.

Lowie, Robert H.

The Crow Indians. 1935. Reprint. Lincoln, NE: Bison Books, University of Nebraska Press, 1963.

Luttig, John C.

Journal of a Fur Trading Expedition on the Upper Missouri. 1920. Reprint. New York: Argosy-Antiquarian, Ltd., 1964.

Meyer, Roy W.

The Village Indians of the Upper Missouri. Lincoln, NE: University of Nebraska Press, 1977.

Miller, Wick R.

Newe Natekwinappeh: Shoshoni Stories and Dictionary. Salt Lake City: University of Utah Anthropological Papers, no. 94, University of Utah Press, 1972.

Moore, Michael

Medicinal Plants of the Mountain West. Santa Fe: Museum of New Mexico Press, 1979.

Morgan, Dale L.

Jedediah Smith and the Opening of the West. Lincoln, NE: University of Nebraska Press, 1953.

Moulton, Gary E., ed.

The Journals of the Lewis and Clark Expedition. Vols. II and III. Lincoln, NE: University of Nebraska Press, 1986.

Nute, Grace Lee

The Voyageur. 1931. Reprint. St. Paul, MN: Minnesota Historical Society, 1953.

Oglesby, Richard Edward

Manuel Lisa and the Opening of the Missouri Fur Trade. Norman, OK: University of Oklahoma Press, 1963.

Powers, William K.

Sacred Language: The Nature of Supernatural Discourse in Lakota. Norman, OK: University of Oklahoma Press, 1986.

Primm, James Neal

Lion of the Valley: St. Louis, Missouri. Boulder, CO: Pruett Press, 1981.

Rogers, Daniel J.

Objects of Change, the Archaeology and History of Arikara Contact with Europeans. Washington, DC: Smithsonian Institution Press, 1990.

Ruxton, George F.
Life in the Far West Among the Indians and the Mountain Men. 1846–1847. 1849. Reprint. Glorietta, NM: Rio Grande Press, 1972.

Schlesier, Karl H.
Plains Indians, A.D. 500–1500. Norman, OK: University of Oklahoma Press, 1994.

Shimkin, Dimitri B.
Some Interactions of Culture Needs and Personalities Among the Wind River Shoshone. Ph.D. dissertation, University of California Library, Berkeley, 1938.

Wind River Shoshone Ethnogeography. Berkeley, CA: University of California Anthropological Records, no. 5 (4), 1947.

Smith, Anne M.
Shoshone Tales. Salt Lake City: University of Utah Press, 1993.

Steffen, Jerome O.
William Clark, Jeffersonian Man on the Frontier. Norman, OK: University of Oklahoma Press, 1977.

Thomas, David, and Karin Ronnefeldt, eds.
People of the First Man. New York: E. P. Dutton, 1976.

Trenholm, Virginia Cole, and Maurine Carley
The Shoshonis: Sentinels of the Rockies. Norman, OK: University of Oklahoma Press, 1964.

WarCloud, Paul
Sioux Indian Dictionary. Sissiton, SD: Paul WarCloud, 1971.

Weeks, Rupert
Pachee Goyo: History and Legends from the Shoshone. Laramie, WY: Jelm Mountain Press, 1981.

Weltfish, Gene
The Lost Universe: Pawnee Life and Culture. 1965. Reprint. Lincoln, NE: Bison Books, University of Nebraska Press, 1977.